GREAT
SHORT
STORIES
OF
THE
WORLD

GREAT SHORT STORIES OF THE WORLD

*Selected
by the Editors
of
The Reader's
Digest*

—

The Reader's Digest Association
Montreal, Sydney, Cape Town
Pleasantville, New York

The stories in this volume
appear substantially at their original length except
for the following, which have been condensed:
Young Archimedes, The Open Boat,
The Brute, Babylon Revisited, Fireworks for Elspeth,
Who Cares?, The Huntsmen, A Priest in the Family
and *The Nightingale*
. Acknowledgments to copyright holders
appear on pages 797 through 799

Library of Congress Catalog Card Number: 72-81158
Printed in the United States of America

Fourth Printing, August 1978

CONTENTS

9   THE LEADER OF THE PEOPLE / John Steinbeck

24   MR. KNOW-ALL / W. Somerset Maugham

31   VANKA / Anton Chekhov

35   THE HAPPY PRINCE / Oscar Wilde

44   THE OLD DEMON / Pearl S. Buck

56   THE SAILOR-BOY'S TALE / Isak Dinesen

67   YOUNG ARCHIMEDES / Aldous Huxley

92   BUTCH MINDS THE BABY / Damon Runyon

105   SUSPICION / Dorothy L. Sayers

121   HAUTOT AND HIS SON / Guy de Maupassant

134   THE OPEN BOAT / Stephen Crane

153   MY ŒDIPUS COMPLEX / Frank O'Connor

165   THE SNOWS OF KILIMANJARO / Ernest Hemingway

188   A LETTER TO GOD / Gregorio López y Fuentes

191   THE LITTLE BOUILLOUX GIRL / Colette

196   THE RUBY / Corrado Alvaro

201   SIX FEET OF THE COUNTRY / Nadine Gordimer

213   THE BOARDING HOUSE / James Joyce

220   THE BRUTE / Joseph Conrad

237   A DOUBLE GAME / Alberto Moravia

244   MATERNITY / Lilika Nakos

248   LEAD HER LIKE A PIGEON / Jessamyn West

256   GOD SEES THE TRUTH, BUT WAITS / Leo Tolstoy

264   THE WALKER-THROUGH-WALLS / Marcel Aymé

274   THE LOTTERY / Shirley Jackson

283   THE McWILLIAMSES AND THE BURGLAR ALARM / Mark Twain

290   THE AUGSBURG CHALK CIRCLE / Bertolt Brecht

303   THE OVERCOAT / Sally Benson

307   BLIND MacNAIR / Thomas H. Raddall

322   THE PROCURATOR OF JUDAEA / Anatole France

336   THE OPEN WINDOW / Saki (H. H. Munro)

339   MARÍA CONCEPCIÓN / Katherine Anne Porter

359   MY LORD, THE BABY / Rabindranath Tagore

367   THE END OF THE PARTY / Graham Greene

376   MODERN CHILDREN / Sholom Aleichem

393   BABYLON REVISITED / F. Scott Fitzgerald

412   CARRION SPRING / Wallace Stegner

428   JUST LATHER, THAT'S ALL / Hernando Téllez

433   THE SECRET LIFE OF WALTER MITTY / James Thurber

438   THE ROCKING-HORSE WINNER / D. H. Lawrence

454   THE SUNDAY MENACE / Robert Benchley

458   THE MEZZOTINT / Montague Rhodes James

469   THE ALLIGATORS / John Updike

476   PELAGEYA / Mikhail Zoshchenko

479   HAIRCUT / Ring Lardner

490   THE BURNING CITY / Hjalmar Söderberg

494   FIREWORKS FOR ELSPETH / Rumer Godden

511   THE OLD CHIEF MSHLANGA / Doris Lessing

524   WHO CARES? / Santha Rama Rau

544   OVER THE RIVER AND THROUGH THE WOOD / John O'Hara

550   DENTAL OR MENTAL, I SAY IT'S SPINACH / S. J. Perelman

554   THE DROVER'S WIFE / Henry Lawson

562   THE HUNTSMEN / Paul Horgan

579   THE GUEST / Albert Camus

593   PATIENCE / Nigel Balchin

612   AMONG THE PATHS TO EDEN / Truman Capote

625   ADMIRAL'S NIGHT / Machado de Assis

632   THE BET / Anton Chekhov

639   THE MAN WHO COULD WORK MIRACLES / H. G. Wells

656   A COUNTRY LOVE STORY / Jean Stafford

669   A WORN PATH / Eudora Welty

678   THE OUTSTATION / W. Somerset Maugham

709   A PRIEST IN THE FAMILY / Leo Kennedy

717   THE COP AND THE ANTHEM / O. Henry

723   MARRIAGE À LA MODE / Katherine Mansfield

734   THE NIGHTINGALE / Maxim Gorky

740   THE LAUNCH / Max Aub

745   THE WREATH / Luigi Pirandello

754   THE EIGHTY-YARD RUN / Irwin Shaw

768   YOU WERE PERFECTLY FINE / Dorothy Parker

772   LUZINA TAKES A HOLIDAY / Gabrielle Roy

789   BIOGRAPHICAL NOTES

797   ACKNOWLEDGMENTS

THE LEADER OF
THE PEOPLE
JOHN STEINBECK / UNITED STATES

John Steinbeck

ON SATURDAY AFTERNOON Billy Buck, the ranch hand, raked together the last of the old year's haystack and pitched small forkfuls over the wire fence to a few mildly interested cattle. High in the air small clouds like puffs of cannon smoke were driven eastward by the March wind. The wind could be heard *whish*ing in the brush on the ridge crests, but no breath of it penetrated down into the ranch cup.

The little boy, Jody, emerged from the house eating a thick piece of buttered bread. He saw Billy working on the last of the haystack. Jody tramped down scuffing his shoes in a way he had been told was destructive to good shoe leather. A flock of white pigeons flew out of the black cypress tree as Jody passed, and circled the tree and landed again. A half-grown tortoiseshell cat leaped from the bunk-house porch, galloped on stiff legs across the road, whirled and galloped back again. Jody picked up a stone to help the game along, but he was too late, for the cat was under the porch before the stone could be discharged. He threw the stone into the cypress tree and started the white pigeons on another whirling flight.

Arriving at the used-up haystack, the boy leaned against the barbed-wire fence. "Will that be all of it, do you think?" he asked.

The middle-aged ranch hand stopped his careful raking and stuck his fork into the ground. He took off his black hat and smoothed down his hair. "Nothing left of it that isn't soggy from ground moisture," he said. He replaced his hat and rubbed his dry leathery hands together.

"Ought to be plenty mice," Jody suggested.

"Lousy with them," said Billy. "Just crawling with mice."

"Well, maybe, when you get all through, I could call the dogs and hunt the mice."

"Sure, I guess you could," said Billy Buck. He lifted a forkful of the damp ground hay and threw it into the air. Instantly three mice leaped out and burrowed frantically under the hay again.

Jody sighed with satisfaction. Those plump, sleek, arrogant mice were doomed. For eight months they had lived and multiplied in the haystack. They had been immune from cats, from traps, from poison, and from Jody. They had grown smug in their security, overbearing and fat. Now the time of disaster had come; they would not survive another day.

Billy looked up at the top of the hills that surrounded the ranch. "Maybe you better ask your father before you do it," he suggested.

"Well, where is he? I'll ask him now."

"He rode up to the ridge ranch after dinner. He'll be back pretty soon."

Jody slumped against the fence post. "I don't think he'd care."

As Billy went back to his work he said ominously, "You'd better ask him anyway. You know how he is."

Jody did know. His father, Carl Tiflin, insisted upon giving permission for anything that was done on the ranch, whether it was important or not. Jody sagged farther against the post until he was sitting on the ground. He looked up at the little puffs of wind-driven cloud. "Is it like to rain, Billy?"

"It might. The wind's good for it, but not strong enough."

"Well, I hope it don't rain until after I kill those damn mice." He looked over his shoulder to see whether Billy had noticed the mature profanity. Billy worked on without comment.

Jody turned back and looked at the side hill where the road from the outside world came down. The hill was washed with lean March sunshine. Silver thistles, blue lupins and a few poppies bloomed among the sage bushes. Halfway up the hill Jody could see Doubletree Mutt, the black dog, digging in a squirrel hole. He paddled for a while and then paused to kick bursts of dirt out between his hind legs, and he dug with an earnestness which belied the knowledge he must have had that no dog had ever caught a squirrel by digging in a hole.

Suddenly, while Jody watched, the black dog stiffened, and backed out of the hole and looked up the hill toward the cleft in the ridge where the road came through. Jody looked up too. For a moment Carl Tiflin on horseback stood out against the pale sky and then he moved down the road toward the house. He carried something white in his hand.

The boy started to his feet. "He's got a letter," Jody cried. He trotted away toward the ranch house, for the letter would probably be read aloud and he wanted to be there. He reached the house before his father did, and ran in. He heard Carl dismount from his creaking saddle and slap the horse on the side to send it to the barn where Billy would unsaddle it and turn it out.

Jody ran into the kitchen. "We got a letter!" he cried.

His mother looked up from a pan of beans. "Who has?"

"Father has. I saw it in his hand."

Carl strode into the kitchen then, and Jody's mother asked, "Who's the letter from, Carl?"

He frowned quickly. "How did you know there was a letter?"

She nodded her head in the boy's direction. "Big-Britches Jody told me."

Jody was embarrassed.

His father looked down at him contemptuously. "He is getting to be a Big-Britches," Carl said. "He's minding everybody's business but his own. Got his big nose into everything."

Mrs. Tiflin relented a little. "Well, he hasn't enough to keep him busy. Who's the letter from?"

Carl still frowned on Jody. "I'll keep him busy if he isn't careful." He held out a sealed letter. "I guess it's from your father."

Mrs. Tiflin took a hairpin from her head and slit open the flap. Her lips pursed judiciously. Jody saw her eyes snap back and forth over the lines. "He says," she translated, "he says he's going to drive out Saturday to stay for a little while. Why, this is Saturday. The letter must have been delayed." She looked at the postmark. "This was mailed day before yesterday. It should have been here yesterday."

She looked questioningly at her husband, and then her face darkened angrily. "Now what have you got that look on you for? He doesn't come often."

Carl turned his eyes away from her anger. He could be stern with her most of the time, but when occasionally her temper arose, he could not combat it.

"What's the matter with you?" she demanded again.

In his explanation there was a tone of apology Jody himself might have used. "It's just that he talks," Carl said lamely. "Just talks."

"Well, what of it? You talk yourself."

"Sure I do. But your father only talks about one thing."

"Indians!" Jody broke in excitedly. "Indians and crossing the plains!"

Carl turned fiercely on him. "You get out, Mr. Big-Britches! Go on, now! Get out!"

Jody went miserably out the back door and closed the screen with elaborate quietness. Under the kitchen window his shamed, downcast eyes fell upon a curiously shaped stone, a stone of such fascination that he squatted down and picked it up and turned it over in his hands.

The voices came clearly to him through the open kitchen window. "Jody's damn well right," he heard his father say. "Just Indians and crossing the plains. I've heard that story about how the horses got driven off about a thousand times. He just goes on and on, and he never changes a word in the things he tells."

When Mrs. Tiflin answered her tone was so changed that Jody, outside the window, looked up from his study of the stone. Her voice had become soft and explanatory. Jody knew how her face would have changed to match the tone. She said quietly, "Look at it this way, Carl. That was the big thing in my father's life. He led a wagon train clear across the plains to the coast, and when it was finished, his life was done. It was a big thing to do, but it didn't last long enough. Look!" she continued, "it's as though he was born to do that, and after he finished it, there wasn't anything more for him to do but think about it and talk about it. If there'd been any farther west to go, he'd have gone. He's told me so himself. But at last there was the ocean. He lives right by the ocean where he had to stop."

She had caught Carl, caught him and entangled him in her soft tone.

"I've seen him," he agreed quietly. "He goes down and stares off west over the ocean." His voice sharpened a little. "And then he goes up to the Horseshoe Club in Pacific Grove, and he tells people how the Indians drove off the horses."

She tried to catch him again. "Well, it's everything to him. You might be patient with him and pretend to listen."

Carl turned impatiently away. "Well, if it gets too bad, I can always go down to the bunkhouse and sit with Billy," he said irritably. He walked through the house and slammed the front door after him.

Jody ran to his chores. He dumped the grain to the chickens without chasing any of them. He gathered the eggs from the nests. He trotted into the house with the wood and interlaced it so carefully in the woodbox that two armloads seemed to fill it to overflowing.

His mother had finished the beans by now. She stirred up the fire and brushed off the stove top with a turkey wing. Jody peered cautiously at her to see whether any rancor toward him remained. "Is he coming today?" Jody asked.

"That's what his letter said."

"Maybe I better walk up the road to meet him."

Mrs. Tiflin clanged the stove lid shut. "That would be nice," she said. "He'd probably like to be met."

"I guess I'll just do it then."

Outside, Jody whistled shrilly to the dogs. "Come on up the hill," he commanded. The two dogs waved their tails and ran ahead. Along the roadside the sage had tender new tips. Jody tore off some pieces and rubbed them on his hands until the air was filled with the sharp wild smell. With a rush the dogs leaped from the road and yapped into the brush after a rabbit. That was the last Jody saw of them, for when they failed to catch the rabbit, they went back home.

Jody plodded on up the hill toward the ridgetop. When he reached the little cleft where the road came through, the afternoon wind struck him and blew up his hair and ruffled his shirt. He looked down on the little hills and ridges below and then out at the huge green Salinas

Valley. He could see the white town of Salinas far out in the flat and the flash of its windows under the waning sun. Directly below him, in an oak tree, a crow congress had convened. The tree was black with crows all cawing at once.

Then Jody's eyes followed the wagon road down from the ridge where he stood, and lost it behind a hill, and picked it up again on the other side. On that distant stretch he saw a cart slowly pulled by a bay horse. It disappeared behind the hill. Jody sat down on the ground and watched the place where the cart would reappear. The wind sang on the hilltops and the puffball clouds hurried eastward.

Then the cart came into sight and stopped. A man dressed in black dismounted from the seat and walked to the horse's head. Although it was so far away, Jody knew he had unhooked the checkrein, for the horse's head dropped forward. The horse moved on, and the man walked slowly up the hill beside it. Jody gave a glad cry and ran down the road toward them. The squirrels bumped along off the road, and a roadrunner flirted its tail and raced over the edge of the hill and sailed out like a glider.

Jody tried to leap into the middle of his shadow at every step. A stone rolled under his foot and he went down. Around a little bend he raced, and there, a short distance ahead, were his grandfather and the cart. The boy dropped from his unseemly running and approached at a dignified walk.

The horse plodded stumble-footedly up the hill and the old man walked beside it. In the lowering sun their giant shadows flickered darkly behind them. The grandfather was dressed in a black broadcloth suit and he wore kid congress gaiters and a black tie on a short, hard collar. He carried his black slouch hat in his hand. His white beard was cropped close and his white eyebrows overhung his eyes like mustaches. The blue eyes were sternly merry. About the whole face and figure there was a granite dignity, so that every motion seemed an impossible thing. Once at rest, it seemed the old man would be stone, would never move again. His steps were slow and certain. Once made, no step could ever be retraced; once headed in a direction, the path would never bend nor the pace increase nor slow.

When Jody appeared around the bend, Grandfather waved his hat slowly in welcome, and he called, "Why, Jody! Come down to meet me, have you?"

Jody sidled near and turned and matched his step to the old man's step and stiffened his body and dragged his heels a little. "Yes, sir," he said. "We got your letter only today."

"Should have been here yesterday," said Grandfather. "It certainly should. How are all the folks?"

"They're fine, sir." He hesitated and then suggested shyly, "Would you like to come on a mouse hunt tomorrow, sir?"

"Mouse hunt, Jody?" Grandfather chuckled. "Have the people of this generation come down to hunting mice? They aren't very strong, the new people, but I hardly thought mice would be game for them."

"No, sir. It's just play. The haystack's gone. I'm going to drive out the mice to the dogs. And you can watch, or even beat the hay a little."

The stern, merry eyes turned down on him. "I see. You don't eat them, then. You haven't come to that yet."

Jody explained, "The dogs eat them, sir. It wouldn't be much like hunting Indians, I guess."

"No, not much—but then later, when the troops were hunting Indians and shooting children and burning teepees, it wasn't much different from your mouse hunt."

They topped the rise and started down into the ranch cup, and they lost the sun from their shoulders. "You've grown," Grandfather said. "Nearly an inch, I should say."

"More," Jody boasted. "Where they mark me on the door, I'm up more than an inch since Thanksgiving even."

Grandfather's rich throaty voice said, "Maybe you're getting too much water and turning to pith and stalk. Wait until you head out, and then we'll see."

Jody looked quickly into the old man's face to see whether his feelings should be hurt, but there was no will to injure, no punishing nor putting-in-your-place light in the keen blue eyes. "We might kill a pig," Jody suggested.

"Oh, no! I couldn't let you do that. You're just humoring me. It isn't the time and you know it."

"You know Riley, the big boar, sir?"

"Yes. I remember Riley well."

"Well, Riley ate a hole into that same haystack, and it fell down on him and smothered him."

"Pigs do that when they can," said Grandfather.

"Riley was a nice pig, for a boar, sir. I rode him sometimes, and he didn't mind."

A door slammed at the house below them, and they saw Jody's mother standing on the porch waving her apron in welcome. And they saw Carl Tiflin walking up from the barn to be at the house for the arrival. The sun had disappeared from the hills by now. The blue smoke from the house chimney hung in flat layers in the purpling ranch cup. The puffball clouds, dropped by the falling wind, hung listlessly in the sky.

Billy Buck came out of the bunkhouse and flung a washbasin of soapy water on the ground. He had been shaving in midweek, for Billy held Grandfather in reverence, and Grandfather said that Billy was one of the few men of the new generation who had not gone soft. Although Billy was in middle age, Grandfather considered him a boy. Now Billy was hurrying toward the house too.

When Jody and Grandfather arrived, the three were waiting for them in front of the yard gate.

Carl said, "Hello, sir. We've been looking for you."

Mrs. Tiflin kissed Grandfather on the side of his beard, and stood still while his big hand patted her shoulder. Billy shook hands solemnly, grinning under his straw mustache.

"I'll put up your horse," said Billy, and he led the rig away.

Grandfather watched him go, and then, turning back to the group, he said as he had said a hundred times before, "There's a good boy. I knew his father, old Mule-tail Buck. I never knew why they called him Mule-tail except he packed mules."

Mrs. Tiflin turned and led the way into the house. "How long are you going to stay, Father? Your letter didn't say."

"Well, I don't know. I thought I'd stay about two weeks. But I never stay as long as I think I'm going to."

In a short while they were sitting at the white oilcloth table eating their supper. The lamp with the tin reflector hung over the table. Outside the dining-room windows the big moths battered softly against the glass.

Grandfather cut his steak into tiny pieces and chewed slowly. "I'm hungry," he said. "Driving out here got my appetite up. It's like when we were crossing. We all got so hungry every night we could hardly wait to let the meat get done. I could eat about five pounds of buffalo meat every night."

"It's moving around does it," said Billy. "My father was a government packer. I helped him when I was a kid. Just the two of us could clean up a deer's ham."

"I knew your father, Billy," said Grandfather. "A fine man he was. They called him Mule-tail Buck. I don't know why except he packed mules."

"That was it," Billy agreed. "He packed mules."

Grandfather put down his knife and fork and looked around the table. "I remember one time we ran out of meat—" His voice dropped to a curious low singsong, dropped into a tonal groove the story had worn for itself. "There was no buffalo, no antelope, not even rabbits. The hunters couldn't even shoot a coyote. That was the time for the leader to be on the watch. I was the leader, and I kept my eyes open. Know why? Well, just the minute the people began to get hungry they'd start slaughtering the team oxen. Do you believe that? I've heard of parties that just ate up their draft cattle. Started from the middle and worked toward the ends. Finally they'd eat the lead pair, and then the wheelers. The leader of a party had to keep them from doing that."

In some manner a big moth got into the room and circled the hanging kerosene lamp. Billy got up and tried to clap it between his hands. Carl struck with a cupped palm and caught the moth and broke it. He walked to the window and dropped it out.

"As I was saying," Grandfather began again, but Carl interrupted him. "You'd better eat some more meat. All the rest of us are ready for our pudding." Jody saw a flash of anger in his mother's eyes.

Grandfather picked up his knife and fork. "I'm pretty hungry, all right," he said. "I'll tell you about that later."

When supper was over, when the family and Billy Buck sat in front of the fireplace in the other room, Jody anxiously watched Grandfather. He saw the signs he knew. The bearded head leaned forward; the eyes lost their sternness and looked wonderingly into the fire; the big lean fingers laced themselves on the black knees. "I wonder," he began, "I just wonder whether I ever told you how those thieving Piutes drove off thirty-five of our horses."

"I think you did," Carl interrupted. "Wasn't it just before you went up into the Tahoe country?"

Grandfather turned quickly toward his son-in-law. "That's right. I guess I must have told you that story."

"Lots of times," Carl said cruelly, and he avoided his wife's eyes. But he felt the angry eyes on him, and he said, "'Course I'd like to hear it again."

Grandfather looked back at the fire. His fingers unlaced and laced again. Jody knew how he felt, how his insides were collapsed and empty. Hadn't Jody been called a Big-Britches that very afternoon? He arose to heroism and opened himself to the term Big-Britches again. "Tell about Indians," he said softly.

Grandfather's eyes grew stern again. "Boys always want to hear about Indians. It was a job for men, but boys want to hear about it. Well, let's see. Did I ever tell you how I wanted each wagon to carry a long iron plate?"

Everyone but Jody remained silent.

Jody said, "No. You didn't."

"Well, when the Indians attacked, we always put the wagons in a circle and fought from between the wheels. I thought that if every wagon carried a long plate with rifle holes, the men could stand the plates on the outside of the wheels when the wagons were in the circle and they would be protected. It would save lives and that would make up for the extra weight of the iron. But of course the party wouldn't do it. No party had done it before and they couldn't see why they should go to the expense. They lived to regret it, too."

Jody looked at his mother, and knew from her expression that she was not listening at all. Carl picked at a callus on his thumb and Billy Buck watched a spider crawling up the wall.

Grandfather's tone dropped into its narrative groove again. Jody knew in advance exactly what words would fall. The story droned on, speeded up for the attack, grew sad over the wounds, struck a dirge at the burials on the great plains. Jody sat quietly watching Grandfather. The stern blue eyes were detached. He looked as though he were not very interested in the story himself.

When it was finished, when the pause had been politely respected as the frontier of the story, Billy Buck stood up and stretched and hitched his trousers. "I guess I'll turn in," he said. Then he faced Grandfather. "I've got an old powder horn and a cap-and-ball pistol down to the bunkhouse. Did I ever show them to you?"

Grandfather nodded slowly. "Yes, I think you did, Billy. Reminds me of a pistol I had when I was leading the people across." Billy stood politely until the little story was done, and then he said, "Good night," and went out of the house.

Carl Tiflin tried to turn the conversation then. "How's the country between here and Monterey? I've heard it's pretty dry."

"It is dry," said Grandfather. "There's not a drop of water in the Laguna Seca. But it's a long pull from '87. The whole country was powder then, and in '61 I believe all the coyotes starved to death. We had fifteen inches of rain this year."

"Yes, but it all came too early. We could do with some now." Carl's eye fell on Jody. "Hadn't you better be getting to bed?"

Jody stood up obediently. "Can I kill the mice in the old hay-stack, sir?"

"Mice? Oh! Sure, kill them all off. Billy said there isn't any good hay left."

Jody exchanged a secret and satisfying look with Grandfather. "I'll kill every one tomorrow," he promised.

Jody lay in his bed and thought of the impossible world of Indians and buffaloes, a world that had ceased to be forever. He wished he could have been living in the heroic time, but he knew he was not of heroic timber. No one living now, save possibly Billy Buck, was worthy to do the things that had been done. A race of giants had lived then, fearless men, men of a staunchness unknown in this day. Jody thought of the wide plains and of the wagons moving across like centipedes. He thought of Grandfather on a huge white horse, marshaling the people. Across his mind marched the great phantoms, and they marched off the earth and they were gone.

He came back to the ranch for a moment, then. He heard the dull rushing sound that space and silence make. He heard one of the dogs, out in the doghouse, scratching a flea and bumping his elbow against the floor with every stroke. Then the wind arose again and the black cypress groaned and Jody went to sleep.

He was up half an hour before the triangle sounded for breakfast. His mother was rattling the stove to make the flames roar when Jody went through the kitchen. "You're up early," she said. "Where are you going?"

"Out to get a good stick. We're going to kill the mice today."

"Who is 'we'?"

"Why, Grandfather and I."

"So you've got him in it. You always like to have someone in with you in case there's blame to share."

"I'll be right back," said Jody. "I just want to have a good stick ready for after breakfast."

He closed the screen door after him and went out into the cool blue morning. The birds were noisy in the dawn and the ranch cats came down from the hill like blunt snakes. They had been hunting gophers in the dark, and although the four cats were full of gopher meat, they sat in a semicircle at the back door and mewed piteously for milk. Doubletree Mutt and Smasher moved sniffing along the edge of the brush, performing the duty with rigid ceremony, but when Jody whistled, their heads jerked up and their tails waved. They plunged down to him, wriggling their skins and yawning. Jody patted their heads seriously, and moved on to the weathered scrap pile. He selected an old broom handle and a short piece of inch-square scrap wood. From his pocket he took a shoelace and tied the ends of the sticks loosely together to make a flail. He whistled his new weapon through the air and struck the ground experimentally, while the dogs leaped aside and whined with apprehension.

Jody turned and started down past the house toward the old haystack ground to look over the field of slaughter, but Billy Buck, sitting patiently on the back steps, called to him, "You better come back. It's only a couple of minutes till breakfast."

Jody changed his course and moved toward the house. He leaned his flail against the steps. "That's to drive the mice out," he said. "I'll bet they're fat. I'll bet they don't know what's going to happen to them today."

"No, nor you either," Billy remarked philosophically, "nor me, nor anyone."

Jody was staggered by this thought. He knew it was true. His imagination twitched away from the mouse hunt. Then his mother came out on the back porch and struck the triangle, and all thoughts fell in a heap.

Grandfather hadn't appeared at the table when they sat down. Billy nodded at his empty chair. "He's all right? He isn't sick?"

"He takes a long time to dress," said Mrs. Tiflin. "He combs his whiskers and rubs up his shoes and brushes his clothes."

Carl scattered sugar on his mush. "A man that's led a wagon train across the plains has got to be pretty careful how he dresses."

Mrs. Tiflin turned on him. "Don't do that, Carl! Please don't!" There was more of threat than of request in her tone. And the threat irritated Carl.

"Well, how many times do I have to listen to the story of the iron plates, and the thirty-five horses? That time's done. Why can't he forget it, now it's done?" He grew angrier while he talked, and his voice rose. "Why does he have to tell them over and over? He came across the plains. All right! Now it's finished. Nobody wants to hear about it over and over."

The door into the kitchen closed softly. The four at the table sat frozen. Carl laid his mush spoon on the table and touched his chin with his fingers.

Then the kitchen door opened and Grandfather walked in. His mouth smiled tightly and his eyes were squinted. "Good morning," he said, and he sat down and looked at his mush dish.

Carl could not leave it there. "Did—did you hear what I said?" Grandfather jerked a little nod.

"I don't know what got into me, sir. I didn't mean it. I was just being funny." Jody glanced in shame at his mother, and he saw that she was looking at Carl, and that she wasn't breathing. It was an awful thing that he was doing. He was tearing himself to pieces to talk like that. It was a terrible thing to him to retract a word, but to retract it in shame was infinitely worse.

Grandfather looked sidewise. "I'm trying to get right side up," he said gently. "I'm not being mad. I don't mind what you said, but it might be true, and I would mind that."

"It isn't true," said Carl. "I'm not feeling well this morning. I'm sorry I said it."

"Don't be sorry, Carl. An old man doesn't see things sometimes. Maybe you're right. The crossing is finished. Maybe it should be forgotten, now it's done."

Carl got up from the table. "I've had enough to eat. I'm going to work. Take your time, Billy!" He walked quickly out of the dining room. Billy gulped the rest of his food and followed soon after. But Jody could not leave his chair.

"Won't you tell any more stories?" Jody asked.

"Why, sure I'll tell them, but only when—I'm sure people want to hear them."

"I like to hear them, sir."

"Oh! Of course you do, but you're a little boy. It was a job for men, but only little boys like to hear about it."

Jody got up from his place. "I'll wait outside for you, sir. I've got a good stick for those mice."

He waited by the gate until the old man came out on the porch. "Let's go down and kill the mice now," Jody called.

"I think I'll just sit in the sun, Jody. You go kill the mice."

"You can use my stick if you like."

"No, I'll just sit here a while."

Jody turned disconsolately away, and walked down toward the old haystack. He tried to whip up his enthusiasm with thoughts of the fat juicy mice. He beat the ground with his flail. The dogs coaxed and whined about him, but he could not go. Back at the house he could see Grandfather sitting on the porch, looking small and thin and black.

Jody gave up and went to sit on the steps at the old man's feet. "Back already? Did you kill the mice?"

"No, sir. I'll kill them some other day."

The morning flies buzzed close to the ground and the ants dashed about in front of the steps. The heavy smell of sage slipped down the hill. The porch boards grew warm in the sunshine.

Jody hardly knew when Grandfather started to talk. "I shouldn't stay here, feeling the way I do." He examined his strong old hands. "I feel as though the crossing wasn't worth doing." His eyes moved up the side hill and stopped on a motionless hawk perched on a dead limb. "I tell those old stories, but they're not what I want to tell. I only know how I want people to feel when I tell them.

"It wasn't Indians that were important, nor adventures, nor even getting out here. It was a whole bunch of people made into one big crawling beast. And I was the head. It was westering and westering. Every man wanted something for himself, but the big beast that was all of them wanted only westering. I was the leader, but if I hadn't been there, someone else would have been the head. The thing had to have a head.

"Under the little bushes the shadows were black at white noonday. When we saw the mountains at last, we cried—all of us. But it wasn't getting here that mattered, it was movement and westering.

"We carried life out here and set it down the way those ants carry eggs. And I was the leader. The westering was as big as God, and the slow steps that made the movement piled up and piled up until the continent was crossed.

"Then we came down to the sea, and it was done." He stopped and wiped his eyes until the rims were red. "That's what I should be telling instead of stories."

When Jody spoke, Grandfather started and looked down at him. "Maybe I could lead the people someday," Jody said.

The old man smiled. "There's no place to go. There's the ocean to stop you. There's a line of old men along the shore hating the ocean because it stopped them."

"In boats I might, sir."

"No place to go, Jody. Every place is taken. But that's not the worst—no, not the worst. Westering has died out of the people. Westering isn't a hunger anymore. It's all done. Your father is right. It is finished." He laced his fingers on his knee and looked at them.

Jody felt very sad. "If you'd like a glass of lemonade I could make it for you."

Grandfather was about to refuse, and then he saw Jody's face. "That would be nice," he said. "Yes, it would be nice to drink a lemonade."

Jody ran into the kitchen where his mother was wiping the last of the breakfast dishes. "Can I have a lemon to make a lemonade for Grandfather?"

His mother mimicked—"And another lemon to make a lemonade for you."

"No, ma'am. I don't want one."

"Jody! You're sick!" Then she stopped suddenly. "Take a lemon out of the cooler," she said softly. "Here, I'll reach the squeezer down to you."

MR. KNOW-ALL
W. SOMERSET MAUGHAM / GREAT BRITAIN

W.S. Maugham

I WAS PREPARED to dislike Max Kelada even before I knew him. The war had just finished and the passenger traffic in the oceangoing liners was heavy. Accommodation was very hard to get and you had to put up with whatever the agents chose to offer you. You could not hope for a cabin to yourself and I was thankful to be given one in which there were only two berths. But when I was told the name of my companion my heart sank. It suggested closed portholes and the night air rigidly excluded. It was bad enough to share a cabin for fourteen days with anyone (I was going from San Francisco to

Yokohama), but I should have looked upon it with less dismay if my fellow passenger's name had been Smith or Brown.

When I went on board I found Mr. Kelada's luggage already below. I did not like the look of it; there were too many labels on the suitcases, and the wardrobe trunk was too big. He had unpacked his toilet things, and I observed that he was a patron of the excellent Monsieur Coty; for I saw on the washing stand his scent, his hair wash and his brilliantine. Mr. Kelada's brushes, ebony with his monogram in gold, would have been all the better for a scrub. I did not at all like Mr. Kelada. I made my way into the smoking room. I called for a pack of cards and began to play patience. I had scarcely started before a man came up to me and asked me if he was right in thinking my name was so-and-so.

"I am Mr. Kelada," he added, with a smile that showed a row of flashing teeth, and sat down.

"Oh, yes, we're sharing a cabin, I think."

"Bit of luck, I call it. You never know who you're going to be put in with. I was jolly glad when I heard you were English. I'm all for us English sticking together when we're abroad, if you understand what I mean."

I blinked. "Are you English?" I asked, perhaps tactlessly.

"Rather. You don't think I look like an American, do you? British to the backbone, that's what I am."

To prove it, Mr. Kelada took out of his pocket a passport and airily waved it under my nose.

King George has many strange subjects. Mr. Kelada was short and of a sturdy build, clean-shaven and darkskinned, with a fleshy, hooked nose and very large, lustrous and liquid eyes. His long black hair was sleek and curly. He spoke with a fluency in which there was nothing English and his gestures were exuberant. I felt pretty sure that a closer inspection of that British passport would have betrayed the fact that Mr. Kelada was born under a bluer sky than is generally seen in England.

"What will you have?" he asked me.

I looked at him doubtfully. Prohibition was in force and to all appearances the ship was bone-dry. When I am not thirsty I do not know which I dislike more, ginger ale or lemon squash. But Mr. Kelada flashed an oriental smile at me.

"Whisky and soda or a dry martini, you have only to say the word."

From each of his hip pockets he fished a flask and laid them on the table before me. I chose the martini, and calling the steward he ordered a tumbler of ice and a couple of glasses.

"A very good cocktail," I said.

"Well, there are plenty more where that came from, and if you've got any friends on board, you tell them you've got a pal who's got all the liquor in the world."

Mr. Kelada was chatty. He talked of New York and San Francisco. He discussed plays, pictures, and politics. He was patriotic. The Union Jack is an impressive piece of drapery, but when it is flourished by a gentleman from Alexandria or Beirut, I cannot but feel that it loses somewhat in dignity. Mr. Kelada was familiar. I do not wish to put on airs, but I cannot help feeling that it is seemly in a total stranger to put mister before my name when he addresses me. Mr. Kelada, doubtless to set me at my ease, used no such formality. I did not like Mr. Kelada. I had put aside the cards when he sat down, but now, thinking that for this first occasion our conversation had lasted long enough, I went on with my game.

"The three on the four," said Mr. Kelada.

There is nothing more exasperating when you are playing patience than to be told where to put the card you have turned up before you have had a chance to look for yourself.

"It's coming out, it's coming out," he cried. "The ten on the knave." With rage and hatred in my heart I finished. Then he seized the pack.

"Do you like card tricks?"

"No, I hate card tricks," I answered.

"Well, I'll just show you this one."

He showed me three. Then I said I would go down to the dining room and get my seat at table.

"Oh, that's all right," he said. "I've already taken a seat for you. I thought that as we were in the same stateroom we might just as well sit at the same table."

I did not like Mr. Kelada.

I not only shared a cabin with him and ate three meals a day at the same table, but I could not walk round the deck without his joining me. It was impossible to snub him. It never occurred to him that he was not wanted. He was certain that you were as glad to see him as he was to see you. In your own house you might have kicked him downstairs and slammed the door in his face without the suspicion dawning on him that he was not a welcome visitor. He was a good mixer, and in three days knew everyone on board. He ran everything. He managed the sweeps, conducted the auctions, collected money for prizes at the sports, got up quoit and golf matches, organized the concert and arranged the fancy dress ball. He was everywhere and always. He was certainly the best-hated man in the ship. We called him Mr. Know-All, even to his face. He took it as a compliment. But it was at mealtimes that he was most intolerable. For the better part of an hour then he had us at his mercy. He was hearty, jovial, loquacious and argumentative. He knew everything better than anybody else, and it was an affront to his overweening vanity that you should disagree with him. He would not drop a subject, however unimportant, till he had brought you round to his way of thinking. The possibility that he could be mistaken never occurred to him. He was the chap who knew. We sat at the doctor's table. Mr. Kelada would certainly have had it all his own way, for the doctor was lazy and I was frigidly indifferent, except for a man called Ramsay who sat there also. He was as dogmatic as Mr. Kelada and resented bitterly the Levantine's cocksureness. The discussions they had were acrimonious and interminable.

Ramsay was in the American Consular Service, and was stationed at Kobe. He was a great heavy fellow from the Middle West, with loose fat under a tight skin, and he bulged out of his ready-made clothes. He was on his way back to resume his post, having been on a flying visit to New York to fetch his wife, who had been spending a year at home. Mrs. Ramsay was a very pretty little thing, with pleasant manners and a sense of humor. The Consular Service is ill paid, and she was dressed always very simply; but she knew how to wear her clothes. She achieved an effect of quiet distinction. I should not have paid any particular attention to her but that she possessed a quality that may be common enough in women, but nowadays is not obvious in their demeanor. You could not look at her without being struck by her modesty. It shone in her like a flower on a coat.

One evening at dinner the conversation by chance drifted to the subject of pearls. There had been in the papers a good deal of talk about the cultured pearls which the cunning Japanese were making, and the doctor remarked that they must inevitably diminish the value of real ones. They were very good already; they would soon be perfect. Mr. Kelada, as was his habit, rushed the new topic. He told us all that was to be known about pearls. I do not believe Ramsay knew anything about them at all, but he could not resist the opportunity to have a fling at the Levantine, and in five minutes we were in the middle of a heated argument. I had seen Mr. Kelada vehement and voluble before, but never so voluble and vehement as now. At last something that Ramsay said stung him, for he thumped the table and shouted:

"Well, I ought to know what I am talking about. I'm going to Japan just to look into this Japanese pearl business. I'm in the trade and there's not a man in it who won't tell you that what I say about pearls goes. I know all the best pearls in the world, and what I don't know about pearls isn't worth knowing."

Here was news for us, for Mr. Kelada, with all his loquacity, had never told anyone what his business was. We only knew vaguely that he was going to Japan on some commercial errand. He looked round the table triumphantly.

"They'll never be able to get a cultured pearl that an expert like me can't tell with half an eye." He pointed to a necklace that Mrs. Ramsay wore. "You take my word for it, Mrs. Ramsay, that necklace you're wearing will never be worth a cent less than it is now."

Mrs. Ramsay in her modest way flushed a little and slipped the necklace inside her dress. Ramsay leaned forward. He gave us all a look, and a smile flickered in his eyes.

"That's a pretty necklace of Mrs. Ramsay's, isn't it?"

"I noticed it at once," answered Mr. Kelada. "Gee, I said to myself, those are pearls, all right."

"I didn't buy it myself, of course. I'd be interested to know how much you think it cost."

"Oh, in the trade somewhere round fifteen thousand dollars. But if it was bought on Fifth Avenue I shouldn't be surprised to hear that anything up to thirty thousand was paid for it."

Ramsay smiled grimly.

"You'll be surprised to hear that Mrs. Ramsay bought that string at a department store the day before we left New York, for eighteen dollars."

Mr. Kelada flushed.

"Rot. It's not only real, but it's as fine a string for its size as I've ever seen."

"Will you bet on it? I'll bet you a hundred dollars it's imitation."

"Done."

"Oh, Elmer, you can't bet on a certainty," said Mrs. Ramsay. She had a little smile on her lips and her tone was gently deprecating.

"Can't I? If I get a chance of easy money like that I should be all sorts of a fool not to take it."

"But how can it be proved?" she continued. "It's only my word against Mr. Kelada's."

"Let me look at the necklace, and if it's imitation I'll tell you quickly enough. I can afford to lose a hundred dollars," said Mr. Kelada.

"Take it off, dear. Let the gentleman look at it as much as he wants."

Mrs. Ramsay hesitated a moment. She put her hands to the clasp.

"I can't undo it," she said. "Mr. Kelada will just have to take my word for it."

I had a sudden suspicion that something unfortunate was about to occur, but I could think of nothing to say.

Ramsay jumped up. "I'll undo it."

He handed the necklace to Mr. Kelada. The Levantine took a magnifying glass from his pocket and closely examined it. A smile of triumph spread over his smooth and swarthy face. He handed back the necklace. He was about to speak. Suddenly he caught sight of Mrs. Ramsay's face. It was so white that she looked as though she were about to faint. She was staring at him with wide and terrified eyes. They held a desperate appeal; it was so clear that I wondered why her husband did not see it.

Mr. Kelada stopped with his mouth open. He flushed deeply. You could almost *see* the effort he was making over himself.

"I was mistaken," he said. "It's a very good imitation, but of course as soon as I looked through my glass I saw that it wasn't real. I think eighteen dollars is just about as much as the damned thing's worth."

He took out his pocketbook and from it a hundred-dollar note. He handed it to Ramsay without a word.

"Perhaps that'll teach you not to be so cocksure another time, my young friend," said Ramsay as he took the note.

I noticed that Mr. Kelada's hands were trembling.

The story spread over the ship as stories do, and he had to put up with a good deal of chaff that evening. It was a fine joke that Mr. Know-All had been caught out. But Mrs. Ramsay retired to her stateroom with a headache.

Next morning I got up and began to shave. Mr. Kelada lay on his bed smoking a cigarette. Suddenly there was a small scraping sound and I saw a letter pushed under the door. I opened the door and looked out. There was nobody there. I picked up the letter and saw that it was addressed to Max Kelada. The name was written in block letters. I handed it to him.

"Who's this from?" He opened it. "Oh!"

He took out of the envelope, not a letter, but a hundred-dollar note. He looked at me and again he reddened. He tore the envelope into little bits and gave them to me.

"Do you mind just throwing them out of the porthole?"

I did as he asked, and then I looked at him with a smile.

"No one likes being made to look a perfect damned fool," he said.

"Were the pearls real?"

"If I had a pretty little wife I shouldn't let her spend a year in New York while I stayed at Kobe," said he.

At that moment I did not entirely dislike Mr. Kelada. He reached out for his pocketbook and carefully put in it the hundred-dollar note.

VANKA

ANTON CHEKHOV / RUSSIA

А. Чеховъ

Translated by Robert Payne

NINE-YEAR-OLD Vanka Zhukov, who was apprenticed three months ago to the shoemaker Alyakhin, did not go to bed on Christmas Eve. He waited till the master and mistress and the more senior apprentices had gone to the early service, and then he took a bottle of ink and a pen with a rusty nib from his master's cupboard, and began to write on a crumpled sheet of paper spread out in front of him. Before tracing the shape of the first letter, he looked several times fearfully in the direction of the doors and windows, and then he gazed up at the dark icon, flanked on either side by shelves filled with cobbler's lasts, and then he heaved a broken sigh. With the paper spread over the bench, Vanka knelt on the floor beside it.

"Dear Grandfather Konstantin Makarich," he wrote. "I am writing a letter to you. I wish you a Merry Christmas and all good things from the Lord God. I have no father and mother, and you are all I have left."

Vanka raised his eyes to the dark windowpane, on which there gleamed the reflection of a candle flame, and in his vivid imagination he saw his grandfather Konstantin Makarich standing there. His grandfather was a night watchman on the estate of some gentlefolk called Zhivaryov, a small, thin, unusually lively and nimble old man of about sixty-five, his face always crinkling with laughter, and his eyes bleary from drink. In the daytime the old man slept in the servants' kitchen or cracked jokes with the cooks. At night, wrapped in an ample sheepskin coat, he made the rounds of the estate, shaking his clapper. Two dogs followed him with drooping heads—one was the old bitch Brownie, the other was called Eel because of his black coat and long weaselly body. Eel always seemed to be extraordinarily respectful and endearing, gazing with the same fond eyes on friends and strangers alike; yet no one trusted him. His deference and humility concealed a most jesuitical malice. No one knew better how to creep stealthily behind someone and take a nip at his leg, or how to crawl into the icehouse, or how to scamper off with a peasant's chicken. More than once they just about broke his hind legs, twice a noose was put round his neck, and every week he was beaten until he was only half alive, yet he always managed to survive.

At this very moment Grandfather was probably standing by the gates, screwing up his eyes at the bright red windows of the village church, stamping about in his felt boots and cracking jokes with the servants. His clapper hung from his belt. He would be throwing out his arms and then hugging himself against the cold, and, hiccupping as old men do, he would be pinching one of the servant girls or one of the cooks.

"What about a pinch of snuff, eh?" he would say, holding out his snuffbox to the women.

Then the women would take a pinch and sneeze, and the old man would be overcome with indescribable ecstasies, laughing joyously and exclaiming: "Fine for frozen noses, eh!"

The dogs, too, were given snuff. Brownie would sneeze, shake her head, and walk away looking offended, while Eel, too polite to sneeze, only wagged his tail. The weather was glorious. The air was still, transparently clear, and fresh. The night was very dark, but the whole white-roofed village with its snowdrifts and trees silvered with hoar-frost and smoke streaming from the chimneys could be seen clearly. The heavens were sprinkled with gay, glinting stars, and the Milky Way stood out as clearly as if it had been washed and scrubbed with snow for the holidays.

Vanka sighed, dipped his pen in the ink, and went on writing: "Yesterday I was given a thrashing. The master dragged me by the hair into the yard and gave me a beating with a stirrup strap because when I was rocking the baby in the cradle, I misfortunately fell asleep. And then last week the mistress ordered me to gut a herring, and because I began with the tail, she took the head of the herring and rubbed it all over my face. The other apprentices made fun of me, sent me to the tavern for vodka, and made me steal the master's cucumbers for them, and then the master beat me with the first thing that came to hand. And there's nothing to eat. In the morning they give me bread, there is porridge for dinner, and in the evening only bread again. They never give me tea or cabbage soup—they gobble it all up themselves. They make me sleep in the passageway, and when their baby cries, I don't get any sleep at all because I have to rock the cradle. Dear Grandfather, please for God's sake take me away from here, take me to the village, it's more than I can bear. . . . I kneel down before you. I'll pray to God to keep you forever, but take me away from here, or I shall die."

Vanka grimaced, rubbed his eyes with his black fists, and sobbed.

"I'll grind your snuff for you," he went on. "I will pray to God to keep you, and if I ever do anything wrong, you can flog me all you like. If you think there's no place for me, then I'll ask the manager for Christ's sake to let me clean boots or take Fedya's place as a shepherd boy. Dear Grandfather, it's more than I can bear, it will be the death of me. I thought of running away to the village, but I haven't any boots, and I am afraid of the ice. If you'll do this for me, I'll feed you when I grow up, and won't let anyone harm you, and when you die, I'll pray for the repose of your soul, just like I do for my mother, Pelageya.

"Moscow is such a big city. There are so many houses belonging to the gentry, so many horses, but no sheep anywhere, and the dogs aren't vicious. The boys don't go about with the Star of Christmas, and they don't let you sing in the choir, and once I saw fishhooks in the shopwindow with the fishing lines for every kind of fish, very fine ones, even one hook which would hold a skate fish weighing forty pounds. I've seen shops selling guns which are just like the master's at home, and each one must cost a hundred rubles. In the butcher shops they have woodcocks and partridges and hares, but the people in the shop won't tell you where they were shot.

"Dear Grandfather, when they put up the Christmas tree at the big house, please take down a golden walnut for me and hide it in the green chest. Ask the young mistress, Olga Ignatyevna, and say it is for Vanka."

Vanka heaved a convulsive sigh, and once more he gazed in the direction of the window. He remembered it was Grandfather who always went to the forest to cut down a Christmas tree for the gentry, taking his grandson with him. They had a wonderful time together. Grandfather chuckled, the frost crackled, and Vanka, not to be outdone, clucked away cheerfully. Before chopping down the fir tree, Grandfather would smoke a pipe, take a long pinch of snuff, and make fun of Vanka, who was shivering in the cold. The young fir trees, garlanded with hoarfrost, stood perfectly still, waiting to see which of them would die. . . . Suddenly out of nowhere a hare came springing across the snowdrifts, quick as an arrow, and Grandfather would be unable to prevent himself from shouting: "Hold him! Hold him! Hold that bobtailed devil, eh!"

When the tree had been chopped down, Grandfather would drag it to the big house and they would start decorating it. The young mistress, Olga Ignatyevna, Vanka's favorite, was the busiest of all. While Vanka's mother, Pelageya, was alive, serving as a chambermaid, Olga Ignatyevna used to stuff him with sugar candy, and it amused her to teach him to read and write, to count up to a hundred, and even to dance the quadrille. But when Pelageya died, they relegated the orphan Vanka to the servants' kitchen to be with his grandfather, and from there he went to Moscow to the shoemaker Alyakhin. . . .

"Come to me, dear Grandfather," Vanka went on. "I beseech you for Christ's sake, take me away from here! Have pity on me, a poor orphan, they are always beating me, and I am terribly hungry, and so miserable I can't tell you, and I'm always crying. The other day the master hit me on the head with a last, and I fell down and thought I would never get up again. It's worse than a dog's life, and so miserable. I send greetings to Alyona, to one-eyed Yegor, and to the coachman, and don't give my harmonica away. I remain your grandson Ivan Zhukov, dear Grandfather, and come soon!"

Vanka twice folded the sheet of paper and then he put it in an envelope bought the previous day for a kopeck. He reflected for a while, dipped the pen in ink, and wrote the address: *To Grandfather in the Village.* Then he scratched his head and thought for a while, and added the words: *Konstantin Makarich.* Pleased because no one interrupted him when he was writing, he threw on his cap, and without troubling to put on a coat, he ran out into the street in his shirt sleeves.

When he talked to the clerks in the butcher shop the previous day, they told him that letters were dropped in boxes, and from these boxes they were carried all over the world on mail coaches drawn by three horses and driven by drunken drivers, while the bells jingled Vanka ran to the nearest mailbox and thrust his precious letter into the slot.

An hour later, lulled by sweetest hopes, he was fast asleep. He dreamed of a stove. His grandfather was sitting on the stove, bare feet dangling down, while he read the letter aloud to the cooks. Eel was walking round the stove, wagging his tail.

THE HAPPY PRINCE
OSCAR WILDE / IRELAND

HIGH ABOVE the city, on a tall column, stood the statue of the Happy Prince. He was gilded all over with thin leaves of fine gold, for eyes he had two bright sapphires, and a large red ruby glowed on his sword hilt.

He was very much admired indeed. "He is as beautiful as a weathercock," remarked one of the Town Councillors who wished to gain a reputation for having artistic tastes; "only not quite so useful," he added, fearing lest people should think him unpractical, which he really was not.

"Why can't you be like the Happy Prince?" asked a sensible mother of her little boy who was crying for the moon. "The Happy Prince never dreams of crying for anything."

"I am glad there is someone in the world who is quite happy," muttered a disappointed man as he gazed at the wonderful statue.

"He looks just like an angel," said the Charity Children as they came out of the cathedral in their bright scarlet cloaks and their clean white pinafores.

"How do you know?" said the Mathematical Master. "You have never seen one."

"Ah! but we have, in our dreams," answered the children; and the Mathematical Master frowned and looked very severe, for he did not approve of children dreaming.

One night there flew over the city a little Swallow. His friends had gone away to Egypt six weeks before, but he had stayed behind, for he was in love with the most beautiful Reed. He had met her early in the spring as he was flying down the river after a big yellow moth, and had been so attracted by her slender waist that he had stopped to talk to her.

"Shall I love you?" said the Swallow, who liked to come to the point at once, and the Reed made him a low bow. So he flew round and round her, touching the water with his wings, and making silver ripples. This was his courtship, and it lasted all through the summer.

"It is a ridiculous attachment," twittered the other Swallows; "she has no money, and far too many relations"; and indeed the river was quite full of Reeds. Then, when the autumn came they all flew away.

After they had gone he felt lonely, and began to tire of his ladylove. "She has no conversation," he said, "and I am afraid that she is a coquette, for she is always flirting with the wind." And certainly, whenever the wind blew, the Reed made the most graceful curtsies. "I admit that she is domestic," he continued, "but I love traveling, and my wife, consequently, should love traveling also."

"Will you come away with me?" he said finally to her, but the Reed shook her head, she was so attached to her home.

"You have been trifling with me," he cried. "I am off to the Pyramids. Good-by!" and he flew away.

All day long he flew, and at nighttime he arrived at the city.

"Where shall I put up?" he said; "I hope the town has made preparations."

Then he saw the statue on the tall column.

"I will put up there," he cried; "it is a fine position, with plenty of fresh air." So he alighted just between the feet of the Happy Prince.

"I have a golden bedroom," he said softly to himself as he looked round, and he prepared to go to sleep; but just as he was putting his head under his wing a large drop of water fell on him. "What a curious thing!" he cried; "there is not a single cloud in the sky, the stars are quite clear and bright, and yet it is raining. The climate in the north of Europe is really dreadful. The Reed used to like the rain, but that was merely her selfishness."

Then another drop fell.

"What is the use of a statue if it cannot keep the rain off?" he said; "I must look for a good chimney pot," and he determined to fly away.

But before he had opened his wings, a third drop fell, and he looked up, and saw—Ah! what did he see?

The eyes of the Happy Prince were filled with tears, and tears were running down his golden cheeks. His face was so beautiful in the moonlight that the little Swallow was filled with pity.

"Who are you?" he said.

"I am the Happy Prince."

"Why are you weeping then?" asked the Swallow; "you have quite drenched me."

"When I was alive and had a human heart," answered the statue, "I did not know what tears were, for I lived in the Palace of Sans-Souci, where sorrow is not allowed to enter. In the daytime I played with my companions in the garden, and in the evening I led the dance in the Great Hall. Round the garden ran a very lofty wall, but I never cared to ask what lay beyond it, everything about me was so beautiful. My courtiers called me the Happy Prince, and happy indeed I was, if pleasure be happiness. So I lived, and so I died. And now that I am dead they have set me up here so high that I can see all the ugliness and all the misery of my city, and though my heart is made of lead yet I cannot choose but weep."

"What! is he not solid gold?" said the Swallow to himself. He was too polite to make any personal remarks out loud.

"Far away," continued the statue in a low musical voice, "far away in a little street there is a poor house. One of the windows is open, and through it I can see a woman seated at a table. Her face is thin and worn, and she has coarse, red hands, all pricked by the needle, for she is a seamstress. She is embroidering passionflowers on a satin gown for the loveliest of the Queen's maids of honor to wear at the next Court ball. In a bed in the corner of the room her little boy is lying ill. He has a fever, and is asking for oranges. His mother has nothing to give him but river water, so he is crying. Swallow, Swallow, little Swallow, will you not bring her the ruby out of my sword hilt? My feet are fastened to this pedestal and I cannot move."

"I am waited for in Egypt," said the Swallow. "My friends are flying up and down the Nile, and talking to the large lotus flowers. Soon they will go to sleep in the tomb of the great King. The King is there himself in his painted coffin. He is wrapped in yellow linen, and embalmed with spices. Round his neck is a chain of pale green jade, and his hands are like withered leaves."

"Swallow, Swallow, little Swallow," said the Prince, "will you not stay with me for one night, and be my messenger? The boy is so thirsty, and the mother so sad."

"I don't think I like boys," answered the Swallow. "Last summer, when I was staying on the river, there were two rude boys, the miller's sons, who were always throwing stones at me. They never hit me, of course; we swallows fly far too well for that, and besides, I come of a family famous for its agility; but still, it was a mark of disrespect."

But the Happy Prince looked so sad that the little Swallow was sorry. "It is very cold here," he said; "but I will stay with you for one night, and be your messenger."

"Thank you, little Swallow," said the Prince.

So the Swallow picked out the great ruby from the Prince's sword, and flew away with it in his beak over the roofs of the town.

He passed by the cathedral tower, where the white marble angels were sculptured. He passed by the palace and heard the sound of dancing. A beautiful girl came out on the balcony with her lover.

"How wonderful the stars are," he said to her, "and how wonderful is the power of love!"

"I hope my dress will be ready in time for the State ball," she answered; "I have ordered passionflowers to be embroidered on it: but the seamstresses are so lazy."

He passed over the river, and saw the lanterns hanging to the masts of the ships. He passed over the Ghetto, and saw the old Jews bargaining with each other, and weighing out money in copper scales. At last he came to the poor house and looked in. The boy was tossing feverishly on his bed, and the mother had fallen asleep, she was so tired. In he hopped, and laid the great ruby on the table beside the woman's thimble. Then he flew gently round the bed, fanning the boy's forehead with his wings. "How cool I feel!" said the boy, "I must be getting better"; and he sank into a delicious slumber.

Then the Swallow flew back to the Happy Prince, and told him what he had done. "It is curious," he remarked, "but I feel quite warm now, although it is so cold."

"That is because you have done a good action," said the Prince. And the little Swallow began to think, and then he fell asleep. Thinking always made him sleepy.

When day broke he flew down to the river and had a bath. "What a remarkable phenomenon!" said the Professor of Ornithology as he was passing over the bridge. "A swallow in winter!" And he wrote a long letter about it to the local newspaper. Everyone quoted it, it was full of so many words that they could not understand.

"Tonight I go to Egypt," said the Swallow, and he was in high spirits at the prospect. He visited all the public monuments, and sat a long time on top of the church steeple. Wherever he went the Sparrows chirruped, and said to each other, "What a distinguished stranger!" so he enjoyed himself very much.

When the moon rose he flew back to the Happy Prince. "Have you any commissions for Egypt?" he cried; "I am just starting."

"Swallow, Swallow, little Swallow," said the Prince, "will you not stay with me one night longer?"

"I am waited for in Egypt," answered the Swallow. "Tomorrow my friends will fly up to the Second Cataract. The river horse couches there among the bulrushes, and on a great granite throne sits the God Memnon. All night long he watches the stars, and when the morning star shines he utters one cry of joy, and then he is silent. At noon the yellow lions come down to the water's edge to drink. They have eyes like green beryls, and their roar is louder than the roar of the cataract."

"Swallow, Swallow, little Swallow," said the Prince, "far away across the city I see a young man in a garret. He is leaning over a desk covered with papers, and in a tumbler by his side there is a bunch of withered violets. His hair is brown and crisp, and his lips are red as a pomegranate, and he has large and dreamy eyes. He is trying to finish a play for the Director of the Theatre, but he is too cold to write anymore. There is no fire in the grate, and hunger has made him faint."

"I will wait with you one night longer," said the Swallow, who really had a good heart. "Shall I take him another ruby?"

"Alas! I have no ruby now," said the Prince: "my eyes are all that I have left. They are made of rare sapphires, which were brought out of India a thousand years ago. Pluck out one of them and take it to him. He will sell it to the jeweler, and buy firewood, and finish his play."

"Dear Prince," said the Swallow, "I cannot do that"; and he began to weep.

"Swallow, Swallow, little Swallow," said the Prince, "do as I command you."

So the Swallow plucked out the Prince's eye, and flew away to the student's garret. It was easy enough to get in, as there was a hole in the roof. Through this he darted, and came into the room. The young man had his head buried in his hands, so he did not hear the flutter of the bird's wings, and when he looked up he found the beautiful sapphire lying on the withered violets.

"I am beginning to be appreciated," he cried; "this is from some great admirer. Now I can finish my play," and he looked quite happy.

The next day the Swallow flew down to the harbor. He sat on the mast of a large vessel and watched the sailors hauling big chests out of the hold with ropes. "Heave ahoy!" they shouted as each chest came up. "I am going to Egypt!" cried the Swallow, but nobody minded, and when the moon rose he flew back to the Happy Prince.

"I am come to bid you good-by," he cried.

"Swallow, Swallow, little Swallow," said the Prince, "will you not stay with me one night longer?"

"It is winter," answered the Swallow, "and the chill snow will soon be here. In Egypt the sun is warm on the green palm trees, and the crocodiles lie in the mud and look lazily about them. My companions are building a nest in the Temple of Baalbec, and the pink and white doves are watching them, and cooing to each other. Dear Prince, I must leave you, but I will never forget you, and next spring I will bring you back two beautiful jewels in place of those you have given away. The ruby shall be redder than a red rose, and the sapphire shall be as blue as the great sea."

"In the square below," said the Happy Prince, "there stands a little match girl. She has let her matches fall in the gutter, and they are all spoiled. Her father will beat her if she does not bring home some money, and she is crying. She has no shoes or stockings, and her little head is bare. Pluck out my other eye, and give it to her, and her father will not beat her."

"I will stay with you one night longer," said the Swallow, "but I cannot pluck out your eye. You would be quite blind then."

"Swallow, Swallow, little Swallow," said the Prince, "do as I command you."

So he plucked out the Prince's other eye, and darted down with it. He swooped past the match girl, and slipped the jewel into the palm of her hand. "What a lovely bit of glass!" cried the little girl; and she ran home, laughing.

Then the Swallow came back to the Prince. "You are blind now," he said, "so I will stay with you always."

"No, little Swallow," said the poor Prince, "you must go away to Egypt."

"I will stay with you always," said the Swallow, and he slept at the Prince's feet.

All the next day he sat on the Prince's shoulder, and told him stories of what he had seen in strange lands. He told him of the red ibises, who stand in long rows on the banks of the Nile, and catch goldfish in their beaks; of the Sphinx, who is as old as the world itself, and lives in the desert, and knows everything; of the merchants, who walk slowly by the side of their camels and carry amber beads in their hands; of the King of the Mountains of the Moon, who is as black as ebony, and worships a large crystal; of the great green snake that sleeps in a palm tree, and has twenty priests to feed it with honey cakes; and of the pygmies who sail over a big lake on large flat leaves, and are always at war with the butterflies.

"Dear little Swallow," said the Prince, "you tell me of marvelous things, but more marvelous than anything is the suffering of men and of women. There is no Mystery so great as Misery. Fly over my city, little Swallow, and tell me what you see there."

So the Swallow flew over the great city, and saw the rich making merry in their beautiful houses, while the beggars were sitting at the gates. He flew into dark lanes, and saw the white faces of starving children looking out listlessly at the black streets. Under the archway of a bridge two little boys were lying in one another's arms to try and keep themselves warm. "How hungry we are!" they said. "You must not lie here," shouted the watchman, and they wandered out into the rain.

Then he flew back and told the Prince what he had seen.

"I am covered with fine gold," said the Prince, "you must take it off, leaf by leaf, and give it to my poor; the living always think that gold can make them happy."

Leaf after leaf of the fine gold the Swallow picked off, till the Happy Prince looked quite dull and gray. Leaf after leaf of the fine gold he brought to the poor, and the children's faces grew rosier, and they laughed and played in the street. "We have bread now!" they cried.

Then the snow came, and after the snow came the frost. The streets looked as if they were made of silver, they were so bright and glistening; long icicles like crystal daggers hung down from the eaves of the houses, everybody went about in furs, and the little boys wore scarlet caps and skated on the ice.

The poor little Swallow grew colder and colder, but he would not leave the Prince, he loved him too well. He picked up crumbs outside the baker's door when the baker was not looking, and tried to keep himself warm by flapping his wings.

But at last he knew that he was going to die. He had just enough strength to fly up to the Prince's shoulder once more. "Good-by, dear Prince!" he murmured, "will you let me kiss your hand?"

"I am glad that you are going to Egypt at last, little Swallow," said the Prince, "you have stayed too long here; but you must kiss me on the lips, for I love you."

"It is not to Egypt that I am going," said the Swallow. "I am going to the House of Death. Death is the brother of Sleep, is he not?"

And he kissed the Happy Prince on the lips, and fell down dead at his feet.

At that moment a curious crack sounded inside the statue, as if something had broken. The fact is that the leaden heart had snapped right in two. It certainly was a dreadfully hard frost.

Early the next morning the Mayor was walking in the square below in company with the Town Councillors. As they passed the column he looked up at the statue: "Dear me! how shabby the Happy Prince looks!" he said.

"How shabby, indeed!" cried the Town Councillors, who always agreed with the Mayor: and they went up to look at it.

"The ruby has fallen out of his sword, his eyes are gone, and he is golden no longer," said the Mayor; "in fact, he is little better than a beggar!"

"Little better than a beggar," said the Town Councillors.

"And here is actually a dead bird at his feet!" continued the Mayor. "We must really issue a proclamation that birds are not to be allowed to die here." And the Town Clerk made a note of the suggestion.

So they pulled down the statue of the Happy Prince. "As he is no longer beautiful he is no longer useful," said the Art Professor at the University.

Then they melted the statue in a furnace, and the Mayor held a meeting of the Corporation to decide what was to be done with the metal. "We must have another statue, of course," he said, "and it shall be a statue of myself."

"Of myself," said each of the Town Councillors, and they quarreled. When I last heard of them they were quarreling still.

"What a strange thing!" said the overseer of the workmen at the foundry. "This broken lead heart will not melt in the furnace. We must throw it away." So they threw it on a dustheap where the dead Swallow was also lying.

"Bring me the two most precious things in the city," said God to one of His Angels; and the Angel brought Him the leaden heart and the dead bird.

"You have rightly chosen," said God, "for in my garden of Paradise this little bird shall sing forevermore, and in my city of gold the Happy Prince shall praise me."

THE OLD DEMON
PEARL S. BUCK / UNITED STATES

Pearl S. Buch

OLD MRS. WANG knew of course that there was a war. Everybody had known for a long time that there was war going on and that Japanese were killing Chinese. But still it was not real and no more than hearsay since none of the Wangs had been killed. The Village of Three Mile Wangs on the flat banks of the Yellow River, which was old Mrs. Wang's clan village, had never even seen a Japanese. This was how they came to be talking about Japanese at all.

It was evening and early summer, and after her supper Mrs. Wang had climbed the dike steps, as she did every day, to see how high the river had risen. She was much more afraid of the river than of the Japanese. She knew what the river would do. And one by one the villagers had followed her up the dike, and now they stood staring down at the malicious yellow water, curling along like a lot of snakes, and biting at the high dike banks. "I never saw it as high as this so early," Mrs. Wang said. She sat down on a bamboo stool that her grandson, Little Pig, had brought for her, and spat into the water.

"It's worse than the Japanese, this old devil of a river," Little Pig said recklessly.

"Fool!" Mrs. Wang said quickly. "The river god will hear you. Talk about something else."

So they had gone on talking about the Japanese. . . . How, for instance, asked Wang, the baker, who was old Mrs. Wang's nephew twice removed, would they know the Japanese when they saw them?

Mrs. Wang at this point said positively, "You'll know them. I once saw a foreigner. He was taller than the eaves of my house and he had mud-colored hair and eyes the color of a fish's eyes. Anyone who does not look like us—that is a Japanese."

Everybody listened to her since she was the oldest woman in the village and whatever she said settled something.

Then Little Pig spoke up in his disconcerting way. "You can't see them, Grandmother. They hide up in the sky in airplanes."

Mrs. Wang did not answer immediately. Once she would have said positively, "I shall not believe in an airplane until I see it." But so many things had been true which she had not believed—the Empress, for instance, whom she had not believed dead, was dead. The Republic, again, she had not believed in because she did not know what it was. She still did not know, but they had said for a long time there had been one. So now she merely stared quietly about the dike where they all sat around her. It was very pleasant and cool, and she felt nothing mattered if the river did not rise to flood.

"I don't believe in the Japanese," she said flatly. They laughed at her a little, but no one spoke. Someone lit her pipe—it was Little Pig's wife, who was her favorite, and she smoked it.

"Sing, Little Pig!" someone called.

So Little Pig began to sing an old song in a high, quavering voice, and old Mrs. Wang listened and forgot the Japanese. The evening was beautiful, the sky so clear and still that the willows overhanging the dike were reflected even in the muddy water. Everything was at peace. The thirty-odd houses which made up the village straggled along beneath them. Nothing could break this peace. After all, the Japanese were only human beings.

"I doubt those airplanes," she said mildly to Little Pig when he stopped singing.

But without answering her, he went on to another song.

Year in and year out she had spent the summer evenings like this on the dike. The first time she was seventeen and a bride, and her husband had shouted to her to come out of the house and up the dike, and she had come, blushing and twisting her hands together, to hide among the women while the men roared at her and made jokes about her. All the same, they had liked her. "A pretty piece of meat in your bowl," they had said to her husband. "Feet a trifle big," he had answered deprecatingly. But she could see he was pleased, and so gradually her shyness went away.

He, poor man, had been drowned in a flood when he was still young. And it had taken her years to get him prayed out of Buddhist purgatory. Finally she had grown tired of it, what with the child and the land all on her back, and so when the priest said coaxingly, "Another ten pieces of silver and he'll be out entirely," she asked, "What's he got in there yet?"

"Only his right hand," the priest said, encouraging her.

Well, then, her patience broke. Ten dollars! It would feed them for the winter. Besides, she had had to hire labor for her share of repairing the dike, too, so there would be no more floods.

"If it's only one hand, he can pull himself out," she said firmly.

She often wondered if he had, poor silly fellow. As like as not, she had often thought gloomily in the night, he was still lying there, waiting for her to do something about it. That was the sort of man he was. Well, some day, perhaps, when Little Pig's wife had had the first baby safely and she had a little extra, she might go back to finish him out of purgatory. There was no real hurry, though. . . .

"Grandmother, you must go in," Little Pig's wife's soft voice said. "There is a mist rising from the river now that the sun is gone."

"Yes, I suppose I must," old Mrs. Wang agreed. She gazed at the river a moment. That river—it was full of good and evil together. It would water the fields when it was curbed and checked, but then if an inch were allowed it, it crashed through like a roaring dragon. That was how her husband had been swept away—careless, he was, about his bit of the dike. He was always going to mend it, always going to pile more earth on top of it, and then in a night the river rose and broke through. He had run out of the house, and she had climbed on the roof with the child and had saved herself and it while he was drowned. Well, they had pushed the river back again behind its dikes, and it had stayed there this time. Every day she herself walked up and down the length of the dike for which the village was responsible and examined it. The men laughed and said, "If anything is wrong with the dikes, Granny will tell us."

It had never occurred to any of them to move the village away from the river. The Wangs had lived there for generations, and some had always escaped the floods and had fought the river more fiercely than ever afterward.

Little Pig suddenly stopped singing.

"The moon is coming up!" he cried. "That's not good. Airplanes come out on moonlight nights."

"Where do you learn all this about airplanes?" old Mrs. Wang exclaimed. "It is tiresome to me," she added, so severely that no one spoke. In this silence, leaning upon the arm of Little Pig's wife, she descended slowly the earthen steps which led down into the village, using her long pipe in the other hand as a walking stick. Behind her the villagers came down, one by one, to bed. No one moved before she did, but none stayed long after her.

And in her own bed at last, behind the blue cotton mosquito curtains which Little Pig's wife fastened securely, she fell peacefully asleep. She had lain awake a little while thinking about the Japanese and wondering why they wanted to fight. Only very coarse persons wanted wars. In her mind she saw large coarse persons. If they came one must wheedle them, she thought, invite them to drink tea, and explain to them, reasonably—only why should they come to a peaceful farming village . . . ?

So she was not in the least prepared for Little Pig's wife screaming at her that the Japanese had come. She sat up in bed muttering, "The teabowls—the tea—"

"Grandmother, there's no time!" Little Pig's wife screamed. "They're here—they're here!"

"Where?" old Mrs. Wang cried, now awake.

"In the sky!" Little Pig's wife wailed.

They had all run out at that, into the clear early dawn, and gazed up. There, like wild geese flying in autumn, were great birdlike shapes.

"But what are they?" old Mrs. Wang cried.

And then, like a silver egg dropping, something drifted straight down and fell at the far end of the village in a field. A fountain of earth flew up, and they all ran to see it. There was a hole thirty feet across, as big as a pond. They were so astonished they could not speak, and then, before anyone could say anything, another and another egg began to fall and everybody was running, running. . . .

Everybody, that is, but Mrs. Wang. When Little Pig's wife seized her hand to drag her along, old Mrs. Wang pulled away and sat down against the bank of the dike.

"I can't run," she remarked. "I haven't run in seventy years, since before my feet were bound. You go on. Where's Little Pig?" She looked around. Little Pig was already gone. "Like his grandfather," she remarked, "always the first to run."

But Little Pig's wife would not leave her, not, that is, until old Mrs. Wang reminded her that it was her duty.

"If Little Pig is dead," she said, "then it is necessary that his son be born alive." And when the girl still hesitated, she struck at her gently with her pipe. "Go on—go on," she exclaimed.

So unwillingly, because now they could scarcely hear each other speak for the roar of the dipping planes, Little Pig's wife went on with the others.

By now, although only a few minutes had passed, the village was in ruins and the straw roofs and wooden beams were blazing. Everybody was gone. As they passed they had shrieked at old Mrs. Wang to come on, and she had called back pleasantly:

"I'm coming—I'm coming!"

But she did not go. She sat quite alone watching now what was an extraordinary spectacle. For soon other planes came, from where she did not know, but they attacked the first ones. The sun came up over the fields of ripening wheat, and in the clear summery air the planes wheeled and darted and spat at each other. When this was over, she thought, she would go back into the village and see if anything was left. Here and there a wall stood, supporting a roof. She could not see her own house from here. But she was not unused to war. Once bandits had looted their village, and houses had been burned then, too. Well, now it had happened again. Burning houses one could see often, but not this darting silvery shining battle in the air. She understood none of it—not what those things were, nor how they stayed up in the sky. She simply sat, growing hungry, and watching.

"I'd like to see one close," she said aloud. And at that moment, as though in answer, one of them pointed suddenly downward, and, wheeling and twisting as though it were wounded, it fell head down in a field which Little Pig had plowed only yesterday for soybeans. And in an instant the sky was empty again, and there was only this wounded thing on the ground and herself.

She hoisted herself carefully from the earth. At her age she need be afraid of nothing. She could, she decided, go and see what it was. So, leaning on her bamboo pipe, she made her way slowly across the fields. Behind her in the sudden stillness two or three village dogs appeared and followed, creeping close to her in their terror. When they drew near to the fallen plane, they barked furiously. Then she hit them with her pipe.

"Be quiet," she scolded, "there's already been noise enough to split my ears!"

She tapped the airplane.

"Metal," she told the dogs. "Silver, doubtless," she added. Melted up, it would make them all rich.

She walked around it, examining it closely. What made it fly? It seemed dead. Nothing moved or made a sound within it. Then, coming to the side to which it tipped, she saw a young man in it, slumped into a heap in a little seat. The dogs growled, but she struck at them again and they fell back.

"Are you dead?" she inquired politely.

The young man moved a little at her voice, but did not speak.

She drew nearer and peered into the hole in which he sat. His side was bleeding.

"Wounded!" she exclaimed. She took his wrist. It was warm, but inert, and when she let it go, it dropped against the side of the hole. She stared at him. He had black hair and a dark skin like a Chinese and still he did not look like a Chinese.

He must be a Southerner, she thought. Well, the chief thing was, he was alive.

"You had better come out," she remarked. "I'll put some herb plaster on your side."

The young man muttered something dully.

"What did you say?" she asked. But he did not say it again.

I am still quite strong, she decided after a moment. So she reached in and seized him about the waist and pulled him out slowly, panting a good deal. Fortunately he was rather a little fellow and very light. When she had him on the ground, he seemed to find his feet; and he stood shakily and clung to her, and she held him up.

"Now if you can walk to my house," she said, "I'll see if it is there."

Then he said something, quite clearly. She listened and could not understand a word of it. She pulled away from him and stared.

"What's that?" she asked.

He pointed at the dogs. They were standing growling, their ruffs up. Then he spoke again, and as he spoke he crumpled to the ground. The dogs fell on him, so that she had to beat them off with her hands.

"Get away!" she shouted. "Who told *you* to kill him?"

And then, when they had slunk back, she heaved him somehow onto her back; and, trembling, half carrying, half pulling him, she dragged him to the ruined village and laid him in the street while she went to find her house, taking the dogs with her.

Her house was quite gone. She found the place easily enough. This was where it should be, opposite the water gate into the dike. She had always watched that gate herself. Miraculously it was not injured now, nor was the dike broken. It would be easy enough to rebuild the house. Only, for the present, it was gone.

So she went back to the young man. He was lying as she had left him, propped against the dike, panting and very pale. He had opened his coat and he had a little bag from which he was taking out strips of cloth and a bottle of something. And again he spoke, and again she understood nothing. Then he made signs and she saw it was water he wanted, so she took up a broken pot from one of many blown about the street, and, going up the dike, she filled it with river water and brought it down again and washed his wound, and she tore off the strips he made from the rolls of bandaging. He knew how to put the cloth over the gaping wound and he made signs to her, and she followed these signs. All the time he was trying to tell her something, but she could understand nothing.

"You must be from the south, sir," she said. It was easy to see that he had education. He looked very clever. "I have heard your language is different from ours." She laughed a little to put him at his ease, but he only stared at her somberly with dull eyes. So she said brightly, "Now if I could find something for us to eat, it would be nice."

He did not answer. Indeed he lay back, panting still more heavily, and stared into space as though she had not spoken.

"You would be better with food," she went on. "And so would I," she added. She was beginning to feel unbearably hungry.

It occurred to her that in Wang, the baker's, shop there might be some bread. Even if it were dusty with fallen mortar, it would still be bread. She would go and see. But before she went she moved the soldier a little so that he lay in the edge of shadow cast by a willow tree that grew in the bank of the dike. Then she went to the baker's shop. The dogs were gone.

The baker's shop was, like everything else, in ruins. No one was there. At first she saw nothing but the mass of crumpled earthen walls. But then she remembered that the oven was just inside the door, and the doorframe still stood erect, supporting one end of the roof. She stood in this frame, and, running her hand in underneath the fallen roof inside, she felt the wooden cover of the iron caldron. Under this there might be steamed bread. She worked her arm delicately and carefully in. It took quite a long time, but, even so, clouds of lime and dust almost choked her. Nevertheless she was right. She squeezed her hand under the cover and felt the firm smooth skin of the big steamed bread rolls, and one by one she drew out four.

"It's hard to kill an old thing like me," she remarked cheerfully to no one, and she began to eat one of the rolls as she walked back. If she had a bit of garlic and a bowl of tea—but one couldn't have everything in these times.

It was at this moment that she heard voices. When she came in sight of the soldier, she saw surrounding him a crowd of other soldiers, who had apparently come from nowhere. They were staring down at the wounded soldier, whose eyes were now closed.

"Where did you get this Japanese, Old Mother?" they shouted.

"What Japanese?" she asked, coming to them.

"This one!" they shouted.

"Is he a Japanese?" she cried in the greatest astonishment. "But he looks like us—his eyes are black, his skin—"

"Japanese!" one of them shouted at her.

"Well," she said quietly, "he dropped out of the sky."

"Give me that bread!" another shouted.

"Take it," she said, "all except this one for him."

"A Japanese monkey eat good bread?" the soldier shouted.

"I suppose he is hungry also," old Mrs. Wang replied. She began to dislike these men. But then, she had always disliked soldiers.

"I wish you would go away," she said. "What are you doing here? Our village has always been peaceful."

"It certainly looks very peaceful now," one of the men said, grinning, "as peaceful as a grave. Do you know who did that, Old Mother? The Japanese!"

"I suppose so," she agreed. Then she asked, "Why? That's what I don't understand."

"Why? Because they want our land, that's why!"

"Our land!" she repeated. "Why, they can't have our land!"

"Never!" they shouted.

But all this time while they were talking and chewing the bread they had divided among themselves, they were watching the eastern horizon.

"Why do you keep looking east?" old Mrs. Wang now asked.

"The Japanese are coming from there," the man replied who had taken the bread.

"Are you running away from them?" she asked, surprised.

"There are only a handful of us," he said apologetically.

"We were left to guard a village—Pao An, in the county of—"

"I know that village," old Mrs. Wang interrupted. "You needn't tell me. I was a girl there. How is the old Pao who keeps the tea shop in the main street? He's my brother."

"Everybody is dead there," the man replied. "The Japanese have taken it—a great army of men came with their foreign guns and tanks, so what could we do?"

"Of course, only run," she agreed. Nevertheless she felt dazed and sick. So he was dead, that one brother she had left! She was now the last of her father's family.

But the soldiers were straggling away again leaving her alone.

"They'll be coming, those little black dwarfs," they were saying. "We'd best go on."

Nevertheless, one lingered a moment, the one who had taken the bread, to stare down at the young wounded man, who lay with his eyes shut, not having moved at all.

"Is he dead?" he inquired. Then, before Mrs. Wang could answer, he pulled a short knife out of his belt. "Dead or not, I'll give him a punch or two with this—"

But old Mrs. Wang pushed his arm away.

"No, you won't," she said with authority. "If he is dead, then there is no use in sending him into purgatory all in pieces. I am a good Buddhist myself."

The man laughed. "Oh well, he is dead," he answered; and then, seeing his comrades already at a distance, he ran after them.

A Japanese, was he? Old Mrs. Wang, left alone with this inert figure, looked at him tentatively. He was very young, she could see, now that his eyes were closed. His hand, limp in unconsciousness, looked like a boy's hand, unformed and still growing. She felt his wrist but could discern no pulse. She leaned over him and held to his lips the half of her roll which she had not eaten.

"Eat," she said very loudly and distinctly. "Bread!"

But there was no answer. Evidently he was dead. He must have died while she was getting the bread out of the oven.

There was nothing to do then but to finish the bread herself. And when that was done, she wondered if she ought not to follow after Little Pig and his wife and all the villagers. The sun was mounting and it was growing hot. If she were going, she had better go. But first she would climb the dike and see what the direction was. They had gone straight west, and as far as eye could look westward was a great plain. She might even see a good-sized crowd miles away. Anyway, she could see the next village, and they might all be there.

So she climbed the dike slowly, getting very hot. There was a slight breeze on top of the dike and it felt good. She was shocked to see the river very near the top of the dike. Why, it had risen in the last hour!

"You old demon!" she said severely. Let the river god hear it if he liked. He was evil, that he was—so to threaten flood when there had been all this other trouble.

She stooped and bathed her cheeks and her wrists. The water was quite cold, as though with fresh rains somewhere. Then she stood up and gazed around her. To the west there was nothing except in the far distance the soldiers still half running, and beyond them the blur of the next village, which stood on a long rise of ground. She had better set out for that village. Doubtless Little Pig and his wife were there waiting for her.

Just as she was about to climb down and start out, she saw something on the eastern horizon. It was at first only an immense cloud of dust. But, as she stared at it, very quickly it became a lot of black dots and shining spots. Then she saw what it was. It was a lot of men—an army. Instantly she knew what army.

That's the Japanese, she thought. Yes, above them were the buzzing silver planes. They circled about, seeming to search for someone.

"I don't know who you're looking for," she muttered, "unless it's me and Little Pig and his wife. We're the only ones left. You've already killed my brother Pao."

She had almost forgotten that Pao was dead. Now she remembered it acutely. He had such a nice shop—always clean, and the tea good and the best meat dumplings to be had and the price always the same. Pao was a good man. Besides, what about his wife and his seven children? Doubtless they were all killed, too. Now these Japanese were looking for her. It occurred to her that on the dike she could easily be seen. So she clambered hastily down.

It was when she was about halfway down that she thought of the water gate. This old river—it had been a curse to them since time began. Why should it not make up a little now for all the wickedness it had done? It was plotting wickedness again, trying to steal over its banks. Well, why not? She wavered a moment. It was a pity, of course, that the young dead Japanese would be swept into the flood. He was a nice-looking boy, and she had saved him from being stabbed. It was not quite the same as saving his life, of course, but still it was a little the same. If he had been alive, he would have been saved. She went over to him and tugged at him until he lay well near the top of the bank. Then she went down again.

She knew perfectly how to open the water gate. Any child knew how to open the sluice for crops. But she knew also how to swing open the whole gate. The question was, could she open it quickly enough to get out of the way?

"I'm only one old woman," she muttered. She hesitated a second more. Well, it would be a pity not to see what sort of a baby Little Pig's wife would have, but one could not see everything. She had seen a great deal in this life. There was an end to what one could see, anyway.

She glanced again to the east. There were the Japanese coming across the plain. They were a long clear line of black, dotted with thousands of glittering points. If she opened this gate, the impetuous water would roar toward them, rushing into the plains, rolling into a wide lake, drowning them, maybe. Certainly they could not keep on marching nearer and nearer to her and to Little Pig and his wife who were waiting for her. Well, Little Pig and his wife—they would wonder about her—but they would never dream of this. It would make a good story—she would have enjoyed telling it.

She turned resolutely to the gate. Well, some people fought with airplanes and some with guns, but you could fight with a river, too, if it were a wicked one like this one. She wrenched out a huge wooden pin. It was slippery with silvery green moss. The rill of water burst into a strong jet. When she wrenched one more pin, the rest would give way themselves. She began pulling at it, and felt it slip a little from its hole.

I might be able to get myself out of purgatory with this, she thought, and maybe they'll let me have that old man of mine, too. What's a hand of his to all this? Then we'll—

The pin slipped away suddenly, and the gate burst flat against her and knocked her breath away. She had only time to gasp, to the river: "Come on, you old demon!"

Then she felt it seize her and lift her up to the sky. It was beneath her and around her. It rolled her joyfully hither and thither, and then, holding her close and enfolded, it went rushing against the enemy.

THE SAILOR-BOY'S TALE
ISAK DINESEN / DENMARK

Isak Dinesen.

THE BARK *Charlotte* was on her way from Marseille to Athens, in gray weather, on a high sea, after three days' heavy gale. A small sailor-boy, named Simon, stood on the wet, swinging deck, held on to a shroud, and looked up towards the drifting clouds, and to the upper topgallant yard of the mainmast.

A bird that had sought refuge upon the mast had got her feet entangled in some loose tackle yarn on the halyard, and, high up there, struggled to get free. The boy on the deck could see her wings flapping and her head turning from side to side.

Through his own experience of life he had come to the conviction that in this world everyone must look after himself, and expect no help from others. But the mute, deadly fight kept him fascinated for more than an hour. He wondered what kind of bird it would be. These last days a number of birds had come to settle in the bark's rigging: swallows, quails, and a pair of peregrine falcons; he believed that this bird was a peregrine falcon. He remembered how many years ago, in his own country and near his home, he had once seen a peregrine falcon quite close, sitting on a stone and flying straight up from it. Perhaps this was the same bird. He thought, That bird is like me. Then she was there, and now she is here.

At that a fellow feeling rose in him, a sense of common tragedy; he stood looking at the bird with his heart in his mouth. There were none of the sailors about to make fun of him; he began to think out how he might go up by the shrouds to help the falcon out. He brushed his hair back and pulled up his sleeves, gave the deck round him a great glance, and climbed up. He had to stop a couple of times in the swaying rigging.

It was indeed, he found when he got to the top of the mast, a peregrine falcon. As his head was on a level with hers, she gave up her struggle, and looked at him with a pair of angry, desperate yellow eyes. He had to take hold of her with one hand while he got his knife out and cut off the tackle yarn. He was scared as he looked down, but at the same time he felt that he had been ordered up by nobody, but that this was his own venture, and this gave him a proud, steadying sensation, as if the sea and the sky, the ship, the bird and himself were all one. Just as he had freed the falcon, she hacked him in the thumb, so that the blood ran, and he nearly let her go. He grew angry with her, and gave her a clout on the head, then he put her inside his jacket, and climbed down again.

When he reached the deck the mate and the cook were standing there, looking up; they roared to him to ask what he had had to do in the mast. He was so tired that the tears were in his eyes. He took the falcon out and showed her to them, and she kept still within his hands. They laughed and walked off. Simon set the falcon down, stood back and watched her. After a while he reflected that she might not be able to get up from the slippery deck, so he caught her once more, walked away with her and placed her upon a bolt of canvas. A little after, she began to trim her feathers, made two or three sharp jerks forward, and then suddenly flew off. The boy could follow her flight above the troughs of the gray sea. He thought, There flies my falcon.

When the *Charlotte* came home, Simon signed aboard another ship, and two years later he was a light hand on the schooner *Hebe* lying at Bodö, high up on the coast of Norway, to buy herrings.

To the great herring markets of Bodö ships came together from all corners of the world; here were Swedish, Finnish and Russian boats, a forest of masts, and on shore a turbulent, irregular display of life, with many languages spoken, and mighty fights. On the shore booths had been set up, and the Lapps, small yellow people, noiseless in their movements, with watchful eyes, whom Simon had never seen before, came down to sell bead-embroidered leather goods. It was April, the sky and the sea were so clear that it was difficult to hold one's eyes up against them—salt, infinitely wide, and filled with bird shrieks—as if someone were incessantly whetting invisible knives, on all sides, high up in heaven.

Simon was amazed at the lightness of these April evenings. He knew no geography, and did not assign it to the latitude, but he took it as a sign of an unwonted goodwill in the universe, a favor. Simon had been small for his age all his life, but this last winter he had grown, and had become strong of limb. That good luck, he felt, must spring from the very same source as the sweetness of the weather, from a new benevolence in the world. He had been in need of such encouragement, for he was timid by nature; now he asked for no more. The rest he felt to be his own affair. He went about slowly, and proudly.

One evening he was ashore with land leave, and walked up to the booth of a small Russian trader, a Jew who sold gold watches. All the sailors knew that his watches were made from bad metal, and would not go; still they bought them, and paraded them about. Simon looked at these watches for a long time, but did not buy. The old Jew had divers goods in his shop, and amongst others a case of oranges. Simon had tasted oranges on his journeys; he bought one and took it with him. He meant to go up on a hill, from where he could see the sea, and suck it there.

As he walked on, and had got to the outskirts of the place, he saw a little girl in a blue frock, standing at the other side of a fence and looking at him. She was thirteen or fourteen years old, as slim as an eel, but with a round, clear, freckled face, and a pair of long plaits. The two looked at one another.

"Who are you looking out for?" Simon asked, to say something. The girl's face broke into an ecstatic, presumptuous smile, "For the man I am going to marry, of course," she said. Something in her countenance made the boy confident and happy; he grinned a little at her. "That will perhaps be me," he said. "Ha, ha," said the girl, "he is a few years older than you, I can tell you." "Why," said Simon, "you are not grown up yourself." The little girl shook her head solemnly. "Nay," she said, "but when I grow up I will be exceedingly beautiful, and wear brown shoes with heels, and a hat." "Will you have an orange?" asked Simon, who could give her none of the things she had named. She looked at the orange and at him. "They are very good to eat," said he. "Why do you not eat it yourself then?" she asked. "I have eaten so many already," said he, "when I was in Athens. Here I had to pay a mark for it." "What is your name?" asked she. "My name is Simon," said he. "What is yours?" "Nora," said the girl. "What do you want for your orange now, Simon?"

When he heard his name in her mouth Simon grew bold. "Will you give me a kiss for the orange?" he asked. Nora looked at him gravely for a moment. "Yes," she said, "I should not mind giving you a kiss." He grew as warm as if he had been running quickly. When she stretched out her hand for the orange he took hold of it. At that moment somebody in the house called out for her. "That is my father," said she, and tried to give him back the orange, but he would not take it. "Then come again tomorrow," she said quickly, "then I will give you a kiss." At that she slipped off. He stood and looked after her, and a little later went back to his ship.

Simon was not in the habit of making plans for the future, and now he did not know whether he would be going back to her or not.

The following evening he had to stay aboard, as the other sailors were going ashore, and he did not mind that either. He meant to sit on the deck with the ship's dog, Balthasar, and to practice upon a concertina that he had purchased some time ago. The pale evening was all round him, the sky was faintly roseate, the sea was quite calm, like milk and water, only in the wake of the boats going inshore it broke into streaks of vivid indigo. Simon sat and played; after a while his own music began to speak to him so strongly that he stopped, got up and looked upwards. Then he saw that the full moon was sitting high on the sky.

The sky was so light that she hardly seemed needed there; it was as if she had turned up by a caprice of her own. She was round, demure and presumptuous. At that he knew that he must go ashore, whatever it was to cost him. But he did not know how to get away, since the others had taken the yawl with them. He stood on the deck for a long time, a small lonely figure of a sailor-boy on a boat, when he caught sight of a yawl coming in from a ship farther out, and hailed her. He found that it was the Russian crew from a boat named *Anna,* going ashore. When he could make himself understood to them, they took him with them; they first asked him for money for his fare, then, laughing, gave it back to him. He thought, These people will be believing that I am going in to town, wenching. And then he felt, with some pride, that they were right, although at the same time they were infinitely wrong, and knew nothing about anything.

When they came ashore they invited him to come in and drink in their company, and he would not refuse, because they had helped him. One of the Russians was a giant, as big as a bear; he told Simon that his name was Ivan. He got drunk at once, and then fell upon the boy with a bearlike affection, pawed him, smiled and laughed into his face, made him a present of a gold watch chain, and kissed him on both cheeks. At that Simon reflected that he also ought to give Nora a present when they met again, and as soon as he could get away from the Russians he walked up to a booth that he knew of, and bought a small blue silk handkerchief, the same color as her eyes.

It was Saturday evening, and there were many people amongst the houses; they came in long rows, some of them singing, all keen to have some fun that night. Simon, in the midst of this rich, bawling life under the clear moon, felt his head light with the flight from the ship and the strong drinks. He crammed the handkerchief in his pocket; it was silk, which he had never touched before, a present for his girl.

He could not remember the path up to Nora's house, lost his way, and came back to where he had started. Then he grew deadly afraid that he should be too late, and began to run. In a small passage between two wooden huts he ran straight into a big man, and found that it was Ivan once more. The Russian folded his arms round him and held him. "Good! Good!" he cried in high glee, "I have found you, my little chicken. I have looked for you everywhere, and poor Ivan has wept because he lost his friend." "Let me go, Ivan," cried Simon. "Oho," said Ivan, "I shall go with you and get you what you want. My heart and my money are all yours, all yours; I have been seventeen years old myself, a little lamb of God, and I want to be so again tonight." "Let me go," cried Simon, "I am in a hurry." Ivan held him so that it hurt, and patted him with his other hand. . . . "Now trust to me, my little friend. Nothing shall part you and me. I hear the others coming; we will have such a night together as you will remember when you are an old grandpapa."

Suddenly he crushed the boy to him, like a bear that carries off a sheep. The odious sensation of male bodily warmth and the bulk of a man close to him made the lean boy mad. He thought of Nora waiting, like a slender ship in the dim air, and of himself, here, in the hot embrace of a hairy animal. He struck Ivan with all his might. "I shall kill you, Ivan," he cried out, "if you do not let me go." "Oh, you will be thankful to me later on," said Ivan, and began to sing. Simon fumbled in his pocket for his knife, and got it opened. He could not lift his hand, but he drove the knife, furiously, in under the big man's arm. Almost immediately he felt the blood spouting out, and running down in his sleeve. Ivan stopped short in the song, let go his hold of the boy and gave two long deep grunts. The next second he tumbled down on his knees. "Poor Ivan, poor Ivan," he groaned. He fell straight on his face. At that moment Simon heard the other sailors coming along, singing, in the bystreet.

He stood still for a minute, wiped his knife, and watched the blood spread into a dark pool underneath the big body. Then he ran. As he stopped for a second to choose his way, he heard the sailors behind him scream out over their dead comrade. He thought, I must get down to the sea, where I can wash my hand. But at the same time he ran the other way. After a little while he found himself on the path that he had walked on the day before, and it seemed as familiar to him, as if he had walked it many hundred times in his life.

He slackened his pace to look round, and suddenly saw Nora standing on the other side of the fence; she was quite close to him when he caught sight of her in the moonlight. Wavering and out of breath he sank down on his knees. For a moment he could not speak. The little girl looked down at him. "Good evening, Simon," she said in her small coy voice. "I have waited for you a long time," and after a moment she added: "I have eaten your orange."

"Oh, Nora," cried the boy. "I have killed a man." She stared at him, but did not move. "Why did you kill a man?" she asked after a moment. "To get here," said Simon. "Because he tried to stop me. But he was my friend." Slowly he got on to his feet. "He loved me!" the boy cried out, and at that burst into tears. "Yes," said she slowly and thoughtfully. "Yes, because you must be here in time." "Can you hide me?" he asked. "For they are after me." "Nay," said Nora, "I cannot hide you. For my father is the parson here at Bodö, and he would be sure to hand you over to them, if he knew that you had killed a man." "Then," said Simon, "give me something to wipe my hands on." "What is the matter with your hands?" she asked, and took a little step forward. He stretched out his hands to her. "Is that your own blood?" she asked. "No," said he, "it is his." She took the step back again. "Do you hate me now?" he asked. "No, I do not hate you," said she. "But do put your hands at your back."

As he did so she came up close to him, at the other side of the fence, and clasped her arms round his neck. She pressed her young body to his, and kissed him tenderly. He felt her face, cool as the moonlight, upon his own, and when she released him, his head swam, and he did not know if the kiss had lasted a second or an hour. Nora stood up straight, her eyes wide open. "Now," she said slowly and proudly, "I promise you that I will never marry anybody, as long as I live." The boy kept standing with his hands on his back, as if she had tied them there. "And now," she said, "you must run, for they are coming." They looked at one another. "Do not forget Nora," said she. He turned and ran.

He leapt over a fence, and when he was down amongst the houses he walked. He did not know at all where to go. As he came to a house, from where music and noise streamed out, he slowly went through the door. The room was full of people; they were dancing in here. A lamp hung from the ceiling, and shone down on them; the air was thick and brown with the dust rising from the floor. There were some women in the room, but many of the men danced with each other, and gravely or laughingly stamped the floor. A moment after Simon had come in, the crowd withdrew to the walls to clear the floor for two sailors, who were showing a dance from their own country.

Simon thought, Now, very soon, the men from the boat will come round to look for their comrade's murderer, and from my hands they will know that I have done it. These five minutes during which he stood by the wall of the dancing room, in the midst of the gay, sweating dancers, were of great significance to the boy. He himself felt it, as if during this time he grew up, and became like other people. He did not entreat his destiny, nor complain. Here he was, he had killed a man, and had kissed a girl. He did not demand any more from life, nor did life now demand more from him. He was Simon, a man like the men round him, and going to die, as all men are going to die.

He only became aware of what was going on outside him, when he saw that a woman had come in, and was standing in the midst of the cleared floor, looking round her. She was a short, broad old woman, in the clothes of the Lapps, and she took her stand with such majesty and fierceness as if she owned the whole place. It was obvious that most of the people knew her, and were a little afraid of her, although a few laughed; the din of the dancing room stopped when she spoke.

"Where is my son?" she asked in a high shrill voice, like a bird's. The next moment her eyes fell on Simon himself, and she steered through the crowd, which opened up before her, stretched out her old skinny, dark hand, and took him by the elbow. "Come home with me now," she said. "You need not dance here tonight. You may be dancing a high enough dance soon."

Simon drew back, for he thought that she was drunk. But as she looked him straight in the face with her yellow eyes, it seemed to him that he had met her before, and that he might do well in listening to her. The old woman pulled him with her across the floor, and he followed her without a word. "Do not birch your boy too badly, Sunniva," one of the men in the room cried to her. "He has done no harm, he only wanted to look at the dance."

At the same moment as they came out through the door, there was an alarm in the street, a flock of people came running down it, and one of them, as he turned into the house, knocked against Simon, looked at him and the old woman, and ran on.

While the two walked along the street, the old woman lifted up her skirt, and put the hem of it into the boy's hand. "Wipe your hand on my skirt," she said. They had not gone far before they came to a small wooden house, and stopped; the door to it was so low that they must bend to get through it. As the Lapp woman went in before Simon, still holding on to his arm, the boy looked up for a moment. The night had grown misty; there was a wide ring round the moon.

The old woman's room was narrow and dark, with but one small window to it; a lantern stood on the floor and lighted it up dimly. It was all filled with reindeer skins and wolf skins, and with reindeer horn, such as the Lapps use to make their carved buttons and knife-handles, and the air in here was rank and stifling. As soon as they were in, the woman turned to Simon, took hold of his head, and with her crooked fingers parted his hair and combed it down in Lapp fashion. She clapped a Lapp cap on him and stood back to glance at him. "Sit down on my stool, now," she said. "But first take out your knife." She was so commanding in voice and manner that the boy could not but choose to do as she told him; he sat down on the stool, and he could not take his eyes off her face, which was flat and brown, and as if smeared with dirt in its net of fine wrinkles.

As he sat there he heard many people come along outside, and stop by the house; then someone knocked at the door, waited a moment and knocked again. The old woman stood and listened, as still as a mouse.

"Nay," said the boy and got up. "This is no good, for it is me that they are after. It will be better for you to let me go out to them." "Give me your knife," said she. When he handed it to her, she stuck it straight into her thumb, so that the blood spouted out, and she let it drip all over her skirt. "Come in, then," she cried.

The door opened, and two of the Russian sailors came and stood in the opening; there were more people outside. "Has anybody come in here?" they asked. "We are after a man who has killed our mate, but he has run away from us. Have you seen or heard anybody this way?" The old Lapp woman turned upon them, and her eyes shone like gold in the lamplight. "Have I seen or heard anyone?" she cried, "I have heard you shriek murder all over the town. You frightened me, and my poor silly boy there, so that I cut my thumb as I was ripping the skin rug that I sew. The boy is too scared to help me, and the rug is all ruined. I shall make you pay me for that. If you are looking for a murderer, come in and search my house for me, and I shall know you when we meet again." She was so furious that she danced where she stood, and jerked her head like an angry bird of prey.

The Russian came in, looked round the room, and at her and her bloodstained hand and skirt. "Do not put a curse on us now, Sunniva," he said timidly. "We know that you can do many things when you like. Here is a mark to pay you for the blood you have spilled." She stretched out her hand, and he placed a piece of money in it. She spat on it. "Then go, and there shall be no bad blood between us," said Sunniva, and shut the door after them. She stuck her thumb in her mouth, and chuckled a little.

The boy got up from his stool, stood up before her and stared into her face. He felt as if he were swaying high up in the air, with but a small hold. "Why have you helped me?" he asked her. "Do you not know?" she answered. "Have you not recognized me yet? But you will remember the peregrine falcon which was caught in the tackle yarn of your boat, the *Charlotte*, as she sailed in the Mediterranean. That day you climbed up by the shrouds of the topgallant mast to help her out, in a stiff wind, and with a high sea. That falcon was me. We Lapps often fly in such a manner, to see the world. When I first met you I was on my way to Africa, to see my younger sister and her children. She is a falcon too, when she chooses. By that time she was living at Takaunga, within an old ruined tower, which down there they call a minaret." She swathed a corner of her skirt round her thumb, and bit at it. "We do not forget," she said. "I hacked your thumb, when you took hold of me; it is only fair that I should cut my thumb for you tonight."

She came close to him, and gently rubbed her two brown, clawlike fingers against his forehead. "So you are a boy," she said, "who will kill a man rather than be late to meet your sweetheart? We hold together, the females of this earth. I shall mark your forehead now, so that the girls will know of that, when they look at you, and they will like you for it." She played with the boy's hair, and twisted it round her finger.

"Listen now, my little bird," said she. "My great grandson's brother-in-law is lying with his boat by the landing place at this moment; he is to take a consignment of skins out to a Danish boat. He will bring you back to your boat, in time, before your mate comes. The *Hebe* is sailing tomorrow morning, is it not so? But when you are aboard, give him back my cap for me." She took up his knife, wiped it in her skirt and handed it to him. "Here is your knife," she said. "You will stick it into no more men; you will not need to, for from now you will sail the seas like a faithful seaman. We have enough trouble with our sons as it is."

The bewildered boy began to stammer his thanks to her. "Wait," said she, "I shall make you a cup of coffee, to bring back your wits, while I wash your jacket." She went and rattled an old copper kettle upon the fireplace. After a while she handed him a hot, strong, black drink in a cup without a handle to it. "You have drunk with Sunniva now," she said; "you have drunk down a little wisdom, so that in the future all your thoughts shall not fall like raindrops into the salt sea."

When he had finished and set down the cup, she led him to the door and opened it for him. He was surprised to see that it was almost clear morning. The house was so high up that the boy could see the sea from it, and a milky mist about it. He gave her his hand to say good-by.

She stared into his face. "We do not forget," she said. "And you, you knocked me on the head there, high up in the mast. I shall give you that blow back." With that she smacked him on the ear as hard as she could, so that his head swam. "Now we are quits," she said, gave him a great, mischievous, shining glance, and a little push down the doorstep, and nodded to him.

In this way the sailor-boy got back to his ship, which was to sail the next morning, and lived to tell the story.

YOUNG ARCHIMEDES
ALDOUS HUXLEY / GREAT BRITAIN

IT was the view which finally made us take the place. True, the house had its disadvantages. It was a long way out of town and had no telephone. The rent was unduly high, the drainage system poor. On windy nights, when the ill-fitting windowpanes were rattling, the electric light, for some mysterious reason, used invariably to go out and leave you in the noisy dark. There was a splendid bathroom; but the electric pump, which was supposed to send up water from the rainwater tanks in the terrace, did not work. Punctually every autumn the drinking well ran dry. And our landlady was a liar and a cheat.

But these are the little disadvantages of every hired house, all over the world. For Italy they were not really at all serious. I have seen plenty of houses which had them all and a hundred others, without possessing the advantages of ours—the southward-facing garden and terrace for the winter and spring, the large cool rooms against the midsummer heat, the hilltop air and freedom from mosquitoes, and finally the view.

And what a view it was! Or rather what a succession of views. For it was different every day. There were autumn days when all the valleys were filled with mist and the crests of Apennines rose darkly out of a flat white lake. There were days when the mist invaded even our hilltop and we were enveloped in a soft vapor, and the only firm and definite things in our small, dim world were the two tall black cypresses growing on a little projecting terrace a hundred feet down the hill. Black, sharp, and solid, they stood there, twin pillars of Hercules at the extremity of the known universe; and beyond them there was only pale cloud.

These were the wintry days; but there were days of spring and autumn, days unchangingly cloudless, or—more lovely still—made various by the huge floating shapes of vapor, gradually unfolding against the pale bright blue sky above the faraway snowcapped mountains. And the sun would come and go behind the clouds; and now the town in the valley would fade and almost vanish in the shadow, and now, like an immense fretted jewel between the hills, it would glow as though by its own light.

There were days when the air was wet with passed or with approaching rain, and all the distances seemed miraculously near and clear. The olive trees detached themselves one from another on the distant slopes; the faraway villages were lovely and pathetic like the most exquisite small toys.

There were days in summertime, days of impending thunder when, bright and sunlit against huge bellying masses of black and purple, the hills and the white houses shone as it were precariously, in a dying splendor, on the brink of some fearful calamity.

How the hills changed and varied! Every day and every hour of the day, almost, they were different. There would be moments when, looking across the plain of Florence, the scene had no depth; there was only a hanging curtain painted flatly with the symbols of mountains. Changeful in its beauty, this wide landscape always preserved a quality of humanness and domestication which made it, to my mind at any rate, the best of all landscapes to live with. Day by day one traveled through its different beauties; but the journey was always a journey through civilization. For all its mountains, its steep slopes and deep valleys, man's traces are across the country. Stripped of its dark woods, planted, terraced, and tilled almost to the mountains' tops, the Tuscan landscape is humanized and safe.

I found that house on the hilltop the ideal dwelling place. For there one could be as solitary as one liked, though our nearest neighbors lived very near. We had two sets of them, as a matter of fact, almost in the same house with us. One was the peasant family, who lived in a long, low building, part dwelling house, part stables, adjoining the villa. Our other neighbors—intermittent neighbors, however, for they only ventured out of Florence to the hilltop every now and then—were the owners of the villa, who had reserved for themselves the smaller wing of the huge L-shaped house.

They were a curious couple, our proprietors. An old husband, gray, listless, tottering, seventy at least; and a *signora* of about forty, short, very plump, with tiny fat hands and feet and a pair of very large, very dark black eyes. Her vitality, if you could have harnessed it, would have supplied a whole town with electric light. Enormous stores of vital energy accumulate in unemployed women of sanguine temperament, which vent themselves in ways that are generally deplorable: in interfering with other people's affairs, in working up emotional scenes, in thinking about love and making it, and in bothering men till they cannot get on with their work.

Signora Bondi got rid of her superfluous energy, among other ways, by "doing in" her tenants. The old gentleman, who was a retired merchant with a reputation for the most perfect rectitude, was allowed to have no dealings with us. When we came to see the house, it was the wife who showed us round. It was she who, with a lavish display of charm, with irresistible rolling of the eyes, expatiated on the merits of the place, sang the praises of the electric pump, glorified the bathroom (considering which, she insisted, the rent was remarkably moderate), and when we suggested calling in a surveyor to look over the house, earnestly begged us not to waste our money unnecessarily. "After all," she said, "we are honest people. I wouldn't dream of letting you the house except in perfect condition. Have confidence." And she looked at me with an appealing, pained expression in her magnificent eyes, as though begging me not to insult her by my coarse suspiciousness. And leaving us no time to pursue the subject, she began assuring us that our little boy was the most beautiful angel she had ever seen. By the time our interview with Signora Bondi was at an end, we had decided to take the house.

"Charming woman," I said, as we left the house. But I think that Elizabeth was not quite so certain of it as I.

Then the pump episode began.

On the evening of our arrival in the house we switched on the electricity. The pump made a very professional whirring noise; but no water came out of the taps in the bathroom. We looked at one another doubtfully.

"Charming woman?" Elizabeth raised her eyebrows.

We asked for interviews; but somehow the old gentleman could never see us, and the *signora* was invariably out or indisposed. We left notes; they were never answered. In the end, we found that the only method of communicating with our landlords, who were now living in the same house with us, was to go down into Florence and send a registered express letter to them. For this they had to sign two separate receipts and there could be no pretending, as there always was with ordinary letters or notes, that the communication had never been received. We began at last to get answers to our complaints. The *signora*, who wrote all the letters, started by telling us that, naturally, the pump didn't work, as the cisterns were empty, owing to the long drought. I had to walk three miles to the post office in order to register my letter reminding her that there had been a violent thunderstorm only last Wednesday, and that the tanks were consequently more than half full. The answer came back; bath water had not been guaranteed in the contract; and if I wanted it, why hadn't I had the pump looked at before I took the house? Another walk into town to inform the *signora* next door that the existence in a house of a bathroom was in itself an implicit guarantee of bath water. The reply to that was that the *signora* couldn't continue to have communications with people who wrote so rudely to her. After that I put the matter into the hands of a lawyer. Two months later the pump was actually replaced. But we had to serve a writ on the lady before she gave in. And the costs were considerable.

One day, towards the end of the episode, I met the old gentleman in the road, taking his big white dog for a walk—or being taken, rather, for a walk by the dog. For where the dog pulled the old gentleman had perforce to follow. And when it stopped the old man had to wait. I passed him patiently standing at the side of the road, while the dog was sniffing at the roots of a big cypress and growling indignantly to itself. Old Signor Bondi, leashed to his dog, was waiting. Leaning on his cane, he stood gazing mournfully and vacantly at the view. The whites of his old eyes were discolored, like ancient billiard balls. His white mustache, ragged and yellowing at the fringes, drooped in a melancholy curve. In his black tie he wore a very large diamond; perhaps that was what Signora Bondi had found so attractive about him.

I took off my hat as I approached. The old man stared at me absently, and it was only when I was already almost past him that he recollected who I was.

"Wait," he called after me, "wait!" And he hastened down the road in pursuit. Taken utterly by surprise, the dog permitted itself to be jerked after him. "Wait!"

I waited.

"My dear sir," the old gentleman said, catching me by the lapel of my coat, "I want to apologize." He looked around him, as though afraid that even here he might be overheard. "I want to apologize," he went on, "about that wretched pump business. I assure you that, if it had been only my affair, I'd have put the thing right as soon as you asked. But my wife"—he lowered his voice—"the fact is that she likes this sort of thing, even when she knows that she's in the wrong and must lose. And besides, she hoped, I daresay, that you'd get tired of asking and have the job done yourself. Still, now she sees that it must be done. In the course of the next two or three days you'll be having your bath water. But I thought I'd just like to tell you how . . ." But the dog, recovered from its surprise, suddenly bounded, growling, up the road. The old gentleman strained at the leash, tottered unsteadily, then gave way and allowed himself to be dragged off. ". . . how sorry I am," he went on, as he receded from me, "that this little misunderstanding . . ." But it was no use. "Good-by." He smiled politely, made a little deprecating gesture, and abandoned himself completely to the dog.

A week later the water really did begin to flow, and the day after our first bath Signora Bondi, dressed in dove-gray satin and wearing all her pearls, came to call.

"Is it peace now?" she asked, with a charming frankness, as she shook hands.

We assured her that, so far as we were concerned, it certainly was.

"But why *did* you write me such dreadfully rude letters?" she said, turning on me a reproachful glance. "And then that writ. How *could* you? To a lady . . ."

I mumbled something about the pump and our wanting baths.

"But how could you expect me to listen to you? Why didn't you set about it differently—politely, charmingly?" She smiled at me and dropped her fluttering eyelids.

I thought it best to change the conversation. It is disagreeable, when one is in the right, to be made to appear in the wrong.

A few weeks later we had a letter—duly registered and by express messenger—in which the *signora* asked us whether we proposed to renew our lease (which was only for six months), and notifying us that, if we did, the rent would be raised twenty-five percent, in consideration of the improvements which had been carried out. We thought ourselves lucky, at the end of much bargaining, to get the lease renewed for a whole year with an increase in the rent of only fifteen percent.

It was chiefly for the sake of the view that we put up with these intolerable extortions. But we had found other reasons, after a few days' residence, for liking the house. Of these the most cogent was that, in the tenant farmer's youngest child, we had discovered what seemed the perfect playfellow for our own small boy. Between little Guido—for that was his name—and the youngest of his brothers and sisters there was a gap of six or seven years. His two elder brothers worked with their father in the fields; since the time of the mother's death, two or three years before we knew them, the eldest sister had ruled the house. The younger sister, who had just left school, kept an eye on Guido, who by this time, however, needed very little looking after; for he was between six and seven years old and as precocious, self-assured, and responsible as the children of the poor, left as they are to themselves almost from the time they can walk, generally are.

Though fully two and a half years older than little Robin—and at that age thirty months are crammed with half a lifetime's experience—Guido took no undue advantage of his superior intelligence and strength. I have never seen a child more patient, tolerant, and untyrannical. He did not tease or bully, but helped his small companion when he was in difficulties and explained when he could not understand. In return, Robin adored him and slavishly imitated him.

Robin's heroic and unsuccessful attempts to perform the feats of strength and skill which Guido could do with ease, were exquisitely comic. And his careful, long-drawn imitations of Guido's habits and mannerisms were no less amusing. Most ludicrous of all, because most incongruous in the imitator, were Robin's impersonations of Guido in the pensive mood. Guido was a thoughtful child, given to brooding and sudden abstractions. One would find him sitting in a corner by himself, chin in hand, elbow on knee, plunged, to all appearances, in the profoundest meditation. And sometimes, even in the midst of his play, he would suddenly break off, to stand, his hands behind his back, frowning and staring at the ground. When this happened, Robin became overawed and a little disquieted. In a puzzled silence he looked at his companion. "Guido," he would say softly, "Guido." But Guido was generally too much preoccupied to answer; and Robin, not venturing to insist, would creep near him, and throwing himself as nearly as possible into Guido's attitude would try to meditate too. But at the end of a minute he began to grow impatient; meditation wasn't his strong point. "Guido," he called again and again and, louder, "Guido!" And he would take him by the hand and try to pull him away. Sometimes Guido roused himself from his reverie and went back to the interrupted game. Sometimes he paid no attention. Melancholy, perplexed, Robin had to take himself off to play by himself. And Guido would go on sitting or standing there, quite still; and his eyes, if one looked into them, were beautiful in their grave and pensive calm.

They were large eyes, set far apart and, what was strange in a dark-haired Italian child, of a luminous pale blue-gray color. They were not always grave and calm. When he was playing, when he talked or laughed, they lit up; and the surface of those clear, pale lakes of thought seemed to be shaken into brilliant sun-flashing ripples. Above those eyes was a beautiful forehead, high and steep and domed in a curve that was like the subtle curve of a rose petal. The nose was straight, the chin small and rather pointed, the mouth drooped a little sadly at the corners.

I have a snapshot of the two children sitting together on the parapet of the terrace. Guido sits almost facing the camera, but looking a little to one side and downwards; his hands are crossed in his lap and his expression is thoughtful, grave, and meditative. It is Guido in one of those moods of abstraction into which he would pass even at the height of laughter and play—quite suddenly and completely, as though he had all at once taken it into his head to go away and had left the silent and beautiful body behind, like an empty house, to wait for his return. And by his side sits little Robin, turning to look up at him, his face half averted from the camera, but the curve of his cheek showing that he is laughing; one little hand clutches at Guido's sleeve, as though he were urging him to come away and play. And the legs dangling from the parapet are in the midst of an impatient wriggle; he is on the point of slipping down and running off to play hide-and-seek in the garden. All the essential characteristics of both the children are in that little snapshot.

"If Robin were not Robin," Elizabeth used to say, "I could almost wish he were Guido."

And I agreed with her. Guido seemed to me one of the most charming little boys I had ever seen.

We were not alone in admiring him. Signora Bondi when, in intervals between quarrels, she came to call, was constantly speaking of him. "Such a beautiful, beautiful child!" she would exclaim with enthusiasm. "It's really a waste that he should belong to peasants who can't afford to dress him properly. If he were mine, I should put him into black velvet; or little white knickers and a white knitted silk jersey; or perhaps a white sailor suit would be pretty. And in winter a little fur coat, and possibly Russian boots . . ." Her imagination was running away with her. "And I'd let his hair grow, like a page's, and have it just curled up a little at the tips. And everyone would turn round and stare after us if I took him out with me in Via Tornabuoni."

What you want, I should have liked to tell her, is not a child; it's a clockwork doll or a performing monkey. But I did not say so—partly because I could not think of the Italian for a clockwork doll and partly because I did not want to risk having the rent raised another fifteen percent.

"Ah, if only I had a little boy like that!" She sighed and modestly dropped her eyelids. "I adore children. I sometimes think of adopting one—that is, if my husband would allow it." She was silent for a moment, as though considering a new idea.

A few days later, when we were sitting in the garden after luncheon, drinking our coffee, Guido's father, instead of passing with a nod and the usual cheerful good-day, halted in front of us and began to talk. He was a fine handsome man, not very tall, but well proportioned, quick and elastic in his movements, and full of life. He had a thin brown face, lit by a pair of the most intelligent-looking gray eyes I ever saw. When, as not infrequently happened, he was trying, with an assumption of perfect frankness and a childlike innocence, to take one in or get something out of one, the intelligence shone there mischievously, delighting in itself.

Today, however, there was no dangerous light in his eyes. He wanted nothing out of us, nothing of any value—only advice, a commodity most people are only too happy to part with. But he wanted advice on what was, for us, rather a delicate subject: on Signora Bondi. Carlo had often complained to us about her. The old man is good, he told us, very good and kind indeed. Which meant, I daresay, among other things, that he could easily be swindled. But his wife . . . He would tell us stories of her insatiable rapacity: she was always claiming more than the half of the produce which, by law, was the proprietor's due. He complained of her suspiciousness: she was forever accusing him of sharp practices, of downright stealing—him, he struck his breast, the soul of honesty. He complained of her shortsighted avarice; she wouldn't spend enough on manure, wouldn't buy him another cow, wouldn't have electric light installed in the stables. And we had sympathized, but cautiously, without expressing too strong an opinion on the subject. The Italians are wonderfully noncommittal in their speech, they will give nothing away to an interested person until they are quite certain that it is right and necessary and, above all, safe to do so. We had lived long enough among them to imitate their caution.

Today Carlo wasn't so much complaining as feeling perplexed. The *signora* had sent for him and asked how he would like it if she were to make an offer—all in the cautious Italian style—to adopt little Guido. Carlo's first instinct had been to say that he wouldn't like it at all. But that would have been too coarsely committal. He had said he would think about it. And now he was asking for our advice.

Do what you think best, was what in effect we replied. But we gave it distantly but distinctly to be understood that we didn't think that Signora Bondi would make a very good foster-mother for the child. And Carlo was inclined to agree. Besides, he was very fond of the boy. "But the thing is," he concluded rather gloomily, "that if she has really set her heart on getting hold of the child, there's nothing she won't do to get him—nothing."

Still, I reflected, as I watched him striding away along the terrace, there was life enough in those elastic limbs, behind those bright gray eyes, to put up a good fight even against the accumulated vital energies of Signora Bondi.

It was a few days after this that my gramophone and two or three boxes of records arrived from England. They were a great comfort to us on the hilltop, providing as they did the only thing in which that spiritually fertile solitude was lacking: music. And that, thanks to the ingenious Edison, can now be taken about in a box and unpacked in whatever solitude one chooses to visit. One can live in the Sahara and still hear Mozart quartets, and selections from the *Well-Tempered Clavier*.

Carlo, who had gone down to the station with his mule and cart to fetch the packing case, was vastly interested in the machine.

"One will hear some music again," he said, as he watched me unpacking the gramophone and the disks. "It is difficult to do much oneself."

Still, I reflected, he managed to do a good deal. On warm nights we used to hear him, where he sat at the door of his house, playing his guitar and softly singing; the eldest boy shrilled out the melody on the mandolin, and sometimes the whole family would join in, and the darkness would be filled with their passionate, throaty singing.

"I used to go and listen to the operas at the Politeama," Carlo went on. "Ah, they were magnificent. But it costs five lire now to get in."

"Too much," I agreed.

"Have you got *Trovatore?*" he asked.

I shook my head.

"*Rigoletto?*"

"I'm afraid not."

"*Bohème? Fanciulla del West? Pagliacci?*"

I had to go on disappointing him.

I put on "La ci darem" out of *Don Giovanni*. He agreed that the singing was good; but I could see that he didn't much like the music.

"It's not like *Pagliacci*," he said at last.

Carlo and his elder children ceased, after the first day or two, to take any interest in the gramophone and the music it played. They preferred the guitar and their own singing.

Guido, on the other hand, was immensely interested. The first record he heard, I remember, was that of the slow movement of Bach's Concerto in D Minor for two violins. That was the disk I put on the turntable as soon as Carlo had left me. It seemed to me, so to speak, the most musical piece of music with which I could refresh my long-parched mind—the coolest and clearest of all draughts. The movement had just got under way and was beginning to unfold its pure and melancholy beauties when the two children, Guido in front and little Robin breathlessly following, came clattering into the room from the loggia.

Guido came to a halt in front of the gramophone and stood there, motionless, listening. His pale blue-gray eyes opened themselves wide. For an instant he looked at me—a questioning, astonished, rapturous look—gave a little laugh, and turned back towards the source of the incredible sounds. Slavishly imitating his elder comrade, Robin had also taken up his stand in front of the gramophone, and in exactly the same position, glancing at Guido from time to time to make sure that he was doing everything in the correct way. But after a minute or so he became bored.

"Soldiers," he said, turning to me; "I want soldiers. Like in London." He remembered the cheerful dance tunes, to whose sharp rhythms he loved to go stamping round and round the room, pretending that he was a whole regiment of soldiers.

I put my fingers to my lips. "Afterwards," I whispered.

Robin managed to remain silent and still for perhaps another twenty seconds. Then he seized Guido by the arm, shouting, *"Vieni, Guido! Soldiers. Soldati. Vieni giuocare soldati."*

It was then, for the first time, that I saw Guido impatient. *"Vai!"* he whispered angrily, slapped at Robin's clutching hand and pushed him roughly away. And he leaned a little closer to the instrument.

Robin looked at him, astonished. Such a thing had never happened before. Then he burst out crying and came to me for consolation.

When the quarrel was made up—and Guido was sincerely repentant when the music had stopped and his mind was free to think of Robin once more—I asked him how he liked the music. He said he thought it was beautiful. But *bello* in Italian is too vague a word to mean very much.

"What did you like best?" I insisted.

He was silent for a moment, pensively frowning. "Well," he said at last, "I liked the bit that went like this." And he hummed a long phrase. "And then there's the other thing singing at the same time—but what are those things," he interrupted himself, "that sing like that?"

"They're called violins," I said.

"Violins." He nodded. "Well, the other violin goes like this." He hummed again. "Why can't one sing both at once? And what is in that box? What makes it make that noise?" The child poured out his questions.

I answered him as best I could, showing him the little spirals on the disk, the needle, the diaphragm. I told him to remember how the string of the guitar trembled when one plucked it; sound is a shaking in the air, I told him, and I tried to explain how those shakings get printed on the black disk. Guido listened gravely, nodding from time to time. I had the impression that he understood perfectly well everything I was saying.

By this time, however, poor Robin was so dreadfully bored that in pity for him I had to send the two children out into the garden to play. Guido went obediently; but I could see that he would have preferred to stay indoors and listen to more music.

After lunch, when Robin had gone upstairs for his afternoon sleep, Guido reappeared. "May I listen now?" he asked. And for an hour he sat there in front of the instrument, his head cocked slightly on one side, listening while I put on one disk after another.

Thenceforward he came every afternoon. Very soon he knew all my library of records, had his preferences and dislikes, and could ask for what he wanted by humming the principal theme.

"I don't like that one," he said of Strauss's *Till Eulenspiegel.* "It's like what we sing in our house. Not really like, you know. But somehow all the same. You understand?" He looked at us perplexedly and appealingly, as though begging us to understand what he meant. We nodded. Guido went on. "And then," he said, "the end doesn't seem to come properly out of the beginning. It's not like the one you played the first time." He hummed a bar or two from the slow movement of Bach's D Minor concerto.

Wagner was among his dislikes; so was Debussy. When I played the record of one of Debussy's arabesques, he said, "Why does he say the same thing over and over again?" Mozart overwhelmed him with delight. The duet from *Don Giovanni*, which his father had found insufficiently palpitating, enchanted Guido. But he preferred the quartets and the orchestral pieces.

"I like music," he said, "better than singing."

Most people, I reflected, like singing better than music; and find the impersonal orchestra less moving than the soloist. The touch of the pianist is the human touch, and the soprano's high C is the personal note. It is for the sake of his touch, that note, that audiences fill the concert halls.

Guido, however, preferred music. The *Figaro* overture was one of his favorites. There is a passage not far from the beginning of the piece, where the first violins suddenly go rocketing up into the heights of loveliness; as the music approached that point, I used always to see a smile developing on Guido's face, and when, punctually, the thing happened, he clapped his hands and laughed with pleasure.

One afternoon, while we were in the middle of one of our concerts, Signora Bondi was ushered in. She began at once to be overwhelmingly affectionate towards the child; kissed him, patted his head, paid him the most outrageous compliments on his appearance. Guido edged away from her.

"And do you like music?" she asked.

The child nodded.

"I think he has a gift," I said. "At any rate, he has a wonderful ear and a power of listening and criticizing such as I've never met with in a child of that age. We're thinking of hiring a piano for him to learn on."

A moment later I was cursing myself for my undue frankness in praising the boy. For Signora Bondi began immediately to protest that, if she could have the upbringing of the child, she would give him the best masters, bring out his talent, make an accomplished *maestro* of him—and, on the way, an infant prodigy. And at that moment, I am sure, she saw herself sitting maternally, in pearls and black satin, in the lee of the huge Steinway, while an angelic Guido, dressed like little Lord Fauntleroy, rattled out Liszt and Chopin, to the loud delight of a thronged auditorium. She saw all the elaborate floral tributes and heard the words with which the veteran *maestri*, touched almost to tears, hailed the coming of the little genius. It became more than ever important for her to acquire the child.

"You've sent her away fairly ravening," said Elizabeth, when Signora Bondi had gone. "Better tell her next time that you made a mistake, and that the boy's got no musical talent whatever."

In due course, the piano arrived. After giving him the minimum of preliminary instruction, I let Guido loose on it. He began by picking out for himself the melodies he had heard, reconstructing the harmonies. After a few lessons, he understood the rudiments of musical notation and could read a simple passage at sight, albeit very slowly. The whole process of reading was still strange to him; he had picked up his letters somehow, but nobody had yet taught him to read whole words and sentences.

I took occasion, next time I saw Signora Bondi, to assure her that Guido had disappointed me. There was nothing in his musical talent, really. She professed to be very sorry to hear it; but I could see that she didn't for a moment believe me. Probably she thought that we were after the child too, and wanted to bag the infant prodigy for ourselves, thus depriving her of what she regarded almost as her feudal right. For, after all, weren't they her peasants? If anyone was to profit by adopting the child it ought to be herself.

Tactfully, diplomatically, she renewed her negotiations with Carlo. The boy, she put it to him, had genius. The foreign gentleman had told her so. If Carlo would let her adopt the child, she'd have him trained. He'd become a great *maestro* and get engagements in the United States, in Paris and in London. He'd earn millions and millions. Part of the millions, she explained, would of course come to Carlo. But first the boy would have to be trained, and training was very expensive. In his own interest, as well as in that of his son, he ought to let her take charge of the child. Carlo said he would think it over, and again applied to us for advice. We suggested that it would be best in any case to wait a little and see what progress the boy made.

He made, in spite of my assertions to Signora Bondi, excellent progress. Every afternoon, while Robin was asleep, he came for his concert and his lesson. He was getting along famously with his reading; his small fingers were acquiring strength and agility. But what to me was more interesting was that he had begun to make up little pieces on his own account. A few of them I took down as he played them and I have them still. Most of them, strangely enough, as I thought then, are canons. He had a passion for canons. When I explained to him the principles of the form he was enchanted.

"It is beautiful," he said, with admiration. "Beautiful, beautiful. And so easy!"

The word surprised me. The canon is not, after all, so conspicuously simple. Thenceforward he spent most of his time at the piano in working out little canons for his own amusement. They were often remarkably ingenious. But in the invention of other kinds of music he did not show himself so fertile as I had hoped. He composed and harmonized one or two solemn little airs like hymn tunes, with a few sprightlier pieces in the spirit of the military march. "He's hardly a Mozart," we agreed, as we played his little pieces over. I felt, it must be confessed, almost aggrieved. Anything less than a Mozart, it seemed to me, was hardly worth thinking about.

He was not a Mozart. No. But he was somebody, as I was to find out, quite as extraordinary. It was one morning in the early summer that I made the discovery. I was sitting in the warm shade of our balcony, working. Guido and Robin were playing in the little enclosed garden below. Absorbed in my work, it was only after a considerable time that I became aware that the children were making remarkably little noise. Knowing by experience that when children are quiet it generally means that they are absorbed in some delicious mischief, I got up from my chair and looked over the balustrade expecting to see them dabbling in water, making a bonfire, covering themselves with tar. But what I actually saw was Guido, with a burnt stick in his hand, demonstrating on the smooth paving stones of the path, that the square of the hypotenuse of a right-angled triangle is equal to the sum of the squares on the other two sides.

Kneeling on the floor, he was drawing with the point of his blackened stick on the flagstones. And Robin, kneeling imitatively beside him, was growing, I could see, rather impatient with this very slow game.

"Guido," he said. But Guido went on with his diagram. "Guido!" The younger child craned his neck so as to look up into Guido's face. "Why don't you draw a train?"

"Afterwards," said Guido. "But I just want to show you this first. It's *so* beautiful," he added cajolingly.

"But I want a train," Robin persisted.

"In a moment. Do just wait a moment." The tone was almost imploring. Robin armed himself with renewed patience. A minute later Guido had finished both his diagrams.

"There!" he said triumphantly, and straightened himself up to look at them. "Now I'll explain."

And he proceeded to prove the theorem of Pythagoras—in the simple and satisfying method which was, in all probability, employed by Pythagoras himself. He had drawn a square and dissected it, by a pair of crossed perpendiculars, into two squares and two equal rectangles. The equal rectangles he divided up by their diagonals into four equal right-angled triangles. The two squares are then seen to be the squares on the two sides of any one of these triangles other than the hypotenuse. So much for the first diagram. In the next he took the four right-angled triangles into which the rectangles had been divided and rearranged them round the original square so that their right angles filled the corners of the square, the hypotenuses looked inwards, and the greater and less sides of the triangles were in continuation along the sides of the square (which are each equal to the sum of these sides). In this way the original square is redissected into four right-angled triangles and the square on the hypotenuse. The four triangles are equal to the two rectangles of the original dissection. Therefore the square on the hypotenuse is equal to the sum of the two squares—the squares on the other two sides—into which, with the rectangles, the original square was first dissected.

In very untechnical language, but clearly and with a relentless logic, Guido expounded his proof. Robin listened, with an expression on his bright, freckled face of perfect incomprehension.

"*Treno,*" he repeated from time to time. "*Treno.* Make a train."

"In a moment," Guido implored. "Wait a moment. But do just look at this. *Do.*" He coaxed and cajoled. "It's so beautiful. It's so easy."

So easy. . . . The theorem of Pythagoras seemed to explain for me Guido's musical predilections. It was not an infant Mozart we had been cherishing; it was a little Archimedes with, like most of his kind, an incidental musical twist.

"*Treno, treno!*" shouted Robin, growing more and more restless as the exposition went on. And when Guido insisted on going on with his proof, he lost his temper. He shouted and began to hit out at him with his fists.

"All right," said Guido resignedly. "I'll make a train." And with his stick of charcoal he began to scribble on the stones.

I looked on for a moment in silence. It was not a very good train. Guido might be able to invent for himself and prove the theorem of Pythagoras; but he was not much of a draftsman.

"Guido!" I called. The two children turned and looked up. "Who taught you to draw those squares?" It was conceivable, of course, that somebody might have taught him.

"Nobody." He shook his head. Then, rather anxiously, he went on to apologize and explain. "You see," he said, "it seemed to me so beautiful. Because those squares"—he pointed at the two small squares in the first figure—"are just as big as this one." And he looked up at me with a deprecating smile.

I nodded. "Yes, it's very beautiful," I said, "it's very beautiful indeed."

An expression of delighted relief appeared on his face; he laughed with pleasure.

"But I want a train," protested Robin.

Leaning on the rail of the balcony, I watched the children below. I thought of the extraordinary thing I had just seen and of what it meant.

I thought of the vast differences between human beings. We classify men by the color of their eyes and hair, the shape of their skulls. Would it not be more sensible to divide them up into intellectual species? There would be even wider gulfs between the extreme mental types than between a Bushman and a Scandinavian. This child, I thought, when he grows up, will be to me, intellectually, what a man is to a dog. And there are other men and women who are, perhaps, almost as dogs to me.

Perhaps the men of genius are the only true men. In all the history of the race there have been only a few thousand real men. And the rest of us—what are we? Teachable animals. Without the help of the real men, we should have found out almost nothing at all. Almost all the ideas with which we are familiar could never have occurred to minds like ours. Plant the seeds there and they will grow; but our minds could never spontaneously have generated them.

There have been whole nations of dogs, I thought; whole epochs in which no Man was born. From the Egyptians the Greeks took crude experience and rules of thumb and made sciences. More than a thousand years passed before Archimedes had a comparable successor. There has been only one Buddha, one Jesus, only one Bach that we know of, one Michelangelo.

Is it by a mere chance, I wondered, that a Man is born from time to time? What causes a whole constellation of them to come contemporaneously into being and from out of a single people? Taine thought that Leonardo, Michelangelo, and Raphael were born when they were because the time was ripe for great painters and the Italian scene congenial. The doctrine is strangely mystical; it may be nonetheless true. But what of those born out of time? What of those? Beethoven born in Greece, I thought, would have had to be content to play thin melodies on the flute or lyre; in those intellectual surroundings it would hardly have been possible for him to imagine the nature of harmony.

This child, I thought, has had the fortune to be born at a time when he will be able to make good use of his capacities. Suppose Guido born while Stonehenge was building; he might have spent a lifetime discovering the rudiments, guessing darkly where now he might have had a chance of proving. Born at the time of the Norman Conquest, he would have had to wrestle with all the preliminary difficulties created by an inadequate symbolism; it would have taken him long years, for example, to learn the art of dividing MMMCCCCLXXXVIII by MCMXIX. In five years, nowadays, he will learn what it took generations of Men to discover.

From drawing trains, the children in the garden below had gone on to playing trains. Robin puff-puffed, and Guido shuffled behind him, tooting. They ran forward, backed, stopped at imaginary stations, shunted, roared over bridges, crashed through tunnels, met with occasional collisions and derailments. The young Archimedes seemed to be just as happy as the little tow-headed barbarian. A few minutes ago he had been busy with the theorem of Pythagoras. Now, tooting indefatigably along imaginary rails, he was perfectly content to shuffle backwards and forwards among the flower beds, between the pillars of the loggia, in and out of the dark tunnels of the laurel tree. The fact that one is going to be Archimedes does not prevent one from being an ordinary cheerful child meanwhile.

In the weeks that followed, I alternated the daily piano lessons with lessons in mathematics. Hints rather than lessons they were; for I only made suggestions, indicated methods, and left the child himself to work out the ideas in detail. Thus I introduced him to algebra by showing him another proof of the theorem of Pythagoras. Guido was as much enchanted by the rudiments of algebra as he would have been if I had given him an engine worked by steam; more enchanted, perhaps—for the engine, remaining always itself, would in any case have lost its charm, while the rudiments of algebra continued to grow and blossom in his mind with an unfailing luxuriance. The new toy was inexhaustible in its potentialities.

In the intervals of applying algebra to the second book of Euclid, we experimented with circles; we stuck bamboos into the parched earth, measured their shadows at different hours of the day, and drew exciting conclusions from our observations. Sometimes, for fun, we cut and folded sheets of paper so as to make cubes and pyramids. One afternoon Guido arrived carrying carefully between his small and rather grubby hands a flimsy dodecahedron.

"È tanto bello!" he said, as he showed us his paper crystal; and when I asked him how he had managed to make it, he merely smiled and said it had been so easy. I looked at Elizabeth and laughed. But it would have been more symbolically to the point, I felt, if I had gone down on all fours and barked my astonished admiration.

It was an uncommonly hot summer. By the beginning of July our little Robin, unaccustomed to these high temperatures, began to look pale and tired; he was listless, had lost his appetite and energy. The doctor advised mountain air. We decided to spend the next ten or twelve weeks in Switzerland. My parting gift to Guido was the first six books of Euclid in Italian. He turned over the pages, looking ecstatically at the figures.

"If only I knew how to read properly," he said. "I'm so stupid. But now I shall really try to learn."

From our hotel near Grindelwald we sent the child, in Robin's name, various postcards of cows, Alp horns, Swiss chalets, edelweiss, and the like. We received no answers to these cards; but then we did not expect answers. Guido scarcely knew how to write, and there was no reason why his father or his sisters should take the trouble to write for him. No news, we took it, was good news. And then one day, early in September, there arrived at the hotel a strange letter. The manager had it stuck up on the glass-fronted notice board in the hall. Passing the board on the way in to lunch, Elizabeth stopped to look at it.

"But it must be from Guido," she said.

I came and looked at the envelope over her shoulder. It was unstamped and black with postmarks. Traced out in pencil, the big uncertain capital letters sprawled across its face. In the first line was written: AL BABBO DI ROBIN, and there followed a travestied version of the name of the hotel and the place. Round the address bewildered postal officials had scrawled suggested emendations. The letter had wandered for a fortnight at least, back and forth across the face of Europe.

"*Al Babbo di Robin.* To Robin's father." I laughed. "Pretty smart of the postmen to have got it here at all." I went to the manager's office, set forth the justice of my claim to the letter and, having paid the fifty-centime surcharge for the missing stamp, had the letter given me. We went in to lunch.

"The writing's magnificent," we agreed, laughing, as we examined the address at close quarters. "Thanks to Euclid," I added. "That's what comes of pandering to the ruling passion."

But when I opened the envelope and looked at its contents I no longer laughed. The letter was brief and almost telegraphical in style. *"Sono dalla Padrona,"* it ran, *"Non mi Piace ha Rubato il mio Libro non Voglio Suonare piu Voglio Tornare a Casa Venga Subito Guido."*

"What is it?"

I handed Elizabeth the letter. "That blasted woman's got hold of him," I said.

BUSTS OF MEN in Homburg hats, statues of little girls, cherubs, veiled figures—the strangest and most diverse idols beckoned and gesticulated as we passed. Printed indelibly on tin and embedded in the living rock, the brown photographs looked out, under glass, from the humbler crosses, headstones, and broken pillars. Dead ladies in the fashions of thirty years ago smiled mournfully out of their marble frames. Men with black mustaches, men with white beards, young clean-shaven men, stared or averted their gaze to show a Roman profile. Children in their stiff best opened wide their eyes, smiled laboriously and obediently because they had been told to. In spiky Gothic cottages of marble the richer dead privately reposed; the less prosperous sections of the majority slept in communities, close-crowded but elegantly housed under smooth continuous marble floors, whose every flagstone was the mouth of a separate grave.

These continental cemeteries, I thought, as Carlo and I made our way among the dead, are more frightful than ours, because these people pay more attention to their dead than we do. There are a hundred gesticulating statues here for every one in an English grave-yard. There are more family vaults, more "luxuriously appointed" (as they say of liners and hotels) than one would find at home. And embedded in every tombstone there are photographs to remind the powdered bones within what form they will have to resume on the Day of Judgment; beside each are little hanging lamps to burn optimistically on All Souls' Day.

"If I had known," Carlo kept repeating, "if only I had known." His voice came to me as though from a distance. "At the time he didn't mind at all. How should I have known that he would take it so much to heart afterwards? And she deceived me, she lied to me."

I assured him yet once more that it wasn't his fault. Though, of course, it was, in part. It was mine too, in part; I ought to have thought of the possibility and somehow guarded against it. And he shouldn't have let the child go, even temporarily and on trial, even though the woman was bringing pressure to bear on him. And the pressure had been considerable. They had worked on the same holding for more than a hundred years, the men of Carlo's family; and now Signora Bondi had made the old man threaten to turn him out. It would be a dreadful thing to leave the place; and besides, another place wasn't so easy to find. It was made quite plain, however, that he could stay if he let her have the child. Only for a little to begin with; just to see how he got on. There would be no compulsion whatever on him to stay if he didn't like it. And it would be all to Guido's advantage; and to his father's, too, in the end. All that the Englishman had said about his not being such a good musician as he had thought at first was obviously untrue—mere jealousy and little-mindedness; the man wanted to take credit for Guido himself, that was all. And the boy, it was obvious, would learn nothing from him. What he needed was a real good professional master.

All the *signora*'s energy went into this campaign. It began the moment we were out of the house. She doubtless thought it was essential to get hold of the child before we could make our bid—for it was obvious to her that we wanted Guido as much as she did.

Day after day she renewed the assault. At the end of a week she sent her husband to complain about the state of the vines; they were in a shocking condition; he had decided, or very nearly decided, to give Carlo notice. Meekly, shamefacedly, in obedience to higher orders, the old gentleman uttered his threats. Next day Signora Bondi returned to the attack. The *padrone*, she declared, had been in a towering passion; but she'd do her best, her very best, to mollify him. And after a significant pause she went on to talk about Guido.

In the end Carlo gave in. The woman was too persistent and she held too many trump cards. The child could go and stay with her for a month or two on trial. After that, if he really expressed a desire to remain with her, she could formally adopt him.

At the idea of going for a holiday to the seaside—and it was to the seaside, Signora Bondi told him, that they were going—Guido was pleased and excited. He had heard a lot about the sea from Robin. *"Tanta acqua!"* And now he was actually to go and see this marvel. Very cheerfully he parted from his family.

But after the holiday by the sea was over, and Signora Bondi had brought him back to her town house in Florence, he began to be homesick. The *signora*, it was true, treated him exceedingly kindly, bought him new clothes, took him out to tea in the Via Tornabuoni, and filled him up with cakes, iced strawberryade, whipped cream, and chocolates. But she made him practice the piano more than he liked, and what was worse, she took away his Euclid, on the score that he wasted too much time with it. And when he said that he wanted to go home, she put him off with promises and excuses and downright lies. She told him that she couldn't take him at once, but that next week, if he were good and worked hard at his piano meanwhile, next week . . . And when the time came she told him that his father didn't want him back. And she redoubled her petting, gave him expensive presents, and stuffed him with yet unhealthier foods. To no purpose. Guido didn't like his new life, didn't want to practice the scales, pined for his book, and longed to be back with his brothers and sisters. Signora Bondi, meanwhile, continued to hope that time and chocolates would eventually make the child hers; and to keep his family at a distance, she wrote to Carlo every few days letters which still purported to come from the seaside (she took the trouble to send them to a friend, who posted them back again to Florence), and in which she painted the most charming picture of Guido's happiness.

It was then that Guido wrote his letter to me. Abandoned, as he supposed, by his family he must have looked to me as his last and only hope. And the letter, with its fantastic address, had been nearly a fortnight on its way. A fortnight—it must have seemed hundreds of years; and as the centuries succeeded one another, gradually, no doubt, the poor child became convinced that I too had abandoned him. There was no hope left.

"Here we are," said Carlo.

I looked up and found myself confronted by an enormous monument. And in bronze letters riveted into the stone was a long legend to the effect that the inconsolable Ernesto Bondi had raised this monument to the memory of his beloved first wife, Annunziata, snatched from him by a premature death.

"They buried him here."

We stood there for a long time in silence. I felt the tears coming into my eyes as I thought of the poor child lying there underground. I thought of those luminous grave eyes, the curve of that beautiful forehead, the droop of the melancholy mouth, of the expression of delight which illumined his face when he learned of some new idea that pleased him, when he heard a piece of music that he liked. And this beautiful small being was dead; and the spirit that inhabited this form, the amazing spirit, that too had been destroyed almost before it had begun to exist.

And the unhappiness that must have preceded the final act, the child's despair, the conviction of his utter abandonment—those were terrible to think of, terrible.

"I think we had better come away now," I said at last, and touched Carlo on the arm. He was standing there like a blind man; from between his closed eyelids the tears welled out, hung for a moment, and trickled down his cheeks. His lips trembled. "Come away," I repeated.

The face which had been still in its sorrow, was suddenly convulsed; he opened his eyes, and through the tears they were bright with a violent anger. "I shall kill her," he said. "I shall kill her. When I think of him throwing himself out, falling through the air . . ." With his two hands he made a violent gesture, bringing them down from over his head and arresting them with a sudden jerk when they were on a level with his breast. "And then crash." He shuddered. "She's as much responsible as though she had pushed him down herself. I shall kill her." He clenched his teeth.

To be angry is easier than to be sad, less painful. It is comforting to think of revenge. "Don't talk like that," I said. "It's no good. It's stupid. And what would be the point?" He had had those fits before, when grief became too painful and he had tried to escape from it. I had had, before this, to persuade him back into the harder path of grief. "It's stupid to talk like that," I repeated, and I led him away through the ghastly labyrinth of tombs, where death seemed more terrible even than it is.

By the time we had left the cemetery, he had become calmer. His anger had subsided again into the sorrow from which it had derived all its strength and its bitterness. We halted for a moment to look down at the city of Florence in the valley below us. It was a day of floating clouds—great shapes, white, golden, and gray; and between them patches of a thin, transparent blue. On the innumerable brown and rosy roofs of the city the afternoon sunlight lay softly, sumptuously, and the towers were as though varnished and enameled with an old gold. I thought of all the Men who had lived here and left the visible traces of their spirit and conceived extraordinary things. I thought of the dead child.

BUTCH MINDS THE BABY
DAMON RUNYON / UNITED STATES

ONE EVENING along about seven o'clock I am sitting in Mindy's restaurant putting on the gefilte fish, which is a dish I am very fond of, when in comes three parties from Brooklyn wearing caps as follows: Harry the Horse, Little Isadore and Spanish John.

Now these parties are not such parties as I will care to have much truck with, because I often hear rumors about them that are very discreditable, even if the rumors are not true. In fact, I hear that many citizens of Brooklyn will be very glad indeed to see Harry the Horse, Little Isadore and Spanish John move away from there, as they are always doing something that is considered a knock to the community, such as robbing people, or maybe shooting or stabbing them, and throwing pineapples, and carrying on generally.

I am really much surprised to see these parties on Broadway, as it is well known that the Broadway coppers just naturally love to shove such parties around, but here they are in Mindy's, and there I am, so of course I give them a very large hello, as I never wish to seem inhospitable, even to Brooklyn parties. Right away they come over to my table and sit down, and Little Isadore reaches out and spears himself a big hunk of my gefilte fish with his fingers, but I overlook this, as I am using the only knife on the table.

Then they all sit there looking at me without saying anything, and the way they look at me makes me very nervous indeed. Finally I figure that maybe they are a little embarrassed being in a high-class spot such as Mindy's, with legitimate people around and about, so I say to them, very polite: "It is a nice night."

"What is nice about it?" asks Harry the Horse, who is a thin man with a sharp face and sharp eyes.

Well, now that it is put up to me in this way, I can see there is nothing so nice about the night, at that, so I try to think of something else jolly to say, while Little Isadore keeps spearing at my gefilte fish with his fingers, and Spanish John nabs one of my potatoes.

"Where does Big Butch live?" Harry the Horse asks.

"Big Butch?" I say, as if I never hear the name before in my life, because in this man's town it is never a good idea to answer any question without thinking it over, as sometime you may give the right answer to the wrong guy, or the wrong answer to the right guy. "Where does Big Butch live?" I ask them again.

"Yes, where does he live?" Harry the Horse says, very impatient. "We wish you to take us to him."

"Now wait a minute, Harry," I say, and I am now more nervous than somewhat. "I am not sure I remember the exact house Big Butch lives in, and furthermore I am not sure Big Butch will care to have me bringing people to see him, especially three at a time, and especially from Brooklyn. You know Big Butch has a very bad disposition, and there is no telling what he may say to me if he does not like the idea of me taking you to him."

"Everything is very kosher," Harry the Horse says. "You need not be afraid of anything whatever. We have a business proposition for Big Butch, so you take us to him at once, or the chances are I will have to put the arm on somebody around here."

Well, as the only one around there for him to put the arm on at this time seems to be me, I can see where it will be good policy for me to take these parties to Big Butch, especially as the last of my gefilte fish is just going down Little Isadore's gullet, and Spanish John is finishing up my potatoes, and is dunking a piece of rye bread in my coffee, so there is nothing more for me to eat.

So I lead them over into West Forty-ninth Street, near Tenth Avenue, where Big Butch lives on the ground floor of an old brownstone-front house, and who is sitting out on the stoop but Big Butch himself. In fact, everybody in the neighborhood is sitting out on the front stoops over there, including women and children, because sitting out on the front stoops is quite a custom in this section.

Big Butch is peeled down to his undershirt and pants, and he has no shoes on his feet, as Big Butch is a guy who likes his comfort. Furthermore, he is smoking a cigar, and laid out on the stoop beside him on a blanket is a little baby with not much clothes on. This baby seems to be asleep, and every now and then Big Butch fans it with a folded newspaper to shoo away the mosquitoes that wish to nibble on the baby. These mosquitoes come across the river from the Jersey side on hot nights and they seem to be very fond of babies.

"Hello, Butch," I say, as we stop in front of the stoop.

"Sh-h-h-h!" Butch says, pointing at the baby, and making more noise with his shush than an engine blowing off steam. Then he gets up and tiptoes down to the sidewalk where we are standing, and I am hoping that Butch feels all right, because when Butch does not feel so good he is apt to be very short with one and all. He is a guy of maybe six foot two and a couple of feet wide, and he has big hairy hands and a mean look.

In fact, Big Butch is known all over this man's town as a guy you must not monkey with in any respect, so it takes plenty of weight off of me when I see that he seems to know the parties from Brooklyn, and nods at them very friendly, especially at Harry the Horse. And right away Harry states a most surprising proposition to Big Butch.

It seems that there is a big coal company which has an office in an old building down in West Eighteenth Street, and in this office is a safe, and in this safe is the company payroll of twenty thousand dollars cash money. Harry the Horse knows the money is there because a personal friend of his who is the paymaster for the company puts it there late this very afternoon.

It seems that the paymaster enters into a dicker with Harry the Horse and Little Isadore and Spanish John for them to slug him while he is carrying the payroll from the bank to the office in the afternoon, but something happens that they miss connections on the exact spot, so the paymaster has to carry the sugar on to the office without being slugged, and there it is now in two fat bundles.

Personally it seems to me as I listen to Harry's story that the paymaster must be a very dishonest character to be making deals to hold still while he is being slugged and the company's sugar taken away from him, but of course it is none of my business, so I take no part in the conversation.

Well, it seems that Harry the Horse and Little Isadore and Spanish John wish to get the money out of the safe, but none of them knows anything about opening safes, and while they are standing around over in Brooklyn talking over what is to be done in this emergency Harry suddenly remembers that Big Butch is once in the business of opening safes for a living.

In fact, I hear afterwards that Big Butch is considered the best safe opener east of the Mississippi River in his day, but the law finally takes to sending him to Sing Sing for opening these safes, and after he is in and out of Sing Sing three different times for opening safes Butch gets sick and tired of the place, especially as they pass what is called the Baumes Law in New York, which is a law that says if a guy is sent to Sing Sing four times hand running, he must stay there the rest of his life, without any argument about it.

So Big Butch gives up opening safes for a living, and goes into business in a small way, such as running beer, and handling a little Scotch now and then, and becomes an honest citizen. Furthermore, he marries one of the neighbor's children over on the West Side by the name of Mary Murphy, and I judge the baby on this stoop comes of this marriage between Big Butch and Mary because I can see that it is a very homely baby, indeed. Still, I never see many babies that I consider rose geraniums for looks, anyway.

Well, it finally comes out that the idea of Harry the Horse and Little Isadore and Spanish John is to get Big Butch to open the coal company's safe and take the payroll money out, and they are willing to give him fifty percent of the money for his bother, taking fifty percent for themselves for finding the plant, and paying all the overhead, such as the paymaster, out of their bit, which strikes me as a pretty fair sort of deal for Big Butch. But Butch only shakes his head.

"It is old-fashioned stuff," Butch says. "Nobody opens pete boxes for a living anymore. They make the boxes too good, and they are all wired up with alarms and are a lot of trouble generally. I am in a legitimate business now and going along. You boys know I cannot stand another fall, what with being away three times already, and in addition to this I must mind the baby. My old lady goes to Mrs. Clancy's wake tonight up in the Bronx, and the chances are she will be there all night, as she is very fond of wakes, so I must mind little John Ignatius Junior."

"Listen, Butch," Harry the Horse says, "this is a very soft pete. It is old-fashioned, and you can open it with a toothpick. There are no wires on it, because they never put more than a dime in it before in years. It just happens they have to put the twenty G's in it tonight because my pal the paymaster makes it a point not to get back from the jug with the scratch in time to pay off today, especially after he sees we miss out on him. It is the softest touch you will ever know, and where can a guy pick up ten G's like this?"

I can see that Big Butch is thinking the ten G's over very seriously, at that, because in these times nobody can afford to pass up ten G's, especially a guy in the beer business, which is very, very tough just now. But finally he shakes his head again and says like this:

"No," he says, "I must let it go, because I must mind the baby. My old lady is very, very particular about this, and I dast not leave little John Ignatius Junior for a minute. If Mary comes home and finds I am not minding the baby she will put the blast on me plenty. I like to turn a few honest bobs now and then as well as anybody, but," Butch says, "John Ignatius Junior comes first with me."

Then he turns away and goes back to the stoop as much as to say he is through arguing, and sits down beside John Ignatius Junior again just in time to keep a mosquito from carrying off one of John's legs. Anybody can see that Big Butch is very fond of this baby, though personally I will not give you a dime a dozen for babies, male and female.

Well, Harry the Horse and Little Isadore and Spanish John are very much disappointed, and stand around talking among themselves, and paying no attention to me, when all of a sudden Spanish John, who never has much to say up to this time, seems to have a bright idea. He talks to Harry and Isadore, and they get all pleasured up over what he has to say, and finally Harry goes to Big Butch.

"Sh-h-h-h!" Big Butch says, pointing to the baby as Harry opens his mouth.

"Listen, Butch," Harry says in a whisper, "we can take the baby with us, and you can mind it and work, too."

"Why," Big Butch whispers back, "this is quite an idea indeed. Let us go into the house and talk things over."

So he picks up the baby and leads us into his joint, and gets out some pretty fair beer, though it is needled a little, at that, and we sit around the kitchen chewing the fat in whispers. There is a crib in the kitchen, and Butch puts the baby in his crib, and it keeps on snoozing away first rate while we are talking. In fact, it is sleeping so sound that I am commencing to figure that Butch must give it some of the needled beer he is feeding us, because I am feeling a little dopey myself.

Finally Butch says that as long as he can take John Ignatius Junior with him he sees no reason why he shall not go and open the safe for them, only he says he must have five percent more to put in the baby's bank when he gets back, so as to round himself up with his ever-loving wife in case of a beef from her over keeping the baby out in the night air. Harry the Horse says he considers this extra five percent a little strong, but Spanish John, who seems to be a very square guy, says that after all it is only fair to cut the baby in if it is to be with them when they are making the score, and Little Isadore seems to think this is all right, too. So Harry the Horse gives in, and says five percent it is.

Well, as they do not wish to start out until after midnight, and as there is plenty of time, Big Butch gets out some more needled beer, and then he goes looking for the tools with which he opens safes, and which he says he does not see since the day John Ignatius Junior is born and he gets them out to build the crib.

Now this is a good time for me to bid one and all farewell, and what keeps me there is something I cannot tell you to this day, because personally I never before have any idea of taking part in a safe opening, especially with a baby, as I consider such actions very dishonorable. When I come to think things over afterwards, the only thing I can figure is the needled beer, but I wish to say I am really very much surprised at myself when I find myself in a taxicab along about one o'clock in the morning with these Brooklyn parties and Big Butch and the baby.

Butch has John Ignatius Junior rolled up in a blanket, and John is still pounding his ear. Butch has a satchel of tools, and what looks to me like a big flat book, and just before we leave the house Butch hands me a package and tells me to be very careful with it. He gives Little Isadore a smaller package, which Isadore shoves into his pistol pocket, and when Isadore sits down in the taxi something goes wa-wa, like a sheep, and Big Butch becomes very indignant because it seems Isadore is sitting on John Ignatius Junior's doll, which says "Mamma" when you squeeze it.

It seems Big Butch figures that John Ignatius Junior may wish something to play with in case he wakes up, and it is a good thing for Little Isadore that the mamma doll is not squashed so it cannot say "Mamma" anymore, or the chances are Little Isadore will get a good bust in the snoot.

We let the taxicab go a block away from the spot we are headed for in West Eighteenth Street, between Seventh and Eighth avenues, and walk the rest of the way two by two. I walk with Big Butch, carrying my package, and Butch is lugging the baby and his satchel and the flat thing that looks like a book. It is so quiet down in West Eighteenth Street at such an hour that you can hear yourself think, and in fact I hear myself thinking very plain that I am a big sap to be on a job like this, especially with a baby, but I keep going just the same, which shows you what a very big sap I am, indeed.

There are very few people in West Eighteenth Street when we get there, and one of them is a fat guy who is leaning against a building almost in the center of the block, and who takes a walk for himself as soon as he sees us. It seems that this fat guy is the watchman at the coal company's office and is also a personal friend of Harry the Horse, which is why he takes the walk when he sees us coming.

It is agreed before we leave Big Butch's house that Harry the Horse and Spanish John are to stay outside the place as lookouts, while Big Butch is inside opening the safe, and that Little Isadore is to go with Butch. Nothing whatever is said by anybody about where I am to be at any time, and I can see that, no matter where I am, I will still be an outsider, but, as Butch gives me the package to carry, I figure he wishes me to remain with him.

It is no bother at all getting into the office of the coal company, which is on the ground floor, because it seems the watchman leaves the front door open, this watchman being a most obliging guy, indeed. In fact he is so obliging that by and by he comes back and lets Harry the Horse and Spanish John tie him up good and tight, and stick a handkerchief in his mouth and chuck him in an areaway next to the office, so nobody will think he has anything to do with opening the safe in case anybody comes around asking.

The office looks out on the street, and the safe that Harry the Horse and Little Isadore and Spanish John wish Big Butch to open is standing up against the rear wall of the office facing the street windows. There is one little electric light burning very dim over the safe so that when anybody walks past the place outside, such as a watchman, they can look in through the window and see the safe at all times, unless they are blind. It is not a tall safe, and it is not a big safe, and I can see Big Butch grin when he sees it, so I figure this safe is not much of a safe, just as Harry the Horse claims.

Well, as soon as Big Butch and the baby and Little Isadore and me get into the office, Big Butch steps over to the safe and unfolds what I think is the big flat book, and what is it but a sort of screen painted on one side to look exactly like the front of a safe. Big Butch stands this screen up on the floor in front of the real safe, leaving plenty of space in between, the idea being that the screen will keep anyone passing in the street outside from seeing Butch while he is opening the safe, because when a man is opening a safe he needs all the privacy he can get.

Big Butch lays John Ignatius Junior down on the floor on the blanket behind the phony safe front and takes his tools out of the satchel and starts to work opening the safe, while Little Isadore and me get back in a corner where it is dark, because there is not room for all of us back of the screen. However, we can see what Big Butch is doing, and I wish to say while I never before see a professional safe opener at work, and never wish to see another, this Butch handles himself like a real artist.

He starts drilling into the safe around the combination lock, working very fast and very quiet, when all of a sudden what happens but John Ignatius Junior sits up on the blanket and lets out a squall. Naturally this is most disquieting to me, and personally I am in favor of beaning John Ignatius Junior with something to make him keep still, because I am nervous enough as it is. But the squalling does not seem to bother Big Butch. He lays down his tools and picks up John Ignatius Junior and starts whispering, "There, there, there, my itty oddleums. Da-dad is here."

Well, this sounds very nonsensical to me in such a situation, and it makes no impression whatever on John Ignatius Junior. He keeps on squalling, and I judge he is squalling pretty loud because I see Harry the Horse and Spanish John both walk past the window and look in very anxious. Big Butch jiggles John Ignatius Junior up and down and keeps whispering baby talk to him, which sounds very undignified coming from a high-class safe opener, and finally Butch whispers to me to hand him the package I am carrying.

He opens the package, and what is in it but a baby's nursing bottle full of milk. Moreover, there is a little tin stewpan, and Butch hands the pan to me and whispers to me to find a water tap somewhere in the joint and fill the pan with water. So I go stumbling around in the dark in a room behind the office and bark my shins several times before I find a tap and fill the pan. I take it back to Big Butch, and he squats there with the baby on one arm, and gets a tin of what is called canned heat out of the package, and lights this canned heat with his cigar lighter, and starts heating the pan of water with the nursing bottle in it.

Big Butch keeps sticking his finger in the pan of water while it is heating, and by and by he puts the rubber nipple of the nursing bottle in his mouth and takes a pull at it to see if the milk is warm enough, just like I see dolls who have babies do. Apparently the milk is okay, as Butch hands the bottle to John Ignatius Junior, who grabs hold of it with both hands and starts sucking on the business end. Naturally he has to stop squalling, and Big Butch goes to work on the safe again, with John Ignatius Junior sitting on the blanket, pulling on the bottle and looking wiser than a treeful of owls.

It seems the safe is either a tougher job than anybody figures, or Big Butch's tools are not so good, what with being old and rusty and used for building baby cribs, because he breaks a couple of drills and works himself up into quite a sweat without getting anywhere. Butch afterwards explains to me that he is one of the first guys in this country to open safes without explosives, but he says to do this work properly you have to know the safes so as to drill to the tumblers of the lock just right, and it seems that this particular safe is a new type to him, even if it is old, and he is out of practice.

Well, in the meantime John Ignatius Junior finishes his bottle and starts mumbling again, and Big Butch gives him a tool to play with, and finally Butch needs this tool and tries to take it away from John Ignatius Junior, and the baby lets out such a squawk that Butch has to let him keep it until he can sneak it away from him, and this causes more delay.

Finally Big Butch gives up trying to drill the safe open, and he whispers to us that he will have to put a little shot in it to loosen up the lock, which is all right with us, because we are getting tired of hanging around and listening to John Ignatius Junior's glug-glugging. As far as I am personally concerned, I am wishing I am home in bed.

Well, Butch starts pawing through his satchel looking for some-thing and it seems that what he is looking for is a little bottle of some kind of explosive with which to shake the lock on the safe up some, and at first he cannot find this bottle, but finally he discovers that John Ignatius Junior has it and is gnawing at the cork, and Butch has quite a battle making John Ignatius Junior give it up.

Anyway, he fixes the explosive in one of the holes he drills near the combination lock on the safe, and then he puts in a fuse, and just before he touches off the fuse Butch picks up John Ignatius Junior and hands him to Little Isadore, and tells us to go into the room behind the office. John Ignatius Junior does not seem to care for Little Isadore, and I do not blame him, at that, because he starts to squirm around quite some in Isadore's arms and lets out a squall, but all of a sudden he becomes very quiet indeed, and, while I am not able to prove it, something tells me that Little Isadore has his hand over John Ignatius Junior's mouth.

Well, Big Butch joins us right away in the back room, and sound comes out of John Ignatius Junior again as Butch takes him from Little Isadore, and I am thinking that it is a good thing for Isadore that the baby cannot tell Big Butch what Isadore does to him.

"I put in just a little bit of a shot," Big Butch says, "and it will not make any more noise than snapping your fingers."

But a second later there is a big *whoom* from the office, and the whole joint shakes, and John Ignatius Junior laughs right out loud. The chances are he thinks it is the Fourth of July.

"I guess maybe I put in too big a charge," Big Butch says, and then he rushes into the office with Little Isadore and me after him, and John Ignatius Junior still laughing very heartily for a small baby. The door of the safe is swinging loose, and the whole joint looks somewhat wrecked, but Big Butch loses no time in getting his dukes into the safe and grabbing out two big bundles of cash money, which he sticks inside his shirt.

As we go into the street Harry the Horse and Spanish John come running up much excited, and Harry says to Big Butch like this:

"What are you trying to do," he says, "wake up the whole town?"

"Well," Butch says, "I guess maybe the charge is too strong, at that, but nobody seems to be coming, so you and Spanish John walk over to Eighth Avenue, and the rest of us will walk to Seventh, and if you go along quiet, like people minding their own business, it will be all right."

But I judge Little Isadore is tired of John Ignatius Junior's company by this time, because he says he will go with Harry the Horse and Spanish John, and this leaves Big Butch and John Ignatius Junior and me to go the other way. So we start moving, and all of a sudden two cops come tearing around the corner toward which Harry and

Isadore and Spanish John are going. The chances are the cops hear the earthquake Big Butch lets off and are coming to investigate.

But the chances are, too, that if Harry the Horse and the other two keep on walking along very quietly like Butch tells them to, the coppers will pass them up entirely, because it is not likely that coppers will figure anybody to be opening safes with explosives in this neighborhood. But the minute Harry the Horse sees the coppers he loses his nut, and he outs with the old equalizer and starts blasting, and what does Spanish John do but get his out, too, and open up.

The next thing anybody knows, the two coppers are down on the ground with slugs in them, but other coppers are coming from every which direction, blowing whistles and doing a little blasting themselves, and there is plenty of excitement, especially when the coppers who are not chasing Harry the Horse and Little Isadore and Spanish John start poking around the neighborhood and find Harry's pal, the watchman, all tied up nice and tight where Harry leaves him, and the watchman explains that some scoundrels blow open the safe he is watching.

All this time Big Butch and me are walking in the other direction toward Seventh Avenue, and Big Butch has John Ignatius in his arms, and John Ignatius is now squalling very loud, indeed. The chances are he is still thinking of the big *whoom* back there which tickles him so and is wishing to hear some more *whooms*. Anyway, he is beating his own best record for squalling, and as we go walking along Big Butch says to me like this:

"I dast not run," he says, "because if any coppers see me running they will start popping at me and maybe hit John Ignatius Junior, and besides running will joggle the milk up in him and make him sick. My old lady always warns me never to joggle John Ignatius Junior when he is full of milk."

"Well, Butch," I say, "there is no milk in me, and I do not care if I am joggled up, so if you do not mind, I will start doing a piece of running at the next corner."

But just then around the corner of Seventh Avenue toward which we are headed comes two or three coppers with a big fat sergeant with them, and one of the coppers, who is half out of breath as if he has been doing plenty of sprinting, is explaining to the sergeant that somebody blows a safe down the street and shoots a couple of coppers in the getaway.

And there is Big Butch, with John Ignatius Junior in his arms and twenty G's in his shirtfront and a tough record behind him, walking right up to them.

I am feeling very sorry, indeed, for Big Butch, and very sorry for myself, too, and I am saying to myself that if I get out of this I will never associate with anyone but ministers of the gospel as long as I live. I can remember thinking that I am getting a better break than Butch, at that, because I will not have to go to Sing Sing for the rest of my life, like him, and I also remember wondering what they will give John Ignatius Junior, who is still tearing off these squalls, with Big Butch saying: "There, there, there, Daddy's itty woogleums." Then I hear one of the coppers say to the fat sergeant: "We better nail these guys. They may be in on this."

Well, I can see it is good-by to Butch and John Ignatius Junior and me, as the fat sergeant steps up to Big Butch, but instead of putting the arm on Butch, the fat sergeant only points at John Ignatius Junior and asks very sympathetic: "Teeth?"

"No," Big Butch says. "Not teeth. Colic. I just get the doctor here out of bed to do something for him, and we are going to a drugstore to get some medicine."

Well, naturally I am very much surprised at this statement, because of course I am not a doctor, and if John Ignatius Junior has colic it serves him right, but I am only hoping they do not ask for my degree, when the fat sergeant says: "Too bad. I know what it is. I got three of them at home. But," he says, "it acts more like it is teeth than colic."

Then as Big Butch and John Ignatius Junior and me go on about our business I hear the fat sergeant say to the copper, very sarcastic: "Yea, of course a guy is out blowing safes with a baby in his arms! You will make a great detective, you will!"

I do not see Big Butch for several days after I learn that Harry the Horse and Little Isadore and Spanish John get back to Brooklyn all right, except they are a little nicked up here and there from the slugs the coppers toss at them, while the coppers they clip are not damaged so very much. The chances are I will not see Big Butch for several years, if it is left to me, but he comes looking for me one night, and he seems to be all pleasured up about something.

"Say," Big Butch says to me, "you know I never give a copper credit for knowing any too much about anything, but I wish to say that this fat sergeant we run into the other night is a very, very smart duck. He is right about it being teeth that is ailing John Ignatius Junior, for what happens yesterday but John cuts in his first tooth."

SUSPICION
DOROTHY L. SAYERS / GREAT BRITAIN

As THE ATMOSPHERE of the railway carriage thickened with tobacco smoke, Mr. Mummery became increasingly aware that his breakfast had not agreed with him.

There could have been nothing wrong with the breakfast itself. Brown bread, rich in vitamin content, as advised by the *Morning Star*'s health expert; bacon fried to a delicious crispness; eggs just nicely set; coffee made as only Mrs. Sutton knew how to make it. Mrs. Sutton had been a real find, and that was something to be thankful for. For Ethel, since her nervous breakdown in the summer, had really not been fit to wrestle with the untrained girls who had come and gone in tempestuous succession. It took very little to upset Ethel nowadays, poor child. Mr. Mummery, trying hard to ignore his growing internal discomfort, hoped he was not in for an illness. Apart from the trouble it would cause at the office, it would worry Ethel terribly, and Mr. Mummery would cheerfully have laid down his rather uninteresting little life to spare Ethel a moment's uneasiness.

He slipped a digestive tablet into his mouth—he had taken lately to carrying a few tablets about with him—and opened his paper. There did not seem to be very much news. A question had been asked in the House about government typewriters. The Prince of Wales had smilingly opened an all-British exhibition of footwear. A further split had occurred in the Liberal Party. The police were still looking for the woman who was supposed to have poisoned a family in Lincoln. Two girls had been trapped in a burning factory. A film star had obtained her fourth decree nisi.

At Paragon Station, Mr. Mummery descended and took a tram. The internal discomfort was taking the form of a definite nausea. Happily he contrived to reach his office before the worst occurred. He was seated at his desk, pale but in control of himself, when his partner came breezing in.

"'Morning, Mummery," said Mr. Brookes in his loud tones, adding inevitably, "Cold enough for you?"

"Quite," replied Mr. Mummery. "Unpleasantly raw, in fact."

"Beastly, beastly," said Mr. Brookes. "Your bulbs all in?"

"Not quite all," confessed Mr. Mummery. "As a matter of fact I haven't been feeling—"

"Pity," interrupted his partner. "Great pity. Ought to get 'em in early. Mine were in last week. My little place will be a picture in the spring. For a town garden, that is. You're lucky, living in the country. Find it better than Hull, I expect, eh? Though we get plenty of fresh air up in the avenues. How's the missus?"

"Thank you, she's very much better."

"Glad to hear that, very glad. Hope we shall have her about again this winter as usual. Can't do without her in the Drama Society, you know. By Jove! I shan't forget her acting last year in *Romance*. She and young Welbeck positively brought the house down, didn't they? The Welbecks were asking after her only yesterday."

"Thank you, yes. I hope she will soon be able to take up her social activities again. But the doctor says she mustn't overdo it. No worry, he says—that's the important thing. She is to go easy and not rush about or undertake too much."

"Quite right, quite right. Worry's the devil and all. I cut out worrying years ago and look at me! Fit as a fiddle, for all I shan't see fifty again. *You're* not looking altogether the thing, by the way."

"A touch of dyspepsia," said Mr. Mummery. "Nothing much. Chill on the liver, that's what I put it down to."

"That's what it is," said Mr. Brookes, seizing his opportunity. "Is life worth living? It depends upon the liver. Ha, ha! Well now, well now—we must do a spot of work, I suppose. Where's that lease of Ferraby's?"

Mr. Mummery, who did not feel at his conversational best that morning, rather welcomed this suggestion, and for half an hour was allowed to proceed in peace with the duties of an estate agent. Presently, however, Mr. Brookes burst into speech again.

"By the way," he said abruptly, "I suppose your wife doesn't know of a good cook, does she?"

"Well, no," replied Mr. Mummery. "They aren't so easy to find nowadays. In fact, we've only just got suited ourselves. But why? Surely your old Cookie isn't leaving you?"

"Good lord, no!" Mr. Brookes laughed heartily. "It would take an earthquake to shake off old Cookie. No. It's for the Philipsons. Their girl's getting married. That's the worst of girls. I said to Philipson, 'You mind what you're doing,' I said. 'Get somebody you know something about, or you may find yourself landed with this poisoning woman—what's her name—Andrews. Don't want to be sending wreaths to your funeral yet awhile,' I said. He laughed, but it's no laughing matter and so I told him. What we pay the police for I simply don't know. Nearly a month now, and they can't seem to lay hands on the woman. All they say is, they think she's hanging about the neighborhood and 'may seek a situation as cook.' As cook! Now I ask you!"

"You don't think she committed suicide, then?" suggested Mr. Mummery.

"Suicide my foot!" retorted Mr. Brookes coarsely. "Don't you believe it, my boy. That coat found in the river was all eyewash. *They* don't commit suicide, that sort don't."

"What sort?"

"Those arsenic maniacs. They're too damned careful of their own skins. Cunning as weasels, that's what they are. It's only to be hoped they'll manage to catch her before she tries her hand on anybody else. As I told Philipson—"

"You think Mrs. Andrews did it, then?"

"Did it? Of course she did it. It's plain as the nose on your face. Looked after her old father, and he died suddenly—left her a bit of money, too. Then she keeps house for an elderly gentleman, and *he* dies suddenly. Now there's this husband and wife—man dies and woman taken very ill, of arsenic poisoning. Cook runs away, and you ask, did she do it? I don't mind betting that when they dig up the father and the other old bird they'll find *them* bung-full of arsenic, too. Once that sort gets started, they don't stop. Grows on 'em, as you might say."

"I suppose it does," said Mr. Mummery. He picked up his paper again and studied the photograph of the missing woman. "She looks harmless enough," he remarked. "Rather a nice, motherly-looking kind of woman."

"She's got a bad mouth," pronounced Mr. Brookes. He had a theory that character showed in the mouth. "I wouldn't trust that woman an inch."

AS THE DAY went on, Mr. Mummery felt better. He was rather nervous about his lunch, choosing carefully a little boiled fish and custard pudding and being particular not to rush about immediately after the meal. To his great relief, the fish and custard remained where they were put, and he was not visited by that tiresome pain which had become almost habitual in the last fortnight. By the end of the day he became quite lighthearted. The bogey of illness and doctor's bills ceased to haunt him. He bought a bunch of bronze chrysanthemums to carry home to Ethel, and it was with a feeling of pleasant anticipation that he left the train and walked up the garden path of Mon Abri.

He was a little dashed by not finding his wife in the sitting room. Still clutching the bunch of chrysanthemums he pattered down the passage and pushed open the kitchen door.

Nobody was there but the cook. She was sitting at the table with her back to him, and started up almost guiltily as he approached.

"Lor', sir," she said, "you give me quite a start. I didn't hear the front door go."

"Where is Mrs. Mummery? Not feeling bad again, is she?"

"Well, sir, she's got a bit of a headache, poor lamb. I made her lay down and took her up a nice cup o' tea at half past four. I think she's dozing nicely now."

"Dear, dear," said Mr. Mummery.

"It was turning out the dining room done it, if you ask me," said Mrs. Sutton. "'Now, don't you overdo yourself, ma'am,' I says to her, but you know how she is, sir. She gets that restless, she can't abear to be doing nothing."

"I know," said Mr. Mummery. "It's not your fault, Mrs. Sutton. I'm sure you look after us both admirably. I'll just run up and have a peep at her. I won't disturb her if she's asleep. By the way, what are we having for dinner?"

"Well, I *had* made a nice steak-and-kidney pie," said Mrs. Sutton, in accents suggesting that she would readily turn it into a pumpkin or a coach-and-four if it was not approved of.

"Oh!" said Mr. Mummery. "Pastry? Well, I—"

"You'll find it beautiful and light," protested the cook, whisking open the oven door for Mr. Mummery to see. "And it's made with butter, sir, you having said that you found lard indigestible."

"Thank you, thank you," said Mr. Mummery. "I'm sure it will be most excellent. I haven't been feeling altogether the thing just lately, and lard does not seem to suit me nowadays."

"Well, it don't suit some people, and that's a fact," agreed Mrs. Sutton. "I shouldn't wonder if you've got a bit of a chill on the liver. I'm sure this weather is enough to upset anybody."

She bustled to the table and cleared away the picture paper which she had been reading.

"Perhaps the mistress would like her dinner sent up to her?" she suggested.

Mr. Mummery said he would go and see, and tiptoed his way upstairs.

Ethel was lying snuggled under the eiderdown and looked very small and fragile in the big double bed. She stirred as he came in and smiled up at him.

"Hullo, darling!" said Mr. Mummery.

"Hullo! You back? I must have been asleep. I got tired and headachy, and Mrs. Sutton packed me off upstairs."

"You've been doing too much, sweetheart," said her husband, taking her hand in his and sitting down on the edge of the bed.

"Yes—it was naughty of me. What lovely flowers, Harold. All for me?"

"All for you, Tiddleywinks," said Mr. Mummery tenderly. "Don't I deserve something for that?"

Mrs. Mummery smiled, and Mr. Mummery took his reward several times over.

"That's quite enough, you sentimental old thing," said Mrs. Mummery. "Run away, now, I'm going to get up."

"Much better go to bed, my precious, and let Mrs. Sutton send your dinner up," said her husband.

Ethel protested, but he was firm with her. If she didn't take care of herself, she wouldn't be allowed to go to the Drama Society meetings. And everybody was so anxious to have her back. The Welbecks had been asking after her and saying that they really couldn't get on without her.

"Did they?" said Ethel with some animation. "It's very sweet of them to want me. Well, perhaps I'll go to bed after all. And how has my old hubby been all day?"

"Not too bad, not too bad."

"No more tummyaches?"

"Well, just a *little* tummyache. But it's quite gone now. Nothing for Tiddleywinks to worry about."

MR. MUMMERY experienced no more distressing symptoms the next day or the next. Following the advice of the newspaper expert, he took to drinking orange juice, and was delighted with the results of the treatment. On Thursday, however, he was taken so ill in the night that Ethel was alarmed and insisted on sending for the doctor. The doctor felt his pulse and looked at his tongue and appeared to take the matter lightly. An inquiry into what he had been eating elicited the fact that dinner had consisted of pigs' trotters, followed by a milk pudding, and that, before retiring, Mr. Mummery had consumed a large glass of orange juice, according to his new regime.

"There's your trouble," said Dr. Griffiths cheerfully. "Orange juice is an excellent thing, and so are trotters, but not in combination. Pig and oranges together are extraordinarily bad for the liver. I don't know why they should be, but there's no doubt that they are. Now I'll send you round a little prescription and you stick to slops for a day or two and keep off pork. And don't you worry about him, Mrs. Mummery, he's as sound as a trout. *You're* the one we've got to look after. I don't want to see those black rings under the eyes, you know. Disturbed night, of course—yes. Taking your tonic regularly? That's right. Well, don't be alarmed about your hubby. We'll soon have him out and about again."

The prophecy was fulfilled, but not immediately. Mr. Mummery, though confining his diet to baby food, bread and milk, and beef tea skillfully prepared by Mrs. Sutton and brought to his bedside by Ethel, remained very seedy all through Friday, and was only able to stagger rather shakily downstairs on Saturday afternoon. He had evidently suffered a "thorough upset." However, he was able to attend to a few papers which Brookes had sent down from the office for his signature, and to deal with the household books. Ethel was not a businesswoman, and Mr. Mummery always ran over the accounts with her. Having settled up with the butcher, the baker, the dairy and the coal merchant, Mr. Mummery looked up inquiringly.

"Anything more, darling?"

"Well, there's Mrs. Sutton. This is the end of her month, you know."

"So it is. Well, you're quite satisfied with her, aren't you, darling?"

"Yes, rather—aren't you? She's a good cook, and a sweet, motherly old thing, too. Don't you think it was a real brain wave of mine, engaging her like that, on the spot?"

"I do, indeed," said Mr. Mummery.

"It was a perfect providence, her turning up like that, just after that wretched Jane had gone off without even giving notice. I was in absolute *despair*. It was a little bit of a gamble, of course, taking her without any references, but naturally, if she'd been looking after a widowed mother, you couldn't expect her to give references."

"N-no," said Mr. Mummery. At the time he had felt uneasy about the matter, though he had not liked to say much because, of course, they simply had to have somebody. And the experiment had justified itself so triumphantly in practice that one couldn't say much about it now. He had once rather tentatively suggested writing to the clergyman of Mrs. Sutton's parish but, as Ethel had said, the clergyman wouldn't have been able to tell them anything about cooking, and cooking, after all, was the chief point.

Mr. Mummery counted out the month's money.

"And by the way, my dear," he said, "you might just mention to Mrs. Sutton that if she *must* read the morning paper before I come down, I should be obliged if she would fold it neatly afterwards."

"What an old fussbox you are, darling," said his wife.

Mr. Mummery sighed. He could not explain that it was somehow important that the morning paper should come to him fresh and prim, like a virgin. Women did not feel these things.

On Sunday, Mr. Mummery felt very much better—quite his old self, in fact. He enjoyed the *News of the World* over breakfast in bed, reading the murders rather carefully. Mr. Mummery got quite a lot of pleasure out of murders—they gave him an agreeable thrill of vicarious adventure, for, naturally, they were matters quite remote from daily life in the outskirts of Hull.

He noticed that Brookes had been perfectly right. Mrs. Andrews' father and former employer had been "dug up" and had, indeed, proved to be "bung-full" of arsenic.

He came downstairs for dinner—roast sirloin, with the potatoes done under the meat and Yorkshire pudding of delicious lightness, and an apple tart to follow. After three days of invalid diet, it was delightful to savor the crisp fat and underdone lean. He ate moderately, but with a sensuous enjoyment. Ethel, on the other hand, seemed a little lacking in appetite, but then, she had never been a great meat eater. She was fastidious and, besides, she was (quite unnecessarily) afraid of getting fat.

It was a fine afternoon, and at three o'clock, when he was quite certain that the roast beef was "settling" properly, it occurred to Mr. Mummery that it would be a good thing to put the rest of those bulbs in. He slipped on his old gardening coat and wandered out to the potting shed. Here he picked up a bag of tulips and a trowel, and then, remembering that he was wearing his good trousers, decided that it would be wise to take a mat to kneel on. When had he had the mat last? He could not recollect, but he rather fancied he had put it away in the corner under the potting shelf. Stooping down, he felt about in the dark among the flowerpots. Yes, there it was, but there was a tin of something in the way. He lifted the tin carefully out. Of course, yes—the remains of the weed killer.

Mr. Mummery glanced at the pink label, printed in staring letters with the legend: ARSENICAL WEED KILLER. *POISON*, and observed, with a mild feeling of excitement, that it was the same brand of stuff that had been associated with Mrs. Andrews' latest victim. He was rather pleased about it. It gave him a sensation of being remotely but definitely in touch with important events. Then he noticed, with surprise and a little annoyance, that the stopper had been put in quite loosely.

"However'd I come to leave it like that?" he grunted. "Shouldn't wonder if all the goodness has gone off." He removed the stopper and squinted into the can, which appeared to be half full. Then he rammed the thing home again, giving it a sharp thump with the handle of the trowel for better security. After that he washed his hands carefully at the scullery tap, for he did not believe in taking risks.

He was a trifle disconcerted, when he came in after planting the tulips, to find visitors in the sitting room. He was always pleased to see Mrs. Welbeck and her son, but he would rather have had warning, so that he could have scrubbed the garden mold out of his nails more thoroughly. Not that Mrs. Welbeck appeared to notice. She was a talkative woman and paid little attention to anything but her own conversation. Much to Mr. Mummery's annoyance, she chose to prattle about the Lincoln poisoning case. A most unsuitable subject for the tea table, thought Mr. Mummery, at the best of times. His own "upset" was vivid enough in his memory to make him queasy over the discussion of medical symptoms, and besides, this kind of talk was not good enough for Ethel. After all, the poisoner was still supposed to be in the neighborhood. It was enough to make even a strong-nerved woman uneasy. A glance at Ethel showed him that she was looking quite white and tremulous. He must stop Mrs. Welbeck somehow, or there would be a repetition of one of the old, dreadful, hysterical scenes.

He broke into the conversation with violent abruptness.

"Those forsythia cuttings, Mrs. Welbeck," he said. "Now is just about the time to take them. If you care to come down the garden I will get them for you."

He saw a relieved glance pass between Ethel and young Welbeck. Evidently the boy understood the situation and was chafing at his mother's tactlessness. Mrs. Welbeck, brought up all standing, gasped slightly and then veered off with obliging readiness on the new tack. She accompanied her host down the garden and chattered cheerfully about horticulture while he selected and trimmed the cuttings. She complimented Mr. Mummery on the immaculacy of his gravel paths. "I simply *cannot* keep the weeds down," she said.

Mr. Mummery mentioned the weed killer and praised its efficacy.

"That stuff!" Mrs. Welbeck stared at him. Then she shuddered. "I wouldn't have it in my place for a thousand pounds," she said, with emphasis.

Mr. Mummery smiled. "Oh, we keep it well away from the house," he said. "Even if I were a careless sort of person—"

He broke off. The recollection of the loosened stopper had come to him suddenly, and it was as though, deep down in his mind, some obscure assembling of ideas had taken place. He left it at that, and went into the kitchen to fetch a newspaper to wrap up the cuttings.

Their approach to the house had evidently been seen from the sitting-room window, for when they entered, young Welbeck was already on his feet and holding Ethel's hand in the act of saying good-by. He maneuvered his mother out of the house with tactful promptness and Mr. Mummery returned to the kitchen to clear up the newspapers he had fished out of the drawer. To clear them up and to examine them more closely. Something had struck him about them, which he wanted to verify. He turned them over very carefully, sheet by sheet. Yes—he had been right. Every portrait of Mrs. Andrews, every paragraph and line about the Lincoln poisoning case, had been carefully cut out.

Mr. Mummery sat down by the kitchen fire. He felt as though he needed warmth. There seemed to be a curious cold lump of something at the pit of his stomach—something that he was chary of investigating.

He tried to recall the appearance of Mrs. Andrews as shown in the newspaper photographs, but he had not a good visual memory. He remembered having remarked to Brookes that it was a "motherly" face. Then he tried counting up the time since the disappearance. Nearly a month, Brookes had said—and that was a week ago. Must be over a month now. A month. He had just paid Mrs. Sutton her month's money.

Ethel! was the thought that hammered at the door of his brain. At all costs, he must cope with this monstrous suspicion on his own. He must spare her any shock or anxiety. And he must be sure of his ground. To dismiss the only decent cook they had ever had out of sheer, unfounded panic, would be wanton cruelty to both women. If he did it at all, it would have to be done arbitrarily, preposterously—he could not suggest horrors to Ethel. However it was done, there would be trouble. Ethel would not understand and he dared not tell her.

But if by any chance there was anything in this ghastly doubt—how could he expose Ethel to the appalling danger of having the woman in the house a moment longer? He thought of the family at Lincoln—the husband dead, the wife escaped by a miracle with her life. Was not any shock, any risk, better than that?

Mr. Mummery felt suddenly very lonely and tired. His illness had taken it out of him. Those illnesses—they had begun, when? Three weeks ago he had had the first attack. Yes, but then he had always been rather subject to gastric troubles. Bilious attacks. Not so violent, perhaps, as these last, but undoubted bilious attacks.

He pulled himself together and went, rather heavily, into the sitting room. Ethel was tucked up in a corner of the chesterfield.

"Tired, darling?"

"Yes, a little."

"That woman has worn you out with talking. She oughtn't to talk so much."

"No." Her head shifted wearily in the cushions. "All about that horrible case. I don't like hearing about such things."

"Of course not. Still, when a thing like that happens in the neighborhood, people will gossip and talk. It would be a relief if they caught the woman. One doesn't like to think—"

"I don't want to think of anything so hateful. She must be a horrible creature."

"Horrible. Brookes was saying the other day—"

"I don't want to hear what he said. I don't want to hear about it at all. I want to be quiet. I want to be quiet!"

He recognized the note of rising hysteria.

"Tiddleywinks shall be quiet. Don't worry, darling. We won't talk about horrors."

No. It would not do to talk about them.

Ethel went to bed early. It was understood that on Sundays Mr. Mummery should sit up till Mrs. Sutton came in. Ethel was a little anxious about this, but he assured her that he felt quite strong enough. In body, indeed, he did; it was his mind that felt weak and confused. He had decided to make a casual remark about the mutilated newspapers—just to see what Mrs. Sutton would say.

He allowed himself the usual indulgence of a whisky and soda as he sat waiting. At a quarter to ten he heard the familiar click of the garden gate. Footsteps passed up the gravel—squeak, squeak, to the back door. Then the sound of the latch, the shutting of the door, the rattle of the bolts being shot home. Then a pause. Mrs. Sutton would be taking off her hat. The moment was coming.

The step sounded in the passage. The door opened. Mrs. Sutton in her neat black dress stood on the threshold. He was aware of a reluctance to face her. Then he looked up. A plump-faced woman, her eyes obscured by thick horn-rimmed spectacles. Was there, perhaps, something hard about the mouth? Or was it just that she had lost most of her front teeth?

"Would you be requiring anything tonight, sir, before I go up?"

"No, thank you, Mrs. Sutton."

"I hope you are feeling better, sir." Her eager interest in his health seemed to him almost sinister, but the eyes, behind the thick glasses, were inscrutable.

"Quite better, thank you, Mrs. Sutton."

"Mrs. Mummery is not indisposed, is she, sir? Should I take her up a glass of hot milk or anything?"

"No, thank you, no." He spoke hurriedly, and fancied that she looked disappointed.

"Very well, sir. Good night, sir."

"Good night. Oh! by the way, Mrs. Sutton—"

"Yes, sir?"

"Oh, nothing," said Mr. Mummery, "nothing."

NEXT MORNING Mr. Mummery opened his paper eagerly. He would have been glad to learn that an arrest had been made over the weekend. But there was no news for him. The chairman of a trust company had blown out his brains, and the headlines were all occupied with tales about lost millions and ruined shareholders. Both in his own paper and in those he purchased on the way to the office, the Lincoln poisoning tragedy had been relegated to an obscure paragraph on a back page, which informed him that the police were still baffled.

The next few days were the most uncomfortable that Mr. Mummery had ever spent. He developed a habit of coming down early in the morning and prowling about the kitchen. This made Ethel nervous, but Mrs. Sutton offered no remark. She watched him tolerantly, even, he thought, with something like amusement. After all, it was ridiculous. What was the use of supervising the breakfast, when he had to be out of the house every day between half past nine and six?

At the office, Brookes rallied him on the frequency with which he rang up Ethel. Mr. Mummery paid no attention. It was reassuring to hear her voice and to know that she was safe and well.

Nothing happened, and by the following Thursday he began to think that he had been a fool. He came home late that night. Brookes had persuaded him to go with him to a little bachelor dinner for a friend who was about to get married. He left the others at eleven o'clock, however, refusing to make a night of it. The household was in bed when he got back but a note from Mrs. Sutton lay on the table, informing him that there was cocoa for him in the kitchen, ready for hotting up. He hotted it up accordingly in the little saucepan where it stood. There was just one good cupful.

He sipped it thoughtfully, standing by the kitchen stove. After the first sip, he put the cup down. Was it his fancy, or was there something queer about the taste? He sipped it again, rolling it upon his tongue. It seemed to him to have a faint tang, metallic and unpleasant. In a sudden dread he ran out to the scullery and spat the mouthful into the sink.

After this, he stood quite still for a moment or two. Then, with a curious deliberation, as though his movements had been dictated to him, he fetched an empty medicine bottle from the pantry shelf, rinsed it under the tap and tipped the contents of the cup carefully into it. He slipped the bottle into his coat pocket and moved on tiptoe to the back door. The bolts were difficult to draw without noise, but he managed it at last. Still on tiptoe, he stole across the garden to the potting shed. Stooping down, he struck a match. He knew exactly where he had left the tin of weed killer, under the shelf behind the pots at the back. Cautiously he lifted it out. The match flared up and burnt his fingers, but before he could light another his sense of touch had told him what he wanted to know. The stopper was loose again.

Panic seized Mr. Mummery, standing there in the earthy-smelling shed, in his dress suit and overcoat, holding the tin in one hand and the matchbox in the other. He wanted very badly to run and tell somebody what he had discovered.

Instead, he replaced the tin exactly where he had found it and went back to the house. As he crossed the garden again, he noticed a light in Mrs. Sutton's bedroom window. This terrified him more than anything which had gone before. Was she watching him? Ethel's window was dark. If she had drunk anything deadly there would be lights everywhere, movements, calls for the doctor, just as when he himself had been attacked. Attacked—that was the right word.

Still with the same odd presence of mind and precision, he went in, washed out the utensils and made a second brew of cocoa, which he left standing in the saucepan. He crept quietly to his bedroom. Ethel's voice greeted him on the threshold.

"How late you are, Harold. Naughty old boy! Have a good time?"

"Not bad. You all right, darling?"

"Quite all right. Did Mrs. Sutton leave something hot for you? She said she would."

"Yes, but I wasn't thirsty."

Ethel laughed. "Oh! it was *that* sort of party, was it?"

Mr. Mummery did not attempt any denials. He undressed and got into bed and clutched his wife to him as though defying death and hell to take her from him. Next morning he would act. He thanked God that he was not too late.

MR. DIMTHORPE, the chemist, was a great friend of Mr. Mummery's. They had often sat together in the untidy little shop on Spring Bank and exchanged views on greenfly and clubroot. Mr. Mummery told his story frankly to Mr. Dimthorpe and handed over the bottle of cocoa. Mr. Dimthorpe congratulated him on his prudence and intelligence. "I will have it ready for you by this evening," he said, "and if it's what you think it is, then we shall have a clear case on which to take action."

Mr. Mummery thanked him, and was extremely vague and inattentive at business all day. But that hardly mattered, for Mr. Brookes, who had seen the party through to a riotous end in the small hours, was in no very observant mood. At half past four, Mr. Mummery shut up his desk decisively and announced that he was off early, he had a call to make.

Mr. Dimthorpe was ready for him.

"No doubt about it," he said. "I used the Marsh test. It's a heavy dose—no wonder you tasted it. There must be four or five grains of pure arsenic in that bottle. Look, here's the test tube. You can see the mirror for yourself."

Mr. Mummery gazed at the little glass tube with its ominous purple-black stain.

"Will you ring up the police from here?" asked the chemist.

"No," said Mr. Mummery. "No—I want to get home. God knows what's happening there. And I've only just time to catch my train."

"All right," said Mr. Dimthorpe. "Leave it to me. I'll ring them up for you."

The local train was not fast enough for Mr. Mummery. Ethel—poisoned—dying—dead—Ethel—poisoned—dying—dead—the wheels drummed in his ears. He almost ran out of the station and along the road. A car was standing at his door. He saw it from the end of the street and broke into a gallop. It had happened already. The doctor was there. Fool, murderer that he was, to have left things so late.

Then, while he was still a hundred and fifty yards off, he saw the front door open. A man came out followed by Ethel herself. The visitor got into his car and was driven away. Ethel went in again. She was safe—safe!

He could hardly control himself to hang up his hat and coat and go in looking reasonably calm. His wife had returned to the armchair by the fire and greeted him in some surprise. There were tea things on the table.

"Back early, aren't you?"

"Yes—business was slack. Somebody been to tea?"

"Yes, young Welbeck. About the arrangements for the Drama Society." She spoke briefly but with an undertone of excitement.

A qualm came over Mr. Mummery. Would a guest be any protection? His face must have shown his feelings, for Ethel stared at him in amazement.

"What's the matter, Harold, you look so queer."

"Darling," said Mr. Mummery, "there's something I want to tell you about." He sat down and took her hand in his. "Something a little unpleasant, I'm afraid—"

"Oh, ma'am!"

The cook was in the doorway.

"I beg your pardon, sir—I didn't know you was in. Will you be taking tea or can I clear away? And oh, ma'am, there was a young man at the fishmonger's and he's just come from Grimsby and they've caught that dreadful woman—that Mrs. Andrews. Isn't it a good thing? It's worritted me dreadful to think she was going about like that, but they've caught her. Taken a job as housekeeper she had to two elderly ladies and they found the wicked poison on her. Girl as spotted her will get a reward. I been keeping my eyes open for her, but it's at Grimsby she was all the time."

Mr. Mummery clutched at the arm of his chair. It had all been a mad mistake then. He wanted to shout or cry. He wanted to apologize to this foolish, pleasant, excited woman. All a mistake.

But there had been the cocoa. Mr. Dimthorpe. The Marsh test. Five grains of arsenic. Who, then—?

He glanced around at his wife, and in her eyes he saw something that he had never seen before. . . .

HAUTOT AND
HIS SON

GUY DE MAUPASSANT / FRANCE

Translated by Anthony Bonner

THE HOUSE, half farm and half manor, was one of those rural dwellings which had once been almost baronial but which was now occupied by wealthy farmers. Outside the door, the dogs tied to the apple trees in the courtyard barked and howled when they saw the game bags being carried past by the keeper and some boys. In the big dining-room-kitchen Hautot, his son, Monsieur Bermont the tax collector, and Monsieur Mondaru the notary were having a snack and a glass of wine before going out hunting. It was the opening day of the season.

Hautot was proud of his possessions and was already boasting of the game his guests would find on his property. He was a big Norman, one of those powerful, ruddy, large-framed men who can lift apple carts on their shoulders. Part farmer and part gentleman, he was rich, respected, influential and authoritarian. He had made his son César Hautot go to school until the tenth grade, and had stopped him there for fear of his growing up with no interest in the land.

César Hautot was almost as tall as his father, but thinner; he was a good boy, docile, always cheerful, and full of admiration, respect and deference for the wishes and opinions of his father.

Monsieur Bermont the tax collector was a short, fat man with cheeks marked by thin networks of violet veins resembling the twisting courses of rivers and their tributaries as they appear on maps.

"How about hares," he asked, "are there any hares?"

"As many as you want," answered Hautot, "especially in the Puysatier valley."

"Where do we start?" asked the notary, a stout, pale, easygoing man whose potbellied frame was tightly clothed in a brand-new hunting outfit he had bought in Rouen the week before.

"Well, over there, in the valley. We'll drive the partridge out into the fields and then go after them."

Hautot got up. The others followed suit, took their guns from the corners of the room, examined their batteries, and before going out stamped their feet to make them snug inside boots which were still somewhat stiff and as yet unsoftened by the warmth of their circulation. The dogs stood up at the end of their chains, letting out piercing howls and waving their front paws in the air.

The men started off toward the valley. It was a little dale, or rather a large undulation of land of poor quality which had therefore remained uncultivated. It was furrowed with ravines, covered with ferns, and an excellent game preserve.

The hunters spread out, Hautot on the right, his son on the left, and the two guests in the middle. The keeper and men carrying the game bags followed. This was the solemn moment when hunters await the first gunshot, when their hearts beat a little faster and when they nervously finger their safety catches.

Then suddenly the first shot was heard! Hautot had fired. They all stopped and saw a partridge detach itself from a swiftly flying group and fall into a ravine beneath dense undergrowth. The excited hunter began running with long strides, tearing out the brambles in his path, and then he in turn disappeared into the thicket, in search of the bird he had shot.

Almost at once a second shot rang out.

"Ah, ah! The rascal," cried Monsieur Bermont, "he flushed a rabbit over there."

They all waited, their eyes fixed on the mass of branches through which they could see nothing.

The notary, cupping his hands over his mouth, shouted, "Did you get them?"

Hautot did not answer. Then César turned toward the keeper and said, "Go help him, Joseph. We have to walk in line; we'll wait."

Joseph, a dried-up, knotty old man, built like a tree trunk, all his joints protruding, walked off at a calm pace and went down into the ravine, choosing his footholds with all the care of a fox. Then suddenly he cried: "Come quickly; something's happened!"

They all rushed to the spot and dived through the brambles. Hautot was lying on his side unconscious, holding both hands over his stomach from which long trickles of blood were running over his bullet-torn vest. He had let go of his gun in order to pick up the dead partridge, and as the gun fell it had gone off again, ripping a hole in his intestine. They dragged him out of the ditch, undressed him, and saw the horrible wound with entrails spilling out of it. After they had sewn it up as best they could, they carried him to his house, sent for the doctor and a priest, and then waited.

When the doctor arrived, he shook his head gravely and turned toward the son who was sobbing in a chair: "My poor boy," he said, "things look bad."

But when the wound had been dressed, the patient moved his fingers, opened his mouth and then his eyes. He looked about with a disturbed, haggard expression, and then seemed to search about in his memory, to remember and understand.

"Good God," he murmured, "this is the end!"

"No, no," said the doctor as he held his hand, "a couple of days of rest and you'll be fine."

"This is the end," repeated Hautot. "My stomach's ripped open.

I know it is." Then suddenly, "I want to talk to the boy, if there's still time."

"Papa, Papa, poor Papa!"

"Come now, no more crying," said the father in a firmer tone, "this isn't the time for that. I've got to talk to you. Stand there, next to me. It'll only take a moment, and it'll make me rest easier. The rest of you—for just a minute, please."

They all went out, leaving the son alone with his father.

The moment they were alone, the father said, "Son, you're twenty-four—I can talk to you like a man. And besides, all this isn't as mysterious as we pretend it is. You know that your mother died seven years ago—right?—and that I'm no more than forty-five years old, since I was married when I was nineteen. Right?"

"Yes," stammered the son, "that's right."

"So, your mother died seven years ago and left me a widower. Well now, a man like me can't stay a widower at the age of thirty-seven, right?"

"Yes, that's right," answered the son.

"God, it hurts," said the father, out of breath, his face pale and contorted. "So, you understand. A man isn't made to live alone, but I didn't want to have a successor to your mother, since I'd promised her that. Well . . . do you understand?"

"Yes, Father."

"So I took up with a little girl in Rouen, on the Rue de l'Eperlan, number eighteen, on the fourth floor, the second door—I'm telling you all this so you won't forget it—a girl who's been very nice to me, loving, devoted, a real wife. Huh? You understand?"

"Yes, Father."

"She's a good girl, I tell you, really good; and if it wasn't for you, the memory of your mother and this house in which the three of us lived together, I would have brought her here and married her, there's no doubt about it. . . . Listen . . . listen . . . my boy . . . I could have made a will . . . but I didn't. I didn't want to . . . because these things shouldn't be written down . . . these things . . . they're too harmful to the rightful heirs . . . and then they get everything in a mess . . . they ruin everyone! Don't have anything to do with official documents; I never did. If I'm rich, it's because I never used them in my whole life. You understand, son?"

"Yes, Father."

"Now listen . . . listen carefully. . . . So, I didn't make any will . . . I didn't want to . . . and besides I know I can trust you, you've got a good heart, you're not mean or stingy. I told myself that when my time was up, I'd tell you everything and ask you not to forget the girl—Caroline Donet, on the Rue de l'Eperlan, number eighteen, on the fourth floor, the second door, don't forget. Now, one more thing. When I'm done for, go there right away—and fix things up so she won't have any reason to complain of my memory. You've got the means to do it. You'll be able to do it—I'm leaving you enough. . . . Listen . . . during most of the week you won't find her there. She works at Madame Moreau's on the Rue Beauvoisine. Go there on a Thursday. That's the day she expects me. That's the day I've been going there, for ten years now. The poor girl, how she'll cry! . . . I tell you all this because I know I can trust you, my boy. These things, one doesn't go spreading them around to everyone, not even to the notary or the priest. People do it and everybody knows they do, but no one talks about it except when they have to. So, don't let any outsider in on the secret, no one but the family, because a family's like one person. Understand?"

"Yes, Father."

"You promise?"

"Yes, Father."

"You give me your word?"

"Yes, Father."

"I beg you, I pray you, don't forget. It means a lot to me."

"No, Father."

"You'll go yourself. I want you to make sure of everything."

"Yes, Father."

"And then you'll see . . . you'll see what she says. I can't tell you any more. You give your word?"

"Yes, Father."

"Good, my boy. Kiss me. Good-by. My time's up, I know it is. Tell them to come in."

César Hautot moaned as he embraced his father. Then, obedient as ever, he opened the door and the priest appeared wearing his white surplice and carrying the holy oil.

But the dying man had closed his eyes and refused to open them or answer, or even to show by a gesture that he understood what was going on.

He had talked enough, and now he was at the end of his tether. Moreover, his conscience was at rest and he wanted to die in peace. What need did he have to confess to God's delegate, since he had just confessed to his son, to him, a member of the family!

In the midst of friends and servants all kneeling, the priest administered extreme unction, purified him and absolved him, without the slightest movement of his face to give any indication that he was still alive.

He died toward midnight, after four hours of trembling amid the most atrocious suffering.

THE HUNTING SEASON had opened on a Sunday, and on the following Tuesday Hautot was buried. After accompanying his father's body to the cemetery, César Hautot returned to his house and spent the rest of the day crying. He scarcely slept the following night, and he felt so sad upon awakening that he wondered how he could go on living.

Nevertheless, all day he thought that in order to carry out his father's last wish he must go to Rouen on the following day and see Caroline Donet of the Rue de l'Eperlan, number eighteen, on the fourth floor, the second door. In a low voice as if muttering a prayer, he had repeated this name and address an incalculable number of times in order not to forget, until his tongue and mind became so possessed by this phrase that he mumbled it on and on without stopping to think of anything.

So, the next day at about eight o'clock, he ordered Graindorge to be harnessed to the gig and he went off down the main road from Ainville to Rouen with his heavy Norman horse at a fast trot. He was wearing his black frock coat, his big silk hat and his trousers with their foot straps. Because of the circumstances he had not wanted to wear his blue smock over his nice suit, the smock that puffed out in the wind and protected his clothes from dust and dirt and which he would take off nimbly upon arriving, as he jumped down from the carriage.

He entered Rouen at ten o'clock and stopped as usual at the Hôtel des Bons-Enfants on the Rue des Trois-Mares. He put up with the embraces of the owner, his wife and five sons, for they had heard the sad news. Then he had to give details of the accident, and this made him cry and turn down their offers of help. They were solicitous because they knew he was rich, but he thwarted them by refusing to have lunch with them.

So he dusted off his hat, brushed his frock coat, wiped his boots and set out in search of the Rue de l'Eperlan, without daring to ask directions of anyone for fear of being recognized and arousing suspicion. Finally, having had no success, he noticed a priest and asked him, trusting in the professional discretion of a churchman.

He had only a short distance to go; it was the second street on the right.

Then he hesitated. Until that moment he had blindly obeyed the dead man's wishes. Now he felt disturbed, confused and humiliated at the idea that he, the son, was about to find himself face-to-face with the woman who had been the mistress of his father. He was upset by those morals which lie within all of us, buried in the depths of our emotions by centuries of hereditary teaching. He was disturbed too by all the catechism had taught him about women of ill repute, by that instinctive disdain which all men carry within them against such women even if they marry one, and by his narrow peasant sense of integrity. All these things held him back, gave him a sense of shame and made him blush.

But he said to himself, "I promised Father. Mustn't go back on my word." The door to the house marked with a number eighteen was ajar; he pushed it open and saw before him a dark staircase. He went up three flights, passed one door and stopped at the second. He found a bellpull and gave it a tug.

The ringing which resounded in the neighboring room made a shudder pass through his body. The door opened and he found himself facing a very well-dressed young lady with brown hair and ruddy complexion, who looked at him with an expression of amazement.

He did not know what to say, and she, who had no idea what was going on and was expecting his father, did not invite him to enter. They looked at each other like this for almost thirty seconds.

Finally she asked, "What can I do for you, Monsieur?"

"I'm Hautot's son," he answered.

She gave a start and became pale. "Monsieur César?" she stammered as if she had known him a long time.

"Yes."

"What did . . . ?"

"My father sent me to talk to you."

"Oh, my God!" she said as she drew back in order to let him enter. He closed the door and followed her.

He then noticed a little boy of four or five sitting on the floor and playing with a cat. Behind him was a stove and steam was rising from the food being kept hot on top of it.

"Sit down," she said.

He sat down.

"Well?" she asked.

He no longer dared speak. His eyes were fixed on the table in the middle of the apartment. It was set with three places, one of which was for the child. He looked at the chair turned with its back to the fire, the plate, the napkin, the glasses, the half-empty bottle of red wine and the unopened bottle of white wine. It was his father's place, in front of the fire! They were expecting him. It was his father's bread that he saw. He recognized it next to the fork, for its crust had been removed on account of Hautot's bad teeth. Then, raising his eyes, he noticed his father's portrait on the wall. It was the big photograph taken in Paris the year of the Exposition, the same one nailed above the bed in his room at Ainville.

"Well, Monsieur César?" the young woman repeated.

He looked at her. Her anguish had drained the color from her face, and she waited fearfully, her hands trembling.

He finally got up the courage. "Well, Mam'selle, Papa died on Sunday, the opening day of the hunting season."

She was so overwhelmed that she did not move. After several

moments of silence, she murmured in an almost inaudible voice: "Oh, no! It can't be!"

Suddenly tears appeared in her eyes; she covered her face with her hands and began to sob.

At this moment the little boy turned his head and began to howl upon seeing his mother in tears. Then, realizing that this sudden sorrow came from the unknown man, he rushed at César, seized his trousers with one hand and with the other slapped his thigh as hard as he could. César was bewildered and filled with compassion at the sight of this woman crying over his father and the boy defending his mother. He felt himself overcome with emotion, and tears welled into his eyes. He began to speak in order to regain his composure.

"Yes," he said, "it happened Sunday morning toward eight o'clock. . . ." He told the story without a thought that she might not be capable of listening. He left out no details, but recounted the most unimportant incidents with the attention to minutiae typical in a peasant. The little boy continued his attack, but now instead of slapping him he was kicking him in the shins.

When he got to the part of his story where Hautot had mentioned her, she heard her name and uncovered her face.

"Excuse me," she said, "but I haven't been following you. I'd like to know if . . . you wouldn't mind starting again."

He started again in exactly the same way: "It happened Sunday morning toward eight o'clock. . . ."

He told the whole story at great length, every now and then stopping to emphasize a point or to interject his own thoughts into the narrative. She listened eagerly; with all her nervous woman's sensibility she caught all the little vicissitudes of the story he recounted, and with shudders of horror, would occasionally say, "Oh, my God!" The little boy, who seemed to think she was calmer, stopped hitting César and took his mother's hand. He too was listening, as if he were capable of understanding.

When the story was over, Hautot's son said, "Now we're going to arrange things between us as he would have wished. Listen, I'm quite well off—he left me some property. I don't want you to have any reason to complain. . . ."

But she interrupted him brusquely.

"Oh! Monsieur César, Monsieur César, not today. My heart's breaking. . . . Some other time, some other day . . . No, not today . . . If I accept, listen . . . it's not for me . . . no, no, no, I give you my word. It's for the little boy. We'll put the property in his name."

César was startled. He guessed the truth and stammered, "Then . . . the boy . . . the boy's his?"

"Why, yes," she said.

Hautot's son looked at his brother with a confused but strong and painful emotion.

There was a long silence, for she was crying again. Afterward, César said in a very embarrassed tone of voice, "Well, then, Mam'selle Donet, I'll be leaving. When would you like to talk about this?"

"Oh, no!" she cried. "Don't go, don't go, don't leave me all alone with Emile. I'll die of sorrow. I've got no one now, no one but my little boy. Oh, what misery, what misery, Monsieur César! Come, sit down. Talk to me some more. Tell me what he did there all week long."

César sat down—he was accustomed to obeying.

She brought a chair near his, in front of the stove where the food was still simmering, took Emile on her knees and asked César all sorts of questions about his father, intimate details by which he could see, or rather feel without reasoning, that she had loved Hautot with all her poor woman's heart.

And, through the natural sequence of his own not-too-numerous thoughts, he came back to the accident and began to recount it again with all the same details.

When he said that the hole in his father's stomach was so big you could have put two fists into it, she let out a kind of shriek and once more broke out sobbing. The contagious atmosphere about him made César also begin to cry, and, since tears always soften the heartstrings, he leaned over Emile and kissed his forehead.

The mother, catching her breath, murmured, "The poor boy, here he is an orphan."

"Me too," said César.

And they didn't say another word.

But suddenly the practical housekeeper's side to her nature, that side accustomed to thinking of everything, reawoke within the young woman.

"You probably haven't eaten a thing all morning, Monsieur César?"

"No, Mam'selle."

"Oh, you must be hungry! Have a bite to eat."

"No, thanks," he said. "I'm not hungry. I've been feeling too miserable."

"In spite of sorrow," she answered, "a man has to live—you can't deny that. Besides, that way you'll stay a bit longer. I don't know what I'll do when you leave."

After a bit more resistance, he yielded and sat down with his back to the fire, facing her. He ate a plate of the tripe which had been sputtering on the stove and had a glass of red wine, but he would not allow her to uncork the white wine.

Several times he wiped the little boy's mouth and chin after it had become smeared with sauce.

As he got up to leave, he asked, "When would you like me to come back to discuss this business, Mam'selle Donet?"

"Next Thursday, if it's all right with you, Monsieur César. That way I won't lose any time. I always have Thursdays off."

"Next Thursday's fine with me."

"You'll come for lunch, won't you?"

"Oh, I couldn't do that."

"People can talk better when they're eating. Besides, it'll give us more time."

"All right then, at noon."

And he left after kissing little Emile again and shaking Mademoiselle Donet's hand.

THE WEEK seemed long to César Hautot. He had never been alone and this isolation seemed intolerable. Until then he had lived beside his father, like a shadow. He would follow him into the fields, seeing that his orders were carried out, and, after having been away from him for a while, would find him again at dinner. They would sit through their evenings facing each other, smoking their pipes and talking about horses, cows and sheep. And the way they shook hands upon arising was like an exchange of deep familial affection.

Now César was alone. He wandered about in the plowed autumn fields always expecting to see the huge, gesticulating silhouette of his father arise at the far end of some open ground. To kill time, he would visit his neighbors and recount the accident to anyone who had not yet heard the details, and sometimes even repeat it over again to the same people. Then, with nothing more to do or occupy his mind, he would sit down at the edge of a road and ask himself how long life could go on like this.

He often thought of Mademoiselle Donet. He had liked her. He had found her respectable, gentle and good, just as his father had said. She was a fine girl—yes, a fine girl. He was determined to do things in a big way: to give her an income of two thousand francs and make the capital over to the child. It even gave him a certain pleasure to think that he would see her on the following Thursday and arrange all this with her. But then the idea of a brother, a little fellow five years old who was the son of his father, bothered him and slightly annoyed him; yet at the same time, it warmed his heart. In that little clandestine urchin who would never bear the name of Hautot he had a kind of family, a family he could take or leave as the spirit moved him, but which would remind him of his father.

So, when he was on the road to Rouen on Thursday morning, carried along by Graindorge's sonorous trot, he felt more lighthearted and relaxed than he had since the accident.

When he entered Mademoiselle Donet's apartment, he found the table set as it had been the previous Thursday, except that the crust had not been removed from the bread.

He shook the young woman's hand, kissed Emile on the cheek and sat down. He already felt at home there, even though his heart was still heavy.

Mademoiselle Donet seemed thinner and paler. She had probably cried a great deal. She acted as though she were now embarrassed in front of him, as if she now understood what she had not grasped the previous week beneath the first blow of her sorrow. Her eyes never left him, she was painfully humble and touchingly solicitous, as if to repay by attention and devotion his kindness toward her. They spent a long time over lunch, discussing the affair which had brought him. She did not want that much money. It was too much, much too much. She earned enough to live and only wanted Emile to have a little something before him when he grew up. César held his ground, and even added a present of a thousand francs for her in view of her bereavement.

After he had taken his coffee, she asked, "Do you smoke?"

"Yes . . . I've got my pipe."

He felt his pocket. Good Lord, he had forgotten it! He would have been very annoyed with himself, but at that moment she offered him his father's pipe which she had put away in a closet. He accepted it, took it in his hand and recognized it as his father's. He sniffed it, proclaimed its excellence with emotion in his voice, filled it with tobacco and lit it. After this he put Emile astride his leg and played horsey with him, while she cleared the table and put the dirty dishes away in the bottom of the sideboard in order to wash them after he had left.

Toward three o'clock he reluctantly got up, dismayed at the idea of having to leave.

"Well, Mam'selle Donet," he said, "good night. Very nice to have seen you again."

She stood in front of him blushing, very moved and thinking of his father as she looked at him.

"Won't we see each other again?" she said.

"Why, yes, Mam'selle," he answered unaffectedly, "if you'd like to."

"Certainly, Monsieur César. Then next Thursday, would that be all right?"

"Yes, Mam'selle Donet."

"You'll come for lunch, without fail?"

"But . . . well, if you'd like it, I won't say no."

"All right then, Monsieur César, next Thursday at noon, like today."

"Thursday at noon, Mam'selle Donet."

THE OPEN BOAT

STEPHEN CRANE / UNITED STATES

Stephen Crane

NONE OF THEM KNEW the color of the sky. Their eyes were fastened upon the waves that swept toward them. These waves were of the hue of slate, save for the tops, which were of foaming white, and all of the men knew the colors of the sea. The horizon narrowed and widened, and dipped and rose, and at all times its edge was jagged with waves thrust up in points like rocks. Many a man ought to have a bathtub larger than the boat which here rode upon the sea. These waves were most wrongfully and barbarously abrupt and tall.

The cook squatted in the bottom, six inches of gunwale separating him from the ocean. His sleeves were rolled over his fat forearms, and two flaps of his unbuttoned vest dangled as he bent to bail out the boat. Often he said: "Gawd! That was a narrow clip."

The oiler, steering with one of the two oars in the boat, sometimes raised himself suddenly to keep clear of water that swirled in over the stern. It was a thin little oar and it seemed often ready to snap.

The correspondent, pulling at the other oar, watched the waves and wondered why he was there.

The injured captain, lying in the bow, was at this time buried in the profound dejection and indifference which comes, temporarily at least, to even the bravest and most enduring when, willy-nilly, the firm fails, the army loses, the ship goes down. The mind of the master of a vessel is rooted deep in her timbers, and this captain had on him the impression of a scene in the grays of dawn of seven turned faces, and later a stump of a topmast with a white ball on it that slashed to and fro at the waves, went low and lower, and down.

Thereafter his voice, although steady, was deep with mourning, and of a quality beyond oration or tears.

"Keep 'er a little more south, Billie," said he.

"A little more south, sir," said the oiler, in the stern.

A seat in this boat was not unlike a seat upon a bucking bronco, and by the same token, a bronco is not much smaller. The craft pranced and reared, and plunged like an animal. As each wave came, and she rose for it, she seemed like a horse making at a fence outrageously high. The manner of her scramble over these walls of water is a mystic thing. Then, after scornfully bumping a crest, she would slide, and race, and splash down a long incline, and arrive bobbing and nodding in front of the next menace.

In a ten-foot dinghy one can get an idea of the resources of the sea in the line of waves that is not probable to the average experience. As each slaty wall of water approached, it shut all else from view, and it was not difficult to imagine that this particular wave was the final outburst of the ocean, the last effort of the grim water. There was a terrible grace in the move of the waves, and they came in silence, save for the snarling of the crests.

In the wan light, the faces of the men must have been gray. Their eyes must have glinted in strange ways as they gazed steadily astern. Viewed from a balcony, the whole thing would doubtless have been weirdly picturesque. But the men in the boat had other things to occupy their minds. The sun swung steadily up the sky, and they knew it was broad day because the color of the waves that rolled toward them changed from slate to emerald green.

In disjointed sentences the cook and the correspondent argued as to the difference between a lifesaving station and a house of refuge. The cook had said: "There's a house of refuge just north of the Mosquito Inlet Light, and as soon as the crew see us, they'll come off in their boat and pick us up."

"Houses of refuge don't have crews," said the correspondent. "They are only places where clothes and grub are stored for the benefit of shipwrecked people. They don't carry crews."

"Oh, yes, they do," said the cook.

"No, they don't," said the correspondent.

"Well, we're not there yet, anyhow," said the oiler, in the stern.

"Well," said the cook, "perhaps it's not a house of refuge that I'm thinking of as being near Mosquito Inlet Light. Perhaps it's a lifesaving station."

"We're not there yet," said the oiler, in the stern.

AS THE BOAT bounced from the top of each wave, the wind tore through the hair of the hatless men, and the spray splashed past them. The crest of each of these waves was a hill, from the top of which the men surveyed, for a moment, a broad tumultuous expanse, shining and wind-riven. It was probably splendid. It was probably glorious, this play of the free sea.

"Bully good thing it's an onshore wind," said the cook. "If not, we wouldn't have a show."

"That's right," said the correspondent.

The busy oiler nodded his assent.

Then the captain, in the bow, chuckled in a way that expressed humor, contempt, tragedy, all in one. "Do you think we've got much of a show now, boys?" said he.

Whereupon the three were silent. To express any particular optimism at this time they felt to be childish and stupid. On the other hand, the ethics of their condition was decidedly against any open suggestion of hopelessness. So they were silent.

"Oh, well," said the captain, soothing his children, "we'll get ashore all right."

But there was that in his tone which made the oiler say: "Yes! If this wind holds!"

The cook was bailing: "Yes! If we don't catch hell in the surf."

Canton flannel gulls flew near and far. Sometimes they sat comfortably down on the sea, near patches of brown seaweed. The birds were envied by some in the dinghy, for the wrath of the sea was no more to them than it was to a covey of prairie chickens a thousand miles inland. Often they came very close and stared at the men with black beadlike eyes, uncanny and sinister in their unblinking scrutiny. The men hooted angrily at them, telling them to be gone. One came, and evidently decided to alight on the top of the captain's head. The bird flew parallel to the boat and made short sidelong jumps in the air. His black eyes were wistfully fixed upon the captain's head.

"Ugly brute," said the oiler to the bird. The cook and the correspondent swore darkly at the creature. The captain naturally wished to knock it away; but anything resembling an emphatic gesture would have capsized this freighted boat, and so with his open hand, the captain gently and carefully waved the gull away. After it had been discouraged from the pursuit the others breathed easier, because the bird struck their minds at this time as being somehow gruesome and ominous.

In the meantime the oiler and the correspondent rowed. They sat together in the same seat, and each rowed an oar. Then the oiler took both oars; then the correspondent took both oars; then the oiler; then the correspondent. They rowed and they rowed. The ticklish part was when the time came for the reclining one in the stern to take his turn at the oars. It is easier to steal eggs from under a hen than it was to change seats in the dinghy. First the man in the stern slid his hand along the thwart and began to move. Then the man in the rowing seat slid his hand along the other thwart. It was all done with the most extraordinary care. As the two sidled past each other, the whole party kept watchful eyes on the coming wave, and the captain cried: "Look out now! Steady there!"

The brown mats of seaweed that appeared from time to time were like islands, bits of earth. They were not traveling, apparently; they were, to all intents, stationary. They informed the men in the boat that it was making progress slowly toward the land.

The captain, rearing cautiously in the bow, after the dinghy soared on a great swell, said that he had seen the lighthouse at Mosquito Inlet. Presently the cook remarked that he had seen it. The correspondent was at the oars then, and he too wished to look, but his back was toward the shore and the waves were important, and for some time he could not seize an opportunity to turn his head. But at last there came a wave more gentle than the others, and when at the crest of it he swiftly scoured the western horizon.

"See it?" said the captain.

"No," said the correspondent slowly, "I didn't see anything."

"Look again," said the captain. He pointed. "It's exactly in that direction."

At the top of another wave, the correspondent did as he was bid, and this time his eyes chanced on a small still thing on the edge of the swaying horizon. It was precisely like the point of a pin. It took an anxious eye to find a lighthouse so tiny.

"Think we'll make it, captain?"

"If this wind holds and the boat don't swamp, we can't do much else," said the captain.

The little boat, lifted by each towering sea, and splashed viciously by the crests, made progress. Occasionally, a great spread of water, like white flames, swarmed into her.

"Bail her, cook," said the captain serenely.

"All right, captain," said the cheerful cook.

THE SUBTLE BROTHERHOOD of men was here established on the seas. No one mentioned it. But it dwelt in the boat, and each man felt it warm him. They were a captain, an oiler, a cook and a correspondent, and they were friends in a curiously ironbound degree. The hurt captain, lying against the water jar in the bow, spoke always in a low voice and calmly, but he could never command a more swiftly obedient crew than the motley three of the dinghy. It was more than a mere recognition of what was best for the common safety. There was surely in it a comradeship that the correspondent, for instance, who had been taught to be cynical of men, knew even at the time was the best experience of his life. But no one said that it was so. No one mentioned it.

"I wish we had a sail," remarked the captain. "We might try my overcoat on the end of an oar and give you two boys a chance to rest." So the cook and the correspondent held the mast and spread wide the overcoat. The oiler steered, and the little boat made good way with her new rig. Sometimes the oiler had to scull sharply to keep a sea from breaking into the boat, but otherwise sailing was a success.

Meanwhile the lighthouse had been growing slowly larger. It had now almost assumed color, and appeared like a little gray shadow on the sky. At last, from the top of each wave the men in the tossing boat could see land, a long black shadow on the sea, thinner than paper. "We must be about opposite New Smyrna," said the cook, who had coasted this shore often in schooners. "Captain, by the way, I believe they abandoned that lifesaving station there about a year ago."

"Did they?" said the captain.

The wind slowly died away. The cook and the correspondent were not now obliged to slave in order to hold high the oar. The little craft, no longer under way, struggled woundily over the waves. The oiler or the correspondent took the oars again.

Shipwrecks are apropos of nothing. If men could only train for them and have them occur when the men had reached pink condition, there would be less drowning at sea. Of the four in the dinghy none had slept any time worth mentioning for two days and two nights previous to embarking in the dinghy, and in the excitement of clambering about the deck of a foundering ship they had also forgotten to eat heartily.

The correspondent now wondered how there could be people who thought it amusing to row a boat. It was not an amusement; it was a diabolical punishment, a horror to the muscles and a crime against the back. He mentioned these thoughts to the boat in general, and the weary-faced oiler smiled in full sympathy. Previous to the foundering, the oiler had worked double watch in the engine room of the ship.

"Take her easy, now, boys," said the captain. "Don't spend yourselves. If we have to run a surf you'll need all your strength, because we'll sure have to swim for it. Take your time."

Slowly the land arose from the sea. From a black line it became a line of black and a line of white, trees and sand. Finally, the captain said that he could make out a house on the shore. "That's the house of refuge, then," said the cook. "They'll see us before long, and come out after us."

The distant lighthouse reared high. "The keeper ought to be able to make us out now, if he's looking through a glass," said the captain. "He'll notify the lifesaving people."

"None of those other boats could have got ashore to give word of the wreck," said the oiler, in a low voice. "Else the lifeboat would be out hunting us."

Slowly and beautifully the land loomed out of the sea. The wind came again. It had veered from the northeast to the southeast. Finally, a new sound struck the ears of the men in the boat. It was the low thunder of the surf on the shore. "Swing her head a little more north, Billie," said the captain.

"A little more north, sir," said the oiler.

Whereupon the little boat turned her nose once more down the wind, and all but the oarsman watched the shore grow. Doubt and direful apprehension were leaving the minds of the men. In an hour, perhaps, they would be ashore.

Their backbones had become thoroughly used to balancing in the boat, and they now rode this wild colt of a dinghy like circus men. The correspondent thought that he had been drenched to the skin, but in the top pocket of his coat he found four perfectly scatheless cigars. After a search, somebody produced three dry matches, and thereupon the four waifs rode impudently in their little boat, and with an assurance of an impending rescue shining in their eyes, puffed at the big cigars. Everybody took a drink of water.

"COOK," REMARKED THE CAPTAIN, "there don't seem to be any signs of life about your house of refuge."

"No," replied the cook. "Funny they don't see us!"

A broad stretch of lowly coast lay before the eyes of the men. It was of dunes topped with dark vegetation. Sometimes they could see the white lip of a wave as it spun up the beach. A tiny house was blocked out black upon the sky. Southward, the slim lighthouse lifted its little gray length.

Tide, wind and waves were swinging the dinghy northward. "Funny they don't see us," said the men.

The surf's roar was dulled, but its tone was thunderous and mighty. As the boat swam over the great rollers, the men sat listening. "We'll swamp sure," said everybody.

It is fair to say here that there was not a lifesaving station within twenty miles in either direction, but they did not know this fact. The lightheartedness had completely faded. Four scowling men sat in the dinghy and made dark and opprobrious remarks concerning the eyesight of the nation's lifesavers. To their sharpened minds it was easy to conjure pictures of all kinds of incompetency and blindness and, indeed, cowardice. There was the shore of the populous land, and it was bitter to them that from it came no sign.

"Well," said the captain, ultimately, "I suppose we'll have to make a try for ourselves. If we stay out here too long, we'll none of us have strength left to swim after the boat swamps."

And so the oiler, who was at the oars, turned the boat straight for the shore. There was a sudden tightening of muscle. There was some thinking.

"If we don't all get ashore—" said the captain. "If we don't all get ashore, I suppose you fellows know where to send news of my finish?"

They then briefly exchanged some addresses and admonitions. As for the reflections of the men, there was a great deal of rage in them, perchance formulated thus: "If I am going to be drowned—if I am going to be drowned, why, in the name of the seven mad gods who rule the sea, was I allowed to come thus far and contemplate sand and trees? If Fate has decided to drown me, why did she not do it in the beginning and save me all this trouble? The whole affair is absurd. . . . But no, she cannot mean to drown me. She dare not drown me. Not after all this work." Afterward the man might have had an impulse to shake his fist at the clouds: "Just you drown me, now, and then hear what I call you!"

The billows that came at this time were more formidable. They seemed always just about to break and roll over the little boat in a turmoil of foam. The shore was still afar. The oiler was a wily surfman. "Boys," he said swiftly, "she won't live three minutes more, and we're too far out to swim. Shall I take her to sea again, captain?"

"Yes! Go ahead!" said the captain.

This oiler, by a series of quick miracles, and fast and steady oarsmanship, turned the boat in the middle of the surf and took her safely to sea again.

There was a considerable silence as the boat bumped over the furrowed sea to deeper water. Then somebody in gloom spoke. "Well, anyhow, they must have seen us from the shore by now."

"What do you think of those lifesaving people? Ain't they peaches?"

"Maybe they think we're out here for sport! Maybe they think we're fishin'. Maybe they think we're damned fools."

It was a long afternoon. A changed tide tried to force them southward, but the wind and wave said northward. And the oiler rowed, and then the correspondent rowed. Then the oiler rowed. It was a weary business. The human back is a limited area, but it can become the theater of innumerable muscular conflicts, tangles, wrenches and other comforts.

"Did you ever like to row, Billie?" asked the correspondent.

"No," said the oiler. "Hang it!"

When one exchanged the rowing seat for a place in the bottom of the boat, he suffered a bodily depression that caused him to be careless of everything. There was cold seawater swashing to and fro in the boat, and he lay in it. Sometimes a particularly obstreperous sea came inboard and drenched him once more. But these matters did not annoy him. It is almost certain that if the boat had capsized he would have tumbled comfortably out upon the ocean as if he felt sure that it was a great soft mattress.

"Look! There's a man on the shore!"

"Where?"

"There! See 'im? See 'im?"

"Yes, sure! He's walking along."

"Now he's stopped. Look! He's facing us!"

"He's waving at us!"

"So he is! By thunder!"

"Ah, now we're all right! Now we're all right! There'll be a boat out here for us in half an hour."

"He's going on. He's running. He's going up to that house there."

The remote beach seemed lower than the sea, and it required a searching glance to discern the little black figure. The captain saw a floating stick and they rowed to it. A bath towel was by some weird chance in the boat, and, tying this on the stick, the captain waved it. The oarsman did not dare turn his head, so he was obliged to ask questions.

"What's he doing now?"

"He's standing still again."

"Is he waving at us?"

"No, not now! He was, though."

"Look! There comes another man!"

"Look at him go, would you."

"Why, he's on a bicycle. Now he's met the other man. They're both waving at us. Look!"

"There comes something up the beach."

"Why it looks like a boat."

"No, it's on wheels."

"Yes, so it is. Well, that must be the lifeboat. They drag them alongshore on a wagon."

"No, by—, it's—it's an omnibus. I can see it plain. See? One of these big hotel omnibuses."

"By thunder, you're right. Maybe they are going around collecting the life crew, hey?"

"That's it, likely. Look! There's a fellow standing on the steps of the omnibus waving a little black flag. There come those other two fellows. Now they're all talking together."

"That ain't a flag, is it? That's his coat."

"So it is. He's taken it off and is waving it around his head. Look at him swing it."

"Oh, say, there isn't any lifesaving station there. That's just a winter resort hotel omnibus that has brought over some of the boarders to see us drown."

"What's that idiot with the coat signaling, anyhow?"

"It looks as if he were trying to tell us to go north. There must be a lifesaving station up there."

"No! He thinks we're fishing. Just giving us a merry hand."

"What do you suppose he means?"

"He don't mean anything. He's just playing."

"Well, if he'd just signal us to try the surf again, or to go to sea and wait, or go north, or go south, or go to hell—there would be some reason in it. But look at him. He just stands there and keeps his coat revolving like a wheel. The ass!"

"There come more people."

"Now there's quite a mob."

"That fellow is still waving his coat."

"Wonder how long he can keep that up. He's been revolving his coat ever since he caught sight of us. He's an idiot. Why aren't they getting men to bring a boat out? Why don't he do something?"

"Oh, it's all right, now."

"They'll have a boat out here for us in less than no time, now that they've seen us."

A faint yellow tone came into the sky over the lowland. The shadows on the sea slowly deepened. The wind bore coldness with it, and the men began to shiver.

"Holy smoke!" said one, "If we've got to flounder out here all night!"

"Oh, we'll never have to stay here all night! Don't you worry. They've seen us now, and they'll come chasing out after us."

The shore grew dusky. The man waving a coat blended gradually into this gloom, and it swallowed in the same manner the omnibus and the group of people. The spray, when it dashed uproariously over the side, made the voyagers shrink and swear like men who were being branded.

"I'd like to catch the chump who waved the coat. I feel like soaking him one. He seemed so damned cheerful."

In the meantime the oiler rowed, and then the correspondent rowed, and then the oiler rowed. Gray-faced and bowed forward, they mechanically, turn by turn, plied the leaden oars. The form of the lighthouse had vanished from the southern horizon, but finally a pale star appeared, just lifting from the sea. The land had vanished, and was expressed only by the low and drear thunder of the surf.

"If I am going to be drowned—if I am going to be drowned, why, in the name of the seven mad gods who rule the sea, was I allowed to come thus far and contemplate sand and trees?"

The patient captain was sometimes obliged to speak to the oarsman.

"Keep her head up! Keep her head up!"

"Keep her head up, sir." The voices were weary and low.

All save the oarsman lay heavily and listlessly in the boat's bottom. As for him, his eyes were just capable of noting the tall black waves that swept forward in a most sinister silence.

The cook's head was on a thwart, and he looked without interest at the water under his nose. Finally he spoke. "Billie," he murmured, dreamily, "what kind of pie do you like best?"

A NIGHT ON THE SEA in an open boat is a long night. As darkness settled finally, the shine of the light, lifting from the sea in the south, changed to full gold. On the northern horizon a new light appeared, a small bluish gleam on the edge of the waters. These two lights were the furniture of the world. Otherwise there was nothing but waves.

Two men huddled in the stern, and distances were so magnificent in the dinghy that the rower was enabled to keep his feet partly warmed by thrusting them under his companions. Sometimes, despite the efforts of the tired oarsman, a wave came piling into the boat, an icy wave of the night, and the chilling water soaked them anew. They would twist their bodies for a moment and groan, and sleep the dead sleep once more.

The oiler plied the oars until his head drooped forward, and the overpowering sleep blinded him. And he rowed yet afterward. Then he touched a man in the bottom of the boat. "Will you spell me for a little while?" he said, meekly.

"Sure, Billie," said the correspondent, awakening and dragging himself to a sitting position. They exchanged places carefully, and the oiler, cuddling down in the seawater at the cook's side, seemed to go to sleep instantly.

The particular violence of the sea had ceased. The waves came without snarling. The obligation of the man at the oars was to keep the boat headed so that the tilt of the rollers would not capsize her, and to preserve her from filling when the crests rushed past.

In a low voice the correspondent addressed the captain. He was not sure that the captain was awake, although this iron man seemed to be always awake. "Captain, shall I keep her making for that light north, sir?"

The same steady voice answered him. "Yes. Keep it about two points off the port bow."

Presently it seemed that even the captain dozed, and the correspondent thought that he was the one man afloat on all the oceans. The wind had a voice as it came over the waves, and it was sadder than the end.

There was a long, loud swishing astern of the boat, and a gleaming trail of phosphorescence, like blue flame, was furrowed on the black waters. It might have been made by a monstrous knife.

Then there came a stillness, until suddenly there was another swish and another long flash of bluish light. This time it was alongside the boat, and might almost have been reached with an oar. The correspondent saw an enormous fin speed like a shadow through the water, hurling the crystalline spray and leaving the long glowing trail.

The correspondent looked over his shoulder at the captain. His face was hidden, and he seemed to be asleep. The others certainly were asleep. So, being bereft of sympathy, he swore softly into the sea.

But ahead or astern, on one side of the boat or the other, at intervals long or short, fled the long sparkling streak, and there was to be heard the *whirroo* of the dark fin. The presence of this biding thing did not affect the man with the same horror that it would if he had been a picnicker. He simply looked at the sea dully and swore in an undertone.

Nevertheless, he did not wish to be alone. He wished one of his companions to awaken and keep him company with it. But the captain hung motionless over the water jar, and the oiler and the cook in the bottom of the boat were plunged in slumber.

"IF I AM GOING to be drowned—if I am going to be drowned, why was I allowed to come thus far and contemplate sand and trees?"

During this dismal night, a man would conclude that it was really the intention of the seven mad gods of the sea to drown him, despite the abominable injustice of it.

When it occurs to a man that nature does not regard him as important, and that she feels she would not maim the universe by disposing of him, he at first wishes to throw bricks at the temple. Any visible expression of nature would surely be pelleted with his jeers.

Then, he feels, perhaps, the desire to confront a personification and indulge in pleas, saying: "Yes, but I love myself."

A high cold star on a winter's night is the word he feels that she says to him. Thereafter he knows the pathos of his situation.

A verse mysteriously entered the correspondent's head. He had even forgotten that he had forgotten this verse.

A soldier of the Legion lay dying in Algiers,
There was lack of woman's nursing, there was dearth of woman's tears;
But a comrade stood beside him, and he took that comrade's hand,
And he said: "I shall never see my own, my native land."

In his childhood, the correspondent had never considered it his affair that a soldier of the Legion lay dying in Algiers, nor had it appeared to him as a matter for sorrow. It was less to him than the breaking of a pencil's point.

Now, however, the correspondent plainly saw the soldier. He lay on the sand with his feet out straight and still. While his pale left hand was upon his chest in an attempt to thwart the going of his life, the blood came between his fingers. The correspondent, plying the oars, was moved by a profound and perfectly impersonal comprehension. He was sorry for the soldier of the Legion who lay dying in Algiers.

The thing which had followed the boat and waited, had evidently grown bored. There was no longer to be heard the slash of the cut water, and there was no longer the flame of the long trail. Sometimes the boom of the surf rang in the correspondent's ears, and he turned the craft seaward then and rowed harder. The wind came stronger, and sometimes a wave suddenly raged out like a mountain cat, and there was to be seen the sheen and sparkle of a broken crest.

The captain, in the bow, moved and sat erect. "Pretty long night," he observed to the correspondent. He looked at the shore. "Those lifesaving people take their time."

"Did you see that shark playing around?"

"Yes, I saw him. He was a big fellow, all right."

"Wish I had known you were awake."

Later the correspondent spoke into the bottom of the boat.

"Billie!" There was a slow and gradual disentanglement. "Billie, will you spell me?"

"Sure," said the oiler.

As soon as the correspondent touched the cold comfortable seawater in the bottom of the boat, he was deep in sleep. This sleep was so good to him that it was but a moment before he heard a voice call his name in a tone that demonstrated the last stages of exhaustion. "Will you spell me?"

"Sure, Billie."

The light in the north had mysteriously vanished, but the correspondent took his course from the wide-awake captain.

Later in the night they took the boat farther out to sea, and the captain directed the cook to take one oar at the stern and keep the boat facing the seas. He was to call out if he should hear the thunder of the surf. This plan enabled the oiler and the correspondent to get respite together.

"We'll give those boys a chance to get into shape again," said the captain. They curled down and slept once more the dead sleep. The ominous slash of the wind and the water affected them as it would have affected mummies.

"Boys," said the cook, with the notes of every reluctance in his voice, "she's drifted in pretty close. I guess one of you had better take her to sea again." The correspondent, aroused, heard the crash of the toppled crests.

As he was rowing, the captain gave him some whisky and water, and this steadied the chills out of him. "If I ever get ashore and anybody shows me even a photograph of an oar—"

At last there was a short conversation.

"Billie. . . . Billie, will you spell me?"

"Sure," said the oiler.

WHEN THE CORRESPONDENT AGAIN opened his eyes, sea and sky were of the gray hue of the dawning. Later, carmine and gold was painted upon the waters. The morning appeared finally, in its splendor, with a sky of pure blue, and the sunlight flamed on the tips of the waves.

On the distant dunes were set many little black cottages, and a tall white windmill reared above them. No man, nor dog, nor bicycle appeared on the beach. The cottages might have formed a deserted village.

The voyagers scanned the shore. "Well," said the captain, "if no help is coming we might better try a run through the surf right away. If we stay out here much longer we will be too weak to do anything for ourselves at all." The others silently acquiesced in this reasoning.

The boat was headed for the beach. The correspondent wondered if none ever ascended the tall wind tower and looked seaward. This tower represented to the correspondent the serenity of nature amid the struggles of the individual. She did not seem cruel to him then, nor beneficent, nor treacherous, nor wise. But she was indifferent, flatly indifferent.

"Now, boys," said the captain, "she is going to swamp, sure. All we can do is to work her in as far as possible, and then when she swamps, pile out and scramble for the beach. Keep cool now, and don't jump until she swamps sure."

The oiler took the oars. Over his shoulders he scanned the surf. "Captain," he said, "I think I'd better bring her about and keep her head-on to the seas and back her in."

"All right, Billie," said the captain. "Back her in." The oiler swung the boat then and, seated in the stern, the cook and the correspondent were obliged to look over their shoulders to contemplate the lonely and indifferent shore.

The monstrous inshore rollers heaved the boat high until the men were again enabled to see the white sheets of water scudding up the slanted beach. "We won't get in very close," said the captain. The correspondent, observing the others, knew that they were not afraid, but the full meaning of their glances was shrouded.

As for himself, he was too tired to grapple fundamentally with the fact. His mind was dominated at this time by his muscles, and the muscles said they did not care. It merely occurred to him that if he should drown it would be a shame.

"Now, remember to get well clear of the boat when you jump," said the captain.

Seaward the crest of a roller suddenly fell with a thunderous crash, and the long white comber came roaring down upon the boat.

"Steady now," said the captain. The men were silent. They turned their eyes from the shore to the comber and waited. The boat slid up the incline, leaped at the furious top, bounced over it, and swung down the long back of the wave. Some water had been shipped and the cook bailed it out.

But the next crashed also. The tumbling, boiling flood of white water swarmed in from all sides. The little boat, drunken with this weight of water, reeled and snuggled deeper into the sea.

"Bail her out, cook! Bail her out," said the captain.

"All right, captain," said the cook.

"Now, boys, the next one will do for us, sure," said the oiler. "Mind to jump clear of the boat."

The third wave moved forward, huge, furious, implacable. It fairly swallowed the dinghy, and almost simultaneously the men tumbled into the sea. A piece of life belt had lain in the bottom of the boat, and as the correspondent went overboard he held this to his chest with his left hand.

The January water was icy, and he reflected immediately that it was colder than he had expected to find it on the coast of Florida. The coldness of the water was sad; it was tragic. Mixed and confused with his opinion of his own situation this fact seemed almost a proper reason for tears. The water was cold.

When he came to the surface he was conscious of little but the noisy water. Afterward he saw his companions in the sea. The oiler was ahead in the race. He was swimming strongly and rapidly. Off to the correspondent's left, the cook's back bulged out of the water, and in the rear the captain was hanging with his one good hand to the keel of the overturned dinghy.

There is a certain immovable quality to a shore. The correspondent knew that it was a long journey, and he paddled leisurely. The piece of life preserver lay under him, and sometimes he whirled down the incline of a wave as if he were on a hand sled.

But finally he arrived at a place in the sea where travel was beset with difficulty. He did not pause swimming to inquire what manner of current had caught him, but there his progress ceased.

As the cook passed, much farther to the left, the captain was calling to him, "Turn over on your back, cook! Turn over on your back and use the oar."

"All right, sir." The cook turned on his back and, paddling with an oar, went ahead as if he were a canoe.

Presently the boat also passed to the left of the correspondent with the captain clinging with one hand to the keel. He would have appeared like a man raising himself to look over a board fence, if it were not for the extraordinary gymnastics of the boat. The correspondent marveled that he could still hold to it.

They passed on, nearer to shore—the oiler, the cook, the captain—and following them went the water jar, bouncing gaily over the seas.

The correspondent remained in the grip of this strange new enemy—a current. The shore, with its white slope of sand and its green bluff, topped with little silent cottages, was spread like a picture before him. It was very near, but he was impressed as one who in a gallery looks at a scene from Brittany or Holland.

He thought: "I am going to drown? Can it be possible? Can it be possible?" Perhaps an individual must consider his own death to be the final phenomenon of nature.

But later a wave perhaps whirled him out of this small, deadly current, for he found suddenly that he could again make progress toward the shore.

Later still, he was aware that the captain, his face turned away from the shore and toward him, was calling his name. "Come to the boat! Come to the boat!"

In his struggle to reach the captain and the boat, he reflected that when one gets properly wearied, drowning must really be a comfortable arrangement, a cessation of hostilities accompanied by a large degree of relief, and he was glad of it. He did not wish to be hurt.

Presently he saw a man running along the shore. He was undressing with most remarkable speed. Coat, trousers, shirt, everything flew magically off him.

"Come to the boat," called the captain.

"All right, captain." As the correspondent paddled, he saw the captain let himself down to bottom and leave the boat. Then the correspondent performed his one little marvel of the voyage. A large wave caught him and flung him with ease and supreme speed completely over the boat and far beyond it. It struck him even then as a true miracle of the sea.

The correspondent arrived in water that reached only to his waist, but he could not stand for more than a moment. Each wave knocked him into a heap, and the undertow pulled at him.

Then he saw the man who had been running and undressing, and undressing and running, come bounding into the water. He dragged the cook ashore, and then waded toward the captain, but the captain waved him away, and sent him to the correspondent. He was naked, naked as a tree in winter, but a halo was about his head, and he shone like a saint. He gave a strong pull, and a long drag, and a bully heave at the correspondent's hand. The correspondent said: "Thanks, old man." But suddenly the man cried: "What's that?" He pointed a swift finger. The correspondent said: "Go."

In the shallows, face downward, lay the oiler. His forehead touched sand that was periodically, between each wave, clear of the sea.

The correspondent did not know all that transpired afterward. When he achieved safe ground he fell, striking the sand with each particular part of his body. It was as if he had dropped from a roof, but the thud was grateful to him.

It seems that instantly the beach was populated with men with blankets, clothes, and flasks, and women with coffee pots and all the remedies sacred to their minds. The welcome of the land to the men from the sea was warm and generous, but a still and dripping shape was carried slowly up the beach, and the land's welcome for it could only be the different and sinister hospitality of the grave.

When it came night, the white waves paced to and fro in the moonlight, and the wind brought the sound of the sea's great voice to the men onshore, and they felt that they could then be interpreters.

MY ŒDIPUS COMPLEX

FRANK O'CONNOR / IRELAND

[signature: Frank O'Connor]

FATHER WAS in the army all through the war—the first war, I mean—so, up to the age of five, I never saw much of him, and what I saw did not worry me. Sometimes I woke and there was a big figure in khaki peering down at me in the candlelight. Sometimes in the early morning I heard the slamming of the front door and the clatter of nailed boots down the cobbles of the lane. These were Father's entrances and exits. Like Santa Claus he came and went mysteriously.

In fact, I rather liked his visits, though it was an uncomfortable squeeze between Mother and him when I got into the big bed in the early morning. He smoked, which gave him a pleasant musty smell, and shaved, an operation of astounding interest. Each time he left a trail of souvenirs—model tanks and Gurkha knives with handles made of bullet cases, and German helmets and cap badges and button sticks, and all sorts of military equipment—carefully stowed away in a long box on top of the wardrobe, in case they ever came in handy. There was a bit of the magpie about Father; he expected everything to come in handy. When his back was turned, Mother let me get a chair and rummage through his treasures. She didn't seem to think so highly of them as he did.

The war was the most peaceful period of my life. The window of my attic faced southeast. My mother had curtained it, but that had small effect. I always woke with the first light and, with all the responsibilities of the previous day melted, feeling myself rather like the sun, ready to illumine and rejoice. Life never seemed so simple and clear and full of possibilities as then. I put my feet out from under the clothes—I called them Mrs. Left and Mrs. Right—and invented dramatic situations for them in which they discussed the problems of the day. At least Mrs. Right did; she was very demonstrative, but I hadn't the same control of Mrs. Left, so she mostly contented herself with nodding agreement.

They discussed what Mother and I should do during the day, what Santa Claus should give a fellow for Christmas, and what steps should be taken to brighten the home. There was that little matter of the baby, for instance. Mother and I could never agree about that. Ours was the only house in the terrace without a new baby, and Mother said we couldn't afford one till Father came back from the war because they cost seventeen and six.

That showed how simple she was. The Geneys up the road had a baby, and everyone knew they couldn't afford seventeen and six. It was probably a cheap baby, and Mother wanted something really good, but I felt she was too exclusive. The Geneys' baby would have done us fine.

Having settled my plans for the day, I got up, put a chair under the attic window, and lifted the frame high enough to stick out my head. The window overlooked the front gardens of the terrace behind ours, and beyond these it looked over a deep valley to the tall, red brick houses terraced up the opposite hillside, which were all still in shadow, while those at our side of the valley were all lit up, though with long strange shadows that made them seem unfamiliar; rigid and painted.

After that I went into Mother's room and climbed into the big bed. She woke and I began to tell her of my schemes. By this time, though I never seemed to have noticed it, I was petrified in my nightshirt, and I thawed as I talked until, the last frost melted, I fell asleep beside her and woke again only when I heard her below in the kitchen, making the breakfast.

After breakfast we went into town; heard Mass at St. Augustine's and said a prayer for Father, and did the shopping. If the afternoon was fine we either went for a walk in the country or a visit to Mother's great friend in the convent, Mother Saint Dominic. Mother had them all praying for Father, and every night, going to bed, I asked God to send him back safe from the war to us. Little, indeed, did I know what I was praying for!

One morning, I got into the big bed, and there, sure enough, was Father in his usual Santa Claus manner, but later, instead of uniform, he put on his best blue suit, and Mother was as pleased as anything. I saw nothing to be pleased about, because, out of uniform, Father was altogether less interesting, but she only beamed, and explained that our prayers had been answered, and off we went to Mass to thank God for having brought Father safely home.

The irony of it! That very day when he came in to dinner he took off his boots and put on his slippers, donned the dirty old cap he wore about the house to save him from colds, crossed his legs, and began to talk gravely to Mother, who looked anxious. Naturally, I disliked her looking anxious, because it destroyed her good looks, so I interrupted him.

"Just a moment, Larry!" she said gently.

This was only what she said when we had boring visitors, so I attached no importance to it and went on talking.

"Do be quiet, Larry!" she said impatiently. "Don't you hear me talking to Daddy?"

This was the first time I had heard those ominous words, "talking to Daddy," and I couldn't help feeling that if this was how God answered prayers, he couldn't listen to them very attentively.

"Why are you talking to Daddy?" I asked with as great a show of indifference as I could muster.

"Because Daddy and I have business to discuss. Now, don't interrupt again!"

In the afternoon, at Mother's request, Father took me for a walk. This time we went into town instead of out in the country, and I thought at first, in my usual optimistic way, that it might be an improvement. It was nothing of the sort. Father and I had quite different notions of a walk in town. He had no proper interest in trams, ships, and horses, and the only thing that seemed to divert him was talking to fellows as old as himself. When I wanted to stop he simply went on, dragging me behind him by the hand; when he wanted to stop I had no alternative but to do the same. I noticed that it seemed to be a sign that he wanted to stop for a long time whenever he leaned against a wall. The second time I saw him do it I got wild. He seemed to be settling himself forever. I pulled him by the coat and trousers, but, unlike Mother who, if you were too persistent, got into a wax and said: "Larry, if you don't behave yourself, I'll give you a good slap," Father had an extraordinary capacity for amiable inattention. I sized him up and wondered would I cry, but he seemed to be too remote to be annoyed even by that. Really, it was like going for a walk with a mountain! He either ignored the wrenching and pummeling entirely, or else glanced down with a grin of amusement from his peak. I had never met anyone so absorbed in himself as he seemed.

At teatime, "talking to Daddy" began again, complicated this time by the fact that he had an evening paper, and every few minutes he put it down and told Mother something new out of it. I felt this was foul play. Man for man, I was prepared to compete with him any time for Mother's attention, but when he had it all made up for him by other people it left me no chance. Several times I tried to change the subject without success.

"You must be quiet while Daddy is reading, Larry," Mother said impatiently.

It was clear that she either genuinely liked talking to Father better than talking to me, or else that he had some terrible hold on her which made her afraid to admit the truth.

"Mummy," I said that night when she was tucking me up, "do you think if I prayed hard God would send Daddy back to the war?"

She seemed to think about that for a moment.

"No, dear," she said with a smile. "I don't think He would."

"Why wouldn't He, Mummy?"

"Because there isn't a war any longer, dear."

"But, Mummy, couldn't God make another war, if He liked?"

"He wouldn't like to, dear. It's not God who makes wars, but bad people."

"Oh!" I said.

I was disappointed about that. I began to think that God wasn't quite what He was cracked up to be.

Next morning I woke at my usual hour, feeling like a bottle of champagne. I put out my feet and invented a long conversation in which Mrs. Right talked of the trouble she had with her own father till she put him in the Home. I didn't quite know what the Home was but it sounded the right place for Father. Then I got my chair and stuck my head out of the attic window. Dawn was just breaking, with a guilty air that made me feel I had caught it in the act. My head bursting with stories and schemes, I stumbled in next door, and in the half-darkness scrambled into the big bed. There was no room at Mother's side so I had to get between her and Father. For the time being I had forgotten about him, and for several minutes I sat bolt upright, racking my brains to know what I could do with him. He was taking up more than his fair share of the bed, and I couldn't get comfortable, so I gave him several kicks that made him grunt and stretch. He made room all right, though. Mother waked and felt for me. I settled back comfortably in the warmth of the bed with my thumb in my mouth.

"Mummy!" I hummed, loudly and contentedly.

"Sssh! dear," she whispered. "Don't wake Daddy!"

This was a new development, which threatened to be even more serious than "talking to Daddy." Life without my early-morning conferences was unthinkable.

"Why?" I asked severely.

"Because poor Daddy is tired."

This seemed to me a quite inadequate reason, and I was sickened by the sentimentality of her "poor Daddy." I never liked that sort of gush; it always struck me as insincere.

"Oh!" I said lightly. Then in my most winning tone: "Do you know where I want to go with you today, Mummy?"

"No, dear," she sighed.

"I want to go down the Glen and fish for thornybacks with my new net, and then I want to go out to the Fox and Hounds, and—"

"Don't-wake-Daddy!" she hissed angrily, clapping her hand across my mouth.

But it was too late. He was awake, or nearly so. He grunted and reached for the matches. Then he stared incredulously at his watch.

"Like a cup of tea, dear?" asked Mother in a meek, hushed voice I had never heard her use before. It sounded almost as though she were afraid.

"Tea?" he exclaimed indignantly. "Do you know what the time is?"

"And after that I want to go up the Rathcooney Road," I said loudly, afraid I'd forget something in all those interruptions.

"Go to sleep at once, Larry!" she said sharply.

I began to snivel. I couldn't concentrate, the way that pair went on, and smothering my early-morning schemes was like burying a family from the cradle.

Father said nothing, but lit his pipe and sucked it, looking out into the shadows without minding Mother or me. I knew he was mad. Every time I made a remark Mother hushed me irritably. I was mortified. I felt it wasn't fair; there was even something sinister in it. Every time I had pointed out to her the waste of making two beds when we could both sleep in one, she had told me it was healthier like that, and now here was this man, this stranger, sleeping with her without the least regard for her health!

He got up early and made tea, but though he brought Mother a cup he brought none for me.

"Mummy," I shouted, "I want a cup of tea, too."

"Yes, dear," she said patiently. "You can drink from Mummy's saucer."

That settled it. Either Father or I would have to leave the house. I didn't want to drink from Mother's saucer; I wanted to be treated as an equal in my own home, so, just to spite her, I drank it all and left none for her. She took that quietly, too.

But that night when she was putting me to bed she said gently: "Larry, I want you to promise me something."

"What is it?" I asked.

"Not to come in and disturb poor Daddy in the morning. Promise?"

"Poor Daddy" again! I was becoming suspicious of everything involving that quite impossible man.

"Why?" I asked.

"Because poor Daddy is worried and tired and he doesn't sleep well."

"Why doesn't he, Mummy?"

"Well, you know, don't you, that while he was at the war Mummy got the pennies from the post office?"

"From Miss MacCarthy?"

"That's right. But now, you see, Miss MacCarthy hasn't any more pennies, so Daddy must go out and find us some. You know what would happen if he couldn't?"

"No," I said, "tell us."

"Well, I think we might have to go out and beg for them like the poor old woman on Fridays. We wouldn't like that, would we?"

"No," I agreed. "We wouldn't."

"So you'll promise not to come in and wake him?"

"Promise."

Mind you, I meant that. I knew pennies were a serious matter, and I was all against having to go out and beg like the old woman on Fridays. Mother laid out all my toys in a complete ring round the bed so that, whatever way I got out, I was bound to fall over one of them.

When I woke I remembered my promise all right. I got up and sat on the floor and played—for hours, it seemed to me. Then I got my chair and looked out the attic window for more hours. I wished it was time for Father to wake; I wished someone would make me a cup of tea. I didn't feel in the least like the sun; instead, I was bored and so very, very cold! I simply longed for the warmth and depth of the big feather bed.

At last I could stand it no longer. I went into the next room. As there was still no room at Mother's side I climbed over her and she woke with a start.

"Larry," she whispered, gripping my arm very tightly, "what did you promise?"

"But I did, Mummy," I wailed, caught in the very act. "I was quiet for ever so long."

"Oh, dear, and you're perished!" she said sadly, feeling me all over. "Now, if I let you stay will you promise not to talk?"

"But I want to talk, Mummy," I wailed.

"That has nothing to do with it," she said with a firmness that was new to me. "Daddy wants to sleep. Now, do you understand that?"

I understood it only too well. I wanted to talk, he wanted to sleep—whose house was it, anyway?

"Mummy," I said with equal firmness, "I think it would be healthier for Daddy to sleep in his own bed."

That seemed to stagger her, because she said nothing for a while.

"Now, once for all," she went on, "you're to be perfectly quiet or go back to your own bed. Which is it to be?"

The injustice of it got me down. I had convicted her out of her own mouth of inconsistency and unreasonableness, and she hadn't even attempted to reply. Full of spite, I gave Father a kick, which she didn't notice but which made him grunt and open his eyes in alarm.

"What time is it?" he asked in a panic-stricken voice, not looking at Mother but at the door, as if he saw someone there.

"It's early yet," she replied soothingly. "It's only the child. Go to sleep again. . . . Now, Larry," she added, getting out of bed, "you've wakened Daddy and you must go back."

This time, for all her quiet air, I knew she meant it, and knew that my principal rights and privileges were as good as lost unless I asserted them at once. As she lifted me, I gave a screech, enough to wake the dead, not to mind Father. He groaned.

"That damn child! Doesn't he ever sleep?"

"It's only a habit, dear," she said quietly, though I could see she was vexed.

"Well, it's time he got out of it," shouted Father, beginning to heave in the bed. He suddenly gathered all the bedclothes about him, turned to the wall, and then looked back over his shoulder with nothing showing only two small, spiteful, dark eyes. The man looked very wicked.

To open the bedroom door, Mother had to let me down, and I broke free and dashed for the farthest corner, screeching. Father sat bolt upright in bed.

"Shut up, you little puppy!" he said in a choking voice.

I was so astonished that I stopped screeching. Never, never had anyone spoken to me in that tone before. I looked at him incredulously and saw his face convulsed with rage. It was only then that I fully realized how God had codded me, listening to my prayers for the safe return of this monster.

"Shut up, you!" I bawled, beside myself.

"What's that you said?" shouted Father, making a wild leap out of the bed.

"Mick, Mick!" cried Mother. "Don't you see the child isn't used to you?"

"I see he's better fed than taught," snarled Father, waving his arms wildly. "He wants his bottom smacked."

All his previous shouting was as nothing to these obscene words referring to my person. They really made my blood boil.

"Smack your own!" I screamed hysterically. "Smack your own! Shut up! Shut up!"

At this he lost his patience and let fly at me. He did it with the lack of conviction you'd expect of a man under Mother's horrified eyes, and it ended up as a mere tap, but the sheer indignity of being struck at all by a stranger, a total stranger who had cajoled his way back from the war into our big bed as a result of my innocent intercession, made me completely dotty. I shrieked and shrieked, and danced in my bare feet, and Father, looking awkward and hairy in nothing but a short gray army shirt, glared down at me like a mountain out for murder. I think it must have been then that I realized he was jealous too. And there stood Mother in her nightdress, looking as if her heart was broken between us. I hoped she felt as she looked. It seemed to me that she deserved it all.

From that morning out my life was a hell. Father and I were enemies, open and avowed. We conducted a series of skirmishes against one another, he trying to steal my time with Mother and I his. When she was sitting on my bed, telling me a story, he took to looking for some pair of old boots which he alleged he had left behind him at the beginning of the war. While he talked to Mother I played loudly with my toys to show my total lack of concern. He created a terrible scene one evening when he came in from work and found me at his box, playing with his regimental badges, Gurkha knives and button sticks. Mother got up and took the box from me.

"You mustn't play with Daddy's toys unless he lets you, Larry," she said severely. "Daddy doesn't play with yours."

For some reason Father looked at her as if she had struck him and then turned away with a scowl.

"Those are not toys," he growled, taking down the box again to see had I lifted anything. "Some of those curios are very rare and valuable."

But as time went on I saw more and more how he managed to alienate Mother and me. What made it worse was that I couldn't grasp his method or see what attraction he had for Mother. In every possible way he was less winning than I. He had a common accent and made noises at his tea. I thought for a while that it might be the newspapers she was interested in, so I made up bits of news of my own to read to her. Then I thought it might be the smoking, which I personally thought attractive, and took his pipes and went round the house dribbling into them till he caught me. I even made noises at my tea, but Mother only told me I was disgusting. It all seemed to hinge round that unhealthy habit of sleeping together, so I made a point of dropping into their bedroom and nosing round, talking to myself, so that they wouldn't know I was watching them, but they were never up to anything that I could see. In the end it beat me. It seemed to depend on being grown-up and giving people rings, and I realized I'd have to wait.

But at the same time I wanted him to see that I was only waiting, not giving up the fight. One evening when he was being particularly obnoxious, chattering away well above my head, I let him have it. "Mummy," I said, "do you know what I'm going to do when I grow up?"

"No, dear," she replied. "What?"

"I'm going to marry you," I said quietly.

Father gave a great guffaw out of him, but he didn't take me in. I knew it must only be pretense. And Mother, in spite of everything, was pleased. I felt she was probably relieved to know that one day

Father's hold on her would be broken. "Won't that be nice?" she said with a smile.

"It'll be very nice," I said confidently. "Because we're going to have lots and lots of babies."

"That's right, dear," she said placidly. "I think we'll have one soon, and then you'll have plenty of company."

I was no end pleased about that because it showed that in spite of the way she gave in to Father she still considered my wishes. Besides, it would put the Geneys in their place.

It didn't turn out like that, though. To begin with, she was very preoccupied—I supposed about where she would get the seventeen and six—and though Father took to staying out late in the evenings it did me no particular good. She stopped taking me for walks, became as touchy as blazes, and smacked me for nothing at all. Sometimes I wished I'd never mentioned the confounded baby—I seemed to have a genius for bringing calamity on myself.

And calamity it was! Sonny arrived in the most appalling hulla-baloo—even that much he couldn't do without a fuss—and from the first moment I disliked him. He was a difficult child—so far as I was concerned he was always difficult—and demanded far too much attention.

Mother was simply silly about him, and couldn't see when he was only showing off. As company he was worse than useless. He slept all day, and I had to go round the house on tiptoe to avoid waking him. It wasn't any longer a question of not waking Father. The slogan now was "Don't-wake-Sonny!" I couldn't understand why the child wouldn't sleep at the proper time, so whenever Mother's back was turned I woke him. Sometimes to keep him awake I pinched him as well. Mother caught me at it one day and gave me a most unmerci-ful flaking.

One evening, when Father was coming in from work, I was playing trains in the front garden.

I let on not to notice him; instead, I pretended to be talking to myself, and said in a loud voice: "If another bloody baby comes into this house, I'm going out."

Father stopped dead and looked at me over his shoulder.

"What's that you said?" he asked sternly.

"I was only talking to myself," I replied, trying to conceal my panic. "It's private."

He turned and went in without a word. Mind you, I intended it as a solemn warning, but its effect was quite different. Father started being quite nice to me. I could understand that, of course. Mother was quite sickening about Sonny. Even at mealtimes she'd get up and gawk at him in the cradle with an idiotic smile, and tell Father to do the same. He was always polite about it, but he looked so puzzled you could see he didn't know what she was talking about. He complained of the way Sonny cried at night, but she only got cross and said that Sonny never cried except when there was something up with him—which was a flaming lie, because Sonny never had anything up with him, and only cried for attention. It was really painful to see how simpleminded she was. Father wasn't attractive, but he had a fine intelligence. He saw through Sonny, and now he knew that I saw through him as well.

One night I woke with a start. There was someone beside me in the bed. For one wild moment I felt sure it must be Mother, having come to her senses and left Father for good, but then I heard Sonny in convulsions in the next room, and Mother saying: "There! There! There!" and I knew it wasn't she. It was Father. He was lying beside me, wide-awake, breathing hard and apparently as mad as hell.

After a while it came to me what he was mad about. It was his turn now. After turning me out of the big bed, he had been turned out himself. Mother had no consideration now for anyone but that poisonous pup, Sonny. I couldn't help feeling sorry for Father. I had been through it all myself, and even at that age I was magnanimous. I began to stroke him down and say: "There! There!" He wasn't exactly responsive.

"Aren't you asleep either?" he snarled.

"Ah, come on and put your arm around us, can't you?" I said, and he did, in a sort of way. Gingerly, I suppose, is how you'd describe it. He was very bony but better than nothing.

At Christmas he went out of his way to buy me a really nice model railway.

THE SNOWS
OF KILIMANJARO

ERNEST HEMINGWAY/UNITED STATES

Kilimanjaro is a snow-covered mountain 19,710 feet high, and is said to be the highest mountain in Africa. Its western summit is called the Masai "Ngàje Ngài," the House of God. Close to the western summit there is the dried and frozen carcass of a leopard. No one has explained what the leopard was seeking at that altitude.

"THE MARVELOUS THING is that it's painless," he said. "That's how you know when it starts."

"Is it really?"

"Absolutely. I'm awfully sorry about the odor though. That must bother you."

"Don't! Please don't."

"Look at them," he said. "Now is it sight or is it scent that brings them like that?"

The cot the man lay on was in the wide shade of a mimosa tree and as he looked out past the shade onto the glare of the plain there were three of the big birds squatted obscenely, while in the sky a dozen more sailed, making quick-moving shadows as they passed.

"They've been there since the day the truck broke down," he said. "Today's the first time any have lit on the ground. I watched the way they sailed very carefully at first in case I ever wanted to use them in a story. That's funny now."

"I wish you wouldn't," she said.

"I'm only talking," he said. "It's much easier if I talk. But I don't want to bother you."

"You know it doesn't bother me," she said. "It's that I've gotten so very nervous not being able to do anything. I think we might make it as easy as we can until the plane comes."

"Or until the plane doesn't come."

"Please tell me what I can do. There must be something I can do."

"You can take the leg off and that might stop it, though I doubt it. Or you can shoot me. You're a good shot now. I taught you to shoot, didn't I?"

"Please don't talk that way. Couldn't I read to you?"

"Read what?"

"Anything in the book bag that we haven't read."

"I can't listen to it," he said. "Talking is the easiest. We quarrel and that makes the time pass."

"I don't quarrel. I never want to quarrel. Let's not quarrel anymore. No matter how nervous we get. Maybe they will be back with another truck today. Maybe the plane will come."

"I don't want to move," the man said. "There is no sense in moving now except to make it easier for you."

"That's cowardly."

"Can't you let a man die as comfortably as he can without calling him names? What's the use of slanging me?"

"You're not going to die."

"Don't be silly, I'm dying now. Ask those bastards." He looked over to where the huge, filthy birds sat, their naked heads sunk in the hunched feathers. A fourth planed down, to run quick-legged and then waddle slowly toward the others.

"They are around every camp. You never notice them. You can't die if you don't give up."

"Where did you read that? You're such a bloody fool."

"You might think about someone else."

"For Christ's sake," he said, "that's been my trade." He lay then and was quiet for a while and looked across the heat shimmer of the plain to the edge of the bush. There were a few Tommies that showed minute and white against the yellow and, far off, he saw a herd of zebra, white against the green of the bush. This was a pleasant camp under big trees against a hill, with good water, and close-by, a nearly dry water hole where sand grouse flighted in the mornings.

"Wouldn't you like me to read?" she asked. She was sitting on a canvas chair beside his cot. "There's a breeze coming up."

"No thanks."

"Maybe the truck will come."

"I don't give a damn about the truck."

"I do."

"You give a damn about so many things that I don't."

"Not so many, Harry."

"What about a drink?"

"It's supposed to be bad for you. It said in Black's to avoid all alcohol. You shouldn't drink."

"Molo!" he shouted.

"Yes Bwana."

"Bring whiskey-soda."

"Yes Bwana."

"You shouldn't," she said. "That's what I mean by giving up. It says it's bad for you. I know it's bad for you."

"No," he said. "It's good for me."

So now it was all over, he thought. So now he would never have a chance to finish it. So this was the way it ended in a bickering over a drink. Since the gangrene started in his right leg he had no pain and with the pain the horror had gone and all he felt now was a great tiredness and anger that this was the end of it. For this, that now was coming, he had very little curiosity. For years it had obsessed him; but now it meant nothing in itself. It was strange how easy being tired enough made it.

Now he would never write the things that he had saved to write until he knew enough to write them well. Well, he would not have to fail at trying to write them either. Maybe you could never write them, and that was why you put them off and delayed the starting. Well, he would never know, now.

"I wish we'd never come," the woman said. She was looking at him holding the glass and biting her lip. "You never would have gotten anything like this in Paris. You always said you loved Paris.

We could have stayed in Paris or gone anywhere. I'd have gone anywhere. I said I'd go anywhere you wanted. If you wanted to shoot we could have gone shooting in Hungary and been comfortable."

"Your bloody money," he said.

"That's not fair," she said. "It was always yours as much as mine. I left everything and I went wherever you wanted to go and I've done what you wanted to do. But I wish we'd never come here."

"You said you loved it."

"I did when you were all right. But now I hate it. I don't see why that had to happen to your leg. What have we done to have that happen to us?"

"I suppose what I did was to forget to put iodine on it when I first scratched it. Then I didn't pay any attention to it because I never infect. Then, later, when it got bad, it was probably using that weak carbolic solution when the other antiseptics ran out that paralyzed the minute blood vessels and started the gangrene." He looked at her. "What else?"

"I don't mean that."

"If we would have hired a good mechanic instead of a half-baked Kikuyu driver, he would have checked the oil and never burned out that bearing in the truck."

"I don't mean that."

"If you hadn't left your own people, your goddamned Old Westbury, Saratoga, Palm Beach people to take me on—"

"Why, I loved you. That's not fair. I love you now. I'll always love you. Don't you love me?"

"No," said the man. "I don't think so. I never have."

"Harry, what are you saying? You're out of your head."

"No. I haven't any head to go out of."

"Don't drink that," she said. "Darling, please don't drink that. We have to do everything we can."

"You do it," he said. "I'm tired."

Now in his mind he saw a railway station at Karagatch and he was standing with his pack and that was the headlight of the Simplon-Orient cutting the dark now and he was leaving Thrace then after the retreat.

That was one of the things he had saved to write, with, in the morning at breakfast, looking out the window and seeing snow on the mountains in Bulgaria and Nansen's secretary asking the old man if it were snow and the old man looking at it and saying, No, that's not snow. It's too early for snow. And the secretary repeating to the other girls, No, you see. It's not snow and them all saying, It's not snow we were mistaken. But it was the snow all right and he sent them on into it when he evolved exchange of populations. And it was snow they tramped along in until they died that winter.

It was snow too that fell all Christmas week that year up in the Gauertal, that year they lived in the woodcutter's house with the big square porcelain stove that filled half the room, and they slept on mattresses filled with beech leaves, the time the deserter came with his feet bloody in the snow. He said the police were right behind him and they gave him woolen socks and held the gendarmes talking until the tracks had drifted over.

In Schrunz, on Christmas Day, the snow was so bright it hurt your eyes when you looked out from the weinstube and saw everyone coming home from church. That was where they walked up the sleigh-smoothed urine-yellowed road along the river with the steep pine hills, skis heavy on the shoulder, and where they ran that great run down the glacier above the Madlener-haus, the snow as smooth to see as cake frosting and as light as powder and he remembered the noiseless rush the speed made as you dropped down like a bird.

They were snowbound a week in the Madlener-haus that time in the blizzard playing cards in the smoke by the lantern light and the stakes were higher all the time as Herr Lent lost more. Finally he lost it all. Everything, the skischule money and all the season's profit and then his capital. He could see him with his long nose, picking up the cards and then opening, "Sans Voir."

There was always gambling then. When there was no snow you gambled and when there was too much you gambled. He thought of all the time in his life he had spent gambling.

But he had never written a line of that, nor of that cold, bright Christmas Day with the mountains showing across the plain that Barker had flown across the lines to bomb the Austrian officers' leave train, machine-gunning them as they scattered and ran. He remembered Barker afterwards coming into the mess and starting to tell about it. And how quiet it got and then somebody saying, "You bloody murderous bastard."

Those were the same Austrians they killed then that he skied with later. No not the same. Hans, that he skied with all that year, had been in the Kaiser-Jägers and when they went hunting hares together up the little valley above the sawmill they had talked of the fighting on Pasubio and of the attack on Pertica and Asalone and he had never written a word of that. Nor of Monte Corno, nor the Siete Commun, nor of Arsiedo.

How many winters had he lived in the Voralberg and the Arlberg? It was four and then he remembered the man who had the fox to sell when they had walked into Bludenz, that time to buy presents, and the cherry-pit taste of good kirsch, the fast-slipping rush of running powder snow on crust, singing "Hi! Ho! said Rolly!" as you ran down the last stretch to the steep drop, taking it straight, then running the orchard in three turns and out across the ditch and onto the icy road behind the inn. Knocking your bindings loose, kicking the skis free and leaning them up against the wooden wall of the inn, the lamplight coming from the window, where inside, in the smoky, new-wine smelling warmth, they were playing the accordion.

"WHERE DID WE STAY in Paris?" he asked the woman who was sitting by him in a canvas chair, now, in Africa.

"At the Crillon. You know that."

"Why do I know that?"

"That's where we always stayed."

"No. Not always."

"There and at the Pavillion Henri-Quatre in St. Germain. You said you loved it there.

"Love is a dunghill," said Harry. "And I'm the cock that gets on it to crow."

"If you have to go away," she said, "is it absolutely necessary to kill off everything you leave behind? I mean do you have to take away everything? Do you have to kill your horse, and your wife and burn your saddle and your armor?"

"Yes," he said. "Your damned money was my armor. My Swift and my Armour."

"Don't."

"All right. I'll stop that. I don't want to hurt you."

"It's a little bit late now."

"All right then. I'll go on hurting you. It's more amusing. The only thing I ever really like to do with you I can't do now."

"No, that's not true. You liked to do many things and everything you wanted to do I did."

"Oh, for Christ sake stop bragging, will you?"

He looked at her and saw her crying.

"Listen," he said. "Do you think that it is fun to do this? I don't know why I'm doing it. It's trying to kill to keep yourself alive, I imagine. I was all right when we started talking. I didn't mean to start this, and now I'm crazy as a coot and being as cruel to you as I can be. Don't pay any attention, darling, to what I say. I love you, really. You know I love you. I've never loved anyone else the way I love you."

He slipped into the familiar lie he made his bread and butter by.

"You're sweet to me."

"You bitch," he said. "You rich bitch. That's poetry. I'm full of poetry now. Rot and poetry. Rotten poetry."

"Stop it. Harry, why do you have to turn into a devil now?"

"I don't like to leave anything," the man said. "I don't like to leave things behind."

—

IT WAS EVENING now and he had been asleep. The sun was gone behind the hill and there was a shadow all across the plain and the small animals were feeding close to camp; quick dropping heads and switching tails, he watched them keeping well out away from the bush now. The birds no longer waited on the ground. They were all perched heavily in a tree. There were many more of them. His personal boy was sitting by the bed.

"Memsahib's gone to shoot," the boy said. "Does Bwana want?"

"Nothing."

She had gone to kill a piece of meat and, knowing how he liked to watch the game, she had gone well away so she would not disturb this little pocket of the plain that he could see. She was always thoughtful, he thought. On anything she knew about, or had read, or that she had ever heard.

It was not her fault that when he went to her he was already over. How could a woman know that you meant nothing that you said; that you spoke only from habit and to be comfortable? After he no longer meant what he said, his lies were more successful with women than when he had told them the truth.

It was not so much that he lied as that there was no truth to tell. He had had his life and it was over and then he went on living it again with different people and more money, with the best of the same places, and some new ones.

You kept from thinking and it was all marvelous. You were equipped with good insides so that you did not go to pieces that way, the way most of them had, and you made an attitude that you cared nothing for the work you used to do, now that you could no longer do it. But, in yourself, you said that you would write about these people; about the very rich; that you were really not of them but a spy in their country; that you would leave it and write of it and for once it would be written by someone who knew what he was writing of. But he would never do it, because each day of not writing, of comfort, of being that which he despised, dulled his ability and softened his will to work so that, finally, he did no work at all. The people he knew now were all much more comfortable when he did not work. Africa was where he had been happiest in the good time of his life, so he had come out here to start again. They had made this safari with the minimum of comfort. There was no hardship; but there was no luxury and he had thought that he could get back into training that way. That in some way he could work the fat off his soul the way a fighter went into the mountains to work and train in order to burn it out of his body.

She had liked it. She said she loved it. She loved anything that was exciting, that involved a change of scene, where there were new people and where things were pleasant. And he had felt the illusion of returning strength of will to work. Now if this was how it ended, and he knew it was, he must not turn like some snake biting itself because its back was broken. It wasn't this woman's fault. If it had not been she it would have been another. If he lived by a lie he should try to die by it. He heard a shot beyond the hill.

She shot very well, this good, this rich bitch, this kindly caretaker and destroyer of his talent. Nonsense. He had destroyed his talent himself. Why should he blame this woman because she kept him well? He had destroyed his talent by not using it, by betrayals of himself and what he believed in, by drinking so much that he blunted the edge of his perceptions, by laziness, by sloth, and by snobbery, by pride and by prejudice, by hook and by crook. What was this? A catalogue of old books? What was his talent anyway? It was a talent all right but instead of using it, he had traded on it. It was never what he had done, but always what he could do. And he had chosen to make his living with something else instead of a pen or a pencil. It was strange, too, wasn't it, that when he fell in love with another woman, that woman should always have more money than the last one? But when he no longer was in love, when he was only lying, as to this woman, now, who had the most money of all, who had all the money there was, who had had a husband and children, who had taken lovers and been dissatisfied with them, and who loved him dearly as a writer, as a man, as a companion and as a proud possession; it was strange that when he did not love her at all and was lying, that he should be able to give her more for her money than when he had really loved.

We must all be cut out for what we do, he thought. However you make your living is where your talent lies. He had sold vitality, in one form or another, all his life and when your affections are not too involved you give much better value for the money. He had found that out but he would never write that, now, either. No, he would not write that, although it was well worth writing.

Now she came in sight, walking across the open toward the camp. She was wearing jodhpurs and carrying her rifle. The two boys had a Tommie slung and they were coming along behind her. She was still a good-looking woman, he thought, and she had a pleasant body. She had a great talent and appreciation for the bed, she was not pretty, but he liked her face, she read enormously, liked to ride and shoot and, certainly, she drank too much. Her husband had died when she was still a comparatively young woman and for a while she had devoted herself to her two just-grown children, who did not need her and were embarrassed at having her about, to her stable of horses, to books, and to bottles. She liked to read in the evening before dinner and she drank Scotch and soda while she read. By dinner she was fairly drunk and after a bottle of wine at dinner she was usually drunk enough to sleep.

That was before the lovers. After she had the lovers she did not drink so much because she did not have to be drunk to sleep. But the lovers bored her. She had been married to a man who had never bored her and these people bored her very much. Then one of her two children was killed in a plane crash and after that was over she did not want the lovers, and drink being no anesthetic she had to make another life. Suddenly, she had been acutely frightened of being alone. But she wanted someone that she respected with her.

It had begun very simply. She liked what he wrote and she had always envied the life he led. She thought he did exactly what he wanted to. The steps by which she had acquired him and the way in which she had finally fallen in love with him were all part of a regular progression in which she had built herself a new life and he had traded away what remained of his old life.

He had traded it for security, for comfort too, there was no denying that, and for what else? He did not know. She would have bought him anything he wanted. He knew that. She was a damned nice woman too. He would as soon be in bed with her as anyone; rather with her, because she was richer, because she was very pleasant and appreciative and because she never made scenes. And now this life that she had built again was coming to a term because he had not used iodine two weeks ago when a thorn had scratched his knee as they moved forward trying to photograph a herd of waterbuck standing, their heads up, peering while their nostrils searched the air, their ears spread wide to hear the first noise that would send them rushing into the bush. They had bolted, too, before he got the picture.

Here she came now. He turned his head on the cot to look toward her. "Hello," he said.

"I shot a Tommy ram," she told him. "He'll make you good broth and I'll have them mash some potatoes with the Klim. How do you feel?"

"Much better."

"Isn't that lovely? You know I thought perhaps you would. You were sleeping when I left."

"I had a good sleep. Did you walk far?"

"No. Just around behind the hill. I made quite a good shot on the Tommy."

"You shoot marvelously, you know."

"I love it. I've loved Africa. Really. If *you're* all right it's the most fun that I've ever had. You don't know the fun it's been to shoot with you. I've loved the country."

"I love it too."

"Darling, you don't know how marvelous it is to see you feeling better. I couldn't stand it when you felt that way. You won't talk to me like that again, will you? Promise me?"

"No," he said. "I don't remember what I said."

"You don't have to destroy me. Do you? I'm only a middle-aged woman who loves you and wants to do what you want to do. I've been destroyed two or three times already. You wouldn't want to destroy me again, would you?"

"I'd like to destroy you a few times in bed," he said.

"Yes. That's the good destruction. That's the way we're made to be destroyed. The plane will be here tomorrow."

"How do you know?"

"I'm sure. It's bound to come. The boys have the wood all ready and the grass to make the smudge. I went down and looked at it again today. There's plenty of room to land and we have the smudges ready at both ends."

"What makes you think it will come tomorrow?"

"I'm sure it will. It's overdue now. Then, in town, they will fix up your leg and then we will have some good destruction. Not that dreadful talking kind."

"Should we have a drink? The sun is down."

"Do you think you should?"

"I'm having one."

"We'll have one together. Molo, *letti dui whiskey-soda!*" she called.

"You'd better put on your mosquito boots," he told her.

"I'll wait till I bathe . . ."

While it grew dark they drank and just before it was dark and there was no longer enough light to shoot, a hyena crossed the open on his way around the hill. "That bastard crosses there every night," the man said. "Every night for two weeks."

"He's the one makes the noise at night. I don't mind it. They're a filthy animal though."

Drinking together, with no pain now except the discomfort of lying in the one position, the boys lighting a fire, its shadow jumping on the tents, he could feel the return of acquiescence in this life of pleasant surrender. She *was* very good to him. He had been cruel and unjust in the afternoon. She was a fine woman, marvelous really. And just then it occurred to him that he was going to die.

It came with a rush; not as a rush of water nor of wind; but of a sudden evil-smelling emptiness and the odd thing was that the hyena slipped lightly along the edge of it.

"What is it, Harry?" she asked him.

"Nothing," he said. "You had better move over to the other side. To windward."

"Did Molo change the dressing?"

"Yes. I'm just using the boric now."

"How do you feel?"

"A little wobbly."

"I'm going in to bathe," she said. "I'll be right out. I'll eat with you and then we'll put the cot in."

So, he said to himself, we did well to stop the quarreling. He had never quarreled much with this woman, while with the women that he loved he had quarreled so much they had finally, always, with the corrosion of the quarreling, killed what they had together. He had loved too much, demanded too much, and he wore it all out.

He thought about alone in Constantinople that time, having quarreled in Paris before he had gone out. He had whored the whole time and then, when that was over, and he had failed to kill his loneliness, but only made

*it worse, he had written her, the first one, the one who left him, a letter
telling her how he had never been able to kill it. . . . How when he thought
he saw her outside the* Regence *one time it made him go all faint and
sick inside, and that he would follow a woman who looked like her in some
way, along the Boulevard, afraid to see it was not she, afraid to lose the
feeling it gave him. How everyone he had slept with had only made him
miss her more. How what she had done could never matter since he knew
he could not cure himself of loving her. He wrote this letter at the Club,
cold sober, and mailed it to New York asking her to write him at the office
in Paris. That seemed safe. And that night missing her so much it made
him feel hollow sick inside, he wandered up past Taxim's, picked a girl
up and took her out to supper. He had gone to a place to dance with her
afterward, she danced badly, and left her for a hot Armenian slut, that
swung her belly against him so it almost scalded. He took her away from
a British gunner subaltern after a row. The gunner asked him outside and
they fought in the street on the cobbles in the dark. He'd hit him twice,
hard, on the side of the jaw and when he didn't go down he knew he was
in for a fight. The gunner hit him in the body, then beside his eye. He
swung with his left again and landed and the gunner fell on him and
grabbed his coat and tore the sleeve off and he clubbed him twice behind
the ear and then smashed him with his right as he pushed him away. When
the gunner went down his head hit first and he ran with the girl because
they heard the M.P.'s coming. They got into a taxi and drove out to Rimmily
Hissa along the Bosphorus, and around, and back in the cool night and
went to bed and she felt as overripe as she looked but smooth, rose-petal,
syrupy, smooth-bellied, big-breasted and needed no pillow under her buttocks,
and he left her before she was awake looking blowsy enough in the first
daylight and turned up at the Pera Palace with a black eye, carrying his
coat because one sleeve was missing.*

*That same night he left for Anatolia and he remembered, later on that
trip, riding all day through fields of the poppies that they raised for opium
and how strange it made you feel, finally, and all the distances seemed wrong,
to where they had made the attack with the newly arrived Constantine officers,
that did not know a goddamned thing, and the artillery had fired into
the troops and the British observer had cried like a child.*

That was the day he'd first seen dead men wearing white ballet skirts and upturned shoes with pompons on them. The Turks had come steadily and lumpily and he had seen the skirted men running and the officers shooting into them and running then themselves and he and the British observer had run too until his lungs ached and his mouth was full of the taste of pennies and they stopped behind some rocks and there were the Turks coming as lumpily as ever. Later he had seen the things that he could never think of and later still he had seen much worse. So when he got back to Paris that time he could not talk about it or stand to have it mentioned. And there in the café as he passed was that American poet with a pile of saucers in front of him and a stupid look on his potato face talking about the Dada movement with a Roumanian who said his name was Tristan Tzara, who always wore a monocle and had a headache, and, back at the apartment with his wife that now he loved again, the quarrel all over, the madness all over, glad to be home, the office sent his mail up to the flat. So then the letter in answer to the one he'd written came in on a platter one morning and when he saw the handwriting he went cold all over and tried to slip the letter underneath another. But his wife said, "Who is that letter from, dear?" and that was the end of the beginning of that.

He remembered the good times with them all, and the quarrels. They always picked the finest places to have the quarrels. And why had they always quarreled when he was feeling best? He had never written any of that because, at first, he never wanted to hurt anyone and then it seemed as though there was enough to write without it. But he had always thought that he would write it finally. There was so much to write. He had seen the world change; not just the events; although he had seen many of them and had watched the people, but he had seen the subtler change and he could remember how the people were at different times. He had been in it and he had watched it and it was his duty to write of it; but now he never would.

"HOW DO YOU FEEL?" she said. She had come out from the tent now after her bath.

"All right."

"Could you eat now?" He saw Molo behind her with the folding table and the other boy with the dishes.

"I want to write," he said.

"You ought to take some broth to keep your strength up."

"I'm going to die tonight," he said. "I don't need my strength up."

"Don't be melodramatic, Harry, please," she said.

"Why don't you use your nose? I'm rotted halfway up my thigh now. What the hell should I fool with broth for? Molo bring whiskey-soda."

"Please take the broth," she said gently.

"All right."

The broth was too hot. He had to hold it in the cup until it cooled enough to take it and then he just got it down without gagging.

"You're a fine woman," he said. "Don't pay any attention to me."

She looked at him with her well-known, well-loved face from *Spur* and *Town and Country*, only a little the worse for drink, only a little the worse for bed, but *Town and Country* never showed those good breasts and those useful thighs and those lightly small-of-back-caressing hands, and as he looked and saw her well-known pleasant smile, he felt death come again. This time there was no rush. It was a puff, as of a wind that makes a candle flicker and the flame go tall.

"They can bring my net out later and hang it from the tree and build the fire up. I'm not going in the tent tonight. It's not worth moving. It's a clear night. There won't be any rain."

So this was how you died, in whispers that you did not hear. Well, there would be no more quarreling. He could promise that. The one experience that he had never had he was not going to spoil now. He probably would. You spoiled everything. But perhaps he wouldn't.

"You can't take dictation, can you?"

"I never learned," she told him.

"That's all right."

There wasn't time, of course, although it seemed as though it telescoped so that you might put it all into one paragraph if you could get it right.

There was a log house, chinked white with mortar, on a hill above the lake. There was a bell on a pole by the door to call the people in to meals. Behind the house were fields and behind the fields was the timber. A line of Lombardy poplars ran from the house to the dock. Other poplars ran along the point. A road went up to the hills along the edge of the timber and along that road he picked blackberries. Then that log house was burned down and all the guns that had been on deer-foot racks above the open fireplace were burned and afterwards their barrels, with the lead melted in the magazines, and the stocks burned away, lay out on the heap of ashes that were used to make lye for the big iron soap kettles, and you asked Grandfather if you could have them to play with, and he said, no. You see they were his guns still and he never bought any others. Nor did he hunt anymore. The house was rebuilt in the same place out of lumber now and painted white and from its porch you saw the poplars and the lake beyond; but there were never any more guns. The barrels of the guns that had hung on the deer feet on the wall of the log house lay out there on the heap of ashes and no one ever touched them.

In the Black Forest, after the war, we rented a trout stream and there were two ways to walk to it. One was down the valley from Triberg and around the valley road in the shade of the trees that bordered the white road, and then up a side road that went up through the hills past many small farms, with the big Schwarzwald houses, until that road crossed the stream. That was where our fishing began.

The other way was to climb steeply up to the edge of the woods and then go across the top of the hills through the pine woods, and then out to the edge of a meadow and down across this meadow to the bridge. There were birches along the stream and it was not big, but narrow, clear and fast, with pools where it had cut under the roots of the birches. At the Hotel in Triberg the proprietor had a fine season. It was very pleasant and we were all great friends. The next year came the inflation and the money he had made the year before was not enough to buy supplies to open the hotel and he hanged himself.

You could dictate that, but you could not dictate the Place Contrescarpe where the flower sellers dyed their flowers in the street and the dye ran over the paving where the autobus started and the old men and the women, always drunk on wine and bad marc; and the children with their noses running in the cold; the smell of dirty sweat and poverty and drunkenness at the Café des Amateurs and the whores at the Bal Musette they lived above. The concierge who entertained the trooper of the Garde Republicaine in her loge, his horsehair-plumed helmet on a chair. The locataire across the hall whose husband was a bicycle racer and her joy that morning at the Crémerie when she had opened L'Auto and seen where he placed third in Paris-Tours, his first big race. She had blushed and laughed and then gone upstairs crying with the yellow sporting paper in her hand. The husband of the woman who ran the Bal Musette drove a taxi and when he, Harry, had to take an early plane the husband knocked upon the door to wake him and they each drank a glass of white wine at the zinc of the bar before they started. He knew his neighbors in that quarter then because they all were poor.

Around that Place there were two kinds; the drunkards and the sportifs. The drunkards killed their poverty that way; the sportifs took it out in exercise. They were the descendants of the Communards and it was no struggle for them to know their politics. They knew who had shot their fathers, their relatives, their brothers, and their friends when the Versailles troops came in and took the town after the Commune and executed anyone they could catch with calloused hands, or who wore a cap, or carried any other sign he was a workingman. And in that poverty, and in that quarter across the street from a Boucherie Chevaline and a wine cooperative he had written the start of all he was to do. There never was another part of Paris that he loved like that, the sprawling trees, the old white plastered houses painted brown below, the long green of the autobus in that round square, the purple flower dye upon the paving, the sudden drop down the hill of the rue Cardinal-Lemoine to the river, and the other way the narrow crowded world of the rue Mouffetard. The street that ran up toward the Panthéon and the other that he always took with the bicycle, the only asphalted street in all that quarter, smooth under the tires, with the high narrow houses and the cheap tall hotel where Paul Verlaine had died. There were only two rooms in the apartments where they lived and he had a room on the top floor of that hotel that cost him sixty francs a month where he did his writing, and from it he could see the roofs and chimney pots and all the hills of Paris.

From the apartment you could only see the wood and coal man's place. He sold wine too, bad wine. The golden horse's head outside the Boucherie Chevaline where the carcasses hung yellow gold and red in the open window, and the green painted cooperative where they bought their wine; good wine and cheap. The rest was plaster walls and the windows of the neighbors.

The neighbors who, at night, when someone lay drunk in the street, moaning and groaning in that typical French ivresse that you were propaganded to believe did not exist, would open their windows and then the murmur of talk.

"Where is the policeman? When you don't want him the bugger is always there. He's sleeping with some concierge. Get the Agent." Till someone threw a bucket of water from a window and the moaning stopped. "What's that? Water. Ah, that's intelligent." And the windows shutting. Marie, his femme de ménage, protesting against the eight-hour day saying, "If a husband works until six he gets only a little drunk on the way home and does not waste too much. If he works only until five he is drunk every night and one has no money. It is the wife of the workingman who suffers from this shortening of hours."

"WOULDN'T YOU LIKE some more broth?" the woman asked him now.

"No, thank you very much. It is awfully good."

"Try just a little."

"I would like a whiskey-soda."

"It's not good for you."

"No. It's bad for me. Cole Porter wrote the words and the music. This knowledge that you're going mad for me."

"You know I like you to drink."

"Oh yes. Only it's bad for me."

When she goes, he thought. I'll have all I want. Not all I want but all there is. Ayee he was tired. Too tired. He was going to sleep a little while. He lay still and death was not there. It must have gone around another street. It went in pairs, on bicycles, and moved absolutely silently on the pavements.

No, he had never written about Paris. Not the Paris that he cared about. But what about the rest that he had never written?

What about the ranch and the silvered gray of the sagebrush, the quick, clear water in the irrigation ditches, and the heavy green of the alfalfa. The trail went up into the hills and the cattle in the summer were shy as deer. The bawling and the steady noise and slow moving mass raising a dust as you brought them down in the fall. And behind the mountains, the clear sharpness of the peak in the evening light and, riding down along the trail in the moonlight, bright across the valley. Now he remembered coming down through the timber in the dark holding the horse's tail when you could not see and all the stories that he meant to write.

About the half-wit chore boy who was left at the ranch that time and told not to let anyone get any hay, and that old bastard from the Forks who had beaten the boy when he had worked for him stopping to get some feed. The boy refusing and the old man saying he would beat him again. The boy got the rifle from the kitchen and shot him when he tried to come into the barn and when they came back to the ranch he'd been dead a week, frozen in the corral, and the dogs had eaten part of him. But what was left you packed on a sled wrapped in a blanket and roped on and you got the boy to help you haul it, and the two of you took it out over the road on skis, and sixty miles down to town to turn the boy over. He having no idea that he would be arrested. Thinking he had done his duty and that you were his friend and he would be rewarded. He'd helped to haul the old man in so everybody could know how bad the old man had been and how he'd tried to steal some feed that didn't belong to him, and when the sheriff put the handcuffs on the boy he couldn't believe it. Then he'd started to cry.

That was one story he had saved to write. He knew at least twenty good stories from out there and he had never written one. Why?

"YOU TELL THEM why," he said.

"Why what, dear?"

"Why nothing."

She didn't drink so much, now, since she had him. But if he lived he would never write about her, he knew that now. Nor about any of them. The rich were dull and they drank too much, or they played too much backgammon. They were dull and they were repetitious. He remembered poor Julian and his romantic awe of them and how he had started a story once that began, "The very rich are different from you and me." And how someone had said to Julian, Yes, they have more money. But that was not humorous to Julian. He thought they were a special glamorous race and when he found they weren't it wrecked him just as much as any other thing that wrecked him.

He had been contemptuous of those who wrecked. You did not have to like it because you understood it. He could beat anything, he thought, because no thing could hurt him if he did not care.

All right. Now he would not care for death. One thing he had always dreaded was the pain. He could stand pain as well as any man, until it went on too long, and wore him out, but here he had something that had hurt frightfully and just when he had felt it breaking him, the pain had stopped.

He remembered long ago when Williamson, the bombing officer, had been hit by a stick bomb someone in a German patrol had thrown as he was coming in through the wire that night and, screaming, had begged everyone to kill him. He was a fat man, very brave, and a good officer, although addicted to fantastic shows. But that night he was caught in the wire, with a flare lighting him up and his bowels spilled out into the wire, so when they brought him in, alive, they had to cut him loose. Shoot me, Harry. For Christ sake shoot me. They had had an argument one time about our Lord never sending you anything you could not bear and someone's theory had been that meant that at a certain time the pain passed you out automatically. But he had always remembered Williamson, that night. Nothing passed out Williamson until he gave him all his morphine tablets that he had always saved to use himself and then they did not work right away.

STILL THIS NOW, that he had, was very easy; and if it was no worse as it went on there was nothing to worry about. Except that he would rather be in better company.

He thought a little about the company that he would like to have.

No, he thought, when everything you do, you do too long, and do too late, you can't expect to find the people still there. The people all are gone. The party's over and you are with your hostess now.

I'm getting as bored with dying as with everything else, he thought.

"It's a bore," he said out loud.

"What is, my dear?"

"Anything you do too bloody long."

He looked at her face between him and the fire. She was leaning back in the chair and the firelight shone on her pleasantly lined face and he could see that she was sleepy. He heard the hyena make a noise just outside the range of the fire.

"I've been writing," he said. "But I got tired."

"Do you think you will be able to sleep?"

"Pretty sure. Why don't you turn in?"

"I like to sit here with you."

"Do you feel anything strange?" he asked her.

"No. Just a little sleepy."

"I do," he said.

He had just felt death come by again.

"You know the only thing I've never lost is curiosity," he said to her.

"You've never lost anything. You're the most complete man I've ever known."

"Christ," he said. "How little a woman knows. What is that? Your intuition?"

Because, just then, death had come and rested its head on the foot of the cot and he could smell its breath.

"Never believe any of that about a scythe and a skull," he told her. "It can be two bicycle policemen as easily, or be a bird. Or it can have a wide snout like a hyena."

It had moved up on him now, but it had no shape anymore. It simply occupied space.

"Tell it to go away."

It did not go away but moved a little closer.

"You've got a hell of a breath," he told it. "You stinking bastard."

It moved up closer to him still and now he could not speak to it, and when it saw he could not speak it came a little closer, and now he tried to send it away without speaking, but it moved in on him so its weight was all upon his chest, and while it crouched there and he could not move, or speak, he heard the woman say, "Bwana is asleep now. Take the cot up very gently and carry it into the tent."

He could not speak to tell her to make it go away and it crouched now, heavier, so he could not breathe. And then, while they lifted the cot, suddenly it was all right and the weight went from his chest.

IT WAS MORNING AND HAD BEEN MORNING for some time and he heard the plane. It showed very tiny and then made a wide circle and the boys ran out and lit the fires, using kerosene, and piled on grass so there were two big smudges at each end of the level place and the morning breeze blew them toward the camp and the plane circled twice more, low this time, and then glided down and leveled off and landed smoothly and, coming walking toward him, was old Compton in slacks, a tweed jacket and a brown felt hat.

"What's the matter, old cock?" Compton said.

"Bad leg," he told him. "Will you have some breakfast?"

"Thanks. I'll just have some tea. It's the Puss Moth you know. I won't be able to take the Memsahib. There's only room for one. Your lorry is on the way."

Helen had taken Compton aside and was speaking to him. Compton came back more cheery than ever.

"We'll get you right in," he said. "I'll be back for the Mem. Now I'm afraid I'll have to stop at Arusha to refuel. We'd better get going."

"What about the tea?"

"I don't really care about it you know."

The boys had picked up the cot and carried it around the green tents and down along the rock and out onto the plain and along past the smudges that were burning brightly now, the grass all consumed, and the wind fanning the fire, to the little plane. It was difficult getting him in, but once in he lay back in the leather seat, and the leg was stuck straight out. to one side of the seat where Compton sat. Compton started the motor and got in. He waved to Helen and to the boys and, as the clatter moved into the old familiar roar, they swung around with Compie watching for warthog holes and roared, bumping, along the stretch between the fires and with the last bump rose and he saw them all standing below, waving, and the camp beside the hill, flattening now, and the plain spreading, clumps of trees, and the bush flattening, while the game trails ran now smoothly to the dry water holes, and there was a new water that he had never known of. The zebra, small rounded backs now, and the wildebeests, big-headed dots seeming to climb as they moved in long fingers across the plain, now scattering as the shadow came toward them, they were tiny now, and the movement had no gallop, and the plain as far as you could see, gray-yellow now and ahead old Compie's tweed back and the brown felt hat. Then they were over the first hills and the wildebeests were trailing up them, and then they were over mountains with sudden depths of green-rising forest and the solid bamboo slopes, and then the heavy forest again, sculptured into peaks and hollows until they crossed, and hills sloped down and then another plain, hot now, and purple brown, bumpy with heat and Compie looking back to see how he was riding. Then there were other mountains dark ahead.

And then instead of going on to Arusha they turned left, he evidently figured that they had the gas, and looking down he saw a pink sifting cloud, moving over the ground, and in the air, like the first snow in a blizzard, that comes from nowhere, and he knew the locusts were coming up from the south. Then they began to climb and they were going to the east it seemed, and then it darkened and they were in a storm, the rain so thick it seemed like flying through a waterfall, and then they were out and Compie turned his head and grinned and pointed and there, ahead, all he could see, as wide as all the world, great, high, and unbelievably white in the sun, was the square top of Kilimanjaro. And then he knew that there was where he was going.

JUST THEN the hyena stopped whimpering in the night and started to make a strange, human, almost crying sound. The woman heard it and stirred uneasily. She did not wake. In her dream she was at the house on Long Island and it was the night before her daughter's début. Somehow her father was there and he had been very rude. Then the noise the hyena made was so loud she woke and for a moment she did not know where she was and she was very afraid. Then she took the flashlight and shone it on the other cot that they had carried in after Harry had gone to sleep. She could see his bulk under the mosquito bar but somehow he had gotten his leg out and it hung down alongside the cot. The dressings had all come down and she could not look at it.

"Molo," she called, "Molo! Molo!"

Then she said, "Harry, Harry!" Then her voice rising, "Harry! Please! Oh Harry!"

There was no answer and she could not hear him breathing.

Outside the tent the hyena made the same strange noise that had awakened her. But she did not hear him for the beating of her heart.

A LETTER TO GOD

GREGORIO LÓPEZ Y FUENTES / MEXICO

Gregorio

Translated by Donald A. Yates

THE HOUSE—the only one in the entire valley—sat on the crest of a low hill. From this height one could see the river and, next to the corral, the field of ripe corn dotted with the kidney-bean flowers that always promised a good harvest.

The only thing the earth needed was a rainfall, or at least a shower. Throughout the morning Lencho—who knew his fields intimately— had done nothing else but scan the sky toward the northeast.

"Now we're really going to get some water, woman."

The woman, who was preparing supper, replied:

"Yes, God willing."

The oldest boys were working in the field, while the smaller ones were playing near the house, until the woman called to them all:

"Come for dinner. . . ."

It was during the meal that, just as Lencho had predicted, big drops of rain began to fall. In the northeast huge mountains of clouds could be seen approaching. The air was fresh and sweet.

The man went out to look for something in the corral for no other reason than to allow himself the pleasure of feeling the rain on his body, and when he returned he exclaimed:

"Those aren't raindrops falling from the sky, they're new coins.

The big drops are ten-centavo pieces and the little ones are fives. . . ."

With a satisfied expression he regarded the field of ripe corn with its kidney-bean flowers, draped in a curtain of rain. But suddenly a strong wind began to blow and together with the rain very large hailstones began to fall. These truly did resemble new silver coins. The boys, exposing themselves to the rain, ran out to collect the frozen pearls.

"It's really getting bad now," exclaimed the man, mortified. "I hope It passes quickly."

It did not pass quickly. For an hour the hail rained on the house, the garden, the hillside, the cornfield, on the whole valley. The field was white, as if covered with salt. Not a leaf remained on the trees. The corn was totally destroyed. The flowers were gone from the kidney-bean plants. Lencho's soul was filled with sadness. When the storm had passed, he stood in the middle of the field and said to his sons:

"A plague of locusts would have left more than this. . . . The hail has left nothing: this year we will have no corn or beans. . . ."

That night was a sorrowful one:

"All our work, for nothing!"

"There's no one who can help us!"

"We'll all go hungry this year. . . ."

But in the hearts of all who lived in that solitary house in the middle of the valley, there was a single hope: help from God.

"Don't be so upset, even though this seems like a total loss. Remember, no one dies of hunger!"

"That's what they say: no one dies of hunger. . . ."

All through the night, Lencho thought only of his one hope: the help of God, whose eyes, as he had been instructed, see everything, even what is deep in one's conscience.

Lencho was an ox of a man, working like an animal in the fields, but still he knew how to write. The following Sunday, at daybreak, after having convinced himself that there is a protecting spirit, he began to write a letter which he himself would carry to town and place in the mail.

It was nothing less than a letter to God.

"God," he wrote, "if you don't help me, my family and I will go hungry this year. I need a hundred pesos in order to resow the field and to live until the crop comes, because the hailstorm . . ."

He wrote "To God" on the envelope, put the letter inside and, still troubled, went to town. At the post office he placed a stamp on the letter and dropped it into the mailbox.

One of the employees, who was a postman and also helped at the post office, went to his boss laughing heartily and showed him the letter to God. Never in his career as a postman had he known that address. The postmaster—a fat, amiable fellow—also broke out laughing, but almost immediately he turned serious and, tapping the letter on his desk, commented:

"What faith! I wish I had the faith of the man who wrote this letter. To believe the way he believes. To hope with the confidence that he knows how to hope with. Starting up a correspondence with God!"

So, in order not to disillusion that prodigy of faith, revealed by a letter that could not be delivered, the postmaster came up with an idea: answer the letter. But when he opened it, it was evident that to answer it he needed something more than goodwill, ink and paper. But he stuck to his resolution: he asked for money from his employee, he himself gave part of his salary, and several friends of his were obliged to give something "for an act of charity."

It was impossible for him to gather together the hundred pesos, so he was able to send the farmer only a little more than half. He put the bills in an envelope addressed to Lencho and with them a letter containing only a single word as a signature: GOD.

The following Sunday Lencho came a bit earlier than usual to ask if there was a letter for him. It was the postman himself who handed the letter to him, while the postmaster, experiencing the contentment of a man who has performed a good deed, looked on from the doorway of his office.

Lencho showed not the slightest surprise on seeing the bills—such was his confidence—but he became angry when he counted the money. . . . God could not have made a mistake, nor could he have denied Lencho what he had requested!

Immediately, Lencho went up to the window to ask for paper and ink. On the public writing table, he started in to write, with much wrinkling of his brow, caused by the effort he had to make to express his ideas. When he finished, he went to the window to buy a stamp which he licked and then affixed to the envelope with a blow of his fist.

The moment that the letter fell into the mailbox the postmaster went to open it. It said:

"God, of the money that I asked for, only seventy pesos reached me. Send me the rest, since I need it very much. But don't send it to me through the mail, because the post-office employees are a bunch of crooks. Lencho."

THE LITTLE BOUILLOUX GIRL
COLETTE / FRANCE

Colette

THE LITTLE BOUILLOUX GIRL was so lovely that even we children noticed it. It is unusual for small girls to recognize beauty in one of themselves and pay homage to it. But there could be no disputing such undeniable loveliness as hers. Whenever my mother met the little Bouilloux girl in the street, she would stop her and bend over her as she was wont to bend over her yellow tea rose, her red flowering cactus or her Azure Blue butterfly trustfully asleep on the scaly bark of the pine tree. She would stroke her curly hair, golden and a half-ripe chestnut, and her delicately tinted cheeks, and watch the incredible lashes flutter over her great dark eyes. She would observe the glimmer of the perfect teeth in her peerless mouth, and when, at last, she let the child go on her way, she would look after her, murmuring, "It's prodigious!"

Several years passed, bringing yet further graces to the little Bouil-loux girl. There were certain occasions recorded by our admiration: a prizegiving at which, shyly murmuring an unintelligible recitation, she glowed through her tears like a peach under a summer shower. The little Bouilloux girl's first communion caused a scandal: the same evening, after vespers, she was seen drinking a half pint at the Café du Commerce, with her father, the sawyer, and that night she danced, already feminine and flirtatious, a little unsteady in her white slippers, at the public ball.

With an arrogance to which she had accustomed us, she informed us later, at school, that she was to be apprenticed.

"Oh! Who to?"

"To Madame Adolphe."

"Oh! And are you to get wages at once?"

"No. I'm only thirteen, I shall start earning next year."

She left us without emotion, and coldly we let her go. Already her beauty isolated her and she had no friends at school, where she learned very little. Her Sundays and her Thursdays brought no inti-macy with us; they were spent with a family that was considered "unsuitable," with girl cousins of eighteen well known for their brazen behavior, and with brothers, cartwright apprentices, who sported ties at fourteen and smoked when they escorted their sister to the Parisian shooting gallery at the fair or to the cheerful bar that the widow Pimolle had made so popular.

The very next morning on my way to school I met the little Bouilloux girl setting out for the dressmaker's workrooms, and I remained motionless, thunderstruck with jealous admiration, at the corner of the Rue des Soeurs, watching Nana Bouilloux's retreating form. She had exchanged her black pinafore and short childish frock for a long skirt and a pleated blouse of pink sateen. She wore a black alpaca apron and her exuberant locks, disciplined and twisted into a "figure of eight," lay close as a helmet about the charming new shape of a round imperious head that retained nothing childish except its freshness and the not yet calculated impudence of a little village adventuress.

That morning the upper forms hummed like a hive.

"I've seen Nana Bouilloux! In a long dress, my dear, would you believe it? And her hair in a chignon! She had a pair of scissors hanging from her belt too!"

At noon I flew home to announce breathlessly: "Mother! I met Nana Bouilloux in the street! She was passing our door. And she had on a long dress! Mother, just imagine, a long dress! And her hair in a chignon! And she had high heels and a pair of . . ."

"Eat, Minet-Chéri, eat, your cutlet will be cold."

"And an apron, mother, such a lovely alpaca apron that looked like silk! Couldn't I possibly . . ."

"No, Minet-Chéri, you certainly couldn't."

"But if Nana Bouilloux can . . ."

"Yes, Nana Bouilloux, at thirteen, can, in fact she should, wear a chignon, a short apron and a long skirt—it's the uniform of all little Bouilloux girls throughout the world, at thirteen—more's the pity."

"But . . ."

"Yes, I know you would like to wear the complete uniform of a little Bouilloux girl. It includes all that you've seen, and a bit more besides: a letter safely hidden in the apron pocket, an admirer who smells of wine and of cheap cigars; two admirers, three admirers and a little later on plenty of tears . . . and a sickly child hidden away, a child that has lain for months crushed by constricting stays. There it is, Minet-Chéri, the entire uniform of the little Bouilloux girls. Do you still want it?"

"Of course not, mother. I only wanted to see if a chignon . . ."

But my mother shook her head, mocking but serious.

"No, no! You can't have the chignon without the apron, the apron without the letter, the letter without the high-heeled slippers, or the slippers without . . . all the rest of it! It's just a matter of choice!"

My envy was soon exhausted. The resplendent little Bouilloux girl became no more than a daily passerby whom I scarcely noticed. Bareheaded in winter and summer, her gaily colored blouses varied from week to week, and in very cold weather she swathed her elegant shoulders in a useless little scarf. Erect, radiant as a thorny rose, her eyelashes sweeping her cheeks or half revealing her dark and dewy eyes, she grew daily more worthy of queening it over crowds, of being gazed at, adorned and bedecked with jewels. The severely smoothed crinkliness of her chestnut hair could still be discerned in little waves that caught the light in the golden mist at the nape of her neck and round her ears. She always looked vaguely offended with her small, velvety nostrils reminding one of a doe.

She was fifteen or sixteen now—and so was I. Except that she laughed too freely on Sundays, in order to show her white teeth, as she hung on the arms of her brothers or her girl cousins, Nana Bouilloux was behaving fairly well. "For a little Bouilloux girl, very well indeed!" was the public verdict.

She was seventeen, then eighteen; her complexion was like a peach on a south wall, no eyes could meet the challenge of hers and she had the bearing of a goddess. She began to take the floor at fetes and fairs, to dance with abandon, to stay out very late at night, wandering in the lanes with a man's arm round her waist. Always unkind, but full of laughter, provoking boldness in those who would have been content merely to love her.

Then came a St. John's Eve when she appeared on the dance floor that was laid down on the Place du Grand-Jeu under the melancholy light of malodorous oil lamps. Hobnailed boots kicked up the dust between the planks of the "floor." All the young men, as was customary, kept their hats on while dancing. Blonde girls became claret-colored in their tight bodices, while the dark ones, sunburned from their work in the fields, looked black. But there, among a band of haughty workgirls, Nana Bouilloux, in a summer dress sprigged with little flowers, was drinking lemonade laced with red wine when the Parisians arrived on the scene.

They were two Parisians such as one sees in the country in summer, friends of a neighboring landowner, and supremely bored; Parisians in tussah and white serge, come for a moment to mock at a village midsummer fete. They stopped laughing when they saw Nana Bouilloux and sat down near the bar in order to see her better. In low voices they exchanged comments which she pretended not to hear, since her pride as a beautiful creature would not let her turn her eyes in their direction and giggle like her companions. She heard the words: "A swan among geese! A Greuze! A crime to let such a wonder bury herself here. . . ." When the young man in the white suit asked the little Bouilloux girl for a waltz she got up without surprise and danced with him gravely, in silence. From time to time her eyelashes, more beautiful than a glance, brushed against her partner's fair mustache.

After the waltz the two Parisians went away, and Nana Bouilloux sat down by the bar, fanning herself. There she was soon approached by young Leriche, by Houette, even by Honce the chemist, and even by Possy the cabinetmaker, who was aging, but nonetheless a good dancer. To all of them she replied, "Thank you, but I'm tired," and she left the ball at half past ten o'clock.

And after that, nothing more ever happened to the little Bouilloux girl. The Parisians did not return, neither they, nor others like them. Houette, Honce, young Leriche, the commercial travelers with their gold watch chains, soldiers on leave and sheriff's clerks vainly climbed our steep street at the hours when the beautifully coiffed seamstress, on her way down it, passed them by stiffly with a distant nod. They looked out for her at dances, where she sat drinking lemonade with an air of distinction and answered their importunities with "Thank you very much, but I'm not dancing, I'm tired." Taking offense, they soon began to snigger: "Tired! Her kind of tiredness lasts for thirty-six weeks!" and they kept a sharp watch on her figure.

But nothing happened to the little Bouilloux girl, neither that nor anything else. She was simply waiting, possessed by an arrogant faith, conscious of the debt owed by the hazard that had armed her too well. She was awaiting . . . not the return of the Parisian in white serge, but a stranger, a ravisher. Her proud anticipation kept her silent and pure; with a little smile of surprise, she rejected Honce, who would have raised her to the rank of chemist's lawful wife, and she would have nothing to say to the sheriff's chief clerk.

With never another lapse, taking back, once and for all, the smiles, the glances, the glowing bloom of her cheeks, the red young lips, the shadowy blue cleft of her breasts which she had so prodigally lavished on mere rustics, she awaited her kingdom and the prince without a name.

Years later, when I passed through my native village, I could not find the shade of her who had so lovingly refused me what she called "the uniform of little Bouilloux girls." But as the car bore me slowly, though not slowly enough—never slowly enough—up a street where I have now no reason to stop, a woman drew back to avoid the wheel. A slender woman, her hair well dressed in a bygone fashion, dressmaker's scissors hanging from a steel chatelaine on her black apron. Large, vindictive eyes, a tight mouth sealed by long silence, the sallow cheeks and temples of those who work by lamplight; a woman of forty-five or . . . Not at all; a woman of thirty-eight, a woman of my own age, of exactly my age, there was no room for doubt. As soon as the car allowed her room to pass, "the little Bouilloux girl" went on her way down the street, erect and indifferent, after one anxious, bitter glance had told her that the car did not contain the long-awaited ravisher.

THE RUBY
CORRADO ALVARO / ITALY

Corrado Alvaro

THE DAILY PAPERS had recorded one of those news items that keep a town in a buzz of excitement for a whole day and finally make a circuit of the world. A ruby as big as a hazelnut, a famous stone, bearing a famous name, and said to be of enormous value, had disappeared. An Indian prince, on a visit to a North American city, had been wearing this jewel as an ornament. He had suddenly become aware of his loss after a journey he had made in a taxi that had set him down—incognito—at a hotel in the suburbs, for he had managed to evade the attention of both his private bodyguard and the police. The flying squad was mobilized, the entire city awoke the following morning to a knowledge of the loss, and right up to midday hundreds of people cherished the hope of finding the celebrated stone in their own street. One of those waves of optimism and excitement had fallen on the town; the kind of feeling you get when the opulence of one individual enriches everybody else's hopes. The prince had not been very forthcoming in his statement to the police, but it ruled out any possibility that the lady accompanying him could have been responsible for the loss. They were not, therefore, to try and locate her. The taxi driver came forward to testify that he had driven the Indian wearing his precious turban, and stated that he had deposited him and the lady in front of a hotel in the suburbs. The lady was a European, and the only thing that distinguished her was a magnificent diamond, the size of a pea, which she wore in her left nostril after the manner of certain wealthy Indians. This detail distracted the attention of the public for a while from the missing ruby and whetted their curiosity still more. The driver, after making a thorough search of the interior of the vehicle, checked up on the fares he had driven during the early hours of the morning in question; they had been a businessman, a foreigner whom he had taken down to the port and who was evidently sailing for Europe, and a woman. The foreigner, recognizable as an Italian, had emerged from one of the houses where emigrants lived in a colony; he had been wearing a pair of trousers of generous width such as are popular with emigrants, rough, thick-soled shoes of a type nowadays seen only among people of that social class, and a hard hat set above a thin, clean-shaven face seamed with wrinkles. His luggage consisted of a heavy suitcase secured with stout cord and one other weighty box which appeared to be made of steel. He had embarked that same day, but any suspicion that might have alighted on him was immediately dispelled when it was realized that he had behaved as though he was riding in a taxi for the first time in his life. He had not managed to close the door properly and had hugged the front window all the time, possibly so as to avoid being suddenly jerked backward into the road, and he had gazed at the streets with the air of one who is leaving a town perhaps forever. The driver reserved his attention rather for the man who, on leaving the suburban hotel, had taken the taxi immediately after the prince and had given orders to be driven to the Italian workmen's quarter, at which point his place had been taken by the foreigner. The fare in question, of whom he had given a description and who must have been a local resident, was searched for in vain. Furthermore the fact that he had failed to answer the appeal published in the newspapers, offering a large reward, was a logical proof that it was not he who had got hold of the famous gem. However, since the missing stone was world-famed and easily recognizable, it was hoped that one day or other it would come to light.

The emigrant, meantime, was on his way home to a country town in southern Italy after five years' absence and was ignorant of all this stir. He had with him the most unusual collections of odds and ends—even for an emigrant. A suitcase, made of artificial leather which he thought was real, contained his blue overalls, pressed and cleaned, twelve fountain pens which he intended to sell to the people of the district, forgetting that most of them were herdsmen and not more than half a dozen of the inhabitants could put pen to paper. In addition, he had some crested table services, a pair of hair clippers which he had used on his fellow workers, a metal object whose function completely mystified him—it had the form of a pistol, but did not fire—twelve squares of American cloth and some novelties to impress and amuse his wife, son and friends. The heavy part of his luggage was the somewhat battered steel strongbox; the lock was operated by a combination, the six-letter name *Annina*. By way of ready cash he took a thousand dollars, which included three hundred to be paid back later to those from whom he had borrowed it for the voyage. In his waistcoat pocket he carried a lump of red crystal; it was many-faceted and as large as a walnut. He had come across it by chance in the taxi that had taken him down to the harbor, but he had no idea what it was for. His fingers had felt it behind the seat cushions. He kept it as a lucky charm for the future; perhaps he would have it attached to his watch chain as a pendant. It seemed odd that it had no hole bored through it. It could not, therefore, be one of those large stones which city ladies have on their necklaces.

The various objects one picks up just before leaving a foreign country are apt to acquire an extraordinary souvenir value, giving one, as it were, a foretaste of distance and nostalgia. It was just such an affection that our emigrant felt for this lump of crystal, so cool to the touch, as translucent and clear as sugar candy.

He had established a small trade with all these different acquisitions. The strongbox, now fixed against the wall, the counter for his transactions, fountain pens in a box, crested table services, squares of American cloth on which were depicted the Statue of Liberty and angels in the corners bearing the portraits of the founders of American independence, each square embroidered with white and blue stars — five long years he had patiently built up his collection against his eventual return; selecting whatever would seem most of a novelty to the folk in a region like his own, though he might have taken his choice from the shabby secondhand goods that come from heaven-knows-where and go the rounds among the emigrant population.

So he who had started life as a day laborer had now become a dealer in various wares. It had been the strongbox that had set him on that train of thought; he had taken to shopkeeping for no other reason. He had felt almost rich because all the money he had in his pockets was in foreign currency and would turn into a larger number of coins when he exchanged them. Mental calculations connected with this engrossed him at all sorts of odd moments. He felt a childish delight every time he fingered the red crystal in his pocket. He began to regard it as a kind of talisman. It became one of those useless objects we cherish all our lives and never have the strength of mind to get rid of, so that in the end they become part of ourselves and even family heirlooms. Whereas important things that we watch over or hide away disappear, objects of the kind referred to never get lost, and our minds hark back to them at intervals. A few days later, for example, the crystal reminded our emigrant of the day when he had embarked for home, the interior of the taxi, and the streets which seemed to roll slowly up like a piece of scenery at the end of a play.

He set up his shop in the upper part of the country town inhabited by peasants and herdsmen. A fortnight after his arrival he had furnished the ground floor of a peasant's cottage with a long counter and shelves, where the blue packets of flour paste and the blue muslin for housewives found a place, and on one side of the shop stood a cask of wine on a couple of trestles, and an earthenware jar of oil. The strongbox had been fixed against the wall, and he felt a great sense of pride when he opened it in the presence of his customers. In it reposed his account ledger and the notebook containing a list of all the goods sold on tick that were to be paid for at harvesttime or after the animal fairs. Gradually his business got to look like any other business; it acquired its own peculiar smell, there were chalk marks made on the wall by his wife—who could not write—recording goods supplied on credit. His young son, however, who attended school, and was now beginning to be able to write customers' names in the register, sometimes took a turn in the shop and managed it quite expertly on hot afternoons when all trade had ceased except that in iced drinks for men recovering from their afternoon siesta.

Slowly, his wife's narrow, American-style slippers acquired more and more creases and she herself the complacent, meticulous air of a shopkeeper's wife. The supply of new material which her husband had brought home had finally ended up among the shop-soiled goods, and only the hard hat, looking almost new, was still left in the wardrobe. The squares of American cloth had been distributed as presents among the important customers; as for the fountain pens, no one had wanted them. Someone had handled them roughly and the fragments still lay in the box. The shopkeeper, who was a boy at heart, often imagined that the pen nibs were of pure gold and he cherished them as a small boy cherishes tinfoil wrapping off chocolates. He also hung on to an old newspaper printed in English. He had refused to part with it even when he was short of wrapping paper. Sometimes he would scrutinize it carefully and the advertisement illustrations would recall to him the people who smoked gold-tipped cigarettes, the street boys, the gramophones, in fact all the life he had seen in the central parts of the city on the rare occasions of his visits there. As for the lump of crystal, he remembered it one day and gave it to his son who was celebrating his birthday with his friends. At that time, boys played a game which consisted of knocking down and conquering castles made of hazelnuts by throwing a heavier one at it; the usual procedure was to select a larger nut, make a small hole in it, patiently scrape out the kernel, then fill it with small lead pellets. The crystal missile was just the thing, it was heavy enough to carry to the mark. Another of the boys used a glass marble of the kind extracted from lemonade bottles, which had the advantage of being round. The shopkeeper's son claimed that his was more beautiful because it came from America and because it was red. He cherished it in the way that boys do who never lose objects of that kind. As his father contemplated this curiosity which had become his child's plaything, his mind would often dwell on the illusions he had once entertained in the days when he traveled about the world, and the world seemed to be filled with valuable things that had been lost which the lucky ones found. That was why he had always felt with his fingers under mattresses of berths on steamers, behind leather cushions on buses and coaches, according to where he happened to be. But he had never found anything. Yes; there had been one occasion. He had found five dollars in the street. It had been raining that day, he remembered.

SIX FEET OF THE COUNTRY
NADINE GORDIMER / SOUTH AFRICA

Nadine Gordimer

My wife and I are not real farmers—not even Lerice, really. We bought our place, ten miles out of Johannesburg on one of the main roads, to change something in ourselves, I suppose; you seem to rattle about so much within a marriage like ours. You long to hear nothing but a deep satisfying silence when you sound a marriage. The farm hasn't managed that for us, of course, but it has done other things, unexpected, illogical. Lerice, who I thought would retire there in Chekhovian sadness for a month or two, and then leave the place to the servants while she tried yet again to get a part she wanted and become the actress she would like to be, has sunk into the business of running the farm with all the serious intensity with which she once imbued the shadows in a playwright's mind. I should have given it up long ago if it had not been for her. Her hands, once small and plain and well kept—she was not the sort of actress who wears red paint and diamond rings—are hard as a dog's pads.

I, of course, am there only in the evenings and on weekends. I am a partner in a luxury-travel agency, which is flourishing—needs to be, as I tell Lerice, in order to carry the farm. Still, though I know we can't afford it, and though the sweetish smell of the fowls Lerice breeds sickens me, so that I avoid going past their runs, the farm is beautiful in a way I had almost forgotten—especially on a Sunday morning when I get up and go out into the paddock and see not the palm trees and fishpond and imitation-stone birdbath of the suburbs but white ducks on the dam, the alfalfa field brilliant as window dresser's grass, and the little, stocky, mean-eyed bull, lustful but bored, having his face tenderly licked by one of his ladies. Lerice comes out with her hair uncombed, in her hand a stick dripping with cattle dip. She will stand and look dreamily for a moment, the way she would pretend to look sometimes in those plays. "They'll mate tomorrow," she will say. "This is their second day. Look how she loves him, my little Napoleon." So that when people come out to see us on Sunday afternoon, I am likely to hear myself saying as I pour out the drinks, "When I drive back home from the city every day, past those rows of suburban houses, I wonder how the devil we ever did stand it. . . . Would you care to look around?" And there I am, taking some pretty girl and her young husband stumbling down to our riverbank, the girl catching her stockings on the mealie-stooks and stepping over cow turds humming with jewel-green flies while she says, ". . . the *tensions* of the damned city. And you're near enough to get into town to a show, too! I think it's wonderful. Why, you've got it both ways!" And for a moment I accept the triumph as if I *had* managed it—the impossibility that I've been trying for all my life—just as if the truth was that you could get it "both ways," instead of finding yourself with not even one way or the other but a third, one you had not provided for at all.

But even in our saner moments, when I find Lerice's earthy enthusiasms just as irritating as I once found her histrionical ones, and she finds what she calls my "jealousy" of her capacity for enthusiasm as big a proof of my inadequacy for her as a mate as ever it was, we do believe that we have at least honestly escaped those tensions peculiar to the city about which our visitors speak. When Johannesburg people speak of "tension," they don't mean hurrying people in crowded streets, the struggle for money, or the general competitive character of city life. They mean the guns under the white men's pillows and the burglar bars on the white men's windows. They mean those strange moments on city pavements when a black man won't stand aside for a white man.

Out in the country, even ten miles out, life is better than that. In the country, there is a lingering remnant of the pretransitional stage; our relationship with the blacks is almost feudal. Wrong, I suppose, obsolete, but more comfortable all around. We have no burglar bars, no gun. Lerice's farm boys have their wives and their piccanins living with them on the land. They brew their sour beer without the fear of police raids. In fact, we've always rather prided ourselves that the poor devils have nothing much to fear, being with us; Lerice even keeps an eye on their children, with all the competence of a woman who has never had a child of her own, and she certainly doctors them all—children and adults—like babies whenever they happen to be sick.

It was because of this that we were not particularly startled one night last winter when the boy Albert came knocking at our window long after we had gone to bed. I wasn't in our bed but sleeping in the little dressing-room-*cum*-linen-room next door, because Lerice had annoyed me and I didn't want to find myself softening toward her simply because of the sweet smell of the talcum powder on her flesh after her bath.

She came and woke me up. "Albert says one of the boys is very sick," she said. "I think you'd better go down and see. He wouldn't get us up at this hour for nothing."

"What time is it?"

"What does it matter?" Lerice is maddeningly logical.

I got up awkwardly as she watched me—how is it I always feel a fool when I have deserted her bed? After all, I know from the way she never looks at me when she talks to me at breakfast the next day that she is hurt and humiliated at my not wanting her—and I went out, clumsy with sleep.

"Which of the boys is it?" I asked Albert as we followed the dance of my torch.

"He's too sick. Very sick, *Baas*," he said.

"But who? Franz?" I remembered Franz had had a bad cough for the past week.

Albert did not answer; he had given me the path, and was walking along beside me in the tall dead grass. When the light of the torch caught his face, I saw that he looked acutely embarrassed. "What's this all about?" I said.

He lowered his head under the glance of the light. "It's not me, *Baas*. I don't know. Petrus he send me."

Irritated, I hurried him along to the huts. And there, on Petrus's iron bedstead, with its brick stilts, was a young man, dead. On his forehead there was still a light, cold sweat; his body was warm. The boys stood around as they do in the kitchen when it is discovered that someone has broken a dish—uncooperative, silent. Somebody's wife hung about in the shadows, her hands wrung together under her apron.

I had not seen a dead man since the war. This was very different. I felt like the others—extraneous, useless. "What was the matter?" I asked.

The woman patted at her chest and shook her head to indicate the painful impossibility of breathing.

He must have died of pneumonia.

I turned to Petrus. "Who was this boy? What was he doing here?" The light of a candle on the floor showed that Petrus was weeping. He followed me out the door.

When we were outside, in the dark, I waited for him to speak. But he didn't. "Now, come on, Petrus, you must tell me who this boy was. Was he a friend of yours?"

"He's my brother, *Baas*. He came from Rhodesia to look for work."

THE STORY STARTLED LERICE AND ME a little. The young boy had walked down from Rhodesia to look for work in Johannesburg, had caught a chill from sleeping out along the way, and had lain ill in his brother Petrus's hut since his arrival three days before. Our boys had been frightened to ask us for help for him because we had never been intended ever to know of his presence. Rhodesian natives are barred from entering the Union unless they have a permit; the young man was an illegal immigrant. No doubt our boys had managed the whole thing successfully several times before; a number of relatives must have walked the seven or eight hundred miles from poverty to the paradise of zoot suits, police raids, and black slum townships that is their *Egoli*, City of Gold—the Bantu name for Johannesburg. It was merely a matter of getting such a man to lie low on our farm until a job could be found with someone who would be glad to take the risk of prosecution for employing an illegal immigrant in exchange for the services of someone as yet untainted by the city.

Well, this was one who would never get up again.

"You would think they would have felt they could tell *us*," said Lerice next morning. "Once the man was ill. You would have thought at least—" When she is getting intense over something, she has a way of standing in the middle of a room as people do when they are shortly to leave on a journey, looking searchingly about her at the most familiar objects as if she had never seen them before. I had noticed that in Petrus's presence in the kitchen, earlier, she had had the air of being almost offended with him, almost hurt.

In any case, I really haven't the time or inclination anymore to go into everything in our life that I know Lerice, from those alarmed and pressing eyes of hers, would like us to go into. She is the kind of woman who doesn't mind if she looks plain, or odd; I don't suppose she would even care if she knew how strange she looks when her whole face is out of proportion with urgent uncertainty. I said, "Now I'm the one who'll have to do all the dirty work, I suppose."

She was still staring at me, trying me out with those eyes—wasting her time, if she only knew. "I'll have to notify the health authorities," I said calmly. "They can't just cart him off and bury him. After all, we don't really know what he died of."

She simply stood there, as if she had given up—simply ceased to see me at all.

I don't know when I've been so irritated. "It might have been something contagious," I said. "God knows." There was no answer.

I am not enamored of holding conversations with myself. I went out to shout to one of the boys to open the garage and get the car ready for my morning drive to town.

AS I HAD EXPECTED, it turned out to be quite a business. I had to notify the police as well as the health authorities, and answer a lot of tedious questions: How was it I was ignorant of the boy's presence? If I did not supervise my native quarters, how did I know that that sort of thing didn't go on all the time? Et cetera, et cetera. And when I flared up and told them that so long as my natives did their work, I didn't think it my right or concern to poke my nose into their private lives, I got from the coarse, dull-witted police sergeant one of those looks that come not from any thinking process going on in the brain but from that faculty common to all who are possessed by the master-race theory—a look of insanely inane certainty. He grinned at me with a mixture of scorn and delight at my stupidity.

Then I had to explain to Petrus why the health authorities had to take away the body for a postmortem—and, in fact, what a postmortem was. When I telephoned the health department some days later to find out the result, I was told that the cause of death was, as we had thought, pneumonia, and that the body had been suitably disposed of. I went out to where Petrus was mixing a mash for the fowls and told him that it was all right, there would be no trouble; his brother had died from that pain in his chest. Petrus put down the paraffin can and said, "When can we go to fetch him, *Baas?*"

"To fetch him?"

"Will the *Baas* please ask them when we must come?"

I went back inside and called Lerice, all over the house. She came down the stairs from the spare bedrooms, and I said, "*Now* what am I going to do? When I told Petrus, he just asked calmly when they could go and fetch the body. They think they're going to bury him themselves."

"Well, go back and tell him," said Lerice. "You must tell him. Why didn't you tell him then?"

When I found Petrus again, he looked up politely. "Look, Petrus," I said. "You can't go to fetch your brother. They've done it already—they've *buried* him, you understand?"

"Where?" he said slowly, dully, as if he thought that perhaps he was getting this wrong.

"You see, he was a stranger. They knew he wasn't from here, and they didn't know he had some of his people here so they thought they must bury him." It was difficult to make a pauper's grave sound like a privilege.

"Please, *Baas*, the *Baas* must ask them." But he did not mean that he wanted to know the burial place. He simply ignored the incomprehensible machinery I told him had set to work on his dead brother; he wanted the brother back.

"But, Petrus," I said, "how can I? Your brother is buried already. I can't ask them now."

"Oh, *Baas!*" he said. He stood with his bran-smeared hands uncurled at his sides, one corner of his mouth twitching.

"Good God, Petrus, they won't listen to me! They can't, anyway. I'm sorry, but I can't do it. You understand?"

He just kept on looking at me, out of his knowledge that white men have everything, can do anything; if they don't, it is because they won't.

And then, at dinner, Lerice started. "You could at least phone," she said.

"Christ, what d'you think I am? Am I supposed to bring the dead back to life?"

But I could not exaggerate my way out of this ridiculous responsibility that had been thrust on me. "Phone them up," she went on. "And at least you'll be able to tell him you've done it and they've explained that it's impossible."

She disappeared somewhere into the kitchen quarters after coffee. A little later she came back to tell me, "The old father's coming down from Rhodesia to be at the funeral. He's got a permit and he's already on his way."

Unfortunately, it was not impossible to get the body back. The authorities said that it was somewhat irregular, but that since the hygiene conditions had been fulfilled, they could not refuse permission for exhumation. I found out that, with the undertaker's charges, it would cost twenty pounds. Ah, I thought, that settles it. On five pounds a month, Petrus won't have twenty pounds—and just as well, since it couldn't do the dead any good. Certainly I should not offer it to him myself. Twenty pounds—or anything else within reason, for that matter—I would have spent without grudging it on doctors or medicines that might have helped the boy when he was alive. Once he was dead, I had no intention of encouraging Petrus to throw away, on a gesture, more than he spent to clothe his whole family in a year.

When I told him, in the kitchen that night, he said, "Twenty pounds?"

I said, "Yes, that's right, twenty pounds."

For a moment, I had the feeling, from the look on his face, that he was calculating. But when he spoke again I thought I must have imagined it.

"We must pay twenty pounds!" he said in the faraway voice in which a person speaks of something so unattainable that it does not bear thinking about.

"All right, Petrus," I said, and went back to the living room.

The next morning before I went to town, Petrus asked to see me. "Please, *Baas*," he said, awkwardly handing me a bundle of notes. They're so seldom on the giving rather than the receiving side, poor devils, that they don't really know how to hand money to a white man. There it was, the twenty pounds, in ones and halves, some creased and folded until they were soft as dirty rags, others smooth and fairly new—Franz's money, I suppose, and Albert's, and Dora the cook's, and Jacob the gardener's, and God knows who else's besides, from all the farms and small holdings round about. I took it in irritation more than in astonishment, really—irritation at the waste, the uselessness of this sacrifice by people so poor. Just like the poor everywhere, I thought, who stint themselves the decencies of life in order to ensure themselves the decencies of death. So incomprehensible to people like Lerice and me, who regard life as something to be spent extravagantly and, if we think about death at all, regard it as the final bankruptcy.

THE SERVANTS don't work on Saturday afternoon anyway, so it was a good day for the funeral. Petrus and his father had borrowed our donkey cart to fetch the coffin from the city, where, Petrus told Lerice on their return, everything was "nice" the coffin waiting for them, already sealed up to save them from what must have been a rather unpleasant sight after two weeks' interment. (It had taken all that time for the authorities and the undertaker to make the final arrangements for moving the body.) All morning, the coffin lay in Petrus's hut, awaiting the trip to the little old burial ground, just outside the eastern boundary of our farm, that was a relic of the days when this was a real farming district rather than a fashionable rural estate. It was pure chance that I happened to be down there near the fence when the procession came past; once again Lerice had forgotten her promise to me and had made the house uninhabitable on a Saturday afternoon. I had come home and been infuriated to find her in a pair of filthy old slacks and with her hair uncombed since the night before, having all the varnish scraped off the living-room floor, if you please. So I had taken my number-8 iron and gone off to practice my approach shots. In my annoyance, I had forgotten about the funeral, and was reminded only when I saw the procession coming up the path along the outside of the fence toward me; from where I was standing, you can see the graves quite clearly, and that day the sun glinted on bits of broken pottery, a lopsided homemade cross, and jam jars brown with rainwater and dead flowers.

I felt a little awkward, and did not know whether to go on hitting my golf ball or stop at least until the whole gathering was decently past. The donkey cart creaks and screeches with every revolution of the wheels, and it came along in a slow, halting fashion somehow peculiarly suited to the two donkeys who drew it, their little potbellies rubbed and rough, their heads sunk between the shafts, and their ears flattened back with an air submissive and downcast; peculiarly suited, too, to the group of men and women who came along slowly behind. The patient ass. Watching, I thought, You can see now why the creature became a Biblical symbol. Then the procession drew level with me and stopped, so I had to put down my club. The coffin was taken down off the cart—it was a shiny, yellow-varnished wood, like cheap furniture—and the donkeys twitched their ears against the flies. Petrus, Franz, Albert, and the old father from Rhodesia hoisted it on their shoulders and the procession moved on, on foot. It was really a very awkward moment. I stood there rather foolishly at the fence, quite still, and slowly they filed past, not looking up, the four men bent beneath the shiny wooden box, and the straggling troop of mourners. All of them were servants or neighbors' servants whom I knew as casual, easygoing gossipers about our lands or kitchen. I heard the old man's breathing.

I had just bent to pick up my club again when there was a sort of jar in the flowing solemnity of their processional mood; I felt it at once, like a wave of heat along the air, or one of those sudden currents of cold catching at your legs in a placid stream. The old man's voice was muttering something; the people had stopped, confused, and they bumped into one another, some pressing to go on, others hissing them to be still. I could see that they were embarrassed, but they could not ignore the voice; it was much the way that the mumblings of a prophet, though not clear at first, arrest the mind. The corner of the coffin the old man carried was sagging at an angle; he seemed to be trying to get out from under the weight of it. Now Petrus expostulated with him.

The little boy who had been left to watch the donkeys dropped the reins and ran to see. I don't know why—unless it was for the same reason people crowd around someone who has fainted in a cinema—but I parted the wires of the fence and went through, after him.

Petrus lifted his eyes to me—to anybody—with distress and horror. The old man from Rhodesia had let go of the coffin entirely, and the three others, unable to support it on their own, had laid it on the ground, in the pathway. Already there was a film of dust lightly wavering up its shiny sides. I did not understand what the old man was saying; I hesitated to interfere. But now the whole seething group turned on my silence. The old man himself came over to me, with his hands outspread and shaking, and spoke directly to me, saying something that I could tell from the tone, without understanding the words, was shocking and extraordinary.

"What is it, Petrus? What's wrong?" I appealed.

Petrus threw up his hands, bowed his head in a series of hysterical shakes, then thrust his face up at me suddenly. "He says, 'My son was not so heavy.'"

Silence. I could hear the old man breathing; he kept his mouth a little open, as old people do.

"My son was young and thin," he said at last, in English.

Again silence. Then babble broke out. The old man thundered against everybody; his teeth were yellowed and few, and he had one of those fine, grizzled, sweeping mustaches that one doesn't often see nowadays, which must have been grown in emulation of early Empire builders. It seemed to frame all his utterances with a special validity, perhaps merely because it was the symbol of the traditional wisdom of age—an idea so fearfully rooted that it carries still something awesome beyond reason. He shocked them; they thought he was mad, but they had to listen to him.

With his own hands he began to prize the lid off the coffin and three of the men came forward to help him. Then he sat down on the ground; very old, very weak, and unable to speak, he merely lifted a trembling hand toward what was there. He abdicated, he handed it over to them; he was no good anymore.

They crowded round to look (and so did I), and now they forgot the nature of this surprise and the occasion of grief to which it belonged, and for a few minutes were carried up in the delightful astonishment of the surprise itself. They gasped and flared noisily with excitement. I even noticed the little boy who had held the donkeys jumping up and down, almost weeping with rage because the backs of the grown-ups crowded him out of his view.

In the coffin was someone no one had ever seen before: a heavily built, rather light-skinned native with a neatly stitched scar on his forehead—perhaps from a blow in a brawl that had also dealt him some other, slower-working injury, which had killed him.

I WRANGLED WITH THE AUTHORITIES for a week over that body. I had the feeling that they were shocked, in a laconic fashion, by their own mistake, but that in the confusion of their anonymous dead they were helpless to put it right. They said to me, "We are trying to find out," and "We are still making inquiries." It was as if at any moment they might conduct me into their mortuary and say, "There! Lift up the sheets; look for him—your poultry boy's brother. There are so many black faces—surely one will do?"

And every evening when I got home, Petrus was waiting in the kitchen. "Well, they're trying. They're still looking. The *Baas* is seeing to it for you, Petrus," I would tell him. "God, half the time I should be in the office I'm driving around the back end of the town chasing after this affair," I added aside, to Lerice, one night.

She and Petrus both kept their eyes turned on me as I spoke, and, oddly, for those moments they looked exactly alike, though it sounds impossible: my wife, with her high, white forehead and her attenuated Englishwoman's body, and the poultry boy, with his horny bare feet below khaki trousers tied at the knee with string and the peculiar rankness of his nervous sweat coming from his skin.

"What makes you so indignant, so determined about this now?" said Lerice suddenly.

I stared at her. "It's a matter of principle. Why should they get away with a swindle? It's time these officials had a jolt from someone who'll bother to take the trouble."

She said, "Oh." And as Petrus slowly opened the kitchen door to leave, sensing that the talk had gone beyond him, she turned away, too.

I continued to pass on assurances to Petrus every evening, but although what I said was the same and the voice in which I said it was the same, every evening it sounded weaker. At last, it became clear that we would never get Petrus's brother back, because nobody really knew where he was. Somewhere in a graveyard as uniform as a housing scheme, somewhere under a number that didn't belong to him, or in the medical school, perhaps, laboriously reduced to layers of muscle and strings of nerve? Goodness knows. He had no identity in this world anyway.

It was only then, and in a voice of shame, that Petrus asked me to try and get the money back.

"From the way he asks, you'd think he was robbing his dead brother," I said to Lerice later. But as I've said, Lerice had got so intense about this business that she couldn't even appreciate a little ironic smile.

I tried to get the money; Lerice tried. We both telephoned and wrote and argued, but nothing came of it. It appeared that the main expense had been the undertaker, and after all he had done his job, So the whole thing was a complete waste, even more of a waste for the poor devils than I had thought it would be.

The old man from Rhodesia was about Lerice's father's size, so she gave him one of her father's old suits, and he went back home rather better off, for the winter, than he had come.

THE BOARDING HOUSE

JAMES JOYCE / IRELAND

James Joyce

MRS. MOONEY was a butcher's daughter. She was a woman who was quite able to keep things to herself: a determined woman. She had married her father's foreman and opened a butcher's shop near Spring Gardens. But as soon as his father-in-law was dead Mr. Mooney began to go to the devil. He drank, plundered the till, ran headlong into debt. It was no use making him take the pledge: he was sure to break out again a few days after. By fighting his wife in the presence of customers and by buying bad meat he ruined his business. One night he went for his wife with the cleaver and she had to sleep in a neighbor's house.

After that they lived apart. She went to the priest and got a separation from him with care of the children. She would give him neither money nor food nor house room; and so he was obliged to enlist himself as a sheriff's man. He was a shabby stooped little drunkard with a white face and a white mustache and white eyebrows, penciled above his little eyes, which were pink-veined and raw; and all day long he sat in the bailiff's room, waiting to be put on a job. Mrs. Mooney, who had taken what remained of her money out of the butcher business and set up a boarding house in Hardwicke Street, was a big imposing woman. Her house had a floating population made up of tourists from Liverpool and the Isle of Man and, occasionally, *artistes* from the music halls. Its resident population was made up of clerks from the city. She governed her house cunningly and firmly, knew when to give credit, when to be stern and when to let things pass. All the resident young men spoke of her as *The Madam*.

Mrs. Mooney's young men paid fifteen shillings a week for board and lodgings (beer or stout at dinner excluded). They shared in common tastes and occupations and for this reason they were very chummy with one another. They discussed with one another the chances of favorites and outsiders. Jack Mooney, the Madam's son, who was clerk to a commission agent in Fleet Street, had the reputation of being a hard case. He was fond of using soldiers' obscenities: usually he came home in the small hours. When he met his friends he had always a good one to tell them and he was always sure to be on to a good thing—that is to say, a likely horse or a likely *artiste*. He was also handy with the mits and sang comic songs. On Sunday nights there would often be a reunion in Mrs. Mooney's front drawing room. The music-hall *artistes* would oblige; and Sheridan played waltzes and polkas and vamped accompaniments. Polly Mooney, the Madam's daughter, would also sing. She sang:

> *I'm a . . . naughty girl.*
> *You needn't sham:*
> *You know I am.*

Polly was a slim girl of nineteen; she had light soft hair and a small full mouth. Her eyes, which were gray with a shade of green through them, had a habit of glancing upwards when she spoke with anyone, which made her look like a little perverse madonna. Mrs. Mooney had first sent her daughter to be a typist in a corn factor's office but, as a disreputable sheriff's man used to come every other day to the office, asking to be allowed to say a word to his daughter, she had taken her daughter home again and set her to do housework. As Polly was very lively the intention was to give her the run of the young men. Besides, young men like to feel that there is a young woman not very far away. Polly, of course, flirted with the young men but Mrs. Mooney, who was a shrewd judge, knew that the young men were only passing the time away: none of them meant business. Things went on so for a long time and Mrs. Mooney began to think of sending Polly back to typewriting when she noticed that something was going on between Polly and one of the young men. She watched the pair and kept her own counsel.

Polly knew that she was being watched, but still her mother's persistent silence could not be misunderstood. There had been no open complicity between mother and daughter, no open understanding but, though people in the house began to talk of the affair, still Mrs. Mooney did not intervene. Polly began to grow a little strange in her manner and the young man was evidently perturbed. At last, when she judged it to be the right moment, Mrs. Mooney intervened. She dealt with moral problems as a cleaver deals with meat; and in this case she had made up her mind.

It was a bright Sunday morning of early summer, promising heat, but with a fresh breeze blowing. All the windows of the boarding house were open and the lace curtains ballooned gently towards the street beneath the raised sashes. The belfry of George's Church sent out constant peals and worshippers, singly or in groups, traversed the little circus before the church, revealing their purpose by their self-contained demeanor no less than by the little volumes in their gloved hands. Breakfast was over in the boarding house and the table of the breakfast room was covered with plates on which lay yellow streaks of eggs with morsels of bacon fat and bacon rind. Mrs. Mooney sat in the straw armchair and watched the servant Mary remove the breakfast things. She made Mary collect the crusts and pieces of broken bread to help to make Tuesday's bread pudding. When the table was cleared, the broken bread collected, the sugar and butter safe under lock and key, she began to reconstruct the interview which she had had the night before with Polly. Things were as she had suspected: she had been frank in her questions and Polly had been frank in her answers. Both had been somewhat awkward, of course. She had been made awkward by her not wishing to receive the news in too cavalier a fashion or to seem to have connived and Polly had been made awkward not merely because allusions of that kind always made her awkward but also because she did not wish it to be thought that in her wise innocence she had divined the intention behind her mother's tolerance.

Mrs. Mooney glanced instinctively at the little gilt clock on the mantelpiece as soon as she had become aware through her revery that the bells of George's Church had stopped ringing. It was seventeen minutes past eleven: she would have lots of time to have the matter out with Mr. Doran and then catch short twelve at Marlborough Street. She was sure she would win. To begin with she had all the weight of social opinion on her side: she was an outraged mother. She had allowed him to live beneath her roof, assuming that he was a man of honor, and he had simply abused her hospitality. He was thirty-four or thirty-five years of age, so that youth could not be pleaded as his excuse; nor could ignorance be his excuse since he was a man who had seen something of the world. He had simply taken advantage of Polly's youth and inexperience; that was evident. The question was: What reparation would he make?

There must be reparation made in such cases. It is all very well for the man: he can go his ways as if nothing had happened, having had his moment of pleasure, but the girl has to bear the brunt. Some mothers would be content to patch up such an affair for a sum of money; she had known cases of it. But she would not do so. For her only one reparation could make up for the loss of her daughter's honor: marriage.

She counted all her cards again before sending Mary up to Mr. Doran's room to say that she wished to speak with him. She felt sure she would win. He was a serious young man, not rakish or loud-voiced like the others. If it had been Mr. Sheridan or Mr. Meade or Bantam Lyons her task would have been much harder. She did not think he would face publicity. All the lodgers in the house knew something of the affair; details had been invented by some. Besides, he had been employed for thirteen years in a great Catholic wine-merchant's office and publicity would mean for him, perhaps, the loss of his job. Whereas if he agreed all might be well. She knew he had a good salary for one thing and she suspected he had a bit of stuff put by.

Nearly the half hour! She stood up and surveyed herself in the pier glass. The decisive expression of her great florid face satisfied her and she thought of some mothers she knew who could not get their daughters off their hands.

Mr. Doran was very anxious indeed this Sunday morning. He had made two attempts to shave but his hand had been so unsteady that he had been obliged to desist. Three days' reddish beard fringed his jaws and every two or three minutes a mist gathered on his glasses so that he had to take them off and polish them with his pocket-handkerchief. The recollection of his confession of the night before was a cause of acute pain to him; the priest had drawn out every ridiculous detail of the affair and in the end had so magnified his sin that he was almost thankful at being afforded a loophole of reparation. The harm was done. What could he do now but marry her or run away? He could not brazen it out. The affair would be sure to be talked of and his employer would be certain to hear of it. Dublin is such a small city: everyone knows everyone else's business. He felt his heart leap warmly in his throat as he heard in his excited imagination old Mr. Leonard calling out in his rasping voice: *Send Mr. Doran here, please.*

All his long years of service gone for nothing! All his industry and diligence thrown away! As a young man he had sown his wild oats, of course; he had boasted of his freethinking and denied the existence of God to his companions in public houses. But that was all passed and done with . . . nearly. He still bought a copy of *Reynolds's Newspaper* every week but he attended to his religious duties and for nine-tenths of the year lived a regular life. He had money enough to settle down on; it was not that. But the family would look down on her. First of all there was her disreputable father and then her mother's boarding house was beginning to get a certain fame. He had a notion that he was being had. He could imagine his friends talking of the affair and laughing. She *was* a little vulgar; sometimes she said *I seen* and *If I had've known*. But what would grammar matter if he really loved her? He could not make up his mind whether to like her or despise her for what she had done. Of course, he had done it too. His instinct urged him to remain free, not to marry. Once you are married you are done for, it said.

While he was sitting helplessly on the side of the bed in shirt and trousers she tapped lightly at his door and entered. She told him all, that she had made a clean breast of it to her mother and that her mother would speak with him that morning. She cried and threw her arms round his neck, saying:

—O Bob! Bob! What am I to do? What am I to do at all?

She would put an end to herself, she said. He comforted her feebly, telling her not to cry, that it would be all right, never fear. He felt against his shirt the agitation of her bosom.

It was not altogether his fault that it had happened. He remembered well, with the curious patient memory of the celibate, the first casual caresses her dress, her breath, her fingers had given him. Then late one night as he was undressing for bed she had tapped at his door, timidly. She wanted to relight her candle at his for hers had been blown out by a gust. It was her bath night. She wore a loose open combing jacket of printed flannel. Her white instep shone in the opening of her furry slippers and the blood glowed warmly behind her perfumed skin. From her hands and wrists too as she lit and steadied her candle a faint perfume arose.

On nights when he came in very late it was she who warmed up his dinner. He scarcely knew what he was eating, feeling her beside him alone, at night, in the sleeping house. And her thoughtfulness! If the night was anyway cold or wet or windy there was sure to be a little tumbler of punch ready for him. Perhaps they could be happy together. . . .

They used to go upstairs together on tiptoe, each with a candle, and on the third landing exchange reluctant good-nights. They used to kiss. He remembered well her eyes, the touch of her hand and his delirium. . . . But delirium passes. He echoed her phrase, applying it to himself: *What am I to do?* The instinct of the celibate warned him to hold back. But the sin was there; even his sense of honor told him that reparation must be made for such a sin.

While he was sitting with her on the side of the bed Mary came to the door and said that the missus wanted to see him in the parlor. He stood up to put on his coat and waistcoat, more helpless than ever. When he was dressed he went over to her to comfort her. It would be all right, never fear. He left her crying on the bed and moaning softly: *O my God!*

Going down the stairs his glasses became so dimmed with moisture that he had to take them off and polish them. He longed to ascend through the roof and fly away to another country where he would never hear again of his trouble, and yet a force pushed him downstairs step by step. The implacable faces of his employer and of the Madam stared upon his discomfiture. On the last flight of stairs he passed Jack Mooney who was coming up from the pantry nursing two bottles of *Bass*. They saluted coldly; and the lover's eyes rested for a second or two on a thick bulldog face and a pair of thick short arms. When he reached the foot of the staircase he glanced up and saw Jack regarding him from the door of the return room.

Suddenly he remembered the night when one of the music-hall *artistes*, a little blond Londoner, had made a rather free allusion to Polly. The reunion had been almost broken up on account of Jack's violence. Everyone tried to quiet him. The music-hall *artiste*, a little paler than usual, kept smiling and saying that there was no harm meant; but Jack kept shouting at him that if any fellow tried that sort of a game on with *his* sister he'd bloody well put his teeth down his throat, so he would.

POLLY SAT for a little time on the side of the bed, crying. Then she dried her eyes and went over to the looking glass. She dipped the end of the towel in the water jug and refreshed her eyes with the cool water. She looked at herself in profile and readjusted a hairpin above her ear. Then she went back to the bed again and sat at the foot. She regarded the pillows for a long time and the sight of them awakened in her mind secret amiable memories. She rested the nape of her neck against the cool iron bed rail and fell into a revery. There was no longer any perturbation visible on her face.

She waited on patiently, almost cheerfully, without alarm, her memories gradually giving place to hopes and visions of the future. Her hopes and visions were so intricate that she no longer saw the white pillows on which her gaze was fixed or remembered that she was waiting for anything. At last she heard her mother calling. She started to her feet and ran to the banisters.

—Polly! Polly!

—Yes, mamma?

—Come down, dear. Mr. Doran wants to speak to you.

Then she remembered what she had been waiting for.

THE BRUTE

JOSEPH CONRAD / GREAT BRITAIN

Dodging in from the rain-swept street, I exchanged a smile and a glance with Miss Blank in the bar of the Three Crows. This exchange was effected with extreme propriety. It is a shock to think that, if still alive, Miss Blank must be something over sixty now. How time passes!

Noticing my gaze directed at the partition of glass and varnished wood, Miss Blank was good enough to say, encouragingly:

"Only Mr. Jermyn and Mr. Stonor in the parlor with another gentleman I've never seen before."

I moved towards the parlor door. A voice discoursing on the other side rose so loudly that the concluding words became quite plain in all their atrocity.

"That fellow Wilmot fairly dashed her brains out, and a good job, too!"

As I opened the parlor door the same voice went on in the same cruel strain:

"I was glad when I heard she got the knock from somebody at last. Sorry enough for poor Wilmot though. That man and I used to be chums at one time. Of course that was the end of him, A clear case if there ever was one. No way out of it. None at all."

The voice belonged to the gentleman Miss Blank had never seen before. He straddled his long legs on the hearthrug. Jermyn, leaning forward, held his pocket-handkerchief spread out before the grate. He looked back dismally over his shoulder, and as I slipped behind one of the little wooden tables, I nodded to him. On the other side of the fire sat Mr. Stonor, jammed tight into a capacious Windsor armchair. There was nothing small about him but his short, white side-whiskers. A man's handbag of the usual size looked like a child's toy on the floor near his feet.

I did not nod to him. He was too big to be nodded to in that parlor. He was a senior Trinity pilot and condescended to take his turn in the cutter only during the summer months. Besides, it's no use nodding to a monument. And he was like one. He didn't speak, he didn't budge. He just sat there, holding his handsome old head up, immovable, and almost bigger than life. It was extremely fine. Mr. Stonor's presence reduced poor old Jermyn to a mere shabby wisp of a man, and made the talkative stranger in tweeds on the hearthrug look absurdly boyish. "I was glad of it," this man repeated, emphatically. "You may be surprised, but then you haven't gone through the experience I've had of her. I can tell you, it was something to remember. Of course, I got off scot-free myself—as you can see. She did her best to break up my pluck for me though. She jolly near drove as fine a fellow as ever lived into a madhouse. What do you say to that—eh?"

Not an eyelid twitched in Mr. Stonor's enormous face. Monumental! The speaker looked straight into my eyes.

"It used to make me sick to think of her going about the world murdering people."

Jermyn held the handkerchief a little nearer to the grate and groaned. It was simply a habit he had.

"She had a house," he declared. "A great, big, ugly, white thing. You could see it from miles away—sticking up."

"So you could," assented the other readily. "It was old Colchester's notion, though he was always threatening to give her up. He couldn't stand her racket anymore. I daresay he would have chucked her, only—it may surprise you—his missus wouldn't hear of it. Funny, eh? But with women, you never know how they will take a thing, and Mrs. Colchester, with her mustaches and big eyebrows, set up for being as strong-minded as they make them. You should have heard her snapping out: 'Rubbish!' or 'Stuff and nonsense!' I daresay she knew when she was well off. They had no children, and had never set up a home anywhere. When in England she just made shift to hang out anyhow in some cheap hotel or boardinghouse. I daresay she liked to get back to the comforts she was used to. She knew very well she couldn't gain by any change. Anyhow, for one reason or another, it was 'Rubbish' and 'Stuff and nonsense' for the good lady. I overheard once young Mr. Apse himself say to her confidentially: 'I assure you, Mrs. Colchester, I am beginning to feel quite unhappy about the name she's getting for herself.' 'Oh,' says she, with her deep little hoarse laugh, 'if one took notice of all the silly talk,' and she showed Apse all her ugly false teeth at once. 'It would take more than that to make me lose my confidence in her, I assure you,' says she."

At this point, without any change of facial expression, Mr. Stonor emitted a short, sardonic laugh. It was very impressive, but I didn't see the fun. I looked from one to another. The stranger on the hearthrug had an ugly smile.

"And Mr. Apse shook both Mrs. Colchester's hands, he was so pleased to hear a good word said for their favorite. All these Apses, young and old you know, were perfectly infatuated with that abominable, dangerous—"

"I beg your pardon," I interrupted, for he seemed to be addressing himself exclusively to me; "but who on earth are you talking about?"

"I am talking of the Apse family," he answered, courteously.

I nearly let out a damn at this. But just then the respected Miss Blank put her head in, and said that the cab was at the door, if Mr. Stonor wanted to catch the eleven-three up.

At once the senior pilot rose in his mighty bulk and began to struggle into his coat. The stranger and I hurried impulsively to his assistance, and directly we laid our hands on him he became perfectly quiescent. We had to raise our arms very high, and to make efforts. It was like caparisoning a docile elephant. With a "Thanks, gentlemen," he dived under and squeezed himself through the door in a great hurry.

We smiled at each other in a friendly way. "Are you a sailor?" I asked the stranger, who had gone back to his position on the rug.

"I used to be till a couple of years ago, when I got married," he answered. "I even went to sea first in that very ship we were speaking of when you came in."

"What ship?" I asked, puzzled. "I never heard you mention a ship."

"I've just told you her name, my dear sir," he replied. "The *Apse Family*. Surely you've heard of the great firm of Apse & Sons, shipowners. They had a pretty big fleet. There was the *Lucy Apse*, and the *Harold Apse*, and *Anne, John, Malcolm, Clara, Juliet*, and so on—no end of *Apse*s. Every brother, sister, aunt, cousin, wife—and grandmother, too, for all I know—of the firm had a ship named after them. Good, solid, old-fashioned craft they were, too, built to carry and to last. None of your newfangled laborsaving appliances in them.

"This last one," he continued, "the *Apse Family*, was to be like the others, only she was to be still stronger, still safer, still more roomy and comfortable. I believe they meant her to last forever. They had her built composite—iron, teakwood, and greenheart, and her scantling was something fabulous. If ever an order was given for a ship in a spirit of pride this one was. Everything of the best. The commodore captain of the employ was to command her, and they planned the accommodation for him like a house on shore under a big, tall poop that went nearly to the mainmast. No wonder Mrs. Colchester wouldn't let the old man give her up.

"The fuss that was made while that ship was building! Let's have this a little stronger, and that a little heavier; and hadn't that other thing better be changed for something a little thicker. The builders entered into the spirit of the game, and there she was, growing into the clumsiest, heaviest ship of her size right before all their eyes, without anybody becoming aware of it somehow. She was to be 2,000 tons register, or a little over; no less on any account. But when they came to measure her she turned out 1,999 tons and a fraction. They say old Mr. Apse was so annoyed when they told him that he took to his bed and died. The old gentleman was ninety-six years old if a day, so his death wasn't, perhaps, so surprising. Still Mr. Lucian Apse was convinced that his father would have lived to a hundred. So we may put the old man at the head of the list. Next comes the poor devil of a shipwright that brute caught and squashed as she went off the ways. They called it a ship launching, but I've heard people say that, from the wailing and yelling and scrambling out of the way, it was more like letting a devil loose upon the river. She snapped all her checks like packthread, and went for the tugs in attendance like a fury. Before anybody could see what she was up to she sent one of them to the bottom, and laid up another for three months' repairs. One of her cables parted, and then, suddenly—you couldn't tell why—she let herself be brought up with the other as quiet as a lamb.

"That's how she was. You could never be sure what she would be up to next. There are ships difficult to handle, but generally you can depend on them behaving rationally. With *that* ship, whatever you did with her you never knew how it would end. She was a wicked beast. Or, perhaps, she was only just insane."

He uttered this supposition in so earnest a tone that I could not refrain from smiling. He left off biting his lower lip to apostrophize me.

"Eh! Why not? Why couldn't there be something in her build, in her lines corresponding to—madness. Why shouldn't there be a mad ship—I mean mad in a shiplike way, so that under no circumstances could you be sure she would do what any other sensible ship would naturally do for you. She was unaccountable. If she wasn't mad, then she was the most evil-minded, underhanded, savage brute that ever went afloat. I've seen her run in a heavy gale beautifully for two days, and on the third broach to twice in the same afternoon. The first time she flung the helmsman clean over the wheel, but as she didn't quite manage to kill him she had another try about three hours afterwards. She swamped herself fore and aft, burst all the canvas we had set, scared all hands into a panic, and even frightened Mrs. Colchester down there in these beautiful stern cabins that she was so proud of. When we mustered the crew there was one man missing. Swept overboard, of course, without being either seen or heard, poor devil! and I only wonder more of us didn't go.

"Always something like that. Always. You could never be certain what would hold her. On the slightest provocation she would start snapping ropes, cables, wire hawsers, like carrots. She was heavy, clumsy, unhandy—but that does not quite explain that power for mischief she had." He looked at me inquisitively. But, of course, I couldn't admit that a ship could be mad.

"In the ports where she was known," he went on, "they dreaded the sight of her. She thought nothing of knocking away twenty feet or so of solid stone facing off a quay or wiping off the end of a wooden wharf. She must have lost miles of chain and hundreds of tons of anchors in her time. When she fell aboard some poor unoffending ship it was the very devil of a job to haul her off again. And she never got hurt herself—just a few scratches or so, perhaps. They had wanted to have her strong. And so she was. Strong enough to ram polar ice with. And as she began so she went on. From the day she was launched she never let a year pass without murdering somebody. I think the owners got very worried about it. But they were a stiff-necked generation, all these Apses; they wouldn't admit there could be anything wrong with the *Apse Family*. They wouldn't even change her name. 'Stuff and nonsense,' as Mrs. Colchester used to say. They ought at least to have shut her up for life in some dry dock or other, away up the river, and never let her smell salt water again. I assure you, my dear sir, that she invariably did kill someone every voyage she made. It was perfectly well-known. She got a name for it, far and wide."

I expressed my surprise that a ship with such a deadly reputation could ever get a crew.

"Then, you don't know what sailors are, my dear sir. Recklessness! The vanity of boasting in the evening to all their chums: 'We've just shipped in that there *Apse Family*. Blow her. She ain't going to scare us.' Sheer sailorlike perversity! A sort of curiosity. Well—a little of all that, no doubt. But I tell you what; there was a sort of fascination about the brute."

Jermyn, who seemed to have seen every ship in the world, broke in sulkily:

"I saw her once out of this very window towing upriver; a great black ugly thing, going along like a big hearse."

"Something sinister about her looks, wasn't there?" said the man in tweeds, looking down at old Jermyn with a friendly eye. "I always had a sort of horror of her. She gave me a beastly shock when I was no more than fourteen, the very first day—nay, hour—I joined her. Father came up to see me off, and was to go down to Gravesend with us. I was his second boy to go to sea. My big brother was already an officer then. We got on board about eleven in the morning, and found the ship ready to drop out of the basin, stern first. She had not moved three times her own length when, at a little pluck the tug gave her to enter the dock gates, she made one of her rampaging starts, and put such a weight on the check rope—a new six-inch hawser—that forward there they had no chance to ease it round in time, and it parted. I saw the broken end fly up high in the air, and the next moment that brute brought her quarter against the pierhead with a jar that staggered everybody about her decks. She didn't hurt herself. Not she! But one of the boys the mate had sent aloft on the mizzen to do something, came down on the poop deck—thump—right in front of me. He was not much older than myself. We had been grinning at each other only a few minutes before. He must have been handling himself carelessly, not expecting to get such a jerk. I heard his startled cry—Oh!—in a high treble as he felt himself going, and looked up in time to see him go limp. He fell within two feet of me, cracking his head on a mooring bitt. Never moved. Stone dead. Ough! Poor Father was remarkably white about the gills when we shook hands in Gravesend. 'Are you all right?' he says, looking hard at me. 'Yes, Father.' 'Quite sure?' 'Yes, Father.' 'Well, then good-by, my boy.' He told me afterwards that for half a word he would have carried me off home with him there and then. I am the baby of the family, you know," he added with an ingenuous smile.

I acknowledged this interesting communication by a sympathetic murmur. He waved his hand carelessly.

"This might have utterly spoiled a chap's nerve for going aloft, you know—utterly. However, that wasn't yet the worst that brute of a ship could do. I served in her three years of my time, and then I got transferred to the *Lucy Apse*, for a year. To me who had known no ship but the *Apse Family*, the *Lucy* was like a sort of magic craft that did what you wanted her to do of her own accord.

"Well, I finished my last year of apprenticeship in that jolly little ship and then just as I was thinking of having three weeks of real good time on shore I got at breakfast a letter asking me the earliest day I could be ready to join the *Apse Family* as third mate. I gave my plate a shove that shot it into the middle of the table; Dad looked up over his paper; Mother raised her hands in astonishment, and I went out bareheaded into our bit of garden, where I walked round and round for an hour.

"When I came in again Mother was out of the dining room, and Dad had shifted berth into his big armchair. The letter was lying on the mantelpiece.

"'It's very creditable to you to get the offer, and very kind of them to make it,' he said. 'And I see also that Charles has been appointed chief mate of that ship for one voyage.'

"There was, overleaf, a P.S. to that effect in Mr. Apse's own handwriting, which I had overlooked. Charley was my big brother.

"'I don't like very much to have two of my boys together in one ship,' Father went on, in his solemn way. 'And I may tell you that I would not mind writing Mr. Apse a letter to that effect.'

"Dear old Dad! He was a wonderful father. What would you have done? The mere notion of going back (and as an officer, too), to be worried and bothered, and kept on the jump night and day by that brute, made me feel sick. But she wasn't a ship you could afford to fight shy of. Besides, the most genuine excuse could not be given without mortally offending Apse & Sons. This was the case for answering 'Ready now' from your very deathbed if you wished to die in their good graces. And that's precisely what I did answer—by wire, to have it over and done with at once.

"The prospect of being shipmates with my big brother cheered me up considerably, though it made me a bit anxious, too. Ever since I remember myself as a little chap he had been very good to me, and I looked upon him as the finest fellow in the world. And so he was. No better officer ever walked the deck of a merchant ship. He was a fine, strong, upstanding, suntanned, young fellow, with his brown hair curling a little, and an eye like a hawk. He was just splendid. We hadn't seen each other for many years, and even this time, though he had been in England three weeks already, he hadn't showed up at home yet, but had spent his spare time in Surrey somewhere making up to Maggie Colchester, old Captain Colchester's niece. Her father, a great friend of Dad's, was in the sugar-broking business, and Charley made a sort of second home of their house. I wondered what my big brother would think of me.

"He received me with a great shout of laughter. He seemed to think my joining as an officer the greatest joke in the world. There was a difference of ten years between us, and I was a kid of four when he first went to sea. It surprised me to find how boisterous he could be.

"'Now we shall see what you are made of,' he cried, and punched my ribs, and hustled me into his berth. 'Sit down, Ned. I am glad of the chance of having you with me. I'll put the finishing touch to you, my young officer, providing you're worth the trouble. And, first of all, get it well into your head that we are not going to let this brute kill anybody this voyage. We'll stop her racket.'

"I perceived he was in dead earnest about it. He talked grimly of the ship, and how we must be careful and never allow this ugly beast to catch us napping with any of her damned tricks.

"He gave me a regular lecture on special seamanship for the use of the *Apse Family;* then changing his tone, he began to talk at large, rattling off the wildest, funniest nonsense, till my sides ached with laughing. I could see he was a bit above himself with high spirits. It couldn't be because of my coming. Not to that extent. But it was all made plain enough a day or two afterwards, when I heard that Miss Maggie Colchester was coming for the voyage. Uncle was giving her a sea trip for the benefit of her health.

"I don't know what could have been wrong with her health. She had a beautiful color, and a deuce of a lot of fair hair. She didn't care a rap for wind, or rain, or spray, or sun, or green seas, or anything. She was a blue-eyed, jolly girl of the very best sort, but the way she cheeked my big brother used to frighten me. I always expected it to end in an awful row. However, nothing decisive happened till after we had been in Sydney for a week. One day, in the men's dinner hour, Charley sticks his head into my cabin. I was stretched out on my back on the settee, smoking in peace.

"'Come ashore with me, Ned,' he says, in his curt way.

"I jumped up, of course, and away after him down the gangway and up George Street. He strode along like a giant, and I at his elbow, panting. It was confoundedly hot. 'Where on earth are you rushing me to, Charley?' I made bold to ask.

"'Here,' he says.

"'Here' was a jeweler's shop. I couldn't imagine what he could want there. It seemed a sort of mad freak. He thrusts under my nose three rings, which looked very tiny on his big, brown palm, growling out:

"'For Maggie! Which?'

"I got a kind of scare at this. I couldn't make a sound, but I pointed at the one that sparkled white and blue. He put it in his waistcoat pocket, paid for it with a lot of sovereigns, and bolted out. When we got on board I was quite out of breath. 'Shake hands, old chap,' I gasped out. He gave me a thump on the back. 'Give what orders you like to the boatswain when the hands turn-to,' says he; 'I am off duty this afternoon.'

"Then he vanished from the deck for a while, but presently he came out of the cabin with Maggie, and these two went over the gangway publicly, before all hands, going for a walk together on that awful, blazing hot day, with clouds of dust flying about. They came back after a few hours looking very staid, but didn't seem to have the slightest idea where they had been. Anyway, that's the answer they both made to Mrs. Colchester's questions at teatime.

"As you may imagine, the fiendish propensities of that cursed ship were never spoken of on board. Not in the cabin, at any rate. Only once on the homeward passage Charley said, incautiously, something about bringing all her crew home this time. Captain Colchester began to look uncomfortable at once; and Mrs. Colchester, that silly, hard-bitten old woman, flew out at Charley as though he had said something indecent. I was quite confounded myself; as to Maggie, she sat completely mystified, opening her blue eyes very wide. Of course, before she was a day older she wormed it all out of me. She was a very difficult person to lie to.

"'How awful,' she said, quite solemn. 'So many poor fellows. I am glad the voyage is nearly over. I won't have a moment's peace about Charley now.'

"I assured her Charley was all right. It took more than that ship knew to get over a seaman like Charley. And she agreed with me.

"Next day we got the tug off Dungeness; and when the towrope was fast Charley rubbed his hands and said to me in an undertone:

"'We've baffled her, Ned.'

"'Looks like it,' I said, with a grin at him. It was beautiful weather, and the sea as smooth as a millpond. We went up the river without a shadow of trouble except once, when off Hole Haven, the brute took a sudden sheer and nearly had a barge anchored just clear of the fairway. But I was aft, looking after the steering, and she did not catch me napping that time. Charley came up on the poop, looking very concerned. 'Close shave,' says he.

"'Never mind, Charley,' I answered, cheerily. 'You've tamed her.'

"We were to tow right up to the dock. The river pilot boarded us below Gravesend, and the first words I heard him say were: 'You may just as well take your port anchor inboard at once, Mr. Mate.'

"This had been done when I went forward. I saw Maggie on the forecastlehead enjoying the bustle and I begged her to go aft, but she took no notice of me, of course. Then Charley, who was very busy with the headgear, caught sight of her and shouted in his biggest voice: 'Get off the forecastlehead, Maggie. You're in the way here.' For an answer she made a funny face at him, and I saw poor Charley turn away, hiding a smile. She was flushed with the excitement of getting home again, and her blue eyes seemed to snap electric sparks as she looked at the river. A collier brig had gone round just ahead of us, and our tug had to stop her engines in a hurry to avoid running into her.

"In a moment, as is usually the case, all the shipping in the reach seemed to get into a hopeless tangle. A schooner and a ketch got up a small collision all to themselves right in the middle of the river. It was exciting to watch, and, meantime, our tug remained stopped. Any other ship than that brute could have been coaxed to keep straight for a couple of minutes—but not she! Her head fell off at once, and she began to drift down, taking her tug along with her. I noticed a cluster of coasters at anchor within a quarter of a mile of us, and I thought I had better speak to the pilot. 'If you let her get amongst that lot,' I said, quietly, 'she will grind some of them to bits before we get her out again.'

"'Don't I know her!' cries he, stamping his foot in a perfect fury. And he out with his whistle to make that bothered tug get the ship's head up again as quick as possible. He blew like mad, waving his arm to port, and presently we could see that the tug's engines had been set going ahead. Her paddles churned the water, but it was as if she had been trying to tow a rock—she couldn't get an inch out of that ship. Again the pilot blew his whistle, and waved his arm to port. We could see the tug's paddles turning faster and faster away, broad on our bow.

"For a moment tug and ship hung motionless in a crowd of moving shipping, and then the terrific strain that evil, stony-hearted brute would always put on everything, tore the towing chock clean out. The towrope surged over, snapping the iron stanchions of the headrail one after another as if they had been sticks of sealing wax. It was only then I noticed that in order to have a better view over our heads, Maggie had stepped upon the port anchor as it lay flat on the forecastle deck. It had been lowered properly into its hardwood beds, but there had been no time to take a turn with it. Anyway, it was quite secure as it was, for going into dock; but I could see directly that the towrope would sweep under the fluke in another second. My heart flew up right into my throat, but not before I had time to yell out: 'Jump clear of that anchor!'

"But I hadn't time to shriek out her name. I don't suppose she heard me at all. The first touch of the hawser against the fluke threw her down; she was up on her feet again quick as lightning, but she was up on the wrong side. I heard a horrid, scraping sound, and then that anchor, tipping over, rose up like something alive; its great, rough iron arm caught Maggie round the waist, seemed to clasp her close with a dreadful hug, and flung itself with her over and down in a terrific clang of iron, followed by heavy ringing blows that shook the ship from stem to stern—because the ring stopper held!"

"How horrible!" I exclaimed.

"I used to dream for years afterwards of anchors catching hold of girls," said the man in tweeds, a little wildly. He shuddered. "With a most pitiful howl Charley was over after her almost on the instant. But, Lord! He didn't see as much as a gleam of her red tam-o'-shanter in the water. Nothing! Nothing whatever! In a moment there were half-a-dozen boats around us, and he got pulled into one. I, with the boatswain and the carpenter, let go the other anchor in a hurry and brought the ship up somehow. The pilot had gone silly. He walked up and down the forecastlehead wringing his hands and muttering to himself: 'Killing women, now! Killing women, now!' Not another word could you get out of him.

"Dusk fell, then a night black as pitch; and peering upon the river I heard a low, mournful hail, 'Ship, ahoy!' Two Gravesend watermen came alongside. They had a lantern in their wherry, and looked up the ship's side, holding on to the ladder without a word. I saw in the patch of light a lot of loose, fair hair down there."

He shuddered again. "After the tide turned poor Maggie's body had floated clear of one of them big mooring buoys," he explained. "I crept aft, feeling half-dead, and managed to send a rocket up—to let the other searchers know, on the river. And then I slunk away forward like a cur, and spent the night sitting on the heel of the bowsprit so as to be as far as possible out of Charley's way."

"Poor fellow!" I murmured.

"Yes. Poor fellow," he repeated, musingly. "That brute wouldn't let him—not even him—cheat her of her prey. But he made her fast in dock next morning. He did. We hadn't exchanged a word—not a single look for that matter. I didn't want to look at him. When the last rope was fast he put his hands to his head and stood gazing down at his feet as if trying to remember something. The men waited on the main dock for the words that end the voyage. Perhaps that is what he was trying to remember. I spoke for him. 'That'll do, men.'

"I never saw a crew leave a ship so quietly. They sneaked over the rail one after another, taking care not to bang their sea chests too heavily. They looked our way, but not one had the stomach to come up and offer to shake hands with the mate as is usual.

"I followed him all over the empty ship to and fro, here and there, with no living soul about but the two of us, because the old shipkeeper had locked himself up in the galley—both doors. Suddenly poor Charley mutters, in a crazy voice: 'I'm done here,' and strides down the gangway with me at his heels, up the dock, out at the gate, on towards Tower Hill."

The man in tweeds nodded at me significantly.

"Ah! There was nothing that could be done with that brute. She had a devil in her."

"Where's your brother?" I asked, expecting to hear he was dead. But he was commanding a smart steamer on the China coast, and never came home now.

Jermyn fetched a heavy sigh, and the handkerchief being now sufficiently dry, put it up tenderly to his red and lamentable nose.

"She was a ravening beast," the man in tweeds started again. "Old Colchester put his foot down and resigned. And would you believe it? Apse & Sons wrote to ask whether he wouldn't reconsider his decision! Anything to save the good name of the *Apse Family!* Old Colchester went to the office then and said that he would take charge again but only to sail her out into the North Sea and scuttle her there. He was nearly off his chump. He used to be darkish iron-gray, but his hair went snow-white in a fortnight.

"They jumped at the first man they could get to take her, for fear

of the scandal of the *Apse Family* not being able to find a skipper.
He was a festive soul, I believe, but he stuck to her grim and hard.
Wilmot was his second mate. A harum-scarum fellow, and pretending
to a great scorn for all the girls. The fact is he was really timid. But
let only one of them do as much as lift her little finger in encouragement, and there was nothing that could hold the beggar.

"It was said that one of the firm had been heard once to express
a hope that this brute of a ship would get lost soon. But not she!
She was going to last forever. She had a nose to keep off the bottom."

Jermyn made a grunt of approval.

"A ship after a pilot's own heart, eh?" jeered the man in tweeds.
"Well, Wilmot managed it. He was the man for it, but even he,
perhaps, couldn't have done the trick without the green-eyed governess, or nurse, or whatever she was to the children of Mr. and Mrs.
Pamphilius.

"Those people were passengers in her from Port Adelaide to the
Cape. Well, the ship went out and anchored outside for the day. The
skipper—hospitable soul—had a lot of guests from town to a farewell
lunch—as usual with him. It was five in the evening before the last
shore boat left the side, and the weather looked ugly and dark in
the gulf. There was no reason for him to get under way. However,
as he had told everybody he was going that day, he imagined it was
proper to do so anyhow. But as he had no mind after all these
festivities to tackle the straits in the dark, he gave orders to keep
the ship under lower topsails and foresail as close as she would lie,
dodging along the land till the morning. Then he sought his couch.
The mate was on deck, having his face washed very clean with hard
rainsqualls. Wilmot relieved him at midnight.

"The *Apse Family* had, as you observed, a house on her poop . . ."

"A big, ugly white thing, sticking up," Jermyn murmured, sadly,
at the fire.

"That's it: a companion for the cabin stairs and a sort of chart
room combined. The rain drove in gusts on the sleepy Wilmot. The
ship was then surging slowly to the southward, close-hauled, with
the coast within three miles or so to windward. There was nothing
to look out for in that part of the gulf, and Wilmot went round

to dodge the squalls under the lee of that chart room, whose door on that side was open. The night was black, like a barrel of coal tar. And then he heard a woman's voice whispering to him.

"That confounded green-eyed girl of the Pamphilius people had put the kids to bed a long time ago, of course, but it seems couldn't get to sleep herself, and she came up into the chart room to cool herself, I daresay. I suppose when she whispered to Wilmot it was as if somebody had struck a match in the fellow's brain. I don't know how it was they had got so very thick. I fancy he had met her ashore a few times before. I couldn't make it out, because, when telling the story, Wilmot would break off to swear something awful at every second word. We had met on the quay in Sydney, and he had an apron of sacking up to his chin, a big whip in his hand. A wagon driver. Glad to do anything not to starve. That's what he had come down to.

"However, there he was, with his head inside the door, on the girl's shoulder as likely as not—officer of the watch! The helmsman, on giving his evidence afterwards, said that he shouted several times that the binnacle lamp had gone out. It didn't matter to him, because his orders were to 'sail her close.' 'I thought it funny,' he said, 'that the ship should keep on falling off in squalls, but I luffed her up every time as close as I was able. It was so dark I couldn't see my hand before my face, and the rain came in bucketfuls on my head.'

"The truth was that at every squall the wind hauled aft a little, till gradually the ship came to be heading straight for the coast, without a single soul in her being aware of it. Wilmot himself confessed that he had not been near the standard compass for an hour. He might well have confessed! The first thing he knew was the man on the lookout shouting blue murder forward there.

"He tore his neck free, he says, and yelled back at him: 'What do you say?'

"'I think I hear breakers ahead, sir,' howled the man, and came rushing aft with the rest of the watch, in the 'awfulest blinding deluge that ever fell from the sky,' Wilmot says. For a second or so he was so scared and bewildered that he could not remember on which side of the gulf the ship was. He wasn't a good officer, but he was a seaman all the same. He pulled himself together in a second, and the right orders sprang to his lips without thinking. They were to hard up with the helm and shiver the main and mizzen topsails.

"It seems that the sails actually fluttered. He couldn't see them, but he heard them rattling and banging above his head. 'No use! She was too slow in going off,' he went on, his dirty face twitching, and the damn'd carter's whip shaking in his hand. 'She seemed to stick fast.' And then the flutter of the canvas above his head ceased. At this critical moment the wind hauled aft again with a gust, filling the sails and sending the ship with a great way upon the rocks on her lee bow. She had overreached herself in her last little game. Her time had come—the hour, the man, the black night, the treacherous gust of wind—the right woman to put an end to her. The brute deserved nothing better. Strange are the instruments of Providence. There's a sort of poetical justice—"

The man in tweeds looked hard at me.

"The first ledge she went over stripped the false keel off her. Rip! The skipper, rushing out of his berth, found a crazy woman, in a red flannel dressing gown, flying round and round the cuddy, screeching like a cockatoo.

"The next bump knocked the woman clean under the cabin table. It also started the sternpost and carried away the rudder, and then that brute ran up a shelving, rocky shore, tearing her bottom out, till she stopped short, and the foremast dropped over the bows like a gangway."

"Anybody lost?" I asked.

"No one, unless that fellow, Wilmot," answered the gentleman, unknown to Miss Blank, looking round for his cap. "And his case was worse than drowning for a man. Everybody got ashore all right. Gale didn't come on till next day, dead from the west, and broke up that brute in a surprisingly short time. It was as though she had been rotten at heart." He changed his tone, "Rain left off? I must get my bike and rush home to dinner. I live in Herne Bay—came out for a spin this morning."

He nodded at me in a friendly way, and went out with a swagger.

"Do you know who he is, Jermyn?" I asked.

The North Sea pilot shook his head, dismally. "Fancy losing a ship in that silly fashion! Oh, dear! Oh dear!" he groaned in lugubrious tones, spreading his damp handkerchief again like a curtain before the glowing grate.

On going out I exchanged a glance and a smile (strictly proper) with the respectable Miss Blank, barmaid of the Three Crows.

A DOUBLE GAME
ALBERTO MORAVIA / ITALY

Alberto Moravia

"U<small>MBERTO DOES THIS</small>; Umberto does that; Umberto's top of his class at school; Umberto's mother says they're giving him a medal; Umberto is working; Umberto brings his money home; Umberto, out of his own money, has bought a motor scooter; Umberto is buying a car." At all ages, from the baby's high chair and bib onwards, I have always found Umberto getting in my way. It was natural: we lived in the same building in Via Candia, and the two small flats, the one belonging to Umberto's father, who kept the poulterer's shop on the ground floor, and our own, gave onto the same landing, and our mothers were friends and we two grew up together. It was natural, I say, that, when I grew up into a shirker and an idler and a loafer, my mother should point to Umberto as a model. I could have said, it is true, that my little finger was worth more than the whole of Umberto, with his sly, priggish, mean character; but what would have been the use? As everyone knows, mothers are all the same, and if the world was made as mothers would like it to be, it would be entirely made up of nonentities, in fact of sly, priggish, mean characters like Umberto.

I had a grudge against Umberto, but our relations were quite polite:

when we met, we greeted each other and exchanged news. The relations, in fact, of a cold war, between people who await the first opportunity to pick a quarrel. This opportunity came on the very same day that I got the sack, for inefficiency, from the vulcanite works in Via Dandolo. As I was going downstairs with my mother's words still in my ears: "My son, you'll break my heart. . . . Now look at Umberto—there's a good son for you. . . . Model yourself on Umberto, my son . . ." I came across Umberto, who was also going out. I at once stopped him and said: "I say, do tell me, I suppose you always do everything well?" "What d'you mean?" "I mean, it never happens to you that you make a mistake, that you do what you oughtn't to do, that—let us say—you gamble away your week's money?" Would you believe it? Anyone else in Umberto's place would have taken offense. But he, his sly face assuming an expression of indulgence, placed his hand on my shoulder and said: "Peppe, do as I do and you'll see you'll be all right." I answered furiously: "Take that hand off my shoulder. . . . Anyhow, I didn't stop you in order to ask your advice. It's I who want to give *you* some advice: keep off Clara; she's practically engaged to *me*." "*Practically* engaged?" "Anyhow, she's my girl and you've got to leave her alone—see?" "What fault is it of mine if . . . ?" "That's enough: forewarned is forearmed."

In order to understand these words of mine you must know that at that time I was running after Clara, a girl who also lived in Via Candia, in a building identical with the one in which I lived, that is to say, old and ugly, with the same huge courtyard as big as a piazza and the same staircases numbered from A to F. On one of these staircases was the little flat belonging to Clara's mother, who was called, or called herself, Dolores, and who practiced the odd profession of palmistry. She was a woman of about fifty, fragile, sickly, white as a ghost, with a face that looked as if it was covered with flour and two black eyes that made this face look like a plaster mask. Poor thing: she had been rich, or so she said, and now she was making shift with fortune-telling by cards and handreading. People say she was good at it, too; and besides the women of Via Candia, ladies, both married and unmarried, used to come to her from the fashionable neighborhoods. As for Clara, she was the exact opposite of her mother. She was healthy, well-groomed, beautiful, with a bright expression, clear, smiling; eyes like two quiet stars, and a lovely pale pink mouth showing, when she smiled, teeth as white as peeled almonds—the mouth of a little girl who has not yet learned to smile coquettishly. Clara worked in an office as a typist and stenographer, and it appears that she was very good at her job. When she was at home and her mother was receiving clients she sat at the table in the kitchen, tapping at her typewriter or studying English grammar. Clara, as I say, was quiet. I can say now, she was so quiet that, much as I loved her, I could not help comparing her secretly to still waters. Not so much the proverbial still waters that run deep; rather, a beautiful calm sea, in August, at night, with the moon and stars reflected in it and making you long to make love in the old-fashioned way, hands clasped together; your arm round her waist, your head on her shoulder. Oh yes, still waters she certainly was—and in both senses.

That same day I told Clara I had confronted Umberto. She started laughing gently: "Is it possible you're jealous of a type like Umberto?" "Well, he's a man, after all." "Yes, but what a man!" Feeling slightly comforted already, I asked her to explain what she meant; and, still laughing in her charming, quiet, childlike way, she went on: "Oh, I don't know. . . . In the first place, physically: he looks like Fagiolino in the puppet theater, the one who always takes the knocks: with that long face and hair like a pincushion. And if you knew what a bore he is! He thinks the world of himself: *he* does everything well, *he's* intelligent, he's this and he's that. . . . He's always talking about himself . . . and besides, he has certain ideas: according to him, a wife must stay at home, do the cooking and look after the children— and woe betide her if she so much as speaks to another man, even if it's her brother. I'd die rather than marry him." In short, she gave such a bad account of Umberto that, in the end, I was completely reassured; and I gave her leave to see him as much as she liked.

From then on, I felt I was avenging myself day by day for all the occasions on which my mother had held up Umberto as a model to me. My mother had placed him upon a pedestal; Clara, on the contrary, threw him off it. "I really don't like that man," she said to me. "I went with him to the yard where he's foreman: he spoke to the workmen as if they were dirt. The engineer arrived, and all at once he became a different person—humble, attentive, fawning." Or: "Let me tell you the latest: he gave a hundred lire to a beggar, and why d'you think it was? Because it was a forged note." Or again: "He has certain habits that I simply can't bear: when he thinks I'm not looking, he starts picking his nose." Clara abused him so much that sometimes I almost reached the point of defending Umberto, if only for the pleasure of hearing her rub it in. "But he's a good son," I would say. And she: "But he treats his mother like a slave." "But," I said, "he takes his money home." "Takes his money home?" she said; "he never does, now; he puts it in the bank." "He works hard," I said. "Works hard?" said she; "he's a shirker. He likes to make other people work and then take advantage of them."

By now I was so sure of Clara that I said to her, one day, that it was fitting that we two should now regularize our position and become officially engaged. She said at once: "I was thinking of that too but I didn't dare say so to you. But these things have to be done properly: you must go and tell Mother; you know her already." So we agreed that I should go and see her mother that same evening; in the meantime she would see Umberto, but for the last time. "I really can't bear to be with him," she said; "he wears me out." I approved this plan, not without a touch of pity for poor Umberto who wasn't expecting it. And at about seven o'clock I left home, crossed Via Candia and entered the main door of Clara's block of flats.

On the third floor of staircase D, Signora Dolores' door was ajar; I pushed it open and went in. I found myself in a tiny waiting room, full of people. There were two or three bareheaded women, fellow inhabitants of Via Candia; there was a good-looking dark girl, who lived in the same quarter and whom I knew by sight; there was a middle-aged lady, rather worn-looking and heavily made-up, wrapped in a brown fur coat. Business, evidently, was good, I thought as I sat down and took an illustrated magazine from the table, and Signora Dolores was doing well, making plenty of money, in fact. I waited for some time and then the door opened and a smart young woman came out, who kissed Signora Dolores effusively on both cheeks, saying: "Thank you, thank you, my dear." Clara's mother, in black silk Japanese pajamas with a colored dragon embroidered on the corner of the jacket and a cigarette holder as long as your arm between her teeth, threw me a glance and said: "Rinaldi, just one moment and then you can come in." She ushered in the middle-aged lady with the fur coat, and disappeared; and it occurred to me, for some reason— possibly from the tone of her voice—that she did not know of the proposal I was going to make to her. Then I had a bright idea: I would make her tell my fortune, to see whether my marriage to Clara was indicated in my hand; and immediately afterwards I would make my declaration. I smiled at this thought and awaited my turn with impatience. After a quarter of an hour the lady with the fur coat slipped out in a mysterious, discreet, hurried manner and went away. And Signora Dolores beckoned me in.

I knew that, for lack of space, she worked in her bedroom; all the same I was surprised. It was a long room, in half-shadow, containing a big double bed covered with a piece of yellow material; and I could not help reflecting that Clara slept in that big bed with her mother. At the window there was a curtain with openwork embroidery of birds and baskets of flowers; near the window, a small table on which lay a pack of cards and a magnifying glass; the whole room was full of little pieces of furniture, knickknacks, photographs with the signatures of important clients, testimonials, souvenirs. Signora Dolores, without a word, sat down at the table and made me sit opposite her. The first thing she did was to take a match, light it and set fire to a small piece of black paper, from which there quickly rose a white, scented smoke. "It's *carta d'Armenia*," she said in her refined, tired voice; "d'you smell the scent of it? Well, Rinaldi, what can I do for you?" I replied that I had come to have my fortune told; and she, having put down her cigarette holder on the ashtray, took my hand, held the magnifying glass over it and examined it at length.

Some moments passed and then, in an almost horrified tone of voice, she asked: "What sort of a man am I speaking to?" Disconcerted, I asked, "Why?" "Well," she said, "because this is the hand

241

of a man who is very fond—altogether too fond—of women." "After all," I said, "I'm a young man." "Yes," she answered, "but there's a limit to these things. And you don't seem to have that limit. Your heart is like an artichoke." "If you say so. . . ." "It's your hand that says so: you're a Don Juan." "Oh well, don't let's exaggerate." "I'm not exaggerating at all; look at your Heart line: it's like a chain—every link a woman." "And otherwise?" "Otherwise—nothing. Little luck in business, little will to work, little seriousness of character, little sense of responsibility." Beginning to be annoyed, I said: "You find nothing but faults in me." "They're not faults," she said, "they're characteristics. Certainly if I were a mother, I wouldn't let my daughter marry you." This made me angry, and I told her: "Well, have a look and see whether there's a marriage line." Scrupulously she took up the magnifying glass again, turned my hand in every direction and then said: "Adventures, as many as you like, but no marriage." "Signora Dolores," I said, "let's understand each other; I didn't come to you to have my hand read but to tell you that your daughter and I love one another and that we decided today to become engaged."

At these words she very calmly put down the magnifying glass and replied: "But, my poor boy. . . ." "What?" "My poor boy, the hand, as always, tells the truth: you're not getting married—not at present, anyhow." "And why, seeing that Clara and I are in agreement?" "You're not in agreement. . . . You think you're in agreement with Clara, but Clara is not in agreement with you." "Who says so?" "*I* say so: Clara is already engaged." "But when . . . ?" "She's been engaged for a week, to Umberto Pompei. Clara hadn't the courage to tell you because she's a shy girl, and besides, she's kindhearted and hates to hurt anybody. But she was worrying; you don't know how worried she's been. And I must say that on this occasion Umberto has shown himself to be a real gentleman: Clara asked his leave to go on seeing you for a few days longer, until there had been a full explanation between you; and he agreed at once. I don't know how many engaged couples, in such a situation, would have acted in this way."

I was dumbfounded. And when she said to me, hypocritically: "Well, now let's have a look at the cards: I bet some more women will turn up," mechanically I took the thousand-lire fee from my pocket, placed it on the table and went out without a word. I felt stunned, as though Signora Dolores, instead of reading my hand, had hit me over the head with a hammer; and into the midst of this stunned feeling there began to creep a number of suspicions, like so many snakes which gradually awake inside a heap of straw, in the warmth of the sun. So, then, while I had thought I was acting generously towards Umberto in letting him see Clara, in reality it had been *he* who acted generously towards *me* in allowing Clara to see me; so, while I had enjoyed hearing Clara abuse Umberto, *he*, perhaps, on his side, had enjoyed hearing Clara abuse *me;* so Clara had, in short, been playing a double game the whole time; only, in the end, it was I who had been fooled.

While these thoughts were going through my head I must have looked thoroughly upset, for all at once the good-looking dark girl who was waiting in the anteroom gave me a "pss pss," as one does to a cat, at the same time beckoning me with a glance. I stooped down and she asked me: "What is it? Does she say nasty things?" "Very nasty," I replied, "for me, anyhow." Promptly she rose to her feet. "Then I shan't go in," she said; "I'm so afraid she might give me some bad news." Mechanically I went out of the door and she followed me.

On the landing, I looked at her sideways. She was very dark, and her hair, cut short almost like a man's, seemed as it were to caress, to encircle her round face, continuing, as it did, in a faint down like a shadow, round her cheeks and chin. I thought her very pretty, and she, as though guessing my thought, turned towards me and said, smiling: "You don't know me, but I know you! We live in the same building."

Suddenly, from the staircase below, there came the sound of a silvery laugh, childish and limpid, Clara's laugh; and at the same time, the rather shrill sound of Umberto's voice. Without hesitating, I put my arm round the girl's waist. "What's your name?" I asked.

"My name's Angela," she said, giving me a bold glance. At that same moment Clara and Umberto passed close to us and I saw that Clara had seen us thus entwined, and that she modestly lowered her eyes. Well, take that, then! I thought to myself bitterly. They went on up the stairs and we went down. I took my arm from Angela's waist and said to her: "Angela dear, let's go and have a drink to celebrate our meeting." She took my arm and we went out together into the street.

MATERNITY
LILIKA NAKOS / GREECE

Lilika Nakos

Translated by Allan Ross Macdougall

IT WAS MORE than a month since they were at Marseille, and the camp of Armenian refugees on the outskirts of the town already looked like a small village. They had settled down in any way they could: the richest under tents; the others in the ruined sheds; but the majority of the refugees, having found nothing better, were sheltered under carpets held up at the four corners by sticks. They thought themselves lucky if they could find a sheet to hang up at the sides and wall them from peering eyes. Then they felt almost at home. The men found work—no matter what—so that in any case they were not racked with hunger and their children had something to eat.

Of all of them, Mikali alone could do nothing. He ate the bread which his neighbors cared to offer and it weighed on him. For he was a big lad of fourteen, healthy and robust. But how could he think of looking for work when he literally bore on his back the burden of a newborn babe? Since its birth, which had caused his mother's death, it had wailed its famine from morn till night. Who would have accepted Mikali's services when his own compatriots had chased him from their quarters because they were unable to bear the uninterrupted howls which kept them awake at night? Mikali himself was dazed by these cries; his head was empty and he wandered about like a lost soul, dying from lack of sleep and weariness, always dragging about with him the deafening burden that had been born for his misfortune—and its own—and that had so badly chosen the moment to appear on this earth. Everybody listened to it with irritation—they had so many troubles of their own—and they all pitifully wished it would die.

But that did not happen for the newborn child sought desperately to live and cry louder its famine. The distracted women stuffed their ears and Mikali went hither and yon like a drunken man. He hadn't a penny in his pocket to buy the infant milk and not one woman in the camp was in a position to give it the breast. Enough to drive one mad!

One day, unable to bear it further, Mikali went to the other side of the place where the Anatolians were: they also had fled from the Turkish massacres in Asia Minor. Mikali had been told that there was a nursing mother there who might take pity on his baby. So there he went full of hope. Their camp was like his—the same misery. Old women were crouched on pallets on the ground; barefooted children played about in pools of dirty water. As he approached, several old women rose to ask what he wanted. But he walked on and stopped only at the opening of a tent where an ikon of the Holy Virgin was hanging; from the interior of the tent came the sound of a wailing infant.

"In the name of the Most Holy Virgin whose ikon you show," he said in Greek, "have pity on this poor orphan and give him a little milk. I am a poor Armenian . . ."

At his appeal, a lovely, dark woman appeared. She held in her arms an infant blissfully sucking the maternal breast, its eyes half closed.

"Let's see the kid. Is't a boy or a girl?"

Mikali's heart trembled with joy. Several neighbors had come closer to see and they helped him to take from his shoulders the sack where the baby brother was held; with curiosity they leaned over. He drew back the cover.

The women gave vent to various cries of horror. The child had no longer anything human about it. It was a monster! The head had become enormous and the body, of an incredible thinness, was all shriveled up. As until then it had sucked only its thumb, it was all swollen and could no longer enter the mouth. It was dreadful to see! Mikali himself drew back in fright.

"Holy Mother!" said one of the old women, "but it's a vampire; a real vampire, that child! Even if I had milk I still wouldn't have the courage to feed it."

"A true Anti-Christ!" said another, crossing herself. "A true son of the Turk!"

An old crone came up. "Hou! Hou!" she screamed, seeing the newborn child. "It's the devil himself!" Then turning to Mikali she yelled: "Get out of here, son of mischance, and never set foot again. You'll bring us bad luck!"

And all of them together chased him away, threatening. His eyes filled with tears, he went off, bearing the little child still wailing its hunger.

There was nothing to be done. The child was condemned to die of hunger. Mikali felt himself immensely alone and lost. A chill ran up his spine at the thought that he was carrying such a monster. He slumped down in the shadow of a shed. It was still very warm. The country spread out before him in arid wasteland, covered with refuse. Noon rang out somewhere. The sound reminded him that he had eaten nothing since the day before. He would have to go sneaking about the streets, round café terraces, filching some half-eaten roll left on a plate; or else rake about in the garbage for what a dog would not have eaten. Suddenly life seemed to him so full of horrors that he covered his face with his hands and began to sob desperately.

When he raised his head a man stood before him gazing down upon him. Mikali recognized the Chinaman who often came to the camp to sell paper knickknacks and charms which no one ever bought from him anyway. Often they mocked him because of his color and his squint eyes; and the children hounded him, shouting: "Lee Link, the stinkin' Chink!"

Mikali saw that he was looking gently down at him and moving his lips as though to speak. Finally the Chinaman said: "You mustn't cry, boy. . . ." Then, timidly: "Come with me. . . ."

Mikali's only answer was to shake his head negatively; he longed to flee. He had heard so many horrors about the cruelty of the Orientals! At the camp they even went so far as to say that they had the habit—like the Jews—of stealing Christian children in order to kill them and drink their blood!

Yet the man remained there and did not budge. So, being in great distress, Mikali followed him. What more awful thing could happen to him? As they walked along he stumbled weakly and almost fell with the child. The Chinaman came to him and taking the baby in his arms, tenderly pressed it to him.

They crossed several empty lots and then the man took the little lane that led them to a sort of wooden cabin surrounded by a very small garden. He stopped before the door and clapped his hands twice. A few light steps inside and a tiny person came to open the door. Seeing the men her face reddened and then a happy smile lit it up. She made a brief curtsy to them. As Mikali remained there, hesitatingly rooted to the threshold, the Chinaman said to him: "Come in, then; do not be afraid. This is my wife."

Mikali went into the room, rather large it seemed, separated in the middle by a colored paper screen. It was all so clean and neat, though very poor looking. In the corner he noticed a wicker cradle.

"That is my baby," said the young woman, cocking her head graciously to one side and smiling to him. "He is very tiny and very beautiful; come and see."

Mikali went up closer and silently admired it. A chubby baby, but lately out of the darkness of the maternal body, slept peacefully, covered with a gold brocade cloth, like a little king.

Then the husband called his wife over, bade her sit on a straw mat, and without a word set down on her lap the little famished one, bowing deeply before her. The woman leaned over with astonishment and drew back the covering in which the child was wrapped. It appeared to her in all its skeletonic horror. She gave a cry—a cry of immense pity—then pressed the babe to her heart, giving it the breast. Then with a gesture of modesty she brought forward a flap of her robe over the milk-swollen breast and the poor, gluttonous infant suckling there.

LEAD HER LIKE
A PIGEON

JESSAMYN WEST / UNITED STATES

Jessamyn West

I T WAS DEEP IN MAY. Fingers had lifted the green strawberry leaves and had found fruit beneath them. The bees had swarmed twice. Cherries, bright as Christmas candles, hung from the trees. Wheat was heading up. The wind was from the south and sent a drift of locust blossoms like summer snow, Mattie thought, through the air.

She left her churn on the back porch and stood for a minute by the springhouse with uplifted face to see how locust snow felt; but the wind died down and no more blossoms fell, so she went back to her churning.

She counted slowly as she moved the dasher up and down. She was keeping track of the least and most strokes it took to bring butter. This at any rate was not going to be a least time. "Eighty-eight, eighty-nine . . ." Josh and Labe were putting horsehairs into the rain barrel to turn into worms. The hired man stuck his head out of the barn door, saw her, and directly pulled it in again.

"Mattie," called her mother, "get finished with thy churning and ride over to the Bents' with some rocks." Mattie could smell the rocks baking: raisins and hickory nuts all bedded down together in sweet dough.

"Lavony Bent's as queer as Dick's hatband," her mother called above the slap and gurgle of the dasher, "half Indian and a newcomer. She needs a token to show she's welcome."

Listening, Mattie slowed her churning. "Bring that butter humping," her mother said. "Thee'll have to get a soon start or it'll get dark on thee." She came to the kitchen door, rosy from the oven's heat, bringing Mattie a new-baked rock. "Day fading so soon," she said. Mattie looked at her mother because of the sadness in her voice, and felt uncertainty and sorrow herself.

"There'll be another to match it tomorrow," her mother promised. "Its equal or better, Mattie. The red sky's a sure sign."

The butter was slow coming—only five strokes short of the most she had ever counted. "Thee'd best go as thee is, Mattie."

"In this?" said Mattie.

"Who's to see?" asked her mother. "None but Bents and hoot owls at this hour."

Mattie wouldn't have named them together—hoot owls and the black-haired, brown-faced boys she had watched walking riverward with fishing poles over their shoulders.

"Once thee starts combing and changing, it'll be nightfall."

So Mattie rode as she was to the Bents', barefoot and in her blue anchor print which had faded until the anchors were almost as pale as the sea that lapped about them.

She carried the rocks in a little wooden box her mother intended to make into a footstool. So far it was only painted white, with cranes and cattails on each side. The brown cattails were set onto the box with so much paint that they curved up plump as real ones beneath Mattie's exploring thumb.

Old Polly walked like a horse in a dream—slow—slow. Tonight, a short way on the pike and then across the woodlot. Mattie ate a rock, pulled down a limb to see it spring back in place, remembered what she had heard about the Bents.

"Never seen a more comfortable sight in my life," her father called one day, and there on a padded chair was Sile Bent riding down the pike in his manure wagon, sitting and reading like a man at ease in his parlor. "Wonderful emancipation," her father said. "Thee mark it, Mattie. The spirit of man's got no limitations."

Sile Bent read and farmed. His boys, all but Gardiner, fished and farmed. "Gardiner's a reader like his pa," said Mattie's father. "Off to normal studying to be a teacher. He figures on getting shut of the manure wagon and having just the book left."

But the day she rode through meant more to Mattie than her

destination. In the woods it was warm and sheltered and the sun, setting, lay like butter on the new green leaves.

At the far edge of the woods she stopped for a minute at the old Wright place. A little white tumbling-down house, empty for years, stood there—a forgotten house; but flowers still came up about it in the patterns in which Mrs. Wright had planted them. It was a sad, beautiful sight, Mattie thought, to see flowers hands had planted growing alone in the woods with not an eye to note whether they did well or not: the snowball bush where the front gate had been, spice pinks still keeping to their circle by the steps, and white flags, gold-powdered now at sunset, by the ruined upping block. A pair of doves, as she watched, slid down from the deep shadows of the woods and wheeled about in the sunlit clearing as if coming home.

Mattie stretched a hand to them. "Thee don't act like wildings," she said.

She slipped down from fat old Polly and, carrying her box of cookies, went to pick some flags. These flowers and buildings have known people for too long, she thought, to be happy alone. They have grown away from their own kind and forgotten the language of woods and doves and long to hear household words again. To hear at bedtime a woman coming to the door for a sight of stars and saying, "There'll be rain before morning. A circle round the moon— and hark to that cock crowing. It's a sure sign." Or a man at morning, scanning the sky as he hitches up his suspenders, "A weather breeder. Have to hustle the hay in."

Mattie talked for the house and flowers to hear as she gathered the flags and laid them across the top of the cookie-filled footstool.

"If it's a dry summer I'll bring thee some water," she said. "I couldn't bear to lie abed a hot night, and you parching here. I'll carry buckets from the branch if the well's dry, and some night I'll come and light a candle in the house so it'll look like olden times. I'll sing a song in the house and it'll be like Mrs. Wright playing on her melodeon again."

"Sing now, why don't you?"

She was bending over the flags, but she wasn't frightened, the voice was so quiet. It was a young man's voice, though, and she dropped the flags in her hand onto her bare feet before she turned to face him. "No human would enjoy my singing—only maybe an old house that can't be choosy."

"I'm not choosy either."

"No, I'm on an errand to take some rocks to Lavony Bent. I only stopped to pick some flags."

"Well, I'm Gard Bent," the boy said, "and I'll walk along home with you. What's your name?"

"Martha Truth Birdwell. Only I'm mostly called Mattie."

"Martha Truth Birdwell. That's as pretty as any song. If he had known you"—and Gardiner Bent held up the book he was carrying—"he'd have written a poem called 'Martha Truth.'"

Mattie saw the name on the book. "He mostly writes of Jeans and Marys," she said. Now maybe this Bent boy wouldn't think she was a know-nothing, barefooted and talking to herself. "Thee take the rocks on to thy ma. I've dallied here so long it'll be dark going home through the woodlot."

"No, I'll walk back with you to the pike. Ma'd never forgive me if I let you go home with your box empty. The boys have been on the river this afternoon. They'll have a fine mess of catfish. Can I help you onto your horse?"

Mattie would dearly have liked being handed onto her horse had she been rightly dressed and old Polly saddled, but that would have to wait for another time. She would not be hoisted like a sack of meal, plopped barefoot onto a saddleless horse. She stood stock-still, the flags covering her feet, and said nothing.

"I'll get the rest of my books," the boy said.

While he was gone Mattie led old Polly to the upping block and settled herself as sedately as if she were riding sidesaddle, one bare foot curled daintily beneath her.

Old Polly stepped slowly along in the dusk down the back road that led to the Bents', and Gard walked beside her. There wasn't much Indian about him, Mattie thought, unless it was his black hair and his quiet, toed-in walk. But his hair wasn't Indian straight, and his eyes weren't black at all, but the color of the sandstone in a go-to-meeting watch fob. It was a pleasing face, a face she did not tire of regarding. Her eyes searched its tenderness and boldness in the May dusk.

"I thought thee was away at Vernon, studying at the normal."

"I was—but it's out. Now I'm studying to take the teachers' examinations. I've got the promise of the school at Rush Branch when I pass. That's why I come to Wrights'—to study where it's quiet. If it gets dark on you, you could see your way home by the fireflies, they're so thick," he finished, as if ashamed of telling so much of himself.

"Fireflies. Is that what thee calls lightning bugs?"

"Elsewhere they're known as fireflies."

It was full sunset before they reached the Bent place. Lavony Bent was cleaning fish on a stump at the edge of the yard. Sile Bent was on the back steps getting the last of the light onto the book he was reading. Two black-haired boys were rolling about on the ground wrestling; a third was trying to bring a tune from a homemade-looking horn. There weren't any flowers or grass about the Bents' house. The yard was trodden flat and swept clean.

Gard called out, "Ma, this is Martha Truth Birdwell come to bring you some cookies."

Mrs. Bent didn't stop her fish cleaning, but looked up kindly enough. "Light down, Martha Truth, light down. I knowed your folks years ago when we's all younger than you are now."

Sile Bent closed his book on his finger and walked over to Mattie. He was a little, plump man with a big head of red hair and a silky red mustache. "If it isn't Spring!" he said. "Spring riding a white horse and with flowers in her hands."

Mattie was too taken aback to answer, but Gard laughed. "She's got a box of cookies under the flowers, Pa."

Mattie handed the box of cookies and the white flags to him. "Spring for looks and Summer for gifts," said Sile Bent, and took a rock in two bites, shaking the crumbs from his mustache like a water-drenched dog. Mattie was afraid to talk to this strange man who carried a book as if it had been a pipe or a jackknife, and spoke of her as though she were absent, or a painted picture.

Mrs. Bent took the head from a still-quivering catfish with a single clean stroke. The boy with the horn started a tune she knew, but he couldn't get far with it. *"Lead her like a pigeon . . . Lead her like a pigeon . . ."* he played over and over. Mattie's ears ached to hear the next notes, to have the piece played through to its ending, not left broken and unfinished. Her mind hummed the tune for him:

> *Lead her like a pigeon,*
> *Bed her like a dove.*
> *Whisper when I'm near her,*
> *"You're my only love."*

But the horn could not follow. *"Lead her like a pigeon,"* it said once more, then gave up.

The wrestlers groaned and strained. They turned up the earth beneath them like a plow. A catfish leaped from the stump and swam again, most pitifully, in the dust.

"I'll have to be turning homewards." Mattie spoke suddenly. "Could I have my box? Ma's fixing to make a footstool of it."

Mrs. Bent sent Gard into the house to empty the cookies; then she lined the footstool with leaves and filled it with fish.

"There's a mess of fish for your breakfast," she said. "Tell your ma she's so clever at sharing I can't hope to keep pace with her."

As they went out of the yard, Mattie once more on old Polly, and Gard walking beside her, Sile Bent called after them, "Persephone and Pluto. Don't eat any pomegranate seeds, Martha Truth."

"What does he mean?" asked Mattie. What Mr. Bent had said didn't sound like English to her.

"Persephone was a girl," Gard said, "the goddess of spring, and Pluto, another god, stole her away to live underground with him. And while she was gone it was winter on earth."

"She's back on earth now, isn't she?" Mattie asked, watching the wink of lightning bugs among the dark leaves.

"Yes, she's back again," Gard said.

They parted at the edge of the woods, where Mattie could see the lights of home glimmering down the road. Supper was over when she brought her box of catfish into the kitchen, and the dishes half washed. "Sit down, child," her mother said, "and have thy supper. What kept thee?"

"The Bents all talk a lot," said Mattie. "It didn't seem polite to go and leave them all talking."

"They'll not be hindered by thy leaving, never fear. Eat, eat. Thy food will lose its savor."

"I can't eat," Mattie said. "I don't seem to have any relish for victuals." She got the dish towel from the rack and started drying.

"Was thee fanciful," asked her mother, who never attributed fright to anything but fancy, "crossing the woodlot?"

"No. Gardiner Bent came with me."

"The normal-school boy?"

"Yes," said Mattie. "He's learned. Flowers. Fireflies. Poetry. Gods and goddesses. It's all one to him," she declared ardently. "He can lay his tongue to anything and give thee a fact about it. Oh, he's full of facts. He's primed for an examination and knows more than he can hold in."

Mattie made the plates she dried fly through her hands like thistledown—as if they were weightless as thistles and as imperishable. Her hands were deft but they had not her mother's flashing grace, and they were silent; they could not play the tune she envied, the tinkling bell-like song of her mother's wedding ring against the china; the constant light clatter of gold against glass and silver that said, "I'm a lady grown and mistress of dishes and cupboards."

Behind were the dark woods, the shadows and bosky places and whatever might slide through them when the sun was set; here the kitchen, the stove still burning, sending a wash of light across the scrubbed floorboards, the known dishes in their rightful stacks, and Ma's ring sounding its quick song of love.

Mattie hummed a little.

"What's thee humming?" her mother asked. "Seems like I've heard it."

"'Lead Her Like a Pigeon,'" Mattie said, smiling.

"Play-party tune." Her mother held her hands above the soapy water and looked far away. "Weevily wheat. Once I was tempted to lift my foot to that."

Lift her foot! Mattie looked at her mother, the Quaker preacher, whose foot now never peeped from beneath her full and seemly skirts. Once tempted . . . The wedding-ring music began again, but Mattie was watching, not drying. A long time ago tempted; yes, there was something in the way her mother would bury her face in a cabbage rose, or run to the door when Father's spring wagon turned off the pike, that showed her the black-haired girl who once listened to that music.

"Who does the Bent boy favor, Mattie?"

"His mother, I reckon. But handsomer. He's got a face to remember," Mattie said earnestly. "A proud, learned face. He's got eyes the color of sandstones. When he walks there isn't any up and down. It's a pleasure to watch him walk."

Mattie's mother put a washed skillet on the still-warm stove to dry. "After a good heart," she said, "the least a woman can do is pick a face she fancies. Men's so much alike and many so sorry, that's the very least. If a man's face pleasures thee, that doesn't change. That is something to bank on. Thy father," she said, "has always been a comely man." She turned back to her dishpan. "Why, Mattie," she said, "what's thee crying about?"

Mattie would not say. Then she burst out: "Pushing me off. Pushing me out of my own home. Thee talking about men that way—as if I would marry one. Anxious to be shut of me." She cried into her already wet dish towel. "My own mother," she sobbed.

"Why, lovey," her mother said, and went to her, but Mattie buried her face more deeply in her dish towel and stumbled up the back stairs.

"My own mother," she wailed.

"What's the trouble? What's Mattie taking on about?"

Eliza Birdwell looked up at her husband, filling the doorway from the sitting room like a staunch timber. "Well, Jess," she said, "I think Mattie got a sudden inkling of what leaving home'll be like."

"Leaving home?" asked Jess. "Getting married? Thee think that's a crying matter, Eliza?"

Eliza looked at the face that had always pleasured her. "Thee knows I don't, Jess," she said.

Jess smiled. "Seems like," he said, "I have a recollection of some few tears thee shed those first—"

But Eliza would have none of that. "Tsk, tsk," she said, her wedding ring beating a lively tattoo against the last kettle, "tsk, tsk, Jess Birdwell."

"Thee happy, now?" Jess asked, smiling.

Eliza wouldn't say, but she hummed a little raveling of a song. "Seems as if I know that," Jess said. "A long time ago."

"Like as not," Eliza agreed, and handed him the pan to empty.

Jess went out with it, trying the tune over. "Tum-te-tum-te-tum. I can't name it," he said when he came back, "but it runs in my mind I know it."

"Thee knows it, Jess, never fear," Eliza said. She took the empty pan from him, her wedding ring making one more musical note.

GOD SEES THE TRUTH, BUT WAITS
LEO TOLSTOY / RUSSIA

IN THE TOWN of Vladimir lived a young merchant named Ivan Dmitrich Aksionov. He had two shops and a house of his own.

Aksionov was a handsome, fair-haired, curly-headed fellow, full of fun, and very fond of singing. When quite a young man he had been given to drink, and was riotous when he had had too much; but after he married he gave up drinking, except now and then.

One summer Aksionov was going to the Nizhny Fair, and as he bade good-by to his family, his wife said to him, "Ivan Dmitrich, do not start today; I have had a bad dream about you."

Aksionov laughed, and said, "You are afraid that when I get to the fair I shall go on a spree."

His wife replied: "I do not know what I am afraid of; all I know is that I had a bad dream. I dreamed you returned from the town, and when you took off your cap I saw that your hair was quite gray."

Aksionov laughed. "That's a lucky sign," said he. "See if I don't sell out all my goods, and bring you some presents from the fair."

So he said good-by to his family, and drove away.

When he had traveled halfway, he met a merchant whom he knew, and they put up at the same inn for the night. They had some tea together, and then went to bed in adjoining rooms.

It was not Aksionov's habit to sleep late, and, wishing to travel while it was still cool, he aroused his driver before dawn, and told him to put in the horses.

Then he made his way across to the landlord of the inn (who lived in a cottage at the back), paid his bill, and continued his journey.

When he had gone about twenty-five miles, he stopped for the horses to be fed. Aksionov rested awhile in the passage of the inn, then he stepped out into the porch, and, ordering a samovar to be heated, got out his guitar and began to play.

Suddenly a troika drove up with tinkling bells, and an official alighted, followed by two soldiers. He came to Aksionov and began to question him, asking him who he was and whence he came. Aksionov answered him fully, and said, "Won't you have some tea with me?" But the official went on cross-questioning him and asking him, "Where did you spend last night? Were you alone, or with a fellow merchant? Did you see the other merchant this morning? Why did you leave the inn before dawn?"

Aksionov wondered why he was asked all these questions, but he described all that had happened, and then added, "Why do you cross-question me as if I were a thief or a robber? I am traveling on business of my own, and there is no need to question me."

Then the official, calling the soldiers, said, "I am the police officer of this district, and I question you because the merchant with whom you spent last night has been found with his throat cut. We must search your things."

They entered the house. The soldiers and the police officer unstrapped Aksionov's luggage and searched it. Suddenly the officer drew a knife out of a bag, crying, "Whose knife is this?" Aksionov looked, and seeing a blood-stained knife taken from his bag, he was frightened.

"How is it there is blood on this knife?"

Aksionov tried to answer, but could hardly utter a word, and only stammered: "I—don't know—not mine."

Then the police officer said: "This morning the merchant was found in bed with his throat cut. You are the only person who could have done it. The house was locked from inside, and no one else was there. Here is this blood-stained knife in your bag, and your face and manner betray you! Tell me how you killed him, and how much money you stole?" Aksionov swore he had not done it; that he had not seen the merchant after they had had tea together; that he had no money except eight thousand rubles of his own, and that the knife was not his. But his voice was broken, his face pale, and he trembled with fear as though he were guilty.

The police officer ordered the soldiers to bind Aksionov and to put him in the cart. As they tied his feet together and flung him into the cart, Aksionov crossed himself and wept. His money and goods were taken from him, and he was sent to the nearest town and imprisoned there. Inquiries as to his character were made in Vladimir. The merchants and other inhabitants of that town said that in former days he used to drink and waste his time, but that he was a good man. Then the trial came on: he was charged with murdering a merchant from Ryazan, and robbing him of twenty thousand rubles.

His wife was in despair, and did not know what to believe. Her children were all quite small; one was a baby at her breast. Taking them all with her, she went to the town where her husband was in jail. At first she was not allowed to see him; but after much begging, she obtained permission from the officials, and was taken to him. When she saw her husband in prison dress and in chains, shut up with thieves and criminals, she fell down, and did not come to her senses for a long time. Then she drew her children to her, and sat down near him. She told him of things at home, and asked about what had happened to him. He told her all, and she asked, "What can we do now?"

"We must petition the czar not to let an innocent man perish."

His wife told him that she had sent a petition to the czar, but it had not been accepted.

Aksionov did not reply, but only looked downcast.

Then his wife said, "It was not for nothing I dreamed your hair had turned gray. You remember? You should not have started that day." And passing her fingers through his hair, she said: "Vanya dearest, tell your wife the truth; was it not you who did it?"

"So you, too, suspect me!" said Aksionov, and, hiding his face in his hands, he began to weep. Then a soldier came to say that the wife and children must go away; and Aksionov said good-by to his family for the last time.

When they were gone, Aksionov recalled what had been said, and when he remembered that his wife also had suspected him, he said to himself, "It seems that only God can know the truth; it is to Him alone we must appeal, and from Him alone expect mercy."

And Aksionov wrote no more petitions, gave up all hope, and only prayed to God.

Aksionov was condemned to be flogged and sent to the mines. So he was flogged with a knout, and when the wounds made by the knout were healed, he was driven to Siberia with other convicts.

For twenty-six years Aksionov lived as a convict in Siberia. His hair turned white as snow, and his beard grew long, thin, and gray. All his mirth went; he stooped; he walked slowly, spoke little, and never laughed, but he often prayed.

In prison Aksionov learned to make boots, and earned a little money, with which he bought *Lives of the Saints*. He read this book when there was light enough in the prison; and on Sundays in the prison church he read the lessons and sang in the choir; for his voice was still good.

The prison authorities liked Aksionov for his meekness, and his fellow prisoners respected him: they called him "Grandfather," and "The Saint." When they wanted to petition the prison authorities about anything, they always made Aksionov their spokesman, and when there were quarrels among the prisoners they came to him to put things right, and to judge the matter.

No news reached Aksionov from his home, and he did not even know if his wife and children were still alive.

One day a fresh gang of convicts came to the prison. In the evening the old prisoners collected round the new ones and asked them what towns or villages they came from, and what they were sentenced for. Among the rest Aksionov sat down near the newcomers, and listened with downcast air to what was said.

One of the new convicts, a tall, strong man of sixty, with a closely cropped gray beard, was telling the others what he had been arrested for. "Well, friends," he said, "I only took a horse that was tied to a sledge, and I was arrested and accused of stealing. I said I had only taken it to get home quicker, and had then let it go; besides, the driver was a personal friend of mine. So I said, 'It's all right.' 'No,' said they, 'you stole it.' But how or where I stole it they could not say. I once really did something wrong, and ought by rights to have come here long ago, but that time I was not found out. Now I have been sent here for nothing at all. . . . Eh, but it's lies I'm telling you; I've been to Siberia before, but I did not stay long."

"Where are you from?" asked someone.

"From Vladimir. My family are of that town. My name is Makar, and they also call me Semyonich."

Aksionov raised his head and said: "Tell me, Semyonich, do you know anything of the merchants Aksionov of Vladimir? Are they still alive?"

"Know them? Of course I do. The Aksionovs are rich, though their father is in Siberia: a sinner like ourselves, it seems! As for you, Granddad, how did you come here?"

Aksionov did not like to speak of his misfortune. He only sighed, and said, "For my sins I have been in prison these twenty-six years."

"What sins?" asked Makar Semyonich.

But Aksionov only said, "Well, well—I must have deserved it!" He would have said no more, but his companions told the newcomers how Aksionov came to be in Siberia; how someone had killed a merchant, and had put the knife among Aksionov's things, and Aksionov had been unjustly condemned.

When Makar Semyonich heard this, he looked at Aksionov, slapped his own knee, and exclaimed, "Well, this is wonderful! Really wonderful! But how old you've grown, Gran'dad!"

The others asked him why he was so surprised, and where he had seen Aksionov before; but Makar Semyonich did not reply. He only said: "It's wonderful that we should meet here, lads!"

These words made Aksionov wonder whether this man knew who had killed the merchant; so he said, "Perhaps, Semyonich, you have heard of that affair, or maybe you've seen me before?"

"How could I help hearing? The world's full of rumors. But it's a long time ago, and I've forgotten what I heard."

"Perhaps you heard who killed the merchant?" asked Aksionov.

Makar Semyonich laughed, and replied: "It must have been him in whose bag the knife was found! If someone else hid the knife there, 'He's not a thief till he's caught,' as the saying is. How could anyone put a knife into your bag while it was under your head? It would surely have woke you up."

When Aksionov heard these words, he felt sure this was the man who had killed the merchant. He rose and went away. All that night Aksionov lay awake. He felt terribly unhappy, and all sorts of images rose in his mind. There was the image of his wife as she was when he parted from her to go to the fair. He saw her as if she were present; her face and her eyes rose before him; he heard her speak and laugh. Then he saw his children, quite little, as they were at that time: one with a little cloak on, another at his mother's breast. And then he remembered himself as he used to be—young and merry. He remembered how he sat playing the guitar in the porch of the inn where he was arrested, and how free from care he had been. He saw, in his mind, the place where he was flogged, the executioner, and the people standing around; the chains, the convicts, all the twenty-six years of his prison life, and his premature old age. The thought of it all made him so wretched that he was ready to kill himself.

And it's all that villain's doing! thought Aksionov. And his anger was so great against Makar Semyonich that he longed for vengeance, even if he himself should perish for it. He kept repeating prayers all night, but could get no peace. During the day he did not go near Makar Semyonich, nor even look at him.

A fortnight passed in this way. Aksionov could not sleep at night, and was so miserable that he did not know what to do.

One night as he was walking about the prison he noticed some earth that came rolling out from under one of the shelves on which the prisoners slept. He stopped to see what it was. Suddenly Makar Semyonich crept out from under the shelf, and looked up at Aksionov with frightened face. Aksionov tried to pass without looking at him, but Makar seized his hand and told him that he had dug a hole under the wall, getting rid of the earth by putting it into his high boots, and emptying it out every day on the road, when the prisoners were driven to their work.

"Just you keep quiet, old man, and you shall get out too. If you blab, they'll flog the life out of me, but I will kill you first."

Aksionov trembled with anger as he looked at his enemy. He drew his hand away, saying, "I have no wish to escape, and you have no need to kill me; you killed me long ago! As to telling of you—I may do so or not, as God shall direct."

Next day, when the convicts were led out to work, the convoy soldiers noticed that one or other of the prisoners emptied some earth out of his boots. The prison was searched and the tunnel found. The governor came and questioned all the prisoners to find out who had dug the hole. They all denied any knowledge of it. Those who knew would not betray Makar Semyonich, knowing he would be flogged almost to death.

At last the governor turned to Aksionov, whom he knew to be a just man, and said: "You are a truthful old man; tell me, before God, who dug the hole?"

Makar Semyonich stood as if he were quite unconcerned, looking at the governor and not so much as glancing at Aksionov. Aksionov's lips and hands trembled, and for a long time he could not utter a word. He thought, Why should I screen him who ruined my life? Let him pay for what I have suffered. But if I tell, they will probably flog the life out of him, and maybe I suspect him wrongly. And, after all, what good would it be to me?

"Well, old man," repeated the governor, "tell me the truth: who has been digging under the wall?"

Aksionov glanced at Makar Semyonich, and said, "I cannot say, your honor. It is not God's will that I should tell! Do what you like with me; I am in your hands."

However much the governor tried, Aksionov would say no more, and so the matter had to be left.

That night, when Aksionov was lying on his bed and just beginning to doze, someone came quietly and sat down on his bed. He peered through the darkness and recognized Makar.

"What more do you want of me?" asked Aksionov. "Why have you come here?"

Makar Semyonich was silent.

So Aksionov sat up and said, "What do you want? Go away, or I will call the guard!"

Makar Semyonich bent close over Aksionov, and whispered, "Ivan Dmitrich, forgive me!"

"What for?" asked Aksionov.

"It was I who killed the merchant and hid the knife among your things. I meant to kill you too, but I heard a noise outside, so I hid the knife in your bag and escaped out of the window."

Aksionov was silent, and did not know what to say. Makar Semyonich slid off the bed-shelf and knelt upon the ground. "Ivan Dmitrich," said he, "forgive me! For the love of God, forgive me! I will confess that it was I who killed the merchant, and you will be released and can go to your home."

"It is easy for you to talk," said Aksionov, "but I have suffered for you these twenty-six years. Where could I go to now? . . . My wife is dead, and my children have forgotten me. I have nowhere to go. . . ."

Makar Semyonich did not rise, but beat his head on the floor. "Ivan Dmitrich, forgive me!" he cried. "When they flogged me with the knout it was not so hard to bear as it is to see you now . . . yet you had pity on me, and did not tell. For Christ's sake forgive me, wretch that I am!" And he began to sob.

When Aksionov heard him sobbing he, too, began to weep.

"God will forgive you!" said he. "Maybe I am a hundred times worse than you." And at these words his heart grew light, and the longing for home left him. He no longer had any desire to leave the prison, but only hoped for his last hour to come.

In spite of what Aksionov had said, Makar Semyonich confessed his guilt. But when the order for his release came, Aksionov was already dead.

THE WALKER-THROUGH-WALLS

MARCEL AYMÉ / FRANCE

Translated by Norman Denny

THERE LIVED in Montmartre, on the third floor of No. 75 *bis*, Rue d'Orchampt, an excellent man named Dutilleul who possessed the singular gift of being able to walk through walls without experiencing any discomfort. He wore pince-nez and a little black beard, and he was a third-grade clerk in the Ministry of Registration. In winter he went by bus to his office, and in summer he went on foot, under his bowler hat.

Dutilleul had just entered his forty-third year when his especial aptitude was revealed to him. One evening, having been caught by a brief failure of the electricity in the vestibule of his small bachelor apartment, he fumbled for a moment in the darkness, and when the lights went on again found himself on the third-floor landing. Since his front door was locked on the inside the incident caused him to reflect, and despite the protests of his reason he resolved to go in as he had come out, by walking through the wall. This strange attainment, which seemed to correspond to none of his aspirations, preyed slightly on his mind, and on the following day, a Saturday, he took advantage of the weekend to call on a neighboring doctor and put the case to him. The doctor, after convincing himself of the truth of his story, discovered upon examination that the cause of the trouble lay in the helicoidal hardening of the strangulatory wall of the thyroid vesicle. He prescribed a regime of intensive exertion, and, at the rate of two tablets a year, the absorption into the system of tetravalent reintegration powder, a mixture of rice flour and centaur's hormones.

After taking the first tablet Dutilleul put the rest away in a drawer and thought no more about them. As for the intensive exertion, his work as a civil servant was ordered by custom which did not permit of any onoooo; neither did his leisure hours, which were devoted to the daily paper and his stamp collection, call for any unreasonable expenditure of energy. So that at the end of a year his knack of walking through walls remained unimpaired; but he never made use of it, except inadvertently, having little love of adventure and being nonreceptive to the lures of the imagination. It did not even occur to him to enter his own apartment otherwise than by the door, after duly turning the key in the lock. Perhaps he would have grown old in his sedate habits, without ever being tempted to put his gift to the test, had not an extraordinary event suddenly occurred to revolutionize his existence. M. Mouron, the head of his subsection at the ministry, was transferred to other duties and replaced by a M. Lécuyer, who was brisk of speech and wore a small military mustache. From the first day this newcomer manifested the liveliest disapproval of the pince-nez which Dutilleul wore attached to a short chain, and of his little black beard, and he elected to treat him as a tiresome and not over-clean elderly encumbrance. Worst of all, he saw fit to introduce into the work of his subsection certain far-reaching reforms which were well calculated to trouble the peace of mind of his subordinate. Dutilleul was accustomed to begin his letters with the following formula: "With reference to your esteemed communication of the such-and-such instant, and having regard to our previous exchange of letters on this subject, I have the honor to inform you . . ." For which M. Lécuyer proposed to substitute a more transatlantic form of words: "Yours of the such-and-such. I beg to state . . ." Dutilleul could not accustom himself to this epistolary terseness. Despite himself he reverted with a machinelike obstinacy to the traditional form, thereby incurring the increasing animosity of his superior. The atmosphere of the Ministry of Registration became almost oppressive to him. He went apprehensively to work in the morning, and at night, after going to bed, he would often lie brooding for as much as a quarter of an hour before falling asleep.

Outraged by reactionary stubbornness which threatened to under-mine the success of his reforms, M. Lécuyer relegated Dutilleul to a small and somber room, scarcely more than a cupboard, next door to his own office. It was entered by a low, narrow door giving on to the corridor, and which bore in capital letters the legend: BACK FILES. Dutilleul resignedly acquiesced in this unprecedented humilia-tion, but when he read some more than usually sanguinary story in his newspaper he found himself dreaming that M. Lécuyer was the victim.

One day his chief burst into his cupboard brandishing a letter and bellowing:

"This must be done again! I insist upon your rewriting this un-speakable document which is a disgrace to my subsection!"

Dutilleul was about to protest, but in a voice of thunder M. Lécuyer informed him that he was a routine-besotted mole, and crumpling the letter flung it in his face. Dutilleul was a modest man, but proud. Left alone in his cupboard he felt his temperature rising, and suddenly he was seized with an inspiration. Leaving his seat he passed into the wall between his chief's room and his own, but he did so with caution, so that only his head emerged on the other side. M. Lécuyer, seated again at his desk, his pen still quivering, was in the act of striking out a comma from the text of a letter submitted by a subordinate for his approval, when he heard the sound of a cough in his room. Looking up he perceived with unspeakable dismay the head of Dutilleul, seemingly affixed to the wall like a trophy of the chase. But this head was alive. Through the pince-nez, with their length of chain, the eyes glared balefully at him. What is more, the head spoke.

"Sir," it said, "you are a scoundrel, a blockhead and a mountebank."

M. Lécuyer, his mouth gaping with horror, had difficulty in with-drawing his gaze from the apparition. At length he heaved himself out of his chair, plunged into the corridor and flung open the door of the cupboard. Dutilleul, pen in hand, was seated in his accustomed place, in an attitude of tranquil and devoted industry. M. Lécuyer stared at him for some time in silence, and then, after muttering a few words, returned to his office. Scarcely had he resumed his seat than the head again appeared on the wall.

"Sir, you are a scoundrel, a blockhead and a mountebank."

In the course of that day alone the terrifying head manifested itself twenty-three times, and on the following days it appeared with a similar frequency. Having acquired a certain skill at the game, Dutilleul was no longer content merely to abuse his chief. He uttered obscure threats, for example proclaiming in a sepulchral voice punctuated with truly demoniac laughter:

"The werewolf is here, the end is near! (*laughter*) Flesh creeps and terror fills the air! (*laughter*)"

Hearing which, the unhappy subsection chief grew yet more pale, yet more breathless, while the hairs stood rigid on his head and the sweat of anguish trickled down his spine. During the first day he lost a pound in weight. In the course of the ensuing week, besides almost visibly melting away, he developed a tendency to eat soup with a fork and to greet the guardians of the law with a military salute. At the beginning of the second week an ambulance called at his dwelling and bore him off to a mental home.

Being thus delivered from the tyranny of M. Lécuyer, Dutilleul could return to his cherished formula—"With reference to your esteemed communication of the such-and-such . . ." Yet he was not satisfied. There was now a yearning in him, a new, imperious impulse which was nothing less than the need to walk through walls. It is true that he had ample opportunities of doing so, in his apartment for example, of which he did not neglect to avail himself. But the man possessing brilliant gifts cannot long be content to squander them on trifles. Moreover, the act of walking through a wall cannot be said to constitute an end in itself. It is a mere beginning, the start of an adventure calling for an outcome, a realization—calling, in short, for a reward. Dutilleul was well aware of this. He felt an inner need to expand, a growing desire to fulfill and surpass himself, and a restless hankering which was in some sort the call of the other side of the wall. But an objective, alas, was lacking. He sought inspiration in his daily paper, particularly in the columns devoted to politics and sport, both of which seemed to him commendable activities; but perceiving finally that these offered no outlet for persons capable of walking through walls, he fell back on the crime columns, which proved to be rich in suggestion.

Dutilleul's first burglary took place in a large credit establishment on the right bank of the Seine. After passing through a dozen walls and partitions he thrust his hand into a number of strongboxes, filled his pockets with bank notes and before leaving signed his crime in red chalk, using the pseudonym of "The Werewolf," adorned with a handsome flourish which was reproduced in all the papers next day. By the end of a week the Werewolf had achieved an extraordinary celebrity. The heart of the public went out unreservedly to this phenomenal burglar who so prettily mocked the police. He drew attention to himself each night by a fresh exploit carried out at the expense, now of a bank, now of a jeweler's shop or of some wealthy individual. In Paris, as in the provinces, there was no woman with romance in her heart who had not a fervent desire to belong body and soul to the terrible Werewolf. After the theft of the famous Burdigala diamond and the robbing of the Crédit Municipal, which occurred during the same week, the enthusiasm of the crowd reached the point of delirium. The Minister of the Interior was compelled to resign, dragging with him in his fall the Minister of Registration. Nevertheless, Dutilleul, now one of the richest men in Paris, never failed to arrive punctually at the office, and was spoken of as a candidate for the *palmes académiques*. And every morning, at the Ministry of Registration, he had the pleasure of hearing his colleagues discuss his exploits of the previous night. "This Werewolf," they said, "is a stupendous fellow, a superman, a genius." Hearing such praise, Dutilleul turned pink with embarrassment and behind the pince-nez his eyes shone with friendship and gratitude. A day came when the atmosphere of sympathy so overwhelmed him that he felt he could keep the secret no longer. Surveying with a last twinge of shyness the group of his colleagues arrayed round a newspaper containing an account of the robbery of the Banque de France, he said in a diffident voice: "As a matter of fact, *I'm* the Werewolf." The confession was received with a huge and interminable burst of laughter, and the nickname of "Werewolf" was at once mockingly bestowed on him. That evening, at the time of leaving the ministry, he was the object of endless pleasantries on the part of his fellow workers, and life seemed to him less rosy.

A few days later the Werewolf allowed himself to be caught by a police patrol in a jeweler's shop on the Rue de la Paix. He had inscribed his signature on the safe and was singing a drinking song while smashing windows with a massive gold tankard. It would have been a simple matter for him to escape by merely slipping through a wall, but everything leads one to suppose that he wished to be arrested, probably for the sole purpose of confounding the colleagues whose incredulity had so mortified him. These were indeed greatly astonished when the newspapers next day published Dutilleul's picture on the front page. They bitterly regretted having underrated their inspired confrere, and did him homage by growing little beards. Some of them, carried away by remorse and admiration, went so far as to try to get their hands on the wallets or watches of their friends and relations.

It may well be considered that to allow oneself to be caught by the police in order to impress a few colleagues is to display an extreme frivolity unworthy of an eminent public figure; but the apparent exercise of free will plays little part in a resolution of this kind. In sacrificing his liberty Dutilleul thought he was yielding to an arrogant desire for revenge, whereas in fact he was merely following the ineluctable course of his destiny. No man who walks through walls can consider his career even moderately fulfilled if he has not had at least one taste of prison. When Dutilleul entered the precincts of the Santé he had a feeling of being the spoiled child of fortune. The thickness of the walls was to him a positive delight. On the very day following his incarceration the warders discovered to their stupefaction that he had driven a nail into the wall of his cell and had hung from it a gold watch belonging to the prison governor. He either could not or would not disclose how the article had come into his possession. The watch was restored to its owner and the next

day was again found at the bedside of the Werewolf, together with
the first volume of *The Three Musketeers*, borrowed from the governor's
library. The whole staff of the prison was on edge. The warders
complained, moreover, of receiving kicks on the bottom coming from
some inexplicable source. It seemed that the walls no longer had ears
but had feet instead. The detention of the Werewolf had lasted a
week when the governor, entering his office one morning, found the
following letter on his desk:

SIR:

    With reference to our interview of the 17th instant, and having
regard to your general instruction of May 15th of last year, I have
the honor to inform you that I have just concluded my perusal of
The Three Musketeers, Vol. II, and that I propose to escape tonight
between 11:25 p.m. and 11:35 p.m.

        I beg to remain, Sir,

            With expressions of the deepest respect,

                Your obedient servant,

                  THE WEREWOLF.

Despite the extremely close watch kept upon him that night,
Dutilleul escaped at 11:30. The news, when it became known to the
public on the following day, occasioned an outburst of tremendous
enthusiasm. Nevertheless, Dutilleul, having achieved another burglary
which set the seal on his popularity, seemed to have little desire to
hide himself and walked freely about Montmartre without taking any
precautions. Three days after his escape he was arrested in the Café
du Rêve on the Rue Clignancourt, where he was drinking a *vin blanc
citron* with a few friends.

Being taken back to the Santé and secured behind triple locks in
a gloomy dungeon, the Werewolf left it the same evening and passed
the night in the guest room of the governor's apartment. At about
nine the next morning he rang for his *petit déjeuner* and allowed
himself to be captured in bed, without offering any resistance, by the
warders summoned for the purpose. The outraged governor caused
a special guard to be posted at the door of his cell and put him on
bread and water. Toward midday he went out and had lunch at a

neighboring restaurant, and, having finished his coffee, telephoned the governor as follows:

"My dear Governor, I am covered with confusion. When I left the prison a short time ago I omitted to take your wallet, so that I am now penniless in a restaurant. Will you be so good as to send someone to pay my bill?"

The governor hurried to the spot in person, and so far forgot himself as to utter threats and abuse. Wounded in his deepest feelings, Dutilleul escaped the following night, never to return. This time he took the precaution of shaving his black tuft of beard and substituting horn-rimmed spectacles for the pince-nez and chain. A sports cap and a suit of plus fours in a loud check completed his transformation. He established himself in a small apartment in the Avenue Junot where, during the period preceding his first arrest, he had installed a part of his furniture and the possessions which he most valued. The notoriety attaching to his name was beginning to weary him, and since his stay in the Santé he had become rather blasé in the matter of walking through walls. The thickest, the proudest of them seemed to him no more than the flimsiest of screens, and he dreamed of thrusting his way into the very heart of some massive pyramid. While meditating on the project of a trip to Egypt he lived the most tranquil of lives, divided between his stamp collection, the cinema and prolonged strolls about Montmartre. So complete was his metamorphosis that, clean-shaven and horn-rimmed-spectacled, he passed his best friends in the street without being recognized. Only the painter, Gen Paul, whom no detail escaped of any change in the physiognomy of an old resident of the quarter, succeeded in the end in penetrating his disguise. Finding himself face-to-face with Dutilleul at the corner of the Rue de l'Abreuvoir, he could not restrain himself from remarking in his crude slang:

"*Dis donc, je vois que tu t'es miché en gigolpince pour tétarer ceux de la sûrepige*"—which roughly means, in common speech: "I see you've got yourself up like a man of fashion to baffle the inspectors of the Sûreté."

"Ah!" murmured Dutilleul. "So you've recognized me!"

He was perturbed by this and resolved to hasten his departure for

Egypt. But it was on the afternoon of this very day that he fell in love with a ravishing blonde whom he twice encountered in the Rue Lepic, at a quarter of an hour's interval. He instantly forgot his stamp collection, Egypt and the Pyramids. The blonde, for her part, had gazed at him with considerable interest. Nothing stirs the imagination of the young women of the present day more than plus fours and horn-rimmed spectacles: they have a flavor of film scripts, they set one dreaming of cocktails and Californian nights. Unfortunately the lady—so Dutilleul was informed by Gen Paul—was married to a violent and jealous man. This suspicious husband, who himself led a dissolute life, regularly forsook his wife between the hours of ten at night and four in the morning; but before doing so he locked her in her bedroom and padlocked all the shutters. During the daytime he kept a close eye on her, even going so far on occasions as to follow her as she went along the streets of Montmartre.

"Always snooping, you see. He's one of those coarse-minded so-and-sos that don't stand for anyone poaching on their preserves."

But Gen Paul's warning served only to inflame Dutilleul's ardor. Encountering the young woman in the Rue Tholozé, on the following day, he boldly followed her into a *crémerie*, and while she was awaiting her turn to be served he told her of his respectful passion and that he knew all—the villainous husband, the locked door and the padlocked shutters—but that he proposed nevertheless to visit her that same evening. The blonde flushed scarlet while the milk jug trembled in her hand. Her eyes melting with tenderness she murmured weakly: "Alas, Monsieur, it is impossible."

On the evening of that glorious day, toward ten o'clock, Dutilleul was at his post in the Rue Norvins, keeping watch on a solid outer wall behind which was situated a small house of which he could see nothing except the weathercock and the chimney stack. A door in this wall opened and a man emerged who, after locking it carefully behind him, went down the hill toward the Avenue Junot. Dutilleul waited until he saw him vanish in the far distance at the turn of the road, after which he counted ten. Then he darted forward, skipped lightly with an athlete's stride into the wall, and running through all obstacles penetrated into the bedroom of the beautiful captive.

She received him with transports of delight and they made love till an advanced hour.

The next day Dutilleul had the vexation to suffer from a severe headache. It was a matter of no importance, and he had no intention of failing to keep his rendezvous for so little. However, chancing to discover a few tablets scattered at the bottom of a drawer, he swallowed one in the morning and another in the afternoon. By the evening his headache was bearable, and his state of exaltation caused him to forget it. The young woman was awaiting him with all the impatience to which her recollections of the previous evening had given rise, and that night they made love until three in the morning. Upon his departure, as he passed through the inner and outer walls of the house, Dutilleul had a sense of unaccustomed friction at his hips and shoulders. However, he did not think this worthy of any particular attention. Only when he came to penetrate the surrounding wall did he become definitely aware of a feeling of resistance. He seemed to be moving in a substance that was still fluid, but which was thickening so that it seemed to gain in consistency with every movement that he made. Having succeeded in thrusting the whole of his body into the thickness of the wall, he found that he could no longer progress, and in terror he recalled the two tablets he had taken during the day. These tablets, which he had mistaken for aspirin, had in reality contained the tetravalent reintegration powder prescribed by the doctor a year before. The medicine, aided by his intensive exertions, was suddenly having its intended effect.

Dutilleul was, as it were, petrified in the interior of the wall. He is there to this day, incorporated in the stone. Night birds descending the Rue Norvins at the hour when the clamor of Paris has died down, may sometimes hear a stifled voice seeming to come from beyond the tomb, which they take to be the moaning of the wind as it whistles at the crossroads of the Butte. It is Werewolf Dutilleul mourning for his glorious career and his too-brief love. Occasionally on a winter's night the painter, Gen Paul, taking down his guitar, ventures forth into the echoing solitude of the Rue Norvins to console the unhappy prisoner with a song; and the notes, flying from his benumbed fingers, pierce to the heart of the stone like drops of moonlight.

THE LOTTERY

SHIRLEY JACKSON / UNITED STATES

Shirley Jackson

THE MORNING of June 27th was clear and sunny, with the fresh warmth of a full-summer day; the flowers were blossoming profusely and the grass was richly green. The people of the village began to gather in the square, between the post office and the bank, around ten o'clock; in some towns there were so many people that the lottery took two days and had to be started on June 26th, but in this village, where there were only about three hundred people, the whole lottery took less than two hours, so it could begin at ten o'clock in the morning and still be through in time to allow the villagers to get home for noon dinner.

The children assembled first, of course. School was recently over for the summer, and the feeling of liberty sat uneasily on most of them; they tended to gather together quietly for a while before they broke into boisterous play, and their talk was still of the classroom and the teacher, of books and reprimands. Bobby Martin had already stuffed his pockets full of stones, and the other boys soon followed his example, selecting the smoothest and roundest stones; Bobby and Harry Jones and Dickie Delacroix—the villagers pronounced this name "Dellacroy"—eventually made a great pile of stones in one corner of the square and guarded it against the raids of the other boys. The girls stood aside, talking among themselves, looking over their shoulders at the boys, and the very small children rolled in the dust or clung to the hands of their older brothers or sisters.

Soon the men began to gather, surveying their own children, speaking of planting and rain, tractors and taxes. They stood together, away from the pile of stones in the corner, and their jokes were quiet and they smiled rather than laughed. The women, wearing faded housedresses and sweaters, came shortly after their menfolk. They greeted one another and exchanged bits of gossip as they went to join their husbands. Soon the women, standing by their husbands, began to call to their children, and the children came reluctantly, having to be called four or five times. Bobby Martin ducked under his mother's grasping hand and ran, laughing, back to the pile of stones. His father spoke up sharply, and Bobby came quickly and took his place between his father and his oldest brother.

The lottery was conducted—as were the square dances, the teen-age club, the Halloween program—by Mr. Summers, who had time and energy to devote to civic activities. He was a round-faced, jovial man and he ran the coal business, and people were sorry for him, because he had no children and his wife was a scold. When he arrived in the square, carrying the black wooden box, there was a murmur of conversation among the villagers, and he waved and called, "Little late today, folks." The postmaster, Mr. Graves, followed him, carrying a three-legged stool, and the stool was put in the center of the square and Mr. Summers set the black box down on it. The villagers kept their distance, leaving a space between themselves and the stool, and when Mr. Summers said, "Some of you fellows want to give me a hand?" there was a hesitation before two men, Mr. Martin and his oldest son, Baxter, came forward to hold the box steady on the stool while Mr. Summers stirred up the papers inside it.

The original paraphernalia for the lottery had been lost long ago, and the black box now resting on the stool had been put into use even before Old Man Warner, the oldest man in town, was born. Mr. Summers spoke frequently to the villagers about making a new box, but no one liked to upset even as much tradition as was represented by the black box. There was a story that the present box had been made with some pieces of the box that had preceded it, the one that had been constructed when the first people settled down to make a village here. Every year, after the lottery, Mr. Summers began talking again about a new box, but every year the subject was allowed to fade off without anything's being done. The black box grew shabbier each year; by now it was no longer completely black but splintered badly along one side to show the original wood color, and in some places faded or stained.

Mr. Martin and his oldest son, Baxter, held the black box securely on the stool until Mr. Summers had stirred the papers thoroughly with his hand. Because so much of the ritual had been forgotten or discarded, Mr. Summers had been successful in having slips of paper substituted for the chips of wood that had been used for generations. Chips of wood, Mr. Summers had argued, had been all very well when the village was tiny, but now that the population was more than three hundred and likely to keep on growing, it was necessary to use something that would fit more easily into the black box. The night before the lottery, Mr. Summers and Mr. Graves made up the slips of paper and put them in the box, and it was then taken to the safe of Mr. Summers's coal company and locked up until Mr. Summers was ready to take it to the square next morning. The rest of the year, the box was put away, sometimes one place, sometimes another; it had spent one year in Mr. Graves's barn and another year underfoot in the post office, and sometimes it was set on a shelf in the Martin grocery and left there.

There was a great deal of fussing to be done before Mr. Summers declared the lottery open. There were the lists to make up—of heads of families, heads of households in each family, members of each household in each family. There was the proper swearing-in of Mr. Summers by the postmaster, as the official of the lottery; at one time, some people remembered, there had been a recital of some sort, performed by the official of the lottery, a perfunctory, tuneless chant that had been rattled off duly each year; some people believed that the official of the lottery used to stand just so when he said or sang it, others believed that he was supposed to walk among the people, but years and years ago this part of the ritual had been allowed to lapse. There had been, also, a ritual salute, which the official of the lottery had had to use in addressing each person who came up to draw from the box, but this also had changed with time, until now it was felt necessary only for the official to speak to each person approaching. Mr. Summers was very good at all this; in his clean white shirt and blue jeans, with one hand resting carelessly on the black box, he seemed very proper and important as he talked interminably to Mr. Graves and the Martins.

Just as Mr. Summers finally left off talking and turned to the assembled villagers, Mrs. Hutchinson came hurriedly along the path to the square, her sweater thrown over her shoulders, and slid into place in the back of the crowd. "Clean forgot what day it was," she said to Mrs. Delacroix, who stood next to her, and they both laughed softly. "Thought my old man was out back stacking wood," Mrs. Hutchinson went on, "and then I looked out the window and the kids was gone, and then I remembered it was the twenty-seventh and came a-running." She dried her hands on her apron, and Mrs. Delacroix said, "You're in time, though. They're still talking away up there."

Mrs. Hutchinson craned her neck to see through the crowd and found her husband and children standing near the front. She tapped Mrs. Delacroix on the arm as a farewell and began to make her way through the crowd. The people separated good-humoredly to let her through; two or three people said, in voices just loud enough to be heard across the crowd, "Here comes your Missus, Hutchinson," and "Bill, she made it after all." Mrs. Hutchinson reached her husband, and Mr. Summers, who had been waiting, said cheerfully, "Thought we were going to have to get on without you, Tessie." Mrs. Hutchinson said, grinning, "Wouldn't have me leave m'dishes in the sink, now, would you, Joe?" and soft laughter ran through the crowd as the people stirred back into position after Mrs. Hutchinson's arrival.

"Well, now," Mr. Summers said soberly, "guess we better get started, get this over with, so's we can go back to work. Anybody ain't here?"

"Dunbar," several people said. "Dunbar, Dunbar."

Mr. Summers consulted his list. "Clyde Dunbar," he said. "That's right. He's broke his leg, hasn't he? Who's drawing for him?"

"Me, I guess," a woman said, and Mr. Summers turned to look at her. "Wife draws for her husband," Mr. Summers said. "Don't you have a grown boy to do it for you, Janey?" Although Mr. Summers and everyone else in the village knew the answer perfectly well, it was the business of the official of the lottery to ask such questions formally. Mr. Summers waited with an expression of polite interest while Mrs. Dunbar answered.

"Horace's not but sixteen yet," Mrs. Dunbar said regretfully. "Guess I gotta fill in for the old man this year."

"Right," Mr. Summers said. He made a note on the list he was holding. Then he asked, "Watson boy drawing this year?"

A tall boy in the crowd raised his hand. "Here," he said. "I'm drawing for m'mother and me." He blinked his eyes nervously and ducked his head as several voices in the crowd said things like "Good fellow, Jack," and "Glad to see your mother's got a man to do it."

"Well," Mr. Summers said, "guess that's everyone. Old Man Warner make it?"

"Here," a voice said, and Mr. Summers nodded.

A SUDDEN HUSH fell on the crowd as Mr. Summers cleared his throat and looked at the list. "All ready?" he called. "Now, I'll read the names—heads of families first—and the men come up and take a paper out of the box. Keep the paper folded in your hand without looking at it until everyone has had a turn. Everything clear?"

The people had done it so many times that they only half listened to the directions; most of them were quiet, wetting their lips, not looking around. Then Mr. Summers raised one hand high and said, "Adams." A man disengaged himself from the crowd and came forward. "Hi, Steve," Mr. Summers said, and Mr. Adams said, "Hi, Joe." They grinned at one another humorlessly and nervously. Then Mr. Adams reached into the black box and took out a folded paper. He held it firmly by one corner as he turned and went hastily back to his place in the crowd, where he stood a little apart from his family, not looking down at his hand.

"Allen," Mr. Summers said. "Anderson. . . . Bentham."

"Seems like there's no time at all between lotteries anymore," Mrs. Delacroix said to Mrs. Graves in the back row. "Seems like we got through with the last one only last week."

"Time sure goes fast," Mrs. Graves said.

"Clark. . . . Delacroix."

"There goes my old man," Mrs. Delacroix said. She held her breath while her husband went forward.

"Dunbar," Mr. Summers said, and Mrs. Dunbar went steadily to the box while one of the women said, "Go on, Janey," and another said, "There she goes."

"We're next," Mrs. Graves said. She watched while Mr. Graves came around from the side of the box, greeted Mr. Summers gravely, and selected a slip of paper from the box. By now, all through the crowd there were men holding the small folded papers in their large hands, turning them over and over nervously. Mrs. Dunbar and her two sons stood together, Mrs. Dunbar holding the slip of paper.

"Harburt. . . . Hutchinson."

"Get up there, Bill," Mrs. Hutchinson said, and the people near her laughed.

"Jones."

"They do say," Mr. Adams said to Old Man Warner, who stood next to him, "that over in the north village they're talking of giving up the lottery."

Old Man Warner snorted. "Pack of crazy fools," he said. "Listening to the young folks, nothing's good enough for *them*. Next thing you know, they'll be wanting to go back to living in caves, nobody work anymore, live *that* way for a while. Used to be a saying about 'Lottery in June, corn be heavy soon.' First thing you know, we'd all be eating stewed chickweed and acorns. There's *always* been a lottery," he added petulantly. "Bad enough to see young Joe Summers up there joking with everybody."

"Some places have already quit lotteries," Mrs. Adams said.

"Nothing but trouble in *that*," Old Man Warner said stoutly. "Pack of young fools."

"Martin." And Bobby Martin watched his father go forward. "Overdyke. . . . Percy."

"I wish they'd hurry," Mrs. Dunbar said to her older son. "I wish they'd hurry."

"They're almost through," her son said.

"You get ready to run tell Dad," Mrs. Dunbar said.

Mr. Summers called his own name and then stepped forward

precisely and selected a slip from the box. Then he called, "Warner."

"Seventy-seventh year I been in the lottery," Old Man Warner said as he went through the crowd. "Seventy-seventh time."

"Watson." The tall boy came awkwardly through the crowd. Someone said, "Don't be nervous, Jack," and Mr. Summers said, "Take your time, son."

"Zanini."

AFTER THAT, there was a long pause, a breathless pause, until Mr. Summers, holding his slip of paper in the air, said, "All right, fellows." For a minute, no one moved, and then all the slips of paper were opened. Suddenly, all the women began to speak at once, saying, "Who is it?" "Who's got it?" "Is it the Dunbars?" "Is it the Watsons?" Then the voices began to say, "It's Hutchinson. It's Bill." "Bill Hutchinson's got it."

"Go tell your father," Mrs. Dunbar said to her older son.

People began to look around to see the Hutchinsons. Bill Hutchinson was standing quiet, staring down at the paper in his hand. Suddenly, Tessie Hutchinson shouted to Mr. Summers. "You didn't give him time enough to take any paper he wanted. I saw you. It wasn't fair!"

"Be a good sport, Tessie," Mrs. Delacroix called, and Mrs. Graves said, "All of us took the same chance."

"Shut up, Tessie," Bill Hutchinson said.

"Well, everyone," Mr. Summers said, "that was done pretty fast, and now we've got to be hurrying a little more to get done in time." He consulted his next list. "Bill," he said, "you draw for the Hutchinson family. You got any other households in the Hutchinsons?"

"There's Don and Eva," Mrs. Hutchinson yelled. "Make *them* take their chance!"

"Daughters draw with their husbands' families, Tessie," Mr. Summers said gently. "You know that as well as anyone else."

"It wasn't *fair*," Tessie said.

"I guess not, Joe," Bill Hutchinson said regretfully. "My daughter draws with her husband's family, that's only fair. And I've got no other family except the kids."

"Then, as far as drawing for families is concerned, it's you," Mr. Summers said in explanation, "and as far as drawing for households is concerned, that's you, too. Right?"

"Right," Bill Hutchinson said.

"How many kids, Bill?" Mr. Summers asked formally.

"Three," Bill Hutchinson said. "There's Bill, Jr., and Nancy, and little Dave. And Tessie and me."

"All right, then," Mr. Summers said. "Harry, you got their tickets back?"

Mr. Graves nodded and held up the slips of paper. "Put them in the box, then," Mr. Summers directed. "Take Bill's and put it in."

"I think we ought to start over," Mrs. Hutchinson said, as quietly as she could. "I tell you it wasn't *fair*. You didn't give him time enough to choose. *Every*body saw that."

Mr. Graves had selected the five slips and put them in the box, and he dropped all the papers but those onto the ground, where the breeze caught them and lifted them off.

"Listen, everybody," Mrs. Hutchinson was saying to the people around her.

"Ready, Bill?" Mr. Summers asked, and Bill Hutchinson, with one quick glance around at his wife and children, nodded.

"Remember," Mr. Summers said, "take the slips and keep them folded until each person has taken one. Harry, you help little Dave." Mr. Graves took the hand of the little boy, who came willingly with him up to the box. "Take a paper out of the box, Davy," Mr. Summers said. Davy put his hand into the box and laughed. "Take just *one* paper," Mr. Summers said. "Harry, you hold it for him." Mr. Graves took the child's hand and removed the folded paper from the tight fist and held it while little Dave stood next to him and looked up at him wonderingly.

"Nancy next," Mr. Summers said. Nancy was twelve, and her school friends breathed heavily as she went forward, switching her skirt, and took a slip daintily from the box. "Bill, Jr.," Mr. Summers said, and Billy, his face red and his feet overlarge, nearly knocked the box over as he got a paper out. "Tessie," Mr. Summers said. She hesitated for a minute, looking around defiantly, and then set her lips and went up to the box. She snatched a paper out and held it behind her.

"Bill," Mr. Summers said, and Bill Hutchinson reached into the box and felt around, bringing his hand out at last with the slip of paper in it.

The crowd was quiet. A girl whispered, "I hope it's not Nancy," and the sound of the whisper reached the edges of the crowd.

"It's not the way it used to be," Old Man Warner said clearly. "People ain't the way they used to be."

"All right," Mr. Summers said. "Open the papers. Harry, you open little Dave's."

Mr. Graves opened the slip of paper and there was a general sigh through the crowd as he held it up and everyone could see that it was blank. Nancy and Bill, Jr., opened theirs at the same time, and both beamed and laughed, turning around to the crowd and holding their slips of paper above their heads.

"Tessie," Mr. Summers said. There was a pause, and then Mr. Summers looked at Bill Hutchinson, and Bill unfolded his paper and showed it. It was blank.

"It's Tessie," Mr. Summers said, and his voice was hushed. "Show us her paper, Bill."

Bill Hutchinson went over to his wife and forced the slip of paper out of her hand. It had a black spot on it, the black spot Mr. Summers had made the night before with the heavy pencil in the coal-company office. Bill Hutchinson held it up, and there was a stir in the crowd.

"All right, folks," Mr. Summers said. "Let's finish quickly."

Although the villagers had forgotten the ritual and lost the original black box, they still remembered to use stones. The pile of stones the boys had made earlier was ready; there were stones on the ground with the blowing scraps of paper that had come out of the box. Mrs. Delacroix selected a stone so large she had to pick it up with both hands and turned to Mrs. Dunbar. "Come on," she said. "Hurry up."

Mrs. Dunbar had small stones in both hands, and she said, gasping for breath, "I can't run at all. You'll have to go ahead and I'll catch up with you."

The children had stones already, and someone gave little Davy Hutchinson a few pebbles.

Tessie Hutchinson was in the center of a cleared space by now, and she held her hands out desperately as the villagers moved in on her. "It isn't fair," she said. A stone hit her on the side of the head.

Old Man Warner was saying, "Come on, come on, everyone." Steve Adams was in the front of the crowd of villagers, with Mrs. Graves beside him.

"It isn't fair, it isn't right," Mrs. Hutchinson screamed, and then they were upon her.

THE McWILLIAMSES
AND THE BURGLAR ALARM
MARK TWAIN / UNITED STATES

Mark Twain

THE CONVERSATION DRIFTED smoothly and pleasantly along from weather to crops, from crops to literature, from literature to scandal, from scandal to religion; then took a random jump, and landed on the subject of burglar alarms. And now for the first time Mr. McWilliams showed feeling. Whenever I perceive this sign on this man's dial, I comprehend it, and lapse into silence, and give him opportunity to unload his heart. Said he, with but ill-controlled emotion:

I DO NOT GO one single cent on burglar alarms, Mr. Twain—not a single cent—and I will tell you why. When we were finishing our house, we found we had a little cash left over, on account of the plumber not knowing it. I was for enlightening the heathen with it, for I was always unaccountably down on the heathen somehow; but Mrs. McWilliams said no, let's have a burglar alarm. I agreed to this compromise. I will explain that whenever I want a thing, and Mrs. McWilliams wants another thing, and we decide upon the thing that Mrs. McWilliams wants—as we always do—she calls that a compromise.

Very well: the man came up from New York and put in the alarm, and charged three hundred and twenty-five dollars for it, and said we could sleep without uneasiness now. So we did for a while—say a month. Then one night we smelled smoke, and I was advised to get up and see what the matter was. I lit a candle, and started toward the stairs, and met a burglar coming out of a room with a basket of tinware, which he had mistaken for solid silver in the dark. He was smoking a pipe. I said, "My friend, we do not allow smoking in this room."

He said he was a stranger, and could not be expected to know the rules of the house: said he had been in many houses just as good as this one, and it had never been objected to before. He added that as far as his experience went, such rules had never been considered to apply to burglars, anyway.

I said: "Smoke along, then, if it is the custom, though I think that the conceding of a privilege to a burglar which is denied to a bishop is a conspicuous sign of the looseness of the times. But waiving all that, what business have you to be entering this house in this furtive and clandestine way, without ringing the burglar alarm?"

He looked confused and ashamed, and said, with embarrassment: "I beg a thousand pardons. I did not know you had a burglar alarm, else I would have rung it. I beg you will not mention it where my parents may hear of it, for they are old and feeble, and such a seemingly wanton breach of the hallowed conventionalities of our Christian civilization might all too rudely sunder the frail bridge which hangs darkling between the pale and evanescent present and the solemn great deeps of the eternities. May I trouble you for a match?"

I said: "Your sentiments do you honor, but if you will allow me to say it, metaphor is not your best hold. Spare your thigh; this kind light only on the box, and seldom there, in fact, if my experience may be trusted. But to return to business: how did you get in here?"

"Through a second-story window."

It was even so. I redeemed the tinware at pawnbroker's rates, less cost of advertising, bade the burglar good-night, closed the window after him, and retired to headquarters to report. Next morning we sent for the burglar-alarm man, and he came up and explained that the reason the alarm did not "go off" was that no part of the house but the first floor was attached to the alarm. This was simply idiotic; one might as well have no armor on at all in battle as to have it only on his legs. The expert now put the whole second story on the alarm, charged three hundred dollars for it, and went his way. By and by, one night, I found a burglar in the third story, about to start down a ladder with a lot of miscellaneous property. My first impulse was to crack his head with a billiard cue; but my second was to refrain from this attention, because he was between me and the cue rack. The second impulse was plainly the soundest, so I refrained, and proceeded to compromise. I redeemed the property at former rates, after deducting ten percent, for the use of ladder, it being my ladder, and next day we sent down for the expert once more, and had the third story attached to the alarm, for three hundred dollars.

By this time the "annunciator" had grown to formidable dimensions. It had forty-seven tags on it, marked with the names of the various rooms and chimneys, and it occupied the space of an ordinary wardrobe. The gong was the size of a washbowl, and was placed above the head of our bed. There was a wire from the house to the coachman's quarters in the stable, and a noble gong alongside his pillow.

We should have been comfortable now but for one defect. Every morning at five the cook opened the kitchen door, in the way of business, and rip went that gong! The first time this happened I thought the last day was come sure. I didn't think it *in* bed—no, but out of it—for the first effect of that frightful gong is to hurl you across the house, and slam you against the wall, and then curl you up, and squirm you like a spider on a stove lid, till somebody shuts the kitchen door. In solid fact, there is no clamor that is even remotely comparable to the dire clamor which that gong makes. Well, this catastrophe happened every morning regularly at five o'clock, and lost us three hours sleep; for, mind you, when that thing wakes you, it doesn't merely wake you in spots; it wakes you all over, conscience and all, and you are good for eighteen hours of wide-awakeness subsequently—eighteen hours of the very most inconceivable wide-awakeness that you ever experienced in your life. A stranger died on our hands one time, and we vacated and left him in our room overnight. Did that stranger wait for the general judgment? *No,* sir; he got up at five the next morning in the most prompt and unostentatious way. I knew he would; I knew it mighty well. He collected his life insurance, and lived happy ever after, for there was plenty of proof as to the perfect squareness of his death.

Well, we were gradually fading toward a better land, on account of the daily loss of sleep; so we finally had the expert up again, and he ran a wire to the outside of the door, and placed a switch there, whereby Thomas, the butler, always made one little mistake—he switched the alarm off at night when he went to bed, and switched it on again at daybreak in the morning, just in time for the cook to open the kitchen door, and enable that gong to slam us across the house, sometimes breaking a window with one or the other of us. At the end of a week we recognized that this switch business was a delusion and a snare. We also discovered that a band of burglars had been lodging in the house the whole time—not exactly to steal, for there wasn't much left now, but to hide from the police, for they were hot pressed, and they shrewdly judged that the detectives would never think of a tribe of burglars taking sanctuary in a house notoriously protected by the most imposing and elaborate burglar alarm in America.

Sent down for the expert again, and this time he struck a most dazzling idea—he fixed the thing so that opening the kitchen door would take off the alarm. It was a noble idea, and he charged accordingly. But you already foresee the result. I switched on the alarm every night at bedtime, no longer trusting on Thomas's frail memory; and as soon as the lights were out the burglars walked in at the kitchen door, thus taking the alarm off without waiting for the cook to do it in the morning.

You see how aggravatingly we were situated. For months we couldn't have any company. Not a spare bed in the house; all occupied by burglars.

Finally, I got up a cure of my own. The expert answered the call, and ran another ground wire to the stable, and established a switch there, so that the coachman could put on and take off the alarm. That worked first rate, and a season of peace ensued, during which we got to inviting company once more and enjoying life.

But by and by the irrepressible alarm invented a new kink. One winter's night we were flung out of bed by the sudden music of that awful gong, and when we hobbled to the annunciator, turned up the gas, and saw the word "Nursery" exposed, Mrs. McWilliams fainted dead away, and I came precious near doing the same thing myself.

I seized my shotgun, and stood timing the coachman whilst that appalling buzzing went on. I knew that his gong had flung him out, too, and that he would be along with his gun as soon as he could jump into his clothes.

When I judged that the time was ripe, I crept to the room next the nursery, glanced through the window, and saw the dim outline of the coachman in the yard below, standing at present arms and waiting for a chance. Then I hopped into the nursery and fired, and in the same instant the coachman fired at the red flash of my gun. Both of us were successful; I crippled a nurse, and he shot off all my back hair. We turned up the gas, and telephoned for a surgeon. There was not a sign of a burglar, and no window had been raised. One glass was absent, but that was where the coachman's charge had come through. Here was a fine mystery—a burglar alarm "going off" at midnight of its own accord, and not a burglar in the neighborhood!

The expert answered the usual call, and explained that it was a "false alarm." Said it was easily fixed. So he overhauled the nursery window, charged a remunerative figure for it, and departed.

What we suffered from false alarms for the next three years no stylographic pen can describe. During the next three months I always flew with my gun to the room indicated, and the coachman always sallied forth with his battery to support me. But there was never anything to shoot at—windows all tight and secure. We always sent down for the expert next day, and he fixed those particular windows so they would keep quiet a week or so, and always remembered to send us a bill about like this:

Wire	$ 2.15
Nipple	.75
Two hours' labor	1.50
Wax	.47
Tape	.34
Screws	.15
Recharging battery	.98
Three hours' labor	2.25
String	.02
Lard	.66
Pond's Extract	1.25
Springs at 50	2.00
Railroad fares	7.25
	$19.77

At length a perfectly natural thing came about—after we had answered three or four hundred false alarms—to wit, we stopped answering them. Yes, I simply rose up calmly, when slammed across the house by the alarm, calmly inspected the annunciator, took note of the room indicated, and then calmly disconnected that room from the alarm, and went back to bed as if nothing had happened. Moreover, I left that room off permanently, and did not send for the expert. Well, it goes without saying that in the course of time *all* the rooms were taken off, and the entire machine was out of service.

It was at this unprotected time that the heaviest calamity of all happened. The burglars walked in one night and carried off the burglar alarm! yes, sir, every hide and hair of it: ripped it out, tooth and nail; springs, bells, gongs, battery, and all; they took a hundred and fifty miles of copper wire; they just cleaned her out, bag and baggage, and never left us a vestige of her to swear at—swear by, I mean.

We had a time of it to get her back; but we accomplished it finally, for money. The alarm firm said that what we needed now was to have her put in right—with their new patent springs in the windows to make false alarms impossible, and their new patent clock attached to take off and put on the alarm morning and night without human assistance. That seemed a good scheme. They promised to have the whole thing finished in ten days. They began work, and we left for the summer. They worked a couple of days; then *they* left for the summer. After which the burglars moved in, and began *their* summer vacation.

When we returned in the fall, the house was as empty as a beer closet in premises where painters have been at work. We refurnished, and then sent down to hurry up the expert. He came up and finished the job, and said: "Now this clock is set to put on the alarm every night at 10:00, and take it off every morning at 5:45. All you've got to do is to wind her up every week, and then leave her alone—she will take care of the alarm herself."

After that we had a most tranquil season during three months. The bill was prodigious, of course, and I had said I would not pay it until the new machinery had proved itself to be flawless. The time stipulated was three months.

So I paid the bill, and the very next day the alarm went to buzzing like ten thousand bee swarms at ten o'clock in the morning. I turned the hands around twelve hours, according to instructions, and this took off the alarm; but there was another hitch at night, and I had to set her ahead twelve hours once more to get her to put the alarm on again.

That sort of nonsense went on a week or two, then the expert came up and put in a new clock. He came up every three months during the next three years, and put in a new clock. But it was always a failure. His clocks all had the same perverse defect: they would put the alarm on in the daytime, and they would *not* put it on at night; and if you forced it on yourself, they *would* take it off again the minute your back was turned.

Now there is the history of that burglar alarm—everything just as it happened; nothing extenuated, and naught set down in malice. Yes, sir,—and when I had slept nine years with burglars, and maintained an expensive burglar alarm the whole time, for their protection, not mine, and at my sole cost—for not a d——d cent could I ever get *them* to contribute—I just said to Mrs. McWilliams that I had had enough of that kind of pie; so with her full consent I took the whole thing out and traded it off for a dog, and shot the dog. I don't know what *you* think about it, Mr. Twain; but *I* think those things are made solely in the interest of the burglars. Yes, sir, a burglar alarm combines in its person all that is objectionable about a fire, a riot, and a harem, and at the same time has none of the compensating advantages, of one sort or another, that customarily belong with that combination. Good-by: I get off here.

THE AUGSBURG CHALK CIRCLE

BERTOLT BRECHT / GERMANY

Translated by Yvonne Kapp

IN THE DAYS of the Thirty Years War a Swiss Protestant by the name of Zingli owned a large tannery and leather business in the free imperial city of Augsburg on the Lech. He was married to an Augsburg woman and had a child by her. As the Catholics marched on the city his friends strongly advised him to flee, but whether it was that his small family held him back or that he did not want to abandon his tannery, he simply could not make up his mind to leave while there was yet time.

Thus he was still there when the imperial troops stormed the city and, while they plundered it that evening, he hid in a pit in the courtyard where the dyes were stored. His wife was to have moved with the child to her relatives on the outskirts, but she spent too much time packing her belongings—dresses, jewelry and bedding—and so it came about that suddenly she saw from a window on the first story a squad of imperial soldiers forcing their way into the courtyard. Beside herself with fear, she dropped everything and fled from the place through a back door.

So the child was left behind in the house. It lay in its cradle in the large hall and played with a wooden ball that hung on a string from the ceiling.

Only a young servant girl was still in the house. She was busy with the copper pots and pans in the kitchen when she heard a noise from the street. Darting to the window she saw soldiers throwing all kinds of loot into the street from the first story of the house opposite. She ran to the hall and was just about to take the child out of the cradle when she heard the sound of heavy blows on the oaken front door. She was seized by panic and flew up the stairs.

The hall was filled with drunken soldiers, who smashed everything to pieces. They knew they were in a Protestant's house. As though by a miracle Anna, the servant girl, remained undiscovered throughout the searching and plundering. The soldiers made off and, scrambling out of the cupboard in which she had been standing, Anna found the child in the hall also unharmed. She snatched it up hastily and stole with it into the courtyard. In the meantime night had fallen, but the red glow from a burning house nearby lit up the courtyard, and with horror she saw the battered corpse of her master. The soldiers had dragged him from his pit and butchered him.

Only now did the girl realize the danger she ran should she be caught in the street with the Protestant's child. With a heavy heart she laid it back in the cradle, gave it a little milk to drink, rocked it to sleep and made her way towards that part of the city where her married sister lived. At about 10 o'clock at night, accompanied by her sister's husband, she elbowed her way through the throng of soldiers celebrating their victory to go to the outskirts and find Frau Zingli, the mother of the child. They knocked on the door of an imposing house, which, after quite a long while, did open slightly. A little old man, Frau Zingli's uncle, stuck his head out. Anna announced breathlessly that Herr Zingli was dead but the child was unharmed in the house. The old man looked at her coldly with fishlike eyes and said his niece was no longer there and he himself washed his hands of the Protestant bastard. With that he shut the door again. As they left, Anna's brother-in-law noticed a curtain move at one of the windows and was convinced that Frau Zingli was there. Apparently she felt no shame in repudiating her child.

Anna and her brother-in-law walked on side by side in silence for a while. Then she declared that she wanted to go back to the tannery and fetch the child. Her brother-in-law, a quiet respectable man, listened to her aghast and tried to talk her out of this dangerous notion. What were these people to her? She had not even been decently treated.

Anna heard him out and promised to do nothing rash. Nevertheless, she must just look in quickly at the tannery to see whether the child needed anything. And she wanted to go alone.

She managed to get her own way. In the midst of the devastated hall the child lay peacefully in its cradle and slept. Wearily Anna sat down by its side and gazed at it. She had not dared to kindle a light, but the nearby house was still burning and by its light she could see the child quite well. It had a tiny mole on its little neck.

When the girl had watched the child breathing and sucking its small fist for some time, maybe an hour, she realized that she had now stayed too long and seen too much to be able to leave without the child. She got to her feet heavily and with slow movements wrapped it in its linen coverlet, tucked it into her arm and left the courtyard with it, looking round furtively like someone with a bad conscience, a thief.

After long consultations with sister and brother-in-law, she took the child to the country two weeks later, to the village of Gross-aitingen, where her elder brother was a peasant. The farm belonged to his wife; he had merely married into it. It had been agreed that perhaps it would be best to tell no one but her brother who the child was, for they had never set eyes on the young wife and did not know how she would receive so dangerous a little guest.

Anna reached the village at about midday. Her brother, his wife and the farm servants were at table. She was not ill received, but one glance at her new sister-in-law decided her to introduce the child then and there as her own. It was not until she had explained that her husband had a job at a mill in a distant village and expected her there with the child in a few weeks that the peasant woman thawed and the child was duly admired.

That afternoon she accompanied her brother to the copse to gather wood. They sat down on tree stumps and Anna made a clean breast of it. She could see that he felt uncomfortable. His position on the farm was still insecure and he commended Anna warmly for having held her tongue in front of his wife. It was plain that he did not credit his young wife with a particularly broadminded attitude towards the Protestant child. He wished the deception to be kept up.

However, that was not so easy as time went on.

Anna joined in the harvesting and tended "her" child betweenwhiles, constantly running back from the fields to the house when the others rested. The little boy thrived and even grew fat, chuckled whenever he saw Anna and made manful efforts to raise his head. But then came winter and the sister-in-law started to make inquiries about Anna's husband.

There was nothing against Anna staying on at the farm; she could make herself useful. The trouble was that the neighbors were growing curious about the father of Anna's boy, since he never came to see how he was getting on. If she could not produce a father for her child, the farm would get itself talked about before long.

One Sunday morning the peasant harnessed the horse and called Anna loudly to come with him to fetch a calf from a neighboring village. As they clattered along the road he told her that he had sought and found a husband for her. It was a dying cottager who, when the two of them stood in his mean hovel, could barely lift his wasted head from the soiled sheet.

He was willing to marry Anna. A yellow-skinned old woman, his mother, stood at the bedside. She was to have a reward for the service rendered to Anna.

The bargain was concluded in ten minutes and Anna and her brother were able to drive on and buy their calf. The wedding took place at the end of that same week. While the priest mumbled the marriage ritual, the lifeless glance of the sick man did not once stray towards Anna. Her brother was in no doubt that she would have the death certificate within a few days. Then Anna's husband, the father of her child, would have died somewhere in a village near Augsburg on his way to her and no one would give the matter another thought if the widow stayed on in her brother's house.

Anna returned joyfully from her strange wedding, at which there had been neither church bells nor a brass band, neither bridesmaids nor guests. By way of a wedding breakfast she ate a piece of bread with a slice of bacon in the larder and then, with her brother, went towards the wooden chest in which lay the child who now had a name. She tucked in the covers more tightly and smiled at her brother.

The death certificate certainly took its time.

Indeed, no word came from the old woman the next nor yet the following week. Anna had given out on the farm that her husband was at present on his way to her. When she was asked what was delaying him now she said that the deep snow must be making the journey difficult. But after another three weeks had gone by, her brother, seriously perturbed, drove to the village near Augsburg.

He came back late at night. Anna was still up and ran to the door as she heard the wheels crunch in the yard. She noticed how slowly the farmer unharnessed and a spasm went through her heart.

He brought bad tidings. On entering the hut he had found the doomed man sitting at the table in shirt-sleeves having supper, chewing away with his mouth full. He was completely restored.

The peasant did not look Anna in the face as he went on telling her. The cottager—his name, by the by, was Otterer—and his mother appeared equally astonished by the turn of events and had probably not yet decided what was to be done. Otterer had not made an unpleasant impression. He had said little, but at one point, when his mother had started lamenting that he was now saddled with an unwanted wife and a stranger's child, he had commanded her to be silent. He went on eating his cheese with deliberation throughout the interview and was still eating when the farmer took his leave.

During the following days Anna was naturally very troubled. In between her housework she taught the boy to walk. When he let go of the distaff and came tottering towards her with little out-stretched arms, she suppressed a dry sob and clasped him tightly to her as she picked him up.

Once she asked her brother: "What sort of a man is he?" She had seen him only on his deathbed and then only in the evening by poor candlelight. Now she learned that her husband was a man in his fifties worn out by toil; was, in fact, what a cottager would be.

Shortly after, she saw him. With a great show of secrecy a peddler had given her a message that "a certain acquaintance" wished to meet her on such-and-such a date at such-and-such a time near such-and-such a village, at the spot where the footpath went off to Landsberg. So the married couple met midway between their villages, like the commanders of old between their battle lines, on open ground, which was covered with snow.

Anna did not take to the man.

He had small gray teeth, looked her up and down—although she was hidden under a thick sheepskin and there was not much to be seen—and then used the words "the sacrament of marriage." She told him curtly that she must still think things over and that he must get some dealer or slaughterer passing through Grossaitingen to tell her in her sister-in-law's hearing that he would soon be coming now and had merely been taken ill on the journey.

Otterer nodded in his deliberate way. He was more than a head taller than she and kept on glancing at the left side of her neck as they talked, which exasperated her.

But the message did not come, and Anna toyed with the idea of simply leaving the farm with the child and looking for work further south, perhaps in Kempten or Sonthofen. Only the perils of the highway, about which there was much talk, and the fact that it was midwinter held her back.

But now her stay at the farm grew difficult. Her sister-in-law put suspicious questions to her about her husband at the dinner table in front of all the farm servants. When on one occasion she went so far as to glance at the child and exclaim loudly in false compassion, "Poor mite!" Anna resolved to go despite everything; but at that point the child fell ill.

He lay restlessly in his wooden chest with a flushed face and clouded eyes, and Anna watched over him for nights on end with fear and hope. When he was on the road to recovery again and his smile had come back, there was a knock on the door one morning and in walked Otterer.

There was no one in the room but Anna and the child, so that she had no need to dissemble, which in any case the shock would have prevented. They stood for quite some time without a word; then

Otterer announced that for his part he had thought the matter over and had come to fetch her. He referred again to the sacrament of marriage. Anna grew angry. In a firm, though low voice she told the man she would not think of living with him, she had entered into the marriage only for the sake of the child and wanted nothing of him beyond giving her and the child his name.

As she mentioned the child Otterer glanced fleetingly towards the chest in which it lay gurgling, without, however, going up to it. This set Anna against him even more.

He voiced a few remarks: she should think things over again; there was scant fare in his home; his mother could sleep in the kitchen. Then the sister-in-law came in, greeted him inquisitively and invited him to dinner. He was already seated at table as he greeted the peasant with a careless nod, neither pretending that he did not know him nor betraying that he did. To the wife's questions he replied in monosyllables, not raising his eyes from his plate, that he had found a job in Mering and Anna could join him. But he no longer suggested that this had to be at once.

During the afternoon he avoided the brother's company and chopped wood behind the house, which no one had asked him to do. After supper, of which he again partook in silence, the sister-in-law herself carried a featherbed into Anna's room so that he could spend the night there; but at that, strange to say, he rose awkwardly to his feet and mumbled that he must get back that night. Before leaving, he gazed with an absentminded expression into the chest where the child lay, but said nothing and did not touch him.

During the night Anna was taken ill and fell into a fever which lasted for weeks. Most of the time she lay apathetically; only now and then towards midday, when the fever abated a little, she crawled to the child's wooden chest and tucked in the covers.

In the fourth week of her illness Otterer drove into the yard in a farm cart and took her and the child away. She let this happen without a word.

Only very slowly did she regain her strength, and small wonder on the cottager's thin soup. But one morning she noticed how dirty and neglected the child looked and resolutely got up.

The little boy received her with his friendly smile in which, her brother had always declared, he took after her. He had grown and now crawled all over the room with lightning speed, slapping his hands on the floor and emitting little screams when he fell on his face. She washed him in a wooden tub and won back her confidence.

A few days later, however, she could stand life in the hovel no longer. She wrapped the little boy in a few blankets, stuck a piece of bread and some cheese in her pocket and ran away.

She intended to reach Sonthofen, but did not get far. She was still very weak in the knees, the highway was covered in slush and, as a result of the war, people in the villages had grown very suspicious and stingy. On the third day of her wayfaring she sprained her foot in a ditch and after many hours, during which she feared for the child, she was brought to a farmstead, where she lay in the barn. The little boy crawled about between the cows' legs and only laughed when she cried out anxiously. In the end she had to tell the farm people her husband's name and he fetched her back again to Mering.

From now on she made no further attempt to escape and accepted her lot. She worked hard. It was difficult to extract anything from the small plot and keep the tiny property going. Yet the man was not unkind to her, and the little boy ate his fill. Also her brother occasionally came over bringing a present of this or that, and once she was even able to have a little coat dyed red for the child. That, she thought, would suit a dyer's child well.

As time passed she grew quite contented and experienced many joys in bringing up the child. Thus several years went by.

But one day she went to the village to buy syrup and on her return the child was not in the hut and her husband told her that a grandly dressed lady had driven up in a coach and taken the child away. She reeled against the wall in horror, and that very evening, carrying nothing but a bundle of food, she set out for Augsburg.

Her first call in the imperial city was at the tannery. She was not admitted and could not catch sight of the child.

Her sister and brother-in-law tried in vain to console her. She ran to the authorities and, beside herself, shouted that her child had been stolen. She went so far as to hint that Protestants had stolen her child. Whereupon she learned that other times now prevailed and that peace had been concluded between Catholics and Protestants.

She would scarcely have accomplished anything had not a singular piece of luck come to her aid. Her case was referred to a judge who was a quite exceptional man.

This was the judge Ignaz Dollinger, famed throughout Swabia for his boorishness and his erudition, known to the elector of Bavaria, whose legal dispute with the free imperial city he had had to settle, as "this Latin clodhopper," but celebrated by the people in a long ballad.

Accompanied by her sister and brother-in-law, Anna came before him. The short but immensely corpulent old man sat in a tiny bare room between piles of documents and listened to her only very briefly. Then he wrote something down, growled: "Step over there, and be quick about it!" and indicated with his small plump hand a spot in the room on which the light fell through the narrow window. For some minutes he studied her face closely, then waved her aside with a snort.

The next day he sent an officer to fetch her and while she was still on the threshold shouted at her: "Why didn't you let on that what you're after is a tannery and the sizable property that goes with it?" Anna said doggedly that what she was after was the child.

"Don't go thinking that you can grab the tannery," shouted the judge. "If the bastard really is yours, the property goes to Zingli's relatives."

Anna nodded without looking at him. Then she said: "He doesn't need the tannery."

"Is he yours?" barked the judge.

"Yes," she said softly. "If I could just keep him until he can say all the words. So far he only knows seven."

The judge coughed and straightened the documents on his table. Then he said more quietly, though still in an irritable tone: "You want the brat and that bitch with her five silk skirts wants him. But he needs the real mother."

"Yes," said Anna, and looked at the judge.

"Be off with you," he growled. "The court sits on Saturday."

On that Saturday the main road and the square outside the town hall by the Perlach Tower were black with people who wanted to attend the proceedings over the Protestant child. This remarkable case had made a great stir from the start, and in dwellings and taverns there were arguments about who was the real and who the false mother. Moreover, old Dollinger was renowned far and wide for his down-to-earth proceedings with their biting remarks and wise sayings. His trials were more popular than minstrels and fairs.

Thus it was not only many Augsburgers who thronged outside the town hall; there were also not a few farmers from the surrounding countryside. Friday was market day and, in anticipation of the lawsuit, they had spent the night in the city.

The hall in which Judge Dollinger heard his cases was the so-called Golden Hall. It was famous as the only hall of its size without pillars in the whole of Germany; the ceiling was suspended from the rafters by chains.

Judge Dollinger sat, a small round mountain of flesh, in front of a closed metal gate along one wall. An ordinary rope cordoned off the public. But the judge sat on the bare floor and had no table before him. He had personally instituted this setting years ago; he strongly believed in staging things properly.

Inside the roped-off enclosure were Frau Zingli with her parents, the newly arrived Swiss relatives of the late Herr Zingli—two well-dressed worthies looking like substantial merchants—and Anna Otterer with her sister. A nurse holding the child could be seen next to Frau Zingli.

Everybody, litigants and witnesses, stood. Judge Dollinger was wont to say that trials tended to be shorter if the participants had to stand. But perhaps, too, he made them stand in order to conceal himself from the public, so that one could only see him if one went on tiptoe and cricked one's neck.

At the start of the proceedings an incident occurred. When Anna caught sight of the child, she uttered a cry and stepped forward, and the child tried to go to her, struggled violently in the nurse's arms and started to scream. The judge ordered him to be taken out of the hall.

Then he called Frau Zingli.

She came rustling forward and described—now and again raising a little handkerchief to her eyes—how the imperial soldiers had snatched the child from her at the time of the looting. That same night the servant girl had come to her father's place and had reported that the child was still in the house, probably in the hope of a tip. One of the father's cooks, on being sent to the tannery, had not, however, found the child, and she assumed that this person (she pointed at Anna) had taken him in order to be able to extort money in some way or other. No doubt she would have come out with such demands sooner or later had she not been deprived of the child beforehand.

Judge Dollinger called Herr Zingli's two relatives and asked them whether they had inquired after Herr Zingli at the time and what Frau Zingli had told them.

They testified that Frau Zingli had let them know her husband had been killed and that she had entrusted the child to a servant girl where it would be in good keeping. They spoke of her in a most unfriendly manner which, indeed, was no wonder, since the property would come to them if Frau Zingli lost the case.

Following their evidence the judge turned again to Frau Zingli and wanted to know from her whether she had not simply lost her head at the time of the attack and abandoned the child.

Frau Zingli looked at him with her pallid blue eyes as if in astonishment and said in injured tones that she had not abandoned her child.

Judge Dollinger cleared his throat and asked her with some interest whether she believed that no mother could abandon her child.

Yes, that was what she believed, she said firmly.

Did she then believe, the judge asked further, that a mother who nevertheless did so ought to have her behind thrashed, regardless of how many skirts she wore over it?

Frau Zingli made no answer and the judge called the former servant girl Anna. She stepped forward quickly and said in a low voice what she had already said at the preliminary inquiry. But she talked as though she were listening at the same time, and every now and again she glanced at the big door through which the child had been taken, as though she were afraid it might still be screaming.

She testified that, although she had called at the house of Frau Zingli's uncle that night, she had not gone back to the tannery, out of fear of the imperial troops and because she was worried about her own illegitimate child which had been placed with good people in the neighboring village of Lechhausen.

Old Dollinger interrupted her rudely and snapped that at least there had been one person in the city who had felt something like fear. He was glad to be able to establish the fact, since it proved that at least one person had had some sense at the time. It was not, of course, very nice of the witness that she had only been concerned about her own child, but on the other hand, as the popular saying went, blood was thicker than water, and anyone who was a proper mother would go to the lengths of stealing for her child, though this was strictly forbidden by law, for property was property, and those who stole also lied, and lying was similarly forbidden by law. And then he gave one of his wise and pungent lectures on the infamy of people who deceived the court till they were black in the face; and after a short digression on peasants who watered the milk of innocent cows and the city council which levied too high market taxes on the peasants—which had absolutely nothing to do with the case—he announced that the examination of witnesses was over and had led nowhere.

Then he made a long pause and showed every sign of being at a loss, gazing about him as though he expected someone or other to suggest how to arrive at a solution.

People looked at one another dumbfounded and some of them craned their necks to catch a glimpse of the helpless judge. But it remained very quiet in the hall; only the crowd in the street below could be heard.

Then, sighing, the judge began to speak again.

"It has not been established who is the real mother," he said. "The child is to be pitied. We have all heard of fathers dodging their duty and not wanting to be fathers—the rogues!—but here are two mothers both laying claim. The court has listened to them as long as they deserve, namely a full five minutes to each, and the court is convinced that both are lying like a book. But, as already said, we still have to think of the child who must have a mother. Therefore it has to be established, without paying attention to mere babble, who the real mother of the child is."

And in a cross voice he called the usher and ordered him to bring a piece of chalk.

The usher went and fetched a piece of chalk.

"Draw a circle with the chalk on the floor big enough for three people to stand in," the judge directed him.

The usher knelt down and drew the circle with the chalk as requested.

"Now fetch the child," ordered the judge.

The child was brought in. He started to howl again and tried to go to Anna. Old Dollinger took no notice of the crying and merely delivered his address in a rather louder voice.

"This test which is now about to be applied," he announced, "I found in an old book and it is considered extremely good. The simple basic idea of the test with the chalk circle is that the real mother will be recognized by her love for the child. Hence the strength of this love must be tested. Usher, place the child in that chalk circle."

The usher took the wailing child from the nurse's hand and led him into the circle. The judge went on, turning towards Frau Zingli and Anna:

"You go and stand in the chalk circle too; each of you take one of the child's hands and when I say 'Go!' try and pull the child out of the circle. Whichever of you has the stronger love will also pull with the greater strength and thus bring the child to her side."

There was a stir in the hall. The spectators stood on tiptoe and had words with those standing in front of them.

But there was dead silence again as the two women stepped into the circle and each grasped one of the child's hands. The child had also fallen silent, as though he sensed what was at stake. He turned his small tear-stained face up to Anna. Then the judge gave the order "Go!".

And with a single violent jerk Frau Zingli tore the child out of the chalk circle. Bewildered and incredulous, Anna's eyes followed him. For fear that he might come to harm if both his little arms were pulled in two directions at once, she had immediately let go.

Old Dollinger stood up.

"And thus we know," he said loudly, "who is the right mother. Take the child away from the slut. She would tear him to pieces in cold blood."

And he nodded to Anna and quickly left the hall to have his breakfast.

And in the following weeks the peasants round about, who were pretty wide-awake, talked of how the judge on awarding the child to the woman from Mering had winked at her.

THE OVERCOAT
SALLY BENSON / UNITED STATES

Sally Benson

IT HAD BEEN noisy and crowded at the Milligans' and Mrs. Bishop had eaten too many little sandwiches and too many iced cakes, so that now, out in the street, the air felt good to her, even if it was damp and cold. At the entrance of the apartment house, she took out her change purse and looked through it and found that by counting the pennies, too, she had just eighty-seven cents, which wasn't enough for a taxi from Tenth Street to Seventy-third. It was horrid never having enough money in your purse, she thought. Playing bridge, when she lost, she often had to give I.O.U.'s and it was faintly embarrassing, although she always managed to make them good. She resented Lila Hardy who could say, "Can anyone change a ten?" and who could take ten dollars from her small, smart bag while the other women scurried about for change.

She decided that it was too late to take a bus and she might as well walk over to the subway, although the air down there would probably make her head ache. It was drizzling a little and the sidewalks were wet. And as she stood on the corner waiting for the traffic lights to change, she felt horribly sorry for herself. She remembered as a young girl she had always assumed she would have lots of money when she was older. She had planned what to do with it—what clothes to buy and what upholstery she would have in her car.

Of course, everybody nowadays talked poor and that was some comfort. But it was one thing to have lost your money and quite another never to have had any. It was absurd, though, to go around with less than a dollar in your purse. Suppose something happened? She was a little vague as to what might happen, but the idea fed her resentment.

Everything for the house, like food and things, she charged. Years ago, Robert had worked out some sort of budget for her, but they had long ago abandoned it. And yet Robert always seemed to have money. That is, when she came to him for five or ten dollars, he managed to give it to her. Men were like that, she thought. They managed to keep money in their pockets but they had no idea you ever needed any. Well, she would insist on having an allowance. Then she would at least know where she stood. When she decided this, she began to walk more briskly and everything seemed simpler.

The air in the subway was worse than usual and she stood on the local side waiting for a train. People who took the expresses seemed to push so and she felt tired and wanted to sit down. When the train came, she took a seat near the door and, although inwardly she was seething with rebellion, her face took on the vacuous look of other faces in the subway. At Eighteenth Street, a great many people got on and she found her vision blocked by a man who had come in and was hanging to the strap in front of her. He was tall and thin and his overcoat which hung loosely on him and swayed with the motion of the train smelled unpleasantly of damp wool. The buttons of the overcoat were of imitation leather and the button directly in front of Mrs. Bishop's eyes evidently had come off and been sewed back on again with black thread, which didn't match the coat at all.

It was what is known as a swagger coat but there was nothing very swagger about it now. The sleeve that she could see was almost threadbare around the cuff and a small shred from the lining hung down over the man's hand. She found herself looking intently at his hand. It was long and pallid and not too clean. The nails were very short as though they had been bitten and there was a discolored callus on his second finger where he probably held his pencil. Mrs. Bishop, who prided herself on her powers of observation, put him in the white-collar class. He most likely, she thought, was the father of a large family and had a hard time sending them all through school. He undoubtedly never spent money on himself. That would account for the shabbiness of his overcoat. And he was probably horribly afraid of losing his job. His house was always noisy and smelled of cooking. Mrs. Bishop couldn't decide whether to make his wife a fat slattern or to have her an invalid. Either would be quite consistent.

She grew warm with sympathy for the man. Every now and then he gave a slight cough, and that increased her interest and her sadness. It was a soft, pleasant sadness and made her feel resigned to life. She decided that she would smile at him when she got off. It would be the sort of smile that couldn't help but make him feel better, as it would be very obvious that she understood and was sorry.

But by the time the train reached Seventy-second Street, the smell of wet wool, the closeness of the air and the confusion of her own worries had made her feelings less poignant, so that her smile, when she gave it, lacked something. The man looked away embarrassed.

HER APARTMENT was too hot and the smell of broiling chops sickened her after the enormous tea she had eaten. She could see Maude, her maid, setting the table in the dining room for dinner. Mrs. Bishop had bought smart little uniforms for her, but there was nothing smart about Maude and the uniforms never looked right.

Robert was lying on the living-room couch, the evening newspaper over his face to shield his eyes. He had changed his shoes, and the gray felt slippers he wore were too short for him and showed the imprint of his toes, and looked depressing. Years ago, when they were first married, he used to dress for dinner sometimes. He would shake up a cocktail for her and things were quite gay and almost the way she had imagined they would be. Mrs. Bishop didn't believe in letting yourself go and it seemed to her that Robert let himself go out of sheer perversity. She hated him as he lay there, resignation in every line of his body. She envied Lila Hardy her husband who drank but who, at least, was somebody. And she felt like tearing the paper from his face because her anger and disgust were more than she could bear.

For a minute she stood in the doorway trying to control herself and then she walked over to a window and opened it roughly. "Goodness," she said. "Can't we ever have any air in here?"

Robert gave a slight start and sat up. "Hello, Mollie," he said. "You home?"

"Yes, I'm home. I came home in the subway."

Her voice was reproachful. She sat down in the chair facing him and spoke more quietly so that Maude couldn't hear what she was saying. "Really, Robert," she said, "it was dreadful. I came out from the tea in all that drizzle and couldn't even take a taxi home. I had just exactly eighty-seven cents. Just eighty-seven cents!"

"Say," he said. "That's a shame. Here." He reached in his pocket and took out a small roll of crumpled bills. "Here," he repeated. And handed her one. She saw that it was five dollars.

Mrs. Bishop shook her head. "No, Robert," she told him. "That isn't the point. The point is that I've really got to have some sort of allowance. It isn't fair to me. I never have any money! Never! It's got so it's positively embarrassing!"

Mr. Bishop fingered the five-dollar bill thoughtfully. "I see," he said. "You want an allowance. What's the matter? Don't I give you money every time you ask for it?"

"Well, yes," Mrs. Bishop admitted. "But it isn't like my own. An allowance would be more like my own."

"Now, Mollie," he reasoned. "If you had an allowance, it would probably be gone by the tenth of the month."

"Don't treat me like a child. I just won't be humiliated anymore."

Mr. Bishop sat turning the five-dollar bill over and over in his hand. "About how much do you think you should have?" he asked.

"Fifty dollars a month," she told him. And her voice was harsh and strained. "That's the very least I can get along on. Why, Lila Hardy would laugh at fifty dollars a month."

"Fifty dollars a month," Mr. Bishop repeated. He coughed a little, nervously, and ran his fingers through his hair. "I've had a lot of things to attend to this month. But, well, maybe if you would be willing to wait until the first of next month, I might manage."

"Oh, next month will be perfectly all right," she said, feeling it wiser not to press her victory. "But don't forget. Because I shan't."

As she walked toward the closet to put away her wraps, she caught sight of Robert's overcoat on the chair near the door. He had tossed it carelessly across the back of the chair as he came in. One sleeve was hanging down and the vibration of her feet on the floor had made it swing gently back and forth. She saw that the cuff was badly worn and a bit of the lining showed. It looked dreadfully like the sleeve of the overcoat she had seen in the subway. And, suddenly, looking at it, she had a horrible sinking feeling, like falling in a dream.

BLIND MacNAIR
THOMAS H. RADDALL / CANADA

Thomas H. Raddall

IN SHARDSTOWN they sing ballads no more. Nor will you hear a chantey, for the chanteymen have vanished and the tall grass shines where once the shipyards lay under a snow of chips and shavings.

It is a village enchanted. There is the yellow dust of the street, the procession of dwellings down to the broad sheltered bay, where a fleet could anchor and only the lone fishing boat flashes a riding sail; and there is the little church and the store and the dry-rotten fish wharf asleep in the sun, all still as death. Half the houses are empty, with blinds drawn and faded and forgotten, and grass in the kitchen path. The people are pleasant but silent. They smile and vanish. Down by the waterside, in the lee of a tottering shed, you may find an old man on a cushion of discarded net, with worn boots thrust out before him, with a frown to shield his old eyes from the shine of the sea, and a dream on his face.

"A ballad? People don't sing ballads now. A chantey? Ha! Where's the need—and no sails to haul?" If you persist he will swear great oaths that have a strong taste of the sea, and he will say, "Och, man, yes; but that's too long ago. That's back in the time of Blind MacNair."

And who was Blind MacNair?

Before Shardstown became enchanted, the village stood pretty much as it stands now, but alive, with a smell of new-sawed wood in the air, and the sounds of hammer and adz, and the *clack-clack* of calking mallets. They built good ships in Shardstown then. The hulls grew by the waterside with their bowsprits reaching over the road. A blockmaker and three families of coopers carried on business in sheds behind their homes, and a busy sailmaker squatted with palm and needle amongst billows of canvas up there in the long sail loft. The village blacksmith made ironwork for vessels three parts of the year; in winter he shod oxen and horses and fitted sled runners and peavey hooks for the loggers.

The tall iron stack of the sawmill poured blue woodsmoke at the sky, and from dawn to dark within its gray wooden walls rang the death scream of logs. There was a wisp in every chimney then, and children played by the dusty road, and women came out of the kitchen doors and set the well windlasses rattling. Too many women; for in those days men went out upon the broad world in the windships and the world did not always give them back. The sea took many, and there was the gold rush to California, and then the gold rush to Australia; and thirty men went to the American war. All that within twenty years.

So there were lonely women in Shardstown. For a time, in one part of the long street lived six widows side by side. Three married again as the years went by; but the others were Bullens and counted unlucky, their husbands gone—blown off a topsail yard, washed overboard, stabbed by a drunken foremast hand—each within fifteen months of the wedding. In a village like Shardstown men could pick safer wives.

There was a fourth Bullen sister, the youngest, but she lived with old Chris on the Bullen farm, a lonely hillside clearing by the Revesport road, fourteen miles out of Shardstown. There was a scandal about Nellie Bullen. She had gone to work in Revesport in '60 or '61, a slim blond girl of two-and-twenty with the self-willed Bullen mouth, and came home late in '62 and had a baby. A fine wagging of tongues there was, to be sure, in that village of too many women. But one Sunday old Chris Bullen came down in his buggy and nailed to the church door a paper for all to see—Nellie Bullen's marriage lines, with a date that defied the gossips' arithmetic.

After that the matter dropped, and nobody even remembered the husband's name, and Nellie Bullen stayed close to the lonely farm with her boy and called herself Nellie Bullen. Things like that happened very easily in the old times, when men came and went from the sea like visitors from the moon.

People sang ballads then, except on Sunday when the minister came over in a buggy from Revesport and there were hymns to be sung. And the best of the singers were chanteymen from the brigs and barks and barkentines, the lovely windships that lay at the waterside. Nowadays men say the windships were hell ships and well lost; and they say the chanteys had no music and the ballads no poetry. Blind they are, more blind than Blind MacNair, who knew the beauty of those things.

Och, yes, Blind MacNair, who came to Shardstown in the fall of 1872 aboard a potato schooner from Prince Edward Island. Square-built he was, with brown hands and a brown face and a curly black beard, and hair long and black as night. He wore a band of green silk across his eyes and carried a stick and bundle. His black frieze trousers were called shag trousers in those days, and he had a pair of stout brown seaboots under their wide bottoms, and a sailor's red shirt tucked in the top, and he wore an old long coat with skirts that hung wrinkled and loose at his knees; but he had no hat and the sea wind stirred the black hairs of his head.

The tide was out and the ship lay low, and Blind MacNair climbed the forerigging to the level of the wharf and a sailor gave him a hand and pointed him for the wharf's end. That was the way Blind MacNair came to Shardstown, with his staff striking a hollow sound from the planks of the wharf, and the sea wind blowing the skirts of his coat, and the long hair streaming about his head, like a blind prophet out of the Bible.

Shardstown folk were shy of strangers, and Blind MacNair was an awesome man to see; so they stood off and watched him up the village street and down, without a word. But children saw the gentleness in him and sang out "Hello," as he passed, and Blind MacNair paused in the dust and asked their names in the deep slow voice he had. And after a time Taggart's wife—Taggart of the forge—called her youngsters to supper and saw them squatted about MacNair in the grass at the wayside.

MacNair was singing softly, and the song was "Fair Margaret and Sweet William." That is a sad song and a sweet song; the children stayed to the end, and Taggart's wife came to the gate and listened, too. At the end she said, "Won't you come in, man, and have a bite with us?"

MacNair rose gravely and bowed. "Thank ye, ma'am, and I will."

After the supper things were cleared Taggart sat with MacNair by the stove in the parlor, and while Mrs. Taggart shushed the children off to their beds the blacksmith said, "Where's your home? If that's a fair question."

"I've none," said Blind MacNair; "no more than the birds."

"It's fall," Taggart said, "and the birds gone to the South for winter."

"South!" said the blind man. "'Tis a great country, the South, but a sad one, and I've had my fill of sadness. Ten years I've been wandering, and there came on me suddenly a great longing to be in my own country. This was my landfall. There's birds must winter in the North, for that is the way of them."

"Ah!" Taggart said. He was a tall man and spare, with a red beard square as a shovel, and his eyes were kind. "Would ye take a bed in the garret the winter?"

"Man, man," said MacNair, "the winter bird's no beggar. The bush by the pasture wall, the red berry left by God on the bare wild rose, a crumb at the kitchen door if it's offered, and chance the rest. That's the winter bird, and that's Blind MacNair."

"You're proud, man, and I respect ye for it," Taggart said. "There's the spare bedroom over the parlor that's fixed up fine for ministers and such."

"Is there no loft to your stable?" demanded MacNair.

"What place is that for a man?" cried Taggart's wife, for she had come into the room and stood by Taggart's chair with her hands on his shoulder.

"I'm only half a man," said MacNair, "and a stable was good enough for the child of God."

SO MacNair slept the winter in Taggart's loft, with the quilts from Taggart's spare bed, and caught his meals as the birds do, a dinner here and a supper there; with Fraser the blockmaker, with Lowrie the fishing captain, with Shard the ship chandler, and now and again at Taggart's—but not often, for "I'm beholden enough for the loft," said Blind MacNair.

He was a welcome guest wherever he went. There was never a speck on his clothes nor a whiff of the stable about him; for he was clean, that man, clean as the brook that fell from the hill, and he ate as neat as a man with eyes. Like everybody in Shardstown he had the Gaelic, and when he said the grace before meat you felt that God was in that house.

After the meal Blind MacNair would sing, with the menfolk at their pipes and the women waiting the dishes, and the children sitting about his feet. A grand strong voice he had, and could roar a chantey with the best of the sailors. But he liked ballads best; for ballads he would drop his voice to the size of the room, till it was like a man speaking music, and his voice was deep and sad on the low notes like the southerly pipes of the Presbyterian organ at Revesport.

Daytime he spent at Taggart's forge. That was Shardstown's club-room in winter, the bellows roaring under the red coals, the old men on the benches that Taggart had made for them, and the teamsters leaning or squatting while their beasts were shod. He loved to get the men singing chanteys, himself giving the by-line in a great round voice and the men roaring in on the chorus. And when they struck up a real rouser like "The Drunken Sailor," Taggart himself would join in, singing free like a man that enjoyed himself, hammering *rang-tang-tang* on the live iron, and the golden fire spurting. Those were singing times, and Shardstown men were great men to sing; but there was never such singing as they had that winter in Taggart's forge.

With the turn of the year the cold grew and there was good snow for the log hauling. Ox bells rang up and down the beaten sled road from the woods, and the birchwood yokes creaked, and the runners squealed on the snow, and the teamsters grinned and cracked their little whips.

When March came the loggers came out of the woods. They had hauled their cut, and a turn of the wind now would bring the thaw and the breakup. And there was work now at the wharves, with schooners to fit out for the spring voyage to the Banks, and a bark from Revesport to load with shooks from McLaughlan's cooperage. There was great singing in the forge then, for the chanteyman of the bark was a big, handsome Negro man with a voice like the sound of great bells, and Singing Johnny Hanigan had come over from Revesport to go in the fishery.

The Negro man had a great store of songs, and Singing Johnny was famous in forty miles of coast, and when the Shardstown men began to brag of Blind MacNair one thing was certain.

It came of a Saturday morning, with the old men sitting each in his place, and sailors and loggers and fishermen and ship carpenters standing or squatting wherever was room for their heels. Taggart's was a big forge and dark, though the sun flamed on the snow outside; for the inside walls and the high gloomy rafters were black with the smoke of a century, and the little windows thick with dust, and the big double doors closed for the sake of the old thin blood on the benches.

There was a smell of hot iron in that place always, and a smell of horses and oxen and scorched hooves; and now such a smell of men and tobacco as the forge had rarely known, for Singing Johnny and the Negro man had set out to sing down Blind MacNair.

Taggart had Donald MacAllan's big ox in the shoeing stall when the singing began, and he went on with it, for he was no man to let pleasure meddle with business. So he thrust the ox down on its knees in the open frame of the stall, and made each foreleg fast with rope to the shoeing ledge, hoof upward, and moored the beast bow and stern like a ship, with a rope to the yoke and a high rope to the off hind foot. And he passed the broad canvas band under the hard brown belly and put the wooden pin in the windlass socket, and hoisted the beast off its hind feet for the shoeing of them.

Each part of that wooden stall was dark and smooth from the grasp of Taggart's hands, and the hands of his father and grandfather before him. The chimney stood at the back of the forge with the brick block of the fireplace waist-high before it, and the black beam of the bellows and the anvil and workbench by the window to the left of it. To the right was a litter of long iron stretched along the floor, and a bench for wheelwright work.

That space was full of men standing, the iron a-clank with the shift of their feet, and the bench laden with sitters. And the space between the fire and the big double doors was full of men too, except the ox stall in the corner where Taggart knelt at his work. And in the midst of it all sat Blind MacNair on a three-legged stool, with his coat skirts in the dust on the floor, and his big hands on his knees. And the smiling Negro sat on the earthen floor, and Johnny Hanigan stood.

They began with chanteys as a matter of course, to get them out of the way, singing the solo lines in turn and chanting the chorus together. The first was "Reuben Ranzo," and they sang twenty verses about that famous dirty sailor who shipped aboard a whaler.

Then it came Johnny Hanigan's turn for the verse. He hesitated, and no wonder, for nobody had ever heard so many verses to "Reuben Ranzo"; but he saved himself in time with a poor patched-up sort of verse out of his own head that fitted the tune badly and rhymed worse.

There was no rule against such, for a good chanteyman could make a new verse to an old tune, and sometimes the verse pleased other ears. That was how chanteys grew. But there was ill taste in offering a trumped-up verse, and a poor one, to sing down another man. Everyone expected MacNair to say something, for he knew no more, but he shrugged and opened his hands; and the Negro man said, "No more here," and the chalk went on the board on the wall with a mark for Singing Johnny.

Then MacNair began "Shenandoah," and the Negro man sang the next verse, and Johnny followed after. That is a great chantey, to be sung slowly, and so they sang it; you could shut your eyes and see sailormen stamping round a capstan with hard brown hands on the bars, and the chanteyman perched on the cathead, and the cable coming in wet from the tide. MacNair had the last of it, for the Negro man grinned and said, "No more here," and Singing Johnny could not say better.

So they went on through "Leave Her Johnny," and "Blow, Boys, Blow," and "Banks of Sacramento," and "Blow the Man Down," and "Paddy Doyle's Boots," and "Stormalong" and the other workaday chanteys, and turned at last to the less familiar ones. And when it came to "Sally Brown," and "Johnny Come to Hilo," and "Bound to Alabama," and those other cotton-rolling songs that drifted out to sea in the bosom of Mississippi, the big Negro man went far ahead in the score, singing verse after verse when the others had dropped out and his mark was up on the wall, singing just for the pleasure of it, and his voice ringing through the crowded forge like a music of hammered brass.

From behind came the sounds of Taggart's work as he tapped home the little half-moon shoes on the ox, snipped the nail points with a twist of the sharp hammer claw, and cast loose the foot lashings, and took the pin from the windlass barrel and lowered the great drooling beast to its new-shod feet. But there the big ox stayed. His owner was part of that listening throng, lost to the world and the waiting sled on the hillside. And Taggart stood on the shoeing ledge of the stall for better hearing, and hung there silent with a hand on the yoke of the ox.

It was strange; the big ox patient in the corner, and the tall red-bearded man above him, and the silence of gathered men, and the singers chanting in the midst, like something barbaric and old as the world.

Outside, the sun stood at noon, but no one in Taggart's forge gave a thought to food. Food was a thing you got three times a day. Singing like this might not come again in a month of Sundays.

They turned to ballads now, as men turn from the morning chores to the real work of the day. Any fool could sing chanteys, and the man with the most verses won the score. But with the ballad it was as with hymns, a proper set of verses handed down from the past, and woe to the man who altered so much as a word. There were keen old ears on the benches, and tongues to chide, and a score to lose on the board of the wall.

Singing Johnny began with "Bold Jack Donohue"; and at the song's end Blind MacNair said quietly, "That is a good ballad and an old one, for it came out of the country of Australia long before the gold-finding; but ye have the names of the bush rangers wrong in the third verse." And the old men nodded and said it was so.

The Negro man had a try at the third verse, but the old men wagged their heads. Then sang MacNair; and the names, Walmsley, Weber, Underwood rang true in the old heads; the blind man's score went up on the board.

And they went on to "The Golden Vanitee," and "Farewell to Ye Spanish Ladies," and "High Barbaree," and other old, old ballads of the sea, and Blind MacNair held his own with Singing Johnny, and the black man held his lead. But when they came to "The Tiger and the Lion," which tells of a sea fight in the olden time, the Negro man dropped a point to Singing Johnny. And they came to "Hame, Dearie, Hame," and the black man dropped a point to Blind MacNair, for he did not know those songs; and from then on the Negro man was lost, for all his fine voice and the good nature of him.

"I never saw the nigger yet could sing ballads!" cried Singing Johnny Hanigan.

"Nor the braggart," answered Blind MacNair, and Singing Johnny laughed; but there was no pleasure on his tongue—then or after.

So the Negro man dropped out of the game, and Johnny and

MacNair went on through "The Chesapeake and Shannon," and then "The Fighting Chance," and the score between them even. Blind MacNair sang "The Captain and the Maiden," and Singing Johnny followed with "Young Johnson": and MacNair sang "Lord Bateman," and Johnny sang "The Banks of Newfoundland."

And Blind MacNair said, "That was a good ballad and well sung, and there's all the sorrow of the sea in the part that goes:

"Oh, when they took us from the wreck we were more like ghosts than men,
They clothed us and they fed us and they took us home again.
But there was few of our company that e'er reached English land,
And the captain lost his limbs by frost on the Banks o' Newfoundland."

And the man with the chalk scored one on the board for Blind MacNair, for Hanigan had it *"The captain died o' frostbite on the Banks o' Newfoundland"*—and all knew that was wrong. And again Singing Johnny laughed, and no pleasure in it.

Then Blind MacNair sang "The Ship Lady Sherbrooke," which is a sad ballad of Irish folk wrecked on the voyage to Quebec. And Johnny Hanigan sang "On the Banks of the Brandywine," a fine tune with romance and scenery and a sailor in it, and popular with the Shardstown men. But MacNair sang "Young Charlotte," the ballad of the frozen bride, for the sad mood was on him; and the fishermen stirred uneasily, for they believed "Young Charlotte" an unlucky song, a Jonah song, and would never hear it sung aboard the vessels.

So Singing Johnny cheered them with "The Rambling Irishman," a jolly thing that set them tapping their feet on the hard earthen floor, and Blind MacNair saw that he must keep his sadness to himself. So he sang "The Braes o' Balquhidder." That song has a lift to its music like the lilting of bagpipes heard afar on the hills in the morning, and the men were glad to see MacNair put his sadness down. And Johnny Hanigan, not to be outdone in a song of old Scotland, sang "The Pride of Glencoe," a grand song about a soldier MacDonald and the lassie that waited home for him. But there was no pleasure in Johnny's singing anymore, because he was behind in the score and he knew he could not sing down Blind MacNair.

The afternoon was far gone, the dinners parching on the stoves of Shardstown and the wives all peering out of doors to know what man-foolishness was afoot in Taggart's forge. The sun drooped low in a patch of mist over the western woods, with queer rays shining out to the four points of the sky's compass. That was a sign of snow; and the wind had come east and fetched now a cold breath from the sea, and set up a shudder in the rigging of ships, and moaned down every chimney in the village. There would be snow before morning.

Singing Johnny was beaten and he was hungry. He stared in the calm face of Blind MacNair and found something terrible about it, the face of an image that could sing, sing forever, and not to be moved by earthquakes. He could not sing that image down; but Johnny Hanigan had made a boast, and a boast is a hard thing to swallow when you are famous in forty miles.

"Can ye sing 'The Blind Sailor'?" asked Singing Johnny.

"I can," said Blind MacNair, and sang it. A verse of that song runs:

Before we reached the mainmast cap a heavier flash came on,
My God, I well remember it, my last glimpse of the sun.
Our main topmast in pieces split, all in a pelting light,
And me and four more seamen bold by lightning lost our sight.

"And," asked Johnny Hanigan, "is that how ye lost yours?"

"'Twas not," said Blind MacNair.

"How then?"

"In war," said Blind MacNair.

"The American war—the Civil War?"

"Call it that if ye like."

"Will ye sing for us 'The Fifer of the Cumberland'?" demanded Johnny Hanigan.

"I will not," said Blind MacNair.

"I wonder ye don't know it. 'Tis the song of a brave boy."

"Ay, a brave boy, and a Yankee boy, and a good brave song."

"I was on the Yankee side in that war," Johnny Hanigan murmured, and ran his glance about the men, for half the gathering had fought in the Northern army in that war.

"No doubt," said Blind MacNair. "The war was across the border and nothing of ours, in a manner of speaking. But our talk was all of the North and the South, and from argument men go to deeds if their heart's in what they say. The war's past and done with now, and they were brave men all; but I fought by the side of the Southern men and I will sing no Yankee song."

And now men noticed that Singing Johnny had come to a stoop, and now he was leaning forward, and his long fingers licking out to the face of Blind MacNair.

"I doubt ye fought in any war and I doubt you're blind!" he cried, and whipped the silk from MacNair's eyes while the whole forge gasped and stared.

MacNair might have been an image of stone. Not a muscle moved. His lips were firm. The lids of his eyes were closed, and white as a woman's, for they had known no sun since the fall of '64. Just beneath the thick black brows ran a scar from side to side, straight as a ruler—straight as a slash of a sword.

Singing Johnny stood dumb, with the green wisp in his fingers.

"I got that," MacNair said quietly, "from Sheridan's cavalry in the Valley of Virginia. A good fight, and my last."

"Sorry," mumbled Johnny Hanigan.

"Sorrow's not enough," said Blind MacNair. He stood up then, a fine strong figure of a man, awesome with the bleached stripe in his dark skin, and the shining scar, and the white closed eyes.

"Many Nova Scotia men went to that war—ten thousand, they say—and some fought for the one side, some for the other, according to their opinions. There's no knowing now which had the right of it, for a brave man makes a brave cause, and blood's the one color, North or South. But whichever jacket he wore, the Bluenose was an honest man and a fighting man and a credit to Nova Scotia. Now there must always be an exception to prove a rule, and there were certain ones that crossed Fundy Bay to pluck what cash they could from the agony of other men. In Boston ye could get two or three hundred dollars from the sons of the rich, to substitute on the draft, and another hundred bounty from the state. And 'twas easy to desert then to another state and 'list again with another name for another shower of Yankee dollars. Some were caught, and some got away home with their blood money—though it couldn't buy enough soap to take the Judas smell from their hands. I'm truly blind, Johnny Hanigan, but the eye of the mind sees through the stones of the wall. I will sing you a Yankee song. 'Tis a good song, and a jolly song, and a fine song for the feet on the road." And he began:

"Come all you fine young fellows, I am going to sing a song:
I pray you give attention and I won't detain you long.
'Tis of a fine young fellow, and Johnny was his name:
He was tried in Alexandria for the doing of this same."

Now that was a song called "The Bounty Jumper," known to every man in the forge, and they joined MacNair in the chorus.

"So come join my humble ditty as from town to town I steer.
Like every real good fellow I am always on the beer;
Like every real good fellow I prefer my whisky clear,
I'm a rambling rake of poverty and the son of a gamboleer."

And Blind MacNair sang on:

"Oh, he jumped in Philadelphy and he jumped into New York;
He jumped in the City of Boston, it was all the people's talk.
Oh, he jumped and he jumped all along the Yankee shore,
But the last place he jumped was in the Town of Baltimore."

It was made for the laughter of marching men, that song; but Blind MacNair sang it with a strange violence, like the chanting of a curse.

Singing Johnny Hanigan stood, white and red by turns, a thin sweat on his long clever face, with the chorus pouring upon him like scalding water. And whenever the tune struck the high note some iron rods vibrated thinly on the beam overhead, as if the old forge itself had come to life for the scorn of Johnny Hanigan.

"Oh, now we'll dig poor Johnny's grave, we'll dig it wide and deep.
We'll bury him in the valley where the bounty jumpers sleep.
We'll put him in his coffin and we'll carry him along,
And we'll all join the chorus of the bounty jumper's song."

But Singing Johnny did not wait for the end. He slunk out of the forge like the shadow of a man, and nobody ever saw him in Shardstown again.

He left one of the big doors open, with a broad wedge of daylight pouring into the forge and blinding them all. There was a great silence. Then a woman's shadow fell across the floor and Nellie Bullen's voice was crying, "Mr. Taggart! Mr. Taggart!"

Taggart stepped down from the shoeing stall and thrust through the blinking men to her.

"The mare's got a loose shoe, Mr. Taggart; will you look at it, please? The road's a glare of ice—and I must get home before the snow."

Taggart went outside and Nellie Bullen turned to follow him, and just then James McCuish said, "Sing us one more song, MacNair, afore we go."

Nellie Bullen paused.

She was a tall woman with gray eyes, and she had the slim proud back of the Bullen women, and thick coils of hair with a dull gold shine like a hempen hawser new from the ropewalk.

"Can ye sing 'The Desolate Widow'?" asked James McCuish, for he was a thoughtless man.

"Not I," said Blind MacNair. He faced the open door with his feet together and his hands at his trouser seams, like a soldier—or a prisoner before judgment. The cold light was full on his face.

"Any song, then! A Gaelic song—we've had no Gaelic songs today."

"I know a song," said Blind MacNair, "but there's no more music in me, and no rhyme to the words. A poor thing it is."

"Give us the hang of it," insisted James McCuish.

"An old tale, James, old as the sorrows of the world. A young man with a hot head, and a young wife with spirit. There's the quarrel, and the young man saying things no lassie of spirit would take, and there's the separation, with the young wife home to her own folk and the young man off to the wars. You see how old a song it is. Now in those old songs always the young man comes home a hero from the wars, and finds the wife forgiving and waiting true, and there's an end of it. But this song of mine goes wrong somehow, for the man comes blind and a beggar, no fit company for man, woman or dog. A judgment on him d'ye see?—for in the parting he'd said, 'May I never see you again!'—and never he will, except with the eye of the mind."

"Cruel judgment, that, for a few foolish words," objected Lowrie the fishing captain.

"The judgment of God?" murmured old John MacLaughlan reprovingly.

"But what's the end of the song?" asked Nellie Bullen from the doorway, and the men pressed back, none knew why, until she was standing alone in the shaft of light that fell upon MacNair, and all the men hushed in the shadows.

"It has no end, it goes on forever," cried Blind MacNair.

"Forever?" she said. "There's only one song goes on forever." There was a flutter of skirts, and suddenly Nellie Bullen had her arms about Blind MacNair and her shining head on his shoulder, and her hat in the dust of the floor.

"Ah, Colin, Colin!" cried Nellie Bullen.

Tears ran down his face, strange and terrible, as if you saw water spring from a barren rock. "I've nothing to give ye, Nellie."

She kissed him then, and the men began stealing out of Taggart's forge with a strange look on their faces, as if they had seen ghosts.

"Will you give your son the sound of his father's voice, Colin?"

"My son!"

"Will you sing for your wife the song that goes without end?"

Och, yes, it was a great singing that day in Taggart's forge, but long ago, and who remembers the old time now? The old Bullen farmhouse, where Nellie MacNair took her husband that night of the big March snow, is gone from the Revesport road, with nothing to mark it but a dent in the green turf.

Some in Shardstown hold the place haunted, and say how on nights of the full May moon you can hear Blind MacNair ploughing the windy hillside behind the old white Bullen horse, and singing the old Gaelic song "Mo Run Geal Dileas"—"My Faithful Fair One." But that is an old wives' tale; and how could they know that song? For in Shardstown only the old men in the sunshine remember, and they sing ballads no more.

THE PROCURATOR OF JUDAEA
ANATOLE FRANCE / FRANCE

A ELIUS LAMIA, born in Italy of illustrious parents, had not yet discarded the *toga praetexta* when he set out for the schools of Athens to study philosophy. Subsequently he took up his residence at Rome, and in his house on the Esquiline, amid a circle of youthful wastrels, abandoned himself to licentious courses. But being accused of engaging in criminal relations with Lepida, the wife of Sulpicius Quirinus, a man of consular rank, and being found guilty, he was exiled by Tiberius Caesar. At that time he was just entering his twenty-fourth year. During the eighteen years that his exile lasted he traversed Syria, Palestine, Cappadocia, and Armenia, and made prolonged visits to Antioch, Caesarea, and Jerusalem. When, after the death of Tiberius, Caius was raised to the purple, Lamia obtained permission to return to Rome. He even regained a portion of his possessions. Adversity had taught him wisdom.

He avoided all intercourse with the wives and daughters of Roman citizens, made no efforts toward obtaining office, held aloof from public honors, and lived a secluded life in his house on the Esquiline. Occupying himself with the task of recording all the remarkable things he had seen during his distant travels, he turned, as he said, the vicissitudes of his years of expiation into a diversion for his hours of rest. In the midst of these calm employments, alternating with assiduous study of the works of Epicurus, he recognized with a mixture of surprise and vexation that age was stealing upon him. In his sixty-second year, being afflicted with an illness which proved in no slight degree troublesome, he decided to have recourse to the waters at Baiae. The coast at that point, once frequented by the halcyon was at this date the resort of the wealthy Roman, greedy of pleasure. For a week Lamia lived alone, without a friend in the brilliant crowd. Then one day, after dinner, an inclination to which he yielded urged him to ascend the incline, which, covered with vines that resembled bacchantes, looked out upon the waves.

Having reached the summit he seated himself by the side of a path beneath a terebinth, and let his glances wander over the lovely landscape. To his left, livid and bare, the Phlegraean plain stretched out toward the ruins of Cumae. On his right, Cape Misenum plunged its abrupt spur beneath the Tyrrhenian sea. Beneath his feet luxurious Baiae, following the graceful outline of the coast, displayed its gardens, its villas thronged with statues, its porticoes, its marble terraces along the shores of the blue ocean where the dolphins sported. Before him, on the other side of the bay, on the Campanian coast, gilded by the already sinking sun, gleamed the temples which far away rose above the laurels of Posilipo, whilst on the extreme horizon Vesuvius looked forth smiling.

Lamia drew from a fold of his toga a scroll containing the *Treatise upon Nature*, extended himself upon the ground, and began to read. But the warning cries of a slave necessitated his rising to allow of the passage of a litter which was being carried along the narrow pathway through the vineyards. The litter being uncurtained, permitted Lamia to see stretched upon the cushions as it was borne nearer to him the figure of an elderly man of immense bulk, who, supporting his head on his hand, gazed out with a gloomy and disdainful expression. His nose, which was aquiline, and his chin, which was prominent, seemed desirous of meeting across his lips, and his jaws were powerful.

From the first moment Lamia was convinced that the face was familiar to him. He hesitated a moment before the name came to him. Then suddenly hastening toward the litter with a display of surprise and delight—

"Pontius Pilate!" he cried. "The gods be praised who have permitted me to see you once again!"

The old man gave a signal to the slaves to stop, and cast a keen glance upon the stranger who had addressed him.

"Pontius, my dear host," resumed the latter, "have twenty years so far whitened my hair and hollowed my cheeks that you no longer recognize your friend Aelius Lamia?"

At this name Pontius Pilate dismounted from the litter as actively as the weight of his years and the heaviness of his gait permitted him, and embraced Aelius Lamia again and again.

"Gods! what a treat it is to me to see you once more! But, alas, you call up memories of those long-vanished days when I was Procurator of Judaea in the province of Syria. Why, it must be thirty years ago that I first met you. It was at Caesarea, whither you came to drag out your weary term of exile. I was fortunate enough to alleviate it a little, and out of friendship, Lamia, you followed me to that depressing place Jerusalem, where the Jews filled me with bitterness and disgust. You remained for more than ten years my guest and my companion, and in converse about Rome and things Roman we both of us managed to find consolation—you for your misfortunes, and I for my burdens of State."

Lamia embraced him afresh.

"You forget two things, Pontius; you are overlooking the facts that you used your influence on my behalf with Herod Antipas, and that your purse was freely open to me."

"Let us not talk of that," replied Pontius, "since after your return to Rome you sent me by one of your freedmen a sum of money which repaid me with usury."

"Pontius, I could never consider myself out of your debt by the mere payment of money. But tell me, have the gods fulfilled your desires? Are you in the enjoyment of all the happiness you deserve? Tell me about your family, your fortunes, your health."

"I have withdrawn to Sicily, where I possess estates, and where I cultivate wheat for the market. My eldest daughter, my best-beloved Pontia, who has been left a widow, lives with me, and directs my household. The gods be praised, I have preserved my mental vigor; my memory is not in the least degree enfeebled. But old age always brings in its train a long procession of griefs and infirmities. I am cruelly tormented with gout. And at this very moment you find me on my way to the Phlegraean plain in search of a remedy for my sufferings. From that burning soil, whence at night flames burst forth, proceed acrid exhalations of sulfur, which, so they say, ease the pains and restore suppleness to the stiffened joints. At least, the physicians assure me that it is so."

"May you find it so in your case, Pontius! But, despite the gout and its burning torments, you scarcely look as old as myself, although in reality you must be my senior by ten years. Unmistakably you have retained a greater degree of vigor than I ever possessed, and I am overjoyed to find you looking so hale. Why, dear friend, did you retire from the public service before the customary age? Why, on resigning your governorship in Judaea, did you withdraw to a voluntary exile on your Sicilian estates? Give me an account of your doings from the moment that I ceased to be a witness of them. You were preparing to suppress a Samaritan rising when I set out for Cappadocia, where I hoped to draw some profit from the breeding of horses and mules. I have not seen you since then. How did that expedition succeed? Pray tell me. Everything interests me that concerns you in any way."

Pontius Pilate sadly shook his head.

"My natural disposition," he said, "as well as a sense of duty, impelled me to fulfill my public responsibilities, not merely with diligence, but even with ardor. But I was pursued by unrelenting hatred. Intrigues and calumnies cut short my career in its prime, and the fruit it should have looked to bear has withered away. You ask me about the Samaritan insurrection. Let us sit down on this hillock. I shall be able to give you an answer in few words. Those occurrences are as vividly present to me as if they had happened yesterday.

"A man of the people, of persuasive speech—there are many such to be met with in Syria—induced the Samaritans to gather together in arms on Mount Gerizim (which in that country is looked upon as a holy place) under the promise that he would disclose to their sight the sacred vessels which in the ancient days of Evander and our father, Aeneas, had been hidden away by an eponymous hero, or rather a tribal deity, named Moses. Upon this assurance the Samaritans rose in rebellion; but having been warned in time to forestall them, I dispatched detachments of infantry to occupy the mountain, and stationed cavalry to keep the approaches to it under observation.

"These measures of prudence were urgent. The rebels were already laying siege to the town of Tyrathaba, situated at the foot of Mount Gerizim. I easily dispersed them, and stifled the as yet scarcely organized revolt. Then, in order to give a forcible example with as few victims as possible, I handed over to execution the leaders of the rebellion. But you are aware, Lamia, in what strait dependence I was kept by the proconsul Vitellius, who governed Syria not in, but against the interests of Rome, and looked upon the provinces of the empire as territories which could be farmed out to tetrarchs. The head-men among the Samaritans, in their resentment against me, came and fell at his feet lamenting. To listen to them, nothing had been further from their thoughts than to disobey Caesar. It was I who had provoked the rising, and it was purely in order to withstand my violence that they had gathered together round Tyrathaba. Vitellius listened to their complaints, and handing over the affairs of Judaea to his friend Marcellus, commanded me to go and justify my proceedings before the Emperor himself. With a heart overflowing with grief and resentment I took ship. Just as I approached the shores of Italy, Tiberius, worn out with age and the cares of the empire, died suddenly on the selfsame Cape Misenum, whose peak we see from this very spot magnified in the mists of evening. I demanded justice of Caius, his successor, whose perception was naturally acute, and who was acquainted with Syrian affairs. But marvel with me, Lamia, at the maliciousness of fortune, resolved on my discomfiture. Caius then had in his suite at Rome the Jew Agrippa, his companion, the friend of his childhood, whom he cherished as his own eyes. Now Agrippa favored Vitellius, inasmuch as Vitellius was the enemy of Antipas, whom Agrippa pursued with his hatred. The Emperor adopted the prejudices of his beloved Asiatic, and refused even to listen to me. There was nothing for me to do but bow beneath the stroke of unmerited misfortune. With tears for my meat and gall for my portion, I withdrew to my estates in Sicily, where I should have died of grief if my sweet Pontia had not come to console her father. I have cultivated wheat, and succeeded in producing the fullest ears in the whole province. But now my life is ended; the future will judge between Vitellius and me."

"Pontius," replied Lamia, "I am persuaded that you acted toward the Samaritans according to the rectitude of your character, and solely in the interests of Rome. But were you not perchance on that occasion a trifle too much influenced by that impetuous courage which has always swayed you? You will remember that in Judaea it often happened that I who, younger than you, should naturally have been more impetuous than you, was obliged to urge you to clemency and suavity."

"Suavity toward the Jews!" cried Pontius Pilate. "Although you have lived amongst them, it seems clear that you ill understand those enemies of the human race. Haughty and at the same time base, combining an invincible obstinacy with a despicably mean spirit, they weary alike your love and your hatred. My character, Lamia, was formed upon the maxims of the divine Augustus. When I was appointed Procurator of Judaea, the world was already penetrated with the majestic ideal of the *pax romana*. No longer, as in the days of our internecine strife, were we witnesses to the sack of a province for the aggrandizement of a proconsul. I knew where my duty lay. I was careful that my actions should be governed by prudence and moderation. The gods are my witnesses that I was resolved upon mildness, and upon mildness only. Yet what did my benevolent intentions avail me? You were at my side, Lamia, when, at the outset of my career as ruler, the first rebellion came to a head. Is there any need for me to recall the details to you? The garrison had been transferred from Caesarea to take up its winter quarters at Jerusalem. Upon the ensigns of the legionaries appeared the presentment of Caesar. The inhabitants of Jerusalem, who did not recognize the indwelling divinity of the Emperor, were scandalized at this, as though, when obedience is compulsory, it were not less abject to obey a god than a man. The priests of their nation appeared before my tribunal imploring me with supercilious humility to have the ensigns removed from within the holy city. Out of reverence for the divine nature of Caesar and the majesty of the empire, I refused to comply. Then the rabble made common cause with the priests, and all around the pretorium portentous cries of supplication arose. I ordered the soldiers to stack their spears in front of the tower of Antonia, and to proceed, armed only with sticks like lictors, to disperse the insolent crowd. But, heedless of blows, the Jews continued their entreaties, and the more obstinate amongst them threw themselves on the ground and, exposing their throats to the rods, deliberately courted death. You were a witness of my humiliation on that occasion, Lamia. By the order of Vitellius I was forced to send the insignia back to Caesarea. That disgrace I had certainly not merited. Before the immortal gods I swear that never once during my term of office did I flout justice and the laws. But I am grown old. My enemies and detractors are dead. I shall die unavenged. Who will now retrieve my character?"

He moaned and lapsed into silence. Lamia replied—

"That man is prudent who neither hopes nor fears anything from the uncertain events of the future. Does it matter in the least what estimate men may form of us hereafter? We ourselves are after all our own witnesses, and our own judges. You must rely, Pontius Pilate, on the testimony you yourself bear to your own rectitude. Be content with your own personal respect and that of your friends. For the rest, we know that mildness by itself will not suffice for the work of government. There is but little room in the actions of public men for that indulgence of human frailty which the philosophers recommend."

"We'll say no more at present," said Pontius. "The sulfureous fumes which rise from the Phlegraean plain are more powerful when the ground which exhales them is still warm beneath the sun's rays. I must hasten on. Adieu! But now that I have rediscovered a friend, I should wish to take advantage of my good fortune. Do me the favor, Aelius Lamia, to give me your company at supper at my house tomorrow. My house stands on the seashore, at the extreme end of the town in the direction of Misenum. You will easily recognize it by the porch which bears a painting representing Orpheus surrounded by tigers and lions, whom he is charming with the strains from his lyre.

"Till tomorrow, Lamia," he repeated, as he climbed once more into his litter. "Tomorrow we will talk about Judaea."

THE FOLLOWING DAY at the supper hour Lamia presented himself at the house of Pontius Pilate. Two couches only were in readiness for occupants. Creditably but simply equipped, the table held a silver service in which were set out beccaficos in honey, thrushes, oysters from the Lucrine lake, and lampreys from Sicily. As they proceeded with their repast, Pontius and Lamia interchanged inquiries with one another about their ailments, the symptoms of which they described at considerable length, mutually emulous of communicating the various remedies which had been recommended to them. Then, congratulating themselves on being thrown together once more at Baiae, they vied with one another in the praise of the beauty of that enchanting coast and the mildness of the climate they enjoyed. Lamia was enthusiastic about the charms of the courtesans who frequented the seashore laden with golden ornaments and trailing draperies of barbaric broidery. But the aged Procurator deplored the ostentation with which by means of trumpery jewels and filmy garments foreigners and even enemies of the empire beguiled the Romans of their gold. After a time they turned to the subject of the great engineering feats that had been accomplished in the country: the prodigious bridge constructed by Caius between Puteoli and Baiae, and the canals which Augustus excavated to convey the waters of the ocean to Lake Avernus and the Lucrine lake.

"I also," said Pontius, with a sigh, "I also wished to set afoot public works of great utility. When, for my sins, I was appointed Governor of Judaea, I conceived the idea of furnishing Jerusalem with an abundant supply of pure water by means of an aqueduct. The elevation of the levels, the proportionate capacity of the various parts, the gradient for the brazen reservoirs to which the distribution pipes were to be fixed—I had gone into every detail, and decided everything for myself with the assistance of mechanical experts. I had drawn up regulations for the superintendents so as to prevent individuals from making unauthorized depredations. The architects and the workmen had their instructions. I gave orders for the commencement of operations. But far from viewing with satisfaction the construction of that conduit, which was intended to carry to their town upon its massive arches not only water but health, the inhabitants of Jerusalem gave vent to lamentable outcries. They gathered tumultuously together, exclaiming against the sacrilege and impiousness, and, hurling themselves upon the workmen, scattered the very foundation stones. Can you picture to yourself, Lamia, a filthier set of barbarians? Nevertheless, Vitellius decided in their favor, and I received orders to put a stop to the work."

"It is a knotty point," said Lamia, "how far one is justified in devising things for the commonweal against the will of the populace."

Pontius Pilate continued as though he had not heard this interruption.

"Refuse an aqueduct! What madness! But whatever is of Roman origin is distasteful to the Jews. In their eyes we are an unclean race, and our very presence appears a profanation to them. You will remember that they would never venture to enter the pretorium for fear of defiling themselves, and that I was consequently obliged to discharge my magisterial functions in an open-air tribunal on that marble pavement your feet so often trod.

"They fear us and they despise us. Yet is not Rome the mother and warden of all those peoples who nestle smiling upon her venerable bosom? With her eagles in the van, peace and liberty have been carried to the very confines of the universe. Those whom we have subdued we look on as our friends, and we leave those conquered races, nay, we secure to them the permanence of their customs and their laws. Did Syria, aforetime rent asunder by its rabble of petty kings, ever even begin to taste of peace and prosperity until it submitted to the armies of Pompey? And when Rome might have reaped a golden harvest as the price of her goodwill, did she lay hands on the hoards that swell the treasuries of barbaric temples? Did she despoil the shrine of Cybele at Pessinus, or the Morimene and Cilician sanctuaries of Jupiter, or the temple of the Jewish god at Jerusalem? Antioch, Palmyra, and Apamea, secure despite their wealth, and no longer in dread of the wandering Arab of the desert, have erected temples to the genius of Rome and the divine Caesar. The Jews alone hate and withstand us. They withhold their tribute till it is wrested from them, and obstinately rebel against military service."

"The Jews," replied Lamia, "are profoundly attached to their ancient customs. They suspected you, unreasonably I admit, of a desire to abolish their laws and change their usages. Do not resent it, Pontius, if I say that you did not always act in such a way as to disperse their unfortunate illusion. It gratified you, despite your habitual self-restraint, to play upon their fears, and more than once have I seen you betray in their presence the contempt with which their beliefs and religious ceremonies inspired you. You irritated them particularly by giving instructions for the sacerdotal garments and ornaments of their high priest to be kept in ward by your legionaries in the Antonine tower. One must admit that though they have never risen like us to an appreciation of things divine, the Jews celebrate rites which their very antiquity renders venerable."

Pontius Pilate shrugged his shoulders.

"They have very little exact knowledge of the nature of the gods," he said. "They worship Jupiter, yet they abstain from naming him or erecting a statue of him. They do not even adore him under the semblance of a rude stone, as certain of the Asiatic peoples are wont to do. They know nothing of Apollo, of Neptune, of Mars, nor of Pluto, nor of any goddess. At the same time, I am convinced that in days gone by they worshipped Venus. For even to this day their women bring doves to the altar as victims; and you know as well as I that the dealers who trade beneath the arcades of their temple supply those birds in couples for sacrifice. I have even been told that on one occasion some madman proceeded to overturn the stalls bearing these offerings, and their owners with them. The priests raised an outcry about it, and looked on it as a case of sacrilege. I am of opinion that their custom of sacrificing turtledoves was instituted in honor of Venus. Why are you laughing, Lamia?"

"I was laughing," said Lamia, "at an amusing idea which, I hardly know how, just occurred to me. I was thinking that perchance some day the Jupiter of the Jews might come to Rome and vent his fury upon you. Why should he not? Asia and Africa have already enriched us with a considerable number of gods. We have seen temples in honor of Isis and the dog-faced Anubis erected in Rome. In the public squares, and even on the racecourses, you may run across the Bona Dea of the Syrians mounted on an ass. And did you never hear how, in the reign of Tiberius, a young patrician passed himself off as the horned Jupiter of the Egyptians, Jupiter Ammon, and in this disguise procured the favors of an illustrious lady who was too virtuous to deny anything to a god? Beware, Pontius, lest the invisible Jupiter of the Jews disembark some day on the quay at Ostia!"

At the idea of a god coming out of Judaea, a fleeting smile played over the severe countenance of the Procurator. Then he replied gravely—

"How would the Jews manage to impose their sacred law on outside peoples when they are in a perpetual state of tumult amongst themselves as to the interpretation of that law? You have seen them yourself, Lamia, in the public squares, split up into twenty rival parties, with staves in their hands, abusing each other and clutching one another by the beard. You have seen them on the steps of the temple, tearing their filthy garments as a symbol of lamentation, with some wretched creature in a frenzy of prophetic exaltation in their midst. They have never realized that it is possible to discuss peacefully and with an even mind those matters concerning the divine which yet are hidden from the profane and wrapped in uncertainty. For the nature of the immortal gods remains hidden from us, and we cannot arrive at a knowledge of it. Though I am of opinion, nonetheless, that it is a prudent thing to believe in the providence of the gods. But the Jews are devoid of philosophy, and cannot tolerate any diversity of opinions. On the contrary, they judge worthy of the extreme penalty all those who on divine subjects profess opinions opposed to their law. And as, since the genius of Rome has towered over them, capital sentences pronounced by their own tribunals can only be carried out with the sanction of the proconsul or the procurator, they harry the Roman magistrate at any hour to procure his signature to their baleful decrees, they besiege the pretorium with their cries of 'Death!' A hundred times, at least, have I known them, mustered, rich and poor together, all united under their priests, make a furious onslaught on my ivory chair, seizing me by the skirts of my robe, by the thongs of my sandals, and all to demand of me—nay, to exact from me—the death sentence on some unfortunate whose guilt I failed to perceive, and as to whom I could only pronounce that he was as mad as his accusers. A hundred times, do I say! Not a hundred, but every day and all day. Yet it was my duty to execute their law as if it were ours, since I was appointed by Rome not for the destruction, but for the upholding of their customs, and over them I had the power of the rod and the axe. At the outset of my term of office I endeavored to persuade them to hear reason; I attempted to snatch their miserable victims from death. But this show of mildness only irritated them the more; they demanded their prey, fighting around me like a horde of vultures with wing and beak. Their priests reported to Caesar that I was violating their law, and their appeals, supported by Vitellius, drew down upon me a severe reprimand. How many times did I long, as the Greeks used to say, to dispatch accusers and accused in one convoy to the crows!

"Do not imagine, Lamia, that I nourish the rancor of the discomfited, the wrath of the superannuated, against a people which in my person has prevailed against both Rome and tranquillity. But I foresee the extremity to which sooner or later they will reduce us. Since we cannot govern them, we shall be driven to destroy them. Never doubt it. Always in a state of insubordination, brewing rebellion in their inflammatory minds, they will one day burst forth upon us with a fury beside which the wrath of the Numidians and the mutterings of the Parthians are mere child's play. They are secretly nourishing preposterous hopes, and madly premeditating our ruin. How can it be otherwise, when, on the strength of an oracle, they are living in expectation of the coming of a prince of their own blood whose kingdom shall extend over the whole earth? There are no half measures with such a people. They must be exterminated. Jerusalem must be laid waste to the very foundation. Perchance, old as I am, it may be granted me to behold the day when her walls shall fall and the flames shall envelop her houses, when her inhabitants shall pass under the edge of the sword, when salt shall be strewn on the place where once the temple stood. And in that day I shall at length be justified."

Lamia exerted himself to lead the conversation back to a less acrimonious note.

"Pontius," he said, "it is not difficult for me to understand both your long-standing resentment and your sinister forebodings. Truly, what you have experienced of the character of the Jews is nothing to their advantage. But I lived in Jerusalem as an interested onlooker, and mingled freely with the people, and I succeeded in detecting certain obscure virtues in these rude folk which were altogether hidden from you. I have met Jews who were all mildness, whose simple manners and faithfulness of heart recalled to me what our poets have related concerning the Spartan lawgiver. And you yourself, Pontius, have seen perish beneath the cudgels of your legionaries simple-minded men who have died for a cause they believed to be just without revealing their names. Such men do not deserve our contempt. I am saying this because it is desirable in all things to preserve moderation and an even mind. But I own that I never experienced any lively sympathy for the Jews. The Jewesses, on the contrary, I found extremely pleasing. I was young then, and the Syrian women stirred all my senses to response. Their ruddy lips, their liquid eyes that shone in the shade, their sleepy gaze pierced me to the very marrow. Painted and stained, smelling of nard and myrrh, steeped in odors, their physical attractions are both rare and delightful."

Pontius listened impatiently to these praises.

"I was not the kind of man to fall into the snares of the Jewish women," he said; "and since you have opened the subject yourself, Lamia, I was never able to approve of your laxity. If I did not express with sufficient emphasis formerly how culpable I held you for having intrigued at Rome with the wife of a man of consular rank, it was because you were then enduring heavy penance for your misdoings. Marriage from the patrician point of view is a sacred tie; it is one of the institutions which are the support of Rome. As to foreign women and slaves, such relations as one may enter into with them would be of little account were it not that they habituate the body to a humiliating effeminacy. Let me tell you that you have been too liberal in your offerings to the Venus of the Marketplace; and what, above all, I blame in you is that you have not married in compliance with the law and given children to the Republic, as every good citizen is bound to do."

But the man who had suffered exile under Tiberius was no longer listening to the venerable magistrate. Having tossed off his cup of Falernian, he was smiling at some image visible to his eye alone.

After a moment's silence he resumed in a very deep voice, which rose in pitch by little and little—

"With what languorous grace they dance, those Syrian women! I knew a Jewess at Jerusalem who used to dance in a poky little room, on a threadbare carpet, by the light of one smoky little lamp, waving her arms as she clanged her cymbals. Her loins arched, her head thrown back, and, as it were, dragged down by the weight of her heavy red hair, her eyes swimming with voluptuousness, eager, languishing, compliant, she would have made Cleopatra herself grow pale with envy. I was in love with her barbaric dances, her voice—a little raucous and yet so sweet—her atmosphere of incense, the semisomnolescent state in which she seemed to live. I followed her everywhere. I mixed with the vile rabble of soldiers, conjurers, and extortioners with which she was surrounded. One day, however, she disappeared, and I saw her no more. Long did I seek her in disreputable alleys and taverns. It was more difficult to learn to do without her than to lose the taste for Greek wine. Some months after I lost sight of her, I learned by chance that she had attached herself to a small company of men and women who were followers of a young Galilean thaumaturgist. His name was Jesus; he came from Nazareth, and he was crucified for some crime, I don't quite know what. Pontius, do you remember anything about the man?"

Pontius Pilate contracted his brows, and his hand rose to his forehead in the attitude of one who probes the deeps of memory. Then after a silence of some seconds—

"Jesus?" he murmured. "Jesus—of Nazareth? I cannot call him to mind."

THE
OPEN WINDOW

SAKI (H.H.MUNRO) / GREAT BRITAIN

"My aunt will be down presently, Mr. Nuttel," said a very self-possessed young lady of fifteen; "in the meantime you must try and put up with me."

Framton Nuttel endeavored to say the correct something which should duly flatter the niece of the moment without unduly discounting the aunt that was to come. Privately he doubted more than ever whether these formal visits on a succession of total strangers would do much towards helping the nerve cure which he was supposed to be undergoing.

"I know how it will be," his sister had said when he was preparing to migrate to this rural retreat; "you will bury yourself down there and not speak to a living soul, and your nerves will be worse than ever from moping. I shall just give you letters of introduction to all the people I know there. Some of them, as far as I can remember, were quite nice." Framton wondered whether Mrs. Sappleton, the lady to whom he was presenting one of the letters of introduction, came into the nice division.

"Do you know many of the people round here?" asked the niece, when she judged that they had had sufficient silent communion.

"Hardly a soul," said Framton. "My sister was staying here, at the rectory, you know, some four years ago, and she gave me letters of introduction to some of the people here."

He made the last statement in a tone of distinct regret.

"Then you know practically nothing about my aunt?" pursued the self-possessed young lady.

"Only her name and address," admitted the caller. He was wondering whether Mrs. Sappleton was in the married or widowed state. An undefinable something about the room seemed to suggest masculine habitation.

"Her great tragedy happened just three years ago," said the child; "that would be since your sister's time."

"Her tragedy?" asked Framton; somehow in this restful country spot tragedies seemed out of place.

"You may wonder why we keep that window wide open on an October afternoon," said the niece, indicating a large French window that opened onto a lawn.

"It is quite warm for the time of the year," said Framton; "but has that window got anything to do with the tragedy?"

"Out through that window, three years ago to a day, her husband and her two young brothers went off for their day's shooting. They never came back. In crossing the moor to their favorite snipe-shooting ground they were all three engulfed in a treacherous piece of bog. It had been that dreadful wet summer, you know, and places that were safe in other years gave way suddenly without warning. Their bodies were never recovered. That was the dreadful part of it." Here the child's voice lost its self-possessed note and became falteringly human. "Poor aunt always thinks that they will come back some day, they and the little brown spaniel that was lost with them, and walk in at that window just as they used to do. That is why the window is kept open every evening till it is quite dusk. Poor dear aunt, she has often told me how they went out, her husband with his white waterproof coat over his arm, and Ronnie, her youngest brother, singing, 'Bertie, why do you bound?' as he always did to tease her, because she said it got on her nerves. Do you know, sometimes on still, quiet evenings like this, I almost get a creepy feeling that they will all walk in through that window—"

She broke off with a little shudder. It was a relief to Framton when the aunt bustled into the room with a whirl of apologies for being late in making her appearance.

"I hope Vera has been amusing you?" she said.

"She has been very interesting," said Framton.

"I hope you don't mind the open window," said Mrs. Sappleton briskly; "my husband and brothers will be home directly from shooting, and they always come in this way. They've been out for snipe in the marshes today, so they'll make a fine mess over my poor carpets. So like you menfolk, isn't it?" She rattled on cheerfully about the shooting and the scarcity of birds, and the prospects for duck in the winter. To Framton it was all purely horrible. He made a desperate effort to turn the talk onto a less ghastly topic; he was conscious that his hostess was giving him only a fragment of her attention, and her eyes were constantly straying past him to the open window and the lawn beyond. It was certainly an unfortunate coincidence that he should have paid his visit on this tragic anniversary.

"The doctors agree in ordering me complete rest, an absence of mental excitement, and avoidance of any violent physical exercise," announced Framton, who labored under the tolerably widespread delusion that total strangers and chance acquaintances are hungry for the least detail of one's ailments and infirmities. "On the matter of diet they are not so much in agreement," he continued.

"No?" said Mrs. Sappleton, in a voice which only replaced a yawn at the last moment. Then she suddenly brightened into alert attention—but not to what Framton was saying.

"Here they are at last!" she cried. "Just in time for tea, and don't they look as if they were muddy up to the eyes!"

Framton shivered slightly and turned towards the niece with a look intended to convey sympathetic comprehension. The child was staring out through the open window with dazed horror in her eyes. In a chill shock of nameless fear Framton swung round in his seat and looked in the same direction.

In the deepening twilight three figures were walking across the lawn towards the window; they all carried guns under their arms, and one of them was additionally burdened with a white coat hung over his shoulders. A tired brown spaniel kept close at their heels. Noiselessly they neared the house, and then a hoarse young voice chanted out of the dusk: "I said, Bertie, why do you bound?"

Framton grabbed wildly at his stick and hat; the hall door, the gravel drive, and the front gate were dimly noted stages in his headlong retreat. A cyclist coming along the road had to run into the hedge to avoid imminent collision.

"Here we are, my dear," said the bearer of the white mackintosh, coming in through the window; "fairly muddy, but most of it's dry. Who was that who bolted out as we came up?"

"A most extraordinary man, a Mr. Nuttel," said Mrs. Sappleton; "could only talk about his illnesses, and dashed off without a word of good-by or apology when you arrived. One would think he had seen a ghost."

"I expect it was the spaniel," said the niece calmly; "he told me he had a horror of dogs. He was once hunted into a cemetery somewhere on the banks of the Ganges by a pack of pariah dogs, and had to spend the night in a newly dug grave with the creatures snarling and grinning and foaming just above him. Enough to make anyone lose their nerve."

Romance at short notice was her speciality.

MARÍA CONCEPCIÓN
KATHERINE ANNE PORTER / UNITED STATES

Katherine Anne Porter

MARÍA CONCEPCIÓN walked carefully, keeping to the middle of the white dusty road, where the maguey thorns and the treacherous curved spines of organ cactus had not gathered so profusely. She would have enjoyed resting for a moment in the dark shade by the roadside, but she had no time to waste drawing cactus needles from her feet. Juan and his chief would be waiting for their food in the damp trenches of the buried city.

She carried about a dozen living fowls slung over her right shoulder, their feet fastened together. Half of them fell upon the flat of her back, the balance dangled uneasily over her breast. They wriggled their benumbed and swollen legs against her neck, they twisted their stupefied eyes and peered into her face inquiringly. She did not see them or think of them. Her left arm was tired with the weight of the food basket, and she was hungry after her long morning's work.

Her straight back outlined itself strongly under her clean bright blue cotton rebozo. Instinctive serenity softened her black eyes, shaped like almonds, set far apart, and tilted a bit endwise. She walked with the free, natural, guarded ease of the primitive woman carrying an unborn child. The shape of her body was easy, the swelling life was not a distortion, but the right inevitable proportions of a woman. She was entirely contented. Her husband was at work and she was on her way to market to sell her fowls.

Her small house sat halfway up a shallow hill, under a clump of pepper trees, a wall of organ cactus enclosing it on the side nearest to the road. Now she came down into the valley, divided by the narrow spring, and crossed a bridge of loose stones near the hut where María Rosa the beekeeper lived with her old godmother, Lupe the medicine woman.

María Concepción had no faith in the charred owl bones, the singed rabbit fur, the cat entrails, the messes and ointments sold by Lupe to the ailing of the village. She was a good Christian, and drank simple herb teas for headache and stomachache, or bought her remedies bottled, with printed directions that she could not read, at the drugstore near the city market, where she went almost daily. But she often bought a jar of honey from young María Rosa, a pretty, shy child only fifteen years old.

María Concepción and her husband, Juan Villegas, were each a little past their eighteenth year. She had a good reputation with the neighbors as an energetic religious woman who could drive a bargain to the end. It was commonly known that if she wished to buy a new rebozo for herself or a shirt for Juan, she could bring out a sack of hard silver coins for the purpose.

She had paid for the license, nearly a year ago, the potent bit of stamped paper which permits people to be married in the church. She had given money to the priest before she and Juan walked together up to the altar the Monday after Holy Week. It had been the adventure of the villagers to go, three Sundays one after another, to hear the banns called by the priest for Juan de Dios Villegas and María Concepción Manríquez, who were actually getting married in the church, instead of behind it, which was the usual custom, less expensive, and as binding as any other ceremony. But María Concepción was always as proud as if she owned a hacienda.

She paused on the bridge and dabbled her feet in the water, her eyes resting themselves from the sunrays in a fixed gaze to the far off mountains, deeply blue under their hanging drift of clouds. It came to her that she would like a fresh crust of honey. The delicious aroma of bees, their slow thrilling hum, awakened a pleasant desire for a flake of sweetness in her mouth.

"If I do not eat it now, I shall mark my child," she thought, peering through the crevices in the thick hedge of cactus that sheered up nakedly, like bared knife blades set protectingly around the small clearing. The place was so silent she doubted if María Rosa and Lupe were at home.

The leaning jacal of dried rush withes and corn sheaves, bound to tall saplings thrust into the earth, roofed with yellowed maguey leaves flattened and overlapping like shingles, hunched drowsy and fragrant in the warmth of noonday. The hives, similarly made, were scattered towards the back of the clearing, like small mounds of clean vegetable refuse. Over each mound there hung a dusty golden shimmer of bees.

A light gay scream of laughter rose from behind the hut; a man's short laugh joined in. "Ah, hahahaha!" went the voices together high and low, like a song.

"So María Rosa has a man!"

María Concepción stopped short, smiling, shifted her burden slightly, and bent forward shading her eyes to see more clearly through the spaces of the hedge.

María Rosa ran, dodging between beehives, parting two stunted jasmine bushes as she came, lifting her knees in swift leaps, looking over her shoulder and laughing in a quivering, excited way. A heavy jar, swung to her wrist by the handle, knocked against her thighs as she ran. Her toes pushed up sudden spurts of dust, her half-raveled braids showered around her shoulders in long crinkled wisps.

Juan Villegas ran after her, also laughing strangely, his teeth set, both rows gleaming behind the small soft black beard growing sparsely on his lips, his chin, leaving his brown cheeks girl-smooth. When he seized her, he clenched so hard her chemise gave way and ripped from her shoulder. She stopped laughing at this, pushed him away and stood silent, trying to pull up the torn sleeve with one hand. Her pointed chin and dark red mouth moved in an uncertain way, as if she wished to laugh again; her long black lashes flickered with the quick-moving lights in her hidden eyes.

María Concepción did not stir nor breathe for some seconds. Her forehead was cold, and yet boiling water seemed to be pouring slowly along her spine. An unaccountable pain was in her knees, as if they were broken. She was afraid Juan and María Rosa would feel her eyes fixed upon them and would find her there, unable to move, spying upon them. But they did not pass beyond the enclosure, nor even glance towards the gap in the wall opening upon the road.

Juan lifted one of María Rosa's loosened braids and slapped her neck with it playfully. She smiled softly, consentingly. Together they moved back through the hives of honeycomb. María Rosa balanced her jar on one hip and swung her long full petticoats with every step. Juan flourished his wide hat back and forth, walking proudly as a gamecock.

María Concepción came out of the heavy cloud which enwrapped her head and bound her throat, and found herself walking onward, keeping the road without knowing it, feeling her way delicately, her ears strumming as if all María Rosa's bees had hived in them. Her careful sense of duty kept her moving toward the buried city where Juan's chief, the American archeologist, was taking his midday rest, waiting for his food.

Juan and María Rosa! She burned all over now, as if a layer of tiny fig-cactus bristles, as cruel as spun glass, had crawled under her skin. She wished to sit down quietly and wait for her death, but not until she had cut the throats of her man and that girl who were laughing and kissing under the cornstalks. Once when she was a young girl she had come back from market to find her jacal burned to a pile of ash and her few silver coins gone. A dark empty feeling had filled her; she kept moving about the place, not believing her eyes, expecting it all to take shape again before her. But it was gone, and though she knew an enemy had done it, she could not find out who it was, and could only curse and threaten the air. Now here was a worse thing, but she knew her enemy. María Rosa, that sinful girl, shameless!

She heard herself saying a harsh, true word about María Rosa, saying it aloud as if she expected someone to agree with her: "Yes, she is a whore! She has no right to live."

At this moment the gray untidy head of Givens appeared over the edges of the newest trench he had caused to be dug in his field of excavations. The long deep crevasses, in which a man might stand without being seen, lay crisscrossed like orderly gashes of a giant scalpel. Nearly all of the men of the community worked for Givens, helping him to uncover the lost city of their ancestors. They worked all the year through and prospered, digging every day for those small clay heads and bits of pottery and fragments of painted walls for which there was no good use on earth, being all broken and encrusted with clay. They themselves could make better ones, perfectly stout and new, which they took to town and peddled to foreigners for real money.

But the unearthly delight of the chief in finding these worn-out things was an endless puzzle. He would fairly roar for joy at times, waving a shattered pot or a human skull above his head, shouting for his photographer to come and make a picture of this!

Now he emerged, and his young enthusiast's eyes welcomed María Concepción from his old-man face, covered with hard wrinkles and burned to the color of red earth.

"I hope you've brought me a nice fat one." He selected a fowl from the bunch dangling nearest him as María Concepción, wordless, leaned over the trench. "Dress it for me, there's a good girl. I'll broil it."

María Concepción took the fowl by the head, and silently, swiftly drew her knife across its throat, twisting the head off with the casual firmness she might use with the top of a beet. "Good God, woman, you do have nerve," said Givens, watching her. "I can't do that. It gives me the creeps."

"My home country is Guadalajara," explained María Concepción, without bravado, as she picked and gutted the fowl.

She stood and regarded Givens condescendingly, that diverting white man who had no woman of his own to cook for him, and moreover appeared not to feel any loss of dignity in preparing his own food.

He squatted now, eyes squinted, nose wrinkled to avoid the smoke, turning the roasting fowl busily on a stick. A mysterious man, undoubtedly rich, and Juan's chief, therefore to be respected, to be placated.

"The tortillas are fresh and hot, señor," she murmured gently. "With your permission I will now go to market."

"Yes, yes, run along; bring me another of these tomorrow." Givens turned his head to look at her again. Her grand manner sometimes reminded him of royalty in exile. He noticed her unnatural paleness. "The sun is too hot, eh?" he asked.

"Yes, sir. Pardon me, but Juan will be here soon?"

"He ought to be here now. Leave his food. The others will eat it."

She moved away; the blue of her rebozo became a dancing spot in the heat waves that rose from the gray-red soil. Givens liked his Indians best when he could feel a fatherly indulgence for their primitive childish ways. He told comic stories of Juan's escapades, of how often he had saved him, in the past five years, from going to jail, and even from being shot, for his varied and always unexpected misdeeds.

"I am never a minute too soon to get him out of one pickle or another," he would say. "Well, he's a good worker, and I know how to manage him."

After Juan was married, he used to twit him, with exactly the right shade of condescension, on his many infidelities to María Concepción. "She'll catch you yet, and God help you!" he was fond of saying, and Juan would laugh with immense pleasure.

IT DID NOT OCCUR TO María Concepción to tell Juan she had found him out. During the day her anger against him died, and her anger against María Rosa grew. She kept saying to herself, "When I was a young girl like María Rosa, if a man had caught hold of me so, I would have broken my jar over his head." She forgot completely that she had not resisted even so much as María Rosa, on the day that Juan had first taken hold of her. Besides she had married him afterwards in the church, and that was a very different thing.

Juan did not come home that night, but went away to war and María Rosa went with him. Juan had a rifle at his shoulder and two pistols at his belt. María Rosa wore a rifle also, slung on her back along with the blankets and the cooking pots. They joined the nearest detachment of troops in the field, and María Rosa marched ahead with the battalion of experienced women of war, which went over the crops like locusts, gathering provisions for the army. She cooked with them, and ate with them what was left after the men had eaten. After battles she went out on the field with the others to salvage clothing and ammunition and guns from the slain before they should begin to swell in the heat. Sometimes they would encounter the women from the other army, and a second battle as grim as the first would take place.

There was no particular scandal in the village. People shrugged, grinned. It was far better that they were gone. The neighbors went around saying that María Rosa was safer in the army than she would be in the same village with María Concepción.

María Concepción did not weep when Juan left her; and when the baby was born, and died within four days, she did not weep. "She is mere stone," said old Lupe, who went over and offered charms to preserve the baby.

"May you rot in hell with your charms," said María Concepción.

If she had not gone so regularly to church, lighting candles before the saints, kneeling with her arms spread in the form of a cross for hours at a time, and receiving holy communion every month, there might have been talk of her being devil-possessed, her face was so changed and blind-looking. But this was impossible when, after all, she had been married by the priest. It must be, they reasoned, that she was being punished for her pride. They decided that this was the true cause for everything: she was altogether too proud. So they pitied her.

During the year that Juan and María Rosa were gone María Concepción sold her fowls and looked after her garden and her sack of hard coins grew. Lupe had no talent for bees, and the hives did not prosper. She began to blame María Rosa for running away, and to praise María Concepción for her behavior. She used to see María Concepción at the market or at church, and she always said that no one could tell by looking at her now that she was a woman who had such a heavy grief.

"I pray God everything goes well with María Concepción from this out," she would say, "for she has had her share of trouble."

When some idle person repeated this to the deserted woman, she went down to Lupe's house and stood within the clearing and called to the medicine woman, who sat in her doorway stirring a mess of her infallible cure for sores: "Keep your prayers to yourself, Lupe, or offer them for others who need them. I will ask God for what I want in this world."

"And will you get it, you think, María Concepción?" asked Lupe, tittering cruelly and smelling the wooden mixing spoon. "Did you pray for what you have now?"

Afterwards everyone noticed that María Concepción went oftener to church, and even seldomer to the village to talk with the other women as they sat along the curb, nursing their babies and eating fruit, at the end of the market day. "She is wrong to take us for enemies," said old Soledad, who was a thinker and a peacemaker. "All women have these troubles. Well, we should suffer together."

But María Concepción lived alone. She was gaunt, as if something were gnawing her away inside, her eyes were sunken, and she would not speak a word if she could help it. She worked harder than ever, and her butchering knife was scarcely ever out of her hand.

JUAN AND MARÍA ROSA, disgusted with military life, came home one day without asking permission of anyone. The field of war had unrolled itself, a long scroll of vexations, until the end had frayed out within twenty miles of Juan's village. So he and María Rosa, now lean as a wolf, burdened with a child daily expected, set out with no farewells to the regiment and walked home.

They arrived one morning about daybreak. Juan was picked up on sight by a group of military police from the small barracks on the edge of town, and taken to prison, where the officer in charge told him with impersonal cheerfulness that he would add one to a catch of ten waiting to be shot as deserters the next morning.

María Rosa, screaming and falling on her face in the road, was taken under the armpits by two guards and helped briskly to her jacal, now sadly run down. She was received with professional importance by Lupe, who helped the baby to be born at once.

Limping with footsoreness, a layer of dust concealing his fine new clothes got mysteriously from somewhere, Juan appeared before the captain at the barracks. The captain recognized him as head digger for his good friend Givens, and dispatched a note to Givens saying: "I am holding the person of Juan Villegas awaiting your further disposition."

When Givens showed up Juan was delivered to him with the urgent request that nothing be made public about so humane and sensible an operation on the part of military authority.

Juan walked out of the rather stifling atmosphere of the drumhead court, a definite air of swagger about him. His hat, of unreasonable dimensions and embroidered with silver thread, hung over one eyebrow, secured at the back by a cord of silver dripping with bright blue tassels. His shirt was of a checkerboard pattern in green and black, his white cotton trousers were bound by a belt of yellow leather tooled in red. His feet were bare, full of stone bruises, and sadly ragged as to toenails.

He removed his cigarette from the corner of his full-lipped wide mouth. He removed the splendid hat. His black dusty hair, pressed moistly to his forehead, sprang up suddenly in a cloudy thatch on his crown. He bowed to the officer, who appeared to be gazing at a vacuum. He swung his arm wide in a free circle upsoaring towards the prison window, where forlorn heads poked over the windowsill, hot eyes following after the lucky departing one. Two or three of the heads nodded, and a half dozen hands were flipped at him in an effort to imitate his own casual and heady manner.

Juan kept up this insufferable pantomime until they rounded the first clump of fig cactus. Then he seized Givens' hand and burst into oratory.

"Blessed be the day your servant Juan Villegas first came under your eyes. From this day my life is yours without condition, ten thousand thanks with all my heart!"

"For God's sake stop playing the fool," said Givens irritably. "Someday I'm going to be five minutes too late."

"Well, it is nothing much to be shot, my chief—certainly you know I was not afraid—but to be shot in a drove of deserters, against a cold wall, just in the moment of my homecoming, by order of that . . ."

Glittering epithets tumbled over one another like explosions of a rocket. All the scandalous analogies from the animal and vegetable worlds were applied in a vivid, unique and personal way to the life, loves, and family history of the officer who had just set him free. When he had quite cursed himself dry, and his nerves were soothed, he added: "With your permission, my chief!"

"What will María Concepción say to all this?" asked Givens. "You are very informal, Juan, for a man who was married in the church."

Juan put on his hat.

"Oh, María Concepción! That's nothing. Look, my chief, to be married in the church is a great misfortune for a man. After that he is not himself anymore. How can that woman complain when I do not drink even at fiestas enough to be really drunk? I do not beat her; never, never. We were always at peace. I say to her, 'Come here,' and she comes straight. I say, 'Go there,' and she goes quickly. Yet sometimes I looked at her and thought, 'Now I am married to that woman in the church,' and I felt a sinking inside, as if something were lying heavy on my stomach. With María Rosa it is all different. She is not silent; she talks. When she talks too much, I slap her and say, 'Silence, thou simpleton!' and she weeps. She is just a girl with whom I do as I please. You know how she used to keep those clean little bees in their hives? She is like their honey to me. I swear it. I would not harm María Concepción because I am married to her in the church; but also, my chief, I will not leave María Rosa, because she pleases me more than any other woman."

"Let me tell you, Juan, things haven't been going as well as you think. You be careful. Someday María Concepción will just take your head off with that carving knife of hers. You keep that in mind."

Juan's expression was the proper blend of masculine triumph and sentimental melancholy. It was pleasant to see himself in the role of hero to two such desirable women. He had just escaped from the threat of a disagreeable end. His clothes were new and handsome, and they had cost him just nothing. María Rosa had collected them for him here and there after battles. He was walking in the early sunshine, smelling the good smells of ripening cactus figs, peaches, and melons, of pungent berries dangling from the pepper trees, and the smoke of his cigarette under his nose. He was on his way to civilian life with his patient chief. His situation was ineffably perfect, and he swallowed it whole.

"My chief," he addressed Givens handsomely, as one man of the world to another, "women are good things, but not at this moment. With your permission, I will now go to the village and eat. My God, *how* I shall eat! Tomorrow morning very early I will come to the buried city and work like seven men. Let us forget María Concepción and María Rosa. Each one in her place. I will manage them when the time comes."

News of Juan's adventure soon got abroad, and Juan found many friends about him during the morning. They frankly commended his way of leaving the army. It was in itself the act of a hero. The new hero ate a great deal and drank somewhat, the occasion being better than a feast day. It was almost noon before he returned to visit María Rosa.

He found her sitting on a clean straw mat, rubbing fat on her three-hour-old son. Before this felicitous vision Juan's emotions so twisted him that he returned to the village and invited every man in the "Death and Resurrection" pulque shop to drink with him.

Having thus taken leave of his balance, he started back to María

Rosa, and found himself unaccountably in his own house, attempting to beat María Concepción by way of reestablishing himself in his legal household.

María Concepción, knowing all the events of that unhappy day, was not in a yielding mood, and refused to be beaten. She did not scream nor implore; she stood her ground and resisted; she even struck at him. Juan, amazed, hardly knowing what he did, stepped back and gazed at her inquiringly through a leisurely whirling film which seemed to have lodged behind his eyes. Certainly he had not even thought of touching her. Oh, well, no harm done. He gave up, turned away, half asleep on his feet. He dropped amiably in a shadowed corner and began to snore.

María Concepción, seeing that he was quiet, began to bind the legs of her fowls. It was market day and she was late. She fumbled and tangled the bits of cord in her haste, and set off across the plowed fields instead of taking the accustomed road. She ran with a crazy panic in her head, her stumbling legs. Now and then she would stop and look about her, trying to place herself, then go on a few steps, until she realized that she was not going towards the market.

At once she came to her senses completely, recognized the thing that troubled her so terribly, was certain of what she wanted. She sat down quietly under a sheltering thorny bush and gave herself over to her long devouring sorrow.

The thing which had for so long squeezed her whole body into a tight dumb knot of suffering suddenly broke with shocking violence. She jerked with the involuntary recoil of one who receives a blow, and the sweat poured from her skin as if the wounds of her whole life were shedding their salt ichor. Drawing her rebozo over her head, she bowed her forehead on her updrawn knees, and sat there in deadly silence and immobility. From time to time she lifted her head where the sweat formed steadily and poured down her face, drenching the front of her chemise, and her mouth had the shape of crying, but there were no tears and no sound. All her being was a dark confused memory of grief burning in her at night, of deadly baffled anger eating at her by day, until her very tongue tasted bitter, and her feet were as heavy as if she were mired in the muddy roads during the time of rains.

After a great while she stood up and threw the rebozo off her face, and set out walking again.

Juan awakened slowly, with long yawns and grumblings, alternated with short relapses into sleep full of visions and clamors. A blur of orange light seared his eyeballs when he tried to unseal his lids. There came from somewhere a low voice weeping without tears, saying meaningless phrases over and over. He began to listen. He tugged at the leash of his stupor, he strained to grasp those words which terrified him even though he could not quite hear them. Then he came awake with frightening suddenness, sitting up and staring at the long sharpened streak of light piercing the cornhusk walls from the level disappearing sun.

María Concepción stood in the doorway, looming colossally tall to his betrayed eyes. She was talking quickly, and calling his name. Then he saw her clearly.

"God's name!" said Juan, frozen to the marrow, "here I am facing my death!" for the long knife she wore habitually at her belt was in her hand. But instead, she threw it away, clear from her, and got down on her knees, crawling toward him as he had seen her crawl many times toward the shrine at Guadalupe Villa. He watched her approach with such horror that the hair of his head seemed to be lifting itself away from him. Falling forward upon her face, she huddled over him, lips moving in a ghostly whisper. Her words became clear, and Juan understood them all.

For a second he could not move nor speak. Then he took her head between both his hands, and supported her in this way, saying swiftly, anxiously reassuring, almost in a babble:

"Oh, thou poor creature! Oh, madwoman! Oh, my María Concepción, unfortunate! Listen. . . . Don't be afraid. Listen to me! I will hide thee away, I thy own man will protect thee! Quiet! Not a sound!"

Trying to collect himself, he held her and cursed under his breath for a few moments in the gathering darkness. María Concepción bent over, face almost on the ground, her feet folded under her, as if she would hide behind him. For the first time in his life Juan was aware of danger. This was danger. María Concepción would be dragged away between two gendarmes, with him following helpless and unarmed, to spend the rest of her days in Belén Prison, maybe. Danger! The night swarmed with threats. He stood up and dragged her up with him. She was silent and perfectly rigid, holding to him with resistless strength, her hands stiffened on his arms.

"Get me the knife," he told her in a whisper. She obeyed, her feet slipping along the hard earth floor, her shoulders straight, her arms close to her side. He lighted a candle. María Concepción held the knife out to him. It was stained and dark even to the handle with drying blood.

He frowned at her harshly, noting the same stains on her chemise and hands.

"Take off thy clothes and wash thy hands," he ordered.

He washed the knife carefully, and threw the water wide of the doorway. She watched him and did likewise with the bowl in which she had bathed.

"Light the brasero and cook food for me," he told her in the same peremptory tone. He took her garments and went out. When he returned, she was wearing an old soiled dress, and was fanning the fire in the charcoal burner.

Seating himself cross-legged near her, he stared at her as a creature unknown to him, who bewildered him utterly, for whom there was no possible explanation. She did not turn her head, but kept silent and still, except for the movements of her strong hands fanning the blaze, which cast sparks and small jets of white smoke, flaring and dying rhythmically with the motion of the fan, lighting her face and darkening it by turns.

Juan's voice barely disturbed the silence: "Listen to me carefully, and tell me the truth, and when the gendarmes come here for us, thou shalt have nothing to fear. But there will be something for us to settle between us afterward."

The light from the charcoal burner shone in her eyes; a yellow phosphorescence glimmered behind the dark iris.

"For me everything is settled now," she answered, in a tone so tender, so grave, so heavy with suffering, that Juan felt his vitals contract. He wished to repent openly, not as a man, but as a very small child. He could not fathom her, nor himself, nor the mysterious fortunes of life grown so instantly confused where all had seemed so gay and simple. He felt too that she had become invaluable, a woman without equal among a million women, and he could not tell why. He drew an enormous sigh that rattled in his chest.

"Yes, yes, it is all settled. I shall not go away again. We must stay here together."

Whispering, he questioned her and she answered whispering, and he instructed her over and over until she had her lesson by heart. The hostile darkness of the night encroached upon them, flowing over the narrow threshold, invading their hearts. It brought with it sighs and murmurs, the pad of secretive feet in the nearby road, the sharp staccato whimper of wind through the cactus leaves. All these familiar, once friendly cadences were now invested with sinister terrors; a dread, formless and uncontrollable, took hold of them both.

"Light another candle," said Juan, loudly, in too resolute, too sharp a tone. "Let us eat now."

They sat facing each other and ate from the same dish, after their old habit. Neither tasted what they ate. With food halfway to his mouth, Juan listened. The sound of voices rose, spread, widened at the turn of the road along the cactus wall. A spray of lantern light shot through the hedge, a single voice slashed the blackness, ripped the fragile layer of silence suspended above the hut.

"Juan Villegas!"

"Pass, friends!" Juan roared back cheerfully.

They stood in the doorway, simple cautious gendarmes from the village, mixed-bloods themselves with Indian sympathies, well known to all the community. They flashed their lanterns almost apologetically upon the pleasant, harmless scene of a man eating supper with his wife.

"Pardon, brother," said the leader. "Someone has killed the woman María Rosa, and we must question her neighbors and friends." He paused, and added with an attempt at severity, "Naturally!"

"Naturally," agreed Juan. "You know that I was a good friend of María Rosa. This is bad news."

They all went away together, the men walking in a group, María Concepción following a few steps in the rear, near Juan. No one spoke.

THE TWO POINTS OF CANDLELIGHT at María Rosa's head fluttered uneasily; the shadows shifted and dodged on the stained darkened walls. To María Concepción everything in the smothering enclosing room shared an evil restlessness. The watchful faces of those called as witnesses, the faces of old friends, were made alien by the look of speculation in their eyes. The ridges of the rose-colored rebozo thrown over the body varied continually, as though the thing it covered was not perfectly in repose. Her eyes swerved over the body in the open painted coffin, from the candle tips at the head to the feet, jutting up thinly, the small scarred soles protruding, freshly washed, a mass of crooked, half-healed wounds, thorn pricks and cuts of sharp stones.

Her gaze went back to the candle flame, to Juan's eyes warning her, to the gendarmes talking among themselves. Her eyes would not be controlled.

With a leap that shook her, her gaze settled upon the face of María Rosa. Instantly her blood ran smoothly again: there was nothing to fear. Even the restless light could not give a look of life to that fixed countenance. She was dead. María Concepción felt her muscles give way softly; her heart began beating steadily without effort. She knew no more rancor against that pitiable thing, lying indifferently in its blue coffin under the fine silk rebozo. The mouth drooped sharply at the corners in a grimace of weeping arrested halfway. The brows were distressed; the dead flesh could not cast off the shape of its last terror. It was all finished. María Rosa had eaten too much honey and had had too much love. Now she must sit in hell, crying over her sins and her hard death forever and ever.

Old Lupe's cackling voice arose. She had spent the morning helping María Rosa, and it had been hard work. The child had spat blood the moment it was born, a bad sign. She thought then that bad luck would come to the house. Well, about sunset she was in the yard at the back of the house grinding tomatoes and peppers. She had left mother and babe asleep. She heard a strange noise in the house, a choking and smothered calling, like someone wailing in sleep. Well, such a thing is only natural. But there followed a light, quick, thudding sound—

"Like the blows of a fist?" interrupted an officer.

"No, not at all like such a thing."

"How do you know?"

"I am well acquainted with that sound, friends," retorted Lupe. "This was something else."

She was at a loss to describe it exactly. A moment later, there came the sound of pebbles rolling and slipping under feet; then she knew someone had been there and was running away.

"Why did you wait so long before going to see?"

"I am old and hard in the joints," said Lupe. "I cannot run after people. I walked as fast as I could to the cactus hedge, for it is only by this way that anyone can enter. There was no one in the road, sir, no one. Three cows, with a dog driving them; nothing else. When I got to María Rosa, she was lying all tangled up, and from her neck to her middle she was full of knife holes. It was a sight to move the Blessed Image Himself! Her eyes were—"

"Never mind. Who came oftenest to her house before she went away? Did you know her enemies?"

Lupe's face congealed, closed. Her spongy skin drew into a network of secretive wrinkles. She turned withdrawn and expressionless eyes upon the gendarmes.

"I am an old woman. I do not see well. I cannot hurry on my feet. I know no enemy of María Rosa. I did not see anyone leave the clearing."

"You did not hear splashing in the spring near the bridge?"

"No, sir."

"Why, then, do our dogs follow a scent there and lose it?"

"God only knows, my friend. I am an old wom—"

"Yes. How did the footfalls sound?"

"Like the tread of an evil spirit!" Lupe broke forth in a swelling oracular tone that startled them. The Indians stirred uneasily, glanced at the dead, then at Lupe. They half expected her to produce the evil spirit among them at once.

The gendarme began to lose his temper.

"No, poor unfortunate; I mean, were they heavy or light? The footsteps of a man or of a woman? Was the person shod or barefoot?"

A glance at the listening circle assured Lupe of their thrilled attention. She enjoyed the dangerous importance of her situation. She could have ruined that María Concepción with a word, but it was even sweeter to make fools of these gendarmes who went about spying on honest people. She raised her voice again. What she had not seen she could not describe, thank God! No one could harm her because her knees were stiff and she could not run even to seize a murderer. As for knowing the difference between footfalls, shod or bare, man or woman, nay, between devil and human, who ever heard of such madness?

"My eyes are not ears, gentlemen," she ended grandly, "but upon my heart I swear those footsteps fell as the tread of the spirit of evil!"

"Imbecile!" yapped the leader in a shrill voice. "Take her away, one of you! Now, Juan Villegas, tell me—"

Juan told his story patiently, several times over. He had returned to his wife that day. She had gone to market as usual. He had helped her prepare her fowls. She had returned about midafternoon, they had talked, she had cooked, they had eaten, nothing was amiss. Then the gendarmes came with the news about María Rosa. That was all. Yes, María Rosa had run away with him, but there had been no bad blood between his wife and María Rosa. Everybody knew that his wife was a quiet woman.

María Concepción heard her own voice answering without a break. It was true at first she was troubled when her husband went away, but after that she had not worried about him. It was the way of men, she believed. She was a church-married woman and knew her place. Well, he had come home at last. She had gone to market, but had come back early, because now she had her man to cook for. That was all.

Other voices broke in. A toothless old man said: "She is a woman of good reputation among us, and María Rosa was not." A smiling young mother, Anita, baby at breast, said: "If no one thinks so, how can you accuse her? It was the loss of her child, and not of her husband that changed her so." Another: "María Rosa had a strange life, apart from us. How do we know who might have come from another place to do her evil?" And old Soledad spoke up boldly: "When I saw María Concepción in the market today, I said, 'Good luck to you,

María Concepción, this is a happy day for you!'" and she gave María Concepción a long easy stare, and the smile of a born wisewoman.

María Concepción suddenly felt herself guarded, surrounded, up-borne by her faithful friends. They were around her, speaking for her, defending her, the forces of life were ranged invincibly with her against the beaten dead. María Rosa had thrown away her share of strength in them, she lay forfeited among them. María Concepción looked from one to the other of the circling, intent faces. Their eyes gave back reassurance, understanding, a secret and mighty sympathy.

The gendarmes were at a loss. They, too, felt that sheltering wall cast impenetrably around her. They were certain she had done it, and yet they could not accuse her. Nobody could be accused; there was not a shred of true evidence. They shrugged their shoulders and snapped their fingers and shuffled their feet. Well, then, good night to everybody. Many pardons for having intruded. Good health!

A small bundle lying against the wall at the head of the coffin squirmed like an eel. A wail, a mere sliver of sound, issued. María Concepción took the son of María Rosa in her arms.

"He is mine," she said clearly, "I will take him with me."

No one assented in words, but an approving nod, a bare breath of complete agreement, stirred among them as they made way for her.

MARÍA CONCEPCIÓN, carrying the child, followed Juan from the clearing. The hut was left with its lighted candles and a crowd of old women who would sit up all night, drinking coffee and smoking and telling ghost stories.

Juan's exaltation had burned out. There was not an ember of excitement left in him. He was tired. The perilous adventure was over. María Rosa had vanished, to come no more forever. Their days of marching, of eating, of quarreling and making love between battles, were all over. Tomorrow he would go back to dull and endless labor, he must descend into the trenches of the buried city as María Rosa must go into her grave. He felt his veins fill up with bitterness, with black unendurable melancholy. Oh, Jesus! what bad luck overtakes a man!

Well, there was no way out of it now. For the moment he craved only to sleep. He was so drowsy he could scarcely guide his feet. The occasional light touch of the woman at his elbow was as unreal, as ghostly as the brushing of a leaf against his face. He did not know why he had fought to save her, and now he forgot her. There was nothing in him except a vast blind hurt like a covered wound.

He entered the jacal, and without waiting to light a candle, threw off his clothing, sitting just within the door. He moved with lagging, half-awake hands, to strip his body of its heavy finery. With a long groaning sigh of relief he fell straight back on the floor, almost instantly asleep, his arms flung up and outward.

María Concepción, a small clay jar in her hand, approached the gentle little mother goat tethered to a sapling, which gave and yielded as she pulled at the rope's end after the farthest reaches of grass about her. The kid, tied up a few feet away, rose bleating, its feathery fleece shivering in the fresh wind. Sitting on her heels, holding his tether, she allowed him to suckle a few moments. Afterward—all her movements very deliberate and even—she drew a supply of milk for the child.

She sat against the wall of her house, near the doorway. The child, fed and asleep, was cradled in the hollow of her crossed legs. The silence overfilled the world, the skies flowed down evenly to the rim of the valley, the stealthy moon crept slantwise to the shelter of the mountains. She felt soft and warm all over; she dreamed that the newly born child was her own, and she was resting deliciously.

María Concepción could hear Juan's breathing. The sound vapored from the low doorway, calmly; the house seemed to be resting after a burdensome day. She breathed, too, very slowly and quietly, each inspiration saturating her with repose. The child's light, faint breath was a mere shadowy moth of sound in the silver air. The night, the earth under her, seemed to swell and recede together with a limitless, unhurried, benign breathing. She drooped and closed her eyes, feeling the slow rise and fall within her own body. She did not know what it was, but it eased her all through. Even as she was falling asleep, head bowed over the child, she was still aware of a strange, wakeful happiness.

MY LORD, THE BABY

RABINDRANATH TAGORE / INDIA

Rabindranath Tagore.

Translated by C. F. Andrews

RAICHARAN WAS twelve years old when he came as a servant to his master's house. He belonged to the same caste as his master, and was given his master's little son to nurse. As time went on the boy left Raicharan's arms to go to school. From school he went on to college, and after college he entered the judicial service. Always, until he married, Raicharan was his sole attendant.

But, when a mistress came into the house, Raicharan found two masters instead of one. All his former influence passed to the new mistress. This was compensated for by a fresh arrival. Anukul had a son born to him, and Raicharan by his unsparing attentions soon got a complete hold over the child. He used to toss him up in his arms, call to him in absurd baby language, put his face close to the baby's and draw it away again with a grin.

Presently the child was able to crawl and cross the doorway. When Raicharan went to catch him, he would scream with mischievous laughter and make for safety. Raicharan was amazed at the profound skill and exact judgment the baby showed when pursued. He would say to his mistress with a look of awe and mystery: "Your son will be a judge some day."

New wonders came in their turn. When the baby began to toddle, that was to Raicharan an epoch in human history. When he called his father Ba-ba and his mother Ma-ma and Raicharan Chan-na, then Raicharan's ecstasy knew no bounds. He went out to tell the news to all the world.

After a while Raicharan was asked to show his ingenuity in other ways. He had, for instance, to play the part of a horse, holding the reins between his teeth and prancing with his feet. He had also to wrestle with his little charge, and if he could not, by a wrestler's trick, fall on his back defeated at the end, a great outcry was certain.

About this time Anukul was transferred to a district on the banks of the Padma. On his way through Calcutta he bought his son a little go-cart. He bought him also a yellow satin waistcoat, a gold-laced cap, and some gold bracelets and anklets. Raicharan was wont to take these out, and put them on his little charge with ceremonial pride, whenever they went for a walk.

Then came the rainy season, and day after day the rain poured down in torrents. The hungry river, like an enormous serpent, swallowed down terraces, villages, cornfields, and covered with its flood the tall grasses and wild casuarinas on the sandbanks. From time to time there was a deep thud, as the riverbanks crumbled. The unceasing roar of the main current could be heard from far away. Masses of foam, carried swiftly past, proved to the eye the swiftness of the stream.

One afternoon the rain cleared. It was cloudy, but cool and bright. Raicharan's little despot did not want to stay in on such a fine afternoon. His lordship climbed into the go-cart. Raicharan, between the shafts, dragged him slowly along till he reached the rice fields on the banks of the river. There was no one in the fields, and no boat on the stream. Across the water, on the farther side, the clouds were rifted in the west. The silent ceremonial of the setting sun was revealed in all its glowing splendor. In the midst of that stillness the child, all of a sudden, pointed with his finger in front of him and cried: "Chan-na! Pitty fow."

Close by on a mud flat stood a large kadamba tree in full flower. My lord, the baby, looked at it with greedy eyes, and Raicharan knew his meaning. Only a short time before he had made, out of these very flower balls, a small go-cart; and the child had been so entirely happy dragging it about with a string, that for the whole day Raicharan was not made to put on the reins at all. He was promoted from a horse into a groom.

But Raicharan had no wish that evening to go splashing knee-deep through the mud to reach the flowers. So he quickly pointed his finger in the opposite direction, calling out: "Oh, look, baby, look! Look at the bird." And with all sorts of curious noises he pushed the go-cart rapidly away from the tree.

But a child, destined to be a judge, cannot be put off so easily. And besides, there was at the time nothing to attract his eyes. And you cannot keep up forever the pretense of an imaginary bird.

The little master's mind was made up, and Raicharan was at his wits' end. "Very well, baby," he said at last, "you sit still in the cart, and I'll go and get you the pretty flower. Only mind you don't go near the water."

As he said this, he made his legs bare to the knee, and waded through the oozing mud towards the tree.

The moment Raicharan had gone, his little master went off at racing speed to the forbidden water. The baby saw the river rushing by, splashing and gurgling as it went. It seemed as though the disobedient wavelets themselves were running away from some greater Raicharan with the laughter of a thousand children. At the sight of their mischief, the heart of the human child grew excited and restless. He got down stealthily from the go-cart and toddled off towards the river. On his way he picked up a small stick, and leant over the bank of the stream pretending to fish. The mischievous fairies of the river with their mysterious voices seemed inviting him into their playhouse.

Raicharan had plucked a handful of flowers from the tree, and was carrying them back in the end of his cloth, with his face wreathed in smiles. But when he reached the go-cart, there was no one there. He looked on all sides and there was no one there. He looked back at the cart and there was no one there.

In that first terrible moment his blood froze within him. Before his eyes the whole universe swam round like a dark mist. From the depth of his broken heart he gave one piercing cry: "Master, master, little master."

But no voice answered "Chan-na." No child laughed mischievously back; no scream of baby delight welcomed his return. Only the river ran on, with its splashing, gurgling noise as before—as though it knew nothing at all, and had no time to attend to such a tiny human event as the death of a child.

As the evening passed by, Raicharan's mistress became very anxious. She sent men out on all sides to search. They went with lanterns in their hands, and reached at last the banks of the Padma. There they found Raicharan rushing up and down the fields, like a stormy wind, shouting the cry of despair: "Master, master, little master!"

When they got Raicharan home at last, he fell prostrate at his mistress's feet. They shook him, and questioned him, and asked him repeatedly where he had left the child; but all he could say was that he knew nothing.

Though everyone held the opinion that the Padma had swallowed the child, there was a lurking doubt left in the mind. For a band of gypsies had been noticed outside the village that afternoon, and some suspicion rested on them. The mother went so far in her wild grief as to think it possible that Raicharan himself had stolen the child. She called him aside with piteous entreaty and said: "Raicharan, give me back my baby. Oh! Give me back my child. Take from me any money you ask, but give me back my child!"

Raicharan only beat his forehead in reply. His mistress ordered him out of the house.

Anukul tried to reason his wife out of this wholly unjust suspicion: "Why on earth," he said, "should he commit such a crime as that?"

The mother only replied: "The baby had gold ornaments on his body. Who knows?"

It was impossible to reason with her after that.

RAICHARAN WENT BACK to his own village. Up to this time he had had no son, and there was no hope that any child would now be born to him. But it came about before the end of a year that his wife gave birth to a son and died.

An overwhelming resentment at first grew up in Raicharan's heart at the sight of this new baby. At the back of his mind was resentful suspicion that it had come as a usurper in place of the little master. He also thought it would be a grave offense to be happy with a son of his own after what had happened to his master's little child. Indeed, if it had not been for a widowed sister, who mothered the new baby, it would not have lived long.

But a change gradually came over Raicharan's mind. A wonderful thing happened. This new baby in turn began to crawl about, and cross the doorway with mischief in its face. It also showed an amusing cleverness in making its escape to safety. Its voice, its sounds of laughter and tears, its gestures, were those of the little master. On some days, when Raicharan listened to its crying, his heart suddenly began thumping wildly against his ribs, and it seemed to him that his former little master was crying somewhere in the unknown land of death because he had lost his Chan-na.

Phailna (for that was the name Raicharan's sister gave to the new baby) soon began to talk. It learnt to say Ba-ba and Ma-ma with a baby accent. When Raicharan heard those familiar sounds the mystery suddenly became clear. The little master could not cast off the spell of his Chan-na, and therefore he had been reborn in his own house.

The arguments in favor of this were, to Raicharan, altogether beyond dispute:

1. The new baby was born soon after his little master's death.
2. His wife could never have accumulated such merit as to give birth to a son in middle age.
3. The new baby walked with a toddle and called out Ba-ba and Ma-ma. There was no sign lacking which marked out the future judge.

Then suddenly Raicharan remembered that terrible accusation of the mother. "Ah," he said to himself with amazement, "the mother's heart was right. She knew I had stolen her child." When once he had come to this conclusion, he was filled with remorse for his past neglect.

He now gave himself over, body and soul, to the new baby, and became its devoted attendant. He began to bring it up as if it were the son of a rich man. He bought a go-cart, a yellow satin waistcoat, and a gold-embroidered cap. He melted down the ornaments of his dead wife, and made gold bangles and anklets. He refused to let the child play with anyone of the neighborhood, and became himself its sole companion day and night.

As the baby grew up to boyhood, he was so petted and spoilt and clad in such finery that the village children would call him "Your Lordship," and jeer at him; and older people regarded Raicharan as unaccountably crazy about the child.

At last the time came for the boy to go to school. Raicharan sold his small piece of land, and went to Calcutta. There he got employment with great difficulty as a servant, and sent Phailna to school. He spared no pains to give him the best education, the best clothes, the best food.

Meanwhile he lived himself on a mere handful of rice, and would say in secret: "Ah! My little master, my dear little master, you loved me so much that you came back to my house. You shall never suffer from any neglect of mine."

Twelve years passed away in this manner. The boy was able to read and write well. He was bright and healthy and good-looking. He paid a great deal of attention to his personal appearance, and was specially careful in parting his hair. He was inclined to extravagance and finery, and spent money freely. He could never quite look on Raicharan as a father, because, though fatherly in affection, he had the manner of a servant. A further fault was this, that Raicharan kept secret from everyone that he was the father of the child.

The students of the hostel, where Phailna was a boarder, were greatly amused by Raicharan's country manners, and I have to confess that behind his father's back Phailna joined in their fun. But, in the bottom of their hearts, all the students loved the innocent and tenderhearted old man, and Phailna was very fond of him also. But, as I have said before, he loved him with a kind of condescension.

Raicharan grew older and older, and his employer was continually finding fault with him for his incompetent work. He had been starving himself for the boy's sake. So he had grown physically weak, and no longer up to his work. He would forget things, and his mind became dull and stupid. But his employer expected a full servant's work out of him, and would not brook excuses. The money that Raicharan had brought with him from the sale of his land was exhausted. The boy was continually grumbling about his clothes, and asking for more money.

RAICHARAN MADE UP HIS MIND. He gave up the situation where he was working as a servant, and left some money with Phailna and said: "I have some business to do at home in my village, and shall be back soon."

He went off at once to Baraset where Anukul was magistrate. Anukul's wife was still broken down with grief. She had had no other child.

One day Anukul was resting after a long and weary day in court. His wife was buying, at an exorbitant price, an herb from a mendicant quack, which was said to ensure the birth of a child. A voice of greeting was heard in the courtyard. Anukul went out to see who was there. It was Raicharan. Anukul's heart was softened when he saw his old servant. He asked him many questions, and offered to take him back into service.

Raicharan smiled faintly, and said in reply: "I want to make obeisance to my mistress."

Anukul went with Raicharan into the house, where the mistress did not receive him as warmly as his old master. Raicharan took no notice of this, but folded his hands, and said: "It was not the Padma that stole your baby. It was I."

Anukul exclaimed: "Great God! Eh! What! Where is he?"

Raicharan replied: "He is with me. I will bring him the day after tomorrow."

It was Sunday. There was no magistrate's court sitting. Both husband and wife were looking expectantly along the road, waiting from early morning for Raicharan's appearance. At ten o'clock he came, leading Phailna by the hand.

Anukul's wife, without a question, took the boy into her lap, and was wild with excitement, sometimes laughing, sometimes weeping, touching him, kissing his hair and his forehead, and gazing into his face with hungry, eager eyes. The boy was very good-looking and dressed like a gentleman's son. The heart of Anukul brimmed over with a sudden rush of affection.

Nevertheless the magistrate in him asked: "Have you any proofs?"

Raicharan said: "How could there be any proof of such a deed? God alone knows that I stole your boy, and no one else in the world."

When Anukul saw how eagerly his wife was clinging to the boy, he realized the futility of asking for proofs. It would be wiser to believe. And then—where could an old man like Raicharan get such a boy from? And why should his faithful servant deceive him for nothing?

"But," he added severely, "Raicharan, you must not stay here."

"Where shall I go, master?" said Raicharan, in a choking voice, folding his hands. "I am old. Who will take in an old man as a servant?"

The mistress said: "Let him stay. My child will be pleased. I forgive him."

But Anukul's magisterial conscience would not allow him. "No," he said, "he cannot be forgiven for what he has done."

Raicharan bowed to the ground, and clasped Anukul's feet. "Master," he cried, "let me stay. It was not I who did it. It was God."

Anukul's conscience was worse stricken than ever, when Raicharan tried to put the blame on God's shoulders.

"No," he said, "I could not allow it. I cannot trust you anymore. You have done an act of treachery."

Raicharan rose to his feet and said: "It was not I who did it."

"Who was it then?" asked Anukul.

Raicharan replied: "It was my fate."

But no educated man could take this for an excuse. Anukul remained obdurate.

When Phailna saw that he was the wealthy magistrate's son, and not Raicharan's, he was angry at first, thinking that he had been cheated all this time of his birthright. But seeing Raicharan in distress, he generously said to his father: "Father, forgive him. Even if you don't let him live with us, let him have a small monthly pension."

After hearing this, Raicharan did not utter another word. He looked for the last time on the face of his son; he made obeisance to his old master and mistress. Then he went out, and was mingled with the numberless people of the world.

At the end of the month Anukul sent him some money to his village. But the money came back. There was no one there of the name of Raicharan.

THE END
OF THE PARTY

GRAHAM GREENE / GREAT BRITAIN

PETER MORTON WOKE with a start to face the first light. Through the window he could see a bare bough dropping across a frame of silver. Rain tapped against the glass. It was January the fifth.

He looked across a table, on which a night-light had guttered into a pool of water, at the other bed. Francis Morton was still asleep, and Peter lay down again with his eyes on his brother. It amused him to imagine that it was himself whom he watched, the same hair, the same eyes, the same lips and line of cheek. But the thought soon palled, and the mind went back to the fact which lent the day importance. It was the fifth of January. He could hardly believe that a year had passed since Mrs. Henne-Falcon had given her last children's party.

Francis turned suddenly upon his back and threw an arm across his face, blocking his mouth. Peter's heart began to beat fast, not with pleasure now but with uneasiness. He sat up and called across the table, "Wake up." Francis's shoulders shook and he waved a clenched fist in the air, but his eyes remained closed. To Peter Morton the whole room seemed suddenly to darken, and he had the impression of a great bird swooping. He cried again, "Wake up," and once more there was silver light and the touch of rain on the windows. Francis rubbed his eyes. "Did you call out?" he asked.

"You are having a bad dream," Peter said with confidence. Already experience had taught him how far their minds reflected each other. But he was the elder, by a matter of minutes, and that brief extra interval of light, while his brother still struggled in pain and darkness,

367

had given him self-reliance and an instinct of protection towards the other who was afraid of so many things.

"I dreamed that I was dead," Francis said.

"What was it like?" Peter asked with curiosity.

"I can't remember," Francis said, and his eyes turned with relief to the silver of day, as he allowed the fragmentary memories to fade.

"You dreamed of a big bird."

"Did I?" Francis accepted his brother's knowledge without question, and for a little the two lay silent in bed facing each other, the same green eyes, the same nose tilting at the tip, the same firm lips parted, and the same premature modeling of the chin. The fifth of January, Peter thought again, his mind drifting idly from the image of cakes to the prizes which might be won. Egg-and-spoon races, spearing apples in basins of water, blindman's buff.

"I don't want to go," Francis said suddenly. "I suppose Joyce will be there . . . Mabel Warren." Hateful to him, the thought of a party shared with those two. They were older than he. Joyce was eleven and Mabel Warren thirteen. Their long pigtails swung superciliously to a masculine stride. Their sex humiliated him, as they watched him fumble with his egg, from under lowered scornful lids. And last year . . . He turned his face away from Peter, his cheeks scarlet.

"What's the matter?" Peter asked.

"Oh, nothing. I don't think I'm well. I've got a cold. I oughtn't to go to the party."

Peter was puzzled. "But, Francis, is it a bad cold?"

"It will be a bad cold if I go to the party. Perhaps I shall die."

"Then you mustn't go," Peter said with decision, prepared to solve all difficulties with one plain sentence, and Francis let his nerves relax in a delicious relief, ready to leave everything to Peter. But though he was grateful he did not turn his face towards his brother. His cheeks still bore the badge of a shameful memory, of the game of hide-and-seek last year in the darkened house, and of how he had screamed when Mabel Warren put her hand suddenly upon his arm. He had not heard her coming. Girls were like that. Their shoes never squeaked. No boards whined under their tread. They slunk like cats on padded claws. When the nurse came in with hot water Francis lay tranquil, leaving everything to Peter. Peter said, "Nurse, Francis has got a cold."

The tall starched woman laid the towels across the cans and said, without turning, "The washing won't be back till tomorrow. You must lend him some of your handkerchiefs."

"But, Nurse," Peter asked, "hadn't he better stay in bed?"

"We'll take him for a good walk this morning," the nurse said. "Wind'll blow away the germs. Get up now, both of you," and she closed the door behind her.

"I'm sorry," Peter said, and then, worried at the sight of a face creased again by misery and foreboding, "Why don't you just stay in bed? I'll tell Mother you felt too ill to get up." But such a rebellion against destiny was not in Francis's power. Besides, if he stayed in bed they would come up and tap his chest and put a thermometer in his mouth and look at his tongue, and they would discover that he was malingering. It was true that he felt ill, a sick empty sensation in his stomach and a rapidly beating heart, but he knew that the cause was only fear, fear of the party, fear of being made to hide by himself in the dark, uncompanioned by Peter and with no night-light to make a blessed breach.

"No, I'll get up," he said, and then with sudden desperation, "But I won't go to Mrs. Henne-Falcon's party. I swear on the Bible I won't." Now surely all would be well, he thought. God would not allow him to break so solemn an oath. He would show him a way. There was all the morning before him and all the afternoon until four o'clock. No need to worry now when the grass was still crisp with the early frost. Anything might happen. He might cut himself or break his leg or really catch a bad cold. God would manage somehow.

He had such confidence in God that when at breakfast his mother said, "I hear you have a cold, Francis," he made light of it. "We should have heard more about it," his mother said with irony, "if there was not a party this evening," and Francis smiled uneasily, amazed and daunted by her ignorance of him. His happiness would have lasted longer if, out for a walk that morning, he had not met Joyce. He was alone with his nurse, for Peter had leave to finish a rabbit hutch in the woodshed. If Peter had been there he would have cared less; the nurse was Peter's nurse also, but now it was as though she were employed only for his sake, because he could not be trusted to go for a walk alone. Joyce was only two years older and she was by herself.

She came striding towards them, pigtails flapping. She glanced scornfully at Francis and spoke with ostentation to the nurse. "Hello, Nurse. Are you bringing Francis to the party this evening? Mabel and I are coming." And she was off again down the street in the direction of Mabel Warren's home, consciously alone and self-sufficient in the long empty road. "Such a nice girl," the nurse said. But Francis was silent, feeling again the jump-jump of his heart, realizing how soon the hour of the party would arrive. God had done nothing for him, and the minutes flew.

They flew too quickly to plan any evasion, or even to prepare his heart for the coming ordeal. Panic nearly overcame him when, all unready, he found himself standing on the doorstep, with coat collar turned up against a cold wind, and the nurse's electric torch making a short luminous trail through the darkness. Behind him were the lights of the hall and the sound of a servant laying the table for dinner, which his mother and father would eat alone. He was nearly overcome by a desire to run back into the house and call out to his mother that he would not go to the party, that he dared not go. They could not make him go. He could almost hear himself saying those final words, breaking down forever, as he knew instinctively, the barrier of ignorance that saved his mind from his parents' knowledge. "I'm afraid of going. I won't go. I daren't go. They'll make me hide in the dark, and I'm afraid of the dark. I'll scream and scream and scream." He could see the expression of amazement on his mother's face, and then the cold confidence of a grown-up's retort. "Don't be silly. You must go. We've accepted Mrs. Henne-Falcon's invitation."

But they couldn't make him go; hesitating on the doorstep while the nurse's feet crunched across the frost-covered grass to the gate, he knew that. He would answer, "You can say I'm ill. I won't go. I'm afraid of the dark." And his mother, "Don't be silly. You know there's nothing to be afraid of in the dark." But he knew the falsity of that reasoning; he knew how they taught also that there was nothing to fear in death, and how fearfully they avoided the idea of it. But they couldn't make him go to the party. "I'll scream. I'll scream."

"Francis, come along." He heard the nurse's voice across the dimly phosphorescent lawn and saw the small yellow circle of her torch wheel from tree to shrub and back to tree again. "I'm coming," he called with despair, leaving the lighted doorway of the house; he couldn't bring himself to lay bare his last secrets and end reserve between his mother and himself, for there was still in the last resort a further appeal possible to Mrs. Henne-Falcon. He comforted himself with that, as he advanced steadily across the hall, very small, towards her enormous bulk. His heart beat unevenly, but he had control now over his voice, as he said with meticulous accent, "Good evening, Mrs. Henne-Falcon. It was very good of you to ask me to your party." With his strained face lifted towards the curve of her breasts, and his polite set speech, he was like an old withered man. For Francis mixed very little with other children. As a twin he was in many ways an only child. To address Peter was to speak to his own image in a mirror, an image a little altered by a flaw in the glass, so as to throw back less a likeness of what he was than of what he wished to be, what he would be without his unreasoning fear of darkness, footsteps of strangers, the flight of bats in dusk-filled gardens.

"Sweet child," said Mrs. Henne-Falcon absentmindedly, before, with a wave of her arms, as though the children were a flock of chickens, she whirled them into her set program of entertainments: egg-and-spoon races, three-legged races, the spearing of apples, games which held for Francis nothing worse than humiliation. And in the frequent intervals when nothing was required of him and he could stand alone in corners as far removed as possible from Mabel Warren's scornful gaze, he was able to plan how he might avoid the approaching terror of the dark. He knew there was nothing to fear until after tea, and not until he was sitting down in a pool of yellow radiance cast by the ten candles on Colin Henne-Falcon's birthday cake did he become fully conscious of the imminence of what he feared. Through the confusion of his brain, now assailed suddenly by a dozen contradictory plans, he heard Joyce's high voice down the table. "After tea we are going to play hide-and-seek in the dark."

"Oh, no," Peter said, watching Francis's troubled face with pity and an imperfect understanding, "don't let's. We play that every year."

"But it's in the program," cried Mabel Warren. "I saw it myself. I looked over Mrs. Henne-Falcon's shoulder. Five o'clock, tea. A quarter to six to half past, hide-and-seek in the dark. It's all written down in the program."

Peter did not argue, for if hide-and-seek had been inserted in Mrs. Henne-Falcon's program, nothing which he could say could avert it. He asked for another piece of birthday cake and sipped his tea slowly. Perhaps it might be possible to delay the game for a quarter of an hour, allow Francis at least a few extra minutes to form a plan, but even in that Peter failed, for children were already leaving the table in twos and threes. It was his third failure, and again, the reflection of an image in another's mind, he saw a great bird darken his brother's face with its wings. But he upbraided himself silently for his folly, and finished his cake encouraged by the memory of that adult refrain, "There's nothing to fear in the dark." The last to leave the table, the brothers came together to the hall to meet the mustering and impatient eyes of Mrs. Henne-Falcon.

"And now," she said, "we will play hide-and-seek in the dark."

Peter watched his brother and saw, as he had expected, the lips tighten. Francis, he knew, had feared this moment from the beginning of the party, had tried to meet it with courage and had abandoned the attempt. He must have prayed desperately for cunning to evade the game, which was now welcomed with cries of excitement by all the other children. "Oh, do let's." "We must pick sides." "Is any of the house out-of-bounds?" "Where shall home be?"

"I think," said Francis Morton, approaching Mrs. Henne-Falcon, his eyes focused unwaveringly on her exuberant breasts, "it will be no use my playing. My nurse will be calling for me very soon."

"Oh, but your nurse can wait, Francis," said Mrs. Henne-Falcon absentmindedly, while she clapped her hands together to summon to her side a few children who were already straying up the wide staircase to upper floors. "Your mother will never mind."

That had been the limit of Francis's cunning. He had refused to believe that so well prepared an excuse could fail. All that he could say now, still in the precise tone which other children hated, thinking it a symbol of conceit, was, "I think I had better not play." He stood motionless, retaining, though afraid, unmoved features. But the knowledge of his terror, of the reflection of the terror itself, reached his brother's brain. For the moment, Peter Morton could have cried aloud with the fear of bright lights going out, leaving him alone in an island of dark surrounded by the gentle lapping of strange footsteps. Then he remembered that the fear was not his own, but his brother's. He said impulsively to Mrs. Henne-Falcon, "Please. I don't think Francis should play. The dark makes him jump so." They were the wrong words. Six children began to sing, "Cowardy, cowardy custard," turning torturing faces with the vacancy of wide sunflowers towards Francis Morton.

Without looking at his brother, Francis said, "Of course I will play. I am not afraid. I only thought . . ." But he was already forgotten by his human tormentors and was able in loneliness to contemplate the approach of the spiritual, the more unbounded, torture. The children scrambled around Mrs. Henne-Falcon, their shrill voices pecking at her with questions and suggestions. "Yes, anywhere in the house. We will turn out all the lights. Yes, you can hide in the cupboards. You must stay hidden as long as you can. There will be no home."

Peter, too, stood apart, ashamed of the clumsy manner in which he had tried to help his brother. Now he could feel, creeping in at the corners of his brain, all Francis's resentment of his championing. Several children ran upstairs, and the lights on the top floor went out. Then darkness came down like the wings of a bat and settled on the landing. Others began to put out the lights at the edge of the hall, till the children were all gathered in the central radiance of the chandelier, while the bats squatted round on hooded wings and waited for that, too, to be extinguished.

"You and Francis are on the hiding side," a tall girl said, and then the light was gone, and the carpet wavered under his feet with the sibilance of footfalls, like small cold drafts, creeping away into corners.

"Where's Francis?" he wondered. "If I join him he'll be less frightened of all these sounds." "These sounds" were the casing of silence. The squeak of a loose board, the cautious closing of a cupboard door, the whine of a finger drawn along polished wood.

Peter stood in the center of the dark deserted floor, not listening but waiting for the idea of his brother's whereabouts to enter his brain. But Francis crouched with fingers on his ears, eyes uselessly closed, mind numbed against impressions, and only a sense of strain could cross the gap of dark. Then a voice called "Coming," and as though his brother's self-possession had been shattered by the sudden cry, Peter Morton jumped with his fear. But it was not his own fear. What in his brother was a burning panic, admitting no ideas except those which added to the flame, was in him an altruistic emotion that left the reason unimpaired. "Where, if I were Francis, should I hide?" Such, roughly, was his thought. And because he was, if not Francis himself, at least a mirror to him, the answer was immediate. "Between the oak bookcase on the left of the study door and the leather settee." Peter Morton was unsurprised by the swiftness of the response. Between the twins there could be no jargon of telepathy. They had been together in the womb, and they could not be parted.

Peter Morton tiptoed towards Francis's hiding place. Occasionally a board rattled, and because he feared to be caught by one of the soft questers through the dark, he bent and untied his laces. A tag struck the floor and the metallic sound set a host of cautious feet moving in his direction. But by that time he was in his stockings and would have laughed inwardly at the pursuit had not the noise of someone stumbling on his abandoned shoes made his heart trip in the reflection of another's surprise. No more boards revealed Peter Morton's progress. On stockinged feet he moved silently and unerringly towards his object. Instinct told him that he was near the wall, and, extending a hand, he laid the fingers across his brother's face.

Francis did not cry out, but the leap of his own heart revealed to Peter a proportion of Francis's terror. "It's all right," he whispered, feeling down the squatting figure until he captured a clenched hand. "It's only me. I'll stay with you." And grasping the other tightly, he listened to the cascade of whispers his utterance had caused to fall. A hand touched the bookcase close to Peter's head and he was aware of how Francis's fear continued in spite of his presence. It was less intense, more bearable, he hoped, but it remained. He knew that it was his brother's fear and not his own that he experienced. The dark to him was only an absence of light; the groping hand that of a familiar child. Patiently he waited to be found.

He did not speak again, for between Francis and himself touch was the most intimate communion. By way of joined hands thought could flow more swiftly than lips could shape themselves round words. He could experience the whole progress of his brother's emotion, from the leap of panic at the unexpected contact to the steady pulse of fear, which now went on and on with the regularity of a heartbeat. Peter Morton thought with intensity, "I am here. You needn't be afraid. The lights will go on again soon. That rustle, that movement is nothing to fear. Only Joyce, only Mabel Warren." He bombarded the drooping form with thoughts of safety, but he was conscious that the fear continued. "They are beginning to whisper together. They are tired of looking for us. The lights will go on soon. We shall have won. Don't be afraid. That was only someone on the stairs. I believe it's Mrs. Henne-Falcon. Listen. They are feeling for the lights." Feet moving on a carpet, hands brushing a wall, a curtain pulled apart, a clicking handle, the opening of a cupboard door. In the case above their heads a loose book shifted under a touch. "Only Joyce, only Mabel Warren, only Mrs. Henne-Falcon," a crescendo of reassuring thought before the chandelier burst, like a fruit tree, into bloom.

The voices of the children rose shrilly into the radiance. "Where's Peter?" "Have you looked upstairs?" "Where's Francis?" but they were silenced again by Mrs. Henne-Falcon's scream. But she was not the first to notice Francis Morton's stillness, where he had collapsed against the wall at the touch of his brother's hand. Peter continued to hold the clenched fingers in an arid and puzzled grief. It was not merely that his brother was dead. His brain, too young to realize the full paradox, yet wondered with an obscure self-pity why it was that the pulse of his brother's fear went on and on, when Francis was now where he had been always told there was no more terror and no more darkness.

MODERN CHILDREN

SHOLOM ALEICHEM / RUSSIA

Translated by Julius and Frances Butwin

MODERN CHILDREN, did you say? Ah, you bring them into the world, sacrifice yourself for them, you slave for them day and night— and what do you get out of it? You think that one way or another it would work out according to your ideas or station. After all, I don't expect to marry them off to millionaires, but then I don't have to be satisfied with just anyone, either. So I figured I'd have at least a little luck with my daughters. Why not? In the first place, didn't the Lord bless me with handsome girls; and a pretty face, as you yourself have said, is half a dowry. And besides, with God's help, I'm not the same Tevye I used to be. Now the best match, even in Yehupetz, is not beyond my reach. Don't you agree with me?

But there is a God in heaven who looks after everything. *"A Lord merciful and compassionate,"* who has His way with me summer and winter, in season and out. And He says to me, "Tevye, don't talk like a fool. Leave the management of the world to Me."

So listen to what can happen in this great world of ours. And to whom does it have to happen? To Tevye, *shlimazl.*

To make a long story short, I had just lost everything I had in a stockmarket investment I had gotten involved in through that relative of mine, Menachem-Mendel (may his name and memory be forever blotted out), and I was very low. It looked as if it was all over with me. No more Tevye, no more dairy business.

"Fool," my wife says to me. "You have worried enough. You'll get nowhere worrying. You'll just eat your heart out. Pretend that robbers had broken in and taken everything away. . . . I'll tell you what," she says to me. "Go out for a while. Go see Lazer-Wolf, the butcher, at Anatevka. He wants to see you about something very important."

"What's the matter?" I asked. "What is he so anxious to see me about? If he is thinking of that milch cow of ours, let him take a stick and knock that idea out of his head."

"What are you so anxious about her for?" she says to me. "The milk that we get out of her, or the cheese or butter?"

"I'm not thinking about that," I answer. "It's just the idea. It would be a sin to give the poor thing away to be slaughtered. You can't do that to a living creature. It is written in the Bible. . . ."

"Oh, enough of that!" she comes back at me. "The whole world knows already that you're a man of learning! You do what I tell you. You go over and see Lazer-Wolf. Every Thursday when our Tzeitl goes there for meat, he won't leave her alone. 'You tell your father,' he keeps saying, 'to come and see me. It's important.'"

Well, once in a while you have to obey your wife. So I let her talk me into it, and I go over to Anatevka, about three miles away. He wasn't home. "Where can he be?" I ask a snub-nosed woman who is bustling around the place.

"They're slaughtering today," says the woman, "and he went down to bring an ox. He'll be coming back pretty soon."

So I wait. And while I'm waiting I look around the house a little. And from what I see, it looks as if Lazer-Wolf has been a good provider. There is a cupboard filled with copperware—at least a hundred and fifty *rubles'* worth; a couple of samovars, some brass trays, silver candlesticks and gilded goblets. And a fancy *Hannukah* lamp and some trinkets made of porcelain and silver and everything.

"Lord Almighty!" I think to myself. "If I can only live to see things like that at my children's homes. . . . What a lucky fellow he is—such wealth, and nobody to support! Both his children are married, and he himself is a widower. . . ."

Well, at last the door opens and in stamps Lazer-Wolf.

"Well, Reb Tevye," he says. "What's the matter? Why is it so hard to get hold of you? How goes it?"

"How should it go?" I say to him. "I go and I go, and I get

nowhere. *'Neither gold nor health nor life itself,'* as the *Torah* says."

"Don't complain, Reb Tevye," he answers me. "Compared with what you were when I first knew you, you're a rich man today."

"May we both have what I still need to make me a rich man," I say. "But I am satisfied, thank God. *'Abracadabra askakudra,'* as the *Talmud* says."

"You're always there with a line of *Talmud*," he comes back. "What a lucky man you are, Reb Tevye, to know all these things. But what does all that wisdom and knowledge have to do with us? We have other things to talk about. Sit down, Tevye." He lets out a yell, "Let's have some tea!" And as if by magic the snub-nosed woman appears, snatches the samovar, and is off to the kitchen.

"Now that we are alone," he says to me, "we can talk business. Here is the story. I've been wanting to talk to you for a long time. I tried to reach you through your daughter. How many times have I begged you to come? You understand, I've been casting an eye . . ."

"I know," I say, "that you have been casting an eye on her, but it's no use. Your pains are wasted, Reb Lazer-Wolf. There is no use talking about it."

"Why not?" he asks, with a frightened look.

"Why yes?" says I. "I can wait. I'm in no hurry. My house isn't on fire."

"But why should you wait, if you can arrange it now?"

"Oh, that's not important," I say. "Besides, I feel sorry for the poor thing."

"Look at him," says Lazer-Wolf with a laugh. "He feels sorry for her. . . . If somebody heard you, Reb Tevye, he'd have sworn that she was the only one you had. It seems to me that you have a few more without her."

"Does it bother you if I keep them?" I say. "If anyone is jealous . . ."

"Jealous? Who is talking of jealousy?" he cries. "On the contrary, I know they're superior, and that is exactly why—you understand? And don't forget, Reb Tevye, that you can get something out of it too!"

"Of course . . . I know all a person can get from you. . . . A piece of ice—in winter. We've known that from way back."

"Forget it," he says to me, sweet as sugar. "That was a long time ago. But now—after all—you and I—we're practically in one family, aren't we?"

"Family? What kind of family? What are you talking about, Reb Lazer-Wolf?"

"You tell me, Reb Tevye. I'm beginning to wonder. . . ."

"What are you wondering about? We're talking about my milch cow. The one you want to buy from me."

Lazer-Wolf throws back his head and lets out a roar. "That's a good one!" he howls at me. "A cow! And a milch cow at that!"

"If not the cow," I say, "then what *were* we talking about? You tell me so I can laugh too."

"Why, about your daughter. We were talking about your daughter Tzeitl the whole time. You know, Reb Tevye, that I have been a widower for quite a while now. So I thought, why do I have to go looking all over the world—get mixed up with matchmakers, those sons of Satan? Here we both are. I know you, you know me. It's not like running after a stranger. I see her in my shop every Thursday. She's made a good impression on me. I've talked with her a few times. She looks like a nice, quiet girl. And as for me—as you see for yourself—I'm pretty well off. I have my own house. A couple of stores, some hides in the attic, a little money in the chest. I live pretty well. . . . Look, Tevye, why do we have to do a lot of bargaining, try to impress each other, bluff each other? Listen to me. Let's shake hands on it and call it a match."

Well, when I heard that I just sat and stared. I couldn't say a word. All I could think was: Lazer-Wolf . . . Tzeitl. . . . He had children as old as she was. But then I reminded myself: what a lucky thing for her. She'll have everything she wants. And if he is not so good-looking? There were other things besides looks. There was only one thing I really had against him: he could barely read his prayers. But then, can everybody be a scholar? There are plenty of wealthy men in Anatevka, in Mazapevka, and even in Yehupetz who don't know one letter from another. Just the same, if it's their luck to have a little money they get all the respect and honor a man could want.

As the saying goes, "There's learning in a strongbox, and wisdom in a purse. . . ."

"Well, Reb Tevye," he says. "Why don't you say something?"

"What do you want me to do? Yell out loud?" I ask mildly, as if not wanting to look anxious. "You understand, don't you, that this is something a person has to think over. It's no trifle. She's my eldest child."

"All the better," he says. "Just because she is your eldest . . . That will give you a chance to marry off your second daughter, too, and then, in time with God's help, the third. Don't you see?"

"Amen. The same to you," I tell him. "Marrying them off is no trick at all. Just let the Almighty send each one her predestined husband."

"No," he says. "That isn't what I mean. I mean something altogether different. I mean the dowry. That you won't need for her. And her clothes I'll take care of too. And maybe you'll find something in your own purse besides. . . ."

"Shame on you!" I shout at him. "You're talking just as if you were in the butcher shop. What do you mean—my purse? Shame! My Tzeitl is not the sort that I'd have to sell for money!"

"Just as you say," he answers. "I meant it all for the best. If you don't like it, let's forget it. If you're happy without that, I'm happy too. The main thing is, let's get it done with. And I mean right away. A house must have a mistress. You know what I mean. . . ."

"Just as you say," I agree. "I won't stand in your way. But I have to talk it over with my wife. In affairs like this she has her say. It's no trifle. As Rashi says: 'A mother is not a dust rag.' Besides, there's Tzeitl herself to be asked. How does the saying go? 'All the kinsmen were brought to the wedding—and the bride was left home. . . .'"

"What foolishness!" says Lazer-Wolf. "Is this something to *ask* her about? *Tell* her, Reb Tevye! Go home. Tell her what is what, and get the wedding canopy ready."

"No, Reb Lazer-Wolf," I say. "That's not the way you treat a young girl."

"All right," he says. "Go home and talk it over. But first, Reb Tevye, let's have a little drink. How about it?"

"Just as you say," I agree. "Why not? How does the saying go? 'Man is human—and a drink is a drink.' There is," I tell him, "a passage in the *Talmud*. . . ." And I give him a passage. I don't know myself what I said. Something from the *Song of Songs* or the *Hagadah*. . . .

Well, we took a drop or two—as it was ordained. In the meantime the woman had brought in the samovar and we made ourselves a glass or two of punch, had a very good time together, exchanged a few toasts—talked—made plans for the wedding— discussed this and that—and then back to the wedding.

"Do you realize, Reb Lazer-Wolf, what a treasure she is?"

"I know. . . . Believe me, I know. . . . If I didn't I would never have suggested anything. . . ."

And we both go on shouting. I: "A jewel! A diamond! I hope you'll know how to treat her! Not like a butcher . . ."

And he: "Don't worry, Reb Tevye. What she'll eat in my house on weekdays she never had in your house on holidays."

"Tut, tut," I said. "Feeding a woman isn't everything. The richest man in the world doesn't eat five-*ruble* gold pieces, and a pauper doesn't eat stones. You're a coarse fellow, Lazer-Wolf. You don't even know how to value her talents—her baking—her cooking! Ah, Lazer-Wolf! The fish she makes! You'll have to learn to appreciate her!"

And he: "Tevye, pardon me for saying it, but you're somewhat befuddled. You don't know your man. You don't know me at all. . . ."

And I: "Put gold on one scale and Tzeitl on the other. . . . Do you hear, Reb Lazer-Wolf, if you had a million *rubles,* you wouldn't be worth her little finger."

And he again: "Believe me, Tevye, you're a big fool, even if you are older than I am."

We yelled away at each other that way for a long time, stopping only for a drink or two, and when I came home, it was late at night and my feet felt as if they had been shackled.

And my wife, seeing right away that I was tipsy, gave me a proper welcome.

"Sh . . . Golde, control yourself," I say to her cheerfully, almost ready to start dancing. "Don't screech like that, my soul. We have congratulations coming."

"Congratulations? For what? For having sold that poor cow to Lazer-Wolf?"

"Worse than that," I say.

"Traded her for another one? And outsmarted Lazer-Wolf—poor fellow?"

"Still worse."

"Talk sense," she pleads. "Look, I have to haggle with him for every word."

"Congratulations, Golde," I say once more. "Congratulations to both of us. Our Tzeitl is engaged to be married."

"If you talk like that then I know you're drunk," she says. "And not slightly, either. You're out of your head. You must have found a real glassful somewhere."

"Yes. I had a glass of whiskey with Lazer-Wolf, and I had some punch with Lazer-Wolf, but I'm still in my right senses. Lo and behold. Golde darling, our Tzeitl has really and truly and officially become betrothed to Lazer-Wolf himself."

And I tell her the whole story from start to finish, how and what and when and why. Everything we discussed, word for word.

"Do you hear, Tevye," my wife finally says, "my heart told me all along that when Lazer-Wolf wanted to see you it was for something. Only I was afraid to think about it. Maybe nothing would come of it. Oh, dear God, I thank Thee, I thank Thee, Heavenly Father. . . . May it all be for the best. May she grow old with him in riches and honor—not like that first wife of his, Fruma-Sarah, whose life with him was none too happy. She was, may she forgive me for saying it, an embittered woman. She couldn't get along with anybody. Not at all like our Tzeitl. . . . Oh, dear God, I thank Thee, dear God . . . Well, Tevye, didn't I tell you, you simpleton. . . . Did you have to worry? If a thing has to happen it will happen. . . ."

"I agree with you," said I. "There is a passage in the *Talmud* that covers that very point. . . ."

"Don't bother me with your passages," she said. "We've got to get ready for the wedding. First of all, make out a list for Lazer-Wolf of all the things Tzeitl will need. She doesn't have a stitch of underwear, not even a pair of stockings. And as for clothes, she'll need a silk dress for the wedding, and a cotton one for summer, a woolen one for winter, and petticoats, and cloaks—she should have at least two—one, a fur-lined cloak for weekdays and a good one with a ruffle for Saturdays. And how about a pair of button-shoes and a corset, gloves, handkerchiefs, a parasol, and all the other things that a girl nowadays has to have?"

"Where, Golde, darling, did you get acquainted with all these riggings?" I ask her.

"Why not?" says she. "Haven't I ever lived among civilized people? And didn't I see, back in Kasrilevka, how ladies dressed themselves? You let me do all the talking with him myself. Lazer-Wolf is, after all, a man of substance. He won't want everybody in the family to come bothering him. Let's do it properly. If a person has to eat pork, let him eat a bellyful. . . ."

So we talked and we talked till it was beginning to get light. "My wife," I said, "it's time to get the cheese and butter together so I can start for Boiberik. It is all very wonderful indeed, but you still have to work for a living."

And so, when it was still barely light I harnessed my little old horse and went off to Boiberik. When I got to the Boiberik marketplace— Oho! Can a person ever keep a secret? Everybody knew about it already, and I was congratulated from all sides.

"Congratulations, congratulations! Reb Tevye, when does the wedding come off?"

"The same to you, the same to you," I tell them. "It looks as if the saying is right: 'The father isn't born yet and the son is dancing on the rooftops. . . .'"

"Forget about that!" they cry out. "You can't get away with that! What we want is treats. Why, how lucky you are, Reb Tevye! An oil well! A gold mine!"

"The well runs dry," I tell them, "and all that's left is a hole in the ground."

Still, you can't be a hog and leave your friends in the lurch. "As soon as I'm through delivering I'll be back," I tell them. "There'll be drinks and a bite to eat. Let's enjoy ourselves. As the Good Book says, *'Even a beggar can celebrate.'*"

So I got through with my work as fast as I could and joined the crowd in a drink or two. We wished each other good luck as people do, and then I got back into my cart and started for home again, happy as could be. It was a beautiful summer day, the sun was hot, but on both sides of the road there was shade, and the odor of the pines was wonderful. Like a prince I stretched myself out in the wagon and eased up on the reins. "Go along," I said to the little old horse, "go your own way. You ought to know it by now." And myself, I clear my throat and start off on some of the old tunes. I am in holiday mood, and the songs I sing are those of *Rosh Hashono* and *Yom Kippur.* As I sing I look up at the sky but my thoughts are concerned with things below. The heavens are the Lord's but the earth He gave to the Children of Adam, for them to brawl around in, to live in such luxury that they have time to tear each other apart for this little honor or that. . . . They don't even understand how one ought to praise the Lord for the good things that He gives them. . . . But we, the poor people, who do not live in idleness and luxury, give us but one good day and we thank the Lord and praise Him; we say, *"Ohavti, I love Him"*—the Highest One—*"for He hears my voice and my prayer, He inclines His ear to me . . . For the waves of death compassed me, the floods of Belial assailed me. . . ."* Here a cow falls down and is injured, there an ill wind brings a kinsman of mine, a good-for-nothing, a Menachem-Mendel from Yehupetz who takes away my last penny; and I am sure that the world has come to an end—there is no truth or justice left anywhere on earth. . . . But what does the Lord do? He moves Lazer-Wolf with the idea of taking my daughter Tzeitl without even a dowry. . . . And therefore I give thanks to Thee, dear God, again and again, for having looked upon Tevye and come to his aid. . . . I shall yet have joy. I shall know what it is to visit my child and find her a mistress of a well-stocked home, with chests full of linens, pantries full of chicken fat and preserves, coops full of chickens, geese and ducks. . . .

Suddenly my horse dashes off downhill, and before I can lift my head to look around I find myself on the ground with all my empty

pots and crocks and my cart on top of me! With the greatest difficulty
I drag myself out from under and pull myself up, bruised and half
dead, and I vent my wrath on the poor little horse. "Sink into the
earth!" I shout. "Who asked you to show that you know how to
run? You almost ruined me altogether, you devil!" And I gave him
as much as he could take. You could see that he realized he had gone
a little too far. He stood there with his head down, humble, ready
to be milked. . . . Still cursing him, I turn the cart upright, gather
up my pots, and off I go. A bad omen, I tell myself, and I wonder
what new misfortunes might be awaiting me. . . .

That's just how it was. About a mile farther on, when I'm getting
close to home, I see someone coming toward me. I drive up closer,
look, and see that it's Tzeitl. At the sight of her my heart sinks, I
don't know why. I jump down from the wagon.

"Tzeitl, is that you? What are you doing here?"

She falls on my neck with a sob. "My daughter, what are you crying
about?" I ask her.

"Oh," she cries, "Father, Father!" And she is choked with tears.

"What is it, daughter? What's happened to you?" I say, putting
my arm around her, patting and kissing her.

"Father, Father, have pity on me. Help me. . . ."

"What are you crying for?" I ask, stroking her head. "Little fool,
what do you have to cry for? For heaven's sake," I say, "if you say
no it's *no*. Nobody is going to force you. We meant it for the best,
we did it for your own sake. But if it doesn't appeal to you, what
are we going to do? Apparently it was not ordained. . . ."

"Oh, thank you, Father, thank you," she cries, and falls on my
neck again and dissolves in tears.

"Look," I say, "you've cried enough for one day. . . . Even eating
pastry becomes tiresome. . . . Climb into the wagon and let's go
home. Lord knows what your mother will be thinking."

So we both get into the cart and I try to calm her down. I tell
her that we had not meant any harm to her. God knows the truth:
all we wanted was to shield our daughter from poverty. "So it was
not meant," I said, "that you should have riches, all the comforts
of life; or that we should have a little joy in our old age after all

our hard work, harnessed, you might say, day and night to a wheel-barrow—no happiness, only poverty and misery and bad luck over and over. . . ."

"Oh, Father," she cries, bursting into tears again. "I'll hire myself out as a servant. I'll carry rocks. I'll dig ditches. . . ."

"What are you crying for, silly child?" I say. "Am I forcing you? Am I complaining? It's just that I feel so wretched that I have to get it off my chest; so I talk it over with Him, with the Almighty, about the way He deals with me. He is, I say, a merciful Father, He has pity on me, but He shows me what He can do, too; and what can I say? Maybe it has to be that way. He is high in heaven, high up, and we are here below, sunk in the earth, deep in the earth. So we must say that He is right and His judgment is right; because if we want to look at it the other way round, who am I? A worm that crawls on the face of the earth, whom the slightest breeze—if God only willed it—could annihilate in the blink of an eye. So who am I to stand up against Him with my little brain and give Him advice on how to run this little world of His? Apparently if He ordains it this way, it has to be this way. What good are complaints? Forty days before you were conceived, the Holy Book tells us, an angel appeared and decreed: 'Let Tevye's daughter Tzeitl take Getzel, the son of Zorach, as her husband; and let Lazer-Wolf the butcher go elsewhere to seek his mate.' And to you, my child, I say this: May God send you your predestined one, one worthy of you, and may he come soon, Amen. And I hope your mother doesn't yell too much. I'll get enough from her as it is."

Well, we came home at last. I unharnessed the little horse and sat down on the grass near the house to think things over, think up some fantastic tale to tell my wife. It was late, the sun was setting; in the distance frogs were croaking; the old horse, tied to a tree, was nibbling at the grass; the cows, just come from pasture, waited in the stalls to be milked. All around me was the heavenly smell of the fresh grass—like the Garden of Eden. I sat there thinking it all over. . . . How cleverly the Eternal One has created this little world of His, so that every living thing, from man to a simple cow, must earn its food. Nothing is free. If you, little cow, wish to eat—then go, let yourself be milked, be the means of livelihood for a man and his wife and children. If you, little horse, wish to chew—then run back and forth every day with the milk to Boiberik. And you, Man, if you want a piece of bread—go labor, milk the cows, carry the pitchers, churn the butter, make the cheese, harness your horse, drag yourself every dawn to the *datchas* of Boiberik, scrape and bow to the rich ones of Yehupetz, smile at them, cater to them, ingratiate yourself with them, see to it that they are satisfied, don't do anything to hurt their pride. . . . Ah, but there still remains the question. '*Mah nish-tano?*' Where is it written that Tevye must labor in their behalf, must get up before daybreak when God Himself is still asleep, just so that they can have a fresh piece of cheese, and butter for their breakfast? Where is it written that I must rupture myself for a pot of thin gruel, a loaf of barley bread, while they—the rich ones of Yehupetz—loll around in their summer homes without so much as lifting a hand, and are served roast ducks and the best of *knishes, blintzes* and *vertutin?* Am I not a man as they are? Would it be a sin, for instance, if Tevye could spend one summer himself in a *datcha* somewhere? But then—where would people get cheese and butter? Who would milk the cows? The Yehupetz aristocrats, maybe? And at the very thought of it I burst out laughing. It's like the old saying: "If God listened to every fool what a different world it would be!"

And then I heard someone call out, "Good evening, Reb Tevye." I looked up and saw a familiar face—Motel Kamzoil, a young tailor from Anatevka.

"Well, well," I say, "you speak of the Messiah and look who's here! Sit down, Motel, on God's green earth. And what brings you here all of a sudden?"

"What brings me here?" he answers. "My two feet."

And he sits down on the grass near me and looks off toward the barn where the girls are moving about with their pots and pitchers. "I have been wanting to come here for a long time, Reb Tevye," he says at last, "only I never seem to have the time. You finish one piece of work and you start the next. I work for myself now, you know, and there is plenty to do, praise the Lord. All of us tailors have as much as we can do right now. It's been a summer of weddings.

Everybody is marrying off his children—everybody, even the widow Trihubecha."

"Everybody," I say. "Everybody except Tevye. Maybe I am not worthy in the eyes of the Lord."

"No," he answers quickly, still looking off where the girls are. "You're mistaken, Reb Tevye. If you only wanted to you could marry off one of your children, too. It all depends on you. . . ."

"So?" I ask. "Maybe you have a match for Tzeitl?"

"A perfect fit!" the tailor answers.

"And," I ask, "is it a good match at least?"

"Like a glove!" he cries in his tailor's language, still looking off at the girls.

I ask, "In whose behalf is it then that you come? If he smells of a butcher shop I don't want to hear another word!"

"God forbid!" he says. "He doesn't begin to smell of a butcher shop!"

"And you really think he's a good match?"

"There never was such a match!" he answers promptly. "There are matches and matches, but this one, I want you to know, was made exactly to measure!"

"And who, may I ask, is the man? Tell me!"

"Who is it?" he says, still looking over yonder. "Who is it? Why, me—myself!"

When he said that I jumped up from the ground as if I had been scalded, and he jumped too, and there we stood facing each other like bristling roosters. "Either you're crazy," I say to him, "or you're simply out of your mind! What are you—everything? The match-maker, the bridegroom, the ushers all rolled into one? I suppose you'll play the wedding march too! I've never heard of such a thing—arranging a match for oneself!"

But he doesn't seem to listen. He goes right on talking.

"Anyone who thinks I'm crazy is crazy himself! No, Reb Tevye, I have all my wits about me. A person doesn't have to be crazy in order to want to marry your Tzeitl. For example, the richest man in our town—Lazer-Wolf, the butcher—wanted her too. Do you think it's a secret? The whole town knows it. And as for being my own matchmaker, I'm surprised at you! After all, Reb Tevye, you're a man of the world. If a person sticks his finger in your mouth you know what to do! So what are we arguing about? Here is the whole story: your daughter Tzeitl and I gave each other our pledge more than a year ago now that we would marry. . . ."

If someone had stuck a knife into my heart it would have been easier to endure than these words. In the first place, how does a stitcher like Motel fit into the picture as my son-in-law? And in the second place, what kind of words are these, "We gave each other our pledge that we would marry"? And where do I come in? . . . I ask him bluntly, "Do I still have the right to say something about my daughter, or doesn't anyone have to ask a father any more?"

"On the contrary," says Motel, "that's exactly why I came to talk with you. I heard that Lazer-Wolf has been discussing a match, and I have loved her now for over a year. More than once I have wanted to come and talk it over with you, but every time I put it off a little. First till I had saved up a few *rubles* for a sewing machine, and then till I got some decent clothes. Nowadays almost everybody has to have two suits and a few good shirts. . . ."

"You and your shirts!" I yell at him. "What childish nonsense is this? And what do you intend to do after you're married? Support your wife with shirts?"

"Why," he says, "why, I'm surprised at you, Reb Tevye! From what I hear, when you got married you didn't have your own brick mansion either, and nevertheless here you are. . . . In any case, if the whole world gets along, I'll get along, too. Besides, I have a trade, haven't I?"

To make a long story short, he talked me into it. For after all—why should we fool ourselves?—how do all Jewish children get married? If we began to be too particular, then no one in our class would ever get married at all. . . . There was only one thing still bothering me, and that I still couldn't understand. What did they mean— pledging their troth? What kind of world has this become? A boy meets a girl and says to her, "Let us pledge our troth." Why, it's just too free-and-easy, that's all!

But when I looked at this Motel standing there with his head bent like a sinner, I saw that he was not trying to get the best of anybody, and I thought: "Now, what am I becoming so alarmed about? What am I putting on such airs for? What is my own pedigree? Reb Tzotzel's grandchild! And what huge dowry can I give my daughter—and what fine clothes? So maybe Motel Kamzoil is only a tailor, but at the same time he is a good man, a worker; he'll be able to make a living. And besides, he's honest too. So what have I got against him?

"Tevye," I said to myself, "don't think up any childish arguments. Let them have their way." Yes . . . but what am I going to do about my Golde? I'll have plenty on my hands there. She'll be hard to handle. How can I make her think it's all right? . . . "You know what, Motel," I said to the young suitor. "You go home. I'll straighten everything out here. I'll talk it over with this one and that one. Everything has to be done right. And tomorrow morning, if you haven't changed your mind by that time, maybe we'll see each other."

"Change my mind!" he yells at me. "You expect me to change my mind? If I do, I hope I never live to go away from here! May I become a stone, a bone, right here in front of you!"

"What's the use of swearing?" I ask him. "I believe you without the oath. Go along, Motel. Good night. And may you have pleasant dreams."

And I myself go to bed, too. But I can't sleep. My head is splitting. I think of one plan and then another, till at last I come upon the right one. And what is that? Listen, I'll tell you. . . .

It's past midnight. All over the house we're sound asleep. This one is snoring, that one is whistling. And suddenly I sit up and let out a horrible yell, as loud as I can: "Help! Help! Help!" It stands to reason that when I let out this yell everybody wakes up, and first of all—Golde.

"May God be with you, Tevye," she gasps, and shakes me. "Wake up! What's the matter with you? What are you howling like this for?"

I open my eyes, look around to see where I am, and call out in terror, "Where is she? Where is she?"

"Where is who?" asks Golde. "What are you talking about?"

I can hardly answer. "Fruma-Sarah. Fruma-Sarah, Lazer-Wolf's first wife . . . She was standing here a minute ago."

"You're out of your head," my wife says to me. "May God save you, Tevye. Do you know how long Fruma-Sarah has been dead?"

"I know that she's dead," I say, "but just the same she was here just a minute ago, right here by the bed, talking to me. Then she grabbed me by the windpipe and started to choke me. . . ."

"What on earth is the matter with you, Tevye?" says my wife. "What are you babbling about? You must have been dreaming. Spit three times and tell me what you dreamt, and I'll tell you what it meant."

"Long may you live, Golde," I tell her. "It's lucky you woke me up or I'd have died of fright right on the spot. Get me a drink of water and I'll tell you my dream. Only I beg you, Golde, don't become frightened: the Holy Books tell us that sometimes only three parts of a dream come true, and the rest means nothing. Absolutely nothing. Well, here is my dream. . . . In the beginning I dreamt that we were having a celebration of some kind, I don't know what. Either an engagement or a wedding. The house was crowded. All the men and women we knew were there—the *rov* and the *shochet* and everybody. And musicians, too. . . . In the midst of the celebration the door opens, and in comes your grandmother Tzeitl, may her soul rest in peace. . . ."

"Grandmother Tzeitl!" my wife shouts, turning pale as a sheet. "How did she look? How was she dressed?"

"How did she look?" I say. "May our enemies look the way she looked. Yellow. A waxen yellow. And she was dressed—how do you expect?—in white. A shroud. She came up to me. 'Congratulations,' she said, 'I am so happy that you picked such a fine young man for your Tzeitl who bears my name. He's a fine, upstanding lad—this Motel Kamzoil. . . . He was named after my uncle Mordecai, and even if he is a tailor he's still an honest boy. . . .'"

"A tailor!" gasps Golde. "Where does a tailor come into our family? In our family we have had teachers, cantors, *shamosim,* undertakers' assistants, and other kinds of poor people. But a tailor—never!"

"Don't interrupt me, Golde," I tell her. "Maybe your grandmother

Tzeitl knows better. . . . When I heard her congratulate me like that, I said to her, 'What is that you said, Grandmother? About Tzeitl's betrothed being a tailor? Did you say Motel? . . . You mean a butcher, don't you? A butcher named Lazer-Wolf?'

"'No,' says your grandmother again. 'No, Tevye. Your daughter is engaged to Motel, and he's a tailor, and she'll grow old with him—if the Lord wills—in comfort and honor.'

"'But Grandmother,' I say again, 'what can we do about Lazer-Wolf? Just yesterday I gave him my word. . . .'

"I had barely finished saying this when I looked up, and your grandmother Tzeitl is gone. In her place is Fruma-Sarah—Lazer-Wolf's first wife—and this is what she says: 'Reb Tevye, I have always considered you an honest man, a man of learning and virtue. But how does it happen that you should do a thing like this—let your daughter take my place, live in my house, carry my keys, wear my clothes, my jewelry, my pearls?'

"'Is it my fault,' I ask her, 'if Lazer-Wolf wanted it that way?'

"'Lazer-Wolf!' she cries. 'Lazer-Wolf will have a terrible fate, and your Tzeitl too, if she marries him. It's a pity, Reb Tevye. I feel sorry for your daughter. She'll live with him no more than three weeks, and when the three weeks are up I'll come to her by night and I'll take her by the throat like this. . . .' And with these words Fruma-Sarah grabs me by the windpipe and begins choking me—so hard that if you hadn't waked me up, by now I'd have been—far, far away. . . ."

"Ptu, ptu, ptu," spits my wife three times. "It's an evil spirit! May it fall into the river; may it sink into the earth; may it climb into attics; may it lie in the forest—but may it never harm us or our children! May that butcher have a dream like that! A dark and horrible dream! Motel Kamzoil's smallest finger is worth more than all of him, even if Motel is only a tailor; for if he was named after my uncle Mordecai he couldn't possibly have been a tailor by birth. And if my grandmother—may she rest in peace—took the trouble to come all the way from the other world to congratulate us, why, all we can do is say that this is all for the best and it couldn't possibly be any better. Amen. *Selah*. . . ."

WELL, WHY SHOULD I go on and on?

The next day they were engaged, and not long after were married. And the two of them, praise the Lord, are happy. He does his own tailoring, goes around in Boiberik from one *datcha* to another picking up work; and she is busy day and night, cooking and baking and washing and tidying and bringing water from the well. . . . They barely make enough for food. If I didn't bring her some of our cheese and butter once in a while--or a few *groschen* sometimes—they would never be able to get by. But if you ask her—my Tzeitl, I mean—she says everything is as good as it could be. Just let Motel stay in good health.

So go complain about modern children. You slave for them, do everything for them! And they tell you that they know better.

And . . . maybe they do. . . .

BABYLON REVISITED
F. SCOTT FITZGERALD/UNITED STATES

F Scott Fitzgerald

"AND WHERE'S Mr. Campbell?" Charlie asked.

"Gone to Switzerland. Mr. Campbell's a sick man, Mr. Wales."

"I'm sorry to hear that. And George Hardt?" Charlie inquired.

"Back in America, gone to work. Anyway, his friend, Mr. Schaeffer, is in Paris."

One familiar name from the long list of a year and a half ago. Charlie scribbled an address in his notebook and tore out the page.

"If you see Mr. Schaeffer, give him this," he said. "It's my brother-in-law's address. I haven't settled on a hotel yet."

He was not really disappointed to find Paris was so empty: But the stillness in the Ritz bar was strange and portentous. It was not an American bar anymore—he felt polite in it, and not as if he owned it. It had gone back into France. He asked for the head barman, Paul, who in the latter days of the bull market had come to work in his own custom-built car. But Paul was at his country house today and Alix giving him information.

"No, no more," Charlie said. "I'm going slow these days."

Alix congratulated him: "You were going pretty strong a couple of years ago."

"I'll stick to it all right," Charlie assured him. "I've stuck to it for over a year and a half now."

"How do you find conditions in America?"

"I haven't been to America for months. I'm in business in Prague, representing a couple of concerns there. They don't know about me down there."

Alix smiled.

"Remember the night of George Hardt's bachelor dinner here?" said Charlie. "By the way, what's become of Claude Fessenden?"

Alix lowered his voice confidentially: "He's in Paris, but he doesn't come here anymore. Paul doesn't allow it. He ran up a bill of thirty thousand francs, charging all his drinks and his lunches, and usually his dinner, for more than a year. And when Paul finally told him he had to pay, he gave him a bad check." Alix shook his head sadly. "I don't understand it, such a dandy fellow. Now he's all bloated up—" He made a plump apple of his hands.

The place oppressed Charlie. He called for the dice and shook with Alix for the drink.

"Here for long, Mr. Wales?"

"I'm here for four or five days to see my little girl."

"Oh-h! You have a little girl?"

Outside, the fire-red, gas-blue, ghost-green signs shone smokily through the tranquil rain. It was late afternoon and the streets were in movement. At the corner of the Boulevard des Capucines he took a taxi.

He directed it to the Avenue de l'Opéra, which was out of his way. But he wanted to see the blue hour spread over the magnificent façade, and imagine that the cab horns were the trumpets of the

Second Empire. They were closing the iron grill in front of Brentano's bookstore, and people were already at dinner behind the trim little bourgeois hedge of Duval's. He had never eaten at a really cheap restaurant in Paris. For some odd reason he wished that he had.

They crossed the Seine, and Charlie felt the sudden provincial quality of the Left Bank. I spoiled this city for myself, he thought. I didn't realize it, but the days came along one after another, and then two years were gone, and everything was gone, and I was gone.

He was thirty-five, and good to look at. The Irish mobility of his face was sobered by a deep wrinkle between his eyes. As he rang his brother-in-law's bell in the Rue Palatine, the wrinkle deepened till it pulled down his brows; he felt a cramping sensation in his belly. From behind the maid who opened the door darted a lovely little girl of nine who shrieked "Daddy!" and flew up, struggling like a fish, into his arms. She pulled his head around by one ear and set her cheek against his.

"My old pie," he said.

"Oh, Daddy, Daddy, Daddy, Daddy, Dads, Dads, Dads!"

She drew him into the salon, where the family waited, a boy and girl his daughter's age, his sister-in-law and her husband. He greeted Marion with his voice pitched carefully to avoid either feigned enthusiasm or dislike, but her response was more frankly tepid, though she minimized her expression of unalterable distrust by directing her regard toward his child. The two men clasped hands in a friendly way and Lincoln Peters rested his for a moment on Charlie's shoulder.

The room was warm and comfortably American. The three children moved intimately about, playing through the yellow oblongs that led to other rooms; the cheer of six o'clock spoke in the eager smacks of the fire and the sounds of French activity in the kitchen. But Charlie did not relax; his heart sat up rigidly in his body and he drew confidence from his daughter, who from time to time came close to him, holding in her arms the doll he had brought.

"Really extremely well," he declared in answer to Lincoln's question. "There's a lot of business there that isn't moving at all, but we're doing better than ever. I'm bringing my sister over from America next month to keep house for me. You see, the Czechs—"

His boasting was for a specific purpose; but after a moment, seeing a faint restiveness in Lincoln's eye, he changed the subject. "Those are fine children of yours, well brought up, good manners."

"We think Honoria's a great little girl too."

Marion Peters came back from the kitchen. She was a tall woman with worried eyes, who had once possessed a fresh American loveliness. Charlie had never been sensitive to it and was always surprised when people spoke of how pretty she had been. From the first there had been an instinctive antipathy between them.

"Well, how do you find Honoria?" she asked.

"Wonderful. I was astonished how much she's grown in ten months. All the children are looking well."

"We haven't had a doctor for a year. How do you like being back in Paris?"

"It seems very funny to see so few Americans around."

"I'm delighted," Marion said vehemently. "Now you can go into a store without their assuming you're a millionaire. We've suffered like everybody, but on the whole it's pleasanter."

"But it was nice while it lasted," Charlie said. "We were a sort of royalty, almost infallible, with a sort of magic around us. In the Ritz bar this afternoon"—he stumbled, seeing his mistake—"there wasn't a man I knew."

She looked at him keenly. "I should think you'd have had enough of bars."

"I only stayed a minute. I take one drink every afternoon, and no more."

"I hope you keep to it," said Marion.

Her dislike was evident in the coldness with which she spoke, but Charlie only smiled; he had larger plans. Her very aggressiveness gave him an advantage, and he knew enough to wait. He wanted them to initiate the discussion of what they knew had brought him to Paris. At dinner he couldn't decide whether Honoria was most like him or her mother. Fortunate if she didn't combine the traits of both that had brought them to disaster. A great wave of protectiveness went over him. He thought he knew what to do for her. He believed in character; he wanted to jump back a whole generation and trust in character again as the eternally valuable element. Everything else wore out.

He left soon after dinner, but not to go home. He was curious to see Paris by night with clearer eyes than those of other days. He strolled toward Montmartre, up the Rue Pigalle into the Place Blanche. The rain had stopped and there were a few people in evening clothes disembarking from taxis in front of cabarets. He passed a lighted door from which issued music, and stopped with the sense of familiarity; it was Bricktop's, where he had parted with so many hours and so much money. A few doors farther on he found another ancient rendezvous and incautiously put his head inside. Immediately an eager orchestra burst into sound, a pair of professional dancers leaped to their feet and a maître d'hôtel swooped toward him, crying, "Crowd just arriving, sir!" But he withdrew quickly.

You have to be damn drunk, he thought.

Zelli's was closed, the bleak and sinister cheap hotels surrounding it were dark. The two great mouths of the Café of Heaven and the Café of Hell still yawned—even devoured, as he watched, the meager contents of a tourist bus—a German, a Japanese, and an American couple who glanced at him with frightened eyes.

So much for the effort and ingenuity of Montmartre. All the catering to vice and waste was on an utterly childish scale, and he suddenly realized the meaning of the word "dissipate"—to dissipate into thin air; to make nothing out of something.

He remembered thousand-franc notes given to an orchestra for playing a single number, hundred-franc notes tossed to a doorman for calling a cab.

But it hadn't been given for nothing. It had been given, even the most wildly squandered sum, as an offering to destiny that he might not remember the things most worth remembering, the things that now he would always remember—his child taken from his control, his wife escaped to a grave in Vermont.

HE WOKE upon a fine fall day. The depression of yesterday was gone and he liked the people on the streets. At noon he sat opposite Honoria at Le Grand Vatel.

"Now, how about vegetables? Oughtn't you to have some vegetables?"

"Well, yes."

"Wouldn't you like to have two vegetables?"

"I usually only have one at lunch."

The waiter was pretending to be inordinately fond of children. *"Qu'elle est mignonne la petite? Elle parle exactement comme une française."*

"How about dessert? Shall we wait and see?"

The waiter disappeared. Honoria looked at her father expectantly.

"What are we going to do?"

"First, we're going to a toy store and buy you anything you like. Then we're going to the vaudeville at the Empire."

She hesitated. "I like it about the vaudeville, but not the toy store."

"Why not?"

"Well, you brought me this doll." She had it with her. "And I've got lots of things. And we're not rich anymore, are we?"

"We never were. But today you are to have anything you want."

"All right," she agreed resignedly.

When there had been her mother and a French nurse he had been inclined to be strict; now he extended himself, reached out for a new tolerance; he must be both parents to her and not shut any of her out of communication.

"I want to get to know you," he said gravely. "First let me introduce myself. My name is Charles J. Wales, of Prague."

"Oh, Daddy!" her voice cracked with laughter.

"And who are you, please?" he persisted, and she accepted a role immediately: "Honoria Wales, Rue Palatine, Paris."

"Married or single?"

"No, not married. Single."

He indicated the doll. "But I see you have a child, madame."

Unwilling to disinherit it, she took it to her heart and thought quickly: "Yes, I've been married, but I'm not married now. My husband is dead."

He went on quickly, "And the child's name?"

"Simone. That's after my best friend at school."

"I'm very pleased that you're doing so well at school."

"I'm third this month," she boasted. "Elsie"—that was her cousin—"is eighteenth, and Richard is about at the bottom."

"You like Richard and Elsie, don't you?"

"Oh, yes. I like him quite well and I like her all right."

Cautiously and casually he asked: "And Aunt Marion and Uncle Lincoln—which do you like best?"

"Oh, Uncle Lincoln, I guess."

He was increasingly aware of her presence. As they came in, a murmur of ". . . adorable" followed them, and now the people at the next table bent all their silences upon her, staring as if she were something no more conscious than a flower.

"Why don't I live with you?" she asked suddenly. "Because Mamma's dead?"

"You must stay here and learn more French. It would have been hard for Daddy to take care of you so well."

"I don't really need much taking care of anymore. I do everything for myself."

Going out of the restaurant, a man and a woman unexpectedly hailed him!

"Well, the old Wales!"

"Hello there, Lorraine. . . . Dunc."

Sudden ghosts out of the past: Duncan Schaeffer, a friend from college. Lorraine Quarrles, a lovely, pale blonde of thirty; one of a crowd who had helped them make months into days in the lavish times of three years ago.

"My husband couldn't come this year," she said. "We're poor as hell. So he gave me two hundred a month, and told me I could do my worst on that. . . . This your little girl?"

"What about coming back and sitting down?" Duncan asked.

"Can't do it." He was glad for an excuse. As always he felt Lorraine's passionate, provocative attraction, but his own rhythm was different now.

"Well, how about dinner?" she asked.

"I'm not free. Give me your address and let me call you."

"Charlie, I believe you're sober," she said judicially. "Pinch him, Dunc, and see if he's sober."

Charlie indicated Honoria with his head. They both laughed.

"What's your address?" said Duncan skeptically.

He hesitated, unwilling to give the name of his hotel.

"I'm not settled yet. I'd better call you. We're going to see the vaudeville at the Empire."

"There! That's what I want to do," Lorraine said. "I want to see some clowns and acrobats and jugglers. That's just what we'll do, Dunc."

"We've got to do an errand first," said Charlie. "Perhaps we'll see you there."

"All right, you snob. . . . Good-by, beautiful little girl."

"Good-by." Honoria bobbed politely.

Somehow, an unwelcome encounter. They liked him because he was functioning, because he was serious; they wanted to see him, because he was stronger than they were now, because they wanted to draw a certain sustenance from his strength.

At the Empire, Honoria proudly refused to sit upon her father's folded coat. She was already an individual with a code of her own, and Charlie was more and more absorbed by the desire of putting a little of himself into her before she crystallized utterly. It was hopeless to try to know her in so short a time.

Between the acts they came upon Duncan and Lorraine in the lobby where the band was playing.

"Have a drink?"

"All right, but not up at the bar. We'll take a table."

"The perfect father."

Listening abstractedly to Lorraine, Charlie watched Honoria's eyes leave their table, and he followed them wistfully about the room, wondering what they saw. He met her glance and she smiled.

"I liked that lemonade," she said.

Going home in a taxi afterward, he pulled her over until her head rested against his chest.

"Darling, do you ever think about your mother?"

"Yes, sometimes," she answered vaguely.

"I don't want you to forget her. Have you got a picture of her?"

"Yes, I think so. Anyhow, Aunt Marion has."

"She loved you very much."

"I loved her too."

They were silent for a moment.

"Daddy, I want to come and live with you," she said suddenly. His heart leaped; he had wanted it to come like this.

"Aren't you perfectly happy?"

"Yes, but I love you better than anybody. And you love me better than anybody, don't you, now that Mummy's dead?"

"Of course I do. But you won't always like me best, honey. You'll grow up and meet somebody your own age and go marry him and forget you ever had a daddy."

"Yes, that's true," she agreed tranquilly.

He didn't go in. He was coming back at nine o'clock and he wanted to keep himself fresh and new for the thing he must say then.

"When you're safe inside, just show yourself in that window."

"All right. Good-by, Dads, Dads, Dads, Dads."

He waited in the dark street until she appeared, all warm and glowing, in the window above and kissed her fingers out into the night.

THEY WERE WAITING. Marion sat behind the coffee service in a dignified black dinner dress that just faintly suggested mourning. Lincoln was walking up and down with the animation of one who had already been talking. Charlie opened the question almost immediately:

"I suppose you know why I really came to Paris."

Marion played with her necklace and frowned.

"I'm awfully anxious to have a home," he continued. "And I'm awfully anxious to have Honoria in it. I appreciate your taking in Honoria for her mother's sake, but things have changed radically with me." He hesitated and then continued more forcibly, "I want to ask you to reconsider the matter. It would be silly for me to deny that three years ago I was acting badly—"

Marion looked up at him with hard eyes.

"—but all that's over. As I told you, I haven't had more than a drink a day for over a year, and I take that drink deliberately, so that the idea of alcohol won't get too big in my imagination. You see the idea?"

"No," said Marion succinctly.

"It's a sort of stunt I set myself. It keeps the matter in proportion."

"I get you," said Lincoln. "You don't want to admit it's got any attraction for you."

"Something like that. Sometimes I forget and don't take it. But I try to take it. Anyhow, I couldn't afford to drink in my position. The people I represent are more than satisfied with what I've done, and I'm bringing my sister over from Burlington to keep house for me, and I want awfully to have Honoria too. You know that even when her mother and I weren't getting along well we never let anything that happened touch Honoria. I know she's fond of me and I know I'm able to take care of her and—well, there you are. How do you feel about it?"

He knew that now he would have to take a beating. It would last an hour or two hours, but if he adopted the chastened attitude of the reformed sinner, he might win his point in the end.

Keep your temper, he told himself. You don't want to be justified. You want Honoria.

Lincoln spoke first: "We've been talking it over ever since we got your letter last month. Honoria's a dear little thing, and we're happy to have her here, but of course that isn't the question—"

Marion interrupted suddenly. "How long are you going to stay sober, Charlie?" she asked.

"Permanently, I hope."

"How can anybody count on that?"

"You know I never did drink heavily until I gave up business and came over here with nothing to do. Then Helen and I began to run around with—"

"Please leave Helen out of it."

He stared at her grimly; he had never been certain how fond of each other the sisters were.

"My drinking only lasted about a year and a half—from the time we came over until I—collapsed."

"It was time enough."

"It was time enough," he agreed.

"My duty is entirely to Helen," she said. "I try to think what she would have wanted me to do. Frankly, from the night you did that terrible thing you haven't really existed for me. I can't help that. She was my sister."

"Yes."

"When she was dying she asked me to look out for Honoria. If you hadn't been in a sanitarium then, it might have helped matters."

He had no answer.

"I'll never in my life be able to forget the morning when Helen knocked at my door, soaked to the skin and shivering, and said you'd locked her out."

Charlie gripped the sides of the chair. He wanted to launch out into a long expostulation and explanation, but he only said: "The night I locked her out—" and she interrupted, "I don't feel up to going over that again."

After a moment's silence Lincoln said: "We're getting off the subject. You want Marion to set aside her legal guardianship and give you Honoria. I think the main point for her is whether she has confidence in you or not."

"I don't blame Marion," Charlie said slowly, "but I think she can have entire confidence in me. I had a good record up to three years ago. Of course, it's within human possibilities I might go wrong anytime. But if we wait much longer I'll lose Honoria's childhood and my chance for a home." He shook his head. "I'll simply lose her, don't you see?"

"Yes, I see," said Lincoln.

"Why didn't you think of all this before?" Marion asked.

"When I consented to the guardianship, I was flat on my back and the market had cleaned me out. I knew I'd acted badly, and I thought if it would bring any peace to Helen, I'd agree to anything. But now it's different. I'm functioning, I'm behaving damn well, so far as—"

"Please don't swear at me," Marion said.

He looked at her, startled. With each remark the force of her dislike became more and more apparent. She had built up all her fear of life into one wall and faced it toward him. Charlie became increasingly alarmed at leaving Honoria in this atmosphere of hostility against himself. But he pulled his temper down out of his face and shut it up inside him; he had won a point, for Lincoln realized the absurdity of Marion's remark and asked her lightly since when she had objected to the word "damn."

"Another thing," Charlie said: "I'm able to give her certain advantages now. I'm going to take a French governess to Prague with me. I've got a lease on a new apartment—"

He stopped, realizing that he was blundering. They couldn't be expected to accept with equanimity the fact that his income was again twice as large as their own.

"I suppose you can give her more luxuries than we can," said Marion. "When you were throwing away money we were watching every ten francs. . . . I suppose you'll start doing it again."

"Oh, no," he said. "I've learned. I worked hard for ten years, you know—until I got lucky in the market, like so many people. It didn't seem any use working anymore, so I quit. It won't happen again."

There was a long silence. All of them felt their nerves straining, and for the first time in a year Charlie wanted a drink. He was sure now that Lincoln Peters wanted him to have his child.

Marion shuddered suddenly; part of her saw that Charlie's feet were planted on the earth now, and her own maternal feeling recognized the naturalness of his desire; but she had lived for a long time with a prejudice—a prejudice founded on a curious disbelief in her sister's happiness, and which, in the shock of one terrible night, had turned to hatred for him.

"I can't help what I think!" she cried out suddenly. "How much you were responsible for Helen's death, I don't know. It's something you'll have to square with your own conscience."

An electric current of agony surged through him; for a moment he was almost on his feet, an unuttered sound echoing in his throat. He hung onto himself for a moment, another moment.

"Hold on there," said Lincoln uncomfortably. "I never thought you were responsible for that."

"Helen died of heart trouble," Charlie said dully.

"Yes, heart trouble." Marion spoke as if the phrase had another meaning for her.

Then, in the flatness that followed her outburst, she saw him plainly and she knew he had somehow arrived at control over the situation. Glancing at her husband, she found no help from him, and as abruptly as if it were a matter of no importance, she threw up the sponge.

"Do what you like!" she cried, springing up from her chair. "She's your child. I'm not the person to stand in your way. I think if it were my child I'd rather see her—" She managed to check herself, "You two decide it. I can't stand this."

She hurried from the room; after a moment Lincoln said:

"This has been a hard day for her. You know how strongly she feels—" His voice was almost apologetic: "When a woman gets an idea in her head."

"Of course."

"It's going to be all right. I think she sees now that you—can provide for the child, and so we can't very well stand in your way or Honoria's way."

"Thank you, Lincoln."

"I'd better go along and see how she is."

"I'm going."

He was still trembling when he reached the street, but a walk down to the quays set him up, and as he crossed the Seine, he felt exultant. But back in his room he couldn't sleep. The image of Helen haunted him. Helen whom he had loved so until they had senselessly begun to abuse each other's love, tear it into shreds. On that terrible February night that Marion remembered so vividly, a slow quarrel had gone on for hours. There was a scene at the Florida, and then he attempted to take her home, and then she kissed young Webb at a table; after that there was what she had hysterically said. When he arrived home alone he turned the key in the lock in wild anger. How could he know she would arrive an hour later alone, that there would be a snowstorm in which she wandered about in slippers, too confused to find a taxi? Then the aftermath, her escaping pneumonia by a miracle, and all the attendant horror. They were "reconciled," but that was the beginning of the end, and Marion, who had imagined it to be one of many scenes from her sister's martyrdom, never forgot.

Going over it again brought Helen nearer, and in the white, soft light that steals upon half sleep near morning he found himself talking to her again. She said that he was perfectly right about Honoria and that she wanted Honoria to be with him. She said she was glad he was being good and doing better. She said a lot of other things—very friendly things—but she was in a swing in a white dress, and swinging faster and faster all the time, so that at the end he could not hear clearly all that she said.

HE WOKE UP feeling happy. The door of the world was open again. He made plans, vistas, futures for Honoria and himself, but suddenly he grew sad, remembering all the plans he and Helen had made. She had not planned to die. The present was the thing—work to do and someone to love. But not to love too much, for he knew the injury that a father can do to a daughter or a mother to a son by attaching them too closely: afterward, out in the world, the child would seek in the marriage partner the same blind tenderness and, failing probably to find it, turn against love and life.

It was another bright, crisp day. He called Lincoln Peters at the bank where he worked and asked if he could take Honoria when he left for Prague. Lincoln agreed that there was no reason for delay. One thing—the legal guardianship. Marion wanted to retain that a while longer. It would oil things if she felt that the situation was still in her control for another year. Charlie agreed, wanting only the tangible, visible child. He lunched with Lincoln Peters at Griffons, trying to keep down his exultation.

"There's nothing quite like your own child," Lincoln said. "But you understand how Marion feels too."

"She's forgotten how hard I worked for seven years there," Charlie said. "She just remembers one night."

"Another thing." Lincoln hesitated. "While you and Helen were tearing around Europe throwing money away, we were just getting along. I think Marion felt there was some kind of injustice in it—you not even working toward the end, and getting richer and richer."

"It went just as quick as it came," said Charlie.

"Yes, a lot of it stayed in the hands of saxophone players and maîtres d'hôtel—well, the big party's over now. I just said that to explain Marion's feeling about those crazy years. If you drop in about six o'clock, we'll settle the details."

Back at his hotel, Charlie found a note that had been redirected from the Ritz bar where Charlie had left his address for the purpose of finding a certain man.

> Dear Charlie: You were so strange when we saw you the other day that I wondered if I did something to offend you. If so, I'm not conscious of it. In fact, I have thought about you too much for the last year, and it's always been in the back of my mind that I might see you if I came over here. We *did* have such good times that crazy spring, like the night you and I stole the butcher's tricycle. Everybody seems so old lately, but I don't feel old a bit. Couldn't we get together for old time's sake? I've got a vile hangover for the moment, but will be feeling better this afternoon and will look for you about five in the sweetshop at the Ritz.
>
> > Always devotedly,
> > Lorraine

His first feeling was one of awe that he had actually, in his mature years, stolen a tricycle and pedaled Lorraine all over the Étoile between the small hours and dawn. In retrospect it was a nightmare. Locking out Helen didn't fit in with any other act of his life, but the tricycle incident did—it was one of many. How many weeks or months of dissipation to arrive at that condition of utter irresponsibility?

He tried to picture how Lorraine had appeared to him then—very attractive; Helen was unhappy about it, though she said nothing. Yesterday, in the restaurant, Lorraine had seemed trite, blurred, worn away. He emphatically did not want to see her. It was a relief to think, instead, of Honoria, to think of Sundays spent with her and of saying good-morning to her and of knowing she was there in his house at night, drawing her breath in the darkness.

At five he took a taxi and bought presents for all the Peters—a piquant cloth doll, a box of Roman soldiers, flowers for Marion, big linen handkerchiefs for Lincoln.

He saw, when he arrived in the apartment, that Marion had accepted the inevitable. She greeted him now as though he were a recalcitrant member of the family, rather than a menacing outsider. Honoria had been told she was going; Charlie was glad to see that her tact made her conceal her excessive happiness. Only on his lap did she whisper her delight and the question "When?" before she slipped away with the other children.

He and Marion were alone for a minute in the room, and on an impulse he spoke out boldly:

"Family quarrels are bitter things. They don't go according to any rules. They're not like aches or wounds; they're more like splits in the skin that won't heal because there's not enough material. I wish you and I could be on better terms."

"Some things are hard to forget," she answered. "It's a question of confidence." There was no answer to this and presently she asked, "When do you propose to take her?"

"As soon as I can get a governess. I hoped the day after tomorrow."

"Not before Saturday. I've got to get her things in shape."

He yielded. Coming back into the room, Lincoln offered him a drink.

"I'll take my daily whisky," he said.

It was warm here, it was a home, people together by a fire. The children felt very safe and important; the mother and father were serious, watchful. They had things to do for the children more important than his visit here. A spoonful of medicine was, after all, more important than the strained relations between Marion and himself. They were not dull people, but they were very much in the grip of life and circumstances. He wondered if he couldn't do something to get Lincoln out of his rut at the bank.

A long peal at the doorbell; the maid-of-all-work passed through and went down the corridor. The door opened upon another long ring, and then voices, and the three in the salon looked up expectantly. Marion rose. Then the maid came back along the corridor, closely followed by the voices, which developed under the light into Duncan Schaeffer and Lorraine Quarrles.

They were gay, they were hilarious, they were roaring with laughter.

For a moment Charlie was astounded; unable to understand how they ferreted out the Peters' address.

"Ah-h-h!" Duncan wagged his finger roguishly at Charlie.

They both slid down another cascade of laughter. Anxious and at a loss, Charlie shook hands with them quickly and presented them to Lincoln and Marion. Marion nodded, scarcely speaking. She had drawn back a step toward the fire; her little girl stood beside her, and Marion put an arm about her shoulder.

With growing annoyance at the intrusion, Charlie waited for them to explain themselves. After some concentration Duncan said:

"We came to invite you out to dinner. Lorraine and I insist that all this cagey business 'bout your address got to stop."

Charlie came closer to them, as if to force them backward down the corridor. "Sorry, but I can't. Tell me where you'll be and I'll phone you in half an hour."

This made no impression. Lorraine sat down suddenly on the side of a chair; and focusing her eyes on Richard, cried, "Oh, what a nice little boy! Come here, little boy." Richard glanced at his mother, but did not move. With a perceptible shrug of her shoulders, Lorraine turned back to Charlie. "Come and dine. Sure your cousins won' mine. See you so sel'om. Or solemn."

"I can't," said Charlie sharply. "You two have dinner and I'll phone you."

Her voice became suddenly unpleasant. "All right. But I remember once when you hammered on my door at four a.m. I was enough of a good sport to give you a drink. Come on, Dunc."

Still in slow motion, with blurred, angry faces, with uncertain feet, they retired along the corridor.

"Good night," Charlie said.

"Good night!" responded Lorraine emphatically.

When he went back into the salon Marion had not moved, only now her son was standing in the circle of her other arm.

"What an outrage!" Charlie broke out. "What an absolute outrage!" Neither Marion nor Lincoln answered. Charlie dropped into an armchair, picked up his drink, set it down again and said:

"People I haven't seen for two years having the colossal nerve—"

He broke off. Marion had made the sound "Oh!" in one swift, furious breath, turned from him with a jerk and left the room.

"You children go in and start your soup," Lincoln said, and when they obeyed, he said to Charlie:

"Marion's not well and she can't stand shocks. That kind of people make her really physically sick."

"I didn't tell them to come here. They wormed your name out of somebody. They deliberately—"

"Well, it doesn't help matters. Excuse me a minute."

Left alone, Charlie sat tense in his chair. In the next room he could hear the children eating, talking in monosyllables, already oblivious to the scene between their elders. He heard a murmur of conversation from a farther room, and in a panic he moved out of earshot.

In a minute Lincoln came back. "Look here, Charlie. I think we'd better call off dinner. Marion's in bad shape."

"Is she angry with me?"

"Sort of," he said, almost roughly. "You mean she's changed her mind about Honoria?"

"You mean she's changed her mind about Honoria?"

"She's pretty bitter right now. I don't know. You phone me at the bank tomorrow."

"I wish you'd explain to her I never dreamed these people would come here. I'm just as sore as you are."

"I couldn't explain anything to her now."

Charlie got up. He took his coat and hat and started down the corridor. Then he opened the door of the dining room and said in a strange voice, "Good night, children."

Honoria rose and ran around the table to hug him.

"Good night, sweetheart," he said vaguely, and then trying to make his voice more tender, trying to conciliate something, "Good night, dear children."

Charlie went directly to the Ritz bar with the furious idea of finding Lorraine and Duncan, but they were not there, and he realized that in any case there was nothing he could do. He had not touched his drink at the Peters' and now he ordered a whisky and soda. Paul came over to say hello.

"It's a great change," he said sadly. "We do about half the business we did. So many fellows I hear about back in the States lost everything, maybe not in the first crash, but then in the second. Your friend George Hardt lost every cent, I hear. Are you back in the States?"

"No, I'm in business in Prague."

"I heard that you lost a lot in the crash."

"I did," and he added grimly, "but I lost everything I wanted in the boom."

Again the memory of those days swept over him like a nightmare— the people they had met traveling; then people who couldn't add a row of figures or speak a coherent sentence. The little man Helen had consented to dance with at the ship's party, who had insulted her ten feet from the table; the women and girls carried screaming with drink or drugs out of public places—

—The men who locked their wives out in the snow, because the snow of twenty-nine wasn't real snow. If you didn't want it to be snow, you just paid some money.

He went to the phone and called Lincoln.

"I called up because this thing is on my mind. Has Marion said anything definite?"

"Marion's sick," Lincoln answered shortly. "I know this thing isn't altogether your fault, but I can't have her go to pieces about it. I'm afraid we'll have to let it slide for six months; I can't chance working her up to this state again."

"I see."

"I'm sorry, Charlie."

He went back to his table. His whisky glass was empty, but he shook his head when Alix looked at it questioningly. There wasn't much he could do now except send Honoria some things; he would send her a lot of things tomorrow. He thought rather angrily that this was just money—he had given so many people money. . . .

"No, no more," he said to another waiter. "What do I owe you?"

He would come back someday; they couldn't make him pay forever. But he wanted his child, and nothing was much good now, beside that fact. He wasn't young anymore, with a lot of nice thoughts and dreams to have by himself. He was absolutely sure Helen wouldn't have wanted him to be so alone.

CARRION SPRING

WALLACE STEGNER / UNITED STATES

THE MOMENT she came to the door she could smell it, not really rotten and not coming from any particular direction, but sweetish, faintly sickening, sourceless, filling the whole air the way a river's water can taste of weeds—the carrion smell of a whole country breathing out in the first warmth across hundreds of square miles.

Three days of chinook had uncovered everything that had been under snow since November. The yard lay discolored and ugly, gray ash pile, rusted cans, spilled lignite, bones. The clinkers that had given them winter footing for the privy and stable lay in raised gray wavers across the mud; the strung lariats they had used for lifelines in blizzardy weather had dried out and sagged to the ground. Muck was knee-deep down in the corrals by the sod-roofed stable, the white-washed logs were yellowed at the corners from dogs lifting their legs against them. Sunken drifts around the hay yard were a reminder of how many times the boys had had to shovel out there to keep the calves from walking into the stacks across the top of the snow. Across the wan and disheveled yard the willows were bare, and beyond them the floodplain hill was brown. The sky was roiled with gray cloud.

Matted, filthy, lifeless, littered, the place of her winter imprisonment was exposed, ugly enough to put gooseflesh up her backbone, and with the carrion smell over all of it. It was like a bad and disgusting wound, infected wire cut, or proud flesh, or the gangrene of frostbite, with the bandage off. With her packed trunk and her telescope bag and two loaded grain sacks behind her, she stood in the door waiting for Ray to come with the buckboard, and she was sick to be gone.

Yet when he did come, with the boys all slopping through the mud behind him, and they threw her trunk and telescope and bags into the buckboard and tied the tarp down and there was nothing left to do but go, she faced them with a sudden desolating desire to cry. She laughed, and caught her lower lip under her teeth and bit down hard on its trembling and went around to shake one hooflike hand after the other, staring into each face in turn and seeing in each something that made it all the harder to say something easy. Good-by, red-bearded, black-bearded, gray-bristled, clean shaven (for her?), two of them with puckered sunken scars on the cheekbones, all of them seedy, mat-haired, weathered, and cracked as old lumber left out for years, they looked sheepish, or sober, or cheerful, and said things like, "Well, Molly, have you a nice trip, now," or "See you in Malta maybe." They had been her family. She had looked after them, fed them, patched their clothes, unraveled old socks to knit them new ones, cut their hair, lanced their boils, tended their wounds. Now it was like the gathered-in family parting at the graveside after someone's funeral.

She had begun to cry quite openly. She pulled her cheeks down, opened her mouth, dabbed at her eyes with her knuckles, laughed. "Now you all take care," she said. "And come see us, you hear? Jesse? Rusty? Slip? Ed? Buck, when you come I'll sure fix you a better patch on your pants than that one. Good-by, Panguingue, you were the best man I had on the coal scuttle. Don't you forget me. Little Horn, I'm sorry we ran out of pie fixings. When you come to Malta I'll make you a peach pie a yard across."

She could not have helped speaking their names, as if to name them were to ensure their permanence. But she knew that though she might see them, or most of them, when Ray brought the drive in to Malta in July, these were friends lost for good. They had already got the word; sweep the range and sell everything—steers, bulls, calves, cows—for whatever it would bring. Put a For Sale sign on the ranch, or simply abandon it. The country had rubbed its lesson in. Like half the outfits between the Milk and the CPR, the T-Down was quitting. As for her, she was quitting first.

She saw Ray slumping, glooming down from the buckboard seat

with the reins wrapped around one gloved hand. Dude and Dinger were hipshot in the harness. As Rusty and Little Horn gave Molly a hand up to climb the wheel, Dude raised his tail and dropped a bundle of dung on the singletree, but she did not even bother to make a face or say something provoked and joking. She was watching Ray, looking right into his gray eyes and his somber dark face and seeing all at once what the winter of disaster had done to him. His cheek, like Ed's and Rusty's, was puckered with frost scars; frost had nibbled at the lobes of his ears; she could see the strain of bone-cracking labor, the bitterness of failure, in the lines from his nose to the corners of his mouth. Making room for her, he did not smile. With her back momentarily to the others, speaking only for him, she said through her tight teeth, "Let's git!"

Promptly—he was always prompt and ready—he plucked whip from whipsocket. The tip snapped on Dinger's haunch, the lurch of the buggy threw her so that she could cling and not have to turn to reveal her face. "Good-by!" she cried, more into the collar of her mackinaw than to them, throwing the words over her shoulder like a flower or a coin, and tossed her left hand in the air and shook it. The single burst of their voices chopped off into silence. She heard only the grate of the tires in gravel; beside her the wheel poured yellow drip. She concentrated on it, fighting her lips that wanted to blubber.

"This could be bad for a minute," Ray said. She looked up. Obediently she clamped thumb and finger over her nose. To their right, filling half of Frying Pan Flat, was the boneyard, two acres of carcasses scattered where the boys had dragged them after skinning them out when they found them dead in the brush. It did not seem that off there they could smell, for the chinook was blowing out in light airs from the west. But when she let go her nose she smelled it rich and rotten, as if it rolled upwind the way water runs upstream in an eddy. Beside her, Ray was silent. The horses were trotting now in the soft sand of the patrol trail. On both sides the willows were gnawed down to stubs, broken and mouthed and gummed off by starving cattle. There was floodwater in the low spots, and the sound of running water under the drifts of every side coulee.

Once Ray said, "Harry Willis says a railroad survey's coming right up the Whitemud Valley this summer. S'pose that'll mean homesteaders in here, maybe a town."

"I s'pose."

"Make it a little easier when you run out of prunes, if there was a store at Eastend."

"Well," she said, "we won't be here to run out," and then immediately, as she caught a whiff that gagged her, "Pee-you! Hurry up!"

Ray did not touch up the team. "What *for?*" he said. "To get to the next one quicker?"

She appraised the surliness of his voice, and judged that some of it was general disgust and some of it was aimed at her. But what did he want? Every time she made a suggestion of some outfit around Malta or Chinook where he might get a job he humped his back and looked as impenetrable as a rock. What *did* he want? To come back here and take another licking? When there wasn't even a cattle outfit left, except maybe the little ones like the Z-X and the Lazy-S? And where one winter could kill you, as it had just killed the T-Down?

She felt like yelling at him, "It isn't *me!* I could stand it. Maybe I wouldn't like it, but I could stand it. But it just makes me sick to see you work yourself to death for nothing. Look at your face. Look at your hands—you can't open them even halfway, for calluses. For what? Maybe three thousand cattle left out of ten thousand, and them skin and bone. Why wouldn't I be glad to get out? Who *cares* if there's a store in Eastend? You're just like an old bulldog with his teeth clinched in somebody's behind, and it'll take a pry bar to make you unclinch!" But she said nothing; she made herself breathe the tainted air evenly.

Floodwater forced them out of the bottoms and up onto the second floodplain. Below them Molly saw the water astonishingly wide, pushing across willow bars and pressing deep into the cutbank bends. She could hear it, when the wheels went quietly—a hushed roar like wind. Cattle were balloonily afloat in the bush where they had died. She saw a brindle longhorn waltz around the deep water of a bend with his legs in the air, and farther on a whiteface that stranded momentarily among flooded rosebushes, and rotated free, and stranded again.

Their bench was cut by a side coulee, and they tipped and rocked down, the rumps of the horses back against the dashboard, Ray's hand on the brake, the shoe screeching mud from the tires. There was brush in the bottom, and stained drifts still unmelted. Their wheels sank in slush, she hung to the seat rail, they righted, the lines cracked across the muscling rumps as the team dug in and lifted them out of the cold, snowbank breath of the draw. Then abruptly, in a hollow on the right, dead eyeballs stared at her from between spraddled legs, horns and tails and legs were tangled in a starved mass of bone and hide not yet, in that cold bottom, puffing with the gases of decay. They must have been three-deep—piled on one another, she supposed, while drifting before some one of the winter's blizzards.

A little later, accosted by a stench so overpowering that she breathed it in deeply as if to sample the worst, she looked to the left and saw a longhorn, its belly blown up ready to pop, hanging by neck and horns from a tight clump of alder and black birch where the snow had left him. She saw the wind make cat's-paws in the heavy winter hair.

"Jesus," Ray said, "when you find 'em in *trees!*"

His boots, worn and whitened by many wettings, were braced against the dash. From the corner of her eye Molly could see his glove, its wrist lace open. His wrist looked as wide as a doubletree, the sleeve of his Levi jacket was tight with forearm. The very sight of his strength made her hate the tone of defeat and outrage in his voice. Yet she appraised the tone cunningly, for she did not want him somehow butting his bullheaded way back into it. There were better things they could do than break their backs and hearts in a hopeless country a hundred miles from anywhere.

With narrowed eyes, caught in an instant vision, she saw the lilac bushes by the front porch of her father's house, heard the screen door bang behind her brother Charley (screen doors!), saw people passing, women in dresses, maybe all going to a picnic or a ball game down in the park by the river. She passed the front of McCabe's General Store and through the window saw the counters and shelves: dried apples, dried peaches, prunes, tapioca, Karo Syrup, everything they had done without for six weeks; and new white-stitched overalls, yellow horsehide gloves, varnished axe handles, barrels of flour and bags of sugar, shiny boots and work shoes, counters full of calico and flowered voile and crepe de chine and curtain net, whole stacks of flypaper stuck sheet to sheet, jars of peppermints and striped candy and horehound. . . . She giggled.

"What?" Ray's neck and shoulders were so stiff with muscle that he all but creaked when he turned his head.

"I was just thinking. Remember the night I used our last sugar to make that batch of divinity, and dragged the boys in after bedtime to eat it?"

"Kind of saved the day," Ray said. "Took the edge off ever'body."

"Kind of left us starving for sugar, though. But I can see them picking up those little bitty dabs of fluff with their fingers like tongs, and stuffing them in among their whiskers and making faces, yum, yum, and wondering what on earth had got into me."

"Nothing got into you. You was just fed up. We all was."

"Remember when Slip picked up that pincushion I was tatting a cover for, and I got sort of hysterical and asked him if he knew what it was? Remember what he said? 'It's a doll piller, ain't it, Molly?' I thought I'd die."

She shook her head angrily and a tear splashed on the dash. Ray was looking sideways at her in alarm. She turned her face away and stared down across the water that spread nearly a half-mile wide in the bottoms. Dirty foam and brush circled in the eddies. She saw a slab cave from an almost drowned cutbank and sink, bubbling. From where they drove, between the water and the outer slope that rolled up to the high prairie, the Cypress Hills made a snow-patched, tree-darkened dome across the west. The wind came off them mild as milk. *Poisoned!* she told herself, and dragged it deep into her lungs.

She was aware again of Ray's gray eye. "Hard on you," he said. For some reason he made her mad, as if he was accusing her of bellyaching. She felt how all the time they bumped and rolled along the shoulder of the river valley they had this antagonism between them like a snarl of barbed wire. You couldn't reach out anywhere without running into it. Did he blame her for going home, or what? What did he expect her to do, come along with a whole bunch of men on that roundup, spend six or eight weeks in pants out among the carcasses? And then what?

A high, sharp whicker came downwind. The team chuckled and surged into their collars. Looking ahead, she saw a horse—picketed, probably, or hobbled—and a man who leaned on something—rifle?—watching them. "Young Schulz," Ray said, and then there came the dogs, four big, bony hounds. The team began to dance. Ray held them in tight and whistled the buggy whip in the air when the hounds got too close.

Young Schulz, Molly saw as they got closer, was leaning on a shovel, not a rifle. He had dug a trench two or three feet deep and ten or twelve long. He dragged a bare forearm across his forehead under a muskrat cap: a sullen-faced boy with eyes like dirty ice. She supposed he had been living all alone since his father had disappeared late in the winter. Somehow he made her want to turn her lips inside out. A wild man, worse than an Indian. She had not liked his father and she did not like him.

The hounds below her were sniffing at the wheels and testing the air up in her direction, wagging slow tails.

"What've you got, wolves?" Ray asked.

"Coyotes."

"Old ones down there?"

"One, anyway. Chased her in."

"Find any escape holes?"

"One. Plugged it."

"You get 'em the hard way," Ray said. "How've you been doing on wolves?"

The boy said a hard, four-letter word, slanted his eyes sideward at Molly in something less than apology—acknowledgment, maybe. "The dogs ain't worth a damn without Puma to kill for 'em. Since he got killed they just catch up with a wolf and run alongside him. I dug out a couple dens."

With his thumb and finger he worked at a pimple under his jaw. The soft wind blew over them, the taint of carrion only a suspicion, perhaps imaginary. The roily sky had begun to break up in patches of blue. Molly felt the solid bump of Ray's shoulder as he twisted to cast a weather eye upward. "Going to be a real spring day," he said. To young Schulz he said, "How far in that burrow go, d'you s'pose?"

"Wouldn't ordinarily go more'n twenty feet or so."

"Need any help diggin'?"

The Schulz boy spat.

"Ray . . ." Molly said. But she stopped when she saw his face.

"Been a long time since I helped dig out a coyote," he said. He watched her as if waiting for a reaction. "Been a long time since I did anything for *fun*."

"Oh, go ahead!" she said. "Long as we don't miss that train."

"I guess we can make Maple Creek by noon tomorrow. And you ain't in such a hurry you have to be there sooner, are you?"

She had never heard so much edge in his voice. He looked at her as if he hated her. She turned so as to keep the Schulz boy from seeing her face, and for just a second she and Ray were all alone up there, eye to eye. She laid a hand on his knee. "I don't know what it is," she said. "Honestly I don't. But you better work it off."

Young Schulz went back to his digging while Ray unhitched and looped the tugs and tied the horses to the wheels. Then Ray took the shovel and began to fill the air with clods. He moved more dirt than the Fresno scrapers she had seen grading the railroad back home; he worked as if exercising his muscles after a long layoff, as if spring had fired him up and set him to running. The soil was sandy and came out in clean brown shovelfuls. The hounds lay back out of range and watched. Ray did not look toward Molly, or say anything to Schulz; he just moved dirt as if dirt was his worst enemy. After a few minutes Molly pulled the buffalo robe out of the buckboard and spread it on the drying prairie. By that time it was getting close to noon. The sun was full out, warm on her face and hands.

The coyote hole ran along about three feet underground. From where she sat she could look right up the trench and see the black opening at the bottom when the shovel broke into it. She could imagine the coyotes, crammed back at the end of their burrow, hearing the noises and seeing the growing light as their death dug toward them, and no way out, nothing to do but wait.

Young Schulz took the shovel and Ray stood out of the trench, blowing. The violent work seemed to have made him more cheerful. He said to Schulz, when the boy stooped and reached a gloved hand up the hole, "She comes out of there in a hurry, she'll run right up your sleeve."

Schulz grunted and resumed his digging. The untroubled sun went over, hanging almost overhead, and an untroubled wind stirred the old grass. Where the terrace of the floodplain rolled up to the prairie the first gopher of the season sat up and looked them over. A dog moved, and he disappeared with a flirt of his tail. Ray was rolling up his sleeves, whistling loosely between his teeth. His forearms were white, his hands blackened and cracked as the charred end of sticks. His eyes touched her—speculatively, she thought. She smiled, making a forgiving, kissing motion of her mouth, but all he did in reply was work his eyebrows, and she could not tell what he was thinking.

Young Schulz was poking up the hole with the shovel handle. Crouching in the trench in his muskrat cap, he looked like some digging animal; she half expected him to put his nose into the hole and sniff and then start throwing dirt out between his hind legs.

Then in a single convulsion of movement Schulz rolled sideward. A naked-gummed thing of teeth and gray fur shot into sight, scrambled at the edge, and disappeared in a pinwheel of dogs. Molly leaped to the heads of the horses, rearing and walleyed and yanking the light buckboard sideways, and with a hand in each bridle steadied them down. Schulz, she saw, was circling the dogs with the shotgun, but it was clear that the dogs had already done it for him. The roaring and snapping tailed off. Schulz kicked the dogs away and with one quick flash and circle and rip tore the scalp and ears off the coyote. It lay there wet, mauled, bloody, with its pink skull bare—a little dog brutally murdered. One of the dogs came up, sniffed with its neck stretched out, sank its teeth in the coyote's shoulder, dragged it a foot or two.

"Ray . . ." Molly said.

He did not hear her; he was blocking the burrow with the shovel blade while Schulz went over to his horse. The boy came back with a red-willow stick seven or eight feet long, forked like a small slingshot at the end. Ray pulled away the shovel and Schulz probed in the hole with the forked end of the stick. A hard grunt came out of him, and he backed up, pulling the stick from the hole. At the last moment he yanked hard, and a squirm of gray broke free and rolled and was pounced on by the hounds.

This time Ray kicked them aside. He picked up the pup by the tail, and it hung down, blood on its fur, and kicked its hind legs a little. Schulz was down again, probing the burrow, twisting, probing again, twisting hard. Again he backed up, working the entangled pup out carefully until it was in the open, and then landing it over his head like a sucker from the river. The pup landed within three feet of the buckboard wheel, and floundered, stunned. In an instant Molly dropped down and smothered it in clothes, hands, arms. There was snarling in her very ear, she was bumped hard, she heard Ray yelling, and then he had her on her feet. From his face, she thought he was going to hit her. Against her middle, held by the scruff and grappled with the other arm, the pup snapped and slavered with needle teeth. She felt the sting of bites on her hands and wrists. The dogs ringed her, kept off by Ray's kicking boot.

"God A'mighty," Ray said, "you want to get yourself killed?"

"I didn't want the dogs to get him."

"No. So maybe they get you. What are you going to do with him now, anyway? We'll just have to knock him in the head."

"I'm going to keep him."

"In Malta?"

"Why not?"

He let go his clutch on her arm. "He'll be a cute pup for a month and then he'll be a chicken thief and then somebody'll shoot him."

"At least he'll have a little bit of a life. Get *away*, you dirty, murdering . . ." She cradled the thudding little body along one arm under her mackinaw, keeping her hold in the scruff with her right hand, and turned herself away from the crowding hounds. "I'm going to tame him," she said. "I don't care what you say."

"Scalp's worth three dollars," Schulz said from the edge of the ditch.

Ray kicked the dogs back. His eyes, ordinarily so cool and gray, looked hot. The digging and the excitement did not seem to have taken the edge off whatever was eating him. He said, "Look, maybe you have to go back home to your folks, but you don't have to take a menagerie along. What are you going to do with him on the train?"

Now it was out. He did blame her. "You think I'm running out on you," she said.

"I just said you can't take a menagerie back to town."

"You said *maybe* I had to go home. Where else would I go? You're going to be on roundup till July. The ranch is going to be sold. Where on earth *would* I go but home?"

"You don't have to stay. You don't have to make me go back to ridin' for some outfit for twenty a month and found."

His dark, battered, scarred face told her to be quiet. Dipping far down in the tight pocket of his Levis he brought up his snap purse and took from it three silver dollars. Young Schulz, who had been probing the den to see if anything else was there, climbed out of the ditch and took the money in his dirty, chapped hand. He gave Molly one infuriatingly cool and knowing look with his dirty-ice eyes, scalped the dead pup, picked up shotgun and twisting stick and shovel, tied them behind the saddle, mounted, whistled at the dogs, and with barely a nod rode off toward the northeastern flank of the hills. The hounds fanned out ahead of him, running loose and easy. In the silence their departure left behind, a clod broke and rolled into the ditch. A gopher piped somewhere. The wind moved quiet as breathing in the grass.

Molly drew a breath that caught a little—a sigh for their quarreling, for whatever bothered him so deeply that he gloomed and grumped and asked something impossible of her—but when she spoke she spoke around it. "No thanks for your digging."

"He don't know much about living with people."

"He's like everything else in this country, wild and dirty and thankless."

In a minute she would really start feeling sorry for herself. But why not? Did it ever occur to him that since November she had seen exactly one woman, for one day and a night? Did he have any idea how she had felt, a bride of ten days, when he went out with the boys and was gone two weeks, through three different blizzards, while she stayed home and didn't know whether he was dead or alive?

"If you mean me," Ray said, "I may be wild and I'm probably dirty, but I ain't thankless, honey."

Shamed, she opened her mouth to reply, but he was already turning away to rummage up a strap and a piece of whang leather to make a collar and leash for her pup.

"Are you hungry?" she said to his shoulders.

"Any time."

"I put up some sandwiches."

"Okay."

"Oh, Ray," she said, "let's not crab at each other. Sure I'm glad we're getting out. Is that so awful? I hate to see you killing yourself bucking this *hopeless* country. But does that mean we have to fight? I thought maybe we could have a picnic like we had coming in, back on that slough where the ducks kept landing on the ice and skidding end over end. I don't know, it doesn't hardly seem we've laughed since."

"Well," he said, "it ain't been much of a laughing winter, for a fact."

He had cut down a cheek strap and tied a rawhide thong to it. Carefully she brought out the pup and he buckled the collar around its neck, but when she set it on the ground it backed up to the end of the thong, cringing and showing its naked gums, so that she picked it up again and let it dig along her arm, hunting darkness under her mackinaw.

"Shall we eat here?" Ray said. "Kind of a lot of chewed-up coyote around."

"Let's go up on the bench."

"Want to tie the pup in the buckboard?"

"I'll take him. I want to get him used to me."

"Okay," he said. "You go on. I'll tie a nose bag on these nags and bring the robe and the lunch box."

She walked slowly, not to scare the pup, until she was up the little bench and onto the prairie. From up there she could see not only the Cypress Hills across the west, but the valley of the Whitemud breaking out of them, and a big slough, spread by floodwater, and watercourses going both ways out of it, marked by thin willows. Just where the Whitemud emerged from the hills were three white dots—the Mountie post, probably, or the Lazy-S, or both. The sun was surprisingly warm, until she counted up and found that it was May 8. It *ought* to be warm.

Ray brought the buffalo robe and spread it, and she sat down. One-handed because she had the thong of the leash wrapped around her palm, she doled out sandwiches and boiled eggs. Ray popped a whole egg in his mouth, and chewing, pointed. "There goes the South Fork of the Swift Current, out of the slough. The one this side, that little scraggle of willows you can see, empties into the Whitemud. That slough sits right on the divide and runs both ways. You don't see that very often."

She appraised his tone. He was feeling better. For that matter, so was she. It had turned out a beautiful day, with big fair-weather clouds coasting over. She saw the flooded river bottoms below them, on the left, darken to winter and then sweep right back to spring again while she could have counted no more than ten. As she moved, the coyote pup clawed and scrambled against her side, and she said, wrinkling her nose in her freckle-faced smile, "If he started eating me, I wonder if I could keep from yelling? Did you ever read that story about the boy that hid the fox under his clothes and the fox started eating a hole in him and the boy never batted an eye, just let himself be chewed?"

"No, I never heard that one," Ray said. "Don't seem very likely, does it?" He lay back and turned his face, shut-eyed, into the sun. Now and then his hand rose to feed bites of sandwich into his mouth.

"The pup's quieter," Molly said. "I wonder if he'd eat a piece of sandwich?"

"Leave him be for a while. I would."

"I guess."

His hand reached over blindly and she put another sandwich into its pincer claws. Chewing, he came up on one elbow, his eyes opened. He stared a long time down into the flooded bottoms and then across toward the slough and the hills. "Soon as the sun comes out, she don't look like the same country, does she?"

Molly said nothing. She watched his nostrils fan in and out as he sniffed. "No smell up here, do you think?" he said.

But she heard the direction he was groping in, the regret that could lead, if they did not watch out, to some renewed and futile hope, and she said tartly, "I can smell it, all right."

He sighed. He lay back and closed his eyes. After about three minutes he said, "Boy, what a day, though. I won't get through on the patrol trail going back. The ice'll be breaking up before tonight, at this rate. Did you hear it crackin' and poppin' a minute ago?"

"I didn't hear it."

"Listen."

They were still. She heard the soft wind move in the prairie wool, and beyond it, filling the background, the hushed and hollow noise of the floodwater, sigh of drowned willows, suck of whirlpools, splash and gurgle as cutbanks caved, and the steady push and swash and ripple of moving water. Into the soft rush of sound came a muffled report like a tree cracking, or a shot a long way off. "Is that it?" she said. "Is that the ice letting loose?"

"Stick around till tomorrow and you'll see that whole channel full of cakes."

Another shadow from one of the big flat-bottomed clouds chilled across them and passed. Ray said into the air, "Harry Willis said this railroad survey will go right through to Medicine Hat. Open up this whole country." Now in fear she sat very still, stroking the soft bulge of the pup through the cloth. "Probably mean a town of Eastend."

"You told me."

"With a store that close we couldn't get quite so snowed in as we did this winter."

Molly said nothing, because she dared not. They were a couple that—like the slough spread out northwest of them—flowed two ways, he to this wild range, she back to town and friends and family. And yet in the thaw of one bright day, their last together up here north of the line, she felt the potential weakening of her resolution. She herself teetered on a divide. She feared the softening that could start her draining toward his side of their never fully articulated argument.

"Molly," Ray said, and made her look at him. She saw him as the country and the winter had left him, weathered and scarred. His eyes were gray and steady, marksman's eyes.

She made a wordless sound that in her own ears seemed almost a groan. "You want awful bad to stay, somehow," she said.

His fingers plucked a strand of grass, he bit it between his teeth, his head went slowly up and down.

"But how?" she said. "Do you want to strike the Z-X for a job, or the Lazy-S, or somebody? Do you want to open a store in Eastend for when the railroad comes through, or what?"

"Haven't you figured that out yet?" he said. "I thought you'd see it in a minute. I want to buy the T-Down."

"You *what?*"

"I want us to buy the T-Down and make her go."

She felt that she went all to pieces. She laughed. She threw her hands around so that the pup scrambled and clawed at her side. "Ray Henry," she said, "you're crazy as a bedbug. Where'd we get the money?"

"Borrow it."

"Go in debt to stay up *here?*"

"Molly," he said, and she heard the slow gather of determination in his voice, "when else could we pick up cattle for twenty dollars a head with sucking calves thrown in? When else could we get a whole ranch layout for a few hundred bucks? The Goodnight herd we were running was the best herd in Canada. This spring roundup we could take our pick of what's left, including bulls, and burn our brand on 'em and turn 'em into summer range and drive everything else to Malta. We wouldn't want more than three, four hundred head. We can swing that much, and we can cut enough hay to bring that many through even a winter like this last one."

She watched him; her eyes groped and slipped.

He said, "We're never going to have another chance like this as long as we live. This country's going to change. There'll be homesteaders in here soon as the railroad comes. Towns, stores, what you've been missing. Womenfolks. We can sit out here on the Whitemud with good hay land and good range and just make this goddarned country holler uncle."

"How long?" she said. "How long have you been thinking this way?"

"Since we got John's letter."

"You never said anything."

"I kept waiting for you to get the idea yourself. But you were hell-bent to get out."

She escaped his eyes, looked down, shifted carefully to accommodate the wild thing snuggled in darkness at her waist, and as she moved her foot scuffed up the scalloped felt edge of the buffalo robe. By her toe was a half-crushed crocus, palely lavender, a thing so tender and unbelievable in the waste of brown grass under the great pour of sky that she cried out, "Why, good land, look at that!"—taking advantage of it both as discovery and as diversion.

"Crocus?" Ray said, bending. "Don't take long, once the snow goes."

It lay in her palm, a thing lucky as a four-leaf clover, and as if it had had some effect in clearing her sight, Molly looked down the south-facing slope and saw it tinged with faintest green. She put the crocus to her nose, but smelled only a mild freshness, an odor no more showy than that of grass. But maybe enough to cover the scent of carrion. Her eyes came up and found Ray's watching her steadily. "You think we could do it?"

"I know we could."

"It's a funny time to start talking that way, when I'm on my way out."

"You don't have to stay out."

Sniffing the crocus, she put her right hand under the mackinaw until her fingers touched fur. The pup stiffened, but did not turn or snap. She moved her fingers softly along his back, willing him tame. For some reason she felt as if she might bust out crying.

"Haven't you got any ambition to be the first white woman in five hundred miles?" Ray said.

Past and below him, three or four miles off, she saw the great slough darken under a driving cloud shadow and then brighten to a blue that flockered with little wind-whipped waves. She wondered what happened to the ice in a slough like that, whether it went on down the little flooded creeks to add to the jams in the Whitemud and Swift Current, or whether it just rose to the surface and gradually melted there. She didn't suppose it would be spectacular like the breakup in the river.

"Mamma and Dad would think we'd lost our minds," she said. "How much would we have to borrow?"

"Maybe six or eight thousand."

"Oh Lord!" She contemplated the sum, a burden of debt heavy enough to pin them down for life. She remembered the winter, six months of unremitting slavery and imprisonment. She lifted the crocus and laid it against Ray's dark scarred cheek.

"You should never wear lavender," she said, and giggled at the very idea, and let her eyes come up to his and stared at him, sick and scared. "All right," she heard herself say. "If it's what you want."

JUST LATHER, THAT'S ALL

HERNANDO TÉLLEZ / COLOMBIA

Translated by Donald A. Yates

HE SAID NOTHING when he entered. I was passing the best of my razors back and forth on a strop. When I recognized him I started to tremble. But he didn't notice. Hoping to conceal my emotion, I continued sharpening the razor. I tested it on the meat of my thumb, and then held it up to the light. At that moment he took off the bullet-studded belt that his gun holster dangled from. He hung it up on a wall hook and placed his military cap over it. Then he turned to me, loosening the knot of his tie, and said, "It's hot as hell. Give me a shave." He sat in the chair.

I estimated he had a four-day beard. The four days taken up by the latest expedition in search of our troops. His face seemed reddened, burned by the sun. Carefully, I began to prepare the soap. I cut off a few slices, dropped them into the cup, mixed in a bit of warm water, and began to stir with the brush. Immediately the foam began to rise. "The other boys in the group should have this much beard, too." I continued stirring the lather.

"But we did all right, you know. We got the main ones. We brought back some dead, and we've got some others still alive. But pretty soon they'll all be dead."

"How many did you catch?" I asked.

"Fourteen. We had to go pretty deep into the woods to find them. But we'll get even. Not one of them comes out of this alive, not one." He leaned back on the chair when he saw me with the lather-covered brush in my hand. I still had to put the sheet on him. No doubt about it, I was upset. I took a sheet out of a drawer and knotted it around my customer's neck. He wouldn't stop talking. He probably thought I was in sympathy with his party.

"The town must have learned a lesson from what we did the other day," he said.

"Yes," I replied, securing the knot at his dark, sweaty neck.

"That was a fine show, eh?"

"Very good," I answered, turning back for the brush. The man closed his eyes with a gesture of fatigue and sat waiting for the cool caress of the soap. I had never had him so close to me. The day he ordered the whole town to file into the patio of the school to see the four rebels hanging there, I came face-to-face with him for an instant. But the sight of the mutilated bodies kept me from noticing the face of the man who had directed it all, the face I was now about to take into my hands. It was not an unpleasant face, certainly. And the beard, which made him seem a bit older than he was, didn't suit him badly at all. His name was Torres. Captain Torres. A man of imagination, because who else would have thought of hanging the naked rebels and then holding target practice on certain parts of their bodies? I began to apply the first layer of soap. With his eyes closed, he continued. "Without any effort I could go straight to sleep," he said, "but there's plenty to do this afternoon." I stopped the lathering and asked with a feigned lack of interest: "A firing squad?" "Something like that, but a little slower." I got on with the job of lathering his beard. My hands started trembling again. The man could not possibly realize it, and this was in my favor. But I would have preferred that he hadn't come. It was likely that many of our faction had seen him enter. And an enemy under one's roof imposes certain conditions. I would be obliged to shave that beard like any other one, carefully, gently, like that of any customer, taking pains to see that no single pore emitted a drop of blood. Being careful to see that the little tufts of hair did not lead the blade astray. Seeing that his skin ended up clean, soft, and healthy, so that passing the back of my hand over it I couldn't feel a hair. Yes, I was secretly a rebel, but I was also a conscientious barber, and proud of the preciseness of my profession. And this four days' growth of beard was a fitting challenge.

I took the razor, opened up the two protective arms, exposed the blade and began the job, from one of the sideburns downward. The razor responded beautifully. His beard was inflexible and hard, not too long, but thick. Bit by bit the skin emerged. The razor rasped along, making its customary sound as fluffs of lather mixed with bits of hair gathered along the blade. I paused a moment to clean it, then took up the strop again to sharpen the razor, because I'm a barber who does things properly. The man, who had kept his eyes closed, opened them now, removed one of his hands from under the sheet, felt the spot on his face where the soap had been cleared off, and said, "Come to the school today at six o'clock." "The same thing as the other day?" I asked, horrified. "It could be better," he replied. "What do you plan to do?" "I don't know yet. But we'll amuse ourselves." Once more he leaned back and closed his eyes. I approached him with the razor poised. "Do you plan to punish them all?" I ventured timidly. "All." The soap was drying on his face. I had to hurry. In the mirror I looked toward the street. It was the same as ever: the grocery store with two or three customers in it. Then I glanced at the clock: two twenty in the afternoon. The razor continued on its downward stroke. Now from the other sideburn down. A thick, blue beard. He should have let it grow like some poets or priests do. It would suit him well. A lot of people wouldn't recognize him. Much to his benefit, I thought, as I attempted to cover the neck area smoothly. There, for sure, the razor had to be handled masterfully, since the hair, although softer, grew into little swirls. A curly beard. One of the tiny pores could be opened up and issue forth its pearl of blood. A good barber such as I prides himself on never allowing this to happen to a client. And this was a first-class client. How many of us had he ordered shot? How many of us had he ordered mutilated? It was better not to think about it. Torres did not know that I was his enemy. He did not know it nor did the rest. It was a secret shared by very few, precisely so that I could inform the revolutionaries of what Torres was doing in the town and of what he was planning each time he undertook a rebel-hunting excursion. So it was going to be very difficult to explain that I had him right in my hands and let him go peacefully—alive and shaved.

The beard was now almost completely gone. He seemed younger, less burdened by years than when he had arrived. I suppose this always happens with men who visit barbershops. Under the stroke of my razor Torres was being rejuvenated—rejuvenated because I am a good barber, the best in the town, if I may say so. A little more lather here, under his chin, on his Adam's apple, on this big vein. How hot it is getting! Torres must be sweating as much as I. But he is not afraid. He is a calm man, who is not even thinking about what he is going to do with the prisoners this afternoon. On the other hand I, with this razor in my hands, stroking and restroking this skin, trying to keep blood from oozing from these pores, can't even think clearly. Damn him for coming, because I'm a revolutionary and not a murderer. And how easy it would be to kill him. And he deserves it. Does he? No! What the devil! No one deserves to have someone else make the sacrifice of becoming a murderer. What do you gain by it? Nothing. Others come along and still others, and the first ones kill the second ones and they the next ones and it goes on like this until everything is a sea of blood. I could cut this throat just so, zip! zip! I wouldn't give him time to complain and since he has his eyes closed he wouldn't see the glistening knife blade or my glistening eyes. But I'm trembling like a real murderer. Out of his neck a gush of blood would spout onto the sheet, on the chair, on my hands, on the floor. I would have to close the door. And the blood would keep inching along the floor, warm, ineradicable, uncontainable, until it reached the street, like a little scarlet stream. I'm sure that one solid stroke, one deep incision, would prevent any pain. He wouldn't suffer. But what would I do with the body? Where would I hide it? I would have to flee, leaving all I have behind, and take refuge far away, far, far away. But they would follow until they found me. "Captain Torres' murderer. He slit his throat while he was shaving him—a coward." And then on the other side. "The avenger of us all. A name to remember. (And here they would mention my name.) He was the town barber. No one knew he was defending our cause."

And what of all this? Murderer or hero? My destiny depends on the edge of this blade. I can turn my hand a bit more, press a little harder on the razor, and sink it in. The skin would give way like silk, like rubber, like the strop. There is nothing more tender than human skin and the blood is always there, ready to pour forth. A blade like this doesn't fail. It is my best. But I don't want to be a murderer, no sir. You came to me for a shave. And I perform my work honorably. . . . I don't want blood on my hands. Just lather, that's all. You are an executioner and I am only a barber. Each person has his own place in the scheme of things. That's right. His own place.

Now his chin had been stroked clean and smooth. The man sat up and looked into the mirror. He rubbed his hands over his skin and felt it fresh, like new.

"Thanks," he said. He went to the hanger for his belt, pistol and cap. I must have been very pale; my shirt felt soaked. Torres finished adjusting the buckle, straightened his pistol in the holster and after automatically smoothing down his hair, he put on the cap. From his pants pocket he took out several coins to pay me for my services. And he began to head toward the door. In the doorway he paused for a moment, and turning to me he said:

"They told me that you'd kill me. I came to find out. But killing isn't easy. You can take my word for it." And he headed on down the street.

THE SECRET LIFE OF WALTER MITTY

JAMES THURBER / UNITED STATES

James Thurber

"WE'RE GOING THROUGH!" The commander's voice was like thin ice breaking. He wore his full-dress uniform with the heavily braided white cap pulled down rakishly over one cold gray eye. "We can't make it, sir. It's spoiling for a hurricane if you ask me." "I'm not asking you, Lieutenant Berg," said the commander. "Throw on the power lights! Rev her up to eighty-five hundred! We're going through!" The pounding of the cylinders increased: ta-pocketa-pocketa-pocketa-*pocketa-pocketa*. The commander stared at the ice forming on the pilot window. He walked over and twisted a row of complicated dials. "Switch on number eight auxiliary!" he shouted. "Switch on number eight auxiliary!" repeated Lieutenant Berg. "Full strength in number three turret!" shouted the commander. "Full strength in number three turret!" The crew, bending to their various tasks in the huge, hurtling eight-engined Navy hydroplane, looked at each other and grinned. "The Old Man'll get us through," they said to one another. "The Old Man ain't afraid of hell!" . . .

"Not so fast! You're driving too fast!" said Mrs. Mitty. "What are you driving so fast for?"

"Hmmm?" said Walter Mitty. He looked at his wife, in the seat beside him, with shocked astonishment. She seemed grossly unfamiliar, like a strange woman who had yelled at him in a crowd. "You were up to fifty-five," she said. "You know I don't like to go more than forty. You were up to fifty-five." Walter Mitty drove on toward Waterbury in silence, the roaring of the SN202 through the worst storm in twenty years of Navy flying fading in the remote, intimate airways of his mind. "You're tensed up again," said Mrs. Mitty. "It's one of your days. I wish you'd let Dr. Renshaw look you over."

Walter Mitty stopped the car in front of the building where his wife went to have her hair done. "Remember to get those overshoes while I'm having my hair done," she said. "I don't need overshoes," said Mitty. She put the mirror back into her bag. "We've been through all that," she said, getting out of the car. "You're not a young man any longer." He raced the engine a little. "Why don't you wear your gloves? Have you lost your gloves?" Walter Mitty reached in a pocket and brought out the gloves. He put them on, but after she had turned and gone into the building and he had driven on to a red light, he took them off again. "Pick it up, brother!" snapped a cop as the light changed, and Mitty hastily pulled on his gloves and lurched ahead. He drove around the streets aimlessly for a time, and then he drove past the hospital on his way to the parking lot. . . .

"It's the millionaire banker, Wellington McMillan," said the pretty nurse. "Yes?" said Walter Mitty, removing his gloves slowly. "Who has the case?" "Dr. Renshaw and Dr. Benbow, but there are two specialists here: Dr. Remington from New York and Dr. Pritchard-Mitford from London. He flew over." A door opened down a long, cool corridor and Dr. Renshaw came out. He looked distraught and haggard. "Hello, Mitty," he said. "We're having the devil's own time with McMillan, the millionaire banker and close personal friend of Roosevelt. Obstreosis of the ductal tract. Tertiary. Wish you'd take a look at him." "Glad to," said Mitty.

In the operating room there were whispered introductions: "Dr. Remington, Dr. Mitty. Dr. Pritchard-Mitford, Dr. Mitty." "I've read your book on streptothricosis," said Pritchard-Mitford, shaking hands. "A brilliant performance, sir." "Thank you," said Walter Mitty. "Didn't know you were in the States, Mitty," grumbled Remington. "Coals to Newcastle, bringing Mitford and me up here for a tertiary." "You are very kind," said Mitty. A huge, complicated machine, connected to the operating table, with many tubes and wires, began at this moment to go pocketa-pocketa-pocketa. "The new anesthetizer is giving way!" shouted an intern. "There is no one in the East who knows how to fix it!" "Quiet, man!" said Mitty, in a low, cool voice. He sprang to the machine, which was now going pocketa-pocketa-queep-pocketa-queep. He began fingering delicately a row of glistening dials. "Give me a fountain pen!" he snapped. Someone handed him a fountain pen. He pulled a faulty piston out of the machine and inserted the pen in its place. "That will hold for ten minutes," he said. "Get on with the operation." A nurse hurried over and whispered to Renshaw. Mitty saw the man turn pale. "Coreopsis has set in," said Renshaw nervously. "If you would take over, Mitty?" Mitty looked at him and at the craven figure of Benbow, who drank, and at the grave, uncertain faces of the two great specialists. "If you wish," he said. They slipped a white gown on him; he adjusted a mask and drew on thin gloves; nurses handed him shining . . .

"Back it up, Mac! Look out for that Buick!" Walter Mitty jammed on the brakes. "Wrong lane, Mac," said the parking-lot attendant, looking at Mitty closely. "Gee. Yeh," muttered Mitty. He began cautiously to back out of the lane marked "Exit Only." "Leave her sit there," said the attendant. "I'll put her away." Mitty got out of the car. "Hey, better leave the key." "Oh," said Mitty, handing the man the ignition key. The attendant vaulted into the car, backed it up with insolent skill, and put it where it belonged.

They're so damn cocky, thought Walter Mitty, walking along Main Street; they think they know everything. Once he had tried to take his chains off, outside New Milford, and he had got them wound around the axles. A man had had to come out in a wrecking car and unwind them, a young, grinning garageman. Since then Mrs. Mitty always made him drive to a garage to have the chains taken off. The next time, he thought, I'll wear my right arm in a sling; they won't grin at me then. I'll have my right arm in a sling and they'll see I couldn't possibly take the chains off myself. He kicked at the slush on the sidewalk. "Overshoes," he said to himself, and he began looking for a shoe store.

When he came out into the street again, with the overshoes in a box under his arm, Walter Mitty began to wonder what the other thing was his wife had told him to get. She had told him, twice before they set out from their house for Waterbury. In a way he hated these weekly trips to town—he was always getting something wrong.

Kleenex, he thought, Squibb's, razor blades? No. Toothpaste, toothbrush, bicarbonate, carborundum, initiative and referendum? He gave it up. But she would remember it. "Where's the what's-its-name?" she would ask. "Don't tell me you forgot the what's-its-name." A newsboy went by shouting something about the Waterbury trial. . . .

"Perhaps this will refresh your memory." The district attorney suddenly thrust a heavy automatic at the quiet figure on the witness stand. "Have you ever seen this before?" Walter Mitty took the gun and examined it expertly. "This is my Webley-Vickers fifty-eighty," he said calmly. An excited buzz ran around the courtroom. The judge rapped for order. "You are a crack shot with any sort of firearm, I believe?" said the district attorney, insinuatingly.

"Objection!" shouted Mitty's attorney. "We have shown that the defendant could not have fired the shot. We have shown that he wore his right arm in a sling on the night of the fourteenth of July." Walter Mitty raised his hand briefly, and the bickering attorneys were stilled. "With any known make of gun," he said evenly, "I could have killed Gregory Fitzhurst at three hundred feet *with my left hand*." Pandemonium broke loose in the courtroom. A woman's scream rose above the bedlam, and suddenly a lovely, dark-haired girl was in Walter Mitty's arms. The district attorney struck at her savagely. Without rising from his chair, Mitty let the man have it on the point of the chin. "You miserable cur!" . . .

"Puppy biscuit," said Walter Mitty. He stopped walking and the buildings of Waterbury rose up out of the misty courtroom and surrounded him again. A woman who was passing laughed. "He said 'puppy biscuit,'" she said to her companion. "That man said 'puppy biscuit' to himself." Walter Mitty hurried on. He went into an A & P, not the first one he came to but a smaller one farther up the street. "I want some biscuit for small, young dogs," he said to the clerk. "Any special brand, sir?" The greatest pistol shot in the world thought a moment. "It says 'Puppies Bark for It' on the box," said Walter Mitty.

His wife would be through at the hairdresser's in fifteen minutes, Mitty saw in looking at his watch, unless they had trouble drying it; sometimes they had trouble drying it. She didn't like to get to the hotel first; she would want him to be there waiting for her as usual. He found a big leather chair in the lobby, facing a window, and he put the overshoes and the puppy biscuit on the floor beside it. He picked up an old copy of *Liberty* and sank down into the chair. "Can Germany Conquer the World Through the Air?" Walter Mitty looked at the pictures of bombing planes and of ruined streets. . . .

"The cannonading has got the wind up in young Raleigh, sir," said the sergeant. Captain Mitty looked up at him through tousled hair. "Get him to bed," he said wearily. "With the others. I'll fly alone." "But you can't, sir," said the sergeant anxiously. "It takes two men to handle that bomber and the Archies are pounding hell out of the air. Von Richtman's circus is between here and Saulier." "Somebody's got to get that ammunition dump," said Mitty. "I'm going over. Spot of brandy?" He poured a drink for the sergeant and one for himself. War thundered and whined around the dugout and battered at the door. There was a rending explosion, and splinters flew through the room. "A bit of a near thing," said Captain Mitty carelessly. "The box barrage is closing in," said the sergeant. "We only live once, sergeant," said Mitty, with his faint, fleeting smile. "Or do we?" He poured another brandy and tossed it off. "I never see a man could hold his brandy like you, sir," said the sergeant. "Begging your pardon, sir." Captain Mitty stood up and strapped on his huge Webley-Vickers automatic. "It's forty kilometers through hell, sir," said the sergeant. Mitty finished one last brandy. "After all," he said softly, "what isn't?" The pounding of the cannon increased; there was the rat-tat-tatting of machine guns, and from somewhere came the menacing pocketa-pocketa-pocketa of the new flamethrowers. Walter Mitty walked to the door of the dugout humming. *"Auprès de ma blonde."* He turned and waved to the sergeant. "Cheerio!" he said. . . .

Something struck his shoulder. "I've been looking all over this hotel for you," said Mrs. Mitty. "Why do you have to hide in this old chair? How did you expect me to find you?" "Things close in," said Walter Mitty vaguely. "What?" Mrs. Mitty said. "Did you get the what's-its-name? The puppy biscuit? What's in that box?" "Overshoes," said Mitty. "Couldn't you have put them on in the store?"

"I was thinking," said Walter Mitty. "Does it ever occur to you that I am sometimes thinking?" She looked at him. "I'm going to take your temperature when I get you home," she said.

They went out through the revolving doors that made a faintly derisive whistling sound when you pushed them. It was two blocks to the parking lot. At the drugstore on the corner she said, "Wait here for me. I forgot something. I won't be a minute." She was more than a minute. Walter Mitty lighted a cigarette. It began to rain, rain with sleet in it. He stood up against the wall of the drugstore, smoking. . . . He put his shoulders back and his heels together. "To hell with the handkerchief," said Walter Mitty scornfully. He took one last drag on his cigarette and snapped it away. Then, with that faint, fleeting smile playing about his lips, he faced the firing squad: erect and motionless, proud and disdainful, Walter Mitty, the Undefeated, inscrutable to the last.

THE ROCKING-HORSE WINNER
D. H. LAWRENCE / GREAT BRITAIN

THERE WAS a woman who was beautiful, who started with all the advantages, yet she had no luck. She married for love, and the love turned to dust. She had bonny children, yet she felt they had been thrust upon her, and she could not love them. They looked at her coldly, as if they were finding fault with her. And hurriedly she felt she must cover up some fault in herself. Yet what it was that she must cover up she never knew. Nevertheless, when her children were present, she always felt the center of her heart go hard. This troubled her, and in her manner she was all the more gentle and anxious for her children, as if she loved them very much. Only she herself knew that at the center of her heart was a hard little place that could not feel love, no, not for anybody. Everybody else said of her: "She is such a good mother. She adores her children." Only she herself, and her children themselves, knew it was not so. They read it in each other's eyes.

There were a boy and two little girls. They lived in a pleasant house, with a garden, and they had discreet servants, and felt themselves superior to anyone in the neighborhood.

Although they lived in style, they felt always an anxiety in the house. There was never enough money. The mother had a small income, and the father had a small income, but not nearly enough for the social position which they had to keep up. The father went into town to some office. But though he had good prospects, these prospects never materialized. There was always the grinding sense of the shortage of money, though the style was always kept up.

At last the mother said: "I will see if _I_ can't make something." But she did not know where to begin. She racked her brains, and tried this thing and the other, but could not find anything successful. The failure made deep lines come into her face. Her children were growing up, they would have to go to school. There must be more money, there must be more money. The father, who was always very handsome and expensive in his tastes, seemed as if he never _would_ be able to do anything worth doing. And the mother, who had a great belief in herself, did not succeed any better, and her tastes were just as expensive.

And so the house came to be haunted by the unspoken phrase: _There must be more money! There must be more money!_ The children could hear it all the time, though nobody said it aloud. They heard it at Christmas, when the expensive and splendid toys filled the nursery. Behind the shining modern rocking horse, behind the smart doll's house, a voice would start whispering: "There _must_ be more money! There _must_ be more money!" And the children would stop playing, to listen for a moment. They would look into each other's eyes, to see if they had all heard. And each one saw in the eyes of the other two that they too had heard. "There _must_ be more money! There _must_ be more money!"

It came whispering from the springs of the still-swaying rocking horse, and even the horse, bending his wooden, champing head, heard it. The big doll, sitting so pink and smirking in her new pram, could hear it quite plainly, and seemed to be smirking all the more self-consciously because of it. The foolish puppy, too, that took the place of the teddy bear, he was looking so extraordinarily foolish for no other reason but that he heard the secret whisper all over the house: "There *must* be more money!"

Yet nobody ever said it aloud. The whisper was everywhere, and therefore no one spoke it. Just as no one ever says: "We are breathing!" in spite of the fact that breath is coming and going all the time.

"Mother," said the boy Paul one day, "why don't we keep a car of our own? Why do we always use Uncle's, or else a taxi?"

"Because we're the poor members of the family," said the mother.

"But why *are* we, Mother?"

"Well—I suppose," she said slowly and bitterly, "it's because your father has no luck."

The boy was silent for some time.

"Is luck money, Mother?" he asked rather timidly.

"No, Paul. Not quite. It's what causes you to have money."

"Oh!" said Paul vaguely. "I thought when Uncle Oscar said *filthy lucker,* it meant money."

"*Filthy lucre* does mean money," said the mother. "But it's lucre, not luck."

"Oh!" said the boy. "Then what *is* luck, Mother?"

"It's what causes you to have money. If you're lucky you have money. That's why it's better to be born lucky than rich. If you're rich, you may lose your money. But if you're lucky, you will always get more money."

"Oh! Will you? And is Father not lucky?"

"Very unlucky, I should say," she said bitterly.

The boy watched her with unsure eyes.

"Why?" he asked.

"I don't know. Nobody ever knows why one person is lucky and another unlucky."

"Don't they? Nobody at all? Does *nobody* know?"

"Perhaps God. But He never tells."

"He ought to, then. And aren't you lucky either, Mother?"

"I can't be, if I married an unlucky husband."

"But by yourself, aren't you?"

"I used to think I was, before I married. Now I think I am very unlucky indeed."

"Why?"

"Well—never mind! Perhaps I'm not really," she said.

The child looked at her, to see if she meant it. But he saw, by the lines of her mouth, that she was only trying to hide something from him.

"Well, anyhow," he said stoutly, "I'm a lucky person."

"Why?" said his mother, with a sudden laugh.

He stared at her. He didn't even know why he had said it.

"God told me," he asserted, brazening it out.

"I hope He did, dear!" she said, again with a laugh, but rather bitter.

"He did, Mother!"

"Excellent!" said the mother.

The boy saw she did not believe him; or, rather, that she paid no attention to his assertion. This angered him somewhat, and made him want to compel her attention.

He went off by himself, vaguely, in a childish way, seeking for the clue to "luck." Absorbed, taking no heed of other people, he went about with a sort of stealth, seeking inwardly for luck. He wanted luck, he wanted it, he wanted it. When the two girls were playing dolls in the nursery, he would sit on his big rocking horse, charging madly into space, with a frenzy that made the little girls peer at him uneasily. Wildly the horse careered, the waving dark hair of the boy tossed, his eyes had a strange glare in them. The little girls dared not speak to him.

When he had ridden to the end of his mad little journey, he climbed down and stood in front of his rocking horse, staring fixedly into its lowered face. Its red mouth was slightly open, its big eye was wide and glassy-bright.

Now! he would silently command the snorting steed. Now, take me to where there is luck! Now take me!

And he would slash the horse on the neck with the little whip he had asked Uncle Oscar for. He *knew* the horse could take him to where there was luck, if only he forced it. So he would mount again, and start on his furious ride, hoping at last to get there. He knew he could get there.

"You'll break your horse, Paul!" said the nurse.

"He's always riding like that! I wish he'd leave off!" said his elder sister Joan.

But he only glared down on them in silence. Nurse gave him up. She could make nothing of him. Anyhow he was growing beyond her.

One day his mother and his uncle Oscar came in when he was on one of his furious rides. He did not speak to them.

"Hallo, you young jockey! Riding a winner?" said his uncle.

"Aren't you growing too big for a rocking horse? You're not a very little boy any longer, you know," said his mother.

But Paul only gave a blue glare from his big, rather close-set eyes. He would speak to nobody when he was in full tilt. His mother watched him with an anxious expression on her face.

At last he suddenly stopped forcing his horse into the mechanical gallop, and slid down.

"Well, I got there!" he announced fiercely, his blue eyes still flaring, and his sturdy long legs straddling apart.

"Where did you get to?" asked his mother.

"Where I wanted to go," he flared back at her.

"That's right, son!" said Uncle Oscar. "Don't you stop till you get there. What's the horse's name?"

"He doesn't have a name," said the boy.

"Gets on without all right?" asked the uncle.

"Well, he has different names. He was called Sansovino last week."

"Sansovino, eh? Won the Ascot. How did you know his name?"

"He always talks about horse races with Bassett," said Joan.

The uncle was delighted to find that his small nephew was posted with all the racing news. Bassett, the young gardener, who had been wounded in the left foot in the war and had got his present job through Oscar Cresswell, whose batman he had been, was a perfect blade of the "turf." He lived in the racing events, and the small boy lived with him.

Oscar Cresswell got it all from Bassett.

"Master Paul comes and asks me, so I can't do more than tell him, sir," said Bassett, his face terribly serious, as if he were speaking of religious matters.

"And does he ever put anything on a horse he fancies?"

"Well—I don't want to give him away—he's a young sport, a fine sport, sir. Would you mind asking him himself? He sort of takes a pleasure in it, and perhaps he'd feel I was giving him away, sir, if you don't mind."

Bassett was serious as a church.

The uncle went back to his nephew and took him off for a ride in the car.

"Say, Paul, old man, do you ever put anything on a horse?" the uncle asked.

The boy watched the handsome man closely.

"Why, do you think I oughtn't to?" he parried.

"Not a bit of it! I thought perhaps you might give me a tip for the Lincoln."

The car sped on into the country, going down to Uncle Oscar's place in Hampshire.

"Honor bright?" said the nephew.

"Honor bright, son!" said the uncle.

"Well, then, Daffodil."

"Daffodil! I doubt it, sonny. What about Mirza?"

"I only know the winner," said the boy. "That's Daffodil."

"Daffodil, eh?"

There was a pause. Daffodil was an obscure horse comparatively.

"Uncle!"

"Yes, son?"

"You won't let it go any further, will you? I promised Bassett."

"Bassett be damned, old man! What's he got to do with it?"

"We're partners. We've been partners from the first. Uncle, he lent me my first five shillings, which I lost. I promised him, honor bright, it was only between me and him; only you gave me that ten-shilling note I started winning with, so I thought you were lucky. You won't let it go any further, will you?"

The boy gazed at his uncle from those big, hot, blue eyes, set rather close together. The uncle stirred and laughed uneasily.

"Right you are, son! I'll keep your tip private. Daffodil, eh? How much are you putting on him?"

"All except twenty pounds," said the boy. "I keep that in reserve."

The uncle thought it a good joke.

"You keep twenty pounds in reserve, do you, you young romancer? What are you betting, then?"

"I'm betting three hundred," said the boy gravely. "But it's between you and me, Uncle Oscar! Honor bright?"

The uncle burst into a roar of laughter.

"It's between you and me all right, you young Nat Gould," he said, laughing. "But where's your three hundred?"

"Bassett keeps it for me. We're partners."

"You are, are you! And what is Bassett putting on Daffodil?"

"He won't go quite as high as I do, I expect. Perhaps he'll go a hundred and fifty."

"What, pennies?" laughed the uncle.

"Pounds," said the child, with a surprised look at his uncle. "Bassett keeps a bigger reserve than I do."

Between wonder and amusement Uncle Oscar was silent. He pursued the matter no further, but he determined to take his nephew with him to the Lincoln races.

"Now, son," he said, "I'm putting twenty on Mirza, and I'll put five for you on any horse you fancy. What's your pick?"

"Daffodil, Uncle."

"No, not the fiver on Daffodil!"

"I should if it was my own fiver," said the child.

"Good! Good! Right you are! A fiver for me and a fiver for you on Daffodil."

The child had never been to a race meeting before, and his eyes were blue fire. He pursed his mouth tight, and watched. A Frenchman just in front had put his money on Lancelot. Wild with excitement, he flailed his arms up and down, yelling *"Lancelot! Lancelot!"* in his French accent.

Daffodil came in first, Lancelot second, Mirza third. The child, flushed and with eyes blazing, was curiously serene. His uncle brought him four five-pound notes, four to one.

"What am I to do with these?" he cried, waving them before the boy's eyes.

"I suppose we'll talk to Bassett," said the boy. "I expect I have fifteen hundred now; and twenty in reserve; and this twenty."

His uncle studied him for some moments.

"Look here, son!" he said. "You're not serious about Bassett and that fifteen hundred, are you?"

"Yes, I am. But it's between you and me, Uncle. Honor bright!"

"Honor bright all right, son! But I must talk to Bassett."

"If you'd like to be a partner, Uncle, with Bassett and me, we could all be partners. Only, you'd have to promise, honor bright, Uncle, not to let it go beyond us three. Bassett and I are lucky, and you must be lucky, because it was your ten shillings I started winning with. . . ."

Uncle Oscar took both Bassett and Paul into Richmond Park for an afternoon, and there they talked.

"It's like this, you see, sir," Bassett said. "Master Paul would get me talking about racing events, spinning yarns, you know, sir. And he was always keen on knowing if I'd made or if I'd lost. It's about a year since, now, that I put five shillings on Blush of Dawn for him—and we lost. Then the luck turned, with that ten shillings he had from you, that we put on Singhalese. And since then, it's been pretty steady, all things considering. What do you say, Master Paul?"

"We're all right when we're sure," said Paul. "It's when we're not quite sure that we go down."

"Oh, but we're careful then," said Bassett.

"But when are you *sure?*" Uncle Oscar smiled.

"It's Master Paul, sir," said Bassett, in a secret, religious voice. "It's as if he had it from heaven. Like Daffodil, now, for the Lincoln. That was as sure as eggs."

"Did you put anything on Daffodil?" asked Oscar Cresswell.

"Yes, sir. I made my bit."

"And my nephew?"

Bassett was obstinately silent, looking at Paul.

"I made twelve hundred, didn't I, Bassett? I told Uncle I was putting three hundred on Daffodil."

"That's right," said Bassett, nodding.

"But where's the money?" asked the uncle.

"I keep it safe locked up, sir. Master Paul he can have it any minute he likes to ask for it."

"What, fifteen hundred pounds?"

"And twenty! And *forty*, that is, with the twenty he made on the course."

"It's amazing!" said the uncle.

"If Master Paul offers you to be partners, sir, I would, if I were you; if you'll excuse me," said Bassett.

Oscar Cresswell thought about it.

"I'll see the money," he said.

They drove home again, and sure enough, Bassett came round to the garden house with fifteen hundred pounds in notes. The twenty pounds reserve was left with Joe Glee, in the Turf Commission deposit.

"You see, it's all right, Uncle, when I'm *sure!* Then we go strong, for all we're worth. Don't we, Bassett?"

"We do that, Master Paul."

"And when are you sure?" said the uncle, laughing.

"Oh, well, sometimes I'm *absolutely* sure, like about Daffodil," said the boy; "and sometimes I have an idea; and sometimes I haven't even an idea, have I, Bassett? Then we're careful, because we mostly go down."

"You do, do you! And when you're sure, like about Daffodil, what makes you sure, sonny?"

"Oh, well, I don't know," said the boy uneasily. "I'm sure, you know, Uncle; that's all."

"It's as if he had it from heaven, sir," Bassett reiterated.

"I should say so!" said the uncle.

But he became a partner. And when the Leger was coming on,

Paul was "sure" about Lively Spark, which was a quite inconsiderable horse. The boy insisted on putting a thousand on the horse, Bassett went for five hundred, and Oscar Cresswell two hundred. Lively Spark came in first, and the betting had been ten to one against him. Paul had made ten thousand.

"You see," he said, "I was absolutely sure of him."

Even Oscar Cresswell had cleared two thousand.

"Look here, son," he said, "this sort of thing makes me nervous."

"It needn't, Uncle! Perhaps I shan't be sure again for a long time."

"But what are you going to do with your money?" asked the uncle.

"Of course," said the boy, "I started it for Mother. She said she had no luck, because Father is unlucky, so I thought if *I* was lucky, it might stop whispering."

"What might stop whispering?"

"Our house. I *hate* our house for whispering."

"What does it whisper?"

"Why—why"—the boy fidgeted—"why, I don't know. But it's always short of money, you know, Uncle."

"I know it, son, I know it."

"You know people send Mother writs, don't you, Uncle?"

"I'm afraid I do," said the uncle.

"And then the house whispers, like people laughing at you behind your back. It's awful, that is! I thought if I was lucky . . ."

"You might stop it," added the uncle.

The boy watched him with big blue eyes, that had an uncanny cold fire in them, and he said never a word.

"Well, then!" said the uncle. "What are we doing?"

"I shouldn't like Mother to know I was lucky," said the boy.

"Why not, son?"

"She'd stop me."

"I don't think she would."

"Oh!"—and the boy writhed in an odd way—"I *don't* want her to know, Uncle."

"All right, son! We'll manage it without her knowing."

They managed it very easily. Paul, at the other's suggestion, handed over five thousand pounds to his uncle, who deposited it with the family lawyer, who was then to inform Paul's mother that a relative had put five thousand pounds into his hands, which sum was to be paid out a thousand pounds at a time, on the mother's birthday, for the next five years.

"So she'll have a birthday present of a thousand pounds for five successive years," said Uncle Oscar. "I hope it won't make it all the harder for her later."

Paul's mother had her birthday in November. The house had been "whispering" worse than ever lately, and, even in spite of his luck, Paul could not bear up against it. He was very anxious to see the effect of the birthday letter, telling his mother about the thousand pounds.

When there were no visitors, Paul now took his meals with his parents, as he was beyond the nursery control. His mother went into town nearly every day. She had discovered that she had an odd knack of sketching furs and dress materials, so she worked secretly in the studio of a friend who was the chief artist for the leading drapers. She drew the figures of ladies in furs and ladies in silk and sequins for the newspaper advertisements. This young woman artist earned several thousand pounds a year, but Paul's mother only made several hundreds, and she was again dissatisfied. She so wanted to be first in something, and she did not succeed, even in making sketches for drapery advertisements.

She was down to breakfast on the morning of her birthday. Paul watched her face as she read her letters. He knew the lawyer's letter. As his mother read it, her face hardened and became more expressionless. Then a cold, determined look came on her mouth. She hid the letter under the pile of others, and said not a word about it.

"Didn't you have anything nice in the post for your birthday, Mother?" said Paul.

"Quite moderately nice," she said, her voice cold and absent.

She went away to town without saying more.

But in the afternoon Uncle Oscar appeared. He said Paul's mother had had a long interview with the lawyer, asking if the whole five thousand could not be advanced at once, as she was in debt.

"What do you think, Uncle?" said the boy.

"I leave it to you, son."

"Oh, let her have it, then! We can get some more with the other," said the boy.

"A bird in the hand is worth two in the bush, laddie!" said Uncle Oscar.

"But I'm sure to *know* for the Grand National; or the Lincolnshire; or else the Derby. I'm sure to know for *one* of them," said Paul.

So Uncle Oscar signed the agreement, and Paul's mother touched the whole five thousand. Then something very curious happened. The voices in the house suddenly went mad, like a chorus of frogs on a spring evening. There were certain new furnishings, and Paul had a tutor. He was *really* going to Eton, his father's school, in the following autumn. There were flowers in the winter, and a blossoming of the luxury Paul's mother had been used to. And yet the voices in the house, behind the sprays of mimosa and almond blossom, and from under the piles of iridescent cushions, simply trilled and screamed in a sort of ecstasy: "There *must* be more money! Oh-h-h; there *must* be more money. Oh, now, now-w! Now-w-w—there *must* be more money!—more than ever! More than ever!"

It frightened Paul terribly. He studied away at his Latin and Greek. But his intense hours were spent with Bassett. The Grand National had gone by: he had not "known," and had lost a hundred pounds. Summer was at hand. He was in agony for the Lincoln. But even for the Lincoln he didn't "know," and he lost fifty pounds. He became wild-eyed and strange, as if something were going to explode in him.

"Let it alone, son! Don't you bother about it!" urged Uncle Oscar. But it was as if the boy couldn't really hear what his uncle was saying.

"I've got to know for the Derby! I've got to know for the Derby!" the child reiterated, his big blue eyes blazing with a sort of madness.

His mother noticed how overwrought he was.

"You'd better go to the seaside. Wouldn't you like to go now to the seaside, instead of waiting? I think you'd better," she said, looking down at him anxiously, her heart curiously heavy because of him.

But the child lifted his uncanny blue eyes. "I couldn't possibly go before the Derby, Mother!" he said. "I couldn't possibly!"

"Why not?" she said, her voice becoming heavy when she was opposed. "Why not? You can still go from the seaside to see the Derby with your uncle Oscar, if that's what you wish. No need for you to wait here. Besides, I think you care too much about these races. It's a bad sign. My family has been a gambling family, and you won't know till you grow up how much damage it has done. But it has done damage. I shall have to send Bassett away, and ask Uncle Oscar not to talk racing to you, unless you promise to be reasonable about it; go away to the seaside and forget it. You're all nerves!"

"I'll do what you like, Mother, so long as you don't send me away till after the Derby," the boy said.

"Send you away from where? Just from this house?"

"Yes," he said, gazing at her.

"Why, you curious child, what makes you care about this house so much, suddenly? I never knew you loved it."

He gazed at her without speaking. He had a secret within a secret, something he had not divulged, even to Bassett or to his uncle Oscar.

But his mother, after standing undecided and a little bit sullen for some moments, said:

"Very well, then! Don't go to the seaside till after the Derby, if you don't wish it. But promise me you won't let your nerves go to pieces. Promise you won't think so much about horse racing and *events*, as you call them!"

"Oh, no," said the boy casually. "I won't think much about them, Mother. You needn't worry. I wouldn't worry, Mother, if I were you."

"If you were me and I were you," said his mother, "I wonder what we *should* do!"

"But you know you needn't worry, Mother, don't you?" the boy repeated.

"I should be awfully glad to know it," she said wearily.

"Oh, well, you *can*, you know. I mean, you *ought* to know you needn't worry," he insisted.

"Ought I? Then I'll see about it," she said.

Paul's secret of secrets was his wooden horse, that which had no name. Since he was emancipated from a nurse and a nursery governess, he had had his rocking horse removed to his own bedroom at the top of the house.

"Surely, you're too big for a rocking horse!" his mother had remonstrated.

"Well, you see, Mother, till I can have a *real* horse, I like to have *some* sort of animal about," had been his quaint answer.

"Do you feel he keeps you company?" She laughed.

"Oh, yes! He's very good, he always keeps me company, when I'm there," said Paul.

So the horse, rather shabby, stood in an arrested prance in the boy's bedroom.

The Derby was drawing near, and the boy grew more and more tense. He hardly heard what was spoken to him, he was very frail, and his eyes were really uncanny. His mother had sudden strange seizures of uneasiness about him. Sometimes, for half an hour, she would feel a sudden anxiety about him that was almost anguish. She wanted to rush to him at once, and know he was safe.

Two nights before the Derby, she was at a big party in town, when one of her rushes of anxiety about her boy, her firstborn, gripped her heart till she could hardly speak. She fought with the feeling, might and main, for she believed in common sense. But it was too strong. She had to leave the dance and go downstairs to telephone to the country. The children's nursery governess was terribly surprised and startled at being rung up in the night.

"Are the children all right, Miss Wilmot?"

"Oh, yes, they are quite all right."

"Master Paul? Is he all right?"

"He went to bed as right as a trivet. Shall I run up and look at him?"

"No," said Paul's mother reluctantly. "No! Don't trouble. It's all right. Don't sit up. We shall be home fairly soon." She did not want her son's privacy intruded upon.

"Very good," said the governess.

It was about one o'clock when Paul's mother and father drove up to their house. All was still. Paul's mother went to her room and slipped off her white fur cloak. She had told her maid not to wait up for her. She heard her husband downstairs, mixing a whisky and soda.

And then, because of the strange anxiety at her heart, she stole upstairs to her son's room. Noiselessly she went along the upper corridor. Was there a faint noise? What was it?

She stood, with arrested muscles, outside his door, listening. There was a strange, heavy, and yet not loud noise. Her heart stood still. It was a soundless noise, yet rushing and powerful. Something huge, in violent, hushed motion. What was it? What in God's name was it? She ought to know. She felt that she knew the noise. She knew what it was.

Yet she could not place it. She couldn't say what it was. And on and on it went, like a madness.

Softly, frozen with anxiety and fear, she turned the door handle.

The room was dark. Yet in the space near the window, she heard and saw something plunging to and fro. She gazed in fear and amazement.

Then suddenly she switched on the light, and saw her son, in his green pajamas, madly surging on the rocking horse. The blaze of light suddenly lit him up, as he urged the wooden horse, and lit her up, as she stood, blonde, in her dress of pale green and crystal, in the doorway.

"Paul!" she cried. "Whatever are you doing?"

"It's Malabar!" he screamed, in a powerful, strange voice. "It's Malabar!"

His eyes blazed at her for one strange and senseless second, as he ceased urging his wooden horse. Then he fell with a crash to the ground, and she, all her tormented motherhood flooding upon her, rushed to gather him up.

But he was unconscious, and unconscious he remained, with some brain fever. He talked and tossed, and his mother sat stonily by his side.

"Malabar! It's Malabar! Bassett, Bassett, I *know!* It's Malabar!"

So the child cried, trying to get up and urge the rocking horse that gave him his inspiration.

"What does he mean by Malabar?" asked the heart-frozen mother.

"I don't know," said the father stonily.

"What does he mean by Malabar?" she asked her brother Oscar.

"It's one of the horses running for the Derby," was the answer.

And, in spite of himself, Oscar Cresswell spoke to Bassett, and himself put a thousand on Malabar: at fourteen to one.

The third day of the illness was critical: they were waiting for a change. The boy, with his rather long, curly hair, was tossing ceaselessly on the pillow. He neither slept nor regained consciousness, and his eyes were like blue stones. His mother sat, feeling her heart had gone, turned actually into a stone.

In the evening, Oscar Cresswell did not come, but Bassett sent a message, saying could he come up for one moment, just one moment? Paul's mother was very angry at the intrusion, but on second thought she agreed. The boy was the same. Perhaps Bassett might bring him to consciousness.

The gardener, a shortish fellow with a little brown mustache, and sharp little brown eyes, tiptoed into the room, touched his imaginary cap to Paul's mother, and stole to the bedside, staring with glittering, smallish eyes at the tossing, dying child.

"Master Paul!" he whispered. "Master Paul! Malabar came in first all right, a clean win. I did as you told me. You've made over seventy thousand pounds, you have; you've got over eighty thousand. Malabar came in all right, Master Paul."

"Malabar! Malabar! Did I say Malabar, Mother? Did I say Malabar? Do you think I'm lucky, Mother? I knew Malabar, didn't I? Over eighty thousand pounds! I call that lucky, don't you, Mother? Over eighty thousand pounds! I knew, didn't I know I knew? Malabar came in all right. If I ride my horse till I'm sure, then I tell you, Bassett, you can go as high as you like. Did you go for all you were worth, Bassett?"

"I went a thousand on it, Master Paul."

"I never told you, Mother, that if I can ride my horse, and *get there*, then I'm absolutely sure—oh, absolutely! Mother, did I ever tell you? I *am* lucky!"

"No, you never did," said the mother.

But the boy died in the night.

And even as he lay dead, his mother heard her brother's voice saying to her: "My God, Hester, you're eighty-odd thousand to the good, and a poor devil of a son to the bad. But, poor devil, poor devil, he's best gone out of a life where he rides his rocking horse to find a winner."

THE SUNDAY MENACE
ROBERT BENCHLEY / UNITED STATES

I AM NOT a gloomy man by nature, nor am I easily depressed. I always say that, no matter how much it looks as if the sun were never going to stop shining and no matter how long the birds carry on their seemingly incessant chatter, there is always a good sleet storm just around the corner and a sniffly head cold in store for those who will only look for it. You can't keep Old Stepmother Nature down for long.

But I frankly see no way out of the problem of Sunday afternoon. For centuries Sunday afternoon has been Old Nell's Curse among the days of the week. Sunday morning may be cheery enough, with its extra cup of coffee and litter of Sunday newspapers, but there is always hanging over it the ominous threat of 3:00 p.m., when the sun gets around to the back windows and Life stops dead in its tracks. No matter where you are—in China, on the high seas, or in a bird's nest—about three o'clock in the afternoon a pall descends over all the world and people everywhere start trying to think of something to do. You might as well try to think of something to do in the death house at Sing Sing, however, because, even if you do it, where does it get you? It is still Sunday afternoon.

The Blue Jeebs begin to drift in along about dessert at Sunday dinner. The last three or four spoonfuls of ice cream somehow lose their flavor and you begin crumbling up your cake instead of eating it. By the time you have finished coffee there is a definite premonition that before long, maybe in forty or fifty minutes, you will be told some bad news, probably involving the death of several favorite people, maybe even yourself. This feeling gives way to one of resignation. What is there to live for, anyway? At this point, your dessert begins to disagree with you.

On leaving the dining room and wandering aimlessly into the living room (living room indeed; there will be precious little living done in that room this afternoon), everyone begins to yawn. The drifts of Sunday papers on the floor which looked so cozy before dinner now are just depressing reminders of the transitory nature of human life. Uncle Ben makes for the sofa and promptly drops off into an unattractive doze. The children start quarreling among themselves and finally involve the grown-ups in what threatens to be a rather nasty brawl.

"Why don't you go out and play?" someone asks.

"Play what?" is their retort, and a good one, too.

This brings up the whole question of what to do and there is a halfhearted attempt at thinking on the part of the more vivacious members of the party. Somebody goes to the window and looks out. He goes back to his chair, and somebody else wanders over to another window and looks out there, pressing the nose against the pane and breathing absentmindedly against the glass. This has practically no effect on the situation.

In an attempt to start conversation, a garrulous one says, "Heigh-ho!" This falls flat, and there is a long silence while you look through the pile of newspapers to see if you missed anything in the morning's perusal. You even read the ship news and the book advertisements.

"This life of Susan B. Anthony looks as if it might be a pretty good book," you say.

"What makes you think so?" queries Ed crossly. Ed came out to dinner because he was alone in town, and now wishes he hadn't. He is already thinking up an excuse to get an early train back.

There being no good reason why you think that the life of Susan

B. Anthony might be interesting, you say nothing. You didn't really think that it might be interesting, anyway.

A walk is suggested, resulting in groans from the rest of the group. The idea of bridge arouses only two out of the necessary four to anything resembling enthusiasm. The time for the arrival of Bad News is rapidly approaching and by now it is pretty fairly certain to involve death. The sun strikes in through the window and you notice that the green chair needs reupholstering. The rug doesn't look any too good, either. There would be no sense in getting a lot of new furniture when everyone is going to be dead before long, anyway.

It is a funny thing about the sunshine on a Sunday afternoon. On other days it is just sunshine and quite cheery in its middle-class way. But on Sunday afternoon it takes on a penetrating harshness which does nothing but show up the furniture. It doesn't make any difference where you are. You may be hanging around the Busy Bee lunch in Hong Kong or polishing brass on a yacht in the North Sea; you may be out tramping across the estate of one of the vice-presidents of a big trust company or teaching Indians to read in Arizona. The Sunday afternoon sunlight makes you dissatisfied with everything it hits. It has got to be stopped.

When the automobile came in it looked as if the Sunday afternoon problem was solved. You could climb in at the back door of the old steamer and puff out into the country, where at least you couldn't hear people playing "Narcissus" on the piano several houses away. (People several houses away are always playing "Narcissus" on the piano on Sunday afternoons. If there is one sound that is typical of Sunday afternoon, it is that of a piano being played several houses away.) It is true, of course, that even out in the country, miles away from everything, you could always tell that it was Sunday afternoon by the strange behavior of the birds, but you could at least pick out an open field and turn somersaults (first taking the small change out of your pockets), or you could run head on into a large oak, causing insensibility. At least, you could in the early days of automobiling.

But, as soon as everybody got automobiles, the first thing they did naturally was to try to run away from Sunday afternoon, with the result that every country road within a hundred miles of any city has now taken the place of the old-time county fair, without the pleasure of the cattle and the jam exhibits. Today the only difference between Sunday afternoon in the city and Sunday afternoon in the country is that, in the country, you don't know the people who are on your lap.

Aside from the unpleasantness of being crowded in with a lot of strangers on a country road and not knowing what to talk about during the long hours while the automobiles are waiting to move ahead, there is the actual danger of an epidemic. Supposing someone took a child out riding in the country on Sunday and while they were jammed in line with hundreds of thousands of other pleasure-riders the child came down with tonsilitis. There she would be, a carrier of disease, in contact with at least two-thirds of the population, giving off germs right and left and perhaps starting an epidemic which would sweep the country before the crowds could get back to their homes and gargle. Subways and crowded tenements have long been recognized as breeding grounds for afflictions of the nose and throat. Are country roads on Sunday afternoons to be left entirely without official regulation?

I really have no remedy for Sunday afternoon, at least none that I have any confidence in. The only one that might work would be to set fire to the house along about 1:30 p.m. If the fire were nursed along, it would cause sufficient excitement to make you forget what day it was, at least until it was time to turn on the lights for the evening. Or you might go down into the cellar right after dinner and take the furnace apart, promising yourself to have it put together again by suppertime. Here, at least, the sunlight couldn't get at you. Or you could rent a diver's suit and go to the nearest body of water and spend the afternoon tottering about under the surface, picking sea anemone and old bits of wreckage.

The method which I myself have tried with considerable success and little expense, however, is to buy a small quantity of Veronal at the nearest druggist's, put it slyly in my coffee on Saturday night, and then bundle off to bed. When you wake up on Monday morning you may not feel crisp, but Sunday will be over.

And that, I take it, is what we are after.

THE MEZZOTINT

MONTAGUE RHODES JAMES / GREAT BRITAIN

M. R. James

SOME TIME AGO I believe I had the pleasure of telling you the story of an adventure which happened to a friend of mine by the name of Dennistoun, during his pursuit of objects of art for the museum at Cambridge.

He did not publish his experiences very widely upon his return to England; but they could not fail to become known to a good many of his friends, and among others to the gentleman who at that time presided over an art museum at another university. It was to be expected that the story should make a considerable impression on the mind of a man whose vocation lay in lines similar to Dennistoun's, and that he should be eager to catch at any explanation of the matter which tended to make it seem improbable that he should ever be called upon to deal with so agitating an emergency. It was, indeed, somewhat consoling to him to reflect that he was not expected to acquire ancient manuscripts for his institution; that was the business of the Shelburnian Library. The authorities of that institution might, if they pleased, ransack obscure corners of the Continent for such matters. He was glad to be obliged at the moment to confine his attention to enlarging the already unsurpassed collection of English topographical drawings and engravings possessed by his museum. Yet, as it turned out, even a department so homely and familiar as this may have its dark corners, and to one of these Mr. Williams was unexpectedly introduced.

Those who have taken even the most limited interest in the acquisition of topographical pictures are aware that there is one

London dealer whose aid is indispensable to their researches. Mr. J. W. Britnell publishes at short intervals very admirable catalogues of a large and constantly changing stock of engravings, plans, and old sketches of mansions, churches, and towns in England and Wales. These catalogues were, of course, the ABC of his subject to Mr. Williams: but as his museum already contained an enormous accumulation of topographical pictures, he was a regular, rather than a copious, buyer; and he rather looked to Mr. Britnell to fill up gaps in the rank and file of his collection than to supply him with rarities.

Now, in February of last year there appeared upon Mr. Williams's desk at the museum a catalogue from Mr. Britnell's emporium, and accompanying it was a typewritten communication from the dealer himself. This latter ran as follows:

Dear Sir,
    We beg to call your attention to No. 978 in our accompanying catalogue, which we shall be glad to send on approval.
Yours faithfully,
J. W. Britnell

To turn to No. 978 in the accompanying catalogue was with Mr. Williams (as he observed to himself) the work of a moment, and in the place indicated he found the following entry:

978.—Unknown. Interesting mezzotint: View of a manor house, early part of the century. 15 by 10 inches; black frame. £2 2s.

It was not specially exciting, and the price seemed high. However, as Mr. Britnell, who knew his business and his customer, seemed to set store by it, Mr. Williams wrote a postcard asking for the article to be sent on approval, along with some other engravings and sketches which appeared in the same catalogue. And so he passed without much excitement of anticipation to the ordinary labors of the day.

A parcel always arrives a day later than you expect it and that of Mr. Britnell proved, as I believe the phrase goes, no exception to the rule. It was delivered at the museum by the afternoon post of Saturday, after Mr. Williams had left his work, and it was accordingly brought round to his rooms in college by the attendant, in order that he might not have to wait over Sunday before looking through it and returning such of the contents as he did not propose to keep. And here he found it when he came in to tea, with a friend.

The only item with which I am concerned was the rather large, black-framed mezzotint of which I have already quoted the short description given in Mr. Britnell's catalogue. Some more details of it will have to be given, though I cannot hope to put before you the look of the picture as clearly as it is present to my own eye. Very nearly the exact duplicate of it may be seen in a good many old inn parlors or in the passages of undisturbed country mansions at the present moment. It was a rather indifferent mezzotint, and an indifferent mezzotint is, perhaps, the worst form of engraving known. It presented a full-face view of a not very large manor house of the last century, with three rows of plain sashed windows with rusticated masonry about them, a parapet with balls or vases at the angles, and a small portico in the center. On either side were trees, and in front a considerable expanse of lawn. The legend *A. W. F. sculpsit* was engraved on the narrow margin; and there was no further inscription. The whole thing gave the impression that it was the work of an amateur. What in the world Mr. Britnell could mean by affixing the price of £2 2s. to such an object was more than Mr. Williams could imagine. He turned it over with a good deal of contempt; upon the back was a paper label, the left-hand half of which had been torn off. All that remained were the ends of two lines of writing: the first had the letters —*ngley Hall;* the second, —*ssex.*

It would, perhaps, be just worthwhile to identify the place represented, which he could easily do with the help of a gazetteer, and then he would send it back to Mr. Britnell, with some remarks reflecting upon the judgment of that gentleman. He lighted the candles, for it was now dark, made the tea, and supplied the friend with whom he had been playing golf (for I believe the authorities of the university I write of indulge in that pursuit by way of relaxation); and tea was taken to the accompaniment of a discussion which golfing persons can imagine for themselves, but which the conscientious writer has no right to inflict upon any nongolfing persons.

The conclusion arrived at was that certain strokes might have been better, and that in certain emergencies neither player had experienced that amount of luck which a human being has a right to expect. It was now that the friend—let us call him Professor Binks—took up the framed engraving, and said: "What's this place, Williams?"

"Just what I am going to try to find out," said Williams, going to the shelf for a gazetteer. "Look at the back. Somethingley Hall, either in Sussex or Essex. Half the name's gone, you see. You don't happen to know it, I suppose?"

"It's from that man Britnell, I suppose, isn't it?" said Binks. "Is it for the museum?"

"Well, I think I should buy it if the price was five shillings," said Williams; "but for some unearthly reason he wants two guineas for it. I can't conceive why. It's a wretched engraving, and there aren't even any figures to give it life."

"It's not worth two guineas, I should think," said Binks; "but I don't think it's so badly done. The moonlight seems rather good to me; and I should have thought there *were* figures, or at least a figure, just on the edge in front."

"Let's look," said Williams. "Well, it's true the light is rather cleverly given. Where's your figure? Oh, yes! Just the head, in the very front of the picture."

And indeed there was—hardly more than a black blot on the extreme edge of the engraving—the head of a man or woman, a good deal muffled up, the back turned to the spectator, and looking towards the house. Williams had not noticed it before. "Still," he said, "though it's a cleverer thing than I thought, I can't spend two guineas of museum money on a picture of a place I don't know."

Professor Binks had his work to do, and soon went; and very nearly up to hall time Williams was engaged in a vain attempt to identify the subject of his picture. If the vowel before the *ng* had only been left, it would have been easy enough, he thought; but as it is, the name may be anything from Guestingley to Langley, and there are many more names ending like this than I thought; and this rotten book has no index of terminations.

Hall in Mr. Williams's college was at seven. It need not be dwelt upon; the less so as he met there colleagues who had been playing golf during the afternoon, and words with which we have no concern were freely bandied across the table—merely golfing words, I would hasten to explain.

I suppose an hour or more to have been spent in what is called common room after dinner. Later in the evening some few retired to Williams's rooms, and I have little doubt that whist was played and tobacco smoked. During a lull in these operations Williams picked up the mezzotint from the table without looking at it, and handed it to a person mildly interested in art, telling him where it had come from, and the other particulars which we already know.

The gentleman took it carelessly, looked at it, then said, in a tone of some interest: "It's really a very good piece of work, Williams; it has quite a feeling of the romantic period. The light is admirably managed, it seems to me, and the figure, though it's rather too grotesque, is somehow very impressive."

"Yes, isn't it?" said Williams, who was just then busy giving whisky and soda to others of the company, and was unable to come across the room to look at the view again.

It was by this time rather late in the evening, and the visitors were on the move. After they went Williams was obliged to write a letter or two and clear up some odd bits of work. At last, sometime past midnight, he was disposed to turn in, and he put out his lamp after lighting his bedroom candle. The picture lay face upwards on the table where the last man who looked at it had put it, and it caught his eye as he turned the lamp down. What he saw made him very nearly drop the candle on the floor, and he declares now that if he had been left in the dark at that moment he would have had a fit. But, as that did not happen, he was able to put down the light on the table and take a good look at the picture. It was indubitable—rankly impossible, no doubt, but absolutely certain. In the middle of the lawn in front of the unknown house there was a figure where no figure had been at five o'clock that afternoon. It was crawling on all fours towards the house, and it was muffled in a strange black garment with a white cross on the back.

I do not know what is the ideal course to pursue in a situation of this kind. I can only tell you what Mr. Williams did. He took the picture by one corner and carried it across the passage to a second set of rooms which he possessed. There he locked it up in a drawer, closed the doors of both sets of rooms, and retired to bed; but first he wrote out and signed an account of the extraordinary change which the picture had undergone since it had come into his possession.

Sleep visited him rather late; but it was consoling to reflect that the behavior of the picture did not depend upon his own unsupported testimony. Evidently the man who had looked at it the night before had seen something of the same kind as he had, otherwise he might have been tempted to think that something gravely wrong was happening either to his eyes or his mind. This possibility being fortunately precluded, two matters awaited him on the morrow. He must take stock of the picture very carefully, and call in a witness for the purpose, and he must make a determined effort to ascertain what house it was that was represented. He would therefore ask his neighbor Nisbet to breakfast with him, and he would subsequently spend a morning over the gazetteer.

Nisbet was disengaged, and arrived about nine thirty. His host was not quite dressed, even at this late hour. During breakfast nothing was said about the mezzotint by Williams, save that he had a picture on which he wished for Nisbet's opinion. But those who are familiar with university life can picture the wide and delightful range of subjects over which the conversation of two Fellows of Canterbury College is likely to extend during a Sunday-morning breakfast. Hardly a topic was left unchallenged, from golf to lawn tennis. Yet I am bound to say that Williams was rather distraught; for his interest naturally centered in that very strange picture which was now reposing, face downwards, in the drawer in the room opposite.

The morning pipe was at last lighted, and the moment had arrived for which he looked. With very considerable—almost tremulous—excitement, he ran across, unlocked the drawer, and, extracting the picture—still face downwards—ran back, and put it into Nisbet's hands. "Now," he said, "Nisbet, I want you to tell me exactly what you see in that picture. Describe it, if you don't mind, rather minutely. I'll tell you why afterwards."

"Well," said Nisbet, "I have here a view of a country house—English, I presume—by moonlight."

"Moonlight? You're sure of that?"

"Certainly. The moon appears to be on the wane, if you wish for details, and there are clouds in the sky."

"All right. Go on. I'll swear," added Williams in an aside, "there was no moon when I saw it first."

"Well, there's not much more to be said," Nisbet continued. "The house has one—two—three rows of windows, five in each row, except at the bottom, where there's a porch instead of the middle one, and—"

"But what about figures?" said Williams, with marked interest.

"There aren't any," said Nisbet; "but—"

"What! No figure on the grass in front?"

"Not a thing."

"You'll swear to that?"

"Certainly I will. But there's just one other thing."

"What?"

"Why, one of the windows on the ground floor—left of the door—is open."

"Is it really so? My goodness! he must have got in," said Williams, with great excitement; and he hurried to the back of the sofa on which Nisbet was sitting, and, catching the picture from him, verified the matter for himself. It was quite true. There was no figure, and there was the open window. Williams, after a moment of speechless surprise, went to the writing table and scribbled for a short time. Then he brought two papers to Nisbet, and asked him first to sign one—it was his own description of the picture, which you have just heard—and then to read the other which was Williams's statement written the night before.

"What can it all mean?" said Nisbet.

"Exactly. Well, one thing I must do—or three things, now I think of it. I must find out from Garwood"—this was his last night's visitor—"what he saw, and then I must get the thing photographed before it goes further, and then I must find out what the place is."

"I can do the photographing myself," said Nisbet, "and I will. But, you know, it looks very much as if we were assisting at the working out of a tragedy somewhere. The question is, Has it happened already, or is it going to come off? You must find out what the place is. Yes," he said, looking at the picture again, "I expect you're right: he has got in. And if I don't mistake there'll be the devil to pay in one of the rooms upstairs."

"I'll tell you what," said Williams; "I'll take the picture across to old Green." (This was the senior Fellow of the college, who had been bursar for many years.) "It's quite likely he'll know it. We have property in Essex and Sussex, and he must have been over the two counties a lot in his time."

"Quite likely he will," said Nisbet; "but just let me take my photograph first. But look here, I rather think Green isn't up today. He wasn't in hall last night, and I think I heard him say he was going down for the Sunday."

"That's true, too," said Williams; "I know he's gone to Brighton. Well, if you'll photograph it now, I'll go across to Garwood and get his statement, and you keep an eye on it while I'm gone. I'm beginning to think two guineas is not a very exorbitant price for it now."

In a short time he had returned, and brought Mr. Garwood with him. Garwood's statement was to the effect that the figure, when he had seen it, was clear of the edge of the picture, but had not got far across the lawn. He remembered a white mark on the back of its drapery, but could not have been sure it was a cross. A document to this effect was then drawn up and signed, and Nisbet proceeded to photograph the picture. "Now what do you mean to do?" he said. "Are you going to sit and watch it all day?"

"Well, no, I think not," said Williams. "I rather imagine we're meant to see the whole thing. You see, between the time I saw it last night and this morning there was time for lots of things to happen, but the creature only got into the house. It could easily have got through its business in the time and gone to its own place again; but the fact of the window being open, I think, must mean that it's in there now. So I feel quite easy about leaving it. And besides, I have a kind of idea that it wouldn't change much, if at all, in the daytime. We might go out for a walk this afternoon, and come in to tea, or whenever it gets dark. I shall leave it out on the table here, and close the door. My skip can get in, but no one else."

The three agreed that this would be a good plan; and, further, that if they spent the afternoon together they would be less likely to talk about the business to other people; for any rumor of such a transaction as was going on would bring the whole of the Phasmatological Society about their ears.

We may give them a respite until five o'clock.

At or near that hour the three were entering Williams's staircase. They were at first slightly annoyed to see that the door of his rooms was ajar; but in a moment it was remembered that on Sunday the skips came for orders an hour or so earlier than on weekdays. However, a surprise was awaiting them. The first thing they saw was the picture leaning up against a pile of books on the table, as it had been left, and the next thing was Williams's skip, seated on a chair opposite, gazing at it with undisguised horror.

How was this? Mr. Filcher (the name is not my own invention) was a servant of considerable standing, and set the standard of etiquette to all his own college and to several neighboring ones, and nothing could be more alien to his practice than to be found sitting on his master's chair, or appearing to take any particular notice of his master's furniture or pictures. Indeed, he seemed to feel this himself. He started violently when the three men were in the room, and got up with a marked effort. Then he said: "I ask your pardon, sir, for taking such a freedom as to set down."

"Not at all, Robert," interposed Mr. Williams. "I was meaning to ask you sometime what you thought of that picture."

"Well, sir, of course I don't set up my opinion again yours, but it ain't the pictur I should 'ang where my little girl could see it."

"Wouldn't you, Robert? Why not?"

"No, sir. Why, the pore child, I recollect once she see a Door Bible, with pictures not 'alf what that is, and we 'ad to set up with her three or four nights afterwards, if you'll believe me; and if she was to ketch a sight of this skelinton here, or whatever it is, carrying off the pore baby, she would be in a taking. You know 'ow it is with children; 'ow nervish they git with a little thing and all. But what I should say, it don't seem a right pictur to be laying about, sir, not where anyone that's liable to be startled could come on it. Should you be wanting anything this evening, sir? Thank you, sir."

With these words the excellent man went to continue the round of his masters, and you may be sure the gentlemen whom he left lost no time in gathering round the engraving. There was the house, as before, under the waning moon and the drifting clouds. The window that had been open was shut, and the figure was once more on the lawn; but not this time crawling cautiously on hands and knees. Now it was erect and stepping swiftly, with long strides, towards the front of the picture. The moon was behind it, and the black drapery hung down over its face so that only hints of that could be seen, and what was visible made the spectators profoundly thankful that they could see no more than a white domelike forehead and a few straggling hairs. The head was bent down, and the arms were tightly clasped over an object which could be dimly seen and identified as a child, whether dead or living it was not possible to say. The legs of the appearance alone could be plainly discerned, and they were horribly thin.

From five to seven the three companions sat and watched the picture by turns. But it never changed. They agreed at last that it would be safe to leave it, and that they would return after hall and await further developments.

When they assembled again, at the earliest possible moment, the engraving was there, but the figure was gone, and the house was quiet under the moonbeams. There was nothing for it but to spend the evening over gazetteers and guidebooks. Williams was the lucky one at last, and perhaps he deserved it. At 11:30 p.m. he read from Murray's *Guide to Essex* the following lines:

> 16½ miles, *Anningley*. The church has been an interesting building of Norman date, but was extensively classicized in the last century. It contains the tomb of the family of Francis, whose mansion, Anningley Hall, a solid Queen Anne house, stands immediately beyond the churchyard in a park of about 80 acres. The family is now extinct, the last heir having disappeared mysteriously in infancy in the year 1802. The father, Mr. Arthur Francis, was locally known as a talented amateur engraver in mezzotint. After his son's disappearance he lived

in complete retirement at the hall, and was found dead in his studio on the third anniversary of the disaster, having just completed an engraving of the house, impressions of which are of considerable rarity.

This looked like business, and, indeed, Mr. Green on his return at once identified the house as Anningley Hall.

"Is there any kind of explanation of the figure, Green?" was the question which Williams naturally asked.

"I don't know, I'm sure, Williams. What used to be said in the place when I first knew it, which was before I came up here, was just this: old Francis was always very much down on these poaching fellows, and whenever he got a chance he used to get a man whom he suspected of it turned off the estate, and by degrees he got rid of them all but one. Squires could do a lot of things then that they daren't think of now. Well, this man that was left was what you find pretty often in that country—the last remains of a very old family. I believe they were lords of the manor at one time. I recollect just the same thing in my own parish."

"Like the man in *Tess of the D'Urbervilles*," Williams put in.

"Yes, I daresay; it's not a book I could ever read myself. But this fellow could show a row of tombs in the church there that belonged to his ancestors, and all that went to sour him a bit; but Francis, they said, could never get at him—he always kept just on the right side of the law—until one night the keepers found him at it in a wood right at the end of the estate. I could show you the place now; it marches with some land that used to belong to an uncle of mine. And you can imagine there was a row; and this man Gawdy (that was the name, to be sure—Gawdy; I thought I should get it—Gawdy), he was unlucky enough, poor chap! to shoot a keeper. Well, that was what Francis wanted, and grand juries—you know what they would have been then—and poor Gawdy was strung up in double-quick time; and I've been shown the place he was buried in, on the north side of the church—you know the way in that part of the world: anyone that's been hanged or made away with themselves, they bury them that side. And the idea was that some friend of Gawdy's—not a relation, because he had none, poor devil! he was the last of his line: kind of *spes ultima gentis*—must have planned to get hold of Francis's boy and put an end to *his* line, too. I don't know—it's rather an out-of-the-way thing for an Essex poacher to think of—but I should say now it looks more as if old Gawdy had managed the job himself. I hate to think of it! have some whisky, Williams!"

The facts were communicated by Williams to Dennistoun, and by him to a mixed company, of which I was one, and the Sadducean Professor of Ophiology another. I am sorry to say that the latter when asked what he thought of it, only remarked: "Oh, those Bridgeford people will say anything"—a sentiment which met with the reception it deserved.

I have only to add that the picture is now in the Ashleian Museum; that it has been treated to discover whether sympathetic ink has been used in it, but without effect; that Mr. Britnell knew nothing of it save that he was sure it was uncommon; and that, though carefully watched, it has never been known to change again.

THE ALLIGATORS
JOHN UPDIKE / UNITED STATES

J OAN EDISON came to their half of the fifth grade from Maryland in March. She had a thin face with something of a grownup's tired expression and long black eyelashes like a doll's. Everybody hated her. That month Miss Fritz was reading to them during homeroom about a girl, Emmy, who was badly spoiled and always telling her parents lies about her twin sister Annie; nobody could believe, it was too amazing, how exactly when they were despising Emmy most Joan should come into the school with her show-off clothes and her hair left hanging down the back of her fuzzy sweater instead of being cut or braided and her having the crust to actually argue with teachers. "Well I'm sorry," she told Miss Fritz, not even rising from her seat, "but I *don't* see what the point is of homework. In Baltimore we never had any, and the *little* kids there knew what's in these books."

Charlie, who in a way enjoyed homework, was ready to join in the angry moan of the others. Little hurt lines had leaped up between Miss Fritz's eyebrows and he felt sorry for her, remembering how when that September John Eberly had half on purpose spilled purple Sho-Card paint on the newly sandpapered floor she had hidden her face in her arms on the desk and cried. She was afraid of the school board. "You're not in Baltimore now, Joan," Miss Fritz said. "You are in Olinger, Pennsylvania."

The children, Charlie among them, laughed, and Joan, blushing a soft brown color and raising her voice excitedly against the current of hatred, got in deeper by trying to explain, "Like there, instead of just *reading* about plants in a book we'd one day all bring in a flower we'd *picked* and cut it open and look at it in a *microscope.*" Because of her saying this, shadows, of broad leaves and wild slashed foreign flowers, darkened and complicated the idea they had of her.

Miss Fritz puckered her orange lips into fine wrinkles, then smiled. "In the upper levels you will be allowed to do that in this school. All things come in time, Joan, to patient little girls." When Joan started to argue *this*, Miss Fritz lifted one finger and said with the extra weight adults always have, held back in reserve, "No. No more, young lady, or you'll be in *serious* trouble with me." It gave the class courage to see that Miss Fritz didn't like her either.

After that, Joan couldn't open her mouth in class without there being a great groan. Outdoors on the macadam playground, at recess or fire drill or waiting in the morning for the buzzer, hardly anybody talked to her except to say "Stuck-up" or "Emmy" or "Whore, whore, from Balti-more." Boys were always yanking open the bow at the back of her fancy dresses and flipping little spitballs into the curls of her hanging hair. Once John Eberly even cut a section of her hair off with a yellow plastic scissors stolen from art class. This was the one time Charlie saw Joan cry actual tears. He was as bad as the others: worse, because what the others did because they felt like it, he did out of a plan, to make himself more popular. In the first and second grade he had been liked pretty well, but somewhere since then he had been dropped. There was a gang, boys and girls both, that met Saturdays—you heard them talk about it on Mondays—in Stuart Morrison's garage, and took hikes and played touch football together, and in winter sledded on Hill Street, and in spring bicycled all over Olinger and did together what else, he couldn't imagine. Charlie had known the chief members since before kindergarten. But after school there seemed nothing for him to do but go home promptly and do his homework and fiddle with his Central American stamps and go to horror movies alone, and on weekends nothing but beat monotonously at marbles or Monopoly or chess Darryl Johns or Marvin Auerbach, who he wouldn't have bothered at all with if they hadn't lived right in the neighborhood, they being at least a year younger and not bright for their age, either. Charlie thought the gang might notice him and take him in if he backed up their policies without being asked.

In Science, which 5A had in Miss Brobst's room across the hall, he sat one seat ahead of Joan and annoyed her all he could, in spite of a feeling that, both being disliked, they had something to share. One fact he discovered was, she wasn't that bright. Her marks on quizzes were always lower than his. He told her, "Cutting up all those flowers didn't do you much good. Or maybe in Baltimore they taught you everything so long ago you've forgotten it in your old age."

Charlie drew; on his tablet where she could easily see over his shoulder he once in a while drew a picture titled "Joan the Dope": the profile of a girl with a lean nose and sad mincemouth, the lashes of her lowered eye as black as the pencil could make them and the hair falling, in ridiculous hooks, row after row, down through the sea-blue cross-lines clear off the bottom edge of the tablet.

March turned into spring. One of the signals was, on the high school grounds, before the cinder track was weeded and when the softball field was still four inches of mud, Happy Lasker came with the elaborate airplane model he had wasted the winter making. It had the American star on the wingtips and a pilot painted inside the cockpit and a miniature motor that burned real gas. The buzzing, off and on all Saturday morning, collected smaller kids from Second Street down to Lynoak. Then it was always the same: Happy shoved the plane into the air, where it climbed and made a razzing noise a minute, then nose-dived and crashed and usually burned in the grass or mud. Happy's father was rich.

In the weeks since she had come, Joan's clothes had slowly grown simpler, to go with the other girls', and one day she came to school with most of her hair cut off, and the rest brushed flat around her head and brought into a little tail behind. The laughter at her was more than she had ever heard. "Ooh. Baldy-paldy!" some idiot girl had exclaimed when Joan came into the cloakroom, and the stupid words went sliding around class all morning. "Baldy-paldy from Baltimore. Why is old Baldy-paldy red in the face?" John Eberly kept making the motion of a scissors with his fingers and its juicy ticking sound with his tongue. Miss Fritz rapped her knuckles on the window sill until she was rubbing the ache with the other hand, and finally she sent two boys to Mr. Lengel's office, delighting Charlie an enormous secret amount.

His own reaction to the haircut had been quiet, to want to draw her, changed. He had kept the other drawings folded in his desk, and one of his instincts was toward complete sets of things, Bat Man comics and A's and Costa Rican stamps. Halfway across the room from him, Joan held very still, afraid, it seemed, to move even a hand, her face a shamed pink. The haircut had brought out her forehead and exposed her neck and made her chin pointier and her eyes larger. Charlie felt thankful once again for having been born a boy, and having no sharp shocks, like losing your curls or starting to bleed, to make growing painful. How much girls suffer had been one of the first thoughts he had ever had. His caricature of her was wonderful, the work of a genius. He showed it to Stuart Morrison behind him; it was too good for him to appreciate, his dull egg eyes just flickered over it. Charlie traced it onto another piece of tablet paper, making her head completely bald. This drawing Stuart grabbed and it was passed clear around the room.

THAT NIGHT HE HAD the dream. He must have dreamed it while lying there asleep in the morning light, for it was fresh in his head when he woke. They had been in a jungle. Joan, dressed in a torn sarong, was swimming in a clear river among alligators. Somehow, as if from a tree, he was looking down, and there was a calmness in the way the slim girl and the green alligators moved, in and out, perfectly visible under the window-skin of the water. Joan's face sometimes showed the horror she was undergoing and sometimes looked numb. Her hair trailed behind and fanned when her face came toward the surface. He shouted silently with grief. Then he had rescued her; without a sense of having dipped his arms in water, he was carrying her in two arms, himself in a bathing suit, and his feet firmly fixed to the knobby back of an alligator which skimmed upstream, through the shadows of high trees and white flowers and hanging vines, like a surfboard in a movie short. They seemed to be heading toward a wooden bridge arching over the stream. He wondered how he would duck it, and the river and the jungle gave way to his bed and his room, but through the change persisted, like a pedalled note on a piano, the sweetness and pride he had felt in saving and carrying the girl.

He loved Joan Edison. The morning was rainy, and under the umbrella his mother made him take this new knowledge, repeated again and again to himself, gathered like a bell of smoke. Love had no taste, but sharpened his sense of smell so that his oilcloth coat, his rubber boots, the red-tipped bushes hanging over the low walls holding back lawns all along Grand Street, even the dirt and moss in the cracks of the pavement each gave off clear odors. He would have laughed, if a wooden weight had not been placed high in his chest, near where his throat joined. He could not imagine himself laughing soon. It seemed he had reached one of those situations his Sunday school teacher, poor Miss West with her little mustache, had been trying to prepare him for. He prayed, *Give me Joan.* With the wet weather a solemn flatness had fallen over everything; an orange bus turning at the Bend and four birds on a telephone wire seemed to have the same importance. Yet he felt firmer and lighter and felt things as edges he must whip around and channels he must rush down. If he carried her off, did rescue her from the others' cruelty, he would have defied the gang and made a new one, his own. Just Joan and he at first, then others escaping from meanness and dumbness, until his gang was stronger and Stuart Morrison's garage was empty every Saturday. Charlie would be a king, with his own touch football game. Everyone would come and plead with him for mercy.

His first step was to tell all those in the cloakroom he loved Joan Edison now. They cared less than he had expected, considering how she was hated. He had more or less expected to have to fight with his fists. Hardly anybody gathered to hear the dream he had pictured himself telling everybody. Anyway that morning it would go around the class that he said he loved her, and though this was what he wanted, to in a way open a space between him and Joan, it felt funny nevertheless, and he stuttered when Miss Fritz had him go to the blackboard to explain something.

At lunch, he deliberately hid in the variety store until he saw her walk by. The homely girl with her he knew turned off at the next street. He waited a minute and then came out and began running to overtake Joan in the block between the street where the other girl turned down and the street where he turned up. It had stopped raining, and his rolled-up umbrella felt like a commando's bayonet. Coming up behind her, he said, "Bang. Bang."

She turned, and under her gaze, knowing she knew he loved her, his face heated and he stared down. "Why, Charlie," her voice said with her Maryland slowness, "what are you doing on this side of the street?" Carl the town cop stood in front of the elementary school to get them on the side of Grand Street where they belonged. Now Charlie would have to cross the avenue again, by himself, at the dangerous five-spoked intersection at the Bend.

"Nothing," he said, and used up the one sentence he had prepared ahead: "I like your hair the new way."

"Thank you," she said, and stopped. In Baltimore she must have had manner lessons. Her eyes looked at his, and his vision jumped back from the rims of her lower lids as if from a brink. Yet in the space she occupied there was a great fullness that lent him height, as if he were standing by a window giving on the first morning after a snow.

"But then I didn't mind it the old way either."

"Yes?"

A peculiar reply. Another peculiar thing was the tan beneath her skin; he had noticed before, though not so closely, how when she colored it came up a gentle dull brown more than red. Also she wore something perfumed.

He asked, "How do you like Olinger?"

"Oh, I think it's nice."

"Nice? I guess. I guess maybe. Nice Olinger. I wouldn't know because I've never been anywhere else."

She luckily took this as a joke and laughed. Rather than risk saying something unfunny, he began to balance the umbrella by its point on one finger and, when this went well, walked backwards, shifting the balanced umbrella, its hook black against the patchy blue sky, from one palm to the other, back and forth. At the corner where they parted he got carried away and in imitating a suave gent leaning on a cane bent the handle hopelessly. Her amazement was worth twice the price of his mother's probable crossness.

He planned to walk her again, and further, after school. All through lunch he kept calculating. His father and he would repaint his bike. At the next haircut he would have his hair parted on the other side to get away from his cowlick. He would change himself totally; everyone would wonder what had happened to him. He would learn to swim, and take her to the dam.

In the afternoon the momentum of the dream wore off somewhat. Now that he kept his eyes always on her, he noticed, with a qualm of his stomach, that in passing in the afternoon from Miss Brobst's to Miss Fritz's room, Joan was not alone, but chattered with others. In class, too, she whispered. So it was with more shame—such shame that he didn't believe he could ever face even his parents again—than surprise that from behind the dark pane of the variety store he saw her walk by in the company of the gang, she and Stuart Morrison throwing back their teeth and screaming and he imitating something and poor moronic John Eberly tagging behind like a thick tail. Charlie watched them walk out of sight behind a tall hedge; relief was as yet a tiny fraction of his reversed world. It came to him that what he had taken for cruelty had been love, that far from hating her everybody had loved her from the beginning, and that even the stupidest knew it weeks before he did. That she was the queen of the class and might as well not exist, for all the good he would get out of it.

PELAGEYA

MIKHAIL ZOSHCHENKO / RUSSIA

Translated by Maria Gordon
and Hugh McLean

PELAGEYA WAS an illiterate woman. She couldn't even write her name.

Pelageya's husband, however, was a responsible Soviet official. Although he had once been a simple peasant, five years of living in the city had taught him an awful lot. Not only how to write his name but a hell of a lot besides.

And he was very much embarrassed to have an illiterate wife.

"You, Pelageyushka, ought at least to learn how to write your name," he used to say to Pelageya. "My last name is an easy one. Two syllables—Kuch-kin. And still you can't write it. It's awkward."

Pelageya used to wave it aside. "There's no use in me trying to learn it now, Ivan Nikolaevich," she would answer. "I'm getting on in years. My fingers are getting stiff. Why should I try to learn to make those letters now? Let the young pioneers learn it. I'll make it to my old age just as I am."

Pelageya's husband was a terribly busy man and couldn't waste much time on his wife. He wagged his head as if to say, "Oh, Pelageya, Pelageya!" But he kept his mouth shut.

But one day Ivan Nikolaevich did bring home a special little book.

"Here, Polya," he said, "is the latest teach-yourself primer, based on the most up-to-date methods. I am going to show you how myself."

Pelageya gave a quiet laugh, took the primer in her hands, turned it over, and hid it in the dresser, as if to say, "Let it lie there. Maybe our grandchildren will have some use for it."

But then one day Pelageya sat down to work. She had to mend a jacket for Ivan Nikolaevich. The sleeve had worn through.

So Pelageya sat down at the table. Took up her needle. Put her hand under the jacket and heard something rustling.

Maybe there's money in there, Pelageya thought.

She looked and found a letter. A nice clean one, with a neat envelope, precise little handwriting, and paper that smelled of perfume or eau de cologne.

Pelageya's heart gave a leap.

Can Ivan Nikolaevich be deceiving me? she thought. Can he be exchanging love letters with well-educated ladies and making fun of his poor, dumb, illiterate wife?

Pelageya looked at the envelope, took out the letter and unfolded it, but since she was illiterate she couldn't make out a word.

For the first time in her life Pelageya was sorry that she couldn't read.

Even though it's somebody else's letter, she thought, I've got to know what's in it. Maybe it will change my whole life, and I'd better go back to the country and work as a peasant.

Pelageya started to cry and began thinking that Ivan Nikolaevich seemed to have changed lately—he seemed to be taking more care of his mustache and washing his hands more often. Pelageya sat looking at the letter and squealing like a stuck pig. But read the letter she couldn't. And to show it to someone else would be embarrassing.

Pelageya hid the letter in the dresser, finished sewing the jacket, and waited for Ivan Nikolaevich to come home.

But when he came Pelageya didn't let on that anything had happened. On the contrary, in calm and even tones she talked to her husband and even hinted that she had nothing against doing a little studying and that she was fed up with being a dark and illiterate peasant.

Ivan Nikolaevich was overjoyed to hear it. "That's just fine," he said. "I'll show you how myself."

"All right, go ahead," said Pelageya.

And she stared fixedly at Ivan Nikolaevich's neat, clipped little mustache.

For two solid months Pelageya studied her reading every day. She patiently pieced together the words from the syllables, learned to form the letters, and memorized sentences. And every evening she took the treasured letter out of the dresser and tried to decipher its secret meaning.

But it was no easy job.

It was the third month before Pelageya mastered the art.

One morning when Ivan Nikolaevich had gone off to work, Pelageya took the letter out of the dresser and started reading it.

It was hard for her to decipher the small handwriting, but the scarcely perceptible scent of perfume from the paper spurred her on. The letter was addressed to Ivan Nikolaevich.

Pelageya read:

Dear Comrade Kuchkin:

I am sending you the primer I promised. I think that your wife should be able to master this vast erudition in two or three months. Promise me, old boy, that you'll make her do it. Explain to her; make her feel how disgusting it is to be an illiterate peasant woman.

To celebrate the anniversary of the Revolution, we are liquidating illiteracy throughout the whole Republic by all possible means; but for some reason we forget about those closest to us.

Be sure to do this, Ivan Nikolaevich.

With Communist greetings,
Maria Blokhina

Pelageya read this letter through twice. Then, pressing her lips together sorrowfully and feeling somehow secretly insulted, she burst into tears.

HAIRCUT

RING LARDNER / UNITED STATES

I GOT ANOTHER BARBER that comes over from Carterville and helps me out Saturdays, but the rest of the time I can get along all right alone. You can see for yourself that this ain't no New York City and besides that, the most of the boys works all day and don't have no leisure to drop in here and get themselves prettied up.

You're a newcomer, ain't you? I thought I hadn't seen you round before. I hope you like it good enough to stay. As I say, we ain't no New York City or Chicago, but we have pretty good times. Not as good, though, since Jim Kendall got killed. When he was alive, him and Hod Meyers used to keep this town in an uproar. I bet they was more laughin' done here than any town its size in America.

Jim was comical, and Hod was pretty near a match for him. Since Jim's gone, Hod tries to hold his end up just the same as ever, but it's tough goin' when you ain't got nobody to kind of work with.

They used to be plenty fun in here Saturdays. This place is jampacked Saturdays, from four o'clock on. Jim and Hod would show up right after their supper, round six o'clock. Jim would set himself down in that big chair, nearest the blue spittoon. Whoever had been settin' in that chair, why they'd get up when Jim come in and give it to him.

You'd of thought it was a reserved seat like they have sometimes in a theayter. Hod would generally always stand or walk up and down, or some Saturdays, of course, he'd be settin' in this chair part of the time, gettin' a haircut.

Well, Jim would set there a w'ile without openin' his mouth only to spit, and then finally he'd say to me, 'Whitey'—my right name, that is, my right first name, is Dick, but everybody round here calls me Whitey—Jim would say, 'Whitey, your nose looks like a rosebud tonight. You must of been drinkin' some of your aw de cologne.'

So I'd say, 'No, Jim, but you look like you'd been drinkin' somethin' of that kind or somethin' worse.'

Jim would have to laugh at that, but then he'd speak up and say, 'No, I ain't had nothin' to drink, but that ain't sayin' I wouldn't like somethin'. I wouldn't even mind if it was wood alcohol.'

Then Hod Meyers would say, 'Neither would your wife.' That would set everybody to laughin' because Jim and his wife wasn't on very good terms. She'd of divorced him only they wasn't no chance to get alimony and she didn't have no way to take care of herself and the kids. She couldn't never understand Jim. He *was* kind of rough, but a good fella at heart.

Him and Hod had all kinds of sport with Milt Sheppard. I don't suppose you've seen Milt. Well, he's got an Adam's apple that looks more like a mushmelon. So I'd be shavin' Milt and when I'd start to shave down here on his neck, Hod would holler, 'Hey, Whitey, wait a minute! Before you cut into it, let's make up a pool and see who can guess closest to the number of seeds.'

And Jim would say, 'If Milt hadn't of been so hoggish, he'd of ordered a half a cantaloupe instead of a whole one and it might not of stuck in his throat.'

All the boys would roar at this and Milt himself would force a smile, though the joke was on him. Jim certainly was a card!

There's his shavin' mug, settin' on the shelf, right next to Charley Vail's. 'Charles M. Vail.' That's the druggist. He comes in regular for his shave, three times a week. And Jim's is the cup next to Charley's. 'James H. Kendall.' Jim won't need no shavin' mug no more, but I'll leave it there just the same for old time's sake. Jim certainly was a character!

Years ago, Jim used to travel for a canned-goods concern over in Carterville. They sold canned goods. Jim had the whole northern half of the State and was on the road five days out of every week.

He'd drop in here Saturdays and tell his experiences for that week. It was rich.

I guess he paid more attention to playin' jokes than makin' sales. Finally the concern let him out and he come right home here and told everybody he'd been fired instead of sayin' he'd resigned like most fellas would of.

It was a Saturday and the shop was full and Jim got up out of that chair and says, 'Gentlemen, I got an important announcement to make. I been fired from my job.'

Well, they asked him if he was in earnest and he said he was and nobody could think of nothin' to say till Jim finally broke the ice himself. He says, 'I been sellin' canned goods and now I'm canned goods myself.'

You see, the concern he'd been workin' for was a factory that made canned goods. Over in Carterville. And now Jim said he was canned himself. He was certainly a card!

Jim had a great trick that he used to play w'ile he was travelin'. For instance, he'd be ridin' on a train and they'd come to some little town like, well, like, we'll say, like Benton. Jim would look out the train window and read the signs on the stores.

For instance, they'd be a sign, 'Henry Smith, Dry Goods.' Well, Jim would write down the name and the name of the town and when he got to wherever he was goin' he'd mail back a postal card to Henry Smith at Benton and not sign no name to it, but he'd write on the card, well, somethin' like 'Ask your wife about that book agent that spent the afternoon last week,' or 'Ask your Missus who kept her from gettin' lonesome the last time you was in Carterville.' And he'd sign the card, 'A Friend.'

Of course, he never knew what really come of none of these jokes, but he could picture what *probably* happened and that was enough.

Jim didn't work very steady after he lost his position with the Carterville people. What he did earn, doin' odd jobs round town, why he spent pretty near all of it on gin and his family might of starved if the stores hadn't of carried them along. Jim's wife tried her hand at dressmakin', but they ain't nobody goin' to get rich makin' dresses in this town.

As I say, she'd of divorced Jim, only she seen that she couldn't support herself and the kids and she was always hopin' that some day Jim would cut out his habits and give her more than two or three dollars a week.

They was a time when she would go to whoever he was workin' for and ask them to give her his wages, but after she done this once or twice, he beat her to it by borrowin' most of his pay in advance. He told it all round town, how he had outfoxed his Missus. He certainly was a caution!

But he wasn't satisfied with just outwittin' her. He was sore the way she had acted, tryin' to grab off his pay. And he made up his mind he'd get even. Well, he waited till Evans's Circus was advertised to come to town. Then he told his wife and two kiddies that he was goin' to take them to the circus. The day of the circus, he told them he would get the tickets and meet them outside the entrance to the tent.

Well, he didn't have no intentions of bein' there or buyin' tickets or nothin'. He got full of gin and laid round Wright's poolroom all day. His wife and the kids waited and waited and of course he didn't show up. His wife didn't have a dime with her, or nowhere else, I guess. So she finally had to tell the kids it was all off and they cried like they wasn't never goin' to stop.

Well, it seems, w'ile they was cryin', Doc Stair came along and he asked what was the matter, but Mrs. Kendall was stubborn and wouldn't tell him, but the kids told him and he insisted on takin' them and their mother in the show. Jim found this out afterwards and it was one reason why he had it in for Doc Stair.

Doc Stair come here about a year and a half ago. He's a mighty handsome young fella and his clothes always look like he has them made to order. He goes to Detroit two or three times a year and w'ile he's there he must have a tailor take his measure and then make him a suit to order. They cost pretty near twice as much, but they fit a whole lot better than if you just bought them in a store.

For a w'ile everybody was wonderin' why a young doctor like Doc Stair should come to a town like this where we already got old Doc Gamble and Doc Foote that's both been here for years and all the practice in town was always divided between the two of them.

Then they was a story got round that Doc Stair's gal had throwed him over, a gal up in the Northern Peninsula somewheres, and the reason he come here was to hide himself away and forget it. He said himself that he thought they wasn't nothin' like general practice in a place like ours to fit a man to be a good all-round doctor. And that's why he'd came.

Anyways, it wasn't long before he was makin' enough to live on, though they tell me that he never dunned nobody for what they owed him, and the folks here certainly has got the owin' habit, even in my business. If I had all that was comin' to me for just shaves alone, I could go to Carterville and put up at the Mercer for a week and see a different picture every night. For instance, they's old George Purdy—but I guess I shouldn't ought to be gossipin'.

Well, last year, our coroner died, died of the flu. Ken Beatty, that was his name. He was the coroner. So they had to choose another man to be coroner in his place and they picked Doc Stair. He laughed at first and said he didn't want it, but they made him take it. It ain't no job that anybody would fight for and what a man makes out of it in a year would just about buy seeds for their garden. Doc's the kind, though, that can't say no to nothin' if you keep at him long enough.

But I was goin' to tell you about a poor boy we got here in town—Paul Dickson. He fell out of a tree when he was about ten years old. Lit on his head and it done somethin' to him and he ain't never been right. No harm in him, but just silly. Jim Kendall used to call him cuckoo; that's a name Jim had for anybody that was off their head, only he called people's head their bean. That was another of his gags, callin' head bean and callin' crazy people cuckoo. Only poor Paul ain't crazy, but just silly.

You can imagine that Jim used to have all kinds of fun with Paul. He'd send him to the White Front Garage for a left-handed monkey wrench. Of course they ain't no such a thing as a left-handed monkey wrench.

And once we had a kind of a fair here and they was a baseball game between the fats and the leans and before the game started Jim called Paul over and sent him way down to Schrader's hardware store to get a key for the pitcher's box.

They wasn't nothin' in the way of gags that Jim couldn't think up, when he put his mind to it.

Poor Paul was always kind of suspicious of people, maybe on account of how Jim had kept foolin' him. Paul wouldn't have much to do with anybody only his own mother and Doc Stair and a girl here in town named Julie Gregg. That is, she ain't a girl no more, but pretty near thirty or over.

When Doc first come to town, Paul seemed to feel like here was a real friend and he hung round Doc's office most the w'ile; the only time he wasn't there was when he'd go home to eat or sleep or when he seen Julie Gregg doin' her shoppin'.

When he looked out Doc's window and seen her, he'd run downstairs and join her and tag along with her to the different stores. The poor boy was crazy about Julie and she always treated him mighty nice and made him feel like he was welcome, though of course it wasn't nothin' but pity on her side.

Doc done all he could to improve Paul's mind and he told me once that he really thought the boy was gettin' better, that they was times when he was as bright and sensible as anybody else.

But I was goin' to tell you about Julie Gregg. Old Man Gregg was in the lumber business, but got to drinkin' and lost the most of his money and when he died, he didn't leave nothin' but the house and just enough insurance for the girl to skimp along on.

Her mother was a kind of a half invalid and didn't hardly ever leave the house. Julie wanted to sell the place and move somewheres else after the old man died, but the mother said she was born here and would die here. It was tough on Julie, as the young people round this town—well, she's too good for them.

She's been away to school and Chicago and New York and different places and they ain't no subject she can't talk on, where you take the rest of the young folks here and you mention anything to them outside of Gloria Swanson or Tommy Meighan and they think you're delirious. Did you see Gloria in *Wages of Virtue?* You missed somethin'!

Well, Doc Stair hadn't been here more than a week when he come in one day to get shaved and I recognized who he was as he had been pointed out to me, so I told him about my old lady. She's been ailin' for a couple years and either Doc Gamble or Doc Foote, neither one, seemed to be helpin' her. So he said he would come out and see her, but if she was able to get out herself, it would be better to bring her to his office where he could make a completer examination.

So I took her to his office and w'ile I was waitin' for her in the reception room, in come Julie Gregg. When somebody comes in Doc Stair's office, they's a bell that rings in his inside office so as he can tell they's somebody to see him.

So he left my old lady inside and come out to the front office and that's the first time him and Julie met and I guess it was what they call love at first sight. But it wasn't fifty-fifty. This young fella was the slickest-lookin' fella she'd ever seen in this town and she went wild over him. To him she was just a young lady that wanted to see the doctor.

She'd came on about the same business I had. Her mother had been doctorin' for years with Doc Gamble and Doc Foote and without no results. So she'd heard they was a new doc in town and decided to give him a try. He promised to call and see her mother that same day.

I said a minute ago that it was love at first sight on her part. I'm not only judgin' by how she acted afterwards but how she looked at him that first day in his office. I ain't no mind reader, but it was wrote all over her face that she was gone.

Now Jim Kendall, besides bein' a jokesmith and a pretty good drinker, well, Jim was quite a lady-killer. I guess he run pretty wild durin' the time he was on the road for them Carterville people, and besides that, he'd had a couple little affairs of the heart right here in town. As I say, his wife could of divorced him, only she couldn't.

But Jim was like the majority of men, and women, too, I guess. He wanted what he couldn't get. He wanted Julie Gregg and worked his head off tryin' to land her. Only he'd of said bean instead of head.

Well, Jim's habits and his jokes didn't appeal to Julie and of course he was a married man, so he didn't have no more chance than, well, than a rabbit. That's an expression of Jim's himself. When somebody didn't have no chance to get elected or somethin', Jim would always say they didn't have no more chance than a rabbit.

He didn't make no bones about how he felt. Right in here, more than once, in front of the whole crowd, he said he was stuck on Julie and anybody that could get her for him was welcome to his house and his wife and kids included. But she wouldn't have nothin' to do with him; wouldn't even speak to him on the street. He finally seen he wasn't gettin' nowheres with his usual line so he decided to try the rough stuff. He went right up to her house one evenin' and when she opened the door he forced his way in and grabbed her. But she broke loose and before he could stop her, she run in the next room and locked the door and phoned to Joe Barnes. Joe's the marshal. Jim could hear who she was phonin' to and he beat it before Joe got there.

Joe was an old friend of Julie's pa. Joe went to Jim the next day and told him what would happen if he ever done it again.

I don't know how the news of this little affair leaked out. Chances is that Joe Barnes told his wife and she told somebody else's wife and they told their husband. Anyways, it did leak out and Hod Meyers had the nerve to kid Jim about it, right here in this shop. Jim didn't deny nothin' and kind of laughed it off and said for us all to wait; that lots of people had tried to make a monkey out of him, but he always got even.

Meanw'ile everybody in town was wise to Julie's bein' wild mad over the Doc. I don't suppose she had any idear how her face changed when him and her was together; of course she couldn't of, or she'd of kept away from him. And she didn't know that we was all noticin' how many times she made excuses to go up to his office or pass it on the other side of the street and look up in his window to see if he was there. I felt sorry for her and so did most other people.

Hod Meyers kept rubbin' it into Jim about how the Doc had cut him out. Jim didn't pay no attention to the kiddin' and you could see he was plannin' one of his jokes.

One trick Jim had was the knack of changin' his voice. He could make you think he was a girl talkin' and he could mimic any man's voice. To show you how good he was along this line, I'll tell you the joke he played on me once.

You know, in most towns of any size, when a man is dead and needs a shave, why the barber that shaves him soaks him five dollars for the job; that is, he don't soak *him,* but whoever ordered the shave. I just charge three dollars because personally I don't mind much shavin' a dead person. They lay a whole lot stiller than live customers. The only thing is that you don't feel like talkin' to them and you get kind of lonesome.

Well, about the coldest day we ever had here, two years ago last winter, the phone rung at the house w'ile I was home to dinner and I answered the phone and it was a woman's voice and she said she was Mrs. John Scott and her husband was dead and would I come out and shave him.

Old John had always been a good customer of mine. But they live seven miles out in the country, on the Streeter road. Still I didn't see how I could say no.

So I said I would be there, but would have to come in a jitney and it might cost three or four dollars besides the price of the shave. So she, or the voice, it said that was all right, so I got Frank Abbott to drive me out to the place and when I got there, who should open the door but old John himself! He wasn't no more dead than, well, than a rabbit.

It didn't take no private detective to figure out who had played me this little joke. Nobody could of thought it up but Jim Kendall. He certainly was a card!

I tell you this incident just to show you how he could disguise his voice and make you believe it was somebody else talkin'. I'd of swore it was Mrs. Scott had called me. Anyways, some woman.

Well, Jim waited till he had Doc Stair's voice down pat; then he went after revenge. He called Julie up on a night when he knew Doc was over in Carterville. She never questioned but what it was Doc's voice. Jim said he must see her that night; he couldn't wait no longer to tell her somethin'. She was all excited and told him to come to the house. But he said he was expectin' an important long-distance call and wouldn't she please forget her manners for once and come to his office. He said they couldn't nothin' hurt her and nobody would see her and he just *must* talk to her a little w'ile. Well, poor Julie fell for it.

Doc always keeps a night-light in his office, so it looked to Julie like they was somebody there.

Meanw'ile Jim Kendall had went to Wright's poolroom, where they was a whole gang amusin' themselves. The most of them had drank plenty of gin, and they was a rough bunch even when sober. They was always strong for Jim's jokes and when he told them to come with him and see some fun they give up their card games and pool games and followed along.

Doc's office is on the second floor. Right outside his door they's a flight of stairs leadin' to the floor above. Jim and his gang hid in the dark behind these stairs.

Well, Julie come up to Doc's door and rung the bell and they was nothin' doin'. She rung it again and she rung it seven or eight times. Then she tried the door and found it locked. Then Jim made some kind of a noise and she heard it and waited a minute, and then she says, 'Is that you, Ralph?' Ralph is Doc's first name.

They was no answer and it must of come to her all of a sudden that she'd been bunked. She pretty near fell downstairs and the whole gang after her. They chased her all the way home, hollerin', 'Is that you, Ralph?' and 'Oh, Ralphie, dear, is that you?' Jim says he couldn't holler it himself, as he was laughin' too hard.

Poor Julie! She didn't show up here on Main Street for a long, long time afterward.

And of course Jim and his gang told everybody in town, everybody but Doc Stair. They was scared to tell him, and he might of never knowed only for Paul Dickson. The poor cuckoo, as Jim called him, he was here in the shop one night when Jim was still gloatin' yet over what he'd done to Julie. And Paul took in as much of it as he could understand and he run to Doc with the story.

It's a cinch Doc went up in the air and swore he'd make Jim suffer. But it was a kind of a delicate thing, because if it got out that he had beat Jim up, Julie was bound to hear of it and then she'd know that Doc knew and of course knowin' that he knew would make it worse for her than ever. He was goin' to do somethin', but it took a lot of figurin'.

Well, it was a couple days later when Jim was here in the shop again, and so was the cuckoo. Jim was goin' duck-shootin' the next day and had came in lookin' for Hod Meyers to go with him. I happened to know that Hod had went over to Carterville and wouldn't be home till the end of the week. So Jim said he hated to go alone and he guessed he would call if off. Then poor Paul spoke up and said if Jim would take him he would go along. Jim thought a w'ile and then he said, well, he guessed a half-wit was better than nothin'.

I suppose he was plottin' to get Paul out in the boat and play some joke on him, like pushin' him in the water. Anyways, he said Paul could go. He asked him had he ever shot a duck and Paul said no, he'd never even had a gun in his hands. So Jim said he could set in the boat and watch him and if he behaved himself, he might lend him his gun for a couple of shots. They made a date to meet in the mornin' and that's the last I seen of Jim alive.

Next mornin', I hadn't been open more than ten minutes when Doc Stair come in. He looked kind of nervous. He asked me had I seen Paul Dickson. I said no, but I knew where he was, out duck-shootin' with Jim Kendall. So Doc says that's what he had heard, and he couldn't understand it because Paul had told him he wouldn't never have no more to do with Jim as long as he lived.

He said Paul had told him about the joke Jim had played on Julie. He said Paul had asked him what he thought of the joke and the Doc had told him that anybody that would do a thing like that ought not to be let live.

I said it had been a kind of a raw thing, but Jim just couldn't resist no kind of a joke, no matter how raw. I said I thought he was all right at heart, but just bubblin' over with mischief. Doc turned and walked out.

At noon he got a phone call from old John Scott. The lake where Jim and Paul had went shootin' is on John's place. Paul had came runnin' up to the house a few minutes before and said they'd been an accident. Jim had shot a few ducks and then give the gun to Paul and told him to try his luck. Paul hadn't never handled a gun and he was nervous. He was shakin' so hard that he couldn't control the gun. He let fire and Jim sunk back in the boat, dead.

Doc Stair, bein' the coroner, jumped in Frank Abbott's flivver and rushed out to Scott's farm. Paul and old John was down on the shore of the lake. Paul had rowed the boat to shore, but they'd left the body in it, waitin' for Doc to come.

Doc examined the body and said they might as well fetch it back to town. They was no use leavin' it there or callin' a jury, as it was a plain case of accidental shootin'.

Personally I wouldn't never leave a person shoot a gun in the same boat I was in unless I was sure they knew somethin' about guns. Jim was a sucker to leave a new beginner have his gun, let alone a half-wit. It probably served Jim right, what he got. But still we miss him round here. He certainly was a card!

Comb it wet or dry?

THE BURNING CITY
HJALMAR SÖDERBERG / SWEDEN

Translated by Charles Wharton Stork

THROUGH THE TWO WINDOWS with their bright lattice-figured curtains the level sunlight of the winter morning falls in two slanting oblong quadrilaterals on the soft green carpet, and in the warm sunny spaces a little boy skips and dances. He knows but little of the world as yet. He knows he is little and is going to be big, but he does not know either that he has been born or that he will die. He knows he is four and will soon be five, but he does not know what is meant by "a year"; he still measures time only into yesterday, today, and tomorrow.

"Papa," he suddenly exclaims to his father, who has just finished breakfast and lighted his first cigar of the day—he being a person to measure time with cigars—"Papa, I dreamed so many things last night! I dreamed about the whole room! I dreamed about the chairs and the green carpet and the mirror and the clock and the stove and the shutters and the cupboards."

With that he skips forward to the stove, where the fire flames and crackles, and turns a somersault. He considers the stove and the place in front of it as the most important and dignified things in the room.

His father nods and laughs at him over the corner of his paper, and the boy laughs back, laughs away uncontrollably. He is at the age when laughter is still only an utterance of joy, not of appreciation for the ridiculous. When he stood at the window some days ago and laughed at the moon, it was not because he found the moon funny, but because it gave him joy with its round bright face.

When he has had his laugh out, he clambers up on a chair and points to one of the pictures on the wall.

"—And I dreamed most of all about that picture," he says.

The picture is a photograph of an old Dutch painting, *A Burning City*.

"Well, and what was it you dreamed?" his father asks.

"I don't know."

"Come, think!"

"Oh yes, I dreamed it was burning and that I patted a doggie."

"But generally you are afraid of doggies."

"Yes, but on pictures I can pat them nicely."

Then he laughs and skips and dances.

At last he comes up to his father and says, "Papa dear, take down the picture. I want Papa to show me the picture again the way he did yesterday."

The picture is a new arrival in the room; it came the day before. With the other pictures around the walls the little boy has acquainted himself long ago: Uncle Strindberg and Uncle Schopaur (i.e., Schopenhauer) and Uncle Napoleon and ugly old Goethe and Grandmother when she was young. But the Burning City is new, and is furthermore in itself a much more amusing picture than the others. The father humors the little boy, takes the picture down from the wall, and they enjoy it together. Over a broad estuary that winds toward the sea and is filled with sloops and rowboats runs an arched bridge with a fortified tower. On the left shore lies the burning city: rows of narrow houses with pointed gables, high roofs, churches, and towers; a throng of people running hither and thither, a sea of fire and flames, clouds of smoke, ladders raised against walls, horses running away with shaking loads, docks crowded with barrels and sacks and all manner of rubbish; on the river a mass of people in a rowboat that is almost ready to capsize, while across the bridge people are running for dear life, and away off in the foreground stand two dogs sniffing at each other. But far in the background, where the estuary widens toward the sea, a much-too-small moon sits on the horizon in a mist of pale clouds, peeping wanly and sadly at all this misery.

"Papa," inquires the little boy, "why is the city burning?"

"Somebody was careless with fire," says the father.

"*Who* was it that was careless?"

"Ah, one can't be sure of that so long afterward."

"How long afterward?"

"It is many hundred years since that city was burned," says the father.

This is a bit puzzling to the little boy, as the father clearly realizes, but he had to answer something. The boy sits quiet a moment and ponders. New thoughts and impressions about things stir in his brain and mingle with the old. He points with his little finger on the glass over the burning city and says:

"Yes, but it was burning yesterday, and now today it's burning too."

The father ventures on an explanation of the difference between pictures and reality.

"That is not a real city," he says, "that is only a picture. The real city was burned up long, long ago. It is gone. The people that run about there waving their arms are dead and don't exist anymore. The houses have been burned up, the towers have fallen. The bridge is gone too."

"Have the towers burned down or tumbled down?" asks the boy.

"They have both burned and tumbled down."

"Are the steamboats dead too?"

"The boats too have been gone long ago," replied the father. "But those are not steamboats, they are sailing vessels. There were no steamboats in those days."

The little boy sticks out his lower lip with a dissatisfied expression.

"But I *see* that they're steamboats," he says. "Papa, what's that steamboat's name?"

He has a mind of his own, the boy does. The father is tired of the labor of instruction and holds his peace. The boy points with his finger to the old Dutch merchantmen and prattles to himself: "That steamer's name is *Bragë*, and that one's is *Hillersea*, and that is the *Princess Ingeborg*. Papa," he cries all of a sudden, "is the moon gone too?"

"No, the moon still exists. It is the one thing of all there that still exists. It is the same moon you laughed at the other day in the nursery window."

Again the little boy sits still and ponders. Then comes yet another question:

"Papa, is it *very* long ago this city was burned? Is it as long ago as when we went away on the *Princess Ingeborg?*"

"It is much, much longer ago," answers the father. "When that city burned, neither you nor I nor Mamma nor Grandma was here."

The boy's face becomes very serious all at once. He looks positively troubled. He sits quiet a long while pondering. But it seems as if things would not work out for him.

"Tell me, Papa," he finally asks, "where was I when that city was burned? Was it when I was at Grenna with Mamma?"

"No, old fellow," replies the father, "when that city burned you didn't yet exist."

The boy sticks out his underlip again with an attitude as much as to say: No, I can't agree to such a thing as that. He then repeats with emphasis:

"Yes, but where was I then?"

His father answers, "You didn't exist at all."

The boy looks at his father with round eyes. Suddenly all the little face brightens, the boy tears himself away from his father, and begins to skip and dance again in the sunny spots on the green carpet, crying at the top of his lungs:

"Oho, yes I did, just the same. I was somewhere, I was somewhere!"

He thought his father was only joking with him. Such an idea was clearly too ridiculous! The maids used sometimes to talk nonsense to him in jest, and he thought his father had done the same.

So he skips and dances in the sunlight.

FIREWORKS FOR ELSPETH
RUMER GODDEN / GREAT BRITAIN

Rumer Godden

WHEN ELSPETH WOKE on the last morning, she was visited by a feeling of extraordinary simplicity. Everything she had to do was done; there was nothing now but to go. She felt as if the doors and windows of the house were already wide open; the sun seemed to make a path from her own window over the lawn to the wood and the sky. I have only to go, thought Elspeth blissfully. Roderick, her black cocker spaniel, lay at the foot of her bed; there was, it was true, a gap in her mind where she must say good-by to Roderick—but that was legitimate grief, nothing disturbing. Nothing disturbing, she thought and stretched herself on the bed. Then Elspeth remembered the lunch party.

How she had pleaded with Mother! "A lunch party! Oh, *Mother,* no! Please no."

"Why not?"

"It wouldn't be—suitable," Elspeth had said, with temerity.

"Elspeth, do I or do I not know what is suitable?"

494

"*Not* a party!"

"Just the family and a few intimate friends."

"But they are the worst."

"Elspeth!"

It's the questions and the looks, Elspeth would have liked to say. Aunt Euphrosyne and Morna and Jean, Lady Bannerman, all of them. They know me so well they take it for granted they can ask things but . . . they have such picking eyes, thought Elspeth in despair. This is whole, in me, but they tatter it to pieces. "Mother," she had begun aloud, but Mother was saying, "Just Aunt Euphrosyne and Uncle Arthur and Morna and Jean. Major Fitzgerald, of course . . ."

"And the Baldocks and Lady Bannerman and Larry and Colin Crump," said Elspeth bitterly.

"They are exactly whom I thought of asking," said Mother; then she had looked at Elspeth and her face had hardened. "Well, Elspeth, why not?"

Elspeth could never say things to Mother; she could have talked to Aunt Bevis but that would have made Mother worse. "Bevis is *not* your mother," Mother often said.

"It—it will all be so complicated," Elspeth had said about the lunch party. "I—I wanted it simple, quiet and—kind of—usual, Mother." She had picked up Roderick and held him tightly to give herself courage while Mother tapped with a pencil on the blotter. "I thought—if I could just leave, as if it were everyday . . ."

"You *cannot* pretend that this kind of thing is everyday."

That had stopped Elspeth, and she could not bear to have the same scene again; instead she had said desperately, "Think of the washing up. Father and I shall have to leave at half past two. I shan't be here to help Marlowe."

"We shall have to get used to that." Mother's voice had been cold as she picked up her pen. "It will be easiest for everybody. If you thought at all, you would know what these last few hours will be like for your father and me, though I must say Father doesn't seem to feel it; *if* you thought, you couldn't do this."

"Oh, *Mother!*" Elspeth had pleaded once again but Mother held up her hand for silence, that thin white peremptory hand that looked fragile and was strong as iron. Elspeth knew how strong it was and her nerves tingled. It was almost time to go but she could still be stopped. The hand was heavy with the rings Mother always wore: diamonds, rubies, sapphires. Elspeth wondered idly what she herself would have done with the rings when they came to her. Now they won't, she thought, with relief. No rings, no Lady Bannerman's emeralds, none of the family silver and pictures and china. Daphne will have them all. I have escaped, thought Elspeth, and her face glowed; she was filled with the inner contentment that was hers now by right—or almost hers—as if it had been given to her, and she thought, It is my gift from God, my jewels and money, my family.

Mother had returned to the subject of the luncheon party. "I won't have people saying we're bundling you off. They might think there was a family rift, or an unhappy love affair."

"Couldn't they think it was choice?" asked Elspeth. At that, Mother's neck had stiffened as it did when she was mortally displeased; she began to write the invitations, but her hand trembled and Elspeth, watching, was smitten. Once again she had hurt Mother—for—for nothing, thought Elspeth. When I'm so happy, why can't I be generous? Why must I always do it? she thought in despair; do what Sister Monica so often said she must not? Trying to impose her own will, instead of accepting? "In these last few days try to do, to be, everything your parents want," Sister Monica had said. "Show them you love them . . ." and I can't be five minutes with Mother before we begin. No wonder they doubt me . . . this rebellious and un-pleasant girl to make a nun!

She had looked helplessly across the room at Aunt Bevis, who had been sewing in the window, and Aunt Bevis had looked back at her and smiled. Never had anyone as clear eyes as Aunt Bevis; they were set a little tilted as if, for all her quietness, Aunt Bevis had an extra private and particular view of the world. Is that what makes her so—large? thought Elspeth now, so without walls? She can see over the wall—but then Mother had caught the look and asked sharply, "Bevis, where's the list? You took it when you went to the telephone. Now it's *lost*."

"It's under the blotter, right-hand side," said Aunt Bevis.

"Thursday, April 2, at a quarter to one," Mother had written. On Thursday, April 2, today, thought Elspeth in bed, she, Elspeth Catherine Mary Erskine, was to enter the Order of the Sisters of Mary at their Convent of St. Faith at Chiswick, where she had already spent two retreats. She was very happy about it.

"What will you be called?" her cousin Morna had asked.

"Reverend Mother has agreed that I shall be Catherine Mary," said Elspeth. "They are saints' names as well as my own."

"Sister Catherine Mary." Morna tried it, and relapsed into helpless giggles.

"Shut up, Morna!" said her sister, Jean, but Morna could not shut up. Soon Jean and then Elspeth herself were giggling too, as they had always giggled when they were together, even though Morna was now twenty and Elspeth and Jean nineteen.

"But a nun *isn't* funny," Elspeth had protested.

"Of c-course not," said Jean, "it's just—you—as a n-nun!"

The giggling had been all right; it was the questions, the—feeling against her—that Elspeth could not face. I wish I belonged to one of those families, in Ireland or America, she thought often, where it's part of family life for a daughter or a sister to enter an Order. In ours you would think no one in the world had ever joined an Order before. "They make it seem so extraordinary," she had said bitterly to Sister Monica, the Mistress of the Novices.

"Wait," said Sister Monica. "Wait and they will see."

For a long time now people had been exhorting Elspeth to wait. "Sixteen is too young. Don't be ridiculous." And, "Eighteen is too young. Wait." She had, of course, needed her parents' consent, and at one time it seemed that Mother, and Father led on by Mother, never would consent. Then at long last there was hope. "If, at the end of a year you still want it . . ."

"I shall still want it," said Elspeth.

"You always were obstinate," said Mother. "Even as a little thing you would rather be sent to bed than give in."

The trouble is, thought Elspeth, that I have always given in—except over this. But, when the year was up, they had given their consent—if Mother's could be called a consent. Even then, Mother never left

Elspeth alone. "Robert killed, Daphne gone, one might think you would realize that you are all we have left."

"But Mother, you didn't mind when Daphne went away to be married. Hong Kong is the other side of the world!"

"That was *quite* different," said Mother. "Marriage is a woman's destiny. I hope I should never be so selfish as to stand between my child and *that*."

"But Mother . . . !"

It was no use. Mother would not listen.

The news had burst suddenly on the family and the family friends. Usually Mother took Aunt Euphrosyne and most of the neighborhood into her strict confidence. Now, until the ultimate decision was taken, Mother had not breathed a word. I suppose she was afraid it would spoil my chances, thought Elspeth. Young men would shy off me if they knew. I mightn't get all my dances! Now young men, dances, chances, did not matter. The news was out and everyone seemed bewildered.

"But how did it happen?" asked Mr. Baldock.

"It began in Paris when she went on the wretched French family-exchange holiday," said Mother. "The daughter . . ."

Yes, there, with dear Jeanne Marie, thought Elspeth.

"What a place to get the idea of being a nun," said Mr. Baldock. A mild little man who grew violets, he was Elspeth's godfather. He looked at her as if he had been given a little seedling to cherish and it had grown into a rampant vine. "It seems so unnatural."

The family were more definite.

"She's out of her mind!" said Uncle Arthur.

"I can't believe it," said Aunt Euphrosyne. "Not *Elspeth!* Why, she was always the naughty, disobedient one."

"Euphrosyne is glad, of course," said Mother afterward. "She was always jealous because you were by far the prettiest. I expect she thinks that now Larry will marry Jean."

"Mother, don't, don't say things like that!"

There had been something a little sadistic about the cousins.

"They give the novices all the worst things," said Morna. "You scrub floors and clean lavatories and shovel coal."

"They bully you and humiliate you to find out what you're made of. I have read about it," said Jean, and she added, "If you like one thing more than another, it's taken away."

"Life does that to you as well," said Aunt Bevis. "As you will find out." Elspeth had looked at Aunt Bevis in surprise. Aunt Bevis's cheeks had been quite pink.

The whole neighborhood was roused.

"A well-plucked girl like that!" said Major Fitzgerald. "You should have seen the way she rode that mare of mine in the Dunbar Hunt Cup; not anyone's ride, I can tell you."

Colin Crump had blinked at Elspeth from behind his glasses and something seemed to boil up in him as if he wanted to speak; no one counted Colin, but there was trouble with Larry.

"I thought you were going to marry Larry," said Lady Bannerman in her gruff voice, and she said, as Elspeth knew she would, "I meant to give you my emeralds."

Elspeth was touched and went to kiss her but Lady Bannerman held her off. "You hurt Larry," she said; the harshness in her voice smote Elspeth. "You led him on, you little—vixen!"

"I didn't," Elspeth retorted before she could stop herself. "Don't answer. Be quiet. Submit," Sister Monica had said, but Elspeth was cut. Led Larry on! She might have said, He was there before I led him, but that would have been to hurt him more.

"You're not listening to me," Lady Bannerman had said. "Hard as nails. You young things don't care how you hurt."

They all said that, thought Elspeth, but she had to put on this front of hardness with them, or give way completely.

"Father is twelve years older than I," said Mother. "When he goes, I shall be left alone. If I get ill . . ."

"Mother, why should you get ill? You're awfully strong."

"You're like marble," said Mother, "like marble."

I'm not. I'm not. If only I were! And Elspeth had thought of Jeanne Marie who was already professed, and of Jeanne Marie's father and mother and brother who were so glad. Elspeth had borrowed the old Rover from Father and driven over to Chiswick to find Sister Monica. "Sister, ought I to give it all up?"

"You must ask yourself that," said Sister Monica. All the sisters were the same; when you asked them, implored them, knelt to them, they put you gently back on your own feet. But perhaps Sister Monica had spoken to Mother Dorothea because the Reverend Mother had sent for Elspeth.

"If you have the least doubt, Elspeth . . ."

"It's not my doubts, Reverend Mother, it's theirs. They make me wonder if I'm selfish. Mother, what should I do?"

"You should read the Commandments," said Mother Dorothea.

"The—the Commandments?"

"Yes. They are in the right order."

Now Elspeth understood. Her firmness shone but she cried, "If only I could *explain* to them, make them see. I—I'm so dumb!"

Reverend Mother was silent before she said, "Perhaps you are given no words because there is no need for words. The action speaks, Elspeth," and she asked, "Isn't that the way of the Cross?"

"But mine's such a little thing," said Elspeth, slightly shocked.

"A little thing but it makes you suffer. I think you have to consent to suffer, Elspeth. On the Cross, our Lord did simply what God asked of Him. He . . . used no fireworks," brought out Mother Dorothea after a hesitation.

Fireworks. That was a funny word for Reverend Mother to use, Elspeth had thought. It seemed almost irreverent. "But . . . the sky darkened," pleaded Elspeth. "The veil was—rent."

Reverend Mother was adamant. "That was given Him," she said. "Sometimes things are given; it's not for us to expect or ask. No. He did not use His power." Her voice grew deep with feeling. "They taunted Him and crowned Him with thorns. They told Him to come down off the Cross and prove Himself God and how did He answer? He let them win; hung there and died." Reverend Mother's face became marvelously kind and she put her hand on Elspeth's head. "He didn't ask for vindication but suffered and died—and lived. That proved Him God."

Elspeth had thought about it every day since.

The second of April remained fixed. Mother's invitations went out and were accepted, and the time went quickly till it came to the last day and Elspeth woke now to that sensation of emptiness and space, the windows and doors open and the sun streaming in. On the borderland of her sleep the birds sounded like the convent choir with children's cherubic singing; she opened her eyes and looked along the sun's path that seemed to go from her bed, across the garden and the copse where she used to play with Robert, to the woods and the far sky. The path might, she thought, have been a vision, only it was the sun; the singing might have been cherubs, only it was the birds; and suddenly, feeling completely happy and rational, she sat up in bed.

Aunt Bevis came in with two cups of tea. In her old paisley dressing gown she sat down on the bed. "Well, I must say, it's refreshing to go away without packing."

In the past weeks Elspeth had given all her things away; her books in the white bookcase, the doll she had had since she was five; all her clothes, ornaments, treasures had gone. The gardener's children had some things, the cousins some. "Would Morna like my pink dress?" "Jean, my tennis racket's for you."

As she gave away her things, her happiness mounted—until other people came in. "Mother, would you and Father mind if I give my brushes to Marlowe? I mean—she's been with us so long and she thinks they're lovely."

"You thought them lovely once," said Mother.

"I—I do now. I love them but I won't need them."

I won't need anything, I shall be free. No more fittings and thinking what I shall wear; and new hats and having things shortened and taken in and cleaned. . . . "No, not even packing," said Elspeth aloud. The new life was breaking through the old, but for this last day it had to be an admixture.

After Aunt Bevis had gone, Elspeth dressed. It was the last time she would put on usual clothes; a gray skirt, gray blouse, pale pink cardigan, stockings, gray shoes. At the convent she would take them off and give them to Sister Monica.

"What will you wear?" Morna had asked, curious about every detail. The Order wore a plain black habit "like a rather full black dress but long," said Elspeth, "and black stockings and shoes."

"Wool stockings, flat shoes?" asked Morna.

"Yes," said Elspeth, and Morna made a face. "Go on," said Morna. "Tell some more."

"For six months I'm on probation. Then I am a novice for two years. Then I change the white veil for a black and am a junior for three more. I'm given a black cord with a crucifix."

"What will you wear at night?" asked Jean.

"A nightgown, I suppose. I didn't ask," said Elspeth, suddenly shy.

Aunt Bevis had rounded on Jean. "What do you think she will wear? A black shroud?"

Aunt Bevis had promised to take Elspeth's few remaining things and send them away with her Relief Committee box.

"You had better wait six months, Bevis," Mother had said. "She has six months in which to change her mind."

"Mother, I shan't change my mind."

"No, you won't," said Mother bitingly.

"Mother, if only you could be glad!"

"Glad!" And for the first time she had said to Elspeth, "What *is* it that draws you, Elspeth? What is it you see?"

Elspeth took heart and cast about for words. "It's as if instead of being blown about with life, with all the days and years, you were rooted whole in a whole place."

"But you have a place, a good home," said Mother.

"Yes, but . . ." Elspeth might have said, It's like finding yourself on a map, knowing where you are, and then you know the direction. But she could only twist her hands helplessly.

"It was that horrid little Jeanne Marie," said Mother.

"It wasn't," said Elspeth hotly. Then she tried painfully for the exact truth. "Jeanne Marie was only a little part. Why, Mother, you taught me," said Elspeth with sudden light. "Think of hymns. Don't you remember how you used to play and we sang?"

"Oh, yes," said Mother, softening. "On Sunday evenings."

"There was that one—'Loving Shepherd of Thy Sheep.'"

Tears had filled Mother's eyes. "It was Robert's favorite hymn."

"But think of what it meant," said Elspeth impatiently, "what it said. Didn't you *mean* us to take it seriously?"

Mother's eyes had flickered. Seriously, but not too seriously, Mother would have said, if she were truthful, but she could not very well say that; instead she had said bitterly, "I never thought I should have to suffer by your being good!"

THERE WERE sausages for breakfast. The room smelled of coffee, hot milk, sausages, toast, marmalade, and apples. "What will they give you to eat in that place?" Marlowe had often asked. She was determined that Elspeth should eat one last good breakfast. Morna and Jean, too, often talked about the food.

"You'll have lentils," said Morna, "and fish. Ugh!"

"Bread and water on Fridays," said Jean.

"No, on Fridays you'll fast, and what about Lent?"

"Listen," said Aunt Bevis. "Have you ever seen a nun who didn't look perfectly well fed?" As a matter of fact, they had not.

Elspeth took up Mother's breakfast tray. Mother was sitting up in bed reading her letters. "Why didn't you let Marlowe bring it?"

"I wanted to," said Elspeth. Mother did not say anything sharp, and by her bed, on the table, was Elspeth's miniature Dresden cup and saucer. Elspeth had brought it to her, the last of her things. Never, thought Elspeth, had she loved people so much, so compassionately, as when she gave away her possessions. She bent down and kissed her mother. "Remember I—I love you just as much," she whispered.

Mother sighed. "That's some consolation." They were, in that moment, closer than they had ever been; then Mother put up her hand to Elspeth's cheek; the rings felt cold and hard. She turned over her letters. "Will they let you have your own post?"

Elspeth was startled. "I—I don't know. I don't see why not."

"Those places are full of taboos," said Mother. "I'm not going to write letters and have them pruned by the Sister Superior."

"I suppose they know best for us, Mother." Elspeth said that tactlessly, but she was trying to convince herself. Mother flushed and said something that linked straight with what Mother Dorothea had said, though Mother would have hated to know that.

"Honoring your father and mother is a Commandment." Mother gave a harsh laugh. "But of course it's a long way down the list."

Things are made clear at last, thought Elspeth, horridly clear, but she could not bear it. She said, as she often had said when she had had to go back to school, "Mother, don't. Not on my last day."

After a moment Mother said, in a normal everyday voice, "What are you going to do this morning?" and Elspeth answered, as she had answered a thousand times, "Oh, all the usual things."

But that was not quite true; after she had helped with the work, she planned to go all around the house and garden and into the copse, with Father perhaps, and take Roderick for a last scamper in the woods. I want to see the house for the last time, thought Elspeth, the old white walls, the flagged path, the lavender bushes, the slated roof brooding among the trees. I shall see it again, of course, but I shall be separated, not quite as I am now. She had meant to go all over it, inside as well as out; see it all: the gleam of silver and brass, the polished mahogany; the crystal vases of cut daffodils, the worn red brocade on the seats of the chairs, the Peter Rabbit frieze in the nursery. But there was the lunch party, of course.

Elspeth dusted the drawing room and put out extra ashtrays and then helped Aunt Bevis with the flowers. Mother was even more fussy than usual about the flowers. "I had thought of primroses. What would *you* like on the table, Elspeth? It's your party."

"Primroses would be lovely."

But when they were done, Mother remembered the pudding was white and the whole effect would be pale. "It will look hideous in this dark room; you must get bright primulas." Elspeth picked orange and rust primulas, dark crimson, vivid blue and magenta, and arranged them in a great bowl.

As she finished, the telephone rang and she went to answer it. "Hallo," said Elspeth, and the voice at the other end said, uncertainly, "Is that—you, Elspeth? Could I speak to your mother?" Since they heard that Elspeth was going to be a nun, their friends seemed to doubt that she could answer the telephone; but nuns telephone, thought Elspeth in irritation; they use typewriters and vacuum cleaners and go in airplanes, and drive cars; they are not medieval idiots.

Everybody's nerves were getting overtaxed. Mother went to lie down, even Aunt Bevis was cross. I didn't mean it to be like this, thought Elspeth unhappily; she looked across the lawn, where the daffodils were bending and bobbing along the hedge by the wicket gate that led into the copse; but time was getting short and she had to help Marlowe make the pudding. It was one of Mother's favorites, mushrooms in grass; the mushrooms were meringue shells, lined with chocolate and turned upside down on fondant stems; they stood on a base of chocolate mousse decorated with fronds of angelica grass. While Elspeth was wearily decorating it in the pantry, her father came and stood by her. "Damned flummery," said Father suddenly.

"Dad, I want to come with you and see what they are doing in the copse," said Elspeth miserably.

He jingled his keys and the silver in his pockets. "The heavy timber's gone," he said, "except the big beech. It took two days to get that down. I should like you to have seen it. Fine tree!" Then he added, "Better do as your mother wants."

Father never made an outcry. "Your mother's a very emotional woman," he had often said to his children. "She feels." Her feelings were so strong that no one paid much attention to his. When Robert was killed, Mother collapsed, but Father only seemed more silent, to grow a little smaller, a little balder; he began to have indigestion, but he was as quiet and gentle as before. Daphne was his favorite, but when she married Cyril, and that had meant Hong Kong, he had only been anxious about her settlement. He had had to sell some of the land and take off some of the timber, as he was doing now in the copse; but he never spoke of bills or worries, except perhaps about the bullfinches that had invaded the fruit; he only took more soda mints. Nowadays he always smelled of soda mints.

When Elspeth had made her decision, he had said, "You really want to do this, Kitten?"

"Yes, Dad."

He had looked at her seriously. "You know what it means? The privations, Elspeth, and the—deprivations."

"Yes. Reverend Mother has explained them clearly"—Elspeth might have said, terribly clearly—"to me."

"I shall have to sell out some shares," said Father. Elspeth was smitten and he said, "Don't look worried. If you had married, you would have had to have a settlement," and he put his hand on her shoulder and said what none of them had said, "This calls for something handsome."

Elspeth, flushed and incoherent with gratitude and tears, had only been able to stammer, "If—if I were marrying a prince or a duke . . . Oh, Dad!"

Now he stayed by her, looking at the pudding. "I suppose your mother wants all that," and he sighed and went away.

There was one thing that Elspeth was determined to do that morning and that was to give Roderick a good brush, leave him clean, fresh, and ordered. As soon as she had finished the pudding she took him into the cloakroom.

"From the moment you come to St. Faith's," Sister Monica had said, "you will own nothing in the world. Here we don't say 'my cell,' 'my bed'; everything belongs to the Order and is lent to you. Not even the handkerchief you use is yours. That isn't hard; you will see. It will come quite naturally."

That had been true of most things—except Roderick. Roderick was not anybody's dog, not like most spaniels; his moods were as dark as his coat; sometimes Elspeth would think there was a being shut up in Roderick, a captured beast, who looked out of his eyes and wrung his heart and made him disagreeable. "He doesn't mean to be cross. He needs understanding, Aunt Bevis."

"I shall try to understand him."

"When he gets a stick and puts his paw on it, it means he only wants you to pretend to take it; he's an actor, Aunt Bevis. When he pretends he doesn't want his food, he wants it very much."

Not even Aunt Bevis could have patience for that! If—if I had known what it was like to leave Roderick, perhaps I shouldn't have gone, thought Elspeth, but that's *disgraceful!* What, mind more about a spaniel than Father, more than Mother or Aunt Bevis? But now, as she brushed him, Elspeth saw that it had been dangerous to go near Roderick; she could not trust herself and tears fell on his head and ran, shining, down his black coat.

"Elspeth!" She whipped around. It was Larry Bannerman, arrived early. He was standing in the doorway of the cloakroom, looking at her with an expression that made her turn back quickly to Roderick. Roderick pierced her, but she pierced Larry.

"Why do you let them make you go?" said Larry angrily.

"No one's making me go. I want to go," said Elspeth.

"Then why are you crying?" said Larry.

"Don't you expect me to feel it?" cried Elspeth, angrily too. "Do you think I'm made of stone?"

"Yes," said Larry tersely.

Stone! Marble! Hard as nails! Oh, I'm not. I'm not.

Larry took one step nearer. "Elspeth, Elspeth! My little love!" His voice shook with feeling.

"Larry, *please* go away."

He came nearer. "You don't want to go. It's an idea that's got hold of you."

"No, Larry! No!" said Elspeth breathlessly between the pent-up sobs that shook her. "It's—it's my life."

"Elspeth, I love you." He stood above her, his eyes pleading.

Elspeth did not know what gave her strength to harden her heart. She whispered, "Larry, couldn't you love Jean?"

His eyes blazed and he said, "You're not the only one who can fix their heart on something."

At that Elspeth burst into sobs, crying, "Oh, Larry! Go aw-a-ay!" He turned on his heel and went, his steps ringing on the tiles. Elspeth cried helplessly, her sobs stifled against Roderick's coat.

"Elspeth! El-speth! Lady Bannerman is here, and Co-lin."

Let me run away, thought Elspeth. She felt hunted. I shall go now. I can't stand any more. There were only two hours or so before the calm, the peace and sanctity would ring her around and she would be safe, attained, achieved. It was near, but it seemed far away with these painful, pricking minutes that lay between. She shut her eyes and the tears ran out under her lids.

"Elspeth, your mother's calling you." Elspeth's eyes flew open and her chin went up. It was Larry's voice, but mercifully he did not come in. She heard the doorbell ring, Marlowe's steps in the hall; then Aunt Euphrosyne's voice shrilled with Mother's. She heard Uncle Arthur's boom. Roderick had a passion for Uncle Arthur. Elspeth put him down and he tore out. She heard Uncle Arthur's "*Hullo,* little dog!" and Mother's "Get down, Roddy," and then, "Elspeth! Elspeth!"

"Just getting tidy," called Elspeth in a loud voice and began splashing her face with cold water, trying to cool her red eyes. Then she heard Mother's quick pattering steps in the passage.

"Elspeth, what are you doing in there?"

"I have been brushing Roddy."

"Brushing Roddy! Everyone's here. You know the men want the cloakroom for washing their hands. Come along. It looks so rude."

Elspeth combed her hair; she would have to leave her face and hope no one would notice. "Now for it," she said and dug her nails into her palms. She saw Mother's slight, tall form in the gray pleated dress at the drawing-room door. Mother bent to pick a thread off the carpet; then she went in. Elspeth heard her saying, "Of course, the poor child has had a great deal to do." Elspeth flinched but she had to go in. Swiftly, breathlessly, she crossed the hall and in a moment she found herself taking glasses around on a tray, as she had a hundred times before; but then she saw that everything was different; different in the way their eyes looked at her; the contrast in their voices as they greeted her; they seemed to edge away, draw together against her.

Then she found herself talking to Colin Crump. Colin had always been a joke to them; he had been asked to every party she could remember, because boys were in short supply; first as a little boy with owlish glasses and sticking-out teeth, who stammered, then as a large boy with even thicker glasses and gold braces and a voice that went up and down; and latterly as this young man, Colin Crump, whose teeth were straight, but whose eyes looked owlish still as they glowed into Elspeth's. She and her cousins had always run away from him, tried to skip his dances, particularly Elspeth; now she could not escape. "I—I think this is splendid of you, El-Elspeth," he said confidentially. "I d-don't know how you found the c-courage to st-ick out for your own way, but of c-course you always d-did."

"Did I?" asked Elspeth uncertainly.

"That's what always made me admire you so t-t-tremendously."

She had never known that Colin Crump could do anything so

positive as admire. She felt she should say something, but she could only smile; the smile felt like a faked simper. She thought everyone in the room was watching her; ostensibly they were talking to one another, laughing, but they never took their eyes off her. How strange that Colin Crump should be the only one to understand her. Colin and perhaps Aunt Bevis. She began to feel hotly rebellious under all these looks, these thoughts that were completely out of sympathy with her. At the least little signal I shall break, Elspeth told herself.

She could see through the door, across the hall to the dining room; the table gleamed with its silver, lace, and the colors of the primulas. She had a sudden vision of the refectory at St. Faith's, the empty, clean room, the tables laid out with a bowl and cup for each sister, who brought her own fork and knife and spoon and helped herself from a side table. She remembered the quiet eating while a young novice stood and read aloud. She saw the colors of the flowers under the statue of the Virgin; the flowers in the convent garden came in their seasons for Her; they did not have to match the pudding. A longing swept over Elspeth; she felt she could not wait.

The guests had fallen into three circles. The young ones were in the window—except Larry, who kept by his mother, tossing down drink after drink. Lady Bannerman was silent but her eyes looked from Elspeth to Jean and back to Elspeth. Jean looked pretty in her new suit. "Is it tomato color?" asked Elspeth.

"They call it spring red," said Jean.

"It's bright tomato," said Elspeth derisively and then remembered Sister Monica and said "It suits you." Jean did not hear her. All of them were listening to their elders.

The men were by the fire, talking jerkily. "That damned bullfinch," said Father.

"There's a spring trap now," said Uncle Arthur.

"Herring nets"—that was Major Fitzgerald, and they began to talk about a glut of cider apples and of Major Fitzgerald's Worcester Pearmains. That was harmless, but on the sofa there was the sound of whispers; the women were on the topic of Elspeth. It was Aunt Euphrosyne who whispered. Mrs. Baldock leaned forward to hear; her blue straw with the white bow met Aunt Euphrosyne's feathers;

Mother's head was in between. "Utterly, utterly, selfish," Elspeth heard; and Jean heard, and Morna and Larry, and Colin Crump, the whole room, and Elspeth felt a burning color flood her neck.

"Ribston Pippins," said Father loudly.

"Can't beat 'em," said Major Fitzgerald.

After all it was Aunt Bevis who precipitated it. Aunt Bevis had been worrying over the food. She had argued with Mother that there was not enough chicken; perhaps if she had not been worrying she would not have spoken so bluntly. "How dare you badger the child," said Aunt Bevis. "Yes, how dare you!"

Elspeth began to tremble and Colin turned. To her horror Colin joined in. "You—you shouldn't," said Colin Crump. "D-do you remember?" he said, and the words seemed to swell with the difficulty he had to get them out. "Do you re-member, Mrs. Ersk-kine, when they c-came to C-Christ and said His mother and His brethren were st-standing without . . . ?"

He could not go on, he was as scarlet as Elspeth, but, "Yes," said Aunt Bevis furiously. "Do you remember what Christ said?"

"I remember, Bevis," said Mother, her voice high. "I remember and I have always thought it was heartless. Heartless!"

There was such a silence that if Roderick had shed one hair on the carpet it would have been heard. Every eye was turned on Elspeth. She had never felt so exposed. Sister Monica had told her not to speak but now it was as if, willy-nilly, through Colin and Aunt Bevis she had been given a voice. Then justify it, thought Elspeth in agony. St. Elizabeth found her apron full of roses. St. Teresa had levitation. The wind changed for St. Joan. O God! prayed Elspeth, her lips silent, her hands sticky. If, through the open window, a wind had swept in and filled all the room with sound; if Elspeth could have been lifted up, even two feet from the carpet, without a hand touching her; if roses had fallen or their scent perfumed the room, even one or two roses—but she was left. There was no help, no vindication.

She had to stand there before them all, helpless and silent. She could feel her heart beating hurtfully; for a moment she could only feel the hurt, the smart, and then it became a tiny echo, echoing down two thousand years—no, nineteen hundred and sixty, thought

Elspeth. The drawing room seemed to swim around her; those near voices faded and Mother Dorothea's, calm, authoritative, directed her: "No fireworks." Elspeth's hands unclenched, and as if she had broken the tension, everyone relaxed. The clock ticked, Uncle Arthur cleared his throat, Mother gave a quick little sob and dabbed her eyes. Everywhere conversation broke out.

"Ribston Pippins? Nothing to beat them," said Mr. Baldock.

"They had a nice brown corduroy skirt with a little checked coat, but I chose this," said Jean.

"Have you heard the S-Simmonses are having a band for their d-dance?" asked Colin Crump of Morna.

"From the Crane Club. It will cost a fortune; quite ridiculous!" called Aunt Euphrosyne.

Lady Bannerman passed her drink to Larry. Larry drank it.

"Bevis, it's a quarter past. Don't you think . . . ?" said Mother, but just then Marlowe sounded the gong.

THE OLD CHIEF MSHLANGA
DORIS LESSING/GREAT BRITAIN

THEY WERE GOOD, the years of ranging the bush over her father's farm which, like every white farm, was largely unused, broken only occasionally by small patches of cultivation. In between, nothing but trees, the long sparse grass, thorn and cactus and gully, grass and outcrop and thorn. And a jutting piece of rock which had been thrust up from the warm soil of Africa unimaginable eras of time ago, washed into hollows and whorls by sun and wind that had travelled so many thousands of miles of space and bush, would hold the weight of a small girl whose eyes were sightless for anything but a pale willowed river, a pale gleaming castle—a small girl singing: "Out flew the web and floated wide, the mirror cracked from side to side . . ."

Pushing her way through the green aisles of the mealie stalks, the leaves arching like cathedrals veined with sunlight far overhead, with the packed red earth underfoot, a fine lace of red starred witchweed would summon up a black bent figure croaking premonitions: the Northern witch, bred of cold Northern forests, would stand before her among the mealie fields, and it was the mealie fields that faded and fled, leaving her among the gnarled roots of an oak, snow falling thick and soft and white, the woodcutter's fire glowing red welcome through crowding tree trunks.

A white child, opening its eyes curiously on a sun-suffused landscape, a gaunt and violent landscape, might be supposed to accept it as her own, to take the msasa trees and the thorn trees as familiars, to feel her blood running free and responsive to the swing of the seasons.

This child could not see a msasa tree, or the thorn, for what they were. Her books held tales of alien fairies, her rivers ran slow and peaceful, and she knew the shape of the leaves of an ash or an oak, the names of the little creatures that lived in English streams, when the words "the veld" meant strangeness, though she could remember nothing else.

Because of this, for many years, it was the veld that seemed unreal; the sun was a foreign sun, and the wind spoke a strange language.

The black people on the farm were as remote as the trees and the rocks. They were an amorphous black mass, mingling and thinning and massing like tadpoles, faceless, who existed merely to serve, to say "Yes, Baas," take their money and go. They changed season by season, moving from one farm to the next, according to their outlandish needs, which one did not have to understand, coming from perhaps hundreds of miles North or East, passing on after a few months—where? Perhaps even as far away as the fabled gold mines of Johannesburg, where the pay was so much better than the few shillings a month and the double handful of mealie meal twice a day which they earned in that part of Africa.

The child was taught to take them for granted: the servants in the house would come running a hundred yards to pick up a book if she dropped it. She was called "Nkosikaas"—Chieftainess, even by the black children her own age.

Later, when the farm grew too small to hold her curiosity, she carried a gun in the crook of her arm and wandered miles a day, from vlei to vlei, from *kopje* to *kopje*, accompanied by two dogs: the dogs and the gun were an armor against fear. Because of them she never felt fear.

If a native came into sight along the kaffir paths half a mile away, the dogs would flush him up a tree as if he were a bird. If he expostulated (in his uncouth language which was by itself ridiculous) that was cheek. If one was in a good mood, it could be a matter for laughter. Otherwise one passed on, hardly glancing at the angry man in the tree.

On the rare occasions when white children met together they could amuse themselves by hailing a passing native in order to make a buffoon of him; they could set the dogs on him and watch him run; they could tease a small black child as if he were a puppy—save that they would not throw stones and sticks at a dog without a sense of guilt.

Later still, certain questions presented themselves in the child's mind; and because the answers were not easy to accept, they were silenced by an even greater arrogance of manner.

It was even impossible to think of the black people who worked about the house as friends, for if she talked to one of them, her mother would come running anxiously: "Come away; you mustn't talk to natives."

It was this instilled consciousness of danger, of something unpleasant, that made it easy to laugh out loud, crudely, if a servant made a mistake in his English or if he failed to understand an order—there is a certain kind of laughter that is fear, afraid of itself.

One evening, when I was about fourteen, I was walking down the side of a mealie field that had been newly ploughed, so that the great red clods showed fresh and tumbling to the vlei beyond, like a choppy red sea; it was that hushed and listening hour, when the birds send long sad calls from tree to tree, and all the colors of earth and sky and leaf are deep and golden. I had my rifle in the curve of my arm, and the dogs were at my heels.

In front of me, perhaps a couple of hundred yards away, a group of three Africans came into sight around the side of a big antheap. I whistled the dogs close in to my skirts and let the gun swing in my hand, and advanced, waiting for them to move aside, off the path, in respect for my passing. But they came on steadily, and the dogs looked up at me for the command to chase. I was angry. It was "cheek" for a native not to stand off a path, the moment he caught sight of you.

In front walked an old man, stooping his weight on to a stick, his hair grizzled white, a dark red blanket slung over his shoulders like a cloak. Behind him came two young men, carrying bundles of pots, assegais, hatchets.

The group was not a usual one. They were not natives seeking work. These had an air of dignity, of quietly following their own purpose. It was the dignity that checked my tongue. I walked quietly on, talking softly to the growling dogs, till I was ten paces away. Then the old man stopped, drawing his blanket close.

"Morning, Nkosikaas," he said, using the customary greeting for any time of the day.

"Good morning," I said. "Where are you going?" My voice was a little truculent.

The old man spoke in his own language, then one of the young men stepped forward politely and said in careful English: "My Chief travels to see his brothers beyond the river."

A Chief! I thought, understanding the pride that made the old man stand before me like an equal—more than an equal, for he showed courtesy, and I showed none.

The old man spoke again, wearing dignity like an inherited garment, still standing ten paces off, flanked by his entourage, not looking at me (that would have been rude) but directing his eyes somewhere over my head at the trees.

"You are the little Nkosikaas from the farm of Baas Jordan?"

"That's right," I said.

"Perhaps your father does not remember," said the interpreter for the old man, "but there was an affair with some goats. I remember seeing you when you were . . ." The young man held his hand at knee level and smiled.

We all smiled.

"What is your name?" I asked.

"This is Chief Mshlanga," said the young man.

"I will tell my father that I met you," I said.

The old man said: "My greetings to your father, little Nkosikaas."

"Good morning," I said politely, finding the politeness difficult, from lack of use.

"Morning, little Nkosikaas," said the old man, and stood aside to let me pass.

I went by, my gun hanging awkwardly, the dogs sniffing and growling, cheated of their favorite game of chasing natives like animals.

Not long afterwards I read in an old explorer's book the phrase: "Chief Mshlanga's country." It went like this: "Our destination was Chief Mshlanga's country, to the north of the river; and it was our desire to ask his permission to prospect for gold in his territory."

The phrase "ask his permission" was so extraordinary to a white child, brought up to consider all natives as things to use, that it revived those questions, which could not be suppressed: they fermented slowly in my mind.

On another occasion one of those old prospectors who still move over Africa looking for neglected reefs, with their hammers and tents, and pans for sifting gold from crushed rock, came to the farm and, in talking of the old days, used that phrase again: "This was the Old Chief's country," he said. "It stretched from those mountains over there way back to the river, hundreds of miles of country." That was his name for our district: "The Old Chief's Country"; he did not use our name for it—a new phrase which held no implication of usurped ownership.

As I read more books about the time when this part of Africa was opened up, not much more than fifty years before, I found Old Chief Mshlanga had been a famous man, known to all the explorers and prospectors. But then he had been young; or maybe it was his father or uncle they spoke of—I never found out.

During that year I met him several times in the part of the farm that was traversed by natives moving over the country. I learned that the path up the side of the big red field where the birds sang was the recognized highway for migrants. Perhaps I even haunted it in the hope of meeting him: being greeted by him, the exchange of courtesies, seemed to answer the questions that troubled me.

Soon I carried a gun in a different spirit; I used it for shooting food and not to give me confidence. And now the dogs learned better manners. When I saw a native approaching, we offered and took greetings; and slowly that other landscape in my mind faded, and my feet struck directly on the African soil, and I saw the shapes of tree and hill clearly, and the black people moved back, as it were, out of my life: it was as if I stood aside to watch a slow intimate dance of landscape and men, a very old dance, whose steps I could not learn.

But I thought: this is my heritage, too; I was bred here; it is my country as well as the black man's country; and there is plenty of room for all of us, without elbowing each other off the pavements and roads.

It seemed it was only necessary to let free that respect I felt when I was talking with old Chief Mshlanga, to let both black and white people meet gently, with tolerance for each other's differences: it seemed quite easy.

Then, one day, something new happened. Working in our house as servants were always three natives: cook, houseboy, garden boy. They used to change as the farm natives changed: staying for a few months, then moving on to a new job, or back home to their kraals. They were thought of as "good" or "bad" natives; which meant: how did they behave as servants? Were they lazy, efficient, obedient, or disrespectful? If the family felt good-humored, the phrase was: "What can you expect from raw black savages?" If we were angry, we said: "These damned niggers, we would be much better off without them."

One day, a white policeman was on his rounds of the district, and he said laughingly: "Did you know you have an important man in your kitchen?"

"What!" exclaimed my mother sharply. "What do you mean?"

"A Chief's son." The policeman seemed amused. "He'll boss the tribe when the old man dies."

"He'd better not put on a Chief's son act with me," said my mother.

When the policeman left, we looked with different eyes at our cook: he was a good worker, but he drank too much at week-ends—that was how we knew him.

He was a tall youth, with very black skin, like black polished metal, his tightly-growing black hair parted white man's fashion at one side, with a metal comb from the store stuck into it; very polite, very distant, very quick to obey an order. Now that it had been pointed out, we said: "Of course, you can see. Blood always tells."

My mother became strict with him now she knew about his birth and prospects. Sometimes, when she lost her temper, she would say: "You aren't the Chief yet, you know." And he would answer her very quietly, his eyes on the ground: "Yes, Nkosikaas."

One afternoon he asked for a whole day off, instead of the customary half-day, to go home next Sunday.

"How can you go home in one day?"

"It will take me half an hour on my bicycle," he explained.

I watched the direction he took; and the next day I went off to look for this kraal; I understood he must be Chief Mshlanga's successor: there was no other kraal near enough our farm.

Beyond our boundaries on that side the country was new to me. I followed unfamiliar paths past *kopjes* that till now had been part of the jagged horizon, hazed with distance. This was Government land, which had never been cultivated by white men; at first I could not understand why it was that it appeared, in merely crossing the boundary, I had entered a completely fresh type of landscape. It was a wide green valley, where a small river sparkled, and vivid water-birds darted over the rushes. The grass was thick and soft to my calves, the trees stood tall and shapely.

I was used to our farm, whose hundreds of acres of harsh eroded soil bore trees that had been cut for the mine furnaces and had grown thin and twisted, where the cattle had dragged the grass flat, leaving innumerable criss-crossing trails that deepened each season into gullies, under the force of the rains.

This country had been left untouched, save for prospectors whose picks had struck a few sparks from the surface of the rocks as they wandered by; and for migrant natives whose passing had left, perhaps, a charred patch on the trunk of a tree where their evening fire had nestled.

It was very silent: a hot morning with pigeons cooing throatily, the midday shadows lying dense and thick with clear yellow spaces of sunlight between and in all that wide green park-like valley, not a human soul but myself.

I was listening to the quick regular tapping of a woodpecker when slowly a chill feeling seemed to grow up from the small of my back to my shoulders, in a constricting spasm like a shudder, and at the roots of my hair a tingling sensation began and ran down over the surface of my flesh, leaving me goosefleshed and cold, though I was damp with sweat. Fever? I thought; then uneasily, turned to look over my shoulder; and realized suddenly that this was fear. It was extraordinary, even humiliating. It was a new fear. For all the years I had walked by myself over this country I had never known a moment's uneasiness; in the beginning because I had been supported by a gun and the dogs, then because I had learnt an easy friendliness for the Africans I might encounter.

I had read of this feeling, how the bigness and silence of Africa, under the ancient sun, grows dense and takes shape in the mind, till even the birds seem to call menacingly, and a deadly spirit comes out of the trees and the rocks. You move warily, as if your very passing disturbs something old and evil, something dark and big and angry that might suddenly rear and strike from behind. You look at groves of entwined trees, and picture the animals that might be lurking there; you look at the river running slowly, dropping from level to level through the vlei, spreading into pools where at night the bucks come to drink, and the crocodiles rise and drag them by their soft noses into underwater caves. Fear possessed me. I found I was turning round and round, because of that shapeless menace behind me that might reach out and take me; I kept glancing at the files of *kopjes* which, seen from a different angle, seemed to change with every step so that even known landmarks, like a big mountain that had sentinelled my world since I first became conscious of it, showed an unfamiliar sunlit valley among its foothills. I did not know where I was. I was lost. Panic seized me. I found I was spinning round and round, staring anxiously at this tree and that, peering up at the sun which appeared to have moved into an eastern slant, shedding the sad yellow light of sunset. Hours must have passed! I looked at my watch and found that this state of meaningless terror had lasted perhaps ten minutes.

The point was that it was meaningless. I was not ten miles from home: I had only to take my way back along the valley to find myself at the fence; away among the foothills of the *kopjes* gleamed the roof of a neighbor's house, and a couple of hours' walking would reach it. This was the sort of fear that contracts the flesh of a dog at night and sets him howling at the full moon. It had nothing to do with what I thought or felt; and I was more disturbed by the fact that I could become its victim than of the physical sensation itself: I walked steadily on, quietened, in a divided mind, watching my own pricking nerves and apprehensive glances from side to side with a disgusted amusement. Deliberately I set myself to think of this village I was seeking, and what I should do when I entered it—if I could find it, which was doubtful, since I was walking aimlessly and it might be anywhere in the hundreds of thousands of acres of bush that stretched about me. With my mind on that village, I realized that a new sensation was added to the fear: loneliness. Now such a terror of isolation invaded me that I could hardly walk; and if it were not that I came over the crest of a small rise and saw a village below me, I should have turned and gone home. It was a cluster of thatched huts in a clearing among trees. There were neat patches of mealies and pumpkins and millet, and cattle grazed under some trees at a distance. Fowls scratched among the huts, dogs lay sleeping on the grass, and goats friezed a *kopje* that jutted up beyond a tributary of the river lying like an enclosing arm round the village.

As I came close I saw the huts were lovingly decorated with patterns of yellow and red and ochre mud on the walls; and the thatch was tied in place with plaits of straw.

This was not at all like our farm compound, a dirty and neglected place, a temporary home for migrants who had no roots in it.

And now I did not know what to do next. I called a small black boy, who was sitting on a lot playing a stringed gourd, quite naked except for the strings of blue beads round his neck, and said: "Tell the Chief I am here." The child stuck his thumb in his mouth and stared shyly back at me.

For minutes I shifted my feet on the edge of what seemed a deserted village, till at last the child scuttled off, and then some women came. They were draped in bright cloths, with brass glinting in their ears and on their arms. They also stared, silently; then turned to chatter among themselves.

I said again: "Can I see Chief Mshlanga?" I saw they caught the name; they did not understand what I wanted. I did not understand myself.

At last I walked through them and came past the huts and saw a clearing under a big shady tree, where a dozen old men sat cross-legged on the ground, talking. Chief Mshlanga was leaning back against the tree, holding a gourd in his hand, from which he had been drinking. When he saw me, not a muscle of his face moved, and I could see he was not pleased: perhaps he was afflicted with my own shyness, due to being unable to find the right forms of courtesy for the occasion. To meet me, on our own farm, was one thing; but I should not have come here. What had I expected? I could not join them socially: the thing was unheard of. Bad enough that I, a white girl, should be walking the veld alone as a white man might: and in this part of the bush where only Government officials had the right to move.

Again I stood, smiling foolishly, while behind me stood the groups of brightly-clad, chattering women, their faces alert with curiosity and interest, and in front of me sat the old men, with old lined faces, their eyes guarded, aloof. It was a village of ancients and children and women. Even the two young men who kneeled beside the Chief were not those I had seen with him previously: the young men were all away working on the white men's farms and mines, and the Chief must depend on relatives who were temporarily on holiday for his attendants.

"The small white Nkosikaas is far from home," remarked the old man at last.

"Yes," I agreed, "it is far." I wanted to say: "I have come to pay you a friendly visit, Chief Mshlanga." I could not say it. I might now be feeling an urgent helpless desire to get to know these men and women as people, to be accepted by them as a friend, but the truth was I had set out in a spirit of curiosity: I had wanted to see the village that one day our cook, the reserved and obedient young man who got drunk on Sundays, would one day rule over.

"The child of Nkosi Jordan is welcome," said Chief Mshlanga.

"Thank you," I said, and could think of nothing more to say. There was a silence, while the flies rose and began to buzz around my head; and the wind shook a little in the thick green tree that spread its branches over the old men.

"Good morning," I said at last. "I have to return now to my home."

"Morning, little Nkosikaas," said Chief Mshlanga.

I walked away from the indifferent village, over the rise past the staring amber-eyed goats, down through the tall stately trees into the great rich green valley where the river meandered and the pigeons cooed tales of plenty and the woodpecker tapped softly.

The fear had gone; the loneliness had set into stiff-necked stoicism; there was now a queer hostility in the landscape, a cold, hard, sullen indomitability that walked with me, as strong as a wall, as intangible as smoke; it seemed to say to me: you walk here as a destroyer. I went slowly homewards, with an empty heart: I had learned that if one cannot call a country to heel like a dog, neither can one dismiss the past with a smile in an easy gush of feeling, saying: I could not help it, I am also a victim.

I only saw Chief Mshlanga once again.

One night my father's big red land was trampled down by small sharp hooves, and it was discovered that the culprits were goats from Chief Mshlanga's kraal. This had happened once before, years ago.

My father confiscated all the goats. Then he sent a message to the old Chief that if he wanted them he would have to pay for the damage.

He arrived at our house at the time of sunset one evening, looking very old and bent now, walking stiffly under his regally-draped blanket, leaning on a big stick. My father sat himself down in his big chair below the steps of the house; the old man squatted carefully on the ground before him, flanked by his two young men.

The palaver was long and painful, because of the bad English of the young man who interpreted, and because my father could not speak dialect, but only kitchen kaffir.

From my father's point of view, at least two hundred pounds' worth of damage had been done to the crop. He knew he could not get the money from the old man. He felt he was entitled to keep the goats. As for the old Chief, he kept repeating angrily: "Twenty goats! My people cannot lose twenty goats! We are not rich, like the Nkosi Jordan, to lose twenty goats at once."

My father did not think of himself as rich, but rather as very poor. He spoke quickly and angrily in return, saying that the damage done meant a great deal to him, and that he was entitled to the goats.

At last it grew so heated that the cook, the Chief's son, was called from the kitchen to be interpreter, and now my father spoke fluently in English, and our cook translated rapidly so that the old man could understand how very angry my father was. The young man spoke without emotion, in a mechanical way, his eyes lowered, but showing how he felt his position by a hostile uncomfortable set of the shoulders.

It was now in the late sunset, the sky a welter of colors, the birds singing their last songs, and the cattle, lowing peacefully, moving past us towards their sheds for the night. It was the hour when Africa is most beautiful; and here was this pathetic, ugly scene, doing no one any good.

At last my father stated finally: "I'm not going to argue about it. I am keeping the goats."

The old Chief flashed back in his own language: "That means that my people will go hungry when the dry season comes."

"Go to the police, then," said my father, and looked triumphant. There was, of course, no more to be said.

The old man sat silent, his head bent, his hands dangling helplessly over his withered knees. Then he rose, the young men helping him, and he stood facing my father. He spoke once again, very stiffly; and turned away and went home to his village.

"What did he say?" asked my father of the young man, who laughed uncomfortably and would not meet his eyes.

"What did he say?" insisted my father.

Our cook stood straight and silent, his brows knotted together. Then he spoke. "My father says: All this land, this land you call yours, is his land, and belongs to our people."

Having made this statement, he walked off into the bush after his father, and we did not see him again.

Our next cook was a migrant from Nyasaland, with no expectations of greatness.

Next time the policeman came on his rounds he was told this story. He remarked: "That kraal has no right to be there; it should have been moved long ago. I don't know why no one has done anything about it. I'll have a chat with the Native Commissioner next week. I'm going over for tennis on Sunday, anyway."

Some time later we heard that Chief Mshlanga and his people had been moved two hundred miles east, to a proper Native Reserve; the Government land was going to be opened up for white settlement soon.

I went to see the village again, about a year afterwards. There was nothing there. Mounds of red mud, where the huts had been, had long swathes of rotting thatch over them, veined with the red galleries of the white ants. The pumpkin vines rioted everywhere, over the bushes, up the lower branches of trees so that the great golden balls rolled underfoot and dangled overhead: it was a festival of pumpkins. The bushes were crowding up, the new grass sprang vivid green.

The settler lucky enough to be allotted the lush warm valley (if he chose to cultivate this particular section) would find, suddenly, in the middle of a mealie field, the plants were growing fifteen feet tall, the weight of the cobs dragging at the stalks, and wonder what unsuspected vein of richness he had struck.

WHO CARES?

SANTHA RAMA RAU / INDIA

Santha Rama Rau

THE ONLY THING, really, that Anand and I had in common was that both of us had been to college in America. Not that we saw much of each other during those four years abroad—he was studying business management or some such thing in Boston and I was taking the usual liberal arts course at Wellesley, and on the rare occasions we met, we hadn't much to say—but when we got back to Bombay, the sense of dislocation we shared was a bond. In our parents' generation that whole malaise was covered by the comprehensive phrase "England-returned," which held good even if you had been studying in Munich or Edinburgh, both popular with Indian students in those days. The term was used as a qualification (for jobs and marriages) and as an explanation of the familiar problems of readjustment. Even after the war, in a particular kind of newspaper, you could find, in the personal columns, advertisements like this: "Wanted: young, fair, educated girl, high caste essential, for England-returned boy. Send photograph." The point is that her family would have to demonstrate her desirability—but "England-returned" would tell them almost everything they needed to know about the boy: that his family was rich enough to send him abroad for his education, that his chances for a good job were better than most, that his wife could probably expect an unorthodox household in which she might be asked to serve meat at meals, entertain foreigners, and even have liquor on the premises. She would also know that it would be a desirable marriage.

The phrase "England-returned" was the kind of Indianism that used to amuse the British very much when it turned up on a job application. To Indians, naturally, it had a serious and precise meaning. But in the course of a generation that became increasingly sensitive to ridicule, it had fallen out of fashion, and by the time Anand and I returned to Bombay we had to find our own description for our uneasy state. We spoke of how our ideas were too advanced for Bombay, or how enterprise could never flourish in India within the deadly grip of the family system, or we made ill-digested psychological comments on the effects of acceptance as a way of life. What we meant, of course, was that we were suffering from the England-returned blues. Mine was a milder case than Anand's, partly because my parents were "liberal"—not orthodox Hindus, that is—and, after fifteen years of wandering about the world in the diplomatic service, were prepared to accept with equanimity and even a certain doubtful approval the idea of my getting a job on a magazine in Bombay. Partly, things were easier for me because I had been through the worst of my readjustments six years before, when I had returned from ten years in English boarding schools.

Anand's England-returned misery was more virulent—his family was orthodox, his mother spoke no English and distrusted foreign ways, he had been educated entirely in Bombay until he had gone to America for postgraduate courses, and his father, a successful contractor in Bombay, insisted that Anand, as the only son, enter the family business.

Our families lived just a few houses from each other, but led very different lives. Among the members of our generation, however, the differences were fading, and Anand and I belonged to the same set, although we had never particularly liked each other. It was a moment of boredom and a fragmentary reminder that both of us had been in America that brought us together.

It was during the monsoon, I remember, and the rain had pelted down all morning. About noon it cleared up, and I decided to spend my lunch hour shopping. I had started walking toward the center of downtown Bombay when the rain began again, ominously gentle at first, then quickly changing into a typical monsoon downpour. I ducked into the first doorway I saw, and ran slap into Anand, a rather short, slender young man, dressed with a certain nattiness. It was the building in which his father's firm had its offices, and Anand stood there staring glumly at the streaming street and scurrying pedestrians. We greeted each other with reserve. Neither was in the mood for a cheery exchange of news. We continued to gaze at the rain, at the tangle of traffic, the wet and shiny cars moving slowly through the dirty water on the road.

At last, without much interest, Anand said, "And what are you up to these days?"

"I *was* going to go shopping," I said coolly, "but I don't see how I can, in this."

"Damn rain," he muttered. I could hardly hear him over the sound of the water rushing along the gutters.

I said, "Mm," and, as a return of politeness, added, "And you? What are you doing?"

"Heaven knows," he said, with a world of depression in his voice. "Working, I suppose." After a pause, he said, "Well, look, since you can't shop and I can't get to the garage for my car, suppose we nip around the corner for a bite of lunch."

"Okay," I said, not knowing quite how to refuse.

Anand looked full at me for the first time and began to smile. "Okay," he repeated. "Haven't heard *that* lately."

We raced recklessly down the street, splashing through puddles and dodging people's umbrellas, until we arrived, soaked and laughing, at the nearest restaurant. It was no more than a snack bar, really, with a counter and stools on one side of the small room and a few tables on the other. We stood between them, breathless, mopping our faces ineffectually with handkerchiefs and slicking back wet hair, still laughing with the silly exhilaration such moments produce. We decided to sit at a table, because Anand said the hard little cakes with pink icing, neatly piled on the counter, looked too unappetizing to be faced all through lunch.

Our explosive entrance had made the other customers turn to stare; but as we settled down at our table, the young men at the counter—clerks, probably, from nearby offices, self-effacing and pathetically tidy in their white drill trousers and white shirts (the inescapable look of Indian clerks)—turned their attention back to their cups of milky coffee and their curry puffs. The Sikhs at the next table, brightly turbaned and expansive of manner, resumed their cheerful conversation. The two Anglo-Indian typists in flowered dresses returned to their whispers and giggles and soda pop.

When the waiter brought us the menu, we discovered that the restaurant was called the Laxmi and Gold Medal Café. This sent Anand into a fresh spasm of laughter, and while we waited for our sandwiches and coffee, he invented equally unlikely combinations for restaurant names—the Venus and Sun Yat-sen Coffee Shoppe, the Cadillac and Red Devil Ice-Cream Parlor, and so on—not very clever, but by that time we were in a good mood and prepared to be amused by almost anything.

At some point, I remember, one of us said, "Well, how do you *really* feel about Bombay?" and the other replied, "Let's face it. Bombay *is* utter hell," and we were launched on the first of our interminable conversations about ourselves, our surroundings, our families, our gloomy predictions for the future. We had a lovely time.

A couple of days later Anand called my office to invite me to lunch again. "I'll make up for the horrors of the Laxmi and Gold Medal," he said. "We'll go to the Taj, which is at least air-conditioned."

He had reserved a table by the windows in the dining room of the Taj Mahal Hotel, where we could sit and look out over the gray, forbidding water of the harbor and watch the massed monsoon clouds above the scattered islands. Cool against the steamy rain outside, we drank a bottle of wine, ate the local *pâté de foie gras*, and felt sorry for ourselves.

Anand said, "I can't think why my father bothered to send me to America, since he doesn't seem interested in anything I learned there."

"Oh, I know, I know," I said, longing to talk about my own concerns.

"Can you believe it, the whole business is run *exactly* the way it was fifty years ago?"

"Of course I can. I mean, take the magazine—"

"I mean, everything done by vague verbal arrangements. Nothing properly filed and accounted for. And such enormous reliance on pull, and influence, and knowing someone in the government who will arrange licenses and import permits and whatever."

"Well, it's a miracle to me that we ever get an issue of the magazine out, considering that none of the typesetters speaks English, and they have to make up the forms in a language they don't know, mirrorwise and by hand."

"But at least you don't have to deal with the family as well. The *amount* of deadwood in the form of aged great-uncles, dimwitted second cousins, who *have* to be employed!"

"Can't you suggest they be pensioned off?"

"Don't think I haven't. My father just smiles and says I'll settle down soon. What's the use?"

Our discussions nearly always ended with one or the other of us saying, with exaggerated weariness, "Well, so it goes. Back to the salt mines now." I never added that I enjoyed my job.

That day we didn't realize until we were on the point of leaving the Taj how many people were lunching in the big dining room whom we knew. On our way out, we smiled and nodded at a number of people and stopped at several tables to exchange greetings. With rising irritation, both of us were aware of the carefully unexpressed curiosity behind the pleasant formalities of speech.

Anand and I sauntered in silence down the wide, shallow staircase of the hotel. And it was only when we reached the road that he exploded. "Damn them," he said. "The prying old cats!"

"It was the wine," I suggested. "Even people who have been abroad a lot don't drink wine at lunchtime."

"So? What's it to them?"

"Well, Dissolute Foreign Ways, and besides you're what they call a catch, so it's only natural that they wonder."

Anand frowned as we crossed the road to where his car was parked against the seawall. He opened the door for me and then climbed in behind the steering wheel. He didn't start the car for a moment, but sat with his hands on the wheel and his head turned away from me, looking at the threatening light of the early afternoon, which would darken into rain any minute. Suddenly he clenched his fingers and said, "Well, the devil with them. Let them talk, if they have nothing better to do."

"Yes. Anyway, who cares?" I said, hoping it didn't sound as though *I* did.

We lunched at the Taj several times after that, but on each occasion a bit more defiantly, a bit more conscious of the appraising looks, always knowing we were the only "unattacheds" lunching together. The others were businessmen, or married couples doing duty entertaining, which, for some reason, they couldn't do at home, or ladies in groups, or foreigners.

Bombay is a big city, but in its life it is more like a conglomeration of villages. In our set, for instance, everyone knew everyone else at least by sight. So, of course, everyone knew that Anand and I lunched together a couple of times a week, and certainly our families must have been told.

My parents never mentioned the matter to me, though there was a certain wariness in their manner whenever Anand's name came up in conversation. If Anand's mother ever lectured him on getting talked about, he evidently didn't think it worth repeating. Of them all, I daresay she was the most troubled, being orthodox, wanting a good, conservative marriage for her only son, being bewildered by what must have appeared to her—it seems astonishing in retrospect— sophistication.

Occasionally Anand would take me home to tea after our offices had closed. I think he did this out of an unadmitted consideration for his mother, to set her mind at rest about the company he was keeping, to show her that I was not a Fast Girl even if I did work on a magazine. I don't know how much I reassured her, with my short hair and lipstick, no *tika* in the middle of my forehead. But she always greeted me politely, bringing her hands together in a *namaskar*, and gave me canny looks when she thought I wasn't noticing. We couldn't even speak to each other, since we came from different communities and she spoke only Gujarati, while my language was Hindi. She would always wait with us in the drawing room until one of the servants brought the tea; then she would lift her comfortable figure out of her chair, nod to me, and leave us alone. We were always conscious of her presence in the next room beyond the curtained archway, and every now and then we would hear her teacup clink on the saucer. Our conversation, even if she didn't understand it, was bound to be pretty stilted.

Perhaps it was this silent pressure, perhaps it was only a sort of restlessness that made Anand and me leave the usual haunts of our set and look for more obscure restaurants for our lunch dates. Liberal as we considered ourselves, I suppose I was beginning to lose my England-returned brashness and intractability. I was not, however, prepared to stop meeting Anand for lunch. I liked him and waited with some impatience for his telephone calls, the rather pleasant voice saying things like "Hello? Is this the career girl?" (This was one of Anand's favorite phrases of defiance—if you came from a respectable family that could support you, you weren't supposed to work for money.) Sometimes he would say, "This is underground agent 507. Are you a fellow resistance fighter?"

In any case, I would laugh and say, "Yes," and he would suggest that we try some Chinese food, or eat dry curried chicken at a certain Irani shop, or, if it was a rainless day, go to Chowpatty beach and eat odds and ends of the delicious, highly spiced mixtures the vendors there concoct. By tacit agreement, he no longer picked me up in his car. Instead, we either met at the corner taxi rank or arrived separately at our rendezvous.

Once, when we were driving to Colaba, the southernmost point of the island, Anand suddenly leaned forward and asked the taxi driver to stop. On an otherwise uninspired-looking street, lined with dingy middle-class houses, he had seen a sign that said "Joe's Place." Anand was entranced, and certainly the sign did look exotic among the bungalows and hibiscus. Joe's Place—named by some homesick American soldier, who had found his way there during the war—quickly became our favorite restaurant. We felt it was our discovery, for one thing, and then it had a Goan cook, which meant that you could order beef. Most Hindus will not allow beef on the premises. It is, as a result, the cheapest meat in Bombay, and we ate a lot of it at Joe's Place.

The proprietor, whom Anand insisted on calling Joe, even though he was a fat and jolly Indian, soon got used to seeing us almost every other day. We couldn't imagine how he made any money, since there never seemed to be anyone there besides Anand and me. Joe waited on table, so there weren't even waiters. Anand said that it was probably a front for black-market activities and that you could expect anything of a man who ran a Joe's Place in Bombay. We came to feel so much at home at Joe's that we bought him a checkered tablecloth, to lend the place a bit of class, and he would spread it ceremoniously over the corner table, invariably pointing out that it had been laundered since our last meal. We kept a bottle of gin at Joe's and taught him to make fresh-lime gimlets with it, so that we could have a cocktail before lunch. He hadn't a license to sell liquor, so he always shook our cocktails in an opaque bottle labeled Stone Ginger, in case anyone came in.

We would sit at our table between the windows, glancing out occasionally at the patch of straggly garden, the jasmine bush, the desultory traffic, and talk. How we talked! On and on. Sometimes it was "In the States, did you ever—" or "Do you remember—" kind of talk. Sometimes it was about incidents at home or in our offices. We talked a lot about Them—a flexible term, including any relatives or friends we considered old-fashioned, interfering, lacking in under-standing. All through the sticky postmonsoon months, into the cooler, brilliant days of early winter, we talked. It seems a miracle to me now that we could have found so much to say about the details of our reasonably pedestrian lives.

If we'd been a bit older or more observant, we would certainly have known that this state of affairs couldn't last much longer. I was dimly aware that every day of life in Bombay relaxed our antagonism a tiny bit and blurred the outlines of our American years. However, I never guessed what Anand's family's counterattack to his England-returned discontent would be. Anand's mother was a direct, uncom-plicated woman, and in her view there was one obvious way to cure the whole disease.

It was at Joe's Place that Anand announced the arrival of Janaki. I had got there early, I remember, and was sitting at our table when Anand came in. He always had a certain tension in his walk, but that day it seemed more pronounced. He held his narrow shoulders stiffly and carried an air of trouble, so I asked him at once whether anything was the matter.

"Matter?" he asked sharply. "Why should anything be the matter?"

"Well, I don't know. You just look funny."

"Well, I don't feel funny," he said, deliberately misunderstanding.

Joe brought him his gimlet and inquired rather despairingly if we wanted steak *again*.

Anand waved a hand at him impatiently and said, "Later. We'll decide later." Then he looked at me with a portentous frown. "Do you *know* what They've gone and done *now?*" he said. "They've invited a cousin—a *distant* cousin—to stay."

This didn't seem to me any great disaster. Cousins, invited or not, were eternally coming to visit. Any relatives had the right to turn up whenever it was convenient for them and stay as long as they liked. But since he seemed so distressed, I asked carefully, "And I suppose you'll be expected to fit him into the firm in some capacity?"

"Her," Anand said. "It's a girl."

"A *girl?* Is *she* going to work in the business?" This was really cataclysmic news.

"Oh, of *course* not. Can't you see what They're up to? They're trying to arrange a marriage for me."

I could think of nothing to say except an unconvincing "Surely not."

He went on without paying any attention. "I daresay They think They're being subtle. Throwing us together, you know, so that my incomprehensible, *foreign*"—he emphasized the word bitterly— "preference for making up my own mind about these things will not be offended. We are to grow imperceptibly fond of each other. Oh, I see the whole plot."

"You must be imagining it all."

"She arrived last night. They didn't even tell me she was coming."

"But people are forever dropping in."

"I know. But she was *invited*. She told me so."

"Poor Anand." I was sorry for him, and angry on his behalf. There had never been any romantic exchanges between Anand and me, so the girl didn't represent any personal threat; but I honestly thought that a matter of principle was involved. We had so often agreed that the system of arranged marriages was the ultimate insult to one's rights as a human being, the final, insupportable interference of domineering families. I tried to think of something comforting to say, but could only produce, feebly, "Well, all you have to do is sit it out."

"And watch her doing little chores around the house? Making herself quietly indispensable?" He added with a sour smile, "As the years roll by. Do you suppose we will grow old gracefully together?"

"Oh, don't be such a fool," I said, laughing. "She'll have to go, sooner or later."

"But will I live that long?" He seemed to be cheering up.

"It's rather unfair to the poor thing," I said, thinking for the first time of the girl. "I mean, if they've got her hopes up."

"Now, don't start sympathizing with *her*. The only way to finish the thing once and for all—to make my position clear—is to marry someone else immediately. I suppose you wouldn't consider marrying me, would you?"

"Heavens, no," I said, startled. "I don't think you need to be as drastic as that."

"Well, perhaps not. We'll see."

At last I thought to ask, "What's she called?"

"Janaki."

"Pretty name."

"It makes me vomit."

I COULD hardly wait for our next lunch date, and when we met a couple of days later at Joe's Place I started questioning Anand eagerly. "Well, how are things? How are you making out with Janaki?"

Anand seemed remote, a bit bored with the subject. "Joe!" he called. "More ice, for Pete's sake. Gimlets aren't supposed to be *mulled*." He tapped his fingers on the table in a familiar, nervous movement. "He'll never learn," he said resignedly. Then, after a pause, "Janaki? Oh, she's all right, I suppose. A minor pest."

"Is she being *terribly* sweet to you?"

"Oh, you know. I will say this for her, she manages to be pretty unobtrusive."

"Oh." I was obscurely disappointed.

"It's just knowing she's always *there* that's so infuriating."

"It would drive me crazy."

In a voice that was suddenly cross, he said, "She's so *womanly.*"

"Hovers about, you mean?"

"Not that, so much, but I can see her *hoping* I'll eat a good dinner or have had a good day at the office, or some damn thing."

"It sounds rather flattering."

"I daresay that's the strategy. It's pathetic, really, how little They know me if They think she's the sort of girl I'd want to marry."

"What sort of girl *would* you want to marry?"

"Heaven knows," Anand said in a hopeless voice. "Someone quite different, anyway. I knew one once."

"Was there a girl in America?" I asked with interest.

"Isn't there always a girl in America? A sort of tradition. In our fathers' time, it used to be the daughter of the landlady somewhere in Earl's Court. Usually blond, always accommodating."

"And yours?"

"Accommodating. But several cuts above the landlady's daughter. She was a senior in college. And she had quite a nice family, if you can stand families, rather timid, but determined to believe that a Good Home Environment was a girl's best protection. I don't think they would have objected if we'd got married."

"Why didn't you marry her, then?"

"Oh, I don't know. I guess I couldn't see her being an Indian daughter-in-law living in a Bombay family—and what a mess that would have made. Hurt feelings and recriminations and disappointment all around. I'm not sentimental about her," he said earnestly, as if it were an important point. "I mean, I know she wasn't particularly good-looking or anything, but I had a separate identity in her mind. I wasn't just somebody's son, or someone to marry, or someone with good business connections."

"And all that is what you are to Janaki?"

"I suppose so. What else could I be?"

As we left Joe's Place after lunch, he said, "I think you'd better come to tea to meet her. Would you like to?"

"I was hoping you'd ask me."

"Okay, then. Tomorrow?"

Full of excitement, the next day, I met Anand and drove home with him. "Is your mother going to be cross about your asking me?"

"Why should she be cross? You've been to tea with us before."

"Oh, don't be so dense," I said, thinking, Poor girl, it's going to be very frustrating for her if he insists on treating her as a casual cousin come for a holiday. "Does your mother tactfully leave you alone with her for tea?"

"Never. The two of them chatter about domestic details. It's really very boring."

To me it was far from boring. For one thing, Anand's mother was more cordial to me than she had been on previous visits, and I wondered whether she could already be so sure of the success of her plan that I was no longer a danger. And then there was the suspense of waiting to see what Janaki would be like.

She came in with the servant who carried the tea tray, holding back the curtain of the dining-room archway so that he could manage more easily. A plump, graceful girl with a very pretty face and a tentative, vulnerable smile, which she seemed ready to cancel at once if you weren't going to smile with her. I saw, instantly, that she was any mother-in-law's ideal—quiet, obedient, helpful. Her hair was drawn back into the conventional knot at the nape of her neck; she had a *tika* on her forehead, wore no makeup except for the faintest touch of lipstick, and even that, I decided, was probably a new experiment for her, a concession to Anand's Westernized tastes.

She spoke mostly to Anand's mother, in Gujarati, and I noticed that she had already assumed some of the duties of a hostess. She poured the tea and asked, in clear, lilting English, whether I took milk and sugar, handed around the plates of Indian savories and sweets.

After the first mouthful, I remarked formally, "This is delicious."

Anand's mother caught the tone, even if she didn't understand the words, and said something in Gujarati to Anand.

He translated, without much interest, "Janaki made them."

Janaki, in embarrassment, wiped her mouth on her napkin, and then gazed in surprise and alarm at the pink smear on the linen.

"How clever you are," I said to Janaki. "I wish I could cook."

"It is very easy to learn," she replied diffidently.

"There never seems to be any time for it."

Entirely without sarcasm or envy she said, "That is true for someone like you who leads such a busy and interesting life."

I felt ashamed of myself, for no reason I could quite put my finger on.

We continued to talk banalities, and Janaki kept up her end admirably, managing to seem interested in the most ordinary comments and still keeping a watchful eye out to see that cups and plates were filled. The conversation gradually fell entirely to Janaki and me, because Anand retreated into a sulky silence. I remember thinking that one couldn't really blame him. It must have been maddening to have to face this sweet and vapid politeness every day after work. At last he jumped up and said abruptly that he had some papers to go through. I left soon after.

Janaki saw me to the front door and, with an unexpected spontaneity, put her hand on my arm. "Please come to tea again," she said. "I mean, if you are not too occupied. I should so much like it. I have no friends in Bombay."

"I'd be delighted, and you must come to tea with me."

"Oh, no, thank you very much. Perhaps later on, but I must learn the ways of this house first. You see that, don't you?"

I walked home, wondering at her mixture of nervousness and confidence, at the fact that she already felt certain she had a permanent place in that house.

At our next lunch date, it was Anand who asked the eager questions. "Well? What did you think of her?"

And I replied noncommittally, "She seemed very pleasant."

"You sound like my mother. She says, 'A good-natured girl. You should count yourself fortunate.' I suppose she asked you to be her friend?"

"How did you know?"

"She's not as stupid as she looks. She said the same to me. 'Will you not allow us to be friendly, Anand?'" He attempted a saccharin, unconvincing falsetto. He frowned. "The thin end of the wedge, don't you see? It would be funny if it weren't so sad."

"Well, at least she's very good-looking," I said defensively.

"She's too fat."

"I think it rather suits her."

"A strong point in her favor, my mother says, to make up for my puniness." Anand was sensitive about his height. He said, in a touchy voice, daring one to sympathize with him, "Eugenically very sound. Strong, healthy girl like Janaki married to a weakling like me, and we have a chance of strong, healthy children that take after her. The children, you see, are the whole point of this stratagem. I'm an only son and must produce some. My mother has a rather simple approach to these things."

"You must admit," I said rather uncomfortably, "that she'd make a very good mother."

"Not a doubt in the world. She's a natural for the part of the Great Earth Mother. But I rather resent being viewed in such an agricultural light."

IN THE WEEKS that followed, Janaki dominated our conversation at lunchtime, and I had tea with them quite frequently. Sometimes, if Anand was kept late at his office or had to attend a board meeting, Janaki and I would have tea alone, and she would ask hundreds of questions about America, trying, I thought, to build up a picture of Anand's life there and the background that seemed to influence him so much. She claimed to be uniformly enthusiastic about everything American, and for me it was rather fun, because it made me feel so superior in experience.

She would question me, sometimes openly and sometimes indirectly, about Anand's tastes and preferences. We had a long session, I remember, about her looks. Should she wear makeup? Should she cut her hair? What about her clothes? I told her she was fine the way she was, but she insisted, "Has he *never* said anything? He must have made *some* remark?"

"Well," I said reluctantly, "he did once mention that he thought you were just a fraction on the chubby side."

Without a trace of rancor, Janaki said, "I will quickly become thin."

"Heavens! Don't take the remark so seriously."

"It is nothing," Janaki assured me. "One need only avoid rice and *ghi*." She did, too. I noticed the difference in a couple of weeks.

When Anand was there, the atmosphere was much more strained. From the frigid politeness of his early days with Janaki, his manner gradually changed to irritation, which expressed itself in angry silence and later in a kind of undercover teasing sometimes laced with malice. For instance, he would greet her with something like, "What have you been up to today? Hemstitching the sheets? Crocheting for the hope chest?" and Janaki would look puzzled and smile, as though she had missed the point of a clever joke. Actually, she was a beautiful needlewoman and did a good deal of exquisitely neat embroidery on all kinds of things—antimacassars, doilies, face towels—infallibly choosing hideous designs of women, in enormous crinolines, watering the flowers in an English garden, or bunches of roses with ribbons streaming from them. Once Janaki answered Anand's inquiry quite seriously with an account of her day, the household jobs she had done, the women who had called on his mother and had been served coffee, and even produced the embroidery she had been working on.

"Wonderfully appropriate for India, don't you think?" Anand remarked to me with rather labored irony. One couldn't help disliking him in this role of tormentor. The fact was, of course, that *I* was getting imperceptibly fonder of Janaki as his impatience with her grew more overt. There was, to me, both gallantry and an appealing innocence in her undaunted conviction that everything would turn out all right. What I didn't recognize was the solid realism behind her attitude. I started to suspect the calculation in her nature one day when Anand had been particularly difficult. He had insisted on talking about books she hadn't read and addressing remarks to her he knew she couldn't answer.

Janaki said nothing for a long time and then admitted, with a becoming lack of pretension, "I'm afraid I read only the stories in the *Illustrated Weekly*. But, Anand, if you would bring me some books you think good, I would read them."

"I'll see if I can find the time," he replied in a surly voice.

When Janaki showed me to the door that evening, I said in considerable exasperation, "Why do you put up with it? He needn't be so disagreeable when he talks to you."

"It is natural that there should be difficulties at first. After his life in America, there are bound to be resentments here."

"Well, I think you are altogether too forbearing. I wouldn't stand it for a second." Privately, I had begun to think she must, after all, be stupid.

Then Janaki said, "What would you do?"

"Leave, of course. Go back." And at that moment I realized what she meant. Go back to what? To another betrothal arranged by her elders? Learning to please some other man? Here, at least, she liked her future mother-in-law.

"And besides," she said, "I know that really he is kind."

In the end, Janaki turned out to be the wisest of us all, and I have often thought how lucky it was that she didn't follow my advice then. Not that Anand capitulated all at once. He remained irritable and carping; but gradually he became enmeshed in that most satisfactory of roles, a reluctant Pygmalion.

I noticed it first one day when he finished his lunch rather hurriedly and said, as we were going back to our offices, "That girl's conversation is driving me nuts. I think I really had better buy her some books. As long as I'm stuck with her company," he added awkwardly.

We parted at the bookshop, and in later conversations I learned that Janaki was doing her homework with diligence and pleasure.

From then on things moved fairly rapidly. I began to anticipate Anand's frequent suggestions that we spend part of the lunch hour shopping—usually rather ungraciously expressed: "We've got to get that girl into some less provincial-looking saris." "That girl listens to nothing but film music. I really must get her some decent classical stuff."

All the same, at home he continued to be offhand or overbearing with her. She remained calm and accepting, a willing pupil who knew that her stupidity was a great trial to her teacher. Still, there wasn't a doubt in my mind about the change of attitude going on in Anand, and I was certain that the Pygmalion story could have only one ending.

Anand's parents were evidently equally confident of the outcome, for one day at tea he announced with exuberance that his father was going to send him to New York on a business trip. He was pleased, he said, because it meant that at last he was to be trusted with some real responsibility.

I said, "And it will be such wonderful fun to be back in America."

"Oh, yes. That, too, naturally. But I don't know how much time I'll have for the bright lights and parties." He had moved so smoothly into the correct businessman's viewpoint that I wanted to laugh.

We became so absorbed in discussing the details of the trip that it came as quite a shock when Janaki suddenly spoke in a flat, decisive voice. "I, too, am leaving. I am going back to my home." Dead silence for a moment. "Tomorrow," she said.

"But *why*—" I began.

"It is my decision," she said.

Anand didn't say anything, just stood up, with all his bright, important planning gone, and walked out of the room. We waited to hear his study door slam.

Then my affection for Janaki (and, of course, curiosity) made me ask, "But why *now*, just when things are going so well?"

"It was your advice, don't you remember?"

"But things were different then."

"Yes." She nodded as though we both recognized some particular truth.

At the time I thought she believed herself defeated. I was surprised and concerned that what seemed so plain to me should remain obscure to her. "Listen," I said cautiously, "don't you see that he—that in spite of everything, he has fallen in love with you?"

I don't know quite what I had expected her response to be—a radiant smile, perhaps, or even a sense of triumph. I hadn't expected her to glare at me as though I were an enemy and say, "Oh, love. I don't want him to *love* me. I want him to marry me."

"It's different for him," I said, as persuasively as I could. "For him it is important."

She looked at me shrewdly, making up her mind about something. "You are sure?" she asked.

"Absolutely sure."

Her voice was hard and impatient. "Love, what books you read, whether you like music, your 'taste'—whatever that may mean. As if all that has anything to do with marriage."

"Well," I said ineffectually.

How can one make the idea of romantic love attractive to someone who wants only a home, a husband, and children? Even if nothing could be done about that, I thought I knew the reason for her sudden despair. The renewing of Anand's American experiences must have seemed to her an overwhelming menace. I tried to reassure her, reminded her that Anand would be gone only a matter of weeks, that he would miss her, that America would look quite different to him now.

But she wouldn't listen, and she kept repeating, "I must pack my things and leave the house tomorrow."

I thought, Poor Janaki. I can see that the tedious business of starting all over again on the unraveling of Anand's England-returned tangles might well seem to be too much to face. It didn't occur to me that I might equally have thought, Clever Janaki, the only one of us who knows exactly what she wants. Leave the house? She would have slit her throat first.

When I think of it, I can't help wondering at the extent of my naïveté then. The fact is that women—or perhaps I mean just the women of a certain kind of world, Janaki's world—have inherited, through bitter centuries, a ruthless sense of self-preservation. It still seems to me ghastly that they should need it; but it would be silly to deny that, in most places on earth, they still do. That cool, subtle determination to find her security and hang on to it, that all's-fair attitude—not in love, which she discounted, but in war, for it *was* war, the gaining or losing of a kingdom—was really no more than the world deserved from Janaki. As in war, victory, conquest, success, call it what you will, was the only virtue. And, of course, the really absurd thing was that nobody would have been more appalled than Janaki if you had called her a feminist.

As it was, I heard with anxiety Anand on the phone the next day, saying, "Let's lunch. I want to talk to you. Joe's Place? One o'clock?"

I was certain that Janaki had gone home, with only the indignities of a few new clothes and a lot of tiresome talk to remember.

As soon as I saw him, I knew I was wrong. He had the conventionally sheepish look that makes the announcing of good news quite pointless. He said, "An eventful evening, wasn't it?"

"Yes, it was, rather."

There was a long pause while he looked embarrassed and then he said all in a rush, "Look, this is going to seem ridiculous. I mean— well, Janaki and I are going to be married."

"You couldn't do a more sensible thing," I said, much relieved.

He looked startled. "Sensible? Perhaps it seems that way to you. Actually, we're in love with each other."

"With *each other?*" I echoed incredulously, and then regretted it.

"I knew it would seem peculiar to you. I daresay you've thought I hated her all this time." He smiled at me in a rather superior way. "I thought so myself for a while. And Janaki, as you well imagine, had every reason to think so. And I must say it certainly took a lot of courage on her part. I mean, when you think—"

"You'd better start at the beginning," I said, suddenly feeling depressed.

"Okay. I heard you leave yesterday, and then I heard Janaki come into the hall—you know that timid way she has of walking—and stand outside my study door. I was in quite a state; but I daresay that I wouldn't have done anything about anything if she hadn't—I mean, if someone hadn't taken the initiative."

"Yes," I said, knowing what was coming but unable to shake off my gloom. "She came to explain why she was going home."

"She said—you see, she isn't the passive girl you think—she told me that quite against her plans or anything she's expected, she'd—I know this will seem silly—but she'd fallen in love with me."

"I see. And that accounted for her behavior. Trying all the time to please you, I mean."

"Well, yes. Then I realized that—"

"All your resentment and bad manners were just that—" I wanted to hurry him through the story.

"Well, yes."

"Well, congratulations," I said uneasily.

"It's funny, isn't it," he said in a confident voice, "that Their plans should have worked out—but so differently. I don't suppose They'll ever understand."

"It wouldn't be worth trying to explain."

"Heavens, no. Look, I'm taking Janaki out to lunch tomorrow. Will you join us?"

"Oh, no, surely—"

"She asked particularly that you come. She likes you very much, you know, and besides, she doesn't feel quite comfortable going out without a chaperon."

"In *that* case—" I said, with a nastiness lost on Anand. And all the time I was thinking, Have we all been made use of? A sympathetic mother-in-law, a man you can flatter, a gullible friend from whom you can learn background and fighting conditions, with whom you can check tactics and their effects. Now that she has won, she must have nothing but contempt for all of us. But simultaneously I was wondering, Is she, after all, really in love? It was a state she didn't know how to cope with, and she could hope only to use the weapon she knew, an ability to please or try to please. Why should she, or how could she, tell me all that herself—a realm of which she was so unsure, which was so far out of her experience?

Now that I have met so many Janakis of the world, I think I know which explanation was right.

"So we'll meet," Anand was saying, "at the Taj, if that's all right with you?"

He had reserved a table by the windows. Janaki was a bit late, to be sure—she explained breathlessly—that we would be there before her, because it would have been agony to sit alone.

We ordered from the Indian menu, and Anand said, with only a fleeting, questioning glance at me, "No wine, I think. There really isn't any wine at all that goes with Indian food, is there?"

OVER THE RIVER AND
THROUGH THE WOOD

JOHN O'HARA / UNITED STATES

M R. WINFIELD'S hat and coat and bag were in the hall of his flat, and when the man downstairs phoned to tell him the car was waiting, he was all ready. He went downstairs and said hello to Robert, the giant Negro chauffeur, and handed Robert the bag and followed him out to the car. For the first time he knew that he and his granddaughter were not to make the trip alone, for there were two girls with Sheila, and she introduced them: "Grandfather, I'd like to have you meet my friends. This is Helen Wales, and this is Kay Farnsworth. My grandfather, Mr. Winfield." The names meant nothing to Mr. Winfield. What did mean something was that he was going to have to sit on the strapontin, or else sit outside with Robert, which was no good. Not that Robert wasn't all right, as chauffeurs go, but Robert was wearing a raccoon coat, and Mr. Winfield had no raccoon coat. So it was sit outside and freeze, or sit on the little seat inside.

Apparently it made no difference to Sheila. He got inside, and when he closed the door behind him, she said, "I wonder what's keeping Robert?"

"He's strapping my bag on that thing in the back," said Mr. Winfield. Sheila obviously was not pleased by the delay, but in a minute or two they got under way, and Mr. Winfield rather admired the way Sheila carried on her conversation with her two friends and at the same time routed and rerouted Robert so that they were out of the city in no time. To Mr. Winfield it was pleasant and a little like old times to have the direction and the driving done for you. Not that he ever drove himself any more, but when he hired a car, he always had to tell the driver just where to turn and where to go straight. Sheila knew.

The girls were of an age, and the people they talked about were referred to by first names only. Ted, Bob, Gwen, Jean, Mary, Liz. Listening with some care, Mr. Winfield discovered that school acquaintances and boys whom they knew slightly were mentioned by their last names.

Sitting where he was, he could not watch the girls' faces, but he formed his opinions of the Misses Wales and Farnsworth. Miss Wales supplied every other word when Sheila was talking. She was smallest of the three girls, and the peppy kind. Miss Farnsworth looked out of the window most of the time, and said hardly anything. Mr. Winfield could see more of her face, and he found himself asking, "I wonder if that child really likes anybody." Well, that was one way to be. Make the world show *you*. You could get away with it, too, if you were as attractive as Miss Farnsworth. The miles streamed by and the weather got colder, and Mr. Winfield listened and soon understood that he was not expected to contribute to the conversation.

"We stop here," said Sheila. It was Danbury, and they came to a halt in front of the old hotel. "Wouldn't you like to stop here, Grandfather?" He understood then that his daughter had told Sheila to stop here; obediently and with no dignity he got out. When he returned to the car, the three girls were finishing their cigarettes, and as he climbed back in the car, he noticed how Miss Farnsworth had been looking at him and continued to look at him, almost as though she were making a point of not helping him—although he wanted no help. He wasn't really an *old* man, an *old man.* Sixty-five.

The interior of the car was filled with cigarette smoke, and Miss Farnsworth asked Mr. Winfield if he'd mind opening a window. He opened it. Then Sheila said one window didn't make any difference; open both windows, just long enough to let the smoke get out. "My! That air feels good," said Miss Wales. Then: "But what about you, Mr. Winfield? You're in a terrible draught there." He replied, for the first use of his voice thus far, that he did not mind. And at that moment the girls thought they saw a car belonging to a boy they knew, and they were in Sheffield, just over the Massachusetts line, before Miss Farnsworth realized that the windows were open and creating a terrible draught. She realized it when the robe slipped off her leg, and she asked Mr. Winfield if he would mind closing the window. But he was unable to get the crank started; his hands were so cold there was no strength in them. "We'll be there soon," said Sheila. Nevertheless, she closed the windows, not even acknowledging Mr. Winfield's shamed apologies.

He had to be first out of the car when they arrived at the house in Lenox, and it was then that he regretted having chosen the strapontin. He started to get out of the car, but when his feet touched the ground, the hard-packed frozen cinders of the driveway flew up at him. His knees had no strength in them, and he stayed there on the ground for a second or two, trying to smile it off. Helpful Robert—almost too helpful; Mr. Winfield wasn't that old—jumped out of the car and put his hands in Mr. Winfield's armpits. The girls were frightened, but it seemed to Mr. Winfield that they kept looking toward the library window, as though they were afraid Sheila's mother would be there and blaming them for his fall. If they only knew . . .

"You go on in, Grandfather, if you're sure you're all right," said Sheila. "I have to tell Robert about the bags."

"I'm all right," said Mr. Winfield. He went in, and hung up his coat and hat in the clothes closet under the stairs. A telephone was there, and in front of the telephone a yellow card of numbers frequently called. Mr. Winfield recognized only a few of the names, but he guessed there was an altogether different crowd of people coming up here these days. Fifteen years makes a difference, even in a place like Lenox. Yes, it was fifteen years since he had been up here in the summertime. These trips, these annual trips for Thanksgiving, you couldn't tell anything about the character of the place from these trips. You never saw anybody but your own family and, like today, their guests.

He went out to the darkened hall and Ula, the maid, jumped in fright. "Ugh. Oh. It's you, Mr. Winfield. You like to scare me."

"Hello, Ula. Glad to see you're still holding the fort. Where's Mrs. Day?"

"Upstairs, I think . . . Here she is now," said Ula.

His daughter came down the steps; her hand on the banister was all he could see at first. "Is that you, Father? I thought I heard the car."

"Hello, Mary," he said. At the foot of the stairs they went through the travesty of a kiss that both knew so well. He leaned forward so that his head was above her shoulder. To Ula, a good Catholic, it must have looked like the kiss of peace. *"Pax tibi,"* Mr. Winfield felt like saying, but he said, "Where have you—"

"Father! You're freezing!" Mrs. Day tried very hard to keep the vexation out of her tone.

"It was a cold ride," he said. "This time of year. We had snow flurries between Danbury and Sheffield, but the girls enjoyed it."

"You go right upstairs and have a bath, and I'll send up—what would you like? Tea? Chocolate? Coffee?"

He was amused. The obvious thing would be to offer him a drink, and it was so apparent that she was talking fast to avoid that. "I think cocoa would be fine, but you'd better have a real drink for Sheila and her friends."

"Now why do you take that tone, Father? You could have a drink if you wanted it, but you're on the wagon, aren't you?"

"Still on it. Up there with the driver."

"Well, and besides, liquor doesn't warm you up the same way something hot does. I'll send up some chocolate. I've put you in your old room, of course. You'll have to share the bathroom with one of Sheila's friends, but that's the best I could do. Sheila wasn't even sure she was coming till the very last minute."

"I'll be all right. It sounds like—I didn't bring evening clothes."

"We're not dressing."

He went upstairs. His room, the room itself, was just about the same; but the furniture was rearranged, his favorite chair not where he liked it best, but it was a good house; you could tell it was being lived in, *this year*, today, tomorrow. Little touches, ashtrays, flowers. It seemed young and white, cool with a warm breath, comfortable— and absolutely strange to him and, more especially, he to it. Whatever of the past this house had held, it was gone now. He sat in the chair and lit a cigarette. In a wave, in a lump, in a gust, the old thoughts came to him. Most of the year they were in the back of his mind, but up here Mr. Winfield held a sort of annual review of far-off, but never-out-of-sight regrets. This house, it used to be his until Mary's husband bought it. A good price, and in 1921 he certainly needed the money. He needed everything, and today he had an income from the money he got for this house, and that was about all. He remembered the day Mary's husband came to him and said, "Mr. Winfield, I hate to have to be the one to do this, but Mary—Mary doesn't—well, she thinks you weren't very nice to Mrs. Winfield. I don't know anything about it myself, of course, but that's what Mary thinks. I expected, naturally, I thought you'd come and live with us now that Mrs. Winfield has died, but—well, the point is, I know you've lost a lot of money, and also I happen to know about Mrs. Winfield's will. So I'm prepared to make you a pretty good offer, strictly legitimate based on current values, for the house in Lenox. I'll pay the delinquent taxes myself and give you a hundred and fifty thousand dollars for the house and grounds. That ought to be enough to pay off your debts and give you a fairly decent income. And, uh, I happen to have a friend who knows Mr. Harding quite well. Fact, he sees the President informally one night a week, and I know he'd be only too glad, if you were interested . . ."

He remembered that had tempted him. Harding might have fixed it so he could go to London, where Enid Walter was. But even then it was too late. Enid had gone back to London because he didn't have the guts to divorce his wife, and the reason he wouldn't divorce his wife was that he wanted to "protect" Mary, and Mary's standing, and Mary's husband's standing, and Mary's little daughter's standing; and now he was "protecting" them all over again, by selling his house so that he would not become a family charge—protecting the very same people from the embarrassment of a poor relation. "You can have the house," he told Day. "It's worth that much, but no more, and I'm grateful to you for not offering me more. About a political job, I think I might like to go to California this winter. I have some friends out there I haven't seen in years." He had known that that was exactly what Mary and her husband wanted, so he'd gone.

There was a knock on the door. It was Ula with a tray. "Why

two cups, Ula?" he said.

"Oh. Di put two cups? So I did. I'm just so used to putting two cups." She had left the door open behind her, and as she arranged the things on the marble-topped table he saw Sheila and the two girls, standing and moving in the hall.

"This is your room, Farnie," said Sheila. "You're down this way, Helen. Remember what I told you, Farnie. Come on, Helen."

"Thank you, Ula," he said. She went out and closed the door, and he stood for a moment, contemplating the chocolate, then poured out a cup and drank it. It made him a little thirsty, but it was good and warming, and Mary was right; it was better than a drink. He poured out another cup and nibbled on a biscuit. He had an idea: Miss Farnsworth might like some. He admired that girl. She had spunk. He bet she knew what she wanted, or seemed to, and no matter how unimportant were the things she wanted, they were the things she wanted, and not someone else. She could damn well thank the Lord, too, that she was young enough to have a whack at whatever she wanted, and not have to wait the way he had. That girl would make up her mind about a man or a fortune or a career, and by God she would attain whatever it was. If she found, as she surely would find, that nothing ever was enough, she'd at least find it out in time; and early disillusionment carried a compensatory philosophical attitude, which in a hard girl like this one would take nothing from her charm. Mr. Winfield felt her charm, and began regarding her as the most interesting person he had met in many dull years. It would be fun to talk to her, to sound her out and see how far she had progressed toward, say, ambition or disillusionment. It would be fun to do, and it would be just plain nice of him, as former master of this house, to invite her to have a cup of cocoa with him. Good cocoa.

He made his choice between going out in the hall and knocking on her door, and knocking on her door to the bathroom. He decided on the second procedure because he didn't want anyone to see him knocking on her door. So he entered the bathroom and tapped on the door that led to her room. "In a minute," he thought he heard her say. But then he knew he must have been wrong. It sounded more like "Come in." He hated people who knocked on doors and had to be told two or three times to come in, and it would make a bad impression if he started the friendship that way.

He opened the door, and immediately he saw how right he had been in thinking she had said "In a minute." For Miss Farnsworth was standing in the middle of the room, standing there all but nude. Mr. Winfield instantly knew that this was the end of any worth-while life he had left. There was cold murder in the girl's eyes, and loathing and contempt and the promise of the thought his name forever would evoke. She spoke to him: "Get out of here you dirty old man."

He returned to his room and his chair. Slowly he took a cigarette out of his case, and did not light it. He did everything slowly. There was all the time in the world, too much of it, for him. He knew it would be hours before he would begin to hate himself. For a while he would just sit there and plan his own terror.

DENTAL OR MENTAL, I SAY IT'S SPINACH

S. J. PERELMAN / UNITED STATES

A FEW days ago, under the heading, MAN LEAPS OUT WINDOW AS DENTIST GETS FORCEPS, The New York Times reported the unusual case of a man who leaped out a window as the dentist got the forceps. Briefly, the circumstances were these. A war worker in Staten Island tottered into a dental parlor and, indicating an aching molar, moaned, "It's killing me. You've got to pull it out." The dentist grinned like a Cheshire cat—The New York Times neglected to say so, but a Cheshire cat who was present at the time grinned like a dentist—and reached for his instruments. "There was a leap and a crash," continues the account. "The astonished dentist saw his patient spring through the closed window and drop ten feet to the sidewalk, where he lay dazed." The casualty was subsequently treated at a near-by hospital for abrasion and shock by Drs. J. G. Abrazian and Walter Shock, and then, like a worm, crept back to the dentist, apologized and offered to pay for the damage. On one point, however, he remained curiously adamant. He still has his tooth.

As a party who recently spent a whole morning with his knees braced against a dentist's chest, whimpering "Don't—don't—I'll do anything, but don't drill!" I am probably the only man in America equipped to sympathize with the poor devil. Ever since Nature presented me at birth with a set of thirty-two flawless little pearls of assorted sizes, I never once relaxed my vigilant stewardship of same. From the age of six onward, I constantly polished the enamel with peanut brittle, massaged the incisors twice daily with lollipops, and chewed taffy and chocolate-covered caramels faithfully to exercise the gums. As for consulting a dentist regularly, my punctuality practically amounted to a fetish. Every twelve years I would drop whatever I was doing and allow wild Caucasian ponies to drag me to a reputable orthodontist. I guess you might say I was hipped on the subject of dental care.

When, therefore, I inadvertently stubbed a tooth on a submerged cherry in an old-fashioned last week and my toupee ricocheted off the ceiling, I felt both dismayed and betrayed. By eleven the next morning, I was seated in the antechamber of one Russell Pipgrass, D.D.S., limply holding a copy of the National Geographic upside down and pretending to be absorbed in Magyar folkways. Through the door communicating with the arena throbbed a thin, blood-curdling whine like a circular saw biting into a green plank. Suddenly an ear-splitting shriek rose above it, receding into a choked gurgle. I nonchalantly tapped out my cigarette in my eardrum and leaned over to the nurse, a Medusa type with serpents writhing out from under her prim white coif.

"Ah—er—pardon me," I observed swallowing a bit of emery paper I had been chewing. "Did you hear anything just then?"

"Why, no," she replied, primly tucking back a snake under her cap. "What do you mean?"

"A—a kind of a scratchy sound," I faltered.

"Oh, that," she sniffed carelessly. "Impacted wisdom tooth. We have to go in through the skull for those, you know." Murmuring some inconsequential excuse about lunching with a man in Sandusky, Ohio, I dropped to the floor and was creeping toward the corridor on all fours when Doctor Pipgrass emerged, rubbing his hands. "Well, here's an unexpected windfall!" he cackled, his eyes gleaming with cupidity. "Look out—slam the door on him!" Before I could dodge past, he pinioned me in a hammerlock and bore me, kicking and struggling, into his web. He was trying to wrestle me into the chair when the nurse raced in, brandishing a heavy glass ash tray.

"Here, hit him with this!" she panted.

"No, no, we mustn't bruise him," muttered Pipgrass. "Their relatives always ask a lot of silly questions." They finally made me comfy by strapping me into the chair with half a dozen towels, tilted my feet up and pried open my teeth with a spoon. "Now then, where are his X-rays?" demanded the doctor.

"We haven't any," returned the nurse. "This is the first time he's been here."

"Well, bring me any X-rays," her employer barked. "What difference does it make? When you've seen one tooth, you've seen them all." He held up the X-rays against the light and examined them critically. "Well, friend, you're in a peck of trouble," he said at length. "You may as well know the worst. These are the teeth of an eighty-year-old man. You got here just in time." Plucking a horrendous nozzle from the rack, he shot compressed air down my gullet that sent me into a strangled paroxysm, and peered curiously at my inlays.

"Who put those in, a steamfitter?" he sneered. "You ought to be arrested for walking around with a job like that." He turned abruptly at the rustle of greenbacks and glared at his nurse. "See here, Miss Smedley, how many times have I told you not to count the patient's money in front of him? Take the wallet outside and go through it there." She nodded shamefacedly and slunk out. "That's the kind of thing that creates a bad impression on the layman," growled Doctor Pipgrass, poking at my tongue with a sharp stick. "Now what seems to be the trouble in there?"

"Ong ong ong," I wheezed.

"H'm'm'm, a cleft palate," he mused. "Just as I feared. And you've got between four and five thousand cavities. While we're at it, I think we'd better tear out those lowers with a jackhammer and put in some nice expensive crowns. Excuse me." He quickly dialed a telephone number. "Is that you, Irene?" he asked. "Russell. Listen, on that white mink coat we were talking about at breakfast—go right ahead, I've changed my mind. . . . No, I'll tell you later. He's filthy with it."

"Look, doctor," I said with a casual yawn. "It's nothing really—just a funny tickling sensation in that rear tooth. I'll be back Tuesday—a year from Tuesday."

"Yes, yes," he interrupted, patting me reassuringly. "Don't be afraid now; this won't hurt a bit." With a slow, cunning smile, he produced from behind his back a hypodermic of the type used on brewery horses and, distending my lip, plunged it into the gum. The tip of my nose instantly froze, and my tongue took on the proportions of a bolt of flannel. I tried to cry out, but my larynx was out to lunch. Seizing the opportunity, Pipgrass snatched up his drill, took a firm purchase on my hair and teed off. A mixture of sensation, roughly comparable to being alternately stilettoed and inflated with a bicycle pump, over-came me; two thin wisps of smoke curled upward slowly from my ears. Fortunately, I had been schooled from boyhood to withstand pain without flinching, and beyond an occasional scream that rattled the windows, I bore myself with the stoicism of a red man. Scarcely ninety minutes later, Doctor Pipgrass thrust aside the drill, wiped his streaming forehead and shook the mass of protoplasm before him.

"Well, we're in the homestretch," he announced brightly, extracting a rubber sheet from a drawer. "We'll put this dam on you and fill her in a jiffy. You don't get claustrophobia, do you?"

"Wh-what's that?" I squeaked.

"Fear of being buried alive," he explained smoothly. "Kind of a stifling feeling. Your heart starts racing and you think you're going crazy. Pure imagination, of course." He pinned the rubber sheet over my face, slipped it over the tooth and left me alone with my thoughts. In less time than it takes to relate, I was a graduate member, *summa cum laude*, of the Claustrophobia Club. My face had turned a stunning shade of green, my heart was going like Big Ben, and a set of castanets in my knees was playing the Malagueña. Summoning my last reserves of strength, I cast off my bonds and catapulted through the anteroom to freedom. I left Pipgrass a fleece-lined overcoat worth sixty-eight dollars, but he's welcome to it; I'll string along nicely with this big wad of chewing gum over my tooth. On me it looks good.

THE DROVER'S WIFE
HENRY LAWSON / AUSTRALIA

Henry Lawson

THE TWO-ROOMED HOUSE is built of round timber, slabs, and stringybark, and floored with split slabs. A big bark kitchen standing at one end is larger than the house itself, veranda included.

Bush all round—bush with no horizon, for the country is flat. No ranges in the distance. The bush consists of stunted, rotten native apple trees. No undergrowth. Nothing to relieve the eye save the darker green of a few she-oaks which are sighing above the narrow, almost waterless creek. Nineteen miles to the nearest sign of civilization—a shanty on the main road.

The drover, an ex-squatter, is away with sheep. His wife and children are left here alone.

Four ragged, dried-up-looking children are playing about the house. Suddenly one of them yells: "Snake! Mother, here's a snake!"

The gaunt, sun-browned bushwoman dashes from the kitchen, snatches her baby from the ground, holds it on her left hip, and reaches for a stick.

"Where is it?"

"Here! Gone into the woodheap!" yells the eldest boy—a sharp-faced urchin of eleven. "Stop there, Mother! I'll have him. Stand back! I'll have the beggar!"

"Tommy, come here, or you'll be bit. Come here at once when I tell you, you little wretch!"

The youngster comes reluctantly, carrying a stick bigger than himself. Then he yells, triumphantly: "There it goes—under the house!" and darts away with club uplifted. At the same time the big, black, yellow-eyed dog-of-all-breeds, who has shown the wildest interest in the proceedings, breaks his chain and rushes after that snake. He is a moment late, however, and his nose reaches the crack in the slabs just as the end of its tail disappears. Almost at the same moment the boy's club comes down and skins the aforesaid nose. Alligator takes small notice of this, and proceeds to undermine the building; but he is subdued after a struggle and chained up. They cannot afford to lose him.

The drover's wife makes the children stand together near the dog house while she watches for the snake. She gets two small dishes of milk and sets them down near the wall to tempt it to come out; but an hour goes by and it does not show itself.

It is near sunset, and a thunderstorm is coming. The children must be brought inside. She will not take them into the house, for she knows the snake is there, and may at any moment come up through a crack in the rough slab floor: so she carries several armfuls of firewood into the kitchen, and then takes the children there. The kitchen has no floor—or, rather an earthen one—called a "ground floor" in this part of the bush. There is a large, roughly made table in the center of the place. She brings the children in, and makes them get on this table. They are two boys and two girls—mere babies. She gives them some supper, and then, before it gets dark, she goes into the house, and snatches up some pillows and bedclothes—expecting to see or lay her hand on the snake any minute. She makes a bed on the kitchen table for the children, and sits down beside it to watch all night.

She has an eye on the corner, and a green sapling club laid in readiness on the dresser by her side; also her sewing basket and a copy of the *Young Ladies' Journal*. She has brought the dog into the room.

Tommy turns in, under protest, but says he'll lie awake all night and smash that blinded snake.

His mother asks him how many times she has told him not to swear.

He has his club with him under the bedclothes, and Jacky protests: "Mummy! Tommy's skinnin' me alive wif his club. Make him take it out."

Tommy: "Shet up, you little—! D'yer want to be bit with the snake?"

Jacky shuts up.

"If yer bit," says Tommy, after a pause, "you'll swell up, an' smell, an' turn red an' green an' blue all over till yer bust. Won't he, Mother?"

"Now then, don't frighten the child. Go to sleep," she says.

The two younger children go to sleep, and now and then Jacky complains of being "skeezed". More room is made for him.

Presently Tommy says: "Mother! listen to them (adjective) little possums. I'd like to screw their blanky necks."

And Jacky protests drowsily.

"But they don't hurt us, the little blanks!"

Mother: "There, I told you you'd teach Jacky to swear." But the remark makes her smile. Jacky goes to sleep.

Presently Tommy asks: "Mother! Do you think they'll ever extricate the (adjective) kangaroo?"

"Lord! How am I to know, child? Go to sleep."

"Will you wake me if the snake comes out?"

"Yes. Go to sleep."

Near midnight. The children are all asleep and she sits there still, sewing and reading by turns. From time to time she glances round the floor and wall plate, and whenever she hears a noise she reaches for the stick. The thunderstorm comes on, and the wind, rushing through the cracks in the slab wall, threatens to blow out her candle. She places it on a sheltered part of the dresser and fixes up a newspaper to protect it. At every flash of lightning the cracks between the slabs gleam like polished silver. The thunder rolls, and the rain comes down in torrents.

Alligator lies at full length on the floor, with his eyes turned towards the partition. She knows by this that the snake is there. There are large cracks in that wall opening under the floor of the house.

She is not a coward, but recent events have shaken her nerves. A little son of her brother-in-law was lately bitten by a snake, and died. Besides, she has not heard from her husband for six months, and is anxious about him.

He was a drover, and started squatting here when they were married. The drought of 18— ruined him. He had to sacrifice the remnant of his flock and go droving again. He intends to move his family into the nearest town when he comes back, and, in the meantime, his brother, who keeps a shanty on the main road, comes over about once a month with provisions. The wife has still a couple of cows, one horse, and a few sheep. The brother-in-law kills one of the latter occasionally, gives her what she needs of it, and takes the rest in return for other provisions.

She is used to being left alone. She once lived like this for eighteen months. As a girl she built the usual castles in the air; but all her girlish hopes and aspirations have long been dead. She finds all the excitement and recreation she needs in the *Young Ladies' Journal*, and—Heaven help her!—takes a pleasure in the fashion plates.

Her husband is an Australian, and so is she. He is careless, but a good enough husband. If he had the means he would take her to the city and keep her there like a princess. They are used to being apart, or at least she is. "No use fretting," she says. He may forget sometimes that he is married; but if he has a good check when he comes back he will give most of it to her. When he had money he took her to the city several times—hired a railway sleeping compartment, and put up at the best hotels. He also bought her a buggy, but they had to sacrifice that along with the rest.

The last two children were born in the bush—one while her husband was bringing a drunken doctor, by force, to attend to her. She was alone on this occasion, and very weak. She had been ill with a fever. She prayed to God to send her assistance. God sent Black Mary—the "whitest" gin in all the land. Or, at least, God sent King Jimmy first, and he sent Black Mary. He put his black face round the door post, took in the situation at a glance, and said cheerfully: "All right, missus—I bring my old woman, she down alonga creek."

One of the children died while she was here alone. She rode nineteen miles for assistance, carrying the dead child.

IT MUST BE near one or two o'clock. The fire is burning low. Alligator lies with his head resting on his paws, and watches the wall. He is not a very beautiful dog, and the light shows numerous old wounds where the hair will not grow. He is afraid of nothing on the face of the earth or under it. He will tackle a bullock as readily as he will tackle a flea. He hates all other dogs—except kangaroo dogs—and has a marked dislike to friends or relations of the family. They seldom call, however. He sometimes makes friends with strangers. He hates snakes and has killed many, but he will be bitten someday and die; most snake dogs end that way.

Now and then the bushwoman lays down her work and watches, and listens, and thinks. She thinks of things in her own life, for there is little else to think about.

The rain will make the grass grow, and this reminds her how she fought a bush fire once while her husband was away. The grass was long, and very dry, and the fire threatened to burn her out. She put on an old pair of her husband's trousers and beat out the flames with a green bough, till great drops of sooty perspiration stood out on her forehead and ran in streaks down her blackened arms. The sight of his mother in trousers greatly amused Tommy, who worked like a little hero by her side, but the terrified baby howled lustily for his "mummy." The fire would have mastered her but for four excited bushmen who arrived in the nick of time. It was a mixed-up affair all round; when she went to take up the baby he screamed and struggled convulsively, thinking it was a "blackman"; and Alligator, trusting more to the child's sense than his own instinct, charged furiously, and (being old and slightly deaf) did not in his excitement at first recognize his mistress's voice, but continued to hang on to the moleskins until choked off by Tommy with a saddle strap. The dog's sorrow for his blunder, and his anxiety to let it be known that it was all a mistake, was as evident as his ragged tail and twelve-inch grin could make it. It was a glorious time for the boys; a day to look back to, and talk about, and laugh over for many years.

She thinks how she fought a flood during her husband's absence. She stood for hours in the drenching downpour, and dug an overflow gutter to save the dam across the creek. But she could not save it. There are things that a bushwoman cannot do. Next morning the dam was broken, and her heart was nearly broken too, for she thought how her husband would feel when he came home and saw the result of years of labor swept away. She cried then.

She also fought the pleuropneumonia—dosed and bled the few remaining cattle, and wept again when her two best cows died.

Again, she fought a mad bullock that besieged the house for a day. She made bullets and fired at him through cracks in the slabs with an old shotgun. He was dead in the morning. She skinned him and got seventeen-and-sixpence for the hide.

She also fights the crows and eagles that have designs on her chickens. Her plan of campaign is very original. The children cry "Crows, Mother!" and she rushes out and aims a broomstick at the birds as though it were a gun, and says "Bung!" The crows leave in a hurry; they are cunning, but a woman's cunning is greater.

Occasionally a bushman in the horrors, or a villainous-looking sundowner, comes and nearly scares the life out of her. She generally tells the suspicious-looking stranger that her husband and two sons are at work below the dam, or over at the yard, for he always cunningly inquires for the boss.

Only last week a gallows-faced swagman—having satisfied himself that there were no men on the place—threw his swag down on the veranda, and demanded tucker. She gave him something to eat; then he expressed his intention of staying for the night. It was sundown then. She got a batten from the sofa, loosened the dog, and confronted the stranger, holding the batten in one hand and the dog's collar with the other. "Now you go!" she said. He looked at her and at the dog, said "All right, mum," in a cringing tone, and left. She was a determined-looking woman, and Alligator's yellow eyes glared unpleasantly—besides, the dog's chawing-up apparatus greatly resembled that of the reptile he was named after.

She has few pleasures to think of as she sits here alone by the fire, on guard against a snake. All days are much the same to her; but on Sunday afternoon she dresses herself, tidies the children, smartens up baby, and goes for a lonely walk along the bush track, pushing an old perambulator in front of her. She does this every Sunday. She takes as much care to make herself and the children look smart as she would if she were going to do the block in the city. There is nothing to see, however, and not a soul to meet. You might walk twenty miles along this track without being able to fix a point in your mind, unless you are a bushman. This is because of the everlasting, maddening sameness of the stunted trees—that monotony which makes a man long to break away and travel as far as trains can go, and sail as far as ship can sail—and further.

But this bushwoman is used to the loneliness of it. As a girl-wife she hated it, and now she would feel strange away from it.

She is glad when her husband returns, but she does not gush or make a fuss about it. She gets him something good to eat, and tidies up the children.

She seems contented with her lot. She loves her children, but has no time to show it. She seems harsh to them. Her surroundings are not favorable to the development of the "womanly" or sentimental side of nature.

IT MUST BE near morning now; but the clock is in the dwelling house. Her candle is nearly done; she forgot that she was out of candles. Some more wood must be got to keep the fire up, and so she shuts the dog inside and hurries round to the woodheap. The rain has cleared off. She seizes a stick, pulls it out, and—crash! the whole pile collapses.

Yesterday she bargained with a stray blackfellow to bring her some wood, and while he was at work she went in search of a missing cow. She was absent an hour or so, and the native black made good use of his time. On her return she was so astonished to see a good heap of wood by the chimney that she gave him an extra fig of tobacco, and praised him for not being lazy. He thanked her, and left with head erect and chest well out. He was the last of his tribe and a king; but he had built that woodheap hollow.

She is hurt now, and tears spring to her eyes as she sits down again by the table. She takes up a handkerchief to wipe the tears away, but pokes her eyes with her bare fingers instead. The handkerchief is full of holes, and she finds that she has put her thumb through one, and her forefinger through another.

This makes her laugh, to the surprise of the dog. She has a keen, very keen, sense of the ridiculous; and some time or other she will amuse bushmen with the story.

She had been amused before like that. One day she sat down "to have a good cry," as she said—and the old cat rubbed against her dress and "cried too." Then she had to laugh.

IT MUST BE near daylight now. The room is very close and hot because of the fire. Alligator still watches the wall from time to time. Suddenly he becomes greatly interested; he draws himself a few inches nearer the partition, and a thrill runs through his body. The hair on the back of his neck begins to bristle, and the battle light is in his yellow eyes. She knows what this means, and lays her hand on the stick. The lower end of one of the partition slabs has a large crack on both sides. An evil pair of small bright beadlike eyes glisten at one of these holes. The snake—a black one—comes slowly out, about a foot, and moves its head up and down. The dog lies still, and the woman sits as one fascinated. The snake comes out a foot further. She lifts her stick, and the reptile, as though suddenly aware of danger, sticks his head in through the crack on the other side of the slab, and hurries to get his tail round after him. Alligator springs, and his jaws come together with a snap. He misses, for his nose is large, and the snake's body close down in the angle formed by the slabs and the floor. He snaps again as the tail comes round. He has the snake now, and tugs it out eighteen inches. Thud, thud, comes the woman's club on the ground. Alligator pulls again. Thud, thud. Alligator gives another pull and he has the snake out—a black brute, five feet long. The head rises to dart about, but the dog has the enemy close to the neck. He is a big, heavy dog, but quick as a terrier. He shakes the snake as though he felt the original curse in common with mankind. The eldest boy wakes up, seizes his stick, and tries to get out of bed, but his mother forces him back with a grip of iron. Thud, thud—the snake's back is broken in several places. Thud, thud—its head is crushed, and Alligator's nose skinned again.

She lifts the mangled reptile on the point of her stick, carries it to the fire, and throws it in; then piles on the wood and watches the snake burn. The boy and dog watch too. She lays her hand on the dog's head, and all the fierce, angry light dies out of his yellow eyes. The younger children are quieted, and presently go to sleep. The dirty-legged boy stands for a moment in his shirt, watching the fire. Presently he looks up at her, sees the tears in her eyes, and, throwing his arms round her neck, exclaims: "Mother, I won't never go drovin'; blast me if I do!"

And she hugs him to her worn-out breast and kisses him; and they sit thus together while the sickly daylight breaks over the bush.

THE HUNTSMEN
PAUL HORGAN / UNITED STATES

EAST OF TOWN about a dozen miles ran the river. To a place near its edge before dawn on Saturday came Mr. Pollock and his younger son, Madison, accompanied by their dog, Punch. It was a cold morning in autumn. The boy was hardly awake yet. His father had to nudge him to climb out of the car when they stopped in a clump of rust-brown salt cedar at the end of the sandy road Mr. Pollock knew about. For years it had brought him from the paved highway and through the low dunes of sand and clay to his favorite spot for duck hunting.

Madison left the car, carrying his own new shotgun. Over his bony little shoulder was slung his canvas bag for shells. As they moved forward to walk beside the river to the blind, the father did not have to tell Madison to be as quiet as possible. He merely gave by example a lesson in the caution and delicacy of how to move when there were surely ducks out on the river. Punch, an elderly rat-tailed spaniel, went heavily but silently on the sand, pausing at intervals to be sure the others were following. As they came between two huge clumps of salt cedar that rattled in the faint cold wind before daylight, Mr. Pollock halted and held his freezing fist by his ear. The gesture said, "Listen!" Madison turned his head and held his breath.

Then, yes, how could his father ever have heard it, it was so faint, but now he could hear it too—the reedy, murmurous sound of ducks disturbed and talking over there, out of sight under the high carved clay banks of the red Pecos River earth.

The boy's heart began to pound. He loved his father for this experience. They stood shivering in the graying dark until there was no more sleepy music from the hidden water. Then they walked carefully up the river, keeping away from the bank until Mr. Pollock found the shallow dirt canyon which led to his favorite blind. The bank rose before them a little, making a small peninsula screened at the edge by a spare rank of young willows. Here was the place. They knelt down and allowed the day to come. It was now not far off.

Though nobody knew it, Mr. Pollock came for this as much as for anything else. In the spectacle of the natural world he found his poetry, his music, his art gallery. This was his culture, and what it meant to him he had no way to tell, except through example, for the benefit of his sons. All his feelings were buried, anyhow. He was a short, heavy man who walked leaning backward, to carry his weight evenly. He was a director of the local bank and the manager of a building and loan association. During business hours he was a leading citizen of Main Street. Many people felt about him as they would about a doctor, for he knew and helped with serious problems in their families which had to do with the possession and safety of their homes. His large light eyes saw everything and betrayed nothing. His mouth was small in his big face, and he said little, but when he spoke, he was believed.

Wherever the town showed its mind or strength, you'd see a Pollock. If Mr. Pollock would sit on platforms as a silent endorsement of civic desires or ambitions, his wife was likely to be one of the speakers. Her voice was loud and harsh, somehow inappropriate to her small size; but everyone was always impressed as she struggled to bend the public will to her personal belief. She governed her family in much the same way, overwhelming them with her anxious vitality, which was a happy joke among them all until in some issue she yielded to the tears that always seemed to lie in waiting behind her pinch-nose eyeglasses. But she was as apt to weep for happiness and her good fortune in such a kind, sober husband and in two such wonderful boys, as she was out of "nerves."

The parents embraced so completely their station in middle life that it was hard to imagine either of them as ever having been boy and girl. Especially was this impossible for their sons to do. It was as though Mr. and Mrs. Pollock had ceded to their sons all graces of person and fiber, and were content to lose those beauties which had once served their mindless purpose in the founding of the family.

Edwin was eighteen, his brother Madison twelve. Both were already taller than their parents, and far more communicative than the father. Give either of the boys something to take part in, and, according to their ages, they would fling themselves into it, and pretty soon end up in charge of it. Edwin was a great local athlete. He was also an honor man in high-school studies. Boys and girls alike admired him as a terrible cynic, and the yearbook in his senior year said that if you ever wanted a shock, just ask Edwin Pollock for his honest opinion of anything. But it added that he always grinned when he gave it, which accounted for all the "broken hearts" he left scattered around him. So tribute was already paid in pathetic and heartfelt ways to Edwin's powers of comeliness, strength and warmth in life. He was a junior public figure in the small city, and was loved most of all because he never seemed to know it.

Now, before going to college, he was taking a year to learn the value of a dollar—his father's favorite words—by selling farm-implement machinery up and down the Pecos valley, which lay fertile and prosperous in the wilderness of dry plains all around, graced by the far-distant lift and loom of the southernmost Rocky Mountains.

Madison Pollock at twelve had the energy and the laughable daring of a half-grown cat. Of all the Pollocks, he was the funniest and the most high-spirited. He loved to show off, knowing exactly how to make people delight in his antics. He, too, was a good student, and he had a few pygmy enemies because he seemed to have been born with all the books in his head, for he never studied, or said he didn't. He probably didn't. He was the only blond Pollock. His eyes were dark blue, his cheeks a furious dusky pink, and his whole self, no matter what he did, seemed always to look dry and clean.

The last member of the Pollock family was Punch, the spaniel, who was an actual character because they had all put their characters into him ever since his puppydom. Now, in his privileged later life, Punch was a leading citizen of the alleys of town, and with his mornings to himself, he made his daily tour of inspection and gluttony along the backyards of countless friends. They would hear him coming, with his collar chain and tags tinkling, and would know that this day, like all the others, would pursue its reassuring course, under the great sky whose light, beating upon houses, and streets, and plains, and the long river, could show everything except what the future would bring.

WAITING FOR DAYLIGHT by the river, Mr. Pollock and Madison shivered companionably. Behind them rose the river's eastern bluffs in cold shadow. But they could see the edge of the skyline now, outlined by a faint lift of pearly light. As still as the rest of the river world, they waited. But they waited in growing excitement, for over and about them proceeded the immense arrival of day. The light gained behind them, and turned to the color of embers, and in the dome of the sky came a smoky blue, and then the western sky showed a pale rose against which the curved shadow of the sleeping earth swept a dying image. Little clouds that were lost in the dark now came to show like wisps of flame in the east. What was that now, on the endless western horizon? The rosy light came down, dispelling the blue earth shadow, and struck the tips of the mountains which so remotely faced the coming sun.

It suddenly seemed colder. Madison hugged himself around his gun. The grand vision before them arose in their spirits, too, and their faces were open with the wonder and promise of this splendor. All this was what Mr. Pollock meant and said nothing about. His greatest moment was still to come, and nothing must destroy it.

Down the distant mountains crept the growing light, until soon there was a blade of golden light cutting across the whole plain at the mountain base, and behind the escarpment to the east blazed visible rays of glory as the sun showed itself at last, tearing the long quiet horizon clouds into silken rags of fire.

Just then the air was filled from everywhere with sound as startling as the vision which grew and grew and spilled over the world. Up from the black lazy water rose the birds in salute to the sunrise. Their calls made a chorus that veered and varied like the wind. They wheeled and shuttered, stirring like a strike of life itself, and went off to taste the sky.

Madison was half standing in the big commotion of all nature. His empty gun was raised. His father reached up and pulled him down again. "They'll come back and settle down," he said in his mild, grainy voice, "if we keep still."

Madison subsided. He swallowed. As thoughtlessly as a duck, he himself had saluted the day, out of an excitement older than memory, and a recognition of glory as near as his impassive father.

The light was now drawing eastward across the plains. Farmhouses began to show, little cubicles poured with gold. Trees stood plain. Green fields of winter wheat looked out of the receding twilight. In a few moments there would be no mystery, no startling grandeur, but only daytime, and a forgotten sun climbing overhead showing, common, the red rocks of the cliffs, the endless sweep of the plains, the smoke-defined town, and the mountains with their faint hovering clouds.

THE DUCKS RETURNED. Madison saw them before he heard them, little twinkling specks of black that moved together against the dove-wing colors of the northern sky. Then came their sound again, from everywhere, as though a cloud could be heard.

Mr. Pollock nodded and silently thrust two shells into his gun and then closed it. Madison copied him, watching his father now, instead of the flight. Punch quivered, his nose lifted to the sky.

Mr. Pollock gave Madison a half look and raised his gun in a trial sight. Then he indicated that if the birds flew over them and started to settle on the river beyond the willows, they would shoot.

Here they came, growing specks along the silver reflection of the gun barrels. The air drummed. All sound vanished and only sight was left, tense, as the guns made their arcs with the circle and swift descent of the ducks. Then, by a common power of agreement, they both fired. The shots broke the whole adventure in stunning strike, and dawn, and boy, and father, and sky life, and river world blazed into an instant of ringing silence.

The flight struck upward again and were gone beyond speed. But two fell, and they saw them, and they knew where.

Madison jumped to his feet. He was charged with love for the birds he had helped to kill. All huntsmen from before his own small lifetime stirred in him. His teeth chattered with mindless power and memory. But his father showed him in silent example how to break his gun and lay it for safety's sake on the ground, and lovingly, because of its exciting oily smell, its sweet smooth wood, its power of compressed dominion over living things. With a hand on Punch, Mr. Pollock led the way through the willows to the shallow water and beyond, where their game lay on the long mudbank in midstream.

Madison's belly felt full to bursting with joy. He wished his brother Edwin could see him now. He wanted to be like Edwin in every way—his body, his style, his mind and his famous cynicism. He felt like Edwin right now, and as he walked he spread his legs somewhat as Edwin did, and made a rather hard-boiled expression on his face. This was more like it. None of that childish excitement. Madison did his best to seem offhand; the master of his gun, and of his power to kill, and provide.

LATER THEY MOVED downstream. They had chances to shoot three more times before Mr. Pollock said that they'd better think about getting back, as he intended to be at his office by ten o'clock, where there was other quarry to size up and bring to terms. He had his canvas pouch pockets full of birds, whose inert weight bumped against his stride with the majestic bother of all trophies.

Madison carried three ducks by hand. There was still enough baby in him to want to hold them forever, just as they were, just as he had made them, with their tiny head and neck feathering of green and blue fire, their stripes of white, black and brown, their leathery bills, their dear death. Punch was allowed to carry one bird in his important jaws. He almost pranced in slow dignity as they returned down the river to the hidden car. All three of them felt the same feelings.

Mr. Pollock unlocked the car and opened the back door on the left side. The back seat was covered by heavy brown wrapping paper—Mrs. Pollock's contribution to the good sense and economy of the expedition. There they put down their bleeding ducks.

This was about nine o'clock. There were no mysteries left in the day. True, it was turning a little colder, for low gray clouds were unfolding from the east. But everything stood clear and simple, so far just like another day.

"Mad, you take the guns and put them in the car," said Mr. Pollock. "I counted one more duck that we knocked down last time. I'll take Punch and go back and find him. You wait here."

Madison hadn't seen another duck fall. But one thing that was never done was to question the father—aloud anyhow. He took Mr. Pollock's gun, which was left open at the break, and empty of shells. He saw the man and the dog trudge off. He went around the car to the other side and opened the front door. There he hurriedly put the two shotguns on the seat, side by side, making the same angle with their open chambers and barrels, muzzles outward. He shut the door on them with a vague feeling of forgetting something, but it seemed more desirable at the moment to get around to the other side of the car in a hurry, in order to watch Mr. Pollock and Punch as they rattled and cracked through the tall reeds up the river. There were a few pauses, while the father would halt and reconstruct the angles of flight, sight, fire and fall. Then the search would continue. Finally Punch gave out his wheezing bark, at the very instant Madison was saying to himself, *They'll never find it, because there isn't one.*

As the retrievers walked patiently back toward the car, Punch carried in his proudly lifted jaws one more dead duck.

Well, sure enough.

But Mr. Pollock was short about his triumph. He had a good eye, a faithful sense of numbers, and a lifelong principle of collecting what was due to him. He simply trusted these faculties. Impervious to compliments, he took the duck from Punch, and leaning somewhat backward, walked heavily around the car to the right side and opened the front door to see where the shotguns were.

So it was that everybody else came to find out where Madison had put the guns, and how. Madison's gun was released by the opening of the car door, and slid along the mohair covering of the seat toward the floor of the car. It struck with force. The breech closed as the butt thumped on the floor, and what Madison had half forgotten then took effect. He had not removed the shells from his gun. The impact of the gunstock on the floor jarred the gun sharply. One barrel fired.

Madison was right there, for he had come around the car to watch, and finally to take his place on the front seat.

That flash of color and sound—what did it do—go off?

The duck fell from Mr. Pollock's hand. It trailed a trifle of slimy blood on the dried mud earth. Mr. Pollock bent forward and made a long agonized sound of groan on the word, "Oh-h-h," and fell down, bleeding, too, slowly, until he was humped leaning against the car with his arms around his middle, his head forced back and his eyes closing from the lower lids up, slowly, shutting out the light of the sky and the mind, both.

HE WAS ALONE with his younger son and his weight of authority now passed to the boy. Madison, as if he were being watched by a host of people, pursed his lips and pinched them with his fingers, and said, nearly aloud, "Now let's see."

But his heart was banging with sick hurry in him, and choking him in the throat. He wanted to talk to his father, but his father was gone, for the time being—he could see that—and he was afraid to reach him, for he knew whose fault it was that Mr. Pollock lay there like something else.

He knelt down and put his arms under Mr. Pollock's shoulders, thinking to lift him into the car. He could not budge him.

Plans occurred to him. Perhaps if he waited a little while, Mr. Pollock would wake up refreshed, and they would get into the car and go back to town, and he and Edwin would clean the ducks in the backyard, and Mom would cook them, with an apple and an onion inside each one. Or perhaps Dr. Dave Sessions would come by here duck hunting, and operate at once, with the heroic assistance of young Madison Pollock.

Or perhaps he, too, would simply die. He closed his eyes to feel how this would be. When he opened them again, he was crying and fully aware of what he had done.

As reality returned to him, he saw what he must do. He managed inch by inch to move his father down to earth from the side of the car. Mr. Pollock was breathing wetly. He seemed to shake his head blindly at Madison as the boy moved him. Now the car was free.

Madison put Punch on guard. The dog looked hungrily after the boy, but stayed where he was meant to be, beside his still master. Madison got into the car, and remembered the few times he had stolen rides alone in it, against every law of the household: no boy of twelve should be allowed to drive, think what could happen—and all the rest of Mrs. Pollock's timeless obedience to the whimpering gods of worry.

He pinched his lips and again said, "Now let's see," as he rehearsed the technique of driving. He started the engine, put the gear into reverse and let the clutch go, but too suddenly. The car leaped backward and then stopped, the engine stalled with too much gas. He started over again, this time swinging in a wide arc to turn around and head for the highway over the dunes. Just before he drove forward, Madison glanced back fearfully to see if perhaps his father would sharply call to him, asking, "Where do you think you're going with that car? You know you are not supposed to drive it."

But there was no such threat, and he whined along in second gear, swaying with the lift and boggle of the car over the uneven road.

On the back seat, the inert necks and heads of the dead ducks rolled from side to side in little arcs. Mrs. Pollock's brown paper was moist and stained in places.

When he reached the highway, he stopped the car just off the paving on the shoulder of the road. He sat there, numb, for a little while, as three or four cars went flashing by.

What would he have to say if he stopped someone? How could he ever say it? He hoped nobody would stop.

He looked both ways. The highway was now empty as far as he could see. His heart fell with pity and relief, even as he licked his dry mouth in a panic of disgust over his great betrayal.

But here came a car, way up at the crest of the cliff, where, in a deep cut, the highway took its course across the great wilderness which led to West Texas and beyond. The car came fast down the long slope toward the bridge.

Inviting his own doom, Madison got out and stepped into the near lane. Long before he could see the driver he began to wave his arms. He ended by leaping off the ground a few times.

The driver began to slacken his speed, and when he saw that this was a boy, he slammed on the brakes. Something told him before he stopped that here was bad trouble, which spoke so powerfully through that young, jumping figure alone in that big spread of country. The boy did not come to him, so he left his own car and walked back to find young Madison Pollock, with his teeth chattering and his right arm pointing off up the river and trying to tell.

"What's it, son?" asked the driver. He was Tim Motherwell, of the Soil Conservation Service. He squatted down before Madison and began to chew on a match, not looking at him, but musing in his presence as though they were two men with all the time in the world to decide or exchange something important. He had noticed blood on the boy's field jacket. What might have put it there he was already imagining, when Madison managed to tell him what lay up the sandy road by the river.

Tim nodded mildly, but he lost no time. He pulled his weathered green government pickup truck well off the highway and returned to Mr. Pollock's car. He drove Madison back up the river.

As they went, Madison tried to tell him how it had happened. "I did it," he kept repeating.

"We'll see," Tim replied, and wondered, like so many people in the next few days, what could ever reclaim this boy from this morning.

Madison was awry in every possible way. His thick yellow hair was tangled and upright. His face was white, but square patches of dusky-peach red tried to show on his cheekbones. His eyes were wild. He kept trying to put his hands on his round young thighs in composure, but they would not stay there, and would spring up in the air as though moved by counterweights.

In a moment they came to a halt and got out of the car. Punch was there, trembling with fear and strangeness, and stood up to greet them with a high, stifled yawp, but did not leave his post. They came forward and Tim bent down. Almost at once he saw that the father was dead.

They got to town as soon as they could manage, and in ten minutes the news was everywhere.

IF PEOPLE DID NOT SAY it aloud, they spoke plainly with their eyes. "Oh, that poor boy! He will never get over this!"

In everybody's face, Madison read, "That is the boy who killed his father," and somehow in those who looked at him or talked about him, awe was mingled with pity, and guilt with forgiveness.

After the three days—the rest of Saturday, all day Sunday, until Monday afternoon, when the funeral was held—Madison Pollock was in danger. Edwin knew it. The boy's teeth would chatter suddenly. By turns he longed to be with his mother, and could not bear facing her. "My baby," she would sob, smothering him with crushing sympathy. And then again she would have hours during which she would exile him in silent grief and widowhood. He was afraid most of all that Edwin would not like him anymore. He spent hours awake at night breaking his will on terrible schemes to make everything up to everybody. But an imp of maturity abided in him, and told him how useless were these waking dreams. He must shrink even from them.

Tuesday morning he did not want to go back to school, giving as his reason that someone had let the air out of his bicycle tires. Edwin went to see, and it was true. The brothers looked at each other, both knowing who had done it. They did not discuss it. Instead, Edwin drove Madison over to school in the car, but he could not make him get out of the car and fall in with the tumbling boys who played touch football on the playfield.

"One of these days, you know, Mad," said Edwin, meaning that he'd have to start school again sooner or later.

Madison shook his head. "Never. I can't."

"Why not?"

Madison shrugged. He didn't know.

"How about trying, say just the first period?" asked Edwin. "I'll promise to be here when the bell rings after the first period, and if you still want to then, I'll let you out of it."

Madison shook his head.

"Well, then, what do you want to do?"

"Nothing."

The brothers sat in silence, staring straight ahead through the windshield while Edwin played a little jazzy tune on his teeth with his thumbnail. A couple of boys spotted the car and ran over to get Madison, calling his name. Madison crouched down and said hoarsely, "Come on, come on. Let's go, let's go."

Edwin drove off.

Without further discussion, Edwin simply let Maddy stay with him that day as he went on his business calls down the valley. This made an idle and drowsy day for Madison, and when it was over, and they were home for supper, he was ready to go to bed early.

It was barely half past seven when someone drifted with heavily shod steps up on the wooden porch and knocked once or twice on the beveled plate-glass pane of the front door. Edwin put on the porch light and could see through the white net curtain inside the glass that a familiar figure stood there, slowly spinning his fawn-colored felt hat on his forefinger. It was Tim Motherwell, offhand and mild.

He came in and shook hands, saying that he just happened to be driving up this street, and thought of looking in for a second, to see if there was anything he could do, and to tell Mrs. Pollock that he certainly felt for her. At this, she raised her head with a hazy social smile, as though to say that people like her should not inflict their misfortunes upon others, but the imposture lasted only a moment before her little face with its passionately trembling eye lenses appeared to dissolve like molten glass, and she lay back in her chair, subject to the grief that pounded upon her from without.

Edwin asked Tim to sit down, which he declined to do. In a minute or two, Mrs. Pollock recovered enough to ask Edwin to show Tim the messages of sympathy they had received, and the long list of those who had sent flowers. Tim examined these gravely, while the widow watched him hungrily for signs of dolorous pride in the tribute paid to the stricken family. Tim read what people said about Mr. Pollock, and gave the papers back to Edwin without a word, but with a black sparkling look in his eyes which was like thought itself made manifest. Mrs. Pollock covered her face and wept again. Edwin felt ashamed of her, and then, for feeling so, ashamed of himself.

Well, he had to be going, said Tim. Edwin went out to the pickup truck with him, and the real purpose of the call became clear. They talked for about fifteen minutes, Tim at the wheel, Edwin leaning his chin on his fists on the open windowsill of the car. Their conversation was muted and serious. Tim felt younger, Edwin felt older, and both felt like good men, assembled in honor of what needed to be done for someone—in this case, Madison Pollock.

Edwin said, yes, his brother was in a bad way, and said something had to be worked out. Tim said he suspected as much, and with modesty and diffidence told what he would do about it if it were his kid brother.

When the essential matter was finished, there was a long terminal pause, after which Tim, where he sat, jumped comically, as though he felt an electric shock, and said, "I'd better get a move on or my little woman won't act so little, time I get there. See you, Ed."

"See you, Tim. Sure do thank you."

Tim switched on his car lights and drove off. Edwin watched him round the next corner. The red taillight on the truck spoke for Tim as long as Edwin could see it, admire it and covet the goodly strength it stood for.

The next morning, Mrs. Pollock, in the name of what Dad would have wanted, declared that this time Madison must go to school, and ordered Edwin to drive him there again.

Madison turned white. "No, I can't."

"Yes, you can. Oh, what have I done to deserve— You know how your father slaved to give you boys a good education, and now, here you sit, and won't—" Her brokenhearted righteousness welled up in her, more powerful than grief itself, and she crushed the boys with the very same love which had given them being.

Madison left the table and went to the backyard. There he was violently sick at his stomach. Edwin found him there, shuddering on the back steps like a starving cat.

"Come on, Maddy," he said, and practically dragged the boy to the car. They drove off, heading south toward the school. Madison set his jaws and braced his feet against the floorboards the closer they came to the red brick school building, but Edwin, without a glance, drove right on past and continued on south and out of town down the valley.

"I'd gain his confidence," Tim had said. "I wouldn't hurry."

So once again—this time defying the suffering authority at home —Edwin took his brother with him, and did the same all the rest of the week. They visited farms in the broad flat valley, and while Edwin talked business, Madison was let alone just to fool around. They spent one afternoon tinkering with an ailing tractor. One evening they lingered with a little crowd of itinerant cotton pickers who had a bonfire going under some cottonwoods by an irrigation ditch; and to guitar music, clapped hands and country song, the illimitable twilight came down like forgiveness over Madison and everyone in the world. Sometimes Edwin took him along to have a glass of beer, though Mad drank only soda. Another time they called on a girl Edwin knew in the little town of Dexter, and the conversation, full of evocative memories and half-suggested plans, brought Madison a wondering sense of more trouble, sweeter than his awful kind.

And then on Saturday—one week after Madison's first time out hunting—Edwin, having made a few preparations in private, got up at four in the morning and went in his shivering nakedness to Maddy's sleeping porch and woke him up. "Come on, get up," he said.

Madison was stunned with sleep. "What for?"

"Never mind what for. I've got your clothes. We can dress in the living room, where it's warm. Be quiet. Don't wake Mom."

The boy followed his brother. In the front room they got dressed stealthily. It was exciting. "Where're we going?"

"Never you mind. Come on. We'll get breakfast downtown."

Edwin was dressed first. Waiting for Maddy, he sat down at the dining-room table, and wrote a note which Mrs. Pollock told everybody later she would keep forever.

"Dear Mom," it said, "don't worry. Mad and I have gone off on a job. Back during the day. Taking Punch along for the buggy ride. Be a good girl and don't worry. Love and kisses, E."

He propped it up against the crystal fruit bowl in the center of the table, where she would easily find it. He knew that when she came to his fond, impudent advice to be a good girl, she, in whom there remained no degree of girl whatever, would weep over it with famished pride, to see that the power of the family had passed to him, the firstborn, now escaped into his own life. It was not cruel to make her weep. It was almost a kindness, for in these days it gave her solace to feel anything but the main dream of her shocking loss.

The boys went gently out the front door, and around to the backyard to Punch's house, which they had built together so long ago. He knew them now as they approached, and mildly banged his ugly rattail on the floor of his residence.

"Come on, Punch, old boy," said Edwin softly. The self-important old dog got up slowly and stretched himself, first fore and then aft. And then with a prankish lunge he assumed the gaiety of a puppy, but could not sustain it, and soberly followed his masters to their car, which was parked in the alley. Edwin unlocked it, they all got in, and Edwin drove off. The night was black and empty in the cold streets of town.

They had coffee, canned orange juice and ham and eggs in Charlie the Greek's, without conversation, though not without communication, for Edwin could feel Maddy throbbing beside him with doubtful wonder. Edwin once turned on his swivel stool to face Madison and cuff him near the ear—an action which said that he was not to worry, or be afraid, or in doubt, for this was still the family, doing its best for him, no matter how things might look.

It was still pitch dark when they drove off again and headed out toward the east, where the road forked to go either down the valley or out to the river. Madison looked sidewise to question his brother. Edwin, though he felt the look, did not acknowledge it, but merely drove on in general confidence and repose.

At the crossroads they were slowed down by a traffic light which blinked all night long. Madison looked to the right, along the highway which would take them on one of their familiar days of salesmanship at the valley farms. But Edwin, resuming high gear, drove straight ahead on the other highway, which led to the river. Maddy's teeth began to chatter.

The first pale strips of day now showed ahead of them in the east. Suddenly, it was there. With it came a colder feeling. Edwin speeded up as though to race the dawn.

Where were they going? Maddy put his hand on the door handle beside him with an unformed motion that he might open the door and, speed or no speed, get out right now. Why not? Edwin caught this out of the corner of his eye in the half-light of the instrument panel. He began to whistle a little tune inside his teeth, leaned over and snapped the door handle up to a locked position.

By the time they saw the river, its slow sparse waters were reflecting the faint early light in the midst of heavy shade over the earth. Maddy, in terror, both did and did not believe it when the family car slowed down at the far end of the Pecos River bridge and took the sandy turnoff of the road that ran over the dunes, in the same darkness, by the same willows, in the same cold, to the same screen of salt cedars as a week ago this morning.

EDWIN STOPPED the car and got out. He opened the rear door for Punch, who scrambled forth with his head lifted amid the marshy smells on the faintly stirring air. At the luggage compartment, Edwin unlocked the handle and flung open the lid. He took out two shotguns, a canvas bag full of shells, and two pairs of rubber boots.

"Come on, Mad!" he called.

The front door opened and Madison stepped out, against his wish. Edwin threw Maddy's boots to him. "Put them on."

"What for?"

"Put them on."

Maddy was overwhelmed. He was numb, inside and out. He put the boots on.

Edwin handed him his own gun.

"No."

"Take it. Go on. We're going to get some ducks."

Madison took it. He could hardly feel it in his grasp.

Edwin led the way up the river to the blind where, long ago, he too, had first come with his father. The day was nearing. Again, sky, mountain, plain and earth's own curve evolved toward the moment of glory and revelation.

Once again not only all light but all sound and all space beat upon the senses when the sun rose. The ducks were there again. They fled the shadows and streaked noisily into the lofty light. Like his father, Edwin stayed their fire at the dawn flight. The birds would return. To be ready—

"Load," said Edwin.

Madison fumbled with his gun. He could not handle it. Edwin took it from him and loaded it, closed it, which cocked it, and handed it back. "You take the first one, Mad."

They waited. The older brother set his jaws. He knew what he was doing, and the pain he was causing.

Presently the birds were coming over again. Edwin pointed. Madison saw only a dazzle of flying black specks in the yellowing day.

"Now," whispered Edwin.

Madison raised his gun and tried to sight, leading the flight, which seemed everywhere. He was shaking. He fired alone. Nothing fell. He brought down his gun. His head was ringing. He looked at Edwin.

"Tough," said Edwin.

Madison thrust his gun at Edwin for him to take. "Let me go," he said in pitiful modesty.

Edwin shook his head and pushed the gun back in his brother's grasp. "You'll do better next time."

"I will?"

"Sure."

Edwin, whistling silently, turned his gaze over the sky.

What? thought Madison. And this was astounding: powerfully like a wind, free and lofting, the idea blew through him, and he thought, *Of course I will.*

He looked at Edwin to find an explanation of the excitement which spread so fast in his being. But Edwin was immovable, watching the lower reaches of the sky.

"I will get some next time," whispered Madison. "I got three last Saturday, and I'll get more today."

Edwin nodded briefly. His heart began to thump with relief. He could never have said so, but Edwin knew they had come here to put death in its place, and were going to succeed.

THE GUEST

ALBERT CAMUS / FRANCE

Translated by Justin O'Brien

THE SCHOOLMASTER was watching the two men climb toward him. One was on horseback, the other on foot. They had not yet tackled the abrupt rise leading to the schoolhouse built on the hillside. They were toiling onward, making slow progress in the snow, among the stones, on the vast expanse of the high, deserted plateau. From time to time the horse stumbled. Without hearing anything yet, he could see the breath issuing from the horse's nostrils. One of the men, at least, knew the region. They were following the trail although it had disappeared days ago under a layer of dirty white snow. The schoolmaster calculated that it would take them half an hour to get onto the hill. It was cold; he went back into the school to get a sweater.

He crossed the empty, frigid classroom. On the blackboard the four rivers of France, drawn with four different colored chalks, had been flowing toward their estuaries for the past three days. Snow had suddenly fallen in mid-October after eight months of drought without the transition of rain, and the twenty pupils, more or less, who lived in the villages scattered over the plateau had stopped coming. With fair weather they would return. Daru now heated only the single room that was his lodging, adjoining the classroom and giving also onto the plateau to the east. Like the class windows, his window looked to the south too. On that side the school was a few kilometers from the point where the plateau began to slope toward the south. In clear weather could be seen the purple mass of the mountain range where the gap opened onto the desert.

Somewhat warmed, Daru returned to the window from which he had first seen the two men. They were no longer visible. Hence they must have tackled the rise. The sky was not so dark, for the snow had stopped falling during the night. The morning had opened with a dirty light which had scarcely become brighter as the ceiling of clouds lifted. At two in the afternoon it seemed as if the day were merely beginning. But still this was better than those three days when the thick snow was falling amidst unbroken darkness with little gusts of wind that rattled the double door of the classroom. Then Daru had spent long hours in his room, leaving it only to go to the shed and feed the chickens or get some coal. Fortunately the delivery truck from Tadjid, the nearest village to the north, had brought his supplies two days before the blizzard. It would return in forty-eight hours.

Besides, he had enough to resist a siege, for the little room was cluttered with bags of wheat that the administration left as a stock to distribute to those of his pupils whose families had suffered from the drought. Actually they had all been victims because they were all poor. Every day Daru would distribute a ration to the children. They had missed it, he knew, during these bad days. Possibly one of the fathers or big brothers would come this afternoon and he could supply them with grain. It was just a matter of carrying them over to the next harvest. Now shiploads of wheat were arriving from France and the worst was over. But it would be hard to forget that poverty, that army of ragged ghosts wandering in the sunlight, the plateaus burned to a cinder month after month, the earth shriveled up little by little, literally scorched, every stone bursting into dust under one's foot. The sheep had died then by thousands and even a few men, here and there, sometimes without anyone's knowing.

In contrast with such poverty, he who lived almost like a monk in his remote schoolhouse, nonetheless satisfied with the little he had and with the rough life, had felt like a lord with his whitewashed walls, his narrow couch, his unpainted shelves, his well, and his weekly provision of water and food. And suddenly this snow, without warning, without the foretaste of rain. This is the way the region was, cruel to live in, even without men—who didn't help matters either. But Daru had been born here. Everywhere else, he felt exiled.

He stepped out onto the terrace in front of the schoolhouse. The two men were now halfway up the slope. He recognized the horseman as Balducci, the old gendarme he had known for a long time. Balducci was holding on the end of a rope an Arab who was walking behind him with hands bound and head lowered. The gendarme waved a greeting to which Daru did not reply, lost as he was in contemplation of the Arab dressed in a faded blue jellaba, his feet in sandals but covered with socks of heavy raw wool, his head surmounted by a narrow, short *chèche*. They were approaching. Balducci was holding back his horse in order not to hurt the Arab, and the group was advancing slowly.

Within earshot, Balducci shouted: "One hour to do the three kilometers from El Ameur!" Daru did not answer. Short and square in his thick sweater, he watched them climb. Not once had the Arab raised his head. "Hello," said Daru when they got up onto the terrace. "Come in and warm up." Balducci painfully got down from his horse without letting go the rope. From under his bristling mustache he smiled at the schoolmaster. His little dark eyes, deep-set under a tanned forehead, and his mouth surrounded with wrinkles made him look attentive and studious. Daru took the bridle, led the horse to the shed, and came back to the two men, who were now waiting for him in the school. He led them into his room. "I am going to heat up the classroom," he said. "We'll be more comfortable there." When he entered the room again, Balducci was on the couch. He had undone the rope tying him to the Arab, who had squatted near the stove. His hands still bound, the *chèche* pushed back on his head, he was looking toward the window. At first Daru noticed only his huge lips, fat, smooth, almost Negroid; yet his nose was straight, his eyes were dark and full of fever. The *chèche* revealed an obstinate forehead and, under the weathered skin now rather discolored by the cold, the whole face had a restless and rebellious look that struck Daru when the Arab, turning his face toward him, looked him straight in the eyes. "Go into the other room," said the schoolmaster, "and I'll make you some mint tea." "Thanks," Balducci said. "What a chore! How I long for retirement." And addressing his prisoner in Arabic: "Come on, you." The Arab got up and, slowly, holding his bound wrists in front of him, went into the classroom.

With the tea, Daru brought a chair. But Balducci was already enthroned on the nearest pupil's desk and the Arab had squatted against the teacher's platform facing the stove, which stood between the desk and the window. When he held out the glass of tea to the prisoner, Daru hesitated at the sight of his bound hands. "He might perhaps be untied." "Sure," said Balducci. "That was for the trip." He started to get to his feet. But Daru, setting the glass on the floor, had knelt beside the Arab. Without saying anything, the Arab watched him with his feverish eyes. Once his hands were free, he rubbed his swollen wrists against each other, took the glass of tea, and sucked up the burning liquid in swift little sips.

"Good," said Daru. "And where are you headed?"

Balducci withdrew his mustache from the tea. "Here, son."

"Odd pupils! And you're spending the night?"

"No. I'm going back to El Ameur. And you will deliver this fellow to Tinguit. He is expected at police headquarters."

Balducci was looking at Daru with a friendly little smile.

"What's this story?" asked the schoolmaster. "Are you pulling my leg?"

"No, son. Those are the orders."

"The orders? I'm not . . ." Daru hesitated, not wanting to hurt the old Corsican. "I mean, that's not my job."

"What! What's the meaning of that? In wartime people do all kinds of jobs."

"Then I'll wait for the declaration of war!"

Balducci nodded.

"O.K. But the orders exist and they concern you too. Things are brewing, it appears. There is talk of a forthcoming revolt. We are mobilized, in a way."

Daru still had his obstinate look.

"Listen, son," Balducci said. "I like you and you must understand. There's only a dozen of us at El Ameur to patrol throughout the whole territory of a small department and I must get back in a hurry. I was told to hand this guy over to you and return without delay. He couldn't be kept there. His village was beginning to stir; they wanted to take him back. You must take him to Tinguit tomorrow before the day is over. Twenty kilometers shouldn't faze a husky fellow like you. After that, all will be over. You'll come back to your pupils and your comfortable life."

Behind the wall the horse could be heard snorting and pawing the earth. Daru was looking out the window. Decidedly, the weather was clearing and the light was increasing over the snowy plateau. When all the snow was melted, the sun would take over again and once more would burn the fields of stone. For days, still, the unchanging sky would shed its dry light on the solitary expanse where nothing had any connection with man.

"After all," he said, turning around toward Balducci, "what did he do?" And, before the gendarme had opened his mouth, he asked: "Does he speak French?"

"No, not a word. We had been looking for him for a month, but they were hiding him. He killed his cousin."

"Is he against us?"

"I don't think so. But you can never be sure."

"Why did he kill?"

"A family squabble, I think. One owed the other grain, it seems. It's not at all clear. In short, he killed his cousin with a billhook. You know, like a sheep, *kreezk!*"

Balducci made the gesture of drawing a blade across his throat and the Arab, his attention attracted, watched him with a sort of anxiety. Daru felt a sudden wrath against the man, against all men with their rotten spite, their tireless hates, their blood lust.

But the kettle was singing on the stove. He served Balducci more tea, hesitated, then served the Arab again, who, a second time, drank avidly. His raised arms made the jellaba fall open and the schoolmaster saw his thin, muscular chest.

"Thanks, kid," Balducci said. "And now, I'm off."

He got up and went toward the Arab, taking a small rope from his pocket.

"What are you doing?" Daru asked dryly.

Balducci, disconcerted, showed him the rope.

"Don't bother."

The old gendarme hesitated. "It's up to you. Of course, you are armed?"

"I have my shotgun."

"Where?"

"In the trunk."

"You ought to have it near your bed."

"Why? I have nothing to fear."

"You're crazy, son. If there's an uprising, no one is safe, we're all in the same boat."

"I'll defend myself. I'll have time to see them coming."

Balducci began to laugh, then suddenly the mustache covered the white teeth.

"You'll have time? O.K. That's just what I was saying. You have always been a little cracked. That's why I like you, my son was like that."

At the same time he took out his revolver and put it on the desk.

"Keep it; I don't need two weapons from here to El Ameur."

The revolver shone against the black paint of the table. When the gendarme turned toward him, the schoolmaster caught the smell of leather and horseflesh.

"Listen, Balducci," Daru said suddenly, "every bit of this disgusts me, and first of all your fellow here. But I won't hand him over. Fight, yes, if I have to. But not that."

The old gendarme stood in front of him and looked at him severely.

"You're being a fool," he said slowly. "I don't like it either. You don't get used to putting a rope on a man even after years of it, and you're even ashamed—yes, ashamed. But you can't let them have their way."

"I won't hand him over," Daru said again.

"It's an order, son, and I repeat it."

"That's right. Repeat to them what I've said to you: I won't hand him over."

Balducci made a visible effort to reflect. He looked at the Arab and at Daru. At last he decided.

"No, I won't tell them anything. If you want to drop us, go ahead; I'll not denounce you. I have an order to deliver the prisoner and I'm doing so. And now you'll just sign this paper for me."

"There's no need. I'll not deny that you left him with me."

"Don't be mean with me. I know you'll tell the truth. You're from hereabouts and you are a man. But you must sign, that's the rule."

Daru opened his drawer, took out a little square bottle of purple ink, the red wooden penholder with the "sergeant-major" pen he used for making models of penmanship, and signed. The gendarme carefully folded the paper and put it into his wallet. Then he moved toward the door.

"I'll see you off," Daru said.

"No," said Balducci. "There's no use being polite. You insulted me."

He looked at the Arab, motionless in the same spot, sniffed peevishly, and turned away toward the door. "Good-by, son," he said. The door shut behind him. Balducci appeared suddenly outside the window and then disappeared. His footsteps were muffled by the snow. The horse stirred on the other side of the wall and several chickens fluttered in fright. A moment later Balducci reappeared outside the window leading the horse by the bridle. He walked toward the little rise without turning around and disappeared from sight with the horse following him. A big stone could be heard bouncing down. Daru walked back toward the prisoner, who, without stirring, never took his eyes off him. "Wait," the schoolmaster said in Arabic and went toward the bedroom. As he was going through the door, he had a second thought, went to the desk, took the revolver, and stuck it in his pocket. Then, without looking back, he went into his room.

For some time he lay on his couch watching the sky gradually close over, listening to the silence. It was this silence that had seemed painful to him during the first days here, after the war. He had requested a post in the little town at the base of the foot-hills separating the upper plateaus from the desert. There, rocky walls, green and black to the north, pink and lavender to the south, marked the frontier of eternal summer. He had been named to a post farther north, on the plateau itself. In the beginning, the solitude and the silence had been hard for him on these wastelands peopled only by stones. Occasionally, furrows suggested cultivation, but they had been dug to uncover a certain kind of stone good for building. The only plowing here was to harvest rocks. Elsewhere a thin layer of soil accumulated in the hollows would be scraped out to enrich paltry village gardens. This is the way it was: bare rock covered three quarters of the region. Towns sprang up, flourished, then disappeared; men came by, loved one another or fought bitterly, then died. No one in this desert, neither he nor his guest, mattered. And yet, outside this desert neither of them, Daru knew, could have really lived.

When he got up, no noise came from the classroom. He was amazed at the unmixed joy he derived from the mere thought that the Arab might have fled and that he would be alone with no decision to make. But the prisoner was there. He had merely stretched out between the stove and the desk. With eyes open, he was staring at the ceiling. In that position, his thick lips were particularly noticeable, giving him a pouting look. "Come," said Daru. The Arab got up and followed him. In the bedroom, the schoolmaster pointed to a chair near the table under the window. The Arab sat down without taking his eyes off Daru.

"Are you hungry?"

"Yes," the prisoner said.

Daru set the table for two. He took flour and oil, shaped a cake in a frying-pan, and lighted the little stove that functioned on bottled gas. While the cake was cooking, he went out to the shed to get cheese, eggs, dates, and condensed milk. When the cake was done he set it on the window sill to cool, heated some condensed milk diluted with water, and beat up the eggs into an omelette. In one of his motions he knocked against the revolver stuck in his right pocket. He set the bowl down, went into the classroom, and put the revolver in his desk drawer. When he came back to the room, night was falling. He put on the light and served the Arab. "Eat," he said. The Arab took a piece of the cake, lifted it eagerly to his mouth, and stopped short.

"And you?" he asked.

"After you. I'll eat too."

The thick lips opened slightly. The Arab hesitated, then bit into the cake determinedly.

The meal over, the Arab looked at the schoolmaster. "Are you the judge?"

"No, I'm simply keeping you until tomorrow."

"Why do you eat with me?"

"I'm hungry."

The Arab fell silent. Daru got up and went out. He brought back a folding bed from the shed, set it up between the table and the stove, perpendicular to his own bed. From a large suitcase which, upright in a corner, served as a shelf for papers, he took two blankets and arranged them on the camp bed. Then he stopped, felt useless, and sat down on his bed. There was nothing more to do or to get ready. He had to look at this man. He looked at him, therefore, trying to imagine his face bursting with rage. He couldn't do so. He could see nothing but the dark yet shining eyes and the animal mouth.

"Why did you kill him?" he asked in a voice whose hostile tone surprised him.

The Arab looked away.

"He ran away. I ran after him."

He raised his eyes to Daru again and they were full of a sort of woeful interrogation. "Now what will they do to me?"

"Are you afraid?"

He stiffened, turning his eyes away.

"Are you sorry?"

The Arab stared at him openmouthed. Obviously he did not understand. Daru's annoyance was growing. At the same time he felt awkward and self-conscious with his big body wedged between the two beds.

"Lie down there," he said impatiently. "That's your bed."

The Arab didn't move. He called to Daru:

"Tell me!"

The schoolmaster looked at him.

"Is the gendarme coming back tomorrow?"

"I don't know."

"Are you coming with us?"

"I don't know. Why?"

The prisoner got up and stretched out on top of the blankets, his feet toward the window. The light from the electric bulb shone straight into his eyes and he closed them at once.

"Why?" Daru repeated, standing beside the bed.

The Arab opened his eyes under the blinding light and looked at him, trying not to blink.

"Come with us," he said.

In the middle of the night, Daru was still not asleep. He had gone to bed after undressing completely; he generally slept naked. But when he suddenly realized that he had nothing on, he hesitated. He felt vulnerable and the temptation came to him to put his clothes back on. Then he shrugged his shoulders; after all, he wasn't a child and, if need be, he could break his adversary in two. From his bed he could observe him, lying on his back, still motionless with his eyes closed under the harsh light. When Daru turned out the light, the darkness seemed to coagulate all of a sudden. Little by little, the night came back to life in the window where the starless sky was stirring gently. The schoolmaster soon made out the body lying at his feet. The Arab still did not move, but his eyes seemed open. A faint wind was prowling around the schoolhouse. Perhaps it would drive away the clouds and the sun would reappear.

During the night the wind increased. The hens fluttered a little and then were silent. The Arab turned over on his side with his back to Daru, who thought he heard him moan. Then he listened for his guest's breathing, become heavier and more regular. He listened to that breath so close to him and mused without being able to go to sleep. In this room where he had been sleeping alone for a year, this presence bothered him. But it bothered him also by imposing on him a sort of brotherhood he knew well but refused to accept in the present circumstances. Men who share the same rooms, soldiers or prisoners, develop a strange alliance as if, having cast off their armor with their clothing, they fraternized every evening, over and above their differences, in the ancient community of dream and fatigue. But Daru shook himself; he didn't like such musings, and it was essential to sleep.

A little later, however, when the Arab stirred slightly, the schoolmaster was still not asleep. When the prisoner made a second move, he stiffened, on the alert. The Arab was lifting himself slowly on his arms with almost the motion of a sleepwalker. Seated upright in bed, he waited motionless without turning his head toward Daru, as if he were listening attentively. Daru did not stir; it had just occurred to him that the revolver was still in the drawer of his desk. It was better to act at once. Yet he continued to observe the prisoner, who, with the same slithery motion, put his feet on the ground, waited again, then began to stand up slowly. Daru was about to call out to him when the Arab began to walk, in a quite natural but extraordinarily silent way. He was heading toward the door at the end of the room that opened into the shed. He lifted the latch with precaution and went out, pushing the door behind him but without shutting it. Daru had not stirred. "He is running away," he merely thought. "Good riddance!" Yet he listened attentively. The hens were not fluttering; the guest must be on the plateau. A faint sound of water reached him, and he didn't know what it was until the Arab again stood framed in the doorway, closed the door carefully, and came back to bed without a sound. Then Daru turned his back on him and fell asleep. Still later he seemed, from the depths of his sleep, to hear furtive steps around the schoolhouse. "I'm dreaming! I'm dreaming!" he repeated to himself. And he went on sleeping.

When he awoke, the sky was clear; the loose window let in a cold, pure air. The Arab was asleep, hunched up under the blankets now, his mouth open, utterly relaxed. But when Daru shook him, he started dreadfully, staring at Daru with wild eyes as if he had never seen him and such a frightened expression that the schoolmaster stepped back. "Don't be afraid. It's me. You must eat." The Arab nodded his head and said yes. Calm had returned to his face, but his expression was vacant and listless.

The coffee was ready. They drank it seated together on the folding bed as they munched their pieces of the cake. Then Daru led the Arab under the shed and showed him the faucet where he washed. He went back into the room, folded the blankets and the bed, made his own bed and put the room in order. Then he went through the classroom and out onto the terrace. The sun was already rising in the blue sky; a soft, bright light was bathing the deserted plateau. On the ridge the snow was melting in spots. The stones were about to reappear. Crouched on the edge of the plateau, the schoolmaster looked at the deserted expanse. He thought of Balducci. He had hurt him, for he had sent him off in a way as if he didn't want to be associated with him. He could still hear the gendarme's farewell and, without knowing why, he felt strangely empty and vulnerable. At that moment, from the other side of the schoolhouse, the prisoner coughed. Daru listened to him almost despite himself and then, furious, threw a pebble that whistled through the air before sinking into the snow. That man's stupid crime revolted him, but to hand him over was contrary to honor. Merely thinking of it made him smart with humiliation. And he cursed at one and the same time his own people who had sent him this Arab and the Arab too who had dared to kill and not managed to get away. Daru got up, walked in a circle on the terrace, waited motionless, and then went back into the schoolhouse.

The Arab, leaning over the cement floor of the shed, was washing his teeth with two fingers. Daru looked at him and said: "Come." He went back into the room ahead of the prisoner. He slipped a hunting-jacket on over his sweater and put on walking-shoes. Standing, he waited until the Arab had put on his *chèche* and sandals. They went into the classroom and the schoolmaster pointed to the exit, saying: "Go ahead." The fellow didn't budge. "I'm coming," said Daru. The Arab went out. Daru went back into the room and made a package of pieces of rusk, dates, and sugar. In the classroom, before going out, he hesitated a second in front of his desk, then crossed the threshold and locked the door. "That's the way," he said. He started toward the east, followed by the prisoner. But, a short distance from the schoolhouse, he thought he heard a slight sound behind them. He retraced his steps and examined the surroundings of the house; there was no one there. The Arab watched him without seeming to understand. "Come on," said Daru.

They walked for an hour and rested beside a sharp peak of limestone. The snow was melting faster and faster and the sun was drinking up the puddles at once, rapidly cleaning the plateau, which gradually dried and vibrated like the air itself. When they resumed walking, the ground rang under their feet. From time to time a bird rent the space in front of them with a joyful cry. Daru breathed in deeply the fresh morning light. He felt a sort of rapture before the vast familiar expanse, now almost entirely yellow under its dome of blue sky. They walked an hour more, descending toward the south. They reached a level height made up of crumbly rocks. From there on, the plateau sloped down, eastward, toward a low plain where there were a few spindly trees and, to the south, toward outcroppings of rock that gave the landscape a chaotic look.

Daru surveyed the two directions. There was nothing but the sky on the horizon. Not a man could be seen. He turned toward the Arab, who was looking at him blankly. Daru held out the package to him. "Take it," he said. "There are dates, bread, and sugar. You can hold out for two days. Here are a thousand francs too." The Arab took the package and the money but kept his full hands at chest level as if he didn't know what to do with what was being given him. "Now look," the schoolmaster said as he pointed in the direction of the east, "there's the way to Tinguit. You have a two-hour walk. At Tinguit you'll find the administration and the police. They are expecting you." The Arab looked toward the east, still holding the package and the money against his chest. Daru took his elbow and turned him rather roughly toward the south. At the foot of the height on which they stood could be seen a faint path. "That's the trail across the plateau. In a day's walk from here you'll find pasturelands and the first nomads. They'll take you in and shelter you according to their law." The Arab had now turned toward Daru and a sort of panic was visible in his expression. "Listen," he said. Daru shook his head: "No, be quiet. Now I'm leaving you." He turned his back on him, took two long steps in the direction of the school, looked hesitantly at the motionless Arab, and started off again. For a few minutes he heard nothing but his own step resounding on the cold ground and did not turn his head. A moment later, however, he turned around. The Arab was still there on the edge of the hill, his arms hanging now, and he was looking at the schoolmaster. Daru felt something rise in his throat. But he swore with impatience, waved vaguely, and started off again. He had already gone some distance when he again stopped and looked. There was no longer anyone on the hill.

Daru hesitated. The sun was now rather high in the sky and was beginning to beat down on his head. The schoolmaster retraced his steps, at first somewhat uncertainly, then with decision. When he reached the little hill, he was bathed in sweat. He climbed it as fast as he could and stopped, out of breath, at the top. The rock-fields to the south stood out sharply against the blue sky, but on the plain to the east a steamy heat was already rising. And in that slight haze, Daru, with heavy heart, made out the Arab walking slowly on the road to prison.

A little later, standing before the window of the classroom, the schoolmaster was watching the clear light bathing the whole surface of the plateau, but he hardly saw it. Behind him on the blackboard, among the winding French rivers, sprawled the clumsily chalked-up words he had just read: "You handed over our brother. You will pay for this." Daru looked at the sky, the plateau, and, beyond, the invisible lands stretching all the way to the sea. In this vast landscape he had loved so much, he was alone.

PATIENCE
NIGEL BALCHIN / GREAT BRITAIN

MY SHARE of the meal had been some whitebait, some cheese and a cup of coffee. The bill was for four pounds, three and sixpence.

"You once told me that the last proprietor of this place was executed," I said rather bitterly. "It wasn't by any chance for highway robbery?"

My Uncle Charles shook his head. "No—just ordinary murder. The circumstances were not uninteresting. I will tell you about it some time." He sighed. "If I were a younger man, with less knowledge of the world," he said sadly, "I suppose I should be offering to pay the bill, or at least to split it with you."

"Why?" I said, astonished.

"On the grounds that I have won some money. I won twenty-five pounds at the Marshalls' at bridge last night."

"Well, it's very decent of you. . . ."

"But you and I know," said my Uncle Charles firmly, "that to win a sum of that kind can be the height of misfortune. I do not know the Marshalls well, and have only played with them a couple of times before. But they are a pair of quietly incompetent performers who, properly nursed, would have meant a steady two or three pounds a week to me for the next ten years. As it is, having lost twenty-five pounds in an evening, they will never ask me there again. I tried hard to avoid it. But when I doubled their final ludicrous slam bid in an effort to save them, they merely redoubled. They made two tricks and I went out into the night. The thing may or may not end in a divorce between them. It is certainly the end of bridge with them for me."

"You believe in small profits and steady returns?"

"It is the only possible principle nowadays, in any form of gambling which involves skill. When the Duchess of Devonshire was prepared to lose fifty thousand pounds at a sitting, it was different. But at a mere five shillings a hundred, one must be prepared to consider one's winnings as a modest pension rather than as the making of a fortune."

"Nobody can afford to play high nowadays."

"Nobody ever could." My Uncle Charles smiled gently to himself. "I have, in fact, taken part in a game of cards which ended in one of the players writing a check for eight hundred pounds, and he certainly could not afford it. But even so, it was, in a way, an illustration of my point that to win may be disastrous and to lose profitable."

"I don't quite follow you."

My Uncle Charles glanced round the restaurant. "You have paid the bill," he said. "If you were to order two more brandies, now, it is possible, though not likely, that they will forget to charge you for them. In the meantime, I will clarify my last statement."

—

"I HAVE NEVER been enthusiastic about the French Riviera which, to me, is a place to which all the people I want to avoid go in order to meet each other. I cannot now recall why, some twenty-five years ago, I spent some time at Nice; and the whole incident is made even more baffling by the fact that I appear to have been staying in a hotel. But it was certainly in the bar of a hotel in Nice that I first met Mr. Brander Heavistone. We were sitting at adjoining tables, and were inadvertently introduced by a waiter who spilt a tray of drinks over the pair of us. Mr. Heavistone was not a difficult man to get to know, and by the time we had mopped ourselves up and had made sure that none of the liquid had gone on his companion's dress, he was ordering replacements for all the three of us. Mr. Heavistone was a middle-aged American who wore the type of rather thick spectacles that magnify the eyes of the wearer. He was a quiet, soft-spoken man with a rather slow, courteous manner. The English have a maddening habit of assuming that all Americans of this type are Southerners. In fact, Mr. Heavistone came from Detroit, and I think he had made his money, of which there appeared to be a good deal, in some offshoot of the automobile industry.

"His companion, whom he introduced as Miss Tracey, was obviously English. In fact, in both appearance and manner, she might have sat for a very flattering portrait of The English Girl. I guessed her age at about twenty-five. She had light brown hair, very fine blue eyes, lovely skin, and very nice manners.

"I must say that as casual acquaintances to pick up in a bar in Nice, they were both exceptionally pleasant. How they had first met, I never knew, but they did not know one another very well. Perhaps somebody had spilt a tray of drinks over them somewhat earlier. We spent a pleasant half hour together and then parted.

"Mr. Heavistone was staying in the hotel and so was I, and during the next few days I saw him several times, and exchanged a few words. On a couple of occasions, Miss Tracey was with him, and somewhen during this time I learnt that she lived in a villa just outside the town with her father, who was a retired soldier. From what she said I inferred that they were not well-off, and merely lived in the South of France because of her father's health. She seemed to worry a good deal about the fact that her father was bored and rather lonely, and one evening she asked me to come out to the villa with Mr. Heavistone and herself to meet him. Mr. Heavistone, I gathered, had been there a couple of times before. I had nothing to do, she was a very attractive girl, and I liked both her and Heavistone, so I was glad to accept.

"The villa was a couple of miles to the east of the town, and very much as I expected—comfortable, pleasant, but quite unpretentious. Colonel Tracey more or less completed the picture—a tall, handsome man of about sixty with closely cut iron-gray hair and a bearing of quiet dignity. He was playing patience when we arrived, and I gathered from his daughter that he spent many hours doing so. I am no expert at patience, and did not recognize the form of the game he was playing; but Heavistone did, and insisted that he should finish it. However, the game came out in a few minutes, and the Colonel then joined us, and we sat and chatted very pleasantly. It was obvious that the Colonel and his daughter were devoted to one another, and one could not help feeling that it was a slightly pathetic household in which the elderly man and the young girl both worried a good deal about the other, without the means to do much about it.

"Colonel Tracey and Heavistone talked a good deal about patience, of which they were both fond, and in the course of conversation I was asked if I played. When I said that I did not play patience but was fond of other card games, I saw the Colonel's face light up. He seemed to hesitate for a moment, and I saw him glance almost guiltily at his daughter. Then he said: 'Do you play poker?'

" 'Yes.'

" 'Do you, Mr. Heavistone?'

" 'I have done, Colonel.'

" 'Then we must make up a little school one evening.' He looked at his daughter defiantly. 'I hardly ever get a chance to play poker now, and I'm very fond of it. That would be nice, wouldn't it, Leo?'

"Miss Tracey smiled and said, 'Of course,' without, I thought, much enthusiasm. But the Colonel insisted on going on and arranging for us to come out and play two evenings later. He was obviously delighted at the prospect, and when we were leaving he reminded us both in turn of the engagement.

"By now Mr. Heavistone and I were on terms of considerable friendship, and it was our habit to meet in the bar most evenings before dinner. The evening after our visit to the Colonel's villa we were sitting there when Miss Tracey entered. We, of course, rose to greet her and offered her a drink. She accepted and sat down with us, but it was not difficult to see that she was nervous and ill at ease. After a very few minutes' rather labored conversation Heavistone happened to mention that we should be seeing her the following evening. Miss Tracey hesitated for a moment and then said bluntly:

'Yes. I—I want to talk to you about that. In fact to be quite frank that's what I came about here this evening. I hoped you'd be here and . . . Would you mind if I asked you something?'

"Heavistone said: 'Why sure. Go ahead.'

"She looked at her glass and twirled it by the stem. 'It's about Daddy and—and playing poker.'

"I said gently: 'You don't like him to play, do you?'

"'How did you know that?' she said sharply.

"'I saw your face when he proposed it.'

"'It's not that I don't like him to *play*,' she said slowly. 'In fact I like him to, because he does love it and he's very lonely, and doesn't have much fun. It's just . . .' she looked up, and the blue eyes were very worried. 'Well frankly, I'm always scared that he'll lose more than he can afford.'

"'Does he tend to lose?' said Heavistone.

"'Oh, not particularly. He says he's a very good player and I daresay he is. But once or twice when he's played with people, he's told me after the sort of amounts they were playing for, and I've wondered what would have happened if—if he *had* lost. You see, the poor old darling hasn't a cent except his pension and . . . Once he played and won two hundred pounds in an evening. He was terribly pleased and being Daddy, went straight off and spent it on me, which was very nice, of course. But I couldn't help wondering what would have happened if he'd *lost* the two hundred. He'll never listen to me. He just laughs and says he's too good a player to lose too much. But surely even the best of players do have runs of bad luck . . . ?'

"'They do,' I said with feeling.

"'They certainly do,' said Mr. Heavistone.

"'So what I wanted to ask you,' said Leonora, 'was whether you'd mind not—not playing for much tomorrow. I've no right to ask you, and it may make it awfully dull for you. But you've both been very kind, and I thought perhaps you wouldn't mind . . .' There were tears in her eyes.

"Mr. Heavistone gave her a gentle pat on the arm. 'Don't you worry,' he said in his soft, slow drawl. 'We'll watch it, won't we, Charles?'

"'Of course.'

"'Only he'll try to make you play for a lot. He always does.'

"I said: 'I never play for more than I can afford, and that's practically nothing.'

"'I can't honestly say that,' said Mr. Heavistone, smiling, 'but I certainly never like to play for enough to make any difference to anybody present. And that goes if we play for matches.'

"She said: 'Oh no—you'll have to play for *something* otherwise he'll be hurt. But just—not an awful lot.'

"'Be all right if he lost ten pounds?'

"'Yes. Quite. But not—not much more than that.'

"'O.K.,' said Mr. Heavistone. 'Then we know where we are.'

"She gave us both a small and rather pathetic smile. 'Mind you, he mustn't ever know I asked you. He'd be . . . I don't know what he'd do.'

"'That's all right,' said Mr. Heavistone. 'Hell, we understand, Leo. Have another drink.'

"She said: 'No, thank you. I've got to get back and see to Daddy's dinner. Good-by and thank you very much. See you tomorrow.'

"When she had gone Mr. Heavistone said: 'Now that's a nice girl.'

"'Yes. As a matter of fact if the old boy does like to bang it up I'm glad she told us. Otherwise it might have been a bit awkward.'

"'I doubt the Colonel'd come to much harm, my poker being the way it is. He's probably pretty good. He's certainly a smart patience player.'

"'Can you be a smart patience player? I thought it was pure chance.'

"'Well it is and it isn't. But I'd say the Colonel would be all right. Still, you never know. Something might have gone wrong, and anyhow I wouldn't like that little girl to worry. Might have been awkward, as you say.'

"'I wasn't really thinking of him so much as of me.'

"Mr. Heavistone eyed me. 'Why?'

"'Well, I very rarely play cards for much money. And certainly not with anybody I don't know—even if it's somebody like the Colonel.' Mr. Heavistone smiled his gentle smile. 'Nor me,' he said. 'So now we can all play a shilling limit just for the hell of it.'"

"IN THE EVENT, we didn't play a shilling limit the following evening, but it was certainly a very harmless game. Leonora did not play, but there was a fourth man about whom I can now remember absolutely nothing except that he spoke English like an Italian. As his daughter had prophesied, the Colonel made a couple of attempts to get the stakes to a more interesting level, but when he got no support from Heavistone or me he did not press it. I fancy Leonora had been lecturing him. He struck me as a good player, but not exceptionally so. He was one of those people who go a trifle exaggeratedly calm and expressionless when they bluff, which is an elementary fault, but one which very few people can spot in themselves. However, on the evening, he won about a couple of pounds, and so did I. Mr. Heavistone lost about three pounds. He was a poor player and obviously had not played the game much. It was not an exciting evening, but it was pleasant enough and the Colonel obviously enjoyed it immensely. On the way home Mr. Heavistone said: 'Well I hope the old boy goes out tomorrow and buys Leo a box of candy with his winnings.'"

"THIS WAS the pattern of several evenings that followed. Usually the vague Italian person made a fourth, and on one occasion there were five of us. The Colonel always made some effort to get us to play for real money, but never pressed it when we objected. On the whole, being a reasonable player, he usually won; but in the whole of the three or four occasions we went there I doubt if anybody was more than ten pounds up or down. Mr. Heavistone never said so, but I think he was a trifle bored by the whole business. He did not really like poker much, and would have been happier just to sit and talk to Leonora—as, indeed, I should. But the Colonel liked his game of poker, and on one occasion when we tried playing bridge instead, he clearly felt that it was a waste of valuable time. It was all very peaceful and pleasant if a trifle dull, and so it remained right up until the fatal evening when M. de Grouchy called.

"Four of us were playing as usual—the Colonel, Mr. Heavistone, the Italian and myself. The only unusual thing about the occasion was that Mr. Heavistone, whose game had improved considerably with practice, had been winning. He may have won thirty shillings. Leonora had left the room a few minutes before. We had just finished a hand, when she returned and said: 'Daddy—here's M. de Grouchy.' She said it as though something delightful had happened, but there was something in her face that told me that it wasn't delightful at all. The Colonel, however, seemed genuinely pleased and jumped up saying, 'Well well—just the man we want,' and proceeded to introduce us.

"Presumably, from his name and his appearance, M. de Grouchy was a Frenchman. He was a slim, rather dapper, youngish man with very sleek black hair and a sallow skin. But his English was absolutely perfect, and if he had an accent at all it was very faintly American.

"I cannot say I took to M. de Grouchy at first sight. I noticed that he greeted the Colonel with considerably less warmth than the Colonel showed towards him; and though what he said was polite enough, there was something slightly insolent in his smile and his manner. While he was being introduced to Heavistone, I caught Leonora's eye and she gave me a quick, anxious shake of the head. For a moment I didn't understand what she was trying to say. But it soon became clear.

"De Grouchy was saying: '. . . I happened to be in Nice, and thought I'd just drop in to see if there was any chance of my revenge.'

"'You couldn't have come at a better time,' said the Colonel. He turned to us. 'Last time de Grouchy was here I trimmed him properly. Two hundred pounds, wasn't it?'

"'Something like that,' said de Grouchy, with his smile. 'But you will admit Colonel, that the cards ran for you.'

"'Oh yes. Up to a point anyhow.' The Colonel smiled at him. 'But the cards always *do* run for the good player, you know.'

"'That's exactly what I want to see,' said de Grouchy. He walked over to the table and flicked some cards through his fingers. 'Well—am I allowed to come in?'

"The Italian said quickly: 'You will take my place, sir. I have to go.'

"The Colonel started to protest but the Italian was already bowing to Leonora. He was a remarkably imperceptible little man, and he simply faded himself out of the room firmly, neatly and rapidly. I had a strong impression that he had tried this party before and didn't propose to try it again. As Leonora went out with him the Colonel said: 'Never mind, we're four which is always a nice game.'

"I glanced at Heavistone and he at me. The same thought, of course, had occurred to both of us. If the Colonel had taken two hundred pounds off de Grouchy the last time he had been there, he could hardly offer him a hand in a game where, with a bit of luck, he might win thirty shillings. We had promised Leonora to keep the game small, and I for one didn't particularly relish a big game with a character like de Grouchy, Heavistone who wasn't a good player, and the Colonel to worry about. On the other hand, we could hardly refuse to play, particularly now the Italian had ducked out.

"The Colonel said briskly: 'Well come along, here's de Grouchy panting to give us the money. Let's get going.' He moved towards the table.

"Heavistone said in his quiet way: 'Look, gentlemen I don't want to spoil the fun, but I'm a small-timer at this game, and so's my friend here.'

"'Oh come,' said the Colonel. 'It won't hurt us to bang it up a bit for once.' His eyes were shining with pleasure and excitement. 'We've all been good boys for a long time. Here's a chance to make some cigar money.'

"'It may not hurt you sir, but it might hurt me. I'm a poor player as you know.'

"'You're right in the middle of a streak of luck. Come on—you can't let me down, Heavistone.'

"Leonora had come back and was sitting by the fire very tense and upright. Her face was rather pale.

"I started to say: 'Well, I agree with Heavistone . . .' when de Grouchy cut in.

"'But surely there is no problem,' he said, with the smile that made one want to kick him. 'You and I wish to play poker, Colonel. If these gentlemen do not wish to trust their skill or their luck against us, we can do one of two things. We can play for points, the points between us having a rather higher value, when we come to settle, than the points between them, or between us and them. Or we can play an ordinary game in which, after all, anybody can always throw in his cards if he feels that the risks are becoming excessive.'

"There was no answer to that—particularly said as he said it. I glanced at Leonora and saw her give a tiny helpless shrug of the shoulders and sink wearily back in her chair. Heavistone had gone slightly red at de Grouchy's tone. He hesitated for a moment and then said coldly: 'Very well, Colonel. If you wish it. I only hope I don't spoil your game.' He sat down and so did I.

"It wasn't a very happy start to the game and it didn't continue very happily. De Grouchy made no secret of the fact that he was after the Colonel—and not in any friendly way. And the Colonel knew it and liked it. Heavistone stuck to his guns and played very small, so that he was hardly ever in the game, which was a pity, since his streak of luck was continuing. I compromised. For a while I felt my way very carefully, and during that time I came to two conclusions— that de Grouchy was a first-class player and that the Colonel was a far worse one playing high than he was when playing our friendly game where there was no money in it. In fact, I didn't like the look of it at all.

"As the cards fell, the first half hour was slightly farcical, since Heavistone and I, who weren't seriously in the game, held very good cards, and de Grouchy and the Colonel, who were panting to cut one another's throats, held nothing at all. Even they weren't prepared to go very far on a pair of tens, which was the sort of thing that took the pots—usually after Heavistone had thrown in three aces. Eventually I got tired of it and took ten pounds off de Grouchy, holding a full house to his three kings. When he saw my hand he smiled thinly and said: 'Only a full house? I thought you must have at least fours to be as reckless as that.'

"After that things began to warm up a bit, as he and the Colonel began to get more cards; and right from the start de Grouchy had the edge on him. It wasn't that he was particularly lucky, though he had what little luck was going. It was mainly that he was simply the better player, and that he could spot the Colonel's overexpressionless bluff every time. I had a few cracks at him myself and on balance was slightly up. But he never went very high with me, and once the Colonel was out he barely pretended to be interested. After the first hour I should say he was about fifty pounds up on the Colonel, and a few down to me. Then he had a very good patch and cleaned up a couple of big pots, so that by about eleven o'clock he'd certainly had his revenge for his two hundred pounds, and a bit over.

"I was getting more and more unhappy, and so was Heavistone. We were both remembering what Leonora had said. 'If he'd lost two hundred instead of winning it, I don't know what would have happened.' The Colonel himself seemed much less worried than we were. Perhaps a bit of the sparkle had gone out of him, but he certainly wasn't acting like a man who had lost enough to matter to him.

"At eleven o'clock Heavistone looked at his watch and said: 'Well, gentlemen, I hate to break up a good party but . . .'

"The Colonel said: 'Oh come now Heavistone—we can't let this fellow get away with it. It's only eleven o'clock.'

"I said: 'I'm a bit weary myself.'

"'What are you worrying about, Charles? You're winning.'

"De Grouchy said: 'I am, of course, at everybody's disposal. But last time—on which occasion I was losing—we broke up at four.'

"'Well, if you think *I'm* going on till four in the morning, sir, you're wrong,' said Heavistone. It was the nearest to an acid remark that I ever heard him make to anybody.

"The Colonel sighed and said: 'They've got no stamina these people, have they de Grouchy? Look Heavistone, I tell you what—give it another hour and then we'll stop. At twelve sharp.'

"'I don't really want to, Colonel.'

"'But you must give me a chance to take it back from this fellow. It's been running all his way for the last hour, and now it ought to even out.'

"Mr. Heavistone hesitated and looked at me. But I had nothing to offer. If there was any truth in what Leonora had said, the Colonel was pretty well in already. If he wanted to try to get himself out, at the risk of going in further, one could hardly stop him. Heavistone said helplessly: 'All right. Twelve sharp then,' and on we went.

"If the previous hour had been worrying, the last hour was a nightmare; for de Grouchy went straight into as big a run of luck as I have ever seen. It wasn't only that he held good cards, but that they were always *just* good enough, and at poker that can be heartbreaking. I can even remember an actual occasion when they both held a full house, de Grouchy's being queens and sevens, and the Colonel's being knaves and fives. It was all like that, and there was nothing we could do but sit and watch it. The Colonel didn't play badly. In fact the more he lost the better and more calmly he seemed to play. But there was nothing he could do about it. There was nothing anybody could have done about it. He had reasonable cards—even good ones. He played them reasonably and he lost practically every hand. By midnight, he must have owed de Grouchy at least five hundred pounds.

"As we threw the cards in at five to twelve Heavistone looked at his watch and said: 'Well—that's that.'

"The Colonel smiled and said: 'The verdict of the umpires is that there's time for one more over.' He was still as calm as ever. If the strain was telling, it merely made his face look rather older than usual.

"De Grouchy said: 'In which he hopes to hit many runs.' He was obviously proud of his knowledge of English colloquialism. Nobody else said anything, and the Colonel dealt.

"My cards, I remember, were of no interest. I had a pair of sixes, and drew one more six. Heavistone told me afterwards that he had a pair of queens and a pair of fours. Neither was the sort of hand which was very relevant in the circumstances. But from the very outset, de Grouchy and the Colonel went out against one another. De Grouchy called for two cards and the Colonel took one, and then the fun began. I was pretty sure from the start of it that the Colonel held fours of something, and for a long time my guess was that de Grouchy had a full house. But he went on with complete confidence and eventually I began to wonder. He must guess that the Colonel held fours, after that draw of one card. The question was whether he had drawn the four of something or whether he was bluffing—or indeed whether they both were."

My Uncle Charles paused and tapped the ash off his cigar. I noticed that his hand was trembling slightly. "I have implied," he said, "that the Colonel was not really a very good player. In justice to him, I must say that in his place I should have done exactly what he did. He was a lot of money down, and on his cards he had the right to think he had caught de Grouchy at last. In fact, his nerves held rather better than the other man's, and when eventually de Grouchy raised to three hundred pounds to see him, he was still raising with the air of a man who will do so indefinitely. The Colonel put down four kings and de Grouchy smiled and put down four aces.

"There was a moment's pause and then Mr. Heavistone said: 'Christ!'

"The Colonel smiled and said: 'There's no justice. Moral—never play against the run of the cards.'

"De Grouchy said: 'You *worried* me. I thought you'd picked up the Joker to four.' It was the only thing he said in the course of the evening with no unpleasant edge in it.

"I said nothing, having nothing in particular to say. After a few moments the Colonel gathered up the cards as though he was not altogether sure what he was doing and said: 'Well well—a pleasant game, if mildly disastrous. Add up, will you?' He turned to Leonora who was still sitting staring into the fire. 'Darling, bring me my checkbook, will you?' She brought it, and the end of it was that he made out a check for eight hundred and thirty-odd pounds and gave it to de Grouchy and she stood and watched him. He was an elderly man, but I noticed that he signed the check without a tremor, and turned and smiled at her in a crooked way. I had been sorry for the Colonel before, that evening, but that was the moment I really disliked.

"Heavistone and I were silent in the car going back to Nice, but I remember saying: 'What will the old boy do now? I doubt if he's got eight hundred pounds in the world.'

"Mr. Heavistone was silent for a moment and then said with sudden and rather startling bitterness: 'No, sir. But he's got a daughter.'"

—

"TO SAY that I lay awake that night worrying about Colonel Tracey's losses would be an exaggeration. I am constitutionally incapable of lying awake at night worrying about anybody's troubles, including my own. But I must confess that I felt very unhappy about the whole affair. Whilst nobody could very well hold Heavistone and myself responsible, the fact remained that Leonora had more or less committed the Colonel to our care, and we had sat by, however excusably, and let him do exactly the thing that she had most feared. I was forcibly reminded of a time when, as an undergraduate, I had been given charge of the only son of a widowed mother on Boat Race night, and at four o'clock the following morning had been forced to lay the body on her doorstep, ring the bell, and run. I was therefore embarrassed, though not at all surprised, when Leonora walked into the lounge of the hotel on the following morning when I was drinking my morning coffee. Mr. Heavistone, unfortunately, had not yet appeared.

"I said all the obvious things—how sorry I was, how unfortunate it had all been, how we had seen no obvious way out, and so on. I then braced myself for the reproaches.

"In this, however, I had underestimated Leonora. She apologized for having given us what she felt must have been a very unpleasant evening, pointed out rather bitterly that it was no responsibility of ours if the Colonel would do these things, and thanked us for our efforts to stop him. She then smiled in a rather strained way and said: 'What I want from you is some advice. What do I do now?'

"'He can't afford to lose the money?'

"'He not only can't afford it—he hasn't got it.'

"'He gave de Grouchy a check.'

"'Anybody can write checks. He hasn't *got* eight hundred pounds.'

"'You're sure?'

"'Absolutely. He's got one hundred and seven pounds, three and eightpence in that account, and the monthly bills are due in a week. When that rat de Grouchy tries to cash that check the bank will refuse it, and Daddy will then talk some nonsense about his honor and shoot himself. Or say he will.' She picked up a couple of lumps of sugar and began to roll them as if they were dice. 'I don't understand about male honor,' she said bitterly. 'It seems that you can play cards for money that ought to pay the tradesmen, or that you haven't got, and as long as you win you're still a gentleman. But if you lose you're a cad and ought to shoot yourself. Is being a gentleman being lucky, or just not being found out?'

"I said: 'Either or both.'

"'Well anyhow, how do I lay hands on seven hundred and fifty pounds in the next few hours? Have *you* got seven hundred and fifty pounds?'

"'No, my dear.'

"'I thought not. Nobody ever has.'

"'Does that villa belong to you?'

"'No. We only rent it.'

"'Anything you can sell? Jewelry or anything?'

"'There's my watch. And my necklace that was mummy's. They're worth a bit, but not as much as that.' She flicked one of the lumps of sugar away impatiently. 'The maddening thing is that in about six months I get a thousand pounds.'

"'How?'

"'Under my aunt's will. When I'm twenty-five. But that isn't till December.'

"'You might borrow on it.'

"'Yes. But not by midday today which is about the latest it's likely to be any good.' She suddenly gave a slightly hysterical giggle. 'Where's Uncle Heavistone? He must have seven hundred and fifty pounds he wouldn't miss.'

"'I shouldn't think so. He's only here on holiday. But you might ask him.'

"'Hardly.'

"'Why not?'

"'How could I?'

"'You asked me.'

"'Only for fun.' She smiled wryly. 'I can hardly go round asking casual acquaintances to pay Daddy's betting losses when I've no security or . . .'

"'How about your aunt's will?'

"'But why should he, anyhow?'

"'I've never seen why anybody should lend anybody money. But in my experience they often do.'

"She hesitated. 'You really think he might?'

"'If he's got it. He was very put out about the whole thing.'

"Leonora sat for a moment in silence. Then she glanced at her watch and sat up. 'Right,' she said quietly. 'It is now ten thirty. I shall go and try to borrow seven hundred and fifty pounds off Mr. Heavistone, if I can find him . . .' She paused. 'You—you wouldn't like to come with me, Charles? I haven't got a lot of experience of this sort of thing.'"

My Uncle Charles paused. "There were tears in her eyes," he said pensively. "I have already said that they were very blue eyes. We found Mr. Heavistone on the terrace."

—

"AS ONE who has borrowed a good deal of money in his time, I am perennially interested in the psychology of the touchee. The experienced borrower, of course, knows his man. He knows whether the poor wretch, in an agony of embarrassment, will mutter 'Of course old man, of course' and press the money into his hand; or whether he will settle for half the amount requested; or whether he will say with artificial firmness that he never lends money but will willingly give it you; or whether he will produce the money and take the opportunity of offering a few words of advice. All these, and many others, are the common coin of borrowing, and in my experience these pitiful defensive techniques are not greatly affected by the sum involved. But I must say that I have never seen anybody borrow five pounds, let alone seven hundred and fifty, as quickly as Leonora borrowed it off Mr. Heavistone. The thing, in fact, struck me as mildly indecent. Mr. Heavistone was sitting in a deck chair on the terrace. I said, with painful jocularity, 'Hallo, Heavistone. Here's Leonora, who wants to borrow some money off you.'

"Mr. Heavistone got up and said: 'Money? How much, my dear?'

"Leonora looked at him and smiled but she couldn't say anything so I said: 'Oh—about seven hundred and fifty.'

"'Pounds or dollars or what?'

"'Pounds.'

"Mr. Heavistone made a mental calculation and clicked his tongue.

'In that case,' he said, 'I shall have to go up to my room. I don't carry that much with me.'

"He was gone about five minutes. When he came down he handed Leonora a thick bundle of notes and said: 'It's in dollars, but maybe it doesn't matter. It's money.'

"Leonora looked at the notes for a moment, and then she stepped forward and kissed Mr. Heavistone on the cheek and turned and ran away. She didn't say anything.

"Mr. Heavistone stood and looked after her and after a while he said: 'I daresay. But what's my chance of ever seeing that back?'

"I said: 'She's got some money coming to her.'

"'So what?'

"'I should think she'll pay you back.'

"Mr. Heavistone said: 'Why seven fifty? The Colonel dropped over eight hundred.'

"'She says there's a hundred in the bank.'

"Mr. Heavistone was still looking in the direction in which Leonora had gone. 'Jeez,' he said softly, 'there are some pretty good people about. You know I wouldn't care a lot if I never saw that back.'"

My Uncle Charles paused and then suddenly whipped round at me and said: "Have I told you this story before?"

"No," I said.

He shook his head. "I can't think why not. One of the most terrifying aspects of growing old is this sudden conviction—usually entirely justified—that one has told people things before. But however—for the next two days I saw nothing of Mr. Heavistone or Leonora, being involved in a visit along the coast. I still don't know what induced me, when returning to Nice on the third day, to go somewhat out of my way to visit the Colonel's villa. Nor why, as soon as I saw it, before I had left my car, I knew it was empty. Perhaps (who knows) some vestige of the brains I was born with had really remained with me throughout the whole affair. I like to think so, and to point to the fact that on the whole transaction I personally was in pocket to the extent of some fourteen pounds. But this is beside the immediate point, which was that the Colonel and Leonora had gone, that they had been gone a couple of days, and that no one appeared to know their next address, and that probably Mr. Heavistone's money had gone too. As I was driven back to Nice, I kept thinking of Mr. Heavistone's face as he looked after Leonora, and I must confess I felt slightly sick. You must remember that I was a good deal younger then than I am now. Indeed, I remember going into the bar and having a large brandy before I went to see Mr. Heavistone, merely because I was not looking forward to telling him what had happened.

"Mr. Heavistone was in his room playing patience. I think the game must have been at a rather critical stage, because he put another card down and considered for a moment before he looked round at me with the curious magnified eyes. 'Hallo,' he said, 'still here? I thought you'd gone.'

"I said: 'No. I've been along the coast. Look here, Heavistone, I'm sorry but I'm afraid I've got a shock for you. We've been swindled.'

"'We?'

"'Well, you have at least.'

"'Who by?'

"'The Colonel and his daughter. They've bolted.'

"Mr. Heavistone took another card from the pack, considered it, and put it down with a little grunt. 'She isn't his daughter,' he said gently, 'she's his wife. Come to that, he isn't a Colonel.'

"'How d'you know?'

"'You find these things out—after.'

"'Did you know they'd gone?'

"'I thought they would be.' He turned and looked at me and gave a little chuckle. 'Tell you the truth, sir, when you didn't show up yesterday, I thought you'd be gone too.'

"'I. Why?'

"'Well, think it over. She was so embarrassed, that poor girl, that she couldn't ask for the money. *You* had to come and . . .'

"I said: 'My God!'

"'Though mind you,' said Mr. Heavistone, 'I wasn't sure about you, any more than about the Italian. Now he may have been in it or he may not. But I doubt it, because then they would have to split the money four ways instead of three.'

"'You mean de Grouchy was in it?'

"'Sure. He had star billing, didn't he?'

"I sat down rather limply and said: 'When did you tumble to all this?'

"'The first time you and I went out there, sir.'

"'Then why on earth did you give her the money?'

"Mr. Heavistone shook his head. 'I hope they don't try to spend that money. The top note was twenty bucks all right. I thought it had been worth that, and maybe the Colonel can buy her a box of candy with it. But the rest cost five dollars the lot at a shop on Madison Avenue. I had a lot more but I gave it to a con man in Paris. They make it for conjurers for that trick where they keep pulling thousands of dollars out of a hat.' He shook his head again. 'It's surprising how few folks in Europe know about what proper American money looks like. You'd think they would by now. They've had enough of it.'

"I said: 'Either I've been so slow that I ought to be in a home, or else you've been damned quick. *How* did you spot it?'

"'Well, you don't play patience. You ought to play patience. It's a great game. Now the Colonel was a smart patience player.'

"'So you said.'

"'Yes. Well the first twice I went out there with the girl, the Colonel was playing patience; and he was playing a sort of patience called Mrs. Kitchner's Ramp, which very few people play. And what is more, sir, he got it out both times. Now I don't know much about poker, as you've seen, but I know a lot about patience, and if you get Mrs. Kitchner's Ramp out once every six months you're lucky. So when you and I went there and he got it out again just conveniently so as to come and talk to us, I knew the Colonel was a smart man with cards, and that they came when he called them.'

"'Then why . . . ?'

"'Why didn't he take us in the ordinary way? Well think it over, sir. I doubt you'd have played him for three thousand dollars, nice as he was. You said you wouldn't to me. Nor would I. Nor would anybody. So the way it went was to build up a big story through the girl, and then have a big loss to a four-letter man like de Grouchy and then it was easy.'

"I said: 'I must have my head attended to. But even now, there's one bit I don't see. Why on earth *should* he cheat himself at patience?'

"Mr. Heavistone smiled. 'If you played patience, you wouldn't ask that question, sir. More people cheat at patience than at anything else.' He pointed to the table. 'Now look at this. If that last card I turned up had been a nine, then it would have come out. The next card in the deck *is* a nine. And I haven't got a game out for a fortnight. See what I mean?' Mr. Heavistone sighed and gathered up the cards. 'Maybe the Colonel just played patience to give him practice with his trick decks. It takes a lot of practice to be as good as that. Or maybe he was like the rest of us and liked to win. After all, he always had to lose when it came to the big hand, and you can see that could be dull, sir.'"

AMONG THE PATHS TO EDEN

TRUMAN CAPOTE / UNITED STATES

Truman Capote

ONE SATURDAY IN MARCH, an occasion of pleasant winds and sailing clouds, Mr. Ivor Belli bought from a Brooklyn florist a fine mass of jonquils and conveyed them, first by subway, then foot, to an immense cemetery in Queens, a site unvisited by him since he had seen his wife buried there the previous autumn. Sentiment could not be credited with returning him today, for Mrs. Belli, to whom he had been married twenty-seven years, during which time she had produced two now-grown and matrimonially-settled daughters, had been a woman of many natures, most of them trying: he had no desire to renew so unsoothing an acquaintance, even in spirit. No; but a hard winter had just passed, and he felt in need of exercise, air, a heart-lifting stroll through the handsome, spring-prophesying weather; of course, rather as an extra dividend, it was nice that he would be able to tell his daughters of a journey to their mother's grave, especially so since it might a little appease the elder girl, who seemed resentful of Mr. Belli's too comfortable acceptance of life as lived alone.

The cemetery was not a reposeful, pretty place; was, in fact, a damned frightening one: acres of fog-colored stone spilled across a sparsely grassed and shadeless plateau. An unhindered view of Manhattan's skyline provided the location with beauty of a stage-prop sort—it loomed beyond the graves like a steep headstone honoring these quiet folk, its used-up and very former citizens: the juxtaposed spectacle made Mr. Belli, who was by profession a tax accountant and therefore equipped to enjoy irony however sadistic, smile, actually chuckle—yet, oh God in heaven, its inferences chilled him, too, deflated the buoyant stride carrying him along the cemetery's rigid, pebbled paths. He slowed until he stopped, thinking: "I ought to have taken Morty to the zoo"; Morty being his grandson, aged three. But it would be churlish not to continue, vengeful: and why waste a bouquet? The combination of thrift and virtue reactivated him; he was breathing hard from hurry when, at last, he stooped to jam the jonquils into a rock urn perched on a rough gray slab engraved with Gothic calligraphy declaring that

Sarah Belli
1901–1959

had been the

DEVOTED WIFE OF IVOR
BELOVED MOTHER OF IVY AND REBECCA.

Lord, what a relief to know the woman's tongue was finally stilled. But the thought, pacifying as it was, and though supported by visions of his new and silent bachelor's apartment, did not relight the suddenly snuffed-out sense of immortality, of glad-to-be-aliveness, which the day had earlier kindled. He had set forth expecting such good from the air, the walk, the aroma of another spring about to be. Now he wished he had worn a scarf; the sunshine was false, without real warmth, and the wind, it seemed to him, had grown rather wild. As he gave the jonquils a decorative pruning, he regretted he could not delay their doom by supplying them with water; relinquishing the flowers, he turned to leave.

A woman stood in his way. Though there were few other visitors to the cemetery, he had not noticed her before, or heard her approach. She did not step aside. She glanced at the jonquils; presently her eyes, situated behind steel-rimmed glasses, swerved back to Mr. Belli.

"Uh. Relative?"

"My wife," he said, and sighed as though some such noise was obligatory.

She sighed, too; a curious sigh that implied gratification. "Gee, I'm sorry."

Mr. Belli's face lengthened. "Well."

"It's a shame."

"Yes."

"I hope it wasn't a long illness. Anything painful."

"No-o-o," he said, shifting from one foot to the other. "In her sleep." Sensing an unsatisfied silence, he added, "Heart condition."

"Gee. That's how I lost my father. Just recently. Kind of gives us something in common. Something," she said, in a tone alarmingly plaintive, "something to talk about."

"—know how you must feel."

"At least they didn't suffer. That's a comfort."

The fuse attached to Mr. Belli's patience shortened. Until now he had kept his gaze appropriately lowered, observing, after his initial glimpse of her, merely the woman's shoes, which were of the sturdy, so-called sensible type often worn by aged women and nurses. "A great comfort," he said, as he executed three tasks: raised his eyes, tipped his hat, took a step forward.

Again the woman held her ground; it was as though she had been employed to detain him. "Could you give me the time? My old clock," she announced, self-consciously tapping some dainty machinery strapped to her wrist, "I got it for graduating high school. That's why it doesn't run so good any more. I mean, it's pretty old. But it makes a nice appearance."

Mr. Belli was obliged to unbutton his topcoat and plow around for a gold watch embedded in a vest pocket. Meanwhile, he scrutinized the lady, really took her apart. She must have been blond as a child, her general coloring suggested so: the clean shine of her Scandinavian skin, her chunky cheeks, flushed with peasant health, and the blueness of her genial eyes—such honest eyes, attractive despite the thin silver spectacles surrounding them; but the hair itself, what could be discerned of it under a drab felt hat, was poorly permanented frizzle of no particular tint. She was a bit taller than Mr. Belli, who was five-foot-eight with the aid of shoe lifts, and she may have weighed more; at any rate he couldn't imagine that she mounted scales too cheerfully. Her hands: kitchen hands; and the nails: not only nibbled ragged, but painted with a pearly lacquer queerly phosphorescent. She wore a plain brown coat and carried a plain black purse. When the student of these components recomposed them he found they assembled themselves into a very decent-looking person whose looks he liked; the nail polish was discouraging; still he felt that here was someone you could trust. As he trusted Esther Jackson, Miss Jackson, his secretary. Indeed, that was who she reminded him of, Miss Jackson; not that the comparison was fair—to Miss Jackson, who possessed, as he had once in the course of a quarrel informed Mrs. Belli, "intellectual elegance and elegance otherwise." Nevertheless, the woman confronting him seemed imbued with that quality of good-will he appreciated in his secretary, Miss Jackson, Esther (as he'd lately, absent-mindedly, called her). Moreover, he guessed them to be about the same age: rather on the right side of forty.

"Noon. Exactly."

"Think of that! Why, you must be famished," she said, and unclasped her purse, peered into it as though it were a picnic hamper crammed with sufficient treats to furnish a smörgåsbord. She scooped out a fistful of peanuts. "I practically live on peanuts since Pop—since I haven't anyone to cook for. I must say, even if I do say so, I miss my own cooking; Pop always said I was better than any restaurant he ever went to. But it's no pleasure cooking just for yourself, even when you *can* make pastries light as a leaf. Go on. Have some. They're fresh-roasted."

Mr. Belli accepted; he'd always been childish about peanuts and, as he sat down on his wife's grave to eat them, only hoped his friend had more. A gesture of his hand suggested that she sit beside him; he was surprised to see that the invitation seemed to embarrass her; sudden additions of pink saturated her cheeks, as though he'd asked her to transform Mrs. Belli's bier into a love bed.

"It's okay for you. A relative. But me. Would she like a stranger sitting on her—resting place?"

"Please. Be a guest. Sarah won't mind," he told her, grateful the dead cannot hear, for it both awed and amused him to consider what Sarah, that vivacious scene-maker, that energetic searcher for lipstick traces and stray blond strands, would say if she could see him shelling peanuts on her tomb with a woman not entirely unattractive.

And then, as she assumed a prim perch on the rim of the grave, he noticed her leg. Her left leg; it stuck straight out like a stiff piece of mischief with which she planned to trip passers-by. Aware of his interest, she smiled, lifted the leg up and down. "An accident. You know. When I was a kid. I fell off a roller coaster at Coney. Honest. It was in the paper. Nobody knows why I'm alive. The only thing is I can't bend my knee. Otherwise it doesn't make any difference. Except to go dancing. Are you much of a dancer?"

Mr. Belli shook his head; his mouth was full of peanuts.

"So that's something else we have in common. Dancing. I *might* like it. But I don't. I like music, though."

Mr. Belli nodded his agreement.

"And flowers," she added, touching the bouquet of jonquils; then her fingers traveled on and, as though she were reading Braille, brushed across the marble lettering on his name. "Ivor," she said, mispronouncing it. "Ivor Belli. My name is Mary O'Meaghan. But I wish *I* were Italian. My sister is; well, she married one. And oh, he's full of fun; happy-natured and outgoing, like all Italians. He says my spaghetti's the best he's ever had. Especially the kind I make with sea-food sauce. You ought to taste it."

Mr. Belli, having finished the peanuts, swept the hulls off his lap. "You've got a customer. But he's not Italian. Belli sounds like that. Only I'm Jewish."

She frowned, not with disapproval, but as if he had mysteriously daunted her.

"My family came from Russia; I was born there."

This last information restored her enthusiasm, accelerated it. "I don't care what they say in the papers. I'm sure Russians are the same as everybody else. Human. Did you see the Bolshoi Ballet on TV? Now didn't that make you proud to be a Russian?"

He thought: she means well; and was silent.

"Red cabbage soup—hot or cold—with sour cream. Hmnn. See," she said, producing a second helping of peanuts, "you *were* hungry. Poor fellow." She sighed. "How you must miss your wife's cooking."

It was true, he did; and the conversational pressure being applied to his appetite made him realize it. Sarah had set an excellent table: varied, on time, and well flavored. He recalled certain cinnamon-scented feast-days. Afternoons of gravy and wine, starchy linen, the "good" silver; followed by a nap. Moreover, Sarah had never asked him to dry a dish (he could hear her calmly humming in the kitchen), had never complained of housework; and she had contrived to make the raising of two girls a smooth series of thought-out, affectionate events; Mr. Belli's contribution to their upbringing had been to be an admiring witness; if his daughters were a credit to him (Ivy living in Bronxville, and married to a dental surgeon; her sister the wife of A. J. Krakower, junior partner in the law firm of Finnegan, Loeb and Krakower), he had Sarah to thank; they were her accomplishment. There was much to be said for Sarah, and he was glad to discover himself thinking so, to find himself remembering not the long hell of hours she had spent honing her tongue on his habits, supposed poker-playing, woman-chasing vices, but gentler episodes: Sarah showing off her self-made hats, Sarah scattering crumbs on snowy window sills for winter pigeons: a tide of visions that towed to sea the junk of harsher recollections. He felt, was all at once happy to feel, mournful, sorry he had not been sorry sooner; but, though he did genuinely value Sarah suddenly, he could not pretend regret that their life together had terminated, for the current arrangement was, on the whole, preferable by far. However, he wished that, instead of jonquils, he had brought her an orchid, the gala sort she'd always salvaged from her daughters' dates and stored in the icebox until they shriveled.

"—aren't they?" he heard, and wondered who had spoken until, blinking, he recognized Mary O'Meaghan, whose voice had been playing along unlistened to: a shy and lulling voice, a sound strangely small and young to come from so robust a figure.

"I said they must be cute, aren't they?"

"Well," was Mr. Belli's safe reply.

"Be modest. But I'm sure they are. If they favor their father; ha ha, don't take me serious, I'm joking. But, seriously, kids just slay me. I'll trade any kid for any grownup that ever lived. My sister has five, four boys and a girl. Dot, that's my sister, she's always after me to baby-sit now that I've got the time and don't have to look after Pop every minute. She and Frank, he's my brother-in-law, the one I mentioned, they say Mary, nobody can handle kids like *you*. At the same time have fun. But it's so easy; there's nothing like hot cocoa and a mean pillow fight to make kids sleepy. Ivy," she said, reading aloud the tombstone's dour script. "Ivy and Rebecca. Sweet names. And I'm sure you do your best. But two little girls without a mother."

"No, no," said Mr. Belli, at last caught up. "Ivy's a mother herself. And Becky's expecting."

Her face restyled momentary chagrin into an expression of disbelief. "A grandfather? You?"

Mr. Belli had several vanities: for example, he thought he was *saner* than other people; also, he believed himself to be a walking compass; his digestion, and an ability to read upside down, were other ego-enlarging items. But his reflection in a mirror aroused little inner applause; not that he disliked his appearance; he just knew that it was very so-what. The harvesting of his hair had begun decades ago; now his head was an almost barren field. While his nose had character, his chin, though it made a double effort, had none. His shoulders were broad; but so was the rest of him. Of course he was neat: kept his shoes shined, his laundry laundered, twice a day scraped and talcumed his bluish jowls; but such measures failed to camouflage, actually they emphasized, his middle-class, middle-aged ordinariness.

Nonetheless, he did not dismiss Mary O'Meaghan's flattery; after all, an undeserved compliment is often the most potent.

"Hell, I'm fifty-one," he said, subtracting four years. "Can't say I feel it." And he didn't; perhaps it was because the wind had subsided, the warmth of the sun grown more authentic. Whatever the reason, his expectations had re-ignited, he was again immortal, a man planning ahead.

"Fifty-one. That's nothing. The prime. Is if you take care of yourself. A man your age needs tending so. Watching after."

Surely in a cemetery one was safe from husband stalkers? The question, crossing his mind, paused midway while he examined her cozy and gullible face, tested her gaze for guile. Though reassured, he thought it best to remind her of their surroundings. "Your father. Is he"—Mr. Belli gestured awkwardly—"near by?"

"Pop? Oh, no. He was very firm; absolutely refused to be buried. So he's at home." A disquieting image gathered in Mr. Belli's head, one that her next words, "His ashes are," did not fully dispel. "Well," she shrugged, "that's how he wanted it. Or—I see—you wondered why *I'm* here? I don't live too far away. It's somewhere to walk, and the view . . ." They both turned to stare at the skyline where the steeples of certain buildings flew pennants of cloud, and sun-dazzled windows glittered like a million bits of mica. Mary O'Meaghan said, "What a perfect day for a parade!"

Mr. Belli thought, *You're a very nice girl;* then he said it, too, and wished he hadn't, for naturally she asked him why. "Because. Well, that was nice what you said. About parades."

"See? So many things in common! I never miss a parade," she told him triumphantly. "The bugles. I play the bugle myself; used to, when I was at Sacred Heart. You said before—" She lowered her voice, as though approaching a subject that required grave tones. "You indicated you were a music lover. Because I have thousands of old records. Hundreds. Pop was in the business and that was his job. Till he retired. Shellacking records in a record factory. Remember Helen Morgan? She slays me, she really knocks me out."

"*Jesus* Christ," he whispered. Ruby Keeler, Jean Harlow: those had been keen but curable infatuations; but Helen Morgan, albino-pale, a sequinned wraith shimmering beyond Ziegfeld footlights—truly, truly he had loved her.

"Do you believe it? That she drank herself to death? On account of a gangster?"

"It doesn't matter. She was lovely."

"Sometimes, like when I'm alone and sort of fed up, I pretend I'm her. Pretend I'm singing in a night club. It's fun; you know?"

"Yes, I know," said Mr. Belli, whose own favorite fantasy was to imagine the adventures he might have if he were invisible.

"May I ask: would you do me a favor?"

"If I can. Certainly."

She inhaled, held her breath as if she were swimming under a wave of shyness; surfacing, she said: "Would you listen to my imitation? And tell me your honest opinion?" Then she removed her glasses: the silver rims had bitten so deeply their shape was permanently printed on her face. Her eyes, nude and moist and helpless, seemed stunned by freedom; the skimpily lashed lids fluttered like long-captive birds abruptly let loose. "There: everything's soft and smoky. Now you've got to use your imagination. So pretend I'm sitting on a piano—gosh, for*give* me, Mr. Belli."

"Forget it. Okay. You're sitting on a piano."

"I'm sitting on a piano," she said, dreamily drooping her head backward until it assumed a romantic posture. She sucked in her cheeks, parted her lips; at the same moment Mr. Belli bit into his. For it was a tactless visit that glamour made on Mary O'Meaghan's filled-out and rosy face; a visit that should not have been paid at all; it was the wrong address. She waited, as though listening for music to cue her; then, *"Don't ever leave me, now that you're here! Here is where you belong. Everything seems so right when you're near, When you're away it's all wrong."* and Mr. Belli was shocked, for what he was hearing was exactly Helen Morgan's voice, and the voice, with its vulnerable sweetness, refinement, its tender quaver toppling high notes, seemed not to be borrowed, but Mary O'Meaghan's own, a natural expression of some secluded identity. Gradually she abandoned theatrical poses, sat upright singing with her eyes squeezed shut: *"—I'm so dependent, When I need comfort, I always run to you. Don't ever leave me! 'Cause if you do, I'll have no one to run to."* Until too late, neither she nor Mr. Belli noticed the coffin-laden entourage invading their privacy: a black caterpillar composed of sedate Negroes who stared at the white couple as though they had stumbled upon a pair of drunken grave robbers—except one mourner, a dry-eyed little girl who started laughing and couldn't stop; her hiccup-like hilarity resounded long after the procession had disappeared around a distant corner.

"If that kid was mine," said Mr. Belli.

"I feel so ashamed."

"Say, listen. What for? That was beautiful. I mean it; you can sing."

"Thanks," she said; and, as though setting up a barricade against impending tears, clamped on her spectacles.

"Believe me, I was touched. What I'd like is, I'd like an encore."

It was as if she were a child to whom he'd handed a balloon, a unique balloon that kept swelling until it swept her upward, danced her along with just her toes now and then touching ground. She descended to say: "Only not here. Maybe," she began, and once more seemed to be lifted, lilted through the air, "maybe sometime you'll let me cook you dinner. I'll plan it really Russian. And we can play records."

The thought, the apparitional suspicion that had previously passed on tiptoe, returned with a heavier tread, a creature fat and foursquare that Mr. Belli could not evict. "Thank you, Miss O'Meaghan. That's something to look forward to," he said. Rising, he reset his hat, adjusted his coat. "Sitting on cold stone too long, you can catch something."

"When?"

"Why, never. You should *never* sit on cold stone."

"When will you come to dinner?"

Mr. Belli's livelihood rather depended upon his being a skilled inventor of excuses. "Any time," he answered smoothly. "Except any time soon. I'm a tax man; you know what happens to us fellows in March. Yes sir," he said, again hoisting out his watch, "back to the grind for me." Still he couldn't—could he?—simply saunter off, leave her sitting on Sarah's grave? He owed her courtesy; for the peanuts, if nothing more, though there was more—perhaps it was due to her that he had remembered Sarah's orchids withering in the icebox. And anyway, she *was* nice, as likeable a woman, stranger, as he'd ever met. He thought to take advantage of the weather but the weather offered none: clouds were fewer, the sun exceedingly visible. "Turned chilly," he observed, rubbing his hands together. "Could be going to rain."

"Mr. Belli. Now I'm going to ask you a very personal question," she said, enunciating each word decisively. "Because I wouldn't want you to think I go about inviting just anybody to dinner. My intentions are—" her eyes wandered, her voice wavered, as though the forthright manner had been a masquerade she could not sustain. "So I'm going to ask you a very personal question. Have you considered marrying again?"

He hummed, like a radio warming up before it speaks; when he did, it amounted to static: "Oh, at *my* age. Don't even want a dog. Just give me TV. Some beer. Poker once a week. Hell. Who the hell would want me?" he said; and, with a twinge, remembered Rebecca's mother-in-law, Mrs. A. J. Krakower, Sr., Dr. Pauline Krakower, a female dentist (retired) who had been an audacious participant in a certain family plot. Or what about Sarah's best friend, the persistent "Brownie" Pollock? Odd, but as long as Sarah lived he had enjoyed, upon occasion taken advantage of, "Brownie's" admiration; afterwards—finally he had *told* her not to telephone him any more (and she had shouted: "Everything Sarah ever said, she was right. You fat little *hairy* little bastard"). Then; and then there was Miss Jackson. Despite Sarah's suspicions, her in fact devout conviction, nothing untoward, very untoward, had transpired between him and the pleasant Esther, whose hobby was bowling. But he had always surmised, and in recent months known, that if one day he suggested drinks, dinner, a workout in some bowling alley . . . He said: "I *was* married. For twenty-seven years. That's enough for any lifetime"; but as he said it, he realized that, in just this moment, he had come to a decision, which was: he *would* ask Esther to dinner, he would take her bowling and buy her an orchid, a gala purple one with a lavender-ribbon bow. And where, he wondered, do couples honeymoon in

April? At the latest May. Miami? Bermuda? Bermuda! "No, I've never considered it. Marrying again."

One would have assumed from her attentive posture that Mary O'Meaghan was raptly listening to Mr. Belli—except that her eyes played hookey, roamed as though she were hunting at a party for a different, more promising face. The color had drained from her own face; and with it had gone most of her healthy charm. She coughed.

He coughed. Raising his hat, he said: "It's been very pleasant meeting you, Miss O'Meaghan."

"Same here," she said, and stood up. "Mind if I walk with you to the gate?"

He did, yes; for he wanted to mosey along alone, devouring the tart nourishment of this spring-shiny, parade-weather, be alone with his many thoughts of Esther, his hopeful, zestful, live-forever mood. "A pleasure," he said, adjusting his stride to her slower pace and the slight lurch her stiff leg caused.

"But it *did* seem like a sensible idea," she said argumentatively. "And there was old Annie Austin: the living proof. Well, nobody had a *better* idea. I mean, everybody was at me: Get married. From the day Pop died, my sister and everybody was saying: Poor Mary, what's to become of her? A girl that can't type. Take shorthand. With her leg and all; can't even wait on table. What happens to a girl—a *grown* woman—that doesn't know anything, never done anything? Except cook and look after her father. All I heard was: Mary, you've got to get married."

"So. Why fight that? A fine person like you, you ought to be married. You'd make some fellow very happy."

"Sure I would. But *who?*" She flung out her arms, extended a hand toward Manhattan, the country, the continents beyond. "So I've looked; I'm not lazy by nature. But honestly, frankly, how does anybody ever find a husband? If they're not very, very pretty; a terrific dancer. If they're just—oh ordinary. Like me."

"No, no, not at all," Mr. Belli mumbled. "Not ordinary, no. Couldn't you make something of your talent? Your voice?"

She stopped, stood clasping and unclasping her purse. "Don't poke fun. Please. My life is at stake." And she insisted: "I *am* ordinary. So is old Annie Austin. And she says the place for me to find a husband—a decent, comfortable man—is in the obituary column."

For a man who believed himself a human compass, Mr. Belli had the anxious experience of feeling he had lost his way; with relief he saw the gates of the cemetery a hundred yards ahead. "She does? She says that? Old Annie Austin?"

"Yes. And she's a very practical woman. She feeds six people on $58.75 a week: food, clothes, everything. And the way she explained it, it certainly *sounded* logical. Because the obituaries are full of unmarried men. Widowers. You just go to the funeral and sort of introduce yourself: sympathize. Or the cemetery: come here on a nice day, or go to Woodlawn, there are always widowers walking around. Fellows thinking how much they miss home life and maybe wishing they were married again."

When Mr. Belli understood that she was in earnest, he was appalled; but he was also entertained: and he laughed, jammed his hands in his pockets and threw back his head. She joined him, spilled a laughter that restored her color, that, in skylarking style, made her rock against him. "Even I—" she said, clutching at his arm "—even *I* can see the humor." But it was not a lengthy vision; suddenly solemn, she said: "But that is how Annie met her husbands. Both of them: Mr. Cruikshank, and then Mr. Austin. So it *must* be a practical idea. Don't you think?"

"Oh, I do think."

She shrugged. "But it hasn't worked out too well. Us, for instance. *We* seemed to have such a lot in common."

"One day," he said, quickening his steps. "With a livelier fellow."

"I don't know. I've met some grand people. But it always ends like this. Like us . . ." she said, and left unsaid something more, for a new pilgrim, just entering through the gates of the cemetery, had attached her interest: an alive little man spouting cheery whistlings and with plenty of snap to his walk. Mr. Belli noticed him, too, observed the black band sewn round the sleeve of the visitor's bright green tweed coat, and commented: "Good luck, Miss O'Meaghan. Thanks for the peanuts."

ADMIRAL'S NIGHT

MACHADO DE ASSIS / BRAZIL

Machado de Assis.

Translated by William L. Grossman

AT THREE O'CLOCK in the afternoon Deolindo the Nostril (a sobriquet given him by his crew mates) left the Navy Yard and walked briskly up the Rua de Bragança. His corvette had just returned from a long training cruise; he came ashore as soon as he could obtain leave. His friends had said to him, laughing: "Hey, Nostril! You're going to have a real Admiral's Night, aren't you? Wine, a guitar, and Genoveva's arms. Genoveva's loving little . . ."

Deolindo had smiled. Exactly so: an Admiral's Night, as the phrase goes, was awaiting him onshore. The passion had begun three months before the corvette's departure. Genoveva was a brown-skinned girl from the country, twenty years old, with dark, knowing eyes. They had met at a friend's house and had fallen madly in love, so madly that they had been on the point of doing a mad thing: he was going to desert the Navy, and she was going to run away with him to the most remote village in the interior.

Old Ignacia, with whom Genoveva lived, had dissuaded them. Hence Deolindo had decided to follow orders and sail on the training cruise. As a mutual guaranty they had decided that they ought to take an oath of fidelity.

"I swear by God in heaven. And you?"

"I also."

"Say it."

"I swear by God in heaven. May the holy light fail me at the hour of death."

The meeting of minds was duly celebrated. No one could doubt their sincerity; she cried like one possessed, he bit his lip to conceal his emotion. Finally they parted. Genoveva watched the corvette sail off and returned home with such tension in her heart that it seemed as though something dreadful was going to happen, but nothing did. The days went by, the weeks, the months, ten months, then the corvette returned and Deolindo with it.

There he goes now, up the Rua de Bragança, through Prainha and Saude, until he comes to Gambôa, where Genoveva lives, just beyond the English cemetery. There he will probably find her leaning on the windowsill, waiting for him. Deolindo prepares a few words with which to greet her. He has already composed this: "I took an oath and I kept it," but he is working on something better. He remembers women he saw all over the world: Italian, Marseillaise, Turkish, many of them pretty or at least so they seemed to him. Not all, he concedes, were exactly his dish, but some of them certainly were, and even so they did not really interest him. He thought only of Genoveva. Her house, her sweet little house, its walls cracked by the sun, and its sparse, old, broken-down furniture, these he remembered when he stood before exotic palaces in distant lands. By considerable abnegation he bought in Trieste a pair of earrings, which he now carries in his pocket together with some less impressive little gifts. And what is she going to give him? Very likely a handkerchief embroidered with his name and with an anchor in the corner, for she is very clever at embroidery.

About this time he arrived in Gambôa, passed the cemetery, and stopped at the house. The door was closed. He knocked and immediately heard a familiar voice, that of old Ignacia, who opened the door with exclamations of great surprise. Deolindo, impatient, asked for Genoveva.

"Don't talk about that crazy girl," said the old woman. "I'm glad about the advice I gave you. See, she's gone off."

"But what was it? What happened?"

The old woman told him to take it easy, it was nothing, just one of those things that happen. It was not worth getting angry about. Genoveva's head was turned . . .

"Who turned it?"

"Did you know José Diogo, the cloth peddler? She's with him. You can't imagine how in love they are. She's like a crazy girl. That's why we had a fight. José Diogo would never go home. They'd whisper and whisper, until one day I said I didn't want my house to get a bad name. Good Father in heaven, it was a day of judgment! Genoveva glared at me with eyes this size, saying that she never gave anyone a bad name and that she didn't need charity. What do you mean, charity, Genoveva? All I said was I don't want whispering at my door until six o'clock at night. . . . Two days later she moved away and never spoke to me again."

"Where is she living?"

"On Formosa Beach, before you come to the quarry. The house has just been painted."

Deolindo had heard enough. Old Ignacia, a little sorry she had spoken so freely, advised prudence, but he did not listen. Off he went. I shall not relate his thoughts on the way, for they were wholly disorganized. Ideas navigated about his brain as in a tempest, amid a confusion of winds and foghorns. Among them gleamed a sailor's knife, vengeful and bloody. He had passed through Gambôa and the Sacco de Alferes, and had entered Formosa Beach. He did not know the number of the house, but knew that it was near the quarry and freshly painted, and with the help of people in the neighborhood he would find it. He had no reason to foresee that chance would take hold of Genoveva and seat her at the window, sewing, at the very moment when he came along. He saw her and stopped. She, seeing the form of a man, raised her eyes and recognized the sailor.

"Of all things!" she exclaimed in surprise. "When did you get back? Come in, Deolindo."

And, rising, she opened the door and let him in. Any man would have become wild with hope, so frank and friendly was the girl's manner. Maybe the old woman had been mistaken or had lied. Maybe, even, the peddler's song had ended. All this indeed passed through Deolindo's mind, without the exact form of reason but swiftly and tumultuously. Genoveva left the door open, had him sit down, asked about the voyage, and said that she thought he had gained weight; no emotion, no intimacy. Deolindo lost all hope. He had no knife with him, but he had his hands; Genoveva was a small piece of woman, he could easily strangle her. For the first few moments he thought of nothing else.

"I know everything," he said.

"Who told you?"

Deolindo shrugged his shoulders.

"Whoever it was," she continued, "did they tell you I was in love with somebody?"

"Yes."

"They told you the truth."

Deolindo started toward her, but the way she looked at him made him stop. Then she said that if she let him in, it was because she thought him an intelligent man. She told him everything, how terribly she had missed him, the propositions the peddler had made, her refusals, until one morning, without knowing how or why, she had awakened in love with him.

"Really, I thought of you a lot. Just ask Ignacia how much I cried. . . . But my heart changed. . . . It changed . . . I'm telling you all this as if I were talking to a priest," she concluded, smiling.

She was not smiling in mockery. Her manner of speech suggested a combination of candor and cynicism, insolence and simplicity; I cannot explain it better. Perhaps the words insolence and cynicism are poorly chosen. Genoveva was not defending herself at all, she had no moral standards to indicate a need for defense. What she was saying, in brief, was that it would have been better not to have changed, that she had really loved him or she would not have been willing to run away with him; but that, as José Diogo had intervened and conquered, one might as well accept the fact. The poor sailor cited the parting oath as an eternal obligation, because of which he had agreed not to desert his ship: "I swear by God in heaven. May the holy light fail me at the hour of death." He had been willing to sail only because she had sworn this oath. With those words in his ears he had gone, traveled, waited, and returned; they had given him the strength to live. I swear by God in heaven. May the holy light fail me at the hour of death . . .

"Yes, all right, Deolindo; it was the truth. When I swore it, it was the truth. I even wanted to run away with you. But then other things happened . . . this fellow came along and I began to like him . . ."

"But that's just why people swear not to, so that they won't like anybody else . . ."

"Stop it, Deolindo. Did you never think of anyone but me? Don't talk nonsense . . ."

"When will José Diogo come back?"

"He's not coming back today."

"No?"

"He's not coming. He's working in Guaratiba. He'll probably be back Friday or Saturday. . . . Why do you want to know? What did he ever do to you?"

Perhaps any other woman would have said substantially the same thing, but few would have expressed it so candidly. See how close to nature we are at this point. What did he ever do to you? What did this rock that fell on your head ever do to you? Any physicist can explain why a rock falls; it has nothing to do with you.

Deolindo declared, with a desperate gesture, that he wanted to kill the peddler. Genoveva looked at him with contempt, smiled slightly, and made a deprecative cluck with her tongue. And when he accused her of ingratitude and lying, she could not conceal her amazement. What lying? What ingratitude? Had she not already told him that what she swore was the truth? The Virgin there on top of the bureau, she knew it was the truth. Is this how he repaid her for her suffering? And he who talked so much about fidelity, had he always thought of her wherever he went?

His answer was to put his hand in his pocket and take out the package he had brought. She opened it, looked at the gifts one by one, and finally came upon the earrings. They were not, they could not be, expensive; they were even in poor taste; but they were glorious to behold. Genoveva took them in her fingers, happy, dazzled, examined one side and then the other, closely and at arm's length, and finally put them on. Then, to appraise their effect, she looked in the ten-cent mirror hanging on the wall between the window and the door. She stepped back, approached the mirror again, turned her head from side to side. "They're very pretty, very!" she said, bowing her thanks. "Where did you buy them?"

He did not reply. Indeed, he had no time to do so, for she fired two or three more questions at him, one right after the other, so confused was she at receiving a wonderful gift in exchange for having fallen out of love with him. Confusion for five or four minutes; maybe two. Then she took off the earrings, contemplated them, and put them in the little box on the round table in the middle of the room. He, for his part, began to think that, just as he had lost her because of his absence, so now the other might lose her; and probably she had sworn no oath at all to the peddler.

"Talking and fooling around all afternoon, and now it's night already," said Genoveva.

Indeed, night was swiftly falling. One could no longer see the Lepers' Hospital and could hardly make out Melon Island; even the rowboats and canoes in front of the house blended with the mud of the beach. Genoveva lit a candle. Then she sat down and asked him to tell her something about the countries he had seen. Deolindo refused. He said he was going; he rose and took a few steps. But the demon of hope was biting the poor devil's heart; he sat down and began to talk about his experiences on the voyage. Genoveva listened attentively. Interrupted by the entrance of a woman friend who lived nearby, Genoveva asked her to sit down, too, and listen to "the pretty stories Deolindo is telling"; there was no other introduction.

The grand lady who lies awake into the morning because she cannot put down the novel she is reading does not live the lives of the characters in it more intimately than the sailor's ex-lover was living the scenes that he narrated; she was as freely absorbed as if there had been nothing between them but the telling of a story. What matters to the grand lady the author of the book? What mattered to this girl the teller of the tales?

Hope, meanwhile, had begun to desert him, and he rose, once and for all, to leave. Genoveva did not want to let him go until her friend had seen the earrings; she showed them to her with comments on their beauty and value. The other woman was enchanted, praised them highly, asked whether he had bought them in France, and requested Genoveva to put them on. "Really, they're beautiful."

I guess the sailor shared this opinion. He liked to look at them, found them to be virtually made for her, and for a few seconds tasted the rare and delicate pleasure of having made a fine gift; but for only a few seconds.

As he was saying good-by, Genoveva accompanied him to the door to thank him once more for the gift and probably to say some politely kind words. Her friend, whom she had left in the room, heard only, "Don't be foolish, Deolindo"; and from the sailor, "You'll see." She could not hear the rest, which was spoken in whispers.

Deolindo walked off along the beach, downcast and slow, no longer the impetuous youth of the afternoon but sorrowful and old or, to use a metaphor common among our sailors, halfway down the deep shore. Genoveva went back indoors, bustling and chatty. She told the woman about her naval romance, praised greatly Deolindo's character and fine manners. Her friend declared that she found him very charming.

"A really nice boy," repeated Genoveva. "Do you know what he just told me?"

"What?"

"That he's going to kill himself."

"Jesus!"

"Don't worry, he won't really. That's how Deolindo is: he says things but he doesn't do them. You'll see, he won't kill himself. Poor thing, he's jealous. . . . The earrings are gorgeous."

"I never saw any like them here in Rio."

"Neither did I," said Genoveva, examining them in the light. Then she put them away and invited the woman to sew with her. "Let's sew awhile, I want to finish my blue camisole . . ."

She was right: the sailor did not kill himself. The next day some of his mates slapped him on the shoulder, congratulating him on his Admiral's Night, and asked about Genoveva, whether she had cried a lot during his absence, whether she was still pretty. . . . He replied to everything with a sly and satisfied smile, the smile of a man tasting inwardly the memories of the night before.

THE BET

ANTON CHEKHOV / RUSSIA

I T WAS a dark autumn night. The old banker was pacing from corner to corner of his study, recalling to his mind the party he gave in the autumn fifteen years before. There were many clever people at the party and much interesting conversation. They talked among other things of capital punishment. The guests, among them not a few scholars and journalists, for the most· part disapproved of capital punishment. They found it obsolete as a means of punishment, unfitted to a Christian state and immoral. Some of them thought that capital punishment should be replaced universally by life imprisonment.

"I don't agree with you," said the host. "I myself have experienced neither capital punishment nor life imprisonment, but if one may judge a priori, then in my opinion capital punishment is more moral and more humane than imprisonment. Execution kills instantly, life imprisonment kills by degrees. Who is the more humane executioner, one who kills you in a few seconds or one who draws the life out of you incessantly, for years?"

"They're both equally immoral," remarked one of the guests, "because their purpose is the same, to take away life. The state is not God. It has no right to take away that which it cannot give back, if it should so desire."

Among the company was a lawyer, a young man of about twenty-five. On being asked his opinion, he said:

"Capital punishment and life imprisonment are equally immoral; but if I were offered the choice between them, I would certainly choose the second. It's better to live somehow than not to live at all."

There ensued a lively discussion. The banker, who was then younger and more nervous, suddenly lost his temper, banged his fist on the table, and turning to the young lawyer, cried out:

"It's a lie. I bet you two millions you wouldn't stick in a cell even for five years."

"If you mean it seriously," replied the lawyer, "then I bet I'll stay not five but fifteen."

"Fifteen! Done!" cried the banker. "Gentlemen, I stake two millions."

"Agreed. You stake two millions, I my freedom," said the lawyer.

So this wild, ridiculous bet came to pass. The banker, who at that time had too many millions to count, spoiled and capricious, was beside himself with rapture. During supper he said to the lawyer jokingly:

"Come to your senses, young man, before it's too late. Two millions are nothing to me, but you stand to lose three or four of the best years of your life. I say three or four, because you'll never stick it out any longer. Don't forget either, you unhappy man, that voluntary is much heavier than enforced imprisonment. The idea that you have the right to free yourself at any moment will poison the whole of your life in the cell. I pity you."

And now the banker, pacing from corner to corner, recalled all this and asked himself:

Why did I make this bet? What's the good? The lawyer loses fifteen years of his life and I throw away two millions. Will it convince people that capital punishment is worse or better than imprisonment for life? No, no! All stuff and rubbish. On my part, it was the caprice of a well-fed man; on the lawyer's pure greed of gold.

He recollected further what happened after the evening party. It was decided that the lawyer must undergo his imprisonment under the strictest observation, in a garden wing of the banker's house. It was agreed that during the period he would be deprived of the right to cross the threshold, to see living people, to hear human voices, and to receive letters and newspapers. He was permitted to have a musical instrument, to read books, to write letters, to drink wine and smoke tobacco. By the agreement he could communicate, but only in silence, with the outside world through a little window specially constructed for this purpose. Everything necessary, books, music, wine, he could receive in any quantity by sending a note through the window. The agreement provided for all the minutest details, which made the confinement strictly solitary, and it obliged the lawyer to remain exactly fifteen years from twelve o'clock of November 14, 1870, to twelve o'clock of November 14, 1885. The least attempt on his part to violate the conditions, to escape if only for two minutes before the time, freed the banker from the obligation to pay him the two millions.

During the first year of imprisonment, the lawyer, as far as it was possible to judge from his short notes, suffered terribly from loneliness and boredom. From his wing day and night came the sound of the piano. He rejected wine and tobacco. "Wine," he wrote, "excites desires, and desires are the chief foes of a prisoner; besides, nothing is more boring than to drink good wine alone, and tobacco spoils the air in his room."

During the first year the lawyer was sent books of a light character; novels with a complicated love interest, stories of crime and fantasy, comedies, and so on.

In the second year the piano was heard no longer and the lawyer asked only for classics. In the fifth year, music was heard again, and the prisoner asked for wine. Those who watched him said that during the whole of that year he was only eating, drinking, and lying on his bed. He yawned often and talked angrily to himself. Books he did not read. Sometimes at nights he would sit down to write. He would write for a long time and tear it all up in the morning. More than once he was heard to weep.

In the second half of the sixth year, the prisoner began zealously to study languages, philosophy, and history. He fell on these subjects so hungrily that the banker hardly had time to get books enough for him. In the space of four years about six hundred volumes were bought at his request.

It was while that passion lasted that the banker received the following letter from the prisoner: "My dear jailer, I am writing these lines in six languages. Show them to experts. Let them read them. If they do not find one single mistake, I beg you to give orders to have a gun fired off in the garden. By the noise I shall know that my efforts have not been in vain. The geniuses of all ages and countries speak in different languages; but in them all burns the same flame. Oh, if you knew my heavenly happiness now that I can understand them!" The prisoner's desire was fulfilled. Two shots were fired in the garden by the banker's order.

Later on, after the tenth year, the lawyer sat immovable before his table and read only the New Testament. The banker found it strange that a man who in four years had mastered six hundred erudite volumes should have spent nearly a year in reading one book, easy to understand and by no means thick. The New Testament was then replaced by the history of religions and theology.

During the last two years of his confinement the prisoner read an extraordinary amount, quite haphazard. Now he would apply himself to the natural sciences, then he would read Byron or Shakespeare. Notes used to come from him in which he asked to be sent at the same time a book on chemistry, a textbook of medicine, a novel, and some treatise on philosophy or theology. He read as though he were swimming in the sea among broken pieces of wreckage, and in his desire to save his life was eagerly grasping one piece after another.

THE BANKER recalled all this, and thought:

Tomorrow at twelve o'clock he receives his freedom. Under the agreement, I shall have to pay him two millions. If I pay, it's all over with me. I am ruined forever. . . .

Fifteen years before, he had too many millions to count, but now he was afraid to ask himself which he had more of, money or debts. Gambling on the stock exchange, risky speculation, and the recklessness of which he could not rid himself even in old age had gradually brought his business to decay; and the fearless, self-confident, proud man of business had become an ordinary banker, trembling at every rise and fall in the market.

"That cursed bet," murmured the old man clutching his head in despair. . . . "Why didn't the man die? He's only forty years old. He will take away my last farthing, marry, enjoy life, gamble on the exchange, and I will look on like an envious beggar and hear the same words from him every day: 'I'm obliged to you for the happiness of my life. Let me help you.' No, it's too much! The only escape from bankruptcy and disgrace is that the man should die."

The clock had just struck three. The banker was listening. In the house everyone was asleep, and one could hear only the frozen trees whining outside the windows. Trying to make no sound, he took out of his safe the key of the door which had not been opened for fifteen years, put on his overcoat, and went out of the house. The garden was dark and cold. It was raining. A damp, penetrating wind howled in the garden and gave the trees no rest.

Though he strained his eyes, the banker could see neither the ground, nor the white statues, nor the garden wing, nor the trees. Approaching the garden wing, he called the watchman twice. There was no answer. Evidently the watchman had taken shelter from the bad weather and was now asleep somewhere in the kitchen or the greenhouse.

If I have the courage to fulfill my intention, thought the old man, the suspicion will fall on the watchman first of all.

In the darkness he groped for the steps and the door and entered the hall of the garden wing, then poked his way into a narrow passage and struck a match. Not a soul was there. Someone's bed, with no bedclothes on it, stood there, and an iron stove loomed dark in the corner. The seals on the door that led into the prisoner's room were unbroken.

When the match went out, the old man, trembling from agitation, peeped into the little window.

In the prisoner's room a candle was burning dimly. The prisoner himself sat by the table. Only his back, the hair on his head, and his hands were visible. Open books were strewn about on the table, the two chairs, and on the carpet near the table.

Five minutes passed and the prisoner never once stirred. Fifteen years' confinement had taught him to sit motionless. The banker tapped on the window with his finger, but the prisoner made no movement in reply. Then the banker cautiously tore the seals from the door and put the key into the lock. The rusty lock gave a hoarse groan and the door creaked. The banker expected instantly to hear a cry of surprise and the sound of steps. Three minutes passed and it was as quiet inside as it had been before. He made up his mind to enter.

Before the table sat a man, unlike an ordinary human being. It was a skeleton, with tight-drawn skin, with long curly hair like a woman's, and a shaggy beard. The color of his face was yellow, of an earthy shade; the cheeks were sunken, the back long and narrow, and the hand upon which he leaned his hairy head was so lean and skinny that it was painful to look upon. His hair was already silvering with gray, and no one who glanced at the senile emaciation of the face would have believed that he was only forty years old. On the table, before his bended head, lay a sheet of paper on which something was written in a tiny hand.

Poor devil, thought the banker, he's asleep and probably seeing millions in his dreams. I have only to take and throw this half-dead thing on the bed, smother him a moment with the pillow, and the most careful examination will find no trace of unnatural death. But, first, let us read what he has written here.

The banker took the sheet from the table and read:

"Tomorrow at twelve o'clock midnight I shall obtain my freedom and the right to mix with people. But before I leave this room and see the sun I think it necessary to say a few words to you. On my own clear conscience and before God who sees me I declare to you that I despise freedom, life, health, and all that your books call the blessings of the world.

"For fifteen years I have diligently studied earthly life. True, I saw neither the earth nor the people, but in your books I drank fragrant wine, sang songs, hunted deer and wild boar in the forests, loved women. . . . And beautiful women, like clouds ethereal, created by the magic of your poets' genius, visited me by night and whispered to me wonderful tales, which made my head drunken.

"In your books I climbed the summits of Elbruz and Mont Blanc and saw from there how the sun rose in the morning, and in the evening suffused the sky, the ocean and the mountain ridges with a purple gold. I saw from there how above me lightnings glimmered cleaving the clouds; I saw green forests, fields, rivers, lakes, cities; I heard sirens singing, and the playing of the pipes of Pan; I touched the wings of beautiful devils who came flying to me to speak of God. . . . In your books I cast myself into bottomless abysses, worked miracles, burned cities to the ground, preached new religions, conquered whole countries. . . .

"Your books gave me wisdom. All that unwearying human thought created in the centuries is compressed to a little lump in my skull. I know that I am cleverer than you all.

"And I despise your books, despise all worldly blessings and wisdom. Everything is void, frail, visionary and delusive as a mirage. Though you be proud and wise and beautiful, yet will death wipe you from the face of the earth like the mice underground; and your posterity, your history, and the immortality of your men of genius will be as frozen slag, burnt down together with the terrestrial globe.

"You are mad, and gone the wrong way. You take falsehood for truth and ugliness for beauty. You would marvel if suddenly apple and orange trees should bear frogs and lizards instead of fruit, and if roses should begin to breathe the odor of a sweating horse. So do I marvel at you, who have bartered heaven for earth. I do not want to understand you.

"That I may show you in deed my contempt for that by which you live, I waive the two millions of which I once dreamed as of paradise, and which I now despise. That I may deprive myself of my right to them, I shall come out from here five minutes before the stipulated term, and thus shall violate the agreement."

When he had read, the banker put the sheet on the table, kissed the head of the strange man, and began to weep. He went out of the wing. Never at any other time, not even after his terrible losses on the exchange, had he felt such contempt for himself as now. Coming home, he lay down on his bed, but agitation and tears kept him a long time from sleeping. . . .

The next morning the poor watchman came running to him and told him that they had seen the man who lived in the wing climb through the window into the garden. He had gone to the gate and disappeared. The banker instantly went with his servants to the wing and established the escape of his prisoner. To avoid unnecessary rumors he took the paper with the renunciation from the table and, on his return, locked it in his safe.

THE MAN WHO COULD WORK MIRACLES

H.G.WELLS / GREAT BRITAIN

I T IS DOUBTFUL whether the gift was innate. For my own part, I think it came to him suddenly. Indeed, until he was thirty he was a skeptic, and did not believe in miraculous powers. And here, since it is the most convenient place, I must mention that he was a little man, and had eyes of a hot brown, very erect red hair, a mustache with ends that he twisted up, and freckles. His name was George McWhirter Fotheringay—not the sort of name by any means to lead to any expectation of miracles—and he was clerk at Gomshott's. He was greatly addicted to assertive argument. It was while he was asserting the impossibility of miracles that he had his first intimation of his extraordinary powers.

This particular argument was being held in the bar of the Long Dragon, and Toddy Beamish was conducting the opposition by a monotonous but effective "So *you* say," that drove Mr. Fotheringay to the very limit of his patience.

There were present, besides these two, a very dusty cyclist, landlord Cox, and Miss Maybridge, the perfectly respectable and rather portly barmaid of the Dragon. Miss Maybridge was standing with her back to Mr. Fotheringay, washing glasses; the others were watching him, more or less amused by the present ineffectiveness of the assertive method. Goaded by the Torres Vedras tactics of Mr. Beamish, Mr. Fotheringay determined to make an unusual rhetorical effort. "Looky here, Mr. Beamish," said Mr. Fotheringay. "Let us clearly understand what a miracle is. It's something contrariwise to the course of nature done by power of Will, something what couldn't happen without being specially willed."

"So *you* say," said Mr. Beamish, repulsing him.

Mr. Fotheringay appealed to the cyclist, who had hitherto been a silent auditor, and received his assent—given with a hesitating cough and a glance at Mr. Beamish. The landlord would express no opinion, and Mr. Fotheringay, returning to Mr. Beamish, received the unexpected concession of a qualified assent to his definition of a miracle.

"For instance," said Mr. Fotheringay, greatly encouraged. "Here would be a miracle. That lamp, in the natural course of nature, couldn't burn like that upsy-down, could it, Beamish?"

"*You* say it couldn't," said Beamish.

"And you?" said Fotheringay. "You don't mean to say—eh?"

"No," said Beamish reluctantly. "No, it couldn't."

"Very well," said Fotheringay. "Then here comes someone, as it might be me, along here, and stands as it might be here, and says to that lamp, as I might do, collecting all my will—'Turn upsy-down without breaking, and go on burning steady.'—Hullo!"

It was enough to make any one say "Hullo!" The impossible, the incredible, was visible to them all. The lamp hung inverted in the air, burning quietly with its flame pointing down. It was as solid, as indisputable as ever a lamp was, the prosaic common lamp of the Long Dragon bar.

Mr. Fotheringay stood with an extended forefinger and the knitted brows of one anticipating a catastrophic smash. The cyclist, who was sitting next the lamp, ducked and jumped across the bar. Everybody jumped more or less. Miss Maybridge turned and screamed. For nearly three seconds the lamp remained still. A faint cry of mental distress came from Mr. Fotheringay. "I can't keep it up," he said, "any longer." He staggered back, and the inverted lamp suddenly flared, fell against the corner of the bar, bounced aside, smashed upon the floor and went out.

It was lucky it had a metal receiver, or the whole place would have been in a blaze. Mr. Cox was the first to speak, and his remark, shorn of needless excrescences, was to the effect that Fotheringay was a fool. Fotheringay was beyond disputing even so fundamental a proposition as that! He was astonished beyond measure at the thing that had occurred. The subsequent conversation threw absolutely no light on the matter so far as Fotheringay was concerned; the general opinion not only followed Mr. Cox very closely but very vehemently. Everyone accused Fotheringay of a silly trick, and presented him to himself as a foolish destroyer of comfort and security. His mind was in a tornado of perplexity, he was himself inclined to agree with them, and he made a remarkably ineffectual opposition to the proposal of his departure.

He went home flushed and heated, coat collar crumpled, eyes smarting and ears red. He watched each of the ten streetlamps nervously as he passed it. It was only when he found himself alone in his little bedroom in Church Row that he was able to grapple seriously with his memories of the occurrence, and ask, "What on earth happened?"

He had removed his coat and boots, and was sitting on the bed with his hands in his pockets repeating the text of his defense for the seventeenth time, "*I* didn't want the confounded thing to upset," when it occurred to him that at the precise moment he had said the commanding words he had inadvertently willed the thing he said, and that when he had seen the lamp in the air he had felt that it depended on him to maintain it there without being clear how this was done. He had not a particularly complex mind, or he might have stuck for a time at that "inadvertently willed," embracing, as it does the abstrusest problems of voluntary action; but as it was, the idea came to him with a quite acceptable haziness. And from that, following, as I must admit, no clear logical path, he came to the test of experiment.

He pointed resolutely to his candle and collected his mind, though he felt he did a foolish thing. "Be raised up," he said. But in a second that feeling vanished. The candle was raised, hung in the air one giddy moment and as Mr. Fotheringay gasped, fell with a smash on his toilet table, leaving him in darkness save for the expiring glow of its wick.

For a time Mr. Fotheringay sat in the darkness, perfectly still. "It did happen, after all," he said. "And 'ow I'm to explain it I *don't* know." He sighed heavily, and began feeling in his pockets for a match. He could find none, and he rose and groped about the toilet table. "I wish I had a match," he said. He resorted to his coat, and there were none there, and then it dawned upon him that miracles were possible even with matches. He extended a hand and scowled at it in the dark. "Let there be a match in that hand," he said. He felt some light object fall across his palm, and his fingers closed upon a match.

After several ineffectual attempts to light this he discovered it was a safety match. He threw it down, and then it occurred to him that he might have willed it lighted. He did, and perceived it burning in the midst of his toilet-table mat. He caught it up hastily, and it went out. His perception of possibilities enlarged, and he felt for and replaced the candle in its candlestick. "Here! *you* be lighted," said Mr. Fotheringay, and forthwith the candle was flaring, and he saw a little black hole in the toilet cover, with a wisp of smoke rising from it. For a time he stared from this to the little flame and back, and then looked up and met his own gaze in the looking glass. By this help he communed with himself in silence for a time.

"How about miracles now?" said Mr. Fotheringay at last, addressing his reflection.

The subsequent meditations of Mr. Fotheringay were of a severe but confused description. So far as he could see, it was case of pure willing with him. The nature of his first experience disinclined him for any further experiments except of the most cautious type. But he lifted a sheet of paper, and turned a glass of water pink and then green, and he created a snail, which he miraculously annihilated, and got himself a miraculous new toothbrush. Somewhere in the small hours he had reached the fact that his willpower must be of a particularly rare and pungent quality, a fact of which he had certainly had inklings before, but no certain assurance. The scare and perplexity of his first discovery was now qualified by pride in this evidence of singularity and by vague intimations of advantage. He became aware that the church clock was striking one, and as it did not occur to him that his daily duties at Gomshott's might be miraculously dispensed with, he resumed undressing, in order to get to bed without further delay. As he struggled to get his shirt over his head, he was struck with a brilliant idea. "Let me be in bed," he said, and found himself so. "Undressed," he stipulated; and, finding the sheets cold, added hastily, "and in my nightshirt—no, in a nice soft woolen nightshirt. Ah!" he said with immense enjoyment, "And now let me be comfortably asleep. . . ."

He awoke at his usual hour and was pensive all through breakfast-time, wondering whether his overnight experience might not be a particularly vivid dream. At length his mind turned again to cautious experiments. For instance, he had three eggs for breakfast; two his landlady had supplied, good, but shoppy, and one was a delicious fresh goose egg, laid, cooked and served by his extraordinary will. He hurried off to Gomshott's in a state of profound but carefully concealed excitement, and only remembered the shell of the third egg when his landlady spoke of it that night. All day he could do no work because of this astonishingly new self-knowledge, but this caused him no inconvenience, because he made up for it miraculously in his last ten minutes.

As the day wore on his state of mind passed from wonder to elation, albeit the circumstances of his dismissal from the Long Dragon were still disagreeable to recall, and a garbled account of the matter that had reached his colleagues led to some badinage. It was evident he must be careful how he lifted frangible articles, but in other ways his gift promised more and more as he turned it over in his mind. He intended among other things to increase his personal property by unostentatious acts of creation. He called into existence a pair of very splendid diamond studs, and hastily annihilated them again as young Gomshott came across the countinghouse to his desk. He was afraid young Gomshott might wonder how he had come by them. He saw quite clearly the gift required caution and watchfulness in its exercise, but so far as he could judge the difficulties attending its mastery would be no greater than those he had already faced in the study of cycling. It was that analogy, perhaps, quite as much as the feeling that he would be unwelcome in the Long Dragon, that drove him out after supper into the lane beyond the gasworks, to rehearse a few miracles in private.

There was possibly a certain want of originality in his attempts, for apart from his willpower Mr. Fotheringay was not a very exceptional man. The miracle of Moses' rod came to his mind, but the night was dark and unfavorable to the proper control of large miraculous snakes. Then he recollected the story of *Tannhäuser* that he had read on the back of the Philharmonic program. That seemed to him singularly attractive and harmless. He stuck his walking stick—a very nice Poonah penang-lawyer—into the turf that edged the footpath, and commanded the dry wood to blossom. The air was immediately full of the scent of roses, and by means of a match he saw for himself that this beautiful miracle was indeed accomplished. His satisfaction was ended by advancing footsteps. Afraid of a premature discovery of his powers, he addressed the blossoming stick hastily: "Go back." What he meant was "Change back"; but of course he was confused. The stick receded at a considerable velocity, and incontinently came a cry of anger and a bad word from the approaching person. "Who are you throwing brambles at, you fool?" cried a voice. "That got me on the shin."

"I'm sorry, old chap," said Mr. Fotheringay, and then realizing the awkward nature of the explanation, caught nervously at his mustache. He saw Winch, one of the three Immering constables, advancing.

"What d'yer mean by it?" asked the constable. "Hullo! It's you, is it? The gent that broke the lamp at the Long Dragon!"

"I don't mean anything by it," said Mr. Fotheringay. "Nothing at all."

"What d'yer do it for then?"

"Oh, bother!" said Mr. Fotheringay.

"Bother, indeed! D'yer know that stick hurt? What d'yer do it for, eh?"

For the moment Mr. Fotheringay could not think what he had done it for. His silence seemed to irritate Mr. Winch. "You've been assaulting the police, young man, this time. That's what *you* done."

"Look here, Mr. Winch," said Mr. Fotheringay, annoyed and confused, "I'm very sorry. The fact is—"

"Well?"

He could think of no way but the truth.

"I was working a miracle." He tried to speak in an offhand way, but try as he would he couldn't.

"Working a—! 'Ere don't you talk rot. Working a miracle, indeed! Miracle! Well, that's downright funny! Why, you's the chap that don't believe in miracles, , , , Fact is, this is another of your silly conjuring tricks—that's what this is. Now, I tell you—"

But Mr. Fotheringay never heard what Mr. Winch was going to tell him. He realized he had given himself away, flung his valuable secret to all the winds of heaven. A violent gust of irritation swept him to action. He turned on the constable swiftly and fiercely. "Here," he said, "I've had enough of this, I have! I'll show you a silly conjuring trick, I will! Go to Hades! Go, now!"

He was alone!

Mr. Fotheringay performed no more miracles that night, nor did he trouble to see what had become of his flowering stick. He returned to the town, scared and very quiet, and went to his bedroom. "Lord!" he said, "it's a powerful gift—an extremely powerful gift. I didn't hardly mean as much as that. Not really. . . . I wonder what Hades is like?"

He sat on the bed taking off his boots. Struck by a happy thought he transferred the constable to San Francisco, and without any more interference with normal causation went soberly to bed. In the night he dreamed of the anger of Winch.

The next day Mr. Fotheringay heard two interesting items of news. Someone had planted a most beautiful climbing rose against the elder Mr. Gomshott's private house in the Lullaborough Road, and the river as far as Rawling's Mill was to be dragged for Constable Winch.

Mr. Fotheringay was abstracted and thoughtful all that day, and performed no miracles except certain provisions for Winch and the miracle of completing his day's work with punctual perfection in spite of all the bee swarm of thoughts that hummed through his mind. And the extraordinary abstractions and meekness of his manner was remarked by several people, and made a matter for jesting. For the most part he was thinking of Winch.

On Sunday evening he went to chapel, and oddly enough, Mr. Maydig, who took a certain interest in occult matters, preached about "things that are not lawful." Mr. Fotheringay was not a regular chapel goer, but the system of assertive skepticism, to which I have already alluded, was now very much shaken. The tenor of the sermon threw an entirely new light on these novel gifts, and he suddenly decided to consult Mr. Maydig immediately after the service. So soon as that was determined, he found himself wondering why he had not done so before.

Mr. Maydig, a lean excitable man with quite remarkably long wrists and neck, was gratified at a request for a private conversation from a young man whose carelessness in religious matters was a subject for general remark in the town. After a few necessary delays, he conducted him to the study of the Manse, which was contiguous to the chapel, seated him comfortably, and standing in front of a cheerful fire—his legs threw a Rhodian arch of shadow on the opposite wall—requested Mr. Fotheringay to state his business.

At first Mr. Fotheringay was a little abashed, and found some difficulty in opening the matter. "You will scarcely believe me, Mr. Maydig, I am afraid"—and so forth for some time. He tried a question at last, and asked Mr. Maydig his opinion of miracles.

Mr. Maydig was still saying "Well" in extremely judicial tone, when Mr. Fotheringay interrupted again: "You don't believe, I suppose that some common sort of person—like myself, for instance—as it might be sitting here now, might have some sort of twist inside him that made him able to do things by his will."

"It's possible," said Mr. Maydig. "Something of the sort, perhaps, is possible."

"If I might make free with something here, I think I might show you by a sort of experiment," said Mr. Fotheringay. "Now that tobacco jar on the table, for instance. What I want to know is whether what I am going to do with it is a miracle or not. Just half a minute, Mr. Maydig, please." He knitted his brows, pointed to the tobacco jar and said: "Be a bowl of vi'lets."

The tobacco jar did as it was ordered.

Mr. Maydig started violently at the change, and stood looking from the thaumaturgist to the bowl of flowers. He said nothing. Presently he ventured to lean over the table and smell the violets; they were fresh picked and very fine ones. Then he stared at Mr. Fotheringay again.

"How did you do that?" he asked.

Mr. Fotheringay pulled his mustache. "Just hold it—and there you are. Is that a miracle, or is it black art, or what is it? And what do you think's the matter with me? That's what I want to ask."

"It's a most extraordinary occurrence."

"And this day last week I knew no more that I could do things like that than you did. It came quite sudden. It's something odd about my will, I suppose, and that's as far as I can see."

"Is *that*—the only thing. Could you do other things besides that?"

"Lord, yes!" said Mr. Fotheringay. "Just anything." He thought, and suddenly recalled a conjuring entertainment he had seen. "Here!" He pointed. "Change into a bowl of fish—no, not that—change into a glass bowl full of water with goldfish swimming in it. That's better! You see that, Mr. Maydig?"

"It's astonishing. It's incredible. You are either a most extraordinary . . . But no—"

"I could change it into anything," said Mr. Fotheringay. "Just anything. Here! be a pigeon, will you?"

In another moment a blue pigeon was fluttering round the room and making Mr. Maydig duck every time it came near him. "Stop there, will you," said Mr. Fotheringay; and the pigeon hung motionless in the air. "I could change it back to a bowl of flowers," he said, and after replacing the pigeon on the table worked that miracle. "I expect you will want your pipe in a bit," he said, and restored the tobacco jar.

Mr. Maydig had followed all these later changes in a sort of ejaculatory silence. He stared at Mr. Fotheringay and, in a very gingerly manner, picked up the tobacco jar, examined it, replaced it on the table. *"Well!"* was the only expression of his feelings.

"Now, after that it's easier to explain what I came about," said

Fotheringay; and proceeded to a lengthy and involved narrative of his strange experiences, beginning with the affair of the lamp in the Long Dragon and complicated by persistent allusions to Winch. As he went on, the transient pride Mr. Maydig's consternation had caused passed away; he became the very ordinary Mr. Fotheringay of everyday intercourse again. Mr. Maydig listened intently, the tobacco jar in his hand, and his bearing changed also with the course of the narrative. Presently, while Mr. Fotheringay was dealing with the miracle of the third egg, the minister interrupted with a fluttering extended hand—

"It is possible," he said. "It is credible. It is amazing, of course, but it reconciles a number of difficulties. The power to work miracles is a gift—a peculiar quality like genius or second sight—hitherto it has come very rarely and to exceptional people. But in this case . . . I have always wondered at the miracles of Mahomet, and at Yogi's miracles, and the miracles of Madame Blavatsky. But, of course! Yes, it is simply a gift! It carries out so beautifully the arguments of that great thinker"—Mr. Maydig's voice sank—"his Grace the Duke of Argyll. Here we plumb some profounder law—deeper than the ordinary laws of nature. Yes—yes. Go on. Go on!"

Mr. Fotheringay proceeded to tell of his misadventure with Winch, and Mr. Maydig, no longer overawed or scared, began to jerk his limbs about and interject astonishment. "It's this what troubled me most," proceeded Mr. Fotheringay; "it's this I'm most mijitly in want of advice for; of course he's at San Francisco—wherever San Francisco may be—but of course it's awkward for both of us, as you'll see, Mr. Maydig. I don't see how he can understand what has happened, and I daresay he's scared and exasperated something tremendous, and trying to get at me. I daresay he keeps on starting off to come here. I send him back, by a miracle, every few hours, when I think of it. And of course, that's a thing he won't be able to understand, and it's bound to annoy him; and, of course, if he takes a ticket every time it will cost him a lot of money. I done the best I could for him, but of course it's difficult for him to put himself in my place. I thought afterward that his clothes might have got scorched, you know—if Hades is all it's supposed to be—before I shifted him. In that case I suppose they'd have locked him up in San Francisco. Of course I willed him a new suit of clothes on him directly I thought of it. But, you see, I'm already in a deuce of a tangle—"

Mr. Maydig looked serious. "I see you are in a tangle. Yes, it's a difficult position. How you are to end it . . ." He became diffuse and inconclusive.

"However, we'll leave Winch for a little and discuss the larger question. I don't think this is a case of the black art or anything of the sort. I don't think there is any taint of criminality about it at all, Mr. Fotheringay—none whatever, unless you are suppressing material facts. No, it's miracles—pure miracles—miracles, if I may say so, of the very highest class."

He began to pace the hearthrug and gesticulate, while Mr. Fotheringay sat with his arm on the table and his head on his arm, looking worried. "I don't see how I'm to manage about Winch," he said.

"A gift of working miracles—apparently a very powerful gift," said Mr. Maydig, "will find a way about Winch—never fear. My dear Sir, you are a most important man—a man of the most astonishing possibilities. As evidence, for example! And in other ways, the things you may do . . ."

"Yes, *I've* thought of a thing or two," said Mr. Fotheringay. "But—some of the things came a bit twisty. You saw that fish at first? Wrong sort of bowl and wrong sort of fish. And I thought I'd ask someone."

"A proper course," said Mr. Maydig, "a very proper course—altogether the proper course." He stopped and looked at Mr. Fotheringay. "It's practically an unlimited gift. Let us test your powers, for instance. If they really *are* . . . if they really are all they seem to be."

And so, incredible as it may seem, in the study of the little house behind the Congregational Chapel, on the evening of Sunday, November 10, 1896, Mr. Fotheringay, egged on and inspired by Mr. Maydig, began to work miracles. The reader's attention is specially and definitely called to the date. He will object, probably has already objected, that certain points in this story are improbable, that if any things of the sort already described had indeed occurred, they would have been in all the papers a year ago. The details immediately following he will find particularly hard to accept, because among other things they involve the conclusion that he or she, the reader in question, must have been killed in a violent unprecedented manner more than a year ago. Now a miracle is nothing if not improbable, and as a matter of fact the reader *was* killed in a violent and unprecedented manner a year ago. In the subsequent course of this story that will become perfectly clear and credible, as every right-minded and reasonable reader will admit. But this is not the place for the end of the story, being but little beyond the hither side of the middle. And at first the miracles worked by Mr. Fotheringay were timid little miracles—little things with the cups and parlor fitments, as feeble as the miracles of theosophists, and feeble as they were, they were received with awe by his collaborator. He would have preferred to settle the Winch business out-of-hand, but Mr. Maydig would not let him. But after they had worked a dozen of these domestic trivialities, their sense of power grew, their imagination began to show signs of stimulation, and their ambition enlarged. Their first larger enterprise was due to hunger and the negligence of Mrs. Minchin, Mr. Maydig's housekeeper. The meal to which the minister conducted Mr. Fotheringay was certainly ill laid and uninviting as refreshment for two industrious miracle workers; but they were seated, and Mr. Maydig was descanting in sorrow rather than in anger upon his housekeeper's shortcomings, before it occurred to Mr. Fotheringay that an opportunity lay before him. "Don't you think, Mr. Maydig," he said, "if it isn't a liberty, I—"

"My dear Mr. Fotheringay! Of course! No—I didn't think."

Mr. Fotheringay waved his hand. "What shall we have?" he said, in a large inclusive spirit, and at Mr. Maydig's order, revised the supper very thoroughly. "As for me," he said, eyeing Mr. Maydig's selection, "I am always particularly fond of a tankard of stout and a nice Welsh rarebit, and I'll order that. I ain't much given to Burgundy," and forthwith stout and Welsh rarebit promptly appeared at his command. They sat long at their supper, talking like equals, as Mr. Fotheringay presently perceived with a glow of surprise and gratification, of all the miracles they would presently do. "And by the way, Mr. Maydig," said Mr. Fotheringay, "I might perhaps be able to help you—in a domestic way."

"Don't quite follow," said Mr. Maydig, pouring out a glass of miraculous old Burgundy.

Mr. Fotheringay helped himself to a second Welsh rarebit out of vacancy, and took a mouthful. "I was thinking," he said, "I might be able (*chum, chum*) to work (*chum, chum*) a miracle with Mrs. Minchin (*chum, chum*)—make her a better woman."

Mr. Maydig put down the glass and looked doubtful. "She's— She strongly objects to interference, you know, Mr. Fotheringay. And—as a matter of fact—it's well past eleven and she's probably in bed and asleep. Do you think, on the whole—"

Mr. Fotheringay considered these objections. "I don't see that it shouldn't be done in her sleep."

For a time Mr. Maydig opposed the idea, and then he yielded. Mr. Fotheringay issued his orders, and a little less at their ease, perhaps, the two gentlemen proceeded with their repast. Mr. Maydig was enlarging on the changes he might expect in his housekeeper next day, with an optimism that seemed even to Mr. Fotheringay's super senses a little forced and hectic, when a series of confused noises from upstairs began. Their eyes exchanged interrogations, and Mr. Maydig left the room hastily. Mr. Fotheringay heard him calling up to his housekeeper and then his footsteps going softly up to her.

In a minute or so the minister returned, his step light, his face radiant. "Wonderful!" he said, "and touching! Most touching!"

He began pacing the hearthrug. "A repentance—a most touching repentance—through the crack of the door. Poor woman! A most wonderful change! She had got up. She must have got up at once. She had got up out of her sleep to smash a private bottle of brandy in her box. And to confess it too! . . . But this gives us—it opens—a most amazing vista of possibilities. If we can work this miraculous change in *her* . . ."

"The thing's unlimited seemingly," said Mr. Fotheringay. "And about Mr. Winch—"

"Altogether unlimited." And from the hearthrug Mr. Maydig, waving the Winch difficulty aside, unfolded a series of wonderful proposals—proposals he invented as he went along.

Now what those proposals were does not concern the essentials of this story. Suffice it that they were designed in a spirit of infinite benevolence, the sort of benevolence that used to be called post-prandial. Suffice it, too, that the problem of Winch remained unsolved. Nor is it necessary to describe how far that series got to its fulfillment. There were astonishing changes. The small hours found Mr. Maydig and Mr. Fotheringay careering across the chilly market square under the still moon, in a sort of ecstasy of thaumaturgy, Mr. Maydig all flap and gesture, Mr. Fotheringay short and bristling, and no longer abashed at his greatness. They had reformed every drunkard in the Parliamentary division, changed all the beer and alcohol to water (Mr. Maydig had overruled Mr. Fotheringay on this point), they had, further, greatly improved the railway communication of the place, drained Flinder's swamp, improved the soil of One Tree Hill, and cured the Vicar's wart. And they were going to see what could be done with the injured pier at South Bridge. "The place," gasped Mr. Maydig, "won't be the same place tomorrow. How surprised and thankful everyone will be!" And just at that moment the church clock struck three.

"I say," said Mr. Fotheringay, "that's three o'clock! I must be getting back. I've got to be at business by eight. And besides, Mrs. Wimms—"

"We're only beginning," said Mr. Maydig, full of the sweetness of unlimited power. "We're only beginning. Think of all the good we're doing. When people wake—"

"But—" said Mr. Fotheringay.

Mr. Maydig gripped his arm suddenly. His eyes were bright and wild. "My dear chap," he said, "there's no hurry. Look"—he pointed to the moon at the zenith—"Joshua!"

"Joshua?" said Mr. Fotheringay.

"Joshua," said Mr. Maydig. "Why not? Stop it."

Mr. Fotheringay looked at the moon.

"That's a bit tall," he said after a pause.

"Why not?" said Mr. Maydig. "Of course it doesn't stop. You stop the rotation of the earth, you know. Time stops. It isn't as if we were doing harm."

"H'm!" said Mr. Fotheringay. "Well." He sighed. "I'll try. Here—"

He buttoned up his jacket and addressed himself to the habitable globe, with as good an assumption of confidence as lay in his power. "Jest stop rotating will you," said Mr. Fotheringay.

Incontinently he was flying head over heels through the air at the rate of dozens of miles a minute. In spite of the innumerable circles he was describing per second, he thought; for thought is wonderful— sometimes as sluggish as flowing pitch, sometimes as instantaneous as light. He thought in a second, and willed. "Let me come down safe and sound. Whatever else happens, let me down safe and sound."

He willed it only just in time, for his clothes, heated by his rapid flight through the air, were already beginning to singe. He came down with a forcible, but by no means injurious bump in what appeared to be a mound of fresh-turned earth. A large mass of metal and masonry, extraordinarily like the clock tower in the middle of the market square, hit the earth near him, ricocheted over him, and flew into stonework, bricks and masonry, like a bursting bomb. A hurtling cow hit one of the larger blocks and smashed like an egg. There was a crash that made all the most violent crashes of his past life seem like the sound of falling dust and this was followed by a descending series of lesser crashes. A vast wind roared throughout earth and heaven, so that he could scarcely lift his head to look. For a while he was too breathless and astonished even to see where he was or what had happened. And his first movement was to feel his head and reassure himself that his streaming hair was still his own.

"Lord!" gasped Mr. Fotheringay, scarce able to speak for the gale, "I've had a squeak! What's gone wrong? Storms and thunder. And only a minute ago a fine night. It's Maydig set me on to this sort of thing. *What* a wind! If I go on fooling in this way I'm bound to have a thundering accident! . . . Where's Maydig? . . . What a confounded mess everything's in!"

He looked about him so far as his flapping jacket would permit. The appearance of things was really extremely strange. "The sky's all right anyhow," said Mr. Fotheringay. "And that's about all that is all right. And even there it looks like a terrific gale coming up. But there's the moon overhead. Just as it was just now. Bright as midday.

But as for the rest— Where's the village? Where's—where's anything? And what on earth set this wind a-blowing? *I* didn't order no wind."

Mr. Fotheringay struggled to get to his feet in vain, and after one failure, remained on all fours, holding on. He surveyed the moonlit world to leeward, with the tails of his jacket streaming over his head. "There's something seriously wrong," said Mr. Fotheringay. "And what it is—goodness knows."

Far and wide nothing was visible in the white glare through the haze of dust that drove before a screaming gale but tumbled masses of earth and heaps of inchoate ruins, no trees, no houses, no familiar shapes, only a wilderness of disorder vanishing at last into the darkness beneath the whirling columns and streamers, the lightnings and thunderings of a swiftly rising storm. Near him in the livid glare was something that might once have been an elm tree, a smashed mass of splinters, shivered from boughs to base, and further a twisted mass of iron girders—only too evidently the viaduct—rose out of the piled confusion.

You see, when Mr. Fotheringay had arrested the rotation of the solid globe, he had made no stipulation concerning the trifling movables upon its surface. And the earth spins so fast that the surface at its equator is traveling at rather more than a thousand miles an hour, and Mr. Maydig, and Mr. Fotheringay, and everybody and everything had been jerked violently forward at about nine miles per second—that is to say, much more violently than if they had been fired out of a cannon. And every human being, every living creature, every house, and every tree—all the world as we know it—had been so jerked and smashed and utterly destroyed. That was all.

These things Mr. Fotheringay did not, of course, fully appreciate. But he perceived that his miracle had miscarried, and with that a great disgust of miracles came upon him. He was in darkness now, for the clouds had swept together and blotted out his momentary glimpse of the moon, and the air was full of fitful struggling tortured wraith of hail. A great roaring of wind and waters filled earth and sky, and peering under his hand through the dust and sleet to windward, he saw by the play of the lightnings a vast wall of water pouring toward him.

"Maydig!" screamed Mr. Fotheringay's feeble voice amid the elemental uproar. "Here!—Maydig!"

"Stop!" cried Mr. Fotheringay to the advancing water. "Oh, for goodness' sake, stop!"

"Just a moment," said Mr. Fotheringay to the lightnings and thunder. "Stop jest a moment while I collect my thoughts. . . . And now what shall I do?" he said. "What *shall* I do? Lord! I wish Maydig was about."

"I know," said Mr. Fotheringay. "And for goodness' sake let's have it right *this* time."

He remained on all fours, leaning against the wind, very intent to have everything right.

"Ah!" he said. "Let nothing what I'm going to order happen until I say 'Off' . . . Lord! I wish I'd thought of that before!"

He lifted his little voice against the whirlwind, shouting louder and louder in the vain desire to hear himself speak. "Now then—here goes! Mind about that what I said just now. In the first place, when all I've got to say is done, let me lose my miraculous power, let my will become just like anybody else's will, and all these dangerous miracles be stopped. I don't like them. I'd rather I didn't work 'em. Ever so much. That's the first thing. And the second is—let me be back just before the blessed lamp turned up. It's a big job, but it's the last. Have you got it? No more miracles, everything as it was—me back in the Long Dragon just before I drank my half-pint. That's it! Yes."

He dug his fingers into the mold, closed his eyes, and said, "Off!"

Everything became perfectly still. He perceived that he was standing erect.

"So *you* say," said a voice.

He opened his eyes. He was in the bar of the Long Dragon, arguing about miracles with Toddy Beamish. He had a vague sense of some great thing forgotten that instantaneously passed. You see, except for the loss of his miraculous powers, everything was back as it had been; his mind and memory therefore were now just as they had been at the time when this story began. So that he knew absolutely nothing of all that is told here, knows nothing of all that is told here to this day. And among other things, of course, he still did not believe in miracles.

"I tell you that miracles, properly speaking, can't possibly happen," he said, "whatever you like to hold. And I'm prepared to prove it up to the hilt."

"That's what *you* think," said Toddy Beamish, and "Prove it if you can."

"Looky here, Mr. Beamish," said Mr. Fotheringay. "Let us clearly understand what a miracle is. It's something contrariwise to the course of nature done by power of Will. . . ."

A COUNTRY LOVE STORY
JEAN STAFFORD / UNITED STATES

Jean Stafford

AN ANTIQUE SLEIGH stood in the yard, snow after snow banked up against its eroded runners. Here and there upon the bleached and splintery seat were wisps of horsehair and scraps of the black leather that had once upholstered it. It bore, with all its jovial curves, an air not so much of desuetude as of slowed-down dash, as if weary horses, unable to go another step, had at last stopped here. The sleigh had come with the house. The former owner, a gifted businesswoman from Castine who bought old houses and sold them again with all their pitfalls still intact, had said when she was showing them the place, "A picturesque detail, I think," and, waving it away, had turned to the well, which, with enthusiasm and at considerable length, she said had never gone dry. Actually, May and Daniel had found the detail more distracting than picturesque, so nearly kin was it to outdoor arts and crafts, and when the woman, as they departed in her car, gestured toward it again and said, "Paint that up a bit with something cheery and it will really add no end to your yard," simultaneous shudders coursed them. They had planned to remove the sleigh before they did anything else.

But partly because there were more important things to be done, and partly because they did not know where to put it (a sleigh could not, in the usual sense of the words, be thrown away), and partly because it seemed defiantly a part of the yard, as entitled to be there permanently as the trees, they did nothing about it. Throughout the summer, they saw birds briefly pause on its rakish front and saw the fresh rains wash its runners; in the autumn they watched the golden leaves fill the seat and nestle dryly down; and now, with the snow, they watched this new accumulation.

The sleigh was visible from the windows of the big, bright kitchen where they ate all their meals and, sometimes too bemused with country solitude to talk, they gazed out at it, forgetting their food in speculating on its history. It could have been driven cavalierly by the scion of some sea captain's family, or it could have been used soberly to haul the household's Unitarians to church or to take the womenfolk around the countryside on errands of good will. They did not speak of what its office might have been, and the fact of their silence was often nettlesome to May, for she felt they were silent too much of the time; a little morosely, she thought, If something as absurd and as provocative as this at which we look together—and which is, even though we didn't want it, our own property—cannot bring us to talk, what can? But she did not disturb Daniel in his private musings; she held her tongue, and out of the corner of her eye she watched him watch the winter cloak the sleigh, and, as if she were computing a difficult sum in her head, she tried to puzzle out what it was that had stilled tongues that earlier, before Daniel's illness, had found the days too short to communicate all they were eager to say.

It had been Daniel's doctor's idea, not theirs, that had brought them to the solemn hinterland to stay after all the summer gentry had departed in their beach wagons. The Northern sun, the pristine air, the rural walks and soundless nights, said Dr. Tellenbach, perhaps pining for his native Switzerland, would do more for the "Professor's" convalescent lung than all the doctors and clinics in the world. Privately he had added to May that after so long a season in the sanitarium (Daniel had been there a year), where everything was tuned to a low pitch, it would be difficult and it might be shattering for "the boy" (not now the "Professor," although Daniel, nearly fifty, was his wife's senior by twenty years and Dr. Tellenbach's by ten) to go back at once to the excitements and the intrigues of the university, to what, with finicking humor, the Doctor called "the omnium-gatherum of the schoolmaster's life." The rigors of a country winter would be as nothing, he insisted, when compared to the strain of feuds and cocktail parties. All professors wanted to write books, didn't they? Surely Daniel, a historian with all the material in the world at his fingertips, must have something up his sleeve that could be the *raison d'être* for this year away? May said she supposed he had, she was not sure. She could hear the reluctance in her voice as she escaped the Doctor's eyes and gazed through his windows at the mountains behind the sanitarium. In the dragging months Daniel had been gone, she had taken solace in imagining the time when they *would* return to just that pandemonium the Doctor so deplored, and because it had been pandemonium on the smallest and most discreet scale, she smiled through her disappointment at the little man's Swiss innocence and explained that they had always lived quietly, seldom dining out or entertaining more than twice a week.

"Twice a week!" He was appalled.

"But I'm afraid," she had protested, "that he would find a second year of inactivity intolerable. He does intend to write a book, but he means to write it in England, and we can't go to England now."

"England!" Dr. Tellenbach threw up his hands. "Good *air* is my recommendation for your husband. Good air and little talk."

She said, "It's talk he needs, I should think, after all this time of communing only with himself except when I came to visit."

He had looked at her with exaggerated patience, and then, courtly but authoritative, he said, "I hope you will not think I importune when I tell you that I am very well acquainted with your husband, and, as his physician, I order this retreat. *He* quite agrees."

Stung to see that there was a greater degree of understanding between Daniel and Dr. Tellenbach than between Daniel and herself, May had objected further, citing an occasion when her husband had put his head in his hands and mourned, "I hear talk of nothing but sputum cups and X-rays. Aren't people interested in the state of the world any more?"

But Dr. Tellenbach had been adamant, and at the end, when she had risen to go, he said, "You are bound to find him changed a little. A long illness removes a thoughtful man from his fellow beings. It is like living with an exacting mistress who is not content with half a man's attention but must claim it all." She had thought his figure of speech absurd and disdained to ask him what he meant.

Actually, when the time came for them to move into the new house and she found no alterations in her husband but found, on the other hand, much pleasure in their country life, she began to forgive Dr. Tellenbach. In the beginning, it was like a second honeymoon, for they had moved to a part of the North where they had never been and they explored it together, sharing its charming sights and sounds. Moreover, they had never owned a house before but had always lived in city apartments, and though the house they bought was old and derelict, its lines and doors and window lights were beautiful, and they were possessed by it. All through the summer, they reiterated, "To think that we own all of this! That it actually belongs to us!" And they wandered from room to room marveling at their windows, from none of which was it possible to see an ugly sight. They looked to the south upon a river, to the north upon a lake; to the west of them were pine woods where the wind forever sighed, voicing a vain entreaty; and to the east a rich man's long meadow that ran down a hill to his old, magisterial house. It was true, even in those bewitched days, that there were times on the lake, when May was gathering water lilies as Daniel slowly rowed, that she had seen on his face a look of abstraction and she had known that he was worlds away, in his memories, perhaps, of his illness and the sanitarium (of which he would never speak) or in the thought of the book he was going to write as soon, he said, as the winter set in and there was nothing to do but work. Momentarily the look frightened her and she remembered the Doctor's words, but then, immediately herself again in the security of married love, she caught at another water lily and pulled at its long stem. Companionably, they gardened, taking special pride in the nicotiana that sent its nighttime fragrance into their bedroom. Together, and with fascination, they consulted carpenters, plasterers, and chimney sweeps. In the blue evenings they read at ease, hearing no sound but that of the night birds—the loons on the lake and the owls in the tops of trees. When the days began to cool and shorten, a cricket came to bless their house, nightly singing behind the kitchen stove. They got two fat and idle tabby cats, who lay insensible beside the fireplace and only stirred themselves to purr perfunctorily.

Because they had not moved in until July and by that time the workmen of the region were already engaged, most of the major repairs of the house were to be postponed until the spring, and in October, when May and Daniel had done all they could by themselves and Daniel had begun his own work, May suddenly found herself without occupation. Whole days might pass when she did nothing more than cook three meals and walk a little in the autumn mist and pet the cats and wait for Daniel to come down from his upstairs study to talk to her. She began to think with longing of the crowded days in Boston before Daniel was sick, and even in the year past, when he had been away and she had gone to concerts and recitals and had done good deeds for crippled children and had endlessly shopped for presents to lighten the tedium of her husband's unwilling exile. And, longing, she was remorseful, as if by desiring another she betrayed this life, and, remorseful, she hid away in sleep. Sometimes she slept for hours in the daytime, imitating the cats, and when at last she got up, she had to push away the dense sleep as if it were a door.

One day at lunch, she asked Daniel to take a long walk with her that afternoon to a farm where the owner smoked his own sausages.

"You never go outdoors," she said, "and Dr. Tellenbach said you must. Besides, it's a lovely day."

"I can't," he said. "I'd like to, but I can't. I'm busy. You go alone."

Overtaken by a gust of loneliness, she cried, "Oh, Daniel, I have nothing to *do!*"

A moment's silence fell, and then he said, "I'm sorry to put you through this, my dear, but you must surely admit that it's not my fault I got sick."

In her shame, her rapid, overdone apologies, her insistence that nothing mattered in the world except his health and peace of mind, she made everything worse, and at last he said shortly to her, "Stop being a child, May. Let's just leave each other alone."

THIS OUTBREAK, the very first in their marriage of five years, was the beginning of a series. Hardly a day passed that they did not bicker over something; they might dispute a question of fact, argue a matter of taste, catch each other out in an inaccuracy, and every quarrel ended with Daniel's saying to her, "Why don't you leave me alone?" Once he said, "I've been sick and now I'm busy and I'm no longer young enough to shift the focus of my mind each time it suits your whim." Afterward, there were always apologies, and then Daniel went back to his study and did not open the door of it again until the next meal. Finally, it seemed to her that love, the very center of their being, was choked off, overgrown, invisible. And silent with hostility or voluble with trivial reproach, they tried to dig it out impulsively and could not—could only maul it in its unkempt grave. Daniel, in his withdrawal from her and from the house, was preoccupied with his research, of which he never spoke except to say that it would bore her, and most of the time, so it appeared to May, he did not worry over what was happening to them. She felt the cold old house somehow enveloping her as if it were their common enemy, maliciously bent on bringing them to disaster. Sunken in faithlessness, they stared, at mealtimes, atrophied within the present hour, at the irrelevant and whimsical sleigh that stood abandoned in the mammoth winter.

May found herself thinking, If we redeemed it and painted it, our house would have something in common with Henry Ford's Wayside Inn. And I might make this very observation to him and he might greet it with disdain and we might once again be able to talk to each other. Perhaps we could talk of Williamsburg and how we disapproved of it. Her mind went toiling on. Williamsburg was part of our honeymoon trip; somewhere our feet were entangled in suckers as we stood kissing under a willow tree. Soon she found that she did not care for this line of thought, nor did she care what his response to it might be. In her imagined conversations with Daniel, she never spoke of the sleigh. To the thin, ill scholar whose scholarship and illness had usurped her place, she had gradually taken a weighty but unviolent dislike.

The discovery of this came, not surprising her, on Christmas Day. The knowledge sank like a plummet, and at the same time she was thinking about the sleigh, connecting it with the smell of the barn on damp days, and she thought perhaps it had been drawn by the very animals who had been stabled there and had pervaded the timbers with their odor. There must have been much life within this house once—but long ago. The earth immediately behind the barn was said by everyone to be extremely rich because of the horses, although there had been none there for over fifty years. Thinking of this soil, which earlier she had eagerly sifted through her fingers, May now realized that she had no wish for the spring to come, no wish to plant a garden, and, branching out at random, she found she had no wish to see the sea again, or children, or favorite pictures, or even her own face on a happy day. For a minute or two, she was almost enraptured in this state of no desire, but then, purged swiftly of her cynicism, she knew it to be false, knew that actually she did have a desire—the desire for a desire. And now she felt that she was stationary in a whirlpool, and at the very moment she conceived the notion a bit of wind brought to the seat of the sleigh the final leaf from the elm tree that stood beside it. It crossed her mind that she might consider the wood of the sleigh in its juxtaposition to the living tree and to the horses, who, although they were long since dead, reminded her of their passionate, sweating, running life every time she went to the barn for firewood.

They sat this morning in the kitchen full of sun, and, speaking not to him but to the sleigh, to icicles, to the dark, motionless pine woods, she said, "I wonder if on a day like this they used to take the pastor home after lunch." Daniel gazed abstractedly at the bright-silver drifts beside the well and said nothing. Presently a wagon went past hauled by two oxen with bells on their yoke. This was the hour they always passed, taking to an unknown destination an aged man in a fur hat and an aged woman in a shawl. May and Daniel listened.

Suddenly, with impromptu anger, Daniel said, "What did you just say?"

"Nothing," she said. And then, after a pause, "It would be lovely at Jamaica Pond today."

He wheeled on her and pounded the table with his fist. "I did not ask for this!" The color rose feverishly to his thin cheeks and his breath was agitated. "You are trying to make me sick again. It was wonderful, wasn't it, for you while I was gone?"

"Oh, no, no! Oh, no, Daniel, it was hell!"

"Then, by the same token, this must be heaven." He smiled, the professor catching out a student in a fallacy.

"Heaven." She said the word bitterly.

"Then why do you stay here?" he cried.

It was a cheap impasse, desolate, true, unfair. She did not answer him.

After a while he said, "I almost believe there's something you haven't told me."

She began to cry at once, blubbering across the table at him. "You have said that before. What am I to say? What have I done?"

He looked at her, impervious to her tears, without mercy and yet without contempt. "I don't know. But you've done something."

It was as if she were looking through someone else's scrambled closets and bureau drawers for an object that had not been named to her, but nowhere could she find her gross offense.

Domestically she asked him if he would have more coffee and he peremptorily refused and demanded, "Will you tell me why it is you must badger me? Is it a compulsion? Can't you control it? Are you going mad?"

FROM THAT DAY ONWARD, May felt a certain stirring of life within her solitude, and now and again, looking up from a book to see if the damper on the stove was right, to listen to a rat renovating its house-within-a-house, to watch the belled oxen pass, she nursed her wound, hugged it, repeated his awful words exactly as he had said them, reproduced the way his wasted lips had looked and his bright, farsighted eyes. She could not read for long at any time, nor could she sew. She cared little now for planning changes in her house; she had meant to sand the painted floors to uncover the wood of the wide boards and she had imagined how the long, paneled windows of the drawing room would look when yellow velvet curtains hung there in the spring. Now, schooled by silence and indifference, she was immune to disrepair and to the damage done by the wind and snow, and she looked, as Daniel did, without dislike upon the old and nasty wallpaper and upon the shabby kitchen floor. One day, she knew that the sleigh would stay where it was so long as they stayed there. From every thought, she returned to her deep, bleeding injury. He had asked her if she were going mad.

She repaid him in the dark afternoons while he was closeted away in his study, hardly making a sound save when he added wood to his fire or paced a little, deep in thought. She sat at the kitchen table looking at the sleigh, and she gave Daniel insult for his injury by imagining a lover. She did not imagine his face, but she imagined his clothing, which would be costly and in the best of taste, and his manner, which would be urbane and anticipatory of her least whim, and his clever speech, and his adept courtship that would begin the moment he looked at the sleigh and said, "I must get rid of that for you at once." She might be a widow, she might be divorced, she might be committing adultery. Certainly there was no need to specify in an affair so securely legal. There was no need, that is, up to a point, and then the point came when she took in the fact that she not only believed in this lover but loved him and depended wholly on his companionship. She complained to him of Daniel and he consoled her; she told him stories of her girlhood, when she had gaily gone to parties, squired by boys her own age; she dazzled him sometimes with the wise comments she made on the books she read. It came to be true that if she so much as looked at the sleigh, she was weakened, failing with starvation.

Often, about her daily tasks of cooking food and washing dishes and tending the fires and shopping in the general store of the village, she thought she should watch her step, that it was this sort of thing that *did* make one go mad; for a while, then, she went back to Daniel's question, sharpening its razor edge. But she could not corral her alien thoughts and she trembled as she bought split peas, fearful that the old men loafing by the stove could see the incubus of her sins beside her. She could not avert such thoughts when they rushed upon her sometimes at tea with one of the old religious ladies of the neighborhood, so that, in the middle of a conversation about a deaconess in Bath, she retired from them, seeking her lover, who came, faceless, with his arms outstretched, even as she sat up straight in a Boston rocker, even as she accepted another cup of tea. She lingered over the cake plates and the simple talk, postponing her return to her own house and to Daniel, whom she continually betrayed.

It was not long after she recognized her love that she began to wake up even before the dawn and to be all day quick to everything, observant of all the signs of age and eccentricity in her husband, and she compared him in every particular—to his humiliation, in her eyes—with the man whom now it seemed to her she had always loved at fever pitch.

Once when Daniel, in a rare mood, kissed her, she drew back involuntarily and he said gently, "I wish I knew what you had done, poor dear." He looked as if for written words in her face.

"You said you knew," she said, terrified.

"I do."

"Then why do you wish you knew?" Her baffled voice was high and frantic. "You don't talk sense!"

"I do," he said sedately. "I talk sense always. It is you who are oblique." Her eyes stole like a sneak to the sleigh. "But I wish I knew your motive," he said impartially.

For a minute, she felt that they were two maniacs answering each other questions that had not been asked, never touching the matter at hand because they did not know what the matter was. But in the next moment, when he turned back to her spontaneously and clasped her head between his hands and said, like a tolerant father, "I forgive you, darling, because you don't know how you persecute me. No one knows except the sufferer what this sickness is," she knew again, helplessly, that they were not harmonious even in their aberrations.

These days of winter came and went, and on each of them, after breakfast and as the oxen passed, he accused her of her concealed misdeed. She could no longer truthfully deny that she was guilty, for she was in love, and she heard the subterfuge in her own voice and felt the guilty fever in her veins. Daniel knew it, too, and watched her. When she was alone, she felt her lover's presence protecting her—when she walked past the stiff spiraea, with icy cobwebs hung between its twigs, down to the lake, where the black, unmeasured water was hidden beneath a lid of ice; when she walked, instead, to the salt river to see the tar-paper shacks where the men caught smelt through the ice; when she walked in the dead dusk up the hill from the store, catching her breath the moment she saw the sleigh. But sometimes this splendid being mocked her when, freezing with fear of the consequences of her sin, she ran up the stairs to Daniel's room and burrowed her head in his shoulder and cried, "Come downstairs! I'm lonely, please come down!" But he would never come, and at last, bitterly, calmed by his calmly inquisitive regard, she went back alone and stood at the kitchen window, coyly half hidden behind the curtains.

For months she lived with her daily dishonor, rattled, ashamed, stubbornly clinging to her secret. But she grew more and more afraid when, oftener and oftener, Daniel said, "Why do you lie to me? What does this mood of yours mean?" and she could no longer sleep. In the raw nights, she lay straight beside him as he slept, and she stared at the ceiling, as bright as the snow it reflected, and tried not to think of the sleigh out there under the elm tree but could think only of it and of the man, her lover, who was connected with it somehow. She said to herself, as she listened to his breathing, "If I confessed to Daniel, he would understand that I was lonely and he would comfort me, saying, 'I am here, May. I shall never let you be lonely again.'" At these times, she was so separated from the world, so far removed from his touch and his voice, so solitary, that she would have sued a stranger for companionship. Daniel slept deeply, having no guilt to make him toss. He slept, indeed, so well that he never even heard the ditcher on snowy nights rising with a groan over the hill, flinging the snow from the road and warning of its approach by lights that first flashed red, then blue. As it passed their house, the hurled snow swashed like flames. All night she heard the squirrels adding up their nuts in the walls and heard the spirit of the house creaking and softly clicking upon the stairs and in the attics.

IN EARLY SPRING, when the whippoorwills begged in the cattails and the marsh reeds, and the northern lights patinated the lake and the tidal river, and the stars were large, and the huge vine of Dutchman's-pipe had started to leaf out, May went to bed late. Each night she sat on the back steps waiting, hearing the snuffling of a dog as it hightailed it for home, the single cry of a loon. Night after night, she waited for the advent of her rebirth while upstairs Daniel, who had spoken tolerantly of her vigils, slept, keeping his knowledge of her to himself. "A symptom," he had said, scowling in concentration, as he remarked upon her new habit. "Let it run its course. Perhaps when this is over, you will know the reason why you torture me with these obsessions and will stop. You know, you may really have a slight disorder of the mind. It would be nothing to be ashamed of; you could go to a sanitarium."

One night, looking out the window, she clearly saw her lover sitting in the sleigh. His hand was over his eyes and his chin was covered by a red silk scarf. He wore no hat and his hair was fair. He was tall and his long legs stretched indolently along the floorboard. He was younger than she had imagined him to be and he seemed rather frail, for there was a delicate pallor on his high, intelligent forehead and there was an invalid's languor in his whole attitude. He wore a white blazer and gray flannels and there was a yellow rosebud in his lapel. Young as he was, he did not, even so, seem to belong to her generation; rather, he seemed to be the reincarnation of someone's uncle as he had been fifty years before. May did not move until he vanished, and then, even though she knew now that she was truly bedeviled, the only emotion she had was bashfulness, mingled with doubt; she was not sure, that is, that he loved her.

That night, she slept a while. She lay near to Daniel, who was smiling in the moonlight. She could tell that the sleep she would have tonight would be as heavy as a coma, and she was aware of the moment she was overtaken.

She was in a canoe in the meadow of water lilies and her lover was tranquilly taking the shell off a hard-boiled egg. "How intimate," he said, "to eat an egg with you." She was nervous lest the canoe tip over, but at the same time she was charmed by his wit and by the way he lightly touched her shoulder with the varnished paddle.

"May? May? I love you, May."

"Oh!" enchanted, she heard her voice replying. "Oh, I love you, too!"

"The winter is over, May. You must forgive the hallucinations of a sick man."

She woke to see Daniel's fair, pale head bending toward her. "He is old! He is ill!" she thought, but through her tears, to deceive him one last time, she cried, "Oh, thank God, Daniel!"

He was feeling cold and wakeful and he asked her to make him a cup of tea; before she left the room, he kissed her hands and arms and said, "If I am ever sick again, don't leave me, May."

Downstairs, in the kitchen, cold with shadows and with the obtrusion of dawn, she was belabored by a chill. "What time is it?" she said aloud, although she did not care. She remembered, not for any reason, a day when she and Daniel had stood in the yard last October wondering whether they should cover the chimneys that would not be used and he decided that they should not, but he had said, "I hope no birds get trapped." She had replied, "I thought they all left at about this time for the South," and he had answered, with an unintelligible reproach in his voice, "The starlings stay." And she remembered, again for no reason, a day when, in pride and excitement, she had burst into the house crying, "I saw an ermine. It was terribly poised and let me watch it quite a while." He had said categorically, "There are no ermines here."

She had not protested; she had sighed as she sighed now and turned to the window. The sleigh was livid in this light and no one was in it; nor had anyone been in it for many years. But at that moment the blacksmith's cat came guardedly across the dewy field and climbed into it, as if by careful plan, and curled up on the seat. May prodded the clinkers in the stove and started to the barn for kindling. But she thought of the cold and the damp and the smell of the horses, and she did not go but stood there, holding the poker and leaning upon it as if it were an umbrella. There was no place warm to go. "What time is it?" she whimpered, heartbroken, and moved the poker, stroking the lion foot of the fireless stove.

She knew now that no change would come, and that she would never see her lover again. Confounded utterly, like an orphan in solitary confinement, she went outdoors and got into the sleigh. The blacksmith's imperturbable cat stretched and rearranged his position, and May sat beside him with her hands locked tightly in her lap, rapidly wondering over and over again how she would live the rest of her life.

A WORN PATH
EUDORA WELTY / UNITED STATES

Eudora Welty

IT WAS DECEMBER—a bright frozen day in the early morning. Far out in the country there was an old Negro woman with her head tied in a red rag, coming along a path through the pinewoods. Her name was Phoenix Jackson. She was very old and small and she walked slowly in the dark pine shadows, moving a little from side to side in her steps, with the balanced heaviness and lightness of a pendulum in a grandfather clock.

She carried a thin, small cane made from an umbrella, and with this she kept tapping the frozen earth in front of her. This made a grave and persistent noise in the still air, that seemed meditative like the chirping of a solitary little bird.

She wore a dark striped dress reaching down to her shoe tops, and an equally long apron of bleached sugar sacks, with a full pocket: all neat and tidy, but every time she took a step she might have fallen over her shoelaces, which dragged from her unlaced shoes. She looked straight ahead. Her eyes were blue with age. Her skin had a pattern all its own of numberless branching wrinkles and as though a whole little tree stood in the middle of her forehead, but a golden color ran underneath, and the two knobs of her cheeks were illumined by a yellow burning under the dark. Under the red rag her hair came down on her neck in the frailest of ringlets, still black, and with an odor like copper.

Now and then there was a quivering in the thicket. Old Phoenix said, "Out of my way, all you foxes, owls, beetles, jackrabbits, coons and wild animals! . . . Keep out from under these feet, little bob-whites. . . . Keep the big wild hogs out of my path. Don't let none of those come running my direction. I got a long way." Under her small black-freckled hand her cane, limber as a buggy whip, would switch at the brush as if to rouse up any hiding things.

On she went. The woods were deep and still. The sun made the pine needles almost too bright to look at, up where the wind rocked. The cones dropped as light as feathers. Down in the hollow was the mourning dove—it was not too late for him.

The path ran up a hill. "Seem like there is chains about my feet, time I get this far," she said, in the voice of argument old people keep to use with themselves. "Something always take a hold of me on this hill—pleads I should stay."

After she got to the top she turned and gave a full, severe look behind her where she had come. "Up through pines," she said at length. "Now down through oaks."

Her eyes opened their widest; and she started down gently. But before she got to the bottom of the hill a bush caught her dress.

Her fingers were busy and intent, but her skirts were full and long, so that before she could pull them free in one place they were caught in another. It was not possible to allow the dress to tear. "I in the thorny bush," she said. "Thorns, you doing your appointed work. Never want to let folks pass, no sir. Old eyes thought you was a pretty little *green* bush."

Finally, trembling all over, she stood free, and after a moment dared to stoop for her cane.

"Sun so high!" she cried, leaning back and looking, while the thick tears went over her eyes. "The time getting all gone here."

At the foot of this hill was a place where a log was laid across the creek.

"Now comes the trial," said Phoenix.

Putting her right foot out, she mounted the log and shut her eyes. Lifting her skirt, leveling her cane fiercely before her, like a festival figure in some parade, she began to march across. Then she opened her eyes and she was safe on the other side.

"I wasn't as old as I thought," she said.

But she sat down to rest. She spread her skirts on the bank around her and folded her hands over her knees. Up above her was a tree in a pearly cloud of mistletoe. She did not dare to close her eyes, and when a little boy brought her a plate with a slice of marble cake on it she spoke to him.

"That would be acceptable," she said. But when she went to take it there was just her own hand in the air.

So she left that tree, and had to go through a barbed-wire fence. There she had to creep and crawl, spreading her knees and stretching her fingers like a baby trying to climb the steps. But she talked loudly to herself: she could not let her dress be torn now, so late in the day, and she could not pay for having her arm or her leg sawed off if she got caught fast where she was.

At last she was safe through the fence and risen up out in the clearing. Big dead trees, like black men with one arm, were standing in the purple stalks of the withered cotton field. There sat a buzzard.

"Who you watching?"

In the furrow she made her way along.

"Glad this not the season for bulls," she said, looking sideways, "and the good Lord made his snakes to curl up and sleep in the winter. A pleasure I don't see no two-headed snake coming around that tree, where it come once. It took a while to get by him, back in the summer."

She passed through the old cotton and went into a field of dead corn. It whispered and shook and was taller than her head. "Through the maze now," she said, for there was no path.

Then there was something tall, black, and skinny there, moving before her.

At first she took it for a man. It could have been a man dancing in the field. But she stood still and listened, and it did not make a sound. It was as silent as a ghost.

"Ghost," she said sharply, "who be you the ghost of? For I have heard of nary death close by."

But there was no answer—only the ragged dancing in the wind.

She shut her eyes, reached out her hand, and touched a sleeve. She found a coat and inside that an emptiness, cold as ice.

"You scarecrow," she said. Her face lighted. "I ought to be shut up for good," she said with laughter. "My senses is gone. I too old. I the oldest people I ever know. Dance, old scarecrow," she said, "while I dancing with you."

She kicked her foot over the furrow, and with mouth drawn down, shook her head once or twice in a little strutting way. Some husks blew down and whirled in streamers about her skirts.

Then she went on, parting her way from side to side with the cane, through the whispering field. At last she came to the end, to a wagon track where the silver grass blew between the red ruts. The quail were walking around like pullets, seeming all dainty and unseen.

"Walk pretty," she said. "This the easy place. This the easy going."

She followed the track, swaying through the quiet bare fields, through the little strings of trees silver in their dead leaves, past cabins silver from weather, with the doors and windows boarded shut, all like old women under a spell sitting there. "I walking in their sleep," she said, nodding her head vigorously.

In a ravine she went where a spring was silently flowing through a hollow log. Old Phoenix bent and drank. "Sweet gum makes the water sweet," she said, and drank more. "Nobody know who made this well, for it was here when I was born."

The track crossed a swampy part where the moss hung as white as lace from every limb. "Sleep on, alligators, and blow your bubbles." Then the track went into the road.

Deep, deep the road went down between the high green-colored banks. Overhead the live oaks met, and it was as dark as a cave.

A black dog with a lolling tongue came up out of the weeds by the ditch. She was meditating, and not ready, and when he came at her she only hit him a little with her cane. Over she went in the ditch, like a little puff of milkweed.

Down there, her senses drifted away. A dream visited her, and she reached her hand up, but nothing reached down and gave her a pull. So she lay there and presently went to talking. "Old woman," she said to herself, "that black dog come up out of the weeds to stall you off, and now there he sitting on his fine tail, smiling at you."

A white man finally came along and found her—a hunter, a young man, with his dog on a chain.

"Well, Granny!" he laughed. "What are you doing there?"

"Lying on my back like a June bug waiting to be turned over, mister," she said, reaching up her hand.

He lifted her up, gave her a swing in the air, and set her down. "Anything broken, Granny?"

"No sir, them old dead weeds is springy enough," said Phoenix, when she had got her breath. "I thank you for your trouble."

"Where do you live, Granny?" he asked, while the two dogs were growling at each other.

"Away back yonder, sir, behind the ridge. You can't even see it from here."

"On your way home?"

"No sir, I going to town."

"Why, that's too far! That's as far as I walk when I come out myself, and I get something for my trouble." He patted the stuffed bag he carried, and there hung down a little closed claw. It was one of the bobwhites, with its beak hooked bitterly to show it was dead. "Now you go on home, Granny!"

"I bound to go to town, mister," said Phoenix. "The time come around."

He gave another laugh, filling the whole landscape. "I know you old colored people! Wouldn't miss going to town to see Santa Claus!"

But something held old Phoenix very still. The deep lines in her face went into a fierce and different radiation. Without warning, she had seen with her own eyes a flashing nickel fall out of the man's pocket onto the ground.

"How old are you, Granny?" he was saying.

"There is no telling, mister," she said, "no telling."

Then she gave a little cry and clapped her hands and said, "Git on away from here, dog! Look! Look at that dog!" She laughed as if in admiration. "He ain't scared of nobody. He a big black dog." She whispered, "Sic him!"

"Watch me get rid of that cur," said the man. "Sic him, Pete! Sic him!"

Phoenix heard the dogs fighting, and heard the man running and throwing sticks. She even heard a gunshot. But she was slowly bending forward by that time, further and further forward, the lids stretched down over her eyes, as if she were doing this in her sleep. Her chin was lowered almost to her knees. The yellow palm of her hand came out from the fold of her apron. Her fingers slid down and along the ground under the piece of money with the grace and care they would have in lifting an egg from under a setting hen. Then she slowly straightened up, she stood erect, and the nickel was in her apron pocket. A bird flew by. Her lips moved. "God watching me the whole time. I come to stealing."

The man came back, and his own dog panted about them. "Well, I scared him off that time," he said, and then he laughed and lifted his gun and pointed it at Phoenix.

She stood straight and faced him.

"Doesn't the gun scare you?" he said, still pointing it.

"No, sir, I seen plenty go off closer by, in my day, and for less than what I done," she said, holding utterly still.

He smiled, and shouldered the gun. "Well, Granny," he said, "you must be a hundred years old, and scared of nothing. I'd give you a dime if I had any money with me. But you take my advice and stay home, and nothing will happen to you."

"I bound to go on my way, mister," said Phoenix. She inclined her head in the red rag. Then they went in different directions, but she could hear the gun shooting again and again over the hill.

She walked on. The shadows hung from the oak trees to the road like curtains. Then she smelled woodsmoke, and smelled the river, and she saw a steeple and the cabins on their steep steps. Dozens of little black children whirled around her. There ahead was Natchez shining. Bells were ringing. She walked on.

In the paved city it was Christmas time. There were red and green electric lights strung and crisscrossed everywhere, and all turned on in the daytime. Old Phoenix would have been lost if she had not distrusted her eyesight and depended on her feet to know where to take her.

She paused quietly on the sidewalk where people were passing by. A lady came along in the crowd, carrying an armful of red-, green- and silver-wrapped presents; she gave off perfume like the red roses in hot summer, and Phoenix stopped her.

"Please, missy, will you lace up my shoe?" She held up her foot.

"What do you want, Grandma?"

"See my shoe," said Phoenix. "Do all right for out in the country, but wouldn't look right to go in a big building."

"Stand still then, Grandma," said the lady. She put her packages down on the sidewalk beside her and laced and tied both shoes tightly.

"Can't lace 'em with a cane," said Phoenix. "Thank you, missy. I doesn't mind asking a nice lady to tie up my shoe, when I gets out on the street."

Moving slowly and from side to side, she went into the big building, and into a tower of steps, where she walked up and around and around until her feet knew to stop.

She entered a door, and there she saw nailed up on the wall the document that had been stamped with the gold seal and framed in the gold frame, which matched the dream that was hung up in her head.

"Here I be," she said. There was a fixed and ceremonial stiffness over her body.

"A charity case, I suppose," said an attendant who sat at the desk before her.

But Phoenix only looked above her head. There was sweat on her face, the wrinkles in her skin shone like a bright net.

"Speak up, Grandma," the woman said. "What's your name? We must have your history, you know. Have you been here before? What seems to be the trouble with you?"

Old Phoenix only gave a twitch to her face as if a fly were bothering her.

"Are you deaf?" cried the attendant.

But then the nurse came in.

"Oh, that's just old Aunt Phoenix," she said. "She doesn't come for herself—she has a little grandson. She makes these trips just as regular as clockwork. She lives away back off the Old Natchez Trace." She bent down. "Well, Aunt Phoenix, why don't you just take a seat? We won't keep you standing after your long trip." She pointed.

The old woman sat down, bolt upright in the chair.

"Now, how is the boy?" asked the nurse.

Old Phoenix did not speak.

"I said, how is the boy?"

But Phoenix only waited and stared straight ahead, her face very solemn and withdrawn into rigidity.

"Is his throat any better?" asked the nurse. "Aunt Phoenix, don't you hear me? Is your grandson's throat any better since the last time you came for the medicine?"

With her hands on her knees, the old woman waited, silent, erect and motionless, just as if she were in armor.

"You mustn't take up our time this way, Aunt Phoenix," the nurse said. "Tell us quickly about your grandson, and get it over. He isn't dead, is he?"

At last there came a flicker and then a flame of comprehension across her face, and she spoke.

"My grandson. It was my memory had left me. There I sat and forgot why I made my long trip."

"Forgot?" The nurse frowned. "After you came so far?"

Then Phoenix was like an old woman begging a dignified forgiveness for waking up frightened in the night. "I never did go to school, I was too old at the Surrender," she said in a soft voice. "I'm an old woman without an education. It was my memory fail me. My little grandson, he is just the same, and I forgot it in the coming."

"Throat never heals, does it?" said the nurse, speaking in a loud, sure voice to old Phoenix. By now she had a card with something written on it, a little list. "Yes. Swallowed lye. When was it?—January—two-three years ago—"

Phoenix spoke unasked now. "No, missy, he not dead, he just the same. Every little while his throat begin to close up again, and he not able to swallow. He not get his breath. He not able to help himself. So the time come around, and I go on another trip for the soothing medicine."

"All right. The doctor said as long as you came to get it, you could have it," said the nurse. "But it's an obstinate case."

"My little grandson, he sit up there in the house all wrapped up, waiting by himself," Phoenix went on. "We is the only two left in the world. He suffer and it don't seem to put him back at all. He got a sweet look. He going to last. He wear a little patch quilt and peep out holding his mouth open like a little bird. I remembers so plain now. I not going to forget him again, no, the whole enduring time. I could tell him from all the others in creation."

"All right." The nurse was trying to hush her now. She brought her a bottle of medicine. "Charity," she said, making a check mark in a book.

Old Phoenix held the bottle close to her eyes, and then carefully put it into her pocket.

"I thank you," she said.

"It's Christmas time, Grandma," said the attendant. "Could I give you a few pennies out of my purse?"

"Five pennies is a nickel," said Phoenix stiffly.

"Here's a nickel," said the attendant.

Phoenix rose carefully and held out her hand. She received the nickel and then fished the other nickel out of her pocket and laid it beside the new one. She stared at her palm closely, with her head on one side.

Then she gave a tap with her cane on the floor.

"This is what come to me to do," she said. "I going to the store and buy my child a little windmill they sells, made out of paper. He going to find it hard to believe there such a thing in the world.

I'll march myself back where he waiting, holding it straight up in this hand."

She lifted her free hand, gave a little nod, turned around, and walked out of the doctor's office. Then her slow step began on the stairs, going down.

THE OUTSTATION
W. SOMERSET MAUGHAM / GREAT BRITAIN

THE NEW assistant arrived in the afternoon. When the Resident, Mr. Warburton, was told that the prahu was in sight he put on his solar topee and went down to the landing stage. The guard, eight little Dyak soldiers, stood to attention as he passed. He noted with satisfaction that their bearing was martial, their uniforms neat and clean, and their guns shining. They were a credit to him. From the landing stage he watched the bend of the river round which in a moment the boat would sweep. He looked very smart in his spotless ducks and white shoes. He held under his arm a gold-headed Malacca cane which had been given him by the Sultan of Perak. He awaited the newcomer with mingled feelings. There was more work in the district than one man could properly do, and during his periodical tours of the country under his charge it had been inconvenient to leave the station in the hands of a native clerk, but he had been so long the only white man there that he could not face the arrival of another without misgiving. He was accustomed to loneliness. During the war he had not seen an English face for three years; and once when he was instructed to put up an afforestation officer he was seized with panic, so that when the stranger was due to arrive, having arranged everything for his reception, he wrote a note telling him he was obliged to go upriver, and fled; he remained away till he was informed by a messenger that his guest had left.

Now the prahu appeared in the broad reach. It was manned by prisoners, Dyaks under various sentences, and a couple of warders were waiting on the landing stage to take them back to jail. They were sturdy fellows, used to the river, and they rowed with a powerful stroke. As the boat reached the side a man got out from under the attap awning and stepped on shore. The guard presented arms.

"Here we are at last. By God, I'm as cramped as the devil. I've brought you your mail."

He spoke with exuberant joviality. Mr. Warburton politely held out his hand.

"Mr. Cooper, I presume?"

"That's right. Were you expecting anyone else?"

The question had a facetious intent, but the Resident did not smile.

"My name is Warburton. I'll show you your quarters. They'll bring your kit along."

He preceded Cooper along the narrow pathway and they entered a compound in which stood a small bungalow.

"I've had it made as habitable as I could, but of course no one has lived in it for a good many years."

It was built on piles. It consisted of a long living room which opened onto a broad veranda, and behind, on each side of a passage, were two bedrooms.

"This'll do me all right," said Cooper.

"I daresay you want to have a bath and a change. I shall be very much pleased if you'll dine with me tonight. Will eight o'clock suit you?"

"Any old time will do for me."

The Resident gave a polite, but slightly disconcerted, smile and withdrew. He returned to the fort where his own residence was. The impression which Allen Cooper had given him was not very favorable, but he was a fair man, and he knew that it was unjust to form an opinion on so brief a glimpse. Cooper seemed to be about thirty. He was a tall, thin fellow, with a sallow face in which there was not a spot of color. It was a face all in one tone. He had a large, hooked nose and blue eyes. When, entering the bungalow, he had taken off his topee and flung it to a waiting boy, Mr. Warburton noticed that his large skull, covered with short, brown hair, contrasted somewhat oddly with a weak, small chin. He was dressed in khaki shorts and a khaki shirt, but they were shabby and soiled; and his battered topee had not been cleaned for days. Mr. Warburton reflected that the young man had spent a week on a coasting steamer and had passed the last forty-eight hours lying in the bottom of a prahu.

"We'll see what he looks like when he comes in to dinner."

He went into his room where his things were as neatly laid out as if he had an English valet, undressed, and, walking down the stairs to the bathhouse, sluiced himself with cool water. The only concession he made to the climate was to wear a white dinner jacket; but otherwise, in a boiled shirt and a high collar, silk socks and patent-leather shoes, he dressed as formally as though he were dining at his club in Pall Mall. A careful host, he went into the dining room to see that the table was properly laid. It was gay with orchids and the silver shone brightly. The napkins were folded into elaborate shapes. Shaded candles in silver candlesticks shed a soft light. Mr. Warburton smiled his approval and returned to the sitting room to await his guest. Presently he appeared. Cooper was wearing the khaki shorts, the khaki shirt, and the ragged jacket in which he had landed. Mr. Warburton's smile of greeting froze on his face.

"Hulloa, you're all dressed up," said Cooper. "I didn't know you were going to do that. I very nearly put on a sarong."

"It doesn't matter at all. I daresay your boys were busy."

"You needn't have bothered to dress on my account, you know."

"I didn't. I always dress for dinner."

"Even when you're alone?"

"Especially when I'm alone," replied Mr. Warburton, with a frigid stare.

He saw a twinkle of amusement in Cooper's eyes, and he flushed an angry red. Mr. Warburton was a hot-tempered man; you might have guessed that from his red face with its pugnacious features and from his red hair, now growing white; his blue eyes, cold as a rule and observing, could flush with sudden wrath; but he was a man of the world and he hoped a just one. He must do his best to get on with this fellow.

"When I lived in London I moved in circles in which it would have been just as eccentric not to dress for dinner every night as not to have a bath every morning. When I came to Borneo I saw no reason to discontinue so good a habit. For three years, during the war, I never saw a white man. I never omitted to dress on a single occasion on which I was well enough to come in to dinner. You have not been very long in this country; believe me, there is no better way to maintain the proper pride which you should have in yourself. When a white man surrenders in the slightest degree to the influences that surround him he very soon loses his self-respect, and when he loses his self-respect you may be quite sure that the natives will soon cease to respect him."

"Well, if you expect me to put on a boiled shirt and a stiff collar in this heat I'm afraid you'll be disappointed."

"When you are dining in your own bungalow you will, of course, dress as you think fit, but when you do me the pleasure of dining with me, perhaps you will come to the conclusion that it is only polite to wear the costume usual in civilized society."

Two Malay boys, in sarongs and *songkoks*, with smart white coats and brass buttons, came in, one bearing gin *pahits*, and the other a tray on which were olives and anchovies. Then they went in to dinner. Mr. Warburton flattered himself that he had the best cook, a Chinese, in Borneo, and he took great trouble to have as good food as in the difficult circumstances was possible. He exercised much ingenuity in making the best of his materials.

"Would you care to look at the menu?" he said, handing it to Cooper.

It was written in French and the dishes had resounding names. They were waited on by the two boys. In opposite corners of the room two more waved immense fans, and so gave movement to the sultry air. The fare was sumptuous and the champagne excellent.

"Do you do yourself like this every day?" said Cooper.

Mr. Warburton gave the menu a careless glance.

"I have not noticed that the dinner is any different from usual," he said. "I eat very little myself, but I make a point of having a proper dinner served to me every night. It keeps the cook in practice and it's good discipline for the boys."

The conversation proceeded with effort. Mr. Warburton was elaborately courteous, and it may be that he found a slightly malicious amusement in the embarrassment which he thereby occasioned in his companion. Cooper had not been more than a few months in Sembulu, and Mr. Warburton's inquiries about friends of his in Kuala Solor were soon exhausted.

"By the way," he said presently, "did you meet a lad called Hennerley? He's come out recently, I believe."

"Oh, yes, he's in the police. A rotten bounder."

"I should hardly have expected him to be that. His uncle is my friend Lord Barraclough. I had a letter from Lady Barraclough only the other day asking me to look out for him."

"I heard he was related to somebody or other. I suppose that's how he got the job. He's been to Eton and Oxford and he doesn't forget to let you know it."

"You surprise me," said Mr. Warburton. "All his family have been at Eton and Oxford for a couple of hundred years. I should have expected him to take it as a matter of course."

"I thought him a damned prig."

"To what school did you go?"

"I was born in Barbados. I was educated there."

"Oh, I see."

Mr. Warburton managed to put so much offensiveness into his brief reply that Cooper flushed. For a moment he was silent.

"I've had two or three letters from Kuala Solor," continued Mr. Warburton, "and my impression was that young Hennerley was a great success. They say he's a first-rate sportsman."

"Oh, yes, he's very popular. He's just the sort of fellow they would like in K.S. I haven't got much use for the first-rate sportsman myself. What does it amount to in the long run that a man can play golf and tennis better than other people? And who cares if he can make a break of seventy-five at billiards? They attach a damned sight too much importance to that sort of thing in England."

"Do you think so? I was under the impression that the first-rate sportsman had come out of the war no worse than anyone else."

"Oh, if you're going to talk of the war then I do know what I'm talking about. I was in the same regiment as Hennerley and I can tell you that the men couldn't stick him at any price."

"How do you know?"

"Because I was one of the men."

"Oh, you hadn't got a commission."

"A fat chance I had of getting a commission. I was what was called a Colonial. I hadn't been to a public school and I had no influence. I was in the ranks the whole damned time."

Cooper frowned. He seemed to have difficulty in preventing himself from breaking into violent invective. Mr. Warburton watched him, his little blue eyes narrowed, watched him and formed his opinion. Changing the conversation, he began to speak to Cooper about the work that would be required of him, and as the clock struck ten he rose.

"Well, I won't keep you any more. I daresay you're tired by your journey."

They shook hands.

"Oh, I say, look here," said Cooper, "I wonder if you can find me a boy. The boy I had before never turned up when I was starting from K.S. He took my kit on board and all that and then disappeared. I didn't know he wasn't there till we were out of the river."

"I'll ask my head boy. I have no doubt he can find you someone."

"All right. Just tell him to send the boy along and if I like the look of him I'll take him."

There was a moon, so that no lantern was needed. Cooper walked across from the fort to his bungalow.

"I wonder why on earth they've sent me a fellow like that?" reflected Mr. Warburton. "If that's the kind of man they're going to get out now I don't think much of it."

He strolled down his garden. The fort was built on the top of a little hill and the garden ran down to the river's edge; on the bank was an arbor, and hither it was his habit to come after dinner to smoke a cheroot. And often from the river that flowed below him a voice was heard, the voice of some Malay too timorous to venture into the light of day; and a complaint or an accusation was softly wafted to his ears, a piece of information was whispered to him or a useful hint, which otherwise would never have come into his official ken. He threw himself heavily into a long rattan chair. Cooper! An envious, ill-bred fellow, bumptious, self-assertive and vain. But Mr. Warburton's irritation could not withstand the silent beauty of the night. The air was scented with the sweet-smelling flowers of a tree that grew at the entrance to the arbor, and the fireflies, sparkling dimly, flew with their slow and silvery flight. The moon made a pathway on the broad river for the light feet of Siva's bride, and on the further bank a row of palm trees was delicately silhouetted against the sky. Peace stole into the soul of Mr. Warburton.

He was a queer creature and he had had a singular career. At the age of twenty-one he had inherited a considerable fortune, a hundred thousand pounds, and when he left Oxford he threw himself into the gay life which in those days (now Mr. Warburton was a man of four and fifty) offered itself to the young man of good family. He had his flat in Mount Street, his private hansom, and his hunting box in Warwickshire. He went to all the places where the fashionable congregate. He was handsome, amusing and generous. He was a figure in the society of London in the early nineties, and society then had not lost its exclusiveness nor its brilliance. The Boer War which shook it was unthought of; the Great War which destroyed it was prophesied only by the pessimists. It was no unpleasant thing to be a rich young man in those days, and Mr. Warburton's chimneypiece during the season was packed with cards for one great function after another. Mr. Warburton displayed them with complacency. For Mr. Warburton was a snob. He was not a timid snob, a little ashamed of being impressed by his betters, nor a snob who sought the intimacy of persons who had acquired celebrity in politics or notoriety in the arts, nor the snob who was dazzled by riches; he was the naked, unadulterated common snob who dearly loved a lord. He was touchy and quick-tempered, but he would much rather have been snubbed by a person of quality than flattered by a commoner. His name figured insignificantly in Burke's Peerage, and it was marvelous to watch the ingenuity he used to mention his distant relationship to the noble family he belonged to; but never a word did he say of the honest Liverpool manufacturer from whom, through his mother, a Miss Gubbins, he had come by his fortune. It was the terror of his fashionable life that at Cowes, maybe, or at Ascot, when he was with a duchess or even with a prince of the blood, one of these relatives would claim acquaintance with him.

His failing was too obvious not soon to become notorious, but its extravagance saved it from being merely despicable. The great whom he adored laughed at him, but in their hearts felt his adoration not unnatural. Poor Warburton was a dreadful snob, of course, but after all he was a good fellow. He was always ready to back a bill for an impecunious nobleman, and if you were in a tight corner you could safely count on him for a hundred pounds. He gave good dinners. He played whist badly, but never minded how much he lost if the company was select. He happened to be a gambler, an unlucky one, but he was a good loser, and it was impossible not to admire the coolness with which he lost five hundred pounds at a sitting. His passion for cards, almost as strong as his passion for titles, was the cause of his undoing. The life he led was expensive and his gambling losses were formidable. He began to plunge more heavily, first on horses, and then on the stock exchange. He had a certain simplicity of character and the unscrupulous found him an ingenuous prey. I do not know if he ever realized that his smart friends laughed at him behind his back, but I think he had an obscure instinct that he could not afford to appear other than careless of his money. He got into the hands of moneylenders. At the age of thirty-four he was ruined.

He was too much imbued with the spirit of his class to hesitate in the choice of his next step. When a man in his set had run through his money he went out to the colonies. No one heard Mr. Warburton repine. He made no complaint because a noble friend had advised a disastrous speculation, he pressed nobody to whom he had lent money to repay it, he paid his debts (if he had only known it, the despised blood of the Liverpool manufacturer came out in him there), .sought help from no one, and, never having done a stroke of work in his life, looked for a means of livelihood. He remained cheerful, unconcerned and full of humor. He had no wish to make anyone with whom he happened to be uncomfortable by the recital of his misfortune. Mr. Warburton was a snob, but he was also a gentleman.

The only favor he asked of any of the great friends in whose daily company he had lived for years was a recommendation. The able man who was at that time Sultan of Sembulu took him into his service. The night before he sailed he dined for the last time at his club.

"I hear you're going away, Warburton," the old Duke of Hereford said to him.

"Yes, I'm going to Borneo."

"Good God, what are you going there for?"

"Oh, I'm broke."

"Are you? I'm sorry. Well, let us know when you come back. I hope you have a good time."

"Oh, yes. Lots of shooting, you know."

The duke nodded and passed on. A few hours later Mr. Warburton watched the coast of England recede into the mist, and he left behind everything which to him made life worth living.

Twenty years had passed since then. He kept up a busy correspondence with various great ladies and his letters were amusing and chatty. He never lost his love for titled persons and paid careful attention to the announcements in *The Times* (which reached him six weeks after publication) of their comings and goings. He perused the column which records births, deaths and marriages, and he was always ready with his letter of congratulation or condolence. The illustrated papers told him how people looked and on his periodical visits to England, able to take up the threads as though they had never been broken, he knew all about any new person who might have appeared on the social surface. His interest in the world of fashion was as vivid as when himself had been a figure in it. It still seemed to him the only thing that mattered.

But insensibly another interest had entered into his life. The position he found himself in flattered his vanity; he was no longer the sycophant craving the smiles of the great, he was the master whose word was law. He was gratified by the guard of Dyak soldiers who presented arms as he passed. He liked to sit in judgment on his fellowmen. It pleased him to compose quarrels between rival chiefs. When the headhunters were troublesome in the old days he set out to chastise them with a thrill of pride in his own behavior. He was too vain not to be of dauntless courage, and a pretty story was told of his coolness in adventuring single-handed into a stockaded village and demanding the surrender of a bloodthirsty pirate. He became a skillful administrator. He was strict, just and honest.

And little by little he conceived a deep love for the Malays. He interested himself in their habits and customs. He was never tired of listening to their talk. He admired their virtues, and with a smile and a shrug of the shoulders condoned their vices.

"In my day," he would say, "I have been on intimate terms with some of the greatest gentlemen in England, but I have never known finer gentlemen than some well-born Malays whom I am proud to call my friends."

He liked their courtesy and their distinguished manners, their gentleness and their sudden passions. He knew by instinct exactly how to treat them. He had a genuine tenderness for them. But he never forgot that he was an English gentleman and he had no patience with the white men who yielded to native customs. He made no surrenders. And he did not imitate so many of the white men in taking a native woman to wife, for an intrigue of this nature, however sanctified by custom, seemed to him not only shocking but undignified. A man who had been called George by Albert Edward, Prince of Wales, could hardly be expected to have any connection with a native. And when he returned to Borneo from his visits to England it was now with something like relief. His friends, like himself, were no longer young, and there was a new generation which looked upon him as a tiresome old man. It seemed to him that the England of today had lost a good deal of what he had loved in the England of his youth. But Borneo remained the same. It was home to him now. He meant to remain in the service as long as was possible, and the hope in his heart was that he would die before at last he was forced to retire. He had stated in his will that wherever he died he wished his body to be brought back to Sembulu and buried among the people he loved within sound of the softly flowing river.

But these emotions he kept hidden from the eyes of men; and no one, seeing this spruce, stout, well-set-up man, with his clean-shaven strong face and his whitening hair, would have dreamed that he cherished so profound a sentiment.

He knew how the work of the station should be done, and during the next few days he kept a suspicious eye on his assistant. He saw very soon that he was painstaking and competent. The only fault he had to find with him was that he was brusque with the natives.

"The Malays are shy and very sensitive," he said to him. "I think you will find that you will get much better results if you take care always to be polite, patient and kindly."

Cooper gave a short, grating laugh.

"I was born in Barbados and I was in Africa in the war. I don't think there's much about niggers that I don't know."

"I know nothing," said Mr. Warburton acidly. "But we were not talking of them. We were talking of Malays."

"Aren't they niggers?"

"You are very ignorant," replied Mr. Warburton.

He said no more.

On the first Sunday after Cooper's arrival he asked him to dinner. He did everything ceremoniously, and though they had met on the previous day in the office and later, on the fort veranda where they drank a gin and bitters together at six o'clock, he sent a polite note across to the bungalow by a boy. Cooper, however unwillingly, came in evening dress and Mr. Warburton, though gratified that his wish was respected, noticed with disdain that the young man's clothes were badly cut and his shirt ill-fitting. But Mr. Warburton was in a good temper that evening.

"By the way," he said to him, as he shook hands, "I've talked to my head boy about finding you someone and he recommends his nephew. I've seen him and he seems a bright and willing lad. Would you like to see him?"

"I don't mind."

"He's waiting now."

Mr. Warburton called his boy and told him to send for his nephew.

In a moment a tall, slender youth of twenty appeared. He had large dark eyes and a good profile. He was very neat in his sarong, a little white coat, and a fez, without a tassel, of plum-colored velvet. He answered to the name of Abas. Mr. Warburton looked on him with approval, and his manner insensibly softened as he spoke to him in fluent and idiomatic Malay. He was inclined to be sarcastic with white people, but with the Malays he had a happy mixture of condescension and kindliness. He stood in the place of the sultan. He knew perfectly how to preserve his own dignity, and at the same time put a native at his ease.

"Will he do?" said Mr. Warburton, turning to Cooper.

"Yes, I daresay he's no more of a scoundrel than any of the rest of them."

Mr. Warburton informed the boy that he was engaged and dismissed him.

"You're very lucky to get a boy like that," he told Cooper. "He belongs to a very good family. They came over from Malacca nearly a hundred years ago."

"I don't much mind if the boy who cleans my shoes and brings me a drink when I want it has blue blood in his veins or not. All I ask is that he should do what I tell him and look sharp about it."

Mr. Warburton pursed his lips, but made no reply.

They went in to dinner. It was excellent, and the wine was good. Its influence presently had its effect on them and they talked not only without acrimony, but even with friendliness. Mr. Warburton liked to do himself well, and on Sunday night he made it a habit to do himself even a little better than usual. He began to think he was unfair to Cooper. Of course he was not a gentleman, but that was not his fault, and when you got to know him it might be that he would turn out a very good fellow. His faults, perhaps, were faults of manner. And he was certainly good at his work, quick, conscientious and thorough. When they reached the dessert Mr. Warburton was feeling kindly disposed towards all mankind.

"This is your first Sunday and I'm going to give you a very special glass of port. I've only got about two dozen of it left and I keep it for special occasions."

He gave his boy instructions and presently the bottle was brought. Mr. Warburton watched the boy open it.

"I got this port from my old friend Charles Hollington. He'd had it for forty years and I've had it for a good many. He was well known to have the best cellar in England."

"Is he a wine merchant?"

"Not exactly," smiled Mr. Warburton. "I was speaking of Lord Hollington of Castle Reagh. He's one of the richest peers in England. A very old friend of mine. I was at Eton with his brother."

This was an opportunity that Mr. Warburton could never resist and he told a little anecdote of which the only point seemed to be that he knew an earl. The port was certainly very good; he drank a glass and then a second. He lost all caution. He had not talked to a white man for months. He began to tell stories. He showed himself in the company of the great. Hearing him you would have thought that at one time ministries were formed and policies decided on his suggestion whispered into the ear of a duchess or thrown over the dinner table to be gratefully acted on by the confidential adviser of the sovereign. The old days at Ascot, Goodwood and Cowes lived again for him. Another glass of port. There were the great house parties in Yorkshire and in Scotland to which he went every year.

"I had a man called Foreman then, the best valet I ever had, and why do you think he gave me notice? You know in the housekeeper's room the ladies' maids and the gentlemen's gentlemen sit according to the precedence of their masters. He told me he was sick of going to party after party at which I was the only commoner. It meant that he always had to sit at the bottom of the table and all the best bits were taken before a dish reached him. I told the story to the old Duke of Hereford and he roared. 'By God, sir,' he said, 'if I were King of England I'd make you a viscount just to give your man a chance.' 'Take him yourself, Duke,' I said. 'He's the best valet I've ever had.' 'Well, Warburton,' he said, 'if he's good enough for you he's good enough for me. Send him along.'"

Then there was Monte Carlo where Mr. Warburton and the Grand Duke Fyodor, playing in partnership, had broken the bank one evening; and there was Marienbad. At Marienbad Mr. Warburton had played baccarat with Edward VII. "He was only Prince of Wales then, of course. I remember him saying to me, 'George, if you draw on a five you'll lose your shirt.' He was right; I don't think he ever said a truer word in his life. He was a wonderful man. I always said he was the greatest diplomatist in Europe. But I was a young fool in those days, I hadn't the sense to take his advice. If I had, if I'd never drawn on a five, I daresay I shouldn't be here today."

Cooper was watching him. His brown eyes, deep in their sockets, were hard and supercilious, and on his lips was a mocking smile. He had heard a good deal about Mr. Warburton in Kuala Solor. Not a bad sort, and he ran his district like clockwork, they said, but by heaven, what a snob! They laughed at him good-naturedly, for it was impossible to dislike a man who was so generous and so kindly, and Cooper had already heard the story of the Prince of Wales and the game of baccarat. But Cooper listened without indulgence. From the beginning he had resented the Resident's manner. He was very sensitive and he writhed under Mr. Warburton's polite sarcasms. Mr. Warburton had a knack of receiving a remark of which he disapproved with a devastating silence. Cooper had lived little in England and he had a peculiar dislike of the English. He resented especially the public-school boy since he always feared that he was going to patronize him. He was so much afraid of others putting on airs with him that, in order as it were to get in first, he put on such airs as to make everyone think him insufferably conceited.

"Well, at all events the war has done one good thing for us," he said at last. "It's smashed up the power of the aristocracy. The Boer War started it, and 1914 put the lid on."

"The great families of England are doomed," said Mr. Warburton with the complacent melancholy of an *émigré* who remembered the court of Louis XV. "They cannot afford any longer to live in their splendid palaces and their princely hospitality will soon be nothing but a memory."

"And a damned good job too in my opinion."

"My poor Cooper, what can you know of the glory that was Greece and the grandeur that was Rome?"

Mr. Warburton made an ample gesture. His eyes for an instant grew dreamy with a vision of the past.

"Well, believe me, we're fed up with all that rot. What we want is a business government by businessmen. I was born in a Crown Colony and I've lived practically all my life in the colonies. I don't give a row of pins for a lord. What's wrong with England is snobbishness. And if there's anything that gets my goat it's a snob."

A snob! Mr. Warburton's face grew purple and his eyes blazed with anger. That was a word that had pursued him all his life. The great ladies whose society he had enjoyed in his youth were not inclined to look upon his appreciation of themselves as unworthy, but even great ladies are sometimes out of temper and more than once Mr. Warburton had had the dreadful word flung in his teeth. He knew, he could not help knowing, that there were odious people who called him a snob. How unfair it was! Why, there was no vice he found so detestable as snobbishness. After all, he liked to mix with people of his own class, he was only at home in their company, and how in heaven's name could anyone say that was snobbish? Birds of a feather.

"I quite agree with you," he answered. "A snob is a man who admires or despises another because he is of a higher social rank than his own. It is the most vulgar failing of our English middle class."

He saw a flicker of amusement in Cooper's eyes. Cooper put up his hand to hide the broad smile that rose to his lips, and so made it more noticeable. Mr. Warburton's hands trembled a little.

Probably Cooper never knew how greatly he had offended his chief. A sensitive man himself he was strangely insensitive to the feelings of others.

Their work forced them to see one another for a few minutes now and then during the day, and they met at six to have a drink on Mr. Warburton's veranda. This was an old-established custom of the country which Mr. Warburton would not for the world have broken. But they ate their meals separately, Cooper in his bungalow and Mr. Warburton at the fort. After the office work was over they walked till dusk fell, but they walked apart. There were but few paths in this country, where the jungle pressed close upon the plantations of the village, and when Mr. Warburton caught sight of his assistant passing along with his loose stride, he would make a circuit in order to avoid him. Cooper, with his bad manners, his conceit in his own judgment and his intolerance, had already got on his nerves; but it was not till Cooper had been on the station for a couple of months that an incident happened which turned the Resident's dislike into bitter hatred.

Mr. Warburton was obliged to go up-country on a tour of inspection, and he left the station in Cooper's charge with more confidence, since he had definitely come to the conclusion that he was a capable fellow. The only thing he did not like was that he had no indulgence. He was honest, just and painstaking, but he had no sympathy for the natives. It bitterly amused Mr. Warburton to observe that this man, who looked upon himself as every man's equal, should look upon so many men as his own inferiors. He was hard, he had no patience with the native mind, and he was a bully. Mr. Warburton very quickly realized that the Malays disliked and feared him. He was not altogether displeased. He would not have liked it very much if his assistant had enjoyed a popularity which might rival his own. Mr. Warburton made his elaborate preparations, set out on his expedition, and in three weeks returned.

Meanwhile the mail had arrived. The first thing that struck his eyes when he entered his sitting room was a great pile of open newspapers. Cooper had met him, and they went into the room together. Mr. Warburton turned to one of the servants who had been left behind and sternly asked him what was the meaning of those open papers. Cooper hastened to explain.

"I wanted to read all about the Wolverhampton murder and so I borrowed your *Times*. I brought them back again. I knew you wouldn't mind."

Mr. Warburton turned on him, white with anger.

"But I do mind. I mind very much."

"I'm sorry," said Cooper, with composure. "The fact is, I simply couldn't wait till you came back."

"I wonder you didn't open my letters as well."

Cooper, unmoved, smiled at his chief's exasperation.

"Oh, that's not quite the same thing. After all, I couldn't imagine you'd mind my looking at your newspapers. There's nothing private in them."

"I very much object to anyone reading my paper before me." He went up to the pile. There were nearly thirty numbers there. "I think it extremely impertinent of you. They're all mixed up."

"We can easily put them in order," said Cooper, joining him at the table.

"Don't touch them," cried Mr. Warburton.

"I say, it's childish to make a scene about a little thing like that."

"How dare you speak to me like that?"

"Oh, go to hell," said Cooper, and he flung out of the room.

Mr. Warburton, trembling with passion, was left contemplating his papers. His greatest pleasure in life had been destroyed by those callous, brutal hands. Most people living in out-of-the-way places when the mail comes tear open impatiently their papers and taking the last ones first glance at the latest news from home. Not so Mr. Warburton. His news agent had instructions to write on the outside of the wrapper the date of each paper he dispatched and when the great bundle arrived Mr. Warburton looked at these dates and with his blue pencil numbered them. His head boy's orders were to place one on the table every morning in the veranda with the early cup of tea, and it was Mr. Warburton's special delight to break the wrapper as he sipped his tea, and read the morning paper. It gave him the illusion of living at home. Every Monday morning he read the Monday *Times* of six weeks back and so went through the week. On Sunday he read *The Observer*. Like his habit of dressing for dinner it was a tie to civilization. And it was his pride that no matter how exciting the news was he had never yielded to the temptation of opening a paper before its allotted time. During the war the suspense sometimes had been intolerable, and when he read one day that a push was begun he had undergone agonies of suspense which he might have saved himself by the simple expedient of opening a later paper which lay waiting for him on a shelf. It had been the severest trial to which he had ever exposed himself, but he victoriously surmounted it. And that clumsy fool had broken open those neat tight packages because he wanted to know whether some horrid woman had murdered her odious husband.

Mr. Warburton sent for his boy and told him to bring wrappers. He folded up the papers as neatly as he could, placed a wrapper round each and numbered it. But it was a melancholy task.

"I shall never forgive him," he said. "Never."

Of course his boy had been with him on his expedition; he never traveled without him, for his boy knew exactly how he liked things, and Mr. Warburton was not the kind of jungle traveler who was prepared to dispense with his comforts; but in the interval since their arrival he had been gossiping in the servants' quarters. He had learned that Cooper had had trouble with his boys. All but the youth Abas had left him. Abas had desired to go too, but his uncle had placed him there on the instructions of the Resident, and he was afraid to leave without his uncle's permission.

"I told him he had done well, tuan," said the boy. "But he is unhappy. He says it is not a good house and he wishes to know if he may go as the others have gone."

"No, he must stay. The tuan must have servants. Have those who went been replaced?"

"No, tuan, no one will go."

Mr. Warburton frowned. Cooper was an insolent fool, but he had an official position and must be suitably provided with servants. It was not seemly that his house should be improperly conducted.

"Where are the boys who ran away?"

"They are in the kampong, tuan."

"Go and see them tonight and tell them that I expect them to be back in Tuan Cooper's house at dawn tomorrow."

"They say they will not go, tuan."

"On my order?"

The boy had been with Mr. Warburton for fifteen years, and he knew every intonation of his master's voice. He was not afraid of him, they had gone through too much together, once in the jungle the Resident had saved his life and once, upset in some rapids, but for him the Resident would have been drowned; but he knew when the Resident must be obeyed without question.

"I will go to the kampong," he said.

Mr. Warburton expected that his subordinate would take the first opportunity to apologize for his rudeness, but Cooper had the ill-bred man's inability to express regret; and when they met next morning in the office he ignored the incident. Since Mr. Warburton had been away for three weeks it was necessary for them to have a somewhat prolonged interview. At the end of it Mr. Warburton dismissed him.

"I don't think there's anything else, thank you." Cooper turned to go, but Mr. Warburton stopped him. "I understand you've been having some trouble with your boys."

Cooper gave a harsh laugh.

"They tried to blackmail me. They had the damned cheek to run away, all except that incompetent fellow Abas—he knew when he was well off—but I just sat tight. They've all come to heel again."

"What do you mean by that?"

"This morning they were all back on their jobs, the Chinese cook and all. There they were, as cool as cucumbers; you would have thought they owned the place. I suppose they'd come to the conclusion that I wasn't such as fool as I looked."

"By no means. They came back on my express order."

Cooper flushed slightly.

"I should be obliged if you wouldn't interfere with my private concerns."

"They're not your private concerns. When your servants run away it makes you ridiculous. You are perfectly free to make a fool of yourself, but I cannot allow you to be made a fool of. It is unseemly that your house should not be properly staffed. As soon as I heard that your boys had left you, I had them told to be back in their places at dawn. That'll do."

Mr. Warburton nodded to signify that the interview was at an end. Cooper took no notice.

"Shall I tell you what I did? I called them and gave the whole bally lot the sack. I gave them ten minutes to get out of the compound."

Mr. Warburton shrugged his shoulders.

"What makes you think you can get others?"

"I've told my own clerk to see about it."

Mr. Warburton reflected for a moment.

"I think you behaved very foolishly. You will do well to remember in future that good masters make good servants."

"Is there anything else you want to teach me?"

"I should like to teach you manners, but it would be an arduous task, and I have not the time to waste. I will see that you get boys."

"Please don't put yourself to any trouble on my account. I'm quite capable of getting them for myself."

Mr. Warburton smiled acidly. He had an inkling that Cooper disliked him as much as he disliked Cooper, and he knew that nothing is more galling than to be forced to accept the favors of a man you detest.

"Allow me to tell you that you have no more chance of getting Malay or Chinese servants here now than you have of getting an English butler or a French chef. No one will come to you except on an order from me. Would you like me to give it?"

"No."

"As you please. Good morning."

Mr. Warburton watched the development of the situation with acrid humor. Cooper's clerk was unable to persuade Malay, Dyak or Chinese to enter the house of such a master. Abas, the boy who remained faithful to him, knew how to cook only native food, and Cooper, a coarse feeder, found his gorge rise against the everlasting rice. There was no water carrier, and in that great heat he needed several baths a day. He cursed Abas, but Abas opposed him with sullen resistance and would not do more than he chose. It was galling to know that the lad stayed with him only because the Resident insisted. This went on for a fortnight and then, one morning, he found in his house the very servants whom he had previously dismissed. He fell into a violent rage, but he had learned a little sense, and this time, without a word, he let them stay. He swallowed his humiliation, but the impatient contempt he had felt for Mr. Warburton's idiosyncrasies changed into a sullen hatred; the Resident with this malicious stroke had made him the laughingstock of all the natives.

The two men now held no communication with one another. They broke the time-honored custom of sharing, notwithstanding personal dislike, a drink at six o'clock with any white man who happened to be at the station. Each lived in his own house as though the other did not exist. Now that Cooper had fallen into the work, it was necessary for them to have little to do with one another in the office. Mr. Warburton used his orderly to send any message he had to give his assistant, and his instructions he sent by formal letter. They saw one another constantly, that was inevitable, but did not exchange half a dozen words in a week. The fact that they could not avoid catching sight of one another got on their nerves. They brooded over their antagonism and Mr. Warburton, taking his daily walk, could think of nothing but how much he detested his assistant.

And the dreadful thing was that in all probability they would remain thus, facing each other in deadly enmity, till Mr. Warburton went on leave. It might be three years. He had no reason to send in a complaint to headquarters: Cooper did his work very well, and at that time men were hard to get. True, vague complaints reached him and hints that the natives found Cooper harsh. There was certainly a feeling of dissatisfaction among them. But when Mr. Warburton looked into specific cases, all he could say was that Cooper had shown severity where mildness would not have been misplaced and had been unfeeling when himself would have been sympathetic. He had done nothing for which he could be taken to task. But Mr. Warburton watched him. Hatred will often make a man clear-sighted, and he had a suspicion that Cooper was using the natives without consideration, yet keeping within the law, because he felt that thus he could exasperate his chief. One day perhaps he would go too far. None knew better than Mr. Warburton how irritable the incessant heat could make a man and how difficult it was to keep one's self-control after a sleepless night. He smiled softly to himself. Sooner or later Cooper would deliver himself into his hand.

When at last the opportunity came Mr. Warburton laughed aloud. Cooper had charge of the prisoners; they made roads, built sheds, rowed when it was necessary to send the prahu up- or down-stream, kept the town clean and otherwise usefully employed themselves. If well-behaved they even on occasion served as houseboys. Cooper kept them hard at it. He liked to see them work. He took pleasure in devising tasks for them; and seeing quickly enough that they were being made to do useless things the prisoners worked badly. He punished them by lengthening their hours. This was contrary to the regulations, and as soon as it was brought to the attention of Mr. Warburton, without referring the matter back to his subordinate, he gave instructions that the old hours should be kept; Cooper, going out for his walk, was astounded to see the prisoners strolling back to the jail; he had given instructions that they were not to knock off till dusk. When he asked the warder in charge why they had left off work he was told that it was the Resident's bidding.

White with rage he strode to the fort. Mr. Warburton, in his spotless white ducks and his neat topee, with a walking stick in his hand, followed by his dogs, was on the point of starting out on his afternoon stroll. He had watched Cooper go and knew that he had taken the road by the river. Cooper jumped up the steps and went straight up to the Resident. "I want to know what the hell you mean by countermanding my order that the prisoners were to work till six," he burst out, beside himself with fury.

Mr. Warburton opened his cold blue eyes very wide and assumed an expression of great surprise.

"Are you out of your mind? Are you so ignorant that you do not know that that is not the way to speak to your official superior?"

"Oh, go to hell. The prisoners are my pidgin and you've got no right to interfere. You mind your business and I'll mind mine. I want to know what the devil you mean by making a damned fool of me. Everyone in the place will know that you've countermanded my order."

Mr. Warburton kept very cool.

"You had no power to give the order you did. I countermanded it because it was harsh and tyrannical. Believe me, I have not made half such a damned fool of you as you have made of yourself."

"You disliked me from the first moment I came here. You've done everything you could to make the place impossible for me because I wouldn't lick your boots for you. You got your knife into me because I wouldn't flatter you."

Cooper, spluttering with rage, was nearing dangerous ground, and Mr. Warburton's eyes grew on a sudden colder and more piercing.

"You are wrong. I thought you were a cad, but I was perfectly satisfied with the way you did your work."

"You snob. You damned snob. You thought me a cad because I hadn't been to Eton. Oh, they told me in K.S. what to expect. Why, don't you know that you're the laughingstock of the whole country? I could hardly help bursting into a roar of laughter when you told your celebrated story about the Prince of Wales. My God, how they shouted at the club when they told it. By God, I'd rather be the cad I am than the snob you are."

He got Mr. Warburton on the raw.

"If you don't get out of my house this minute I shall knock you down," he cried.

The other came a little closer to him and put his face in his.

"Touch me, touch me," he said. "By God, I'd like to see you hit me. Do you want me to say it again? Snob. Snob."

Cooper was three inches taller than Mr. Warburton, a strong, muscular young man. Mr. Warburton was fat and fifty-four. His clenched fist shot out. Cooper caught him by the arm and pushed him back.

"Don't be a damned fool. Remember I'm not a gentleman. I know how to use my hands."

He gave a sort of hoot, and, grinning all over his pale, sharp face, jumped down the veranda steps. Mr. Warburton, his heart in his anger pounding against his ribs, sank exhausted into a chair. His body tingled as though he had prickly heat. For one horrible moment he thought he was going to cry. But suddenly he was conscious that his head boy was on the veranda and instinctively regained control of himself. The boy came forward and filled him a glass of whisky and soda. Without a word Mr. Warburton took it and drank it to the dregs.

"What do you want to say to me?" asked Mr. Warburton, trying to force a smile onto his strained lips.

"Tuan, the assistant tuan is a bad man. Abas wishes again to leave him."

"Let him wait a little. I shall write to Kuala Solor and ask that Tuan Cooper should go elsewhere."

"Tuan Cooper is not good with the Malays."

"Leave me."

The boy silently withdrew. Mr. Warburton was left alone with his thoughts. He saw the club at Kuala Solor, the men sitting round the table in the window in their flannels, when the night had driven them in from golf and tennis, drinking whiskies and gin *pahits* and laughing when they told the celebrated story of the Prince of Wales and himself at Marienbad. He was hot with shame and misery. A snob! They all thought him a snob. And he had always thought them very good fellows, he had always been gentleman enough to let it make no difference to him that they were of very second-rate position. He hated them now. But his hatred for them was nothing compared with his hatred for Cooper. And if it had come to blows Cooper could have thrashed him. Tears of mortification ran down his red, fat face. He sat there for a couple of hours smoking cigarette after cigarette, and he wished he were dead.

At last the boy came back and asked him if he would dress for dinner.

Of course! He always dressed for dinner. He rose wearily from his chair and put on his stiff shirt and the high collar. He sat down at the prettily decorated table and was waited on as usual by the two boys while two others waved their great fans. Over there in the bungalow, two hundred yards away, Cooper was eating a filthy meal clad only in a sarong and a *baju*. His feet were bare and while he ate he probably read a detective story. After dinner Mr. Warburton sat down to write a letter. The sultan was away, but he wrote, privately and confidentially, to his representative. Cooper did his work very well, he said, but the fact was that he couldn't get on with him. They were getting dreadfully on each other's nerves and he would look upon it as a very great favor if Cooper could be transferred to another post.

He dispatched the letter next morning by special messenger. The answer came a fortnight later with the month's mail. It was a private note and ran as follows:

My dear Warburton:

I do not want to answer your letter officially and so I am writing you a few lines myself. Of course if you insist I will put the matter up to the Sultan, but I think you would be much wiser to drop it. I know Cooper is a rough diamond, but he is capable, and he had a pretty thin time in the war, and I think he should be given every chance. I think you are a little too much inclined to attach importance to a man's social position. You must remember that times have changed. Of course it's a very good thing for a man to be a gentleman, but it's better that he should be competent and hardworking. I think if you'll exercise a little tolerance you'll get on very well with Cooper.

Yours very sincerely,

Richard Temple

The letter dropped from Mr. Warburton's hand. It was easy to read between the lines. Dick Temple, whom he had known for twenty years, Dick Temple, who came from quite a good county family, thought him a snob and for that reason had no patience with his request. Mr. Warburton felt on a sudden discouraged with life. The world of which he was a part had passed away, and the future belonged to a meaner generation. Cooper represented it and Cooper he hated with all his heart. He stretched out his hand to fill his glass and at the gesture his head boy stepped forward.

"I didn't know you were there."

The boy picked up the official letter. Ah, that was why he was waiting.

"Does Tuan Cooper go, tuan?"

"No."

"There will be a misfortune."

For a moment the words conveyed nothing to his lassitude. But only for a moment. He sat up in his chair and looked at the boy. He was all attention. "What do you mean by that?"

"Tuan Cooper is not behaving rightly with Abas."

Mr. Warburton shrugged his shoulders. How should a man like Cooper know how to treat servants? Mr. Warburton knew the type: he would be grossly familiar with them at one moment and rude and inconsiderate the next.

"Let Abas go back to his family."

"Tuan Cooper holds back his wages so that he may not run away. He has paid him nothing for three months. I tell him to be patient. But he is angry, he will not listen to reason. If the tuan continues to use him ill there will be a misfortune."

"You were right to tell me."

The fool! Did he know so little of the Malays as to think he could safely injure them? It would serve him damned well right if he got a kris in his back. A kris. Mr. Warburton's heart seemed on a sudden to miss a beat. He had only to let things take their course and one fine day he would be rid of Cooper. He smiled faintly as the phrase, a masterly inactivity, crossed his mind. And now his heart beat a little quicker, for he saw the man he hated lying on his face in a pathway of the jungle with a knife in his back. A fit end for the cad and the bully. Mr. Warburton sighed. It was his duty to warn him and of course he must do it. He wrote a brief and formal note to Cooper asking him to come to the fort at once.

In ten minutes Cooper stood before him. They had not spoken to one another since the day when Mr. Warburton had nearly struck him. He did not now ask him to sit down.

"Did you wish to see me?" Cooper asked.

He was untidy and none too clean. His face and hands were covered with little red blotches where mosquitos had bitten him and he had scratched himself till the blood came. His long, thin face bore a sullen look.

"I understand that you are again having trouble with your servants. Abas, my head boy's nephew, complains that you have held back his wages for three months. I consider it a most arbitrary proceeding. The lad wishes to leave you, and I certainly do not blame him. I must insist on your paying what is due to him."

"I don't choose that he should leave me. I am holding back his wages as a pledge of his good behavior."

"You do not know the Malay character. The Malays are very sensitive to injury and ridicule. They are passionate and revengeful. It is my duty to warn you that if you drive this boy beyond a certain point you run a great risk."

Cooper gave a contemptuous chuckle.

"What do you think he'll do?"

"I think he'll kill you."

"Why should you mind?"

"Oh, I wouldn't," replied Mr. Warburton, with a faint laugh. "I should bear it with the utmost fortitude. But I feel the official obligation to give you a proper warning."

"Do you think I'm afraid of a damned nigger?"

"It's a matter of entire indifference to me."

"Well, let me tell you this, I know how to take care of myself; that boy Abas is a dirty, thieving rascal, and if he tries any monkey tricks on me, by God, I'll wring his bloody neck."

"That was all I wished to say to you," said Mr. Warburton. "Good evening."

Mr. Warburton gave him a little nod of dismissal. Cooper flushed, did not for a moment know what to say or do, turned on his heel and stumbled out of the room. Mr. Warburton watched him go with an icy smile on his lips. He had done his duty. But what would he have thought had he known that when Cooper got back to his bungalow, so silent and cheerless, he threw himself down on his bed and in his bitter loneliness on a sudden lost all control of himself? Painful sobs tore his chest and heavy tears rolled down his thin cheeks.

After this Mr. Warburton seldom saw Cooper, and never spoke to him. He read his *Times* every morning, did his work at the office, took his exercise, dressed for dinner, dined and sat by the river smoking his cheroot. If by chance he ran across Cooper he cut him dead. Each, though never for a moment unconscious of the propinquity, acted as though the other did not exist. Time did nothing to assuage their animosity. They watched one another's actions and each knew what the other did. Though Mr. Warburton had been a keen shot in his youth, with age he had acquired a distaste for killing the wild things of the jungle, but on Sundays and holidays Cooper went out with his gun: if he got something it was a triumph over Mr. Warburton; if not, Mr. Warburton shrugged his shoulders and chuckled. These counter-jumpers trying to be sportsmen!

Christmas was a bad time for both of them: they ate their dinners alone, each in his own quarters, and they got deliberately drunk. They were the only white men within two hundred miles and they lived within shouting distance of each other. At the beginning of the year Cooper went down with fever, and when Mr. Warburton caught sight of him again he was surprised to see how thin he had grown. He looked ill and worn. The solitude, so much more unnatural because it was due to no necessity, was getting on his nerves. It was getting on Mr Warburton's too, and often he could not sleep at night. He lay awake brooding. Cooper was drinking heavily and surely the breaking point was near; but in his dealings with the natives he took care to do nothing that might expose him to his chief's rebuke. They fought a grim and silent battle with one another. It was a test of endurance. The months passed, and neither gave sign of weakening. They were like men dwelling in regions of eternal night, and their souls were oppressed with the knowledge that never would the day dawn for them. It looked as though their lives would continue forever in this dull and hideous monotony of hatred.

And when at last the inevitable happened it came upon Mr. Warburton with all the shock of the unexpected. Cooper accused the boy Abas of stealing some of his clothes, and when the boy denied the theft took him by the scruff of the neck and kicked him down the steps of the bungalow. The boy demanded his wages, and Cooper flung at his head every word of abuse he knew. If he saw him in the compound in an hour he would hand him over to the police. Next morning the boy waylaid him outside the fort when he was walking over to his office, and again demanded his wages. Cooper struck him in the face with his clenched fist. The boy fell to the ground and got up with blood streaming from his nose.

Cooper walked on and set about his work. But he could not attend to it. The blow had calmed his irritation, and he knew that he had gone too far. He was worried. He felt ill, miserable and discouraged. In the adjoining office sat Mr. Warburton, and his impulse was to go and tell him what he had done; he made a movement in his chair, but he knew with what icy scorn he would listen to the story. He could see his patronizing smile. For a moment he had an uneasy fear of what Abas might do. Warburton had warned him all right. He sighed. What a fool he had been! But he shrugged his shoulders impatiently. He did not care; a fat lot he had to live for. It was all Warburton's fault; if he hadn't put his back up nothing like this would have happened. Warburton had made life a hell for him from the start. The snob. But they were all like that: it was because he was a Colonial. It was a damned shame that he had never got his commission in the war; he was as good as anyone else. They were a lot of dirty snobs. He was damned if he was going to knuckle under now. Of course Warburton would hear of what had happened; the old devil knew everything. He wasn't afraid. He wasn't afraid of any Malay in Borneo, and Warburton could go to blazes.

He was right in thinking that Mr. Warburton would know what had happened. His head boy told him when he went in to tiffin.

"Where is your nephew now?"

"I do not know, tuan. He has gone."

Mr. Warburton remained silent. After luncheon as a rule he slept a little, but today he found himself very wide awake. His eyes involuntarily sought the bungalow where Cooper was now resting.

The idiot! Hesitation for a little was in Mr. Warburton's mind. Did the man know in what peril he was? He supposed he ought to send for him. But each time he had tried to reason with Cooper, Cooper had insulted him. Anger, furious anger welled up suddenly in Mr. Warburton's heart, so that the veins on his temples stood out and he clenched his fists. The cad had had his warning. Now let him take what was coming to him. It was no business of his and if anything happened it was not his fault. But perhaps they would wish in Kuala Solor that they had taken his advice and transferred Cooper to another station.

He was strangely restless that night. After dinner he walked up and down the veranda. When the boy went away to his own quarters, Mr. Warburton asked him whether anything had been seen of Abas.

"No, tuan. I think maybe he has gone to the village of his mother's brother."

Mr. Warburton gave him a sharp glance, but the boy was looking down and their eyes did not meet. Mr. Warburton went down to the river and sat in his arbor. But peace was denied him. The river flowed ominously silent. It was like a great serpent gliding with sluggish movement towards the sea. And the trees of the jungle over the water were heavy with a breathless menace. No bird sang. No breeze ruffled the leaves of the cassias. All around him it seemed as though something waited.

He walked across the garden to the road. He had Cooper's bungalow in full view from there. There was a light in his sitting room and across the road floated the sound of ragtime. Cooper was playing his gramophone. Mr. Warburton shuddered; he had never got over his instinctive dislike of that instrument. But for that he would have gone over and spoken to Cooper. He turned and went back to his own house. He read late into the night, and at last he slept. But he did not sleep very long, he had terrible dreams, and he seemed to be awakened by a cry. Of course that was a dream too, for no cry—from the bungalow for instance—could be heard in his room. He lay awake till dawn. Then he heard hurried steps and the sound of voices, his head boy burst suddenly into the room without his fez, and Mr. Warburton's heart stood still.

"Tuan, tuan."

Mr. Warburton jumped out of bed.

"I'll come at once."

He put on his slippers, and in his sarong and pajama jacket walked across his compound and into Cooper's. Cooper was lying in bed, with his mouth open, and a kris sticking in his heart. He had been killed in his sleep. Mr. Warburton started, but not because he had not expected to see just such a sight, he started because he felt in himself a sudden glow of exultation. A great burden had been lifted from his shoulders.

Cooper was quite cold. Mr. Warburton took the kris out of the wound, it had been thrust in with such force that he had to use an effort to get it out, and looked at it. He recognized it. It was a kris that a dealer had offered him some weeks before and which he knew Cooper had bought.

"Where is Abas?" he asked sternly.

"Abas is at the village of his mother's brother."

The sergeant of the native police was standing at the foot of the bed.

"Take two men and go to the village and arrest him."

Mr. Warburton did what was immediately necessary. With set face he gave orders. His words were short and peremptory. Then he went back to the fort. He shaved and had his bath, dressed and went into the dining room. By the side of his plate *The Times* in its wrapper lay waiting for him. He helped himself to some fruit. The head boy poured out his tea while the second handed him a dish of eggs. Mr. Warburton ate with a good appetite. The head boy waited.

"What is it?" asked Mr. Warburton.

"Tuan, Abas, my nephew, was in the house of his mother's brother all night. It can be proved. His uncle will swear that he did not leave the kampong."

Mr. Warburton turned upon him with a frown.

"Tuan Cooper was killed by Abas. You know it as well as I know it. Justice must be done."

"Tuan, you would not hang him?"

Mr. Warburton hesitated an instant, and though his voice remained set and stern a change came into his eyes. It was a flicker which the Malay was quick to notice and across his own eyes flashed an answering look of understanding.

"The provocation was very great. Abas will be sentenced to a term of imprisonment." There was a pause while Mr. Warburton helped himself to marmalade. "When he has served a part of his sentence in prison I will take him into this house as a boy. You can train him in his duties. I have no doubt that in the house of Tuan Cooper he got into bad habits."

"Shall Abas give himself up, tuan?"

"It would be wise of him."

The boy withdrew. Mr. Warburton took his *Times* and neatly slit the wrapper. He loved to unfold the heavy, rustling pages. The morning, so fresh and cool, was delicious and for a moment his eyes wandered out over his garden with a friendly glance. A great weight had been lifted from his mind. He turned to the columns in which were announced the births, deaths and marriages. That was what he always looked at first. A name he knew caught his attention. Lady Ormskirk had had a son at last. By George, how pleased the old dowager must be! He would write her a note of congratulation by the next mail.

Abas would make a very good houseboy.

That fool Cooper!

A PRIEST IN THE FAMILY
LEO KENNEDY / CANADA

Leo Kennedy

Mrs. Halloran had a nephew in the priesthood but that didn't keep her away from the bottle. Her husband, big Flatfoot Halloran, had been a patrolman on the Montreal waterfront, but gin and cahoots with the Black Hook Gang had got him off the cops some years before. Flatfoot then worked as a bouncer in a joint in St. Henri, but gin and a depression laid that job by the heels, and Mrs. Halloran had gone tearfully back to charring.

She charred in an office building and in St. Timothy's Church in Irish Griffintown. Rubbing the warts on her long, lean chin, she frequently lamented that Irish St. Timothy's was plumped down within swearing distance of the tough Italian section. What with blowsy, fat Dago women, pushcarts loaded with red and green peppers, and part-time bad men, Mrs. Halloran found the neighborhood too colorful.

Mrs. Halloran had a concave chest, thin gray hair, and sharp, red elbows. How, with her drinking, this chaste matron managed to keep her place at the church was more than her snooping neighbors could tell. But the curly-haired, plump-cheeked cleric who functioned as bursar for the establishment dealt mildly with sins of the flesh. He was, as he liked to say with a chuckle, always getting parishioners out of jail or into the cops; and the charwoman's cautious tippling on weekdays and flagrant jags on Saturdays never loomed larger than peccadilloes in his tolerant mind. Besides, her nephew was a priest.

Mrs. Halloran's nephew worked for souls in the wilds of British Columbia. As she had never traveled farther than Ahuntsic the good woman was somewhat vague as to the conditions of his employment and habitat, but she never let people forget there was an ordained priest in the family. Gossiping with friends, she liked to bring the talk around to things religious. Then she'd say what a blessing it was to have a nephew who prayed daily for her sins, adding that, though her soul was as scarlet, her Joey's monthly novena to the Holy Virgin for his poor old aunt would bring her still to glory.

She always breathed strongly of gin when she talked about religion. The drink provoked her to thoughts of heavenly ecstasy; the tin crucifix on her scrawny chest heaved and bobbed with the fervor of her devotion. But liquor also brought out a violent distaste for foreign devils. For instance, when she passed her large Italian neighbor, Mrs. Castelano, on the tenement stairs, she would sneer disparagement of all Neapolitan womanhood. She would say in a thin voice to the stairs: "May Jesus, Mary and Holy Joseph put boils on her neck."

At St. Timothy's, Mrs. Halloran's companion in toil was a middle-aged widow with flat, red hair and a squint. Mrs. Scully was a good soul, though rheumatic, and one Thursday, just before Lent, her complaint confined her to bed. Nolan, the sexton, pulled a long face when he heard of it. Mrs. Scully's chapped fists were needed for washing pews that day, and no doubt, he decided, Mrs. Halloran would be tipsy.

Mrs. Castelano came into the refectory that morning with a tale of woe about her husband going to jail again and no money in the house. Father Hoffman called Nolan in.

"Here's a poor soul in distress," he said. "Bandy Castelano has been peddling booze again. They've fixed him with a stretch this time. And it's my wish, and the will of God Almighty, that Bandy's unhappy spouse should have bread on her table. So what can we give her in the way of work?"

Nolan looked critically at Mrs. Castelano's great thews and blowsy costume and said sure she could take Mrs. Scully's place that was ill of the gout.

"There, Mrs. Castelano," Father Hoffman said. "You can work for your children and the Sacred Heart of Jesus at one and the same time. Nolan, tell this woman what to do."

THAT AFTERNOON Mrs. Halloran entered the precincts of St. Timothy's armed with the requisites of her trade—a pail of hot water thinly sudded, a gray cloth for washing the pews, a pail of clear water for the last ablution. She was late for work, having lingered at home to haggle with Flatfoot and tipple strength for her labors. Depositing her pails at the head of the nave, she dropped her jaw to see her loathed Italian neighbor in Mrs. Scully's stead. Mrs. Castelano was already wiping the pew woodwork, and she nodded briefly.

Mrs. Halloran bristled. She stood over her pails with arms akimbo and loosed a tentative broadside:

"An' may I be askin' where Mrs. Scully is at today? An' for what are you workin' in her place?"

"Mrs. Scully, she's sick in her legs," said Mrs. Castelano, her large bosom rising a little. "She don't work. Me, I got the job to wash in the church till she's fine." Her glance took in the other's condition. "When she come back, too, maybe," she added.

"An' is it you who're makin' aspersions at me, Mrs. Castelano? To what end, may I ask? Would you be graftin' my job for your fat self? Would you be keepin' your bootlegger husband on *my* wages?"

Mrs. Castelano breathed deeply and gave her wet cloth a wrench. "Me, I talk to you after," she said, "not now in the holy God's house. I got to work. Better you work, too, yes."

Mrs. Halloran plunged her cloth into soapy water. With a vixenish back turned to the Italian woman, she wiped a pew vigorously. Muttering to herself at intervals, she washed and dried. Savagely, she poked into corners as though stabbing her enemy with a cloth-draped finger.

Miss Brown, the little dried spinster who cared for the altar flowers and linens, entered the church from the sacristy. She always wore somber woolen suits, and hats that excited neither pity nor admiration. She had a brittle, ethereal look and walked with a slight list to the right. One felt that a breath that could flutter a candle would douse her outright.

Miss Brown began to clear the altar. She paid no attention to the two charwomen in the dimly lit aisle; she was thinking timidly of Father Hoffman's curly head and broadish girth. The one comfort of her arid virginity was the occasional nearness of this honest and holy man.

Mrs. Halloran regarded Miss Brown's birdlike movements with disfavor. She resented that social balance which set herself at one end of the church with scrub pails, and this lopsided holier-than-thou at the altar with her paws on the monstrance. She continued to swab down pews.

Watching Miss Brown bobbing about up front, Mrs. Halloran began to think of the duty of women to God and how her sister had done credit to her race and family by presenting nephew Joey to holy orders. She lingered over her own barren lot, and she thought with distaste of Mrs. Castelano's seven. The big sow!

"Mrs. Castelano"—she struck her favorite motif—"did I ever speak of my nephew in orders, my own sister's child? As I always say, a priest in the family should slip me through Purgatory with just the bit of a singe."

"Sure," said Mrs. Castelano, plying her rag, "you told me plenty. For me, I don't like so much those Irish priests. Young one, old one, they are not much priest. Look here, St. Timothy's. What they got? They got no Irish priest. They got Father Hoffman . . . a name for a German fella. For me, I like Italian priest. Like the Pope."

Mrs. Halloran twisted her wash cloth violently. "You'll be sayin' next the Lord Jesus was a Dago! An' Saint Peter and Saint Paul. It was a dark day for the blessed fisher of men when he set up the holy wood in heathen Rome. No good came out of that country . . . for there's no good in it. An' it's the blight and curse of the Catholic Church that the Pope is a wop that can't talk English!"

An outraged madonna flashed black eyes at her antagonist. Ordinarily cowlike and placid, her anger was gathering like clouds before thunder. But Mrs. Halloran spluttered on: "For what are your fat priests good, but to snore at confession and sneeze in the font? It's the likes of them as breaks the heart of his Eminence the Bishop, an' keeps the Irish parishes prayin' for light to array their schemin' hearts!" Her voice screamed up among the organ pipes. "You Dagos, you! Gunmen and whores! Peddlers of bathtub gin!"

Shaking with rage, Mrs. Castelano dropped her wash cloth in the dirty water, retrieved it sopping, and slashed Mrs. Halloran across the mouth. She squealed and struck—again and again.

The Irish woman, spitting filthy water and abuse, fought free of the piston arm. Seizing her own pail of slops, she deluged Mrs. Castelano, who screeched at the shock and was still unrecovered when Mrs. Halloran's wash cloth slapped her stingingly across the eyes.

Half blinded, she whirled to where she dimly saw her antagonist, and struck out with cloth and fist. Mrs. Halloran evaded her blows and delivered what thumps and scratches she might. Their turmoil filled the church.

Miss Brown had been working quietly when pandemonium broke loose in God's tabernacle. She thrilled with horror at the sacrilege and made futile little gestures with her hands. The church was empty of faithful and she prayed that no one would come before the mad women could be quieted.

A bellow from Mrs. Halloran shocked her from the static pose. She swung wide the altar gate and ran screaming to part the women. "Father Hoffman! Mr. Nolan! They'll kill each other!"

"Love of Jesus!" A blow from Mrs. Castelano caught the spinster and bowled her into a pew.

The priest and sexton, busy in the sacristy, were startled to hear muffled cries.

"Father Hoffman! Father Hoffman! A scandal in the church, Father. Oh, hurry, for the love of God."

Again attempting to part the furies, little Miss Brown had her hat dragged off, her hair torn, and one eye damaged. She reeled out of the radius of whirling fists and collapsed in a pew, weeping hysterically.

The charwomen lashed and kicked at one another, howling abuse and panting for breath. Mrs. Halloran's right cheek was channeled with the marks of four clawed fingers; the dress of Mrs. Castelano was torn half off her shoulders, disclosing a shoulder bruised where it had been battered by the pail.

They separated for a moment, then with loud cries flew at each other again. At that moment the priest tore down the aisle with Nolan at his heels; the men dragged the combatants apart and hustled all the women into the sacristy, pausing only behind closed doors to draw a free breath.

"In the name of Judgment, what scandal is this?" The priest's eyes burned. "Would you be murdering each other, and you employed in the house of God? You, Mrs. Halloran, with gin on your breath, and you, Mrs. Castelano, with your dress half off."

The last named, a panting mountain of a woman ready to subside in tears, tried clumsily to fasten her dress.

"What can a Christian say to such business?" the priest continued in righteous wrath. "Such devil's work under Saint Timothy's nose! Mrs. Castelano, did I give you a job this day that you could be tearing and clawing this woman's face, and swabbing her blood with your floor cloth?"

The German cleric's excited accent implied a south-of-Ireland mother. "And Mary Mother, crowned in Heaven, what a battered mess you've made of Miss Brown! Miss Brown, what started this fiendish ruction, that yourself should be clawed like a tomcat? But wait . . . wait . . . this is no case for me . . . Nolan, be calling the cop off his beat!"

At this, the women made great outcry: Miss Brown bleating there was scandal enough; Mrs. Castelano wailing that her man was in the jail already, and what would her children do if she followed; Mrs. Halloran demanding what was religion coming to, when Catholic priests turned their parishioners over to the bulls? Father Hoffman motioned Nolan out nonetheless, and closed the door after the sexton. He asked Miss Brown to tell him calmly how the row began.

Nursing her bruises, Miss Brown said dazedly, "These *ladies* had some kind of argument that turned into a screaming battle. They're *both* wretches, Father, but the skinny one was yelling the *worst* curses.

I didn't see who struck the first blow, but before God, *this* woman is the shame of the parish!"

Father Hoffman sighed his weariness. "Go on," he said.

"Well," Miss Brown babbled, pulling herself together, "it's *true* the Italian lady bleared my eye, but that *other* one would prompt a saint to murder! Yes, her face *is* scratched, but she bashed the big lady with the pail on her . . . well, chest, and she a mother, judging from her figure!"

Mrs. Castelano cried out that she was a mother seven times over with God's help.

Father Hoffman said, "Hush, be still!" and told Miss Brown to go home and tend to her wounds. He swore her to silence, promised to give the women their deserts, and with a friendly pat on the cheek that made her dejected spirit flicker and rise like the phoenix, ushered her out. Then, with an expression of gravity, he confronted the culprits.

"Mrs. Castelano, I'm thinking that, in spite of your actions, you're more sinned against than sinning. God knows His house is no place for a free-for-all, but knowing you both as well as I do, I see fit to make no bother this time. But think of poor Bandy languishing, and your children's hungry mouths, before you go bashing people about the head. I'll be letting you off, and more than that, I'll be letting you keep your job, but not a word of this to a soul, on your honor as a Catholic. Now go tell Mr. Nolan I said you were to stay. And you'd better come and confess to me this night."

Mrs. Castelano went out whimpering, and the priest fixed Mrs. Halloran with a calculating eye. "If I didn't know you and your man so well, I'd be sending you off to the jail now! You're a blot on the roll of the parish, Mrs. Halloran. It's a lot of trouble you're making here, and a power of hellfire you're fixing for the hereafter. And with a priest in the family!"

The woman began to weep with sentimental religious fear.

"The Almighty Lord is forgiving of sin, but bitter to those who make it a habit. You're too fond of the gin."

"Yes, Father."

"A woman of your years should have her eyes set on eternal life.

The pleasures of this life pass like snow before the sun, and Judgment awaits us the other side of the grave. Think well of that when you'd be drinking. Drink, Mrs. Halloran, is one of the Church's greatest enemies, and the devil's own brew!"

He observed her reaction shrewdly. "Are you prepared to burn in hell, my poor woman? Not for the term of your life, but for all eternity, a length of time you can't possibly imagine?"

"No, Father! I swear to Jesus, no!"

"Swearing by the Holy Name will bring you no nearer to glory . . . but confession will. Mrs. Halloran, I'd like to hear your confession now!" He went to a closet and took his stole from a hook, then seated himself in an easy chair and motioned to Mrs. Halloran to kneel. The woman, terror tweaking her bowels, got down beside him and blessed herself.

"Bless me, Father, for I have sinned; I confess to Almighty God and to you, Father . . ."

Her confessor heard her out and pronounced a nominal penance. The man's natural kindliness made him regard her benevolently. "Ah, Mrs. Halloran, the Saviour loves a penitent! Your soul is now as white as the lilies of the field, but keep it so! For your soul's good and for the good of your job in the church, will you promise to quit the liquor? I'm thinking of Father Joseph O'Connaught, and how he'd feel about a drunken aunt. It's for his sake I'm letting you keep your place, though the saints know you've tried me sorely. . . ."

Mrs. Halloran thanked him with fervor. She tucked her hair up under her kerchief and went back into the church. Mrs. Castelano was working already; her broad back was stiff and forbidding. Mrs. Halloran got her pails, filled them, and then commenced working too. In her mind she began to rattle off the prayers of her penance.

Hail, Mary, full of grace, the Lord is with thee, blessed art thou among women an' blessed is the fruit . . .

He said it was because Joey is a priest. Isn't that fine now? He wouldn't fire me because of my nephew. . . .

. . . of thy womb, Jesus. Holy Mary, Mother of God . . .

I always said a priest in the family is God's own blessing. An' Joey makes a monthly novena to Mary for me. . . .

. . . pray for us sinners . . .

Prayer *is* a blessing. Joey's prayers will get me through Purgatory sure as blazes . . . but just the same . . . they've saved my bacon here below as well. . . .

. . . now an' at the hour of our death. Amen.

THE COP AND THE
ANTHEM
O. HENRY / UNITED STATES

O. Henry

ON HIS BENCH in Madison Square Soapy moved uneasily. When wild geese honk high of nights, and when women without sealskin coats grow kind to their husbands, and when Soapy moves uneasily on his bench in the park, you may know that winter is near at hand.

A dead leaf fell in Soapy's lap. That was Jack Frost's card. Jack is kind to the regular denizens of Madison Square, and gives fair warning of his annual call. At the corners of four streets he hands his pasteboard to the North Wind, footman of the mansion of All Outdoors, so that the inhabitants thereof may make ready.

Soapy's mind became cognizant of the fact that the time had come for him to resolve himself into a singular Committee of Ways and Means to provide against the coming rigor. And therefore he moved uneasily on his bench.

The hibernatorial ambitions of Soapy were not of the highest. In them were no considerations of Mediterranean cruises, of soporific Southern skies or drifting in the Vesuvian Bay. Three months on the Island was what his soul craved. Three months of assured board and bed and congenial company, safe from Boreas and bluecoats, seemed to Soapy the essence of things desirable.

For years the hospitable Blackwell's had been his winter quarters.

Just as his more fortunate fellow New Yorkers had bought their tickets to Palm Beach and the Riviera each winter, so Soapy had made his humble arrangements for his annual hegira to the Island. And now the time was come. On the previous night three Sabbath newspapers, distributed beneath his coat, about his ankles and over his lap, had failed to repulse the cold as he slept on his bench near the spurting fountain in the ancient square. So the Island loomed big and timely in Soapy's mind. He scorned the provisions made in the name of charity for the city's dependents. In Soapy's opinion the Law was more benign than Philanthropy. There was an endless round of institutions, municipal and eleemosynary, on which he might set out and receive lodging and food accordant with the simple life. But to one of Soapy's proud spirit the gifts of charity are encumbered. If not in coin you must pay in humiliation of spirit for every benefit received at the hands of philanthropy. As Caesar had his Brutus, every bed of charity must have its toll of a bath, every loaf of bread its compensation of a private and personal inquisition. Wherefore it is better to be a guest of the law, which, though conducted by rules, does not meddle unduly with a gentleman's private affairs.

Soapy, having decided to go to the Island, at once set about accomplishing his desire. There were many easy ways of doing this. The pleasantest was to dine luxuriously at some expensive restaurant; and then, after declaring insolvency, be handed over quietly and without uproar to a policeman. An accommodating magistrate would do the rest. Soapy left his bench and strolled out of the square and across the level sea of asphalt, where Broadway and Fifth Avenue flow together. Up Broadway he turned, and halted at a glittering café, where are gathered together nightly the choicest products of the grape, the silkworm and the protoplasm.

Soapy had confidence in himself from the lowest button of his vest upward. He was shaven, and his coat was decent and his neat black, ready tied four-in-hand had been presented to him by a lady missionary on Thanksgiving Day. If he could reach a table in the restaurant unsuspected success would be his. The portion of him that would show above the table would raise no doubt in the waiter's mind. A roasted mallard duck, thought Soapy, would be about the thing—with a bottle of Chablis, and then Camembert, a demitasse and a cigar. One dollar for the cigar would be enough. The total would not be so high as to call forth any supreme manifestation of revenge from the café management; and yet the meat would leave him filled and happy for the journey to his winter refuge.

But as Soapy set foot inside the restaurant door the headwaiter's eye fell upon his frayed trousers and decadent shoes. Strong and ready hands turned him about and conveyed him in silence and haste to the sidewalk and averted the ignoble fate of the menaced mallard.

Soapy turned off Broadway. It seemed that his route to the coveted Island was not to be an epicurean one. Some other way of entering limbo must be thought of.

At a corner of Sixth Avenue electric lights and cunningly displayed wares behind plate glass made a shopwindow conspicuous. Soapy took a cobblestone and dashed it through the glass. People came running around the corner, a policeman in the lead. Soapy stood still, with his hands in his pockets, and smiled at the sight of brass buttons.

"Where's the man that done that?" inquired the officer, excitedly.

"Don't you figure out that I might have had something to do with it?" said Soapy, not without sarcasm, but friendly, as one greets good fortune.

The policeman's mind refused to accept Soapy even as a clue. Men who smash windows do not remain to parley with the law's minions. They take to their heels. The policeman saw a man halfway down the block running to catch a car. With drawn club he joined in the pursuit. Soapy, with disgust in his heart, loafed along, twice unsuccessful.

On the opposite side of the street was a restaurant of no great pretensions. It catered to large appetites and modest purses. Its crockery and atmosphere were thick; its soup and napery thin. Into this place Soapy took his accusive shoes and telltale trousers without challenge. At a table he sat and consumed beefsteak, flapjacks, doughnuts and pie. And then to the waiter he betrayed the fact that the minutest coin and himself were strangers.

"Now, get busy and call a cop," said Soapy. "And don't keep a gentleman waiting."

"No cop for youse," said the waiter, with a voice like butter cakes and an eye like the cherry in a Manhattan cocktail. "Hey, Con!"

Neatly upon his left ear on the callous pavement two waiters pitched Soapy. He arose joint by joint, as a carpenter's rule opens, and beat the dust from his clothes. Arrest seemed but a rosy dream. The Island seemed very far away. A policeman who stood before a drugstore two doors away laughed and walked down the street.

Five blocks Soapy traveled before his courage permitted him to woo capture again. This time the opportunity presented what he fatuously termed to himself a "cinch." A young woman of a modest and pleasing guise was standing before a show window gazing with sprightly interest at its display of shaving mugs and inkstands, and two yards from the window a large policeman of severe demeanor leaned against a water plug.

It was Soapy's design to assume the role of the despicable and execrated "masher." The refined and elegant appearance of his victim and the contiguity of the conscientious cop encouraged him to believe that he would soon feel the pleasant official clutch upon his arm that would ensure his winter quarters on the right little, tight little isle.

Soapy straightened the lady missionary's ready-made tie, dragged his shrinking cuffs into the open, set his hat at a killing cant and sidled toward the young woman. He made eyes at her, was taken with sudden coughs and "hems," smiled, smirked and went brazenly through the impudent and contemptible litany of the "masher." With half an eye Soapy saw that the policeman was watching him fixedly. The young woman moved away a few steps, and again bestowed her absorbed attention upon the shaving mugs. Soapy followed, boldly stepping to her side, raised his hat and said:

"Ah there, Bedelia! Don't you want to come and play in my yard?"

The policeman was still looking. The persecuted young woman had but to beckon a finger and Soapy would be practically en route for his insular haven. Already he imagined he could feel the cozy warmth of the station house. The young woman faced him and, stretching out a hand, caught Soapy's coat sleeve.

"Sure, Mike," she said, joyfully, "if you'll blow me to a pail of suds. I'd have spoke to you sooner, but the cop was watching."

With the young woman playing the clinging ivy to his oak Soapy walked past the policeman overcome with gloom. He seemed doomed to liberty.

At the next corner he shook off his companion and ran. He halted in the district where by night are found the lightest streets, hearts, vows and librettos. Women in furs and men in greatcoats moved gaily in the wintry air. A sudden fear seized Soapy that some dreadful enchantment had rendered him immune to arrest. The thought brought a little of panic upon it, and when he came upon another policeman lounging grandly in front of a transplendent theater he caught at the immediate straw of "disorderly conduct."

On the sidewalk Soapy began to yell drunken gibberish at the top of his harsh voice. He danced, howled, raved, and otherwise disturbed the welkin. The policeman twirled his club, turned his back to Soapy and remarked to a citizen: "'Tis one of them Yale lads celebratin' the goose egg they give to the Hartford College. Noisy; but no harm. We've instructions to lave them be."

Disconsolate, Soapy ceased his unavailing racket. Would never a policeman lay hands on him? In his fancy the Island seemed an unattainable Arcadia. He buttoned his thin coat against the chilling wind.

In a cigar store he saw a well-dressed man lighting a cigar at a swinging light. His silk umbrella he had set by the door on entering. Soapy stepped inside, secured the umbrella and sauntered off with it slowly. The man at the cigar light followed hastily.

"My umbrella," he said, sternly.

"Oh, is it?" sneered Soapy, adding insult to petit larceny. "Well, why don't you call a policeman? I took it. Your umbrella! Why don't you call a cop? There stands one on the corner."

The umbrella owner slowed his steps. Soapy did likewise, with a presentiment that luck would again run against him. The policeman looked at the two curiously.

"Of course," said the umbrella man—"that is—well, you know how these mistakes occur—I—if it's your umbrella I hope you'll excuse me—I picked it up this morning in a restaurant—If you recognize it as yours, why—I hope you'll——"

"Of course it's mine," said Soapy, viciously.

The ex-umbrella man retreated. The policeman hurried to assist a tall blonde in an opera cloak across the street in front of a streetcar that was approaching two blocks away.

Soapy walked eastward through a street damaged by improvements. He hurled the umbrella wrathfully into an excavation. He muttered against the men who wear helmets and carry clubs. Because he wanted to fall into their clutches, they seemed to regard him as a king who could do no wrong.

At length Soapy reached one of the avenues to the east where the glitter and turmoil was but faint. He set his face down this toward Madison Square, for the homing instinct survives even when the home is a park bench.

But on an unusually quiet corner Soapy came to a standstill. Here was an old church, quaint and rambling and gabled. Through one violet-stained window a soft light glowed, where, no doubt, the organist loitered over the keys, making sure of his mastery of the coming Sabbath anthem. For there drifted out to Soapy's ears sweet music that caught and held him transfixed against the convolutions of the iron fence.

The moon was above, lustrous and serene; vehicles and pedestrians were few; sparrows twittered sleepily in the eaves—for a little while the scene might have been a country churchyard. And the anthem that the organist played cemented Soapy to the iron fence, for he had known it well in the days when his life contained such things as mothers and roses and ambitions and friends and immaculate thoughts and collars.

The conjunction of Soapy's receptive state of mind and the influences about the old church wrought a sudden and wonderful change in his soul. He viewed with swift horror the pit into which he had tumbled, the degraded days, unworthy desires, dead hopes, wrecked faculties and base motives that made up his existence.

And also in a moment his heart responded thrillingly to this novel mood. An instantaneous and strong impulse moved him to battle with his desperate fate. He would pull himself out of the mire; he would make a man of himself again; he would conquer the evil that had taken possession of him. There was time; he was comparatively young yet: he would resurrect his old eager ambitions and pursue them without faltering. Those solemn but sweet organ notes had set up a revolution in him. Tomorrow he would go into the roaring downtown district and find work. A fur importer had once offered him a place as driver. He would find him tomorrow and ask for the position. He would be somebody in the world. He would——

Soapy felt a hand laid on his arm. He looked quickly around into the broad face of a policeman.

"What are you doin' here?" asked the officer.

"Nothin'," said Soapy.

"Then come along," said the policeman.

"Three months on the Island," said the Magistrate in the Police Court the next morning.

MARRIAGE À LA MODE
KATHERINE MANSFIELD / GREAT BRITAIN

Katherine Mansfield

ON HIS WAY to the station William remembered with a fresh pang of disappointment that he was taking nothing down to the kiddies. Poor little chaps! It was hard lines on them. Their first words always were as they ran to greet him, "What have you got for me, daddy?" and he had nothing. He would have to buy them some sweets at the station. But that was what he had done for the past four Saturdays; their faces had fallen last time when they saw the same old boxes produced again.

And Paddy had said, "I had red ribbing on mine *bee*-fore!"

And Johnny had said, "It's always pink on mine. I hate pink."

But what was William to do? The affair wasn't so easily settled.

In the old days, of course, he would have taken a taxi off to a decent toyshop and chosen them something in five minutes. But nowadays they had Russian toys, French toys, Serbian toys—toys from God knows where. It was over a year since Isabel had scrapped the old donkeys and engines and so on because they were so "dreadfully sentimental" and "so appallingly bad for the babies' sense of form."

"It's so important," the new Isabel had explained, "that they should like the right things from the very beginning. It saves so much time later on. Really, if the poor pets have to spend their infant years staring at these horrors, one can imagine them growing up and asking to be taken to the Royal Academy."

And she spoke as though a visit to the Royal Academy was certain immediate death to any one. . . .

"Well, I don't know," said William slowly. "When I was their age I used to go to bed hugging an old towel with a knot in it."

The new Isabel looked at him, her eyes narrowed, her lips apart.

"*Dear* William! I'm sure you did!" She laughed in the new way.

Sweets it would have to be, however, thought William gloomily, fishing in his pocket for change for the taxi-man. And he saw the kiddies handing the boxes round—they were awfully generous little chaps—while Isabel's precious friends didn't hesitate to help themselves. . . .

What about fruit? William hovered before a stall just inside the station. What about a melon each? Would they have to share that, too? Or a pineapple for Pad, and a melon for Johnny? Isabel's friends could hardly go sneaking up to the nursery at the children's meal-times. All the same, as he bought the melon William had a horrible vision of one of Isabel's young poets lapping up a slice, for some reason, behind the nursery door.

With his two very awkward parcels he strode off to his train. The platform was crowded, the train was in. Doors banged open and shut. There came such a loud hissing from the engine that people looked dazed as they scurried to and fro. William made straight for a first-class smoker, stowed away his suit-case and parcels, and taking a huge wad of papers out of his inner pocket, he flung down in the corner and began to read.

"Our client moreover is positive. . . . We are inclined to reconsider . . . in the event of—" Ah, that was better. William pressed back his flattened hair and stretched his legs across the carriage floor. The familiar dull gnawing in his breast quietened down. "With regard to our decision—" He took out a blue pencil and scored a paragraph slowly.

Two men came in, stepped across him, and made for the farther corner. A young fellow swung his golf clubs into the rack and sat down opposite. The train gave a gentle lurch, they were off. William glanced up and saw the hot, bright station slipping away. A red-faced girl raced along by the carriages, there was something strained and almost desperate in the way she waved and called. "Hysterical!" thought William dully. Then a greasy, black-faced workman at the end of the platform grinned at the passing train. And William thought, "A filthy life!" and went back to his papers.

When he looked up again there were fields, and beasts standing for shelter under the dark trees. A wide river, with naked children splashing in the shallows, glided into sight and was gone again. The sky shone pale, and one bird drifted high like a dark fleck in a jewel.

"We have examined our client's correspondence files. . . ." The last sentence he had read echoed in his mind. "We have examined . . ." William hung on to that sentence, but it was no good; it snapped in the middle, and the fields, the sky, the sailing bird, the water, all said, "Isabel." The same thing happened every Saturday afternoon. When he was on his way to meet Isabel there began those countless imaginary meetings. She was at the station, standing just a little apart from everybody else; she was sitting in the open taxi outside; she was at the garden gate; walking across the parched grass; at the door, or just inside the hall.

And her clear, light voice said, "It's William," or "Hillo, William!" or "So William has come!" He touched her cool hand, her cool cheek.

The exquisite freshness of Isabel! When he had been a little boy, it was his delight to run into the garden after a shower of rain and shake the rose-bush over him. Isabel was that rose-bush, petal-soft, sparkling and cool. And he was still that little boy. But there was no running into the garden now, no laughing and shaking. The dull, persistent gnawing in his breast started again. He drew up his legs, tossed the papers aside, and shut his eyes.

"What is it, Isabel? What is it?" he said tenderly. They were in their bedroom in the new house. Isabel sat on a painted stool before the dressing-table that was strewn with little black and green boxes.

"What is what, William?" And she bent forward, and her fine light hair fell over her cheeks.

"Ah, you know!" He stood in the middle of the strange room and he felt a stranger. At that Isabel wheeled round quickly and faced him.

"Oh, William!" she cried imploringly, and she held up the hair-brush: "Please! Please don't be so dreadfully stuffy and—tragic. You're always saying or looking or hinting that I've changed. Just because I've got to know really congenial people, and go about more, and am frightfully keen on—on everything, you behave as though I'd—" Isabel tossed back her hair and laughed—"killed our love or something. It's so awfully absurd"—she bit her lip—"and it's so maddening, William. Even this new house and the servants you grudge me."

"Isabel!"

"Yes, yes, it's true in a way," said Isabel quickly. "You think they are another bad sign. Oh, I know you do. I feel it," she said softly, "every time you come up the stairs. But we couldn't have gone on living in that other poky little hole, William. Be practical, at least! Why, there wasn't enough room for the babies even."

No, it was true. Every morning when he came back from chambers it was to find the babies with Isabel in the back drawing-room. They were having rides on the leopard skin thrown over the sofa back, or they were playing shops with Isabel's desk for a counter, or Pad was sitting on the hearthrug rowing away for dear life with a little brass fire shovel, while Johnny shot at pirates with the tongs. Every evening they each had a pick-a-back up the narrow stairs to their fat old Nanny.

Yes, he supposed it was a poky little house. A little white house with blue curtains and a window-box of petunias. William met their friends at the door with "Seen our petunias? Pretty terrific for London, don't you think?"

But the imbecile thing, the absolutely extraordinary thing was that he hadn't the slightest idea that Isabel wasn't as happy as he. God, what blindness! He hadn't the remotest notion in those days that she really hated that inconvenient little house, that she thought the fat Nanny was ruining the babies, that she was desperately lonely, pining for new people and new music and pictures and so on. If they hadn't gone to that studio party at Moira Morrison's—if Moira Morrison hadn't said as they were leaving, "I'm going to rescue your wife, selfish man. She's like an exquisite little Titania"—if Isabel hadn't gone with Moira to Paris—if—if . . .

The train stopped at another station. Bettingford. Good heavens! They'd be there in ten minutes. William stuffed the papers back into his pockets; the young man opposite had long since disappeared. Now the other two got out. The late afternoon sun shone on women in cotton frocks and little sunburnt, barefoot children. It blazed on a silky yellow flower with coarse leaves which sprawled over a bank of rock. The air ruffling through the window smelled of the sea. Had Isabel the same crowd with her this week-end, wondered William?

And he remembered the holidays they used to have, the four of them, with a little farm girl, Rose, to look after the babies. Isabel wore a jersey and her hair in a plait; she looked about fourteen. Lord! how his nose used to peel! And the amount they ate, and the amount they slept in that immense feather bed with their feet locked together. . . . William couldn't help a grim smile as he thought of Isabel's horror if she knew the full extent of his sentimentality.

"HILLO, William!" She was at the station after all, standing just as he had imagined, apart from the others, and—William's heart leapt—she was alone.

"Hallo, Isabel!" William stared. He thought she looked so beautiful that he had to say something, "You look very cool."

"Do I?" said Isabel. "I don't feel very cool. Come along, your horrid old train is late. The taxi's outside." She put her hand lightly on his arm as they passed the ticket collector. "We've all come to meet you," she said. "But we've left Bobby Kane at the sweet shop, to be called for."

"Oh!" said William. It was all he could say for the moment.

There in the glare waited the taxi, with Bill Hunt and Dennis Green sprawling on one side, their hats tilted over their faces, while on the other, Moira Morrison, in a bonnet like a huge strawberry, jumped up and down.

"No ice! No ice! No ice!" she shouted gaily.

And Dennis chimed in from under his hat. "*Only* to be had from the fishmonger's."

And Bill Hunt, emerging, added, "With *whole* fish in it."

"Oh, what a bore!" wailed Isabel. And she explained to William how they had been chasing round the town for ice while she waited for him. "Simply everything is running down the steep cliffs into the sea, beginning with the butter."

"We shall have to anoint ourselves with the butter," said Dennis. "May thy head, William, lack not ointment."

"Look here," said William, "how are we going to sit? I'd better get up by the driver."

"No, Bobby Kane's by the driver," said Isabel. "You're to sit between Moira and me." The taxi started. "What have you got in those mysterious parcels?"

"De-cap-it-ated heads!" said Bill Hunt, shuddering beneath his hat.

"Oh, fruit!" Isabel sounded very pleased. "Wise William! A melon and a pineapple. How too nice!"

"No, wait a bit," said William, smiling. But he really was anxious. "I brought them down for the kiddies."

"Oh, my dear!" Isabel laughed, and slipped her hand through his arm. "They'd be rolling in agonies if they were to eat them. No"—she patted his hand—"you must bring them something next time. I refuse to part with my pineapple."

"Cruel Isabel! Do let me smell it!" said Moira. She flung her arms across William appealingly. "Oh!" The strawberry bonnet fell forward: she sounded quite faint.

"A Lady in Love with a Pineapple," said Dennis, as the taxi drew up before a little shop with a striped blind. Out came Bobby Kane, his arms full of little packets.

"I do hope they'll be good. I've chosen them because of the colours. There are some round things which really look too divine. And just look at this nougat," he cried ecstatically, "just look at it! It's a perfect little ballet."

But at that moment the shopman appeared. "Oh, I forgot. They're none of them paid for," said Bobby, looking frightened. Isabel gave the shopman a note, and Bobby was radiant again. "Hallo, William! I'm sitting by the driver." And bareheaded, all in white, with his sleeves rolled up to the shoulders, he leapt into his place. "Avanti!" he cried. . . .

After tea the others went off to bathe, while William stayed and made his peace with the kiddies. But Johnny and Paddy were asleep, the rose-red glow had paled, bats were flying, and still the bathers had not returned. As William wandered downstairs, the maid crossed the hall carrying a lamp. He followed her into the sitting-room. It was a long room, coloured yellow. On the wall opposite William some one had painted a young man, over life-size, with very wobbly legs, offering a wide-eyed daisy to a young woman who had one very short arm and one very long, thin one. Over the chairs and sofa there hung strips of black material, covered with big splashes like broken eggs, and everywhere one looked there seemed to be an ash-tray full of cigarette ends. William sat down in one of the arm-chairs. Nowadays, when one felt with one hand down the sides, it wasn't to come upon a sheep with three legs or a cow that had lost one horn, or a very fat dove out of the Noah's Ark. One fished up yet another little paper-covered book of smudged-looking poems. . . . He thought of the wad of papers in his pocket, but he was too hungry and tired to read. The door was open; sounds came from the kitchen. The servants were talking as if they were alone in the house. Suddenly there came a loud screech of laughter and an equally loud "Sh!" They had remembered him. William got up and went through the French windows into the garden, and as he stood there in the shadow he heard the bathers coming up the sandy road; their voices rang through the quiet.

"I think it's up to Moira to use her little arts and wiles."

A tragic moan from Moira.

"We ought to have a gramophone for the week-ends that played 'The Maid of the Mountains.'"

"Oh no! Oh no!" cried Isabel's voice. "That's not fair to William. Be nice to him, my children! He's only staying until tomorrow evening."

"Leave him to me," cried Bobby Kane. "I'm awfully good at looking after people."

The gate swung open and shut. William moved on the terrace; they had seen him. "Hallo, William!" And Bobby Kane, flapping his towel, began to leap and pirouette on the parched lawn. "Pity you didn't come, William. The water was divine. And we all went to a little pub afterwards and had sloe gin."

The others had reached the house. "I say, Isabel," called Bobby, "would you like me to wear my Nijinsky dress to-night?"

"No," said Isabel, "nobody's going to dress. We're all starving. William's starving, too. Come along, *mes amis,* let's begin with sardines."

"I've found the sardines," said Moira, and she ran into the hall, holding a box high in the air.

"A Lady with a Box of Sardines," said Dennis gravely.

"Well, William, and how's London?" asked Bill Hunt, drawing the cork out of a bottle of whisky.

"Oh, London's not much changed," answered William.

"Good old London," said Bobby, very hearty, spearing a sardine.

But a moment later William was forgotten. Moira Morrison began wondering what colour one's legs really were under water.

"Mine are the palest, palest mushroom colour."

Bill and Dennis ate enormously. And Isabel filled glasses, and changed plates, and found matches, smiling blissfully. At one moment she said, "I do wish, Bill, you'd paint it."

"Paint what?" said Bill loudly, stuffing his mouth with bread.

"Us," said Isabel, "round the table. It would be so fascinating in twenty years' time."

Bill screwed up his eyes and chewed. "Light's wrong," he said rudely, "far too much yellow"; and went on eating. And that seemed to charm Isabel, too.

But after supper they were all so tired they could do nothing but yawn until it was late enough to go to bed. . . .

It was not until William was waiting for his taxi the next afternoon that he found himself alone with Isabel. When he brought his suit-case down into the hall, Isabel left the others and went over to him. She stooped down and picked up the suit-case. "What a weight!" she said, and she gave a little awkward laugh. "Let me carry it! To the gate."

"No, why should you?" said William. "Of course not. Give it to me."

"Oh, please do let me," said Isabel. "I want to, really." They walked together silently. William felt there was nothing to say now.

"There," said Isabel triumphantly, setting the suit-case down, and she looked anxiously along the sandy road. "I hardly seem to have seen you this time," she said breathlessly. "It's so short, isn't it? I feel you've only just come. Next time—" The taxi came into sight. "I hope they look after you properly in London. I'm so sorry the babies have been out all day, but Miss Neil had arranged it. They'll hate missing you. Poor William, going back to London." The taxi turned. "Good-bye!" She gave him a little hurried kiss; she was gone.

Fields, trees, hedges streamed by. They shook through the empty, blind-looking little town, ground up the steep pull to the station.

The train was in. William made straight for a first-class smoker, flung back into the corner, but this time he let the papers alone. He folded his arms against the dull, persistent gnawing, and began in his mind to write a letter to Isabel.

—

THE POST was late as usual. They sat outside the house in long chairs under coloured parasols. Only Bobby Kane lay on the turf at Isabel's feet. It was dull, stifling; the day drooped like a flag.

"Do you think there will be Mondays in Heaven?" asked Bobby childishly.

And Dennis murmured, "Heaven will be one long Monday."

But Isabel couldn't help wondering what had happened to the salmon they had for supper last night. She had meant to have fish mayonnaise for lunch and now . . .

Moira was asleep. Sleeping was her latest discovery. "It's *so* wonderful. One simply shuts one's eyes, that's all. It's *so* delicious."

When the old ruddy postman came beating along the sandy road on his tricycle one felt the handlebars ought to have been oars.

Bill Hunt put down his book. "Letters," he said complacently, and they all waited. But, heartless postman—O malignant world! There was only one, a fat one for Isabel. Not even a paper.

"And mine's only from William," said Isabel mournfully.

"From William—already?"

"He's sending you back your marriage lines as a gentle reminder."

"Does everybody have marriage lines? I thought they were only for servants."

"Pages and pages! Look at her! A Lady reading a Letter," said Dennis.

My darling, precious Isabel. Pages and pages there were. As Isabel read on her feeling of astonishment changed to a stifled feeling. What on earth had induced William. . . ? How extraordinary it was. . . . What could have made him. . . ? She felt confused, more and more excited, even frightened. It was just like William. Was it? It was absurd, of course, it must be absurd, ridiculous. "Ha, ha, ha! Oh dear!" What was she to do? Isabel flung back in her chair and laughed till she couldn't stop laughing.

"Do, do tell us," said the others. "You must tell us."

"I'm longing to," gurgled Isabel. She sat up, gathered the letter, and waved it at them. "Gather round," she said. "Listen, it's too marvellous. A love-letter!"

"A love-letter! But how divine!" *Darling, precious Isabel.* But she had hardly begun before their laughter interrupted her.

"Go on, Isabel, it's perfect."

"It's the most marvellous find."

"Oh, do go on, Isabel!"

God forbid, my darling, that I should be a drag on your happiness.

"Oh! oh! oh!"

"Sh! sh! sh!"

And Isabel went on. When she reached the end they were hysterical: Bobby rolled on the turf and almost sobbed.

"You must let me have it just as it is, entire, for my new book," said Dennis firmly. "I shall give it a whole chapter."

"Oh, Isabel," moaned Moira, "that wonderful bit about holding you in his arms!"

"I always thought those letters in divorce cases were made up. But they pale before this."

"Let me hold it. Let me read it, mine own self," said Bobby Kane.

But, to their surprise, Isabel crushed the letter in her hand. She was laughing no longer. She glanced quickly at them all; she looked exhausted. "No, not just now. Not just now," she stammered.

And before they could recover she had run into the house, through the hall, up the stairs into her bedroom. Down she sat on the side of the bed. "How vile, odious, abominable, vulgar," muttered Isabel. She pressed her eyes with her knuckles and rocked to and fro. And again she saw them, but not four, more like forty, laughing, sneering, jeering, stretching out their hands while she read them William's letter. Oh, what a loathsome thing to have done. How could she have done it! *God forbid, my darling, that I should be a drag on your happiness.* William! Isabel pressed her face into the pillow. But she felt that even the grave bedroom knew her for what she was, shallow, tinkling, vain. . . .

Presently from the garden below there came voices.

"Isabel, we're all going for a bathe. Do come!"

"Come, thou wife of William!"

"Call her once before you go, call once yet!"

Isabel sat up. Now was the moment, now she must decide. Would she go with them, or stay here and write to William. Which, which should it be? "I must make up my mind." Oh, but how could there be any question? Of course she would stay here and write.

"Titania!" piped Moira.

"Isa-bel?"

No, it was too difficult. "I'll—I'll go with them, and write to William later. Some other time. Later. Not now. But I shall *certainly* write," thought Isabel hurriedly.

And, laughing in the new way, she ran down the stairs.

THE NIGHTINGALE

MAXIM GORKY / RUSSIA

[signature]

Translated by George Reavey

THE PADDLE STEAMER was proceeding on its way between Kazan and Kozlovka.

It was quiet and fresh on the Volga. Evening was falling. A lilac-colored mist was beginning to envelop the hilly bank of the river; the opposite bank of meadowland had been flooded and pushed far back to the horizon. In places, green islets of submerged trees rose above the water. The noise of the paddles sounded dully in the damp, thick air heavy with the fragrance of fresh foliage. A broad band of foaming water stretched behind the steamer, and waves were sent rolling towards both banks. The sunset was burning down ahead of the steamer, and night was catching up in the rear. Here and there in the darkening sky stars kindled faintly.

A group of first-class passengers on the promenade deck was muted to a minor key under the influence of the melancholy evening, which was nascent on the river. There were four passengers seated there: an old man, tall and stooping, wearing a soft, wide-brimmed hat, the brim of which overshadowed the whole of his face, including the beard; beside him sat a young lady, wrapped closely in a gray shawl, staring dreamily out of her blue eyes at the hilly, wooded bank. Not far from them, on the same bench, sat another pair—a dry-looking gentleman in a gray overcoat and a buxom, shapely lady with regular features and large dark eyes. The gentleman next to her, who was nervously twisting his carefully trimmed French beard, leaned forward slightly and seemed to twitch. The lady, on the other hand, had settled against the back of the bench and sat there as immobile as a statue. The old man, gripping his cane with both hands and resting his chin on them, hunched himself forward and stared fixedly at the deck.

They were all silent. The steamer shuddered as it moved forward rapidly. Somewhere below could be heard the intrusive clatter of dishes, the trampling of feet and peals of laughter; and from the stern floated a subdued, almost sighing song, which was lost every now and again in all the noises that had blended into one smooth, monotonous wave of abrupt and incomplete sounds.

"A bit fresh, isn't it? . . . Shouldn't we go down to our cabins, eh?" the old man suggested, raising his head.

In the meantime, floating from somewhere a good way off, came a strange, husky whistling that resembled a yearning, long-restrained sigh from some small but powerful, and very passionate breast.

The passengers raised their heads.

"A nightingale!" the old man exclaimed with a laugh.

"A little early, isn't it!"

"Let's stay and listen, Papa . . ." the young lady suggested.

"As you wish. You may stay here, and they have no objection either," he answered, rising. "But I'll be off. After all, nightingales are not my . . ." But, leaving his sentence unfinished, the old man sat down again.

The nightingale's ringing, joyful, nerve-stirring trill rang and lilted through the air. The notes rushed so fast, so impetuously one after the other, that it seemed the songster was afraid he would have no time to say everything he wanted to say in his song. Nervously quivering roulades were suddenly interrupted by husky, sighing sounds, somehow very descriptive of a deeply yearning, impassioned heart. Once more the feverish *pizzicato* spattered through the air, vanishing abruptly and giving place to a minor melody, interrupted in its turn by a sort of crackling sound as if the singer were smacking his lips at his own song.

Everything on the steamer grew hushed. Every noise, except for the monotonous thud of the paddle wheels, had vanished somewhere.

The song poured out and ruled both the river and the passengers, who listened to it in silence. The young lady smiled dreamily; the married lady's face lost something of its seriousness and strictness. The old man sighed and said:

"There we have it, the playful and fantastic wisdom of nature! A small, useless bird is endowed with such a wealth of tone . . . but the cow, though a useful animal, is capable only of uttering a single, unpleasant mooing tone. Both in our life and in nature, men find the crude and ugly useful, whereas, what is beautiful and enjoyable . . . touching to the soul . . . man finds useless."

"Don't talk, Papa . . . I can't hear!" the daughter exclaimed tartly.

The father smiled skeptically and growled again: "But you must agree that, if cows sang like nightingales, it wouldn't be at all bad, eh?"

"Do stop it, Papa!" the daughter implored.

"All right . . . all right . . . I'll keep quiet! But he's stopped too . . . that rhapsodist of love. . . . Have you had your fill? Well, shall we go down to the cabins?"

"Let's sit here a little longer. . . ." the married lady said slowly in a hushed voice.

The nightingale was still singing. But now his song had grown faint and dying. . . . The sunset had burned out. The waters of the Volga had grown dark and solid-looking. The moon was climbing; and the hilly bank cast dark shadows upon the calm surface. There was the gleam of a bonfire in the hollow of a hill, and the crimson band of the reflected fire sparkled and quivered on the river. It was wonderfully quiet. . . .

The nightingale's song broke off. . . .

A SAILOR APPEARED on the promenade deck.

For a while he shuffled about on one spot; then he removed his leather cap, looked at the passengers and resolutely approached them.

"You wouldn't like to hear the nightingale, would you?" He inquired rather awkwardly for some reason.

"What's that?" the old man asked squeamishly with a wry expression.

"The nightingale, if you wish? . . . There's a boy here . . . who whistles like a regular nightingale . . . God's truth!" the sailor explained, backing away from the old man's piercing scrutiny.

"Bring him along. . . ." the married lady said curtly. The man beside her began to shift nervously on the bench.

"Is it necessary, Nina?" he demanded, frowning sourly.

The young lady stared at the sailor with wide-open eyes.

"Would you want me to bring him?" the sailor asked again.

"Yes, of course. I told you so," the lady snapped angrily.

"He'll come by himself!" the sailor clarified and then disappeared.

"The devil knows what this is!" the old man explained, raising his brows. "Some sort of a boy who whistles like a regular nightingale. . . . We heard him already, believing he was a real nightingale and, listening to him, one of us began philosophizing. . . . What a wild fowl!" And he shook his head reproachfully, feeling embarrassed by this wild fowl.

A boy of about fourteen appeared on deck.

He was wearing a jacket, narrow trousers and, on his head, a new, visored cap tipped slightly to one side. His freckled face, his rolling gait, his thick, short fingers and his sun-bleached yellow hair, proclaimed him to be a villager. He approached the group, removed his visored cap, bowed, shook his head and, leaving it uncovered, silently began to fidget with the visor as if trying to straighten it. . . . The passengers also scrutinized him in silence. There was a puzzled look in the young lady's eyes. The boy's gray eyes swept boldly over their faces. "Would you have me whistle?" he asked.

"Was it you whistling just now like a nightingale?" the old man inquired.

"Yes, me. The barman had asked me. . . ."

"Is that all you do . . . whistle?"

"Exactly so. . . . I board the steamer and travel as far as Kazan. . . . Then I do the return trip from Kazan. . . ."

"Well, then let's hear you whistle, please!"

"I don't want to hear it," the young lady said in a low voice.

The boy looked at her, puzzled.

"Who taught you this?" the married lady asked the boy in a husky contralto.

"Why, I myself . . . I was a herdsboy . . . I come from hereabouts," he said, waving his hand vaguely towards the river bank, "from a village . . . I'd be minding the herd and listening all day to all sorts of birds. . . . So I began whistling to the birds myself . . . well, and so I learned little by little. . . . I can whistle like a siskin . . . the robin, too. . . . But that's not as rousing as the nightingale. And I've become such a good hand at the nightingale that I even take in the hunters. I'll sit in the bushes and let rip! Just like a real bird, honest!" As he talked, the boy's face glowed with the proud awareness of his mastery and the vanity of an artist.

"When I became such a good hand at it," he went on, "there were village folk who said: 'Just go on, Misha, don't stop. Just go on whistling. . . . You might please the gentry who travel by steamer. Maybe you'll get somewhere.' So off I went. . . . Then I started riding on these here steamers. . . . It's not too bad, I get on. At times they give so much money, my eyes pop. Money's cheap to the gentry—"

He broke off, realizing that he had said too much, and then asked bashfully: "Would you have me whistle now?"

A silence of several seconds ensued before the married lady commanded curtly: "Whistle!"

The boy threw the cap at his feet, put his fingers to his mouth and arched his throat. . . . For some reason his face was smiling, but he took some time to begin. First, he pulled his fingers out of his mouth, wiped his lips, snorted and made all kinds of grimaces.

At last the yearning, sighing whistling resounded again. It rang out and died away. And then suddenly the full lilting trill of a nightingale's roulade rang out in the air. The young lady quivered and sighed sadly. . . . The married lady smiled glumly and contemptuously; her companion hunched himself and grimaced nervously; and the old man stared seriously and intently at the boy's face. This latter had turned very red and swollen from the effort; but his dilated eyes remained dull and inexpressive and did not illumine him in any way. The "nightingale" crackled, trilled and, throbbing, stopped for an instant and then renewed its singing, calling . . . and sighing nostalgically. The imitation was remarkably exact.

"Papa, tell him . . . to stop," the young lady said in a low voice. She suddenly rose and walked away, looking pale and with tears in her eyes.

"Enough!" the old man said with a wave of his hand.

The "nightingale" broke off his song, wiped his lips with his hand, picked up the visored cap and held it out towards the old man's hand. There was a rustling of paper. . . .

"My humble thanks!" the boy said, and quickly disappeared, descending somewhere downstairs. The lady followed him with her eyes and smiled ironically. Her companion growled something to himself and raised the collar of his overcoat. . . . The night deepened, growing thicker and darker. The water looked black now. The banks of the river were lost in the shadow. But the stars were already gleaming in the sky and, as before, the water churned monotonously beneath the paddle wheels of the steamer.

"An artist!" the old man exclaimed, changing his position. "Another victim of the public. . . . That's how it is—the public will swallow anything that gives it pleasure . . . the weight lifting of a circus strong man and a virtuoso playing the violin. And it feels flattered when it observes that a man is ready to do anything in order to merit its attention . . ." But apparently the others were not listening to him, for nobody answered.

"But if that sailor had not come," he began again after a pause, "we would have remained convinced that we had heard a bird famed by the poets rather than a scrubby little village lad, a pretender. H'm . . . yes! To learn the truth is not so great a pleasure . . . when the illusion is more beautiful."

"Let's go," the lady said, rising. They all got up and went to their cabins.

"Lena is probably weeping by now . . . she's such a nervous girl," the old man added. "But that's all right. . . . Gradually she must get used to the trifling, foolish pranks of life. . . . She'll find it easier to deal with larger and more serious issues. . . . Why are you trembling, Sonya? Is it the chill?"

"No, it's nothing. Don't worry," the lady replied softly. Her nervous companion glanced indifferently at her through his colorless and ironically screwed up eyes. Then they all disappeared behind the cabin door.

The moon, ascending, cast her reflections upon the dark waters; and, gleaming faintly, they quivered on the vacillating surface of the waves.

In the distance quivering points of light appeared.

A feeling of sadness hung over the drowsy river.

THE LAUNCH
MAX AUB / SPAIN

Translated by Elizabeth Mantel

He said he was born in Bermeo, but the truth was that he came from a little town across the mouth of the Mundaca River, a settlement which was known by no name, or by many names, which is the same thing.

The beaches and cliffs of this area were all that he knew of the world. For him, the Machichaco, Potorroari and Uguerriz marked Ultima Thule; for him, Sollube was Olympus; Bermeo, Paris; and the Atalaya mall, the Elysian Fields. The wide expanse of his world, his Sahara, was the Laida, and the end of his world to the east was the steep, flat-topped, reddish Ogoño. Beyond was Elanchove and the gentlemen of Lequeitio, in hell.

His mother was the daughter of an overseer in an arms factory in Guernica. His father was a miner from Matamoros; he did not live long. They called him El Chirto, perhaps because he was half-crazy. When he became ill he left the Franco-Belgian mines of Somorrostro, and went to work in a sawmill factory. There, among the wood-planing and dovetailing machines, Erramón Churrimendi grew up.

He was fond of the little steamboats, the tunny boats, the pretty little sardine-fishing smacks; the fishing tackle: the trotlines, the sieves, the fish traps, the nets. The world was the sea, and the only living beings were the hake, the eels, the sea bass, and the tunny. And he loved to catch moving fish in the water with a deep fisherman's net, to fish for anchovies and sardines with a light, or at dusk; and to catch the bonito and tuna with a spinning tackle.

But he no sooner put his feet in a boat than he became seasick. And there was nothing he could do about it. He tried all the official medicines, and all the recondite ones, and all advice, spoken and whispered.

He followed the advice of Don Pablo, of the drugstore; of Don Saturnio, of the City Council; of Cándida, Don Timoteo's maid; of the doctor from Zarauz, who was a native of Bermeo. To no avail. He had only to put one foot in a boat, and he became seasick.

He tried a hundred stratagems: he would get aboard on an empty stomach, or after a good breakfast, sober, or drunk, or without having slept; he even tried the magic cures of Sebastiana, the woman from the edge of town; he tried crosses, lemons, the right foot, the left foot, at 7:00 a.m. on the dot, at low tide and at high tide, on the right day of the week.

He went after Mass, after several "Our Fathers," and he tried pure willpower and even in his sleep he heard: "I'll never be seasick again, I'll never be seasick again. . . ." But nothing helped. As soon as he put his foot on a moving plank his insides turned round and round, he lost all sense of balance, and he was forced to huddle in the corner of the boat to keep out of the others' way, hoping to stay unnoticed.

He spent some terrible moments. But he was not among those who despair, and for many years he repeatedly dared the adventure. Because, naturally, the people were laughing at him—not much, but they were laughing at him. He took to wine. What else could he do? Chacolí wine is a remedy. Erramón never married, the idea never even occurred to him. Who would marry him? He was a good man. Everyone admitted that. He was not even guilty of anything. But he got seasick. The sea made sport of him, and without any right.

He slept in a cabin by the estuary. It belonged to him. There was a beautiful oak there—if I say *there was*, it's for a good reason. It *was* really a splendid tree, with a tall trunk and high branches. A tree the likes of which there are not many. It was his tree, and every day, every morning, every evening, on passing by, the man would touch it as if it were a horse's croup or the side of a beautiful woman. Sometimes he even spoke to it. It seemed to him that the bark was warm and that the tree was grateful to him. The roughness of the tree perfectly matched the rough skin on the man's hand. There was a perfect understanding between him and the tree.

Erramón was a methodical man. So long as there was variety in his work he did whatever he was asked, willingly and tidily. He was asked to do a hundred odd chores: to repair nets, to dig, to help in the sawmill, which had been his father's; to him it was all the same whether he raised a thatch or calked, or earned his few pesetas by helping to bring in the fish. He never said no to anything. Erramón also sang, and sang well. He was greatly respected in the tavern. One of his Basque songs went something like this:

> *All the Basques are alike.*
> *All save one.*
> *And what's the matter with that one?*
> *That's Erramón.*
> *And he's like all the rest.*

One night Erramón dreamed that he was not seasick. He was alone in a little boat, far out on the sea. He could see the coastline clearly in the distance. Only the red Ogoño shone like a fake sun which was sinking in the middle of the earth. Erramón was happier than he had ever been in his life. He lay down in the bottom of the boat and began to watch the clouds. He could feel the incessant rocking motion of the sea. The clouds were flying swiftly by, pushed by a wind which greeted him without stopping; and the circling sea gulls were shouting his welcome:

"Erramón, Erramón!"

And again:

"Erramón, Erramón!"

The clouds were like lace doves. Erramón closed his eyes. He was on the water and he was not seasick. The waves rocked him in their hammock back and forth, back and forth, up and down, in a sweet cradling motion. All his youth was about his neck, and yet, at that moment, Erramón had no memories, no other desire than to continue forever just as he was. He caressed the sides of his boat. Suddenly his hands were speaking to him. Erramón raised his head in surprise. He was not mistaken! His boat was made of the wood of his oak tree!

So shocking was the effect that he woke up.

From that moment on, Erramón's life began to change completely. It entered his head that if he made a boat out of his tree he would never again become seasick. In order to prevent himself from committing this crime, he drank more chacolí than usual; but he could not sleep. He turned over and over in his bed, hounded by the stars. He listened to his dream. He tried to convince himself of the absurdity of all this:

"If I've always been seasick, I'll continue being seasick."

He turned over on his left side.

He got up to look at his tree, and caressed it.

"Will I end by winning or losing?"

But deep inside he knew he should not do it, that it would be a crime. Was it his tree's fault that he got seasick? But Erramón could not resist the temptation for long. One morning he himself, aided by Ignacio, the one from the sawmill, cut down the tree. When the tree fell, Erramón felt very sad and alone as if the most beloved member of his family had died. It was hard for him now to recognize his cabin, it was so lonely. Only with his back to it, facing the estuary, did he feel easy.

Every afternoon he went to see how his tree was changing into a boat. This took place on the beach where his friend Santiago, the boatwright, was building it. The whole thing was made of the trunk; the keel, the floor timbers, the frame, the stem, the beams, even the seats and the oars, and a mast, just in case.

And so it was that one August morning when the sea did not seem like one, it was so calm, Erramón plowed outward on it with his new boat. It was a marvelous boat, it flew at the slightest urging of the man; he dipped the oars gently, throwing back his shoulders before he slightly contracted his arms, which made the boat fly. For the first time Erramón felt drunk, ecstatic. He drew away from the shore.

He dipped the right oar a few times to make a turn, then the other in order to zigzag through the water. Then he drew the oars in and began to caress the wood of his boat. Slowly, the boards were letting in a little water. Erramón raised his hands to his forehead to dampen it a little. The silence was absolute; not a cloud, not a breeze, not even a sea gull. The land had disappeared, submerged. Erramón put his hands on the gunwale to caress it. Again he removed his hands wet. He was a little surprised: splashes on the wood had long since dried in the sun. He glanced over the inside of the boat: from every part water was slowly seeping in. On the bottom there was already a small puddle. Erramón did not know what to do. Again he passed his hands over the sides of his boat. There was no question about it; the wood was gradually letting water in.

Erramón looked around; a slight uneasiness was beginning to gnaw his stomach. He had himself helped in calking the boat and was sure that the work had been well done. He bent down to inspect the seams: they were dry. It was the wood that was letting the water in! Without thinking, he raised his hand to his mouth. The water was sweet!

Desperately, he began to row. But despite his frantic efforts the boat did not move. It seemed to him that his boat was caught among the branches of a giant underwater tree, held as if in a hand. He rowed as hard as he could, but the boat did not budge. And now he could see with his own eyes how the wood of his tree was exuding clean, fresh water!

Erramón fell to his knees and began to bail with his hands, because he had no bucket.

But the hull continued to ooze more and more water. It was already a spring with a thousand holes. And the sea seemed to be sprouting branches.

Erramón crossed himself.

He was never seen again on the shores of Biscay. Some said that he had been seen around San Sebastián, others that he was seen in Bilbao. A sailor spoke of an enormous octopus which had been seen about that time. But no one could give any information about him with any certainty. The oak tree began to grow again. The people shrugged their shoulders. The rumor spread that he was in America. Then, nothing.

THE WREATH

LUIGI PIRANDELLO / ITALY

Translated by Lily Duplaix

Dr. CIMA paused before the entrance to the public gardens which rose on a hill on the outskirts of town. He lingered a moment, looking at the rustic gate, an iron bar suspended between columns. Two melancholy cypress trees loomed behind them, melancholy despite the rambler roses twining in and out of their dark branches. A steep path led from the gate to the top of the hill where a pergola stood out among the trees.

Enjoying the warmth of the early sun, he waited lazily for his inertia to pass so that he could stroll in that old deserted garden. In the cool shade of the northern slope of the hill the air was heavy with the mingled fragrance of mint, sage and wild plum; the birds twittered incessantly in the nearby trees, welcoming the return of spring. The doctor gratefully breathed in the scented air, then started slowly up the path. New green bursting from all the plants, white butterflies fluttering over the flower beds—all gave a misty, dreamlike turn to his unhappy thoughts. How beautiful it was, this peaceful garden where few if any ever came to stroll!

If it were only mine, he thought, and this yearning was echoed by a prolonged sigh.

How many, like himself, had come here to walk and to sigh, If it were only mine? It is fate that whatever belongs to everyone never belongs to anyone in particular. At every turn a sign was posted: DON'T WALK ON THE FLOWER BEDS. DON'T DAMAGE THE PLANTS. DON'T PICK THE FLOWERS. You could take a look in passing! Ownership means "I" not "we," and only one person could say "I" here: the gardener. In a sense, he was the true proprietor and for this he was paid, given a house to live in and allowed to pick the flowers which belonged to everybody and to no one, some of which he sold for his own profit.

The singing notes of one particular bird, soaring high above the others, suddenly reminded the doctor of a long-ago vacation he had spent on a dairy farm lost among trees in open country near the sea. He had been only a small boy, but how he loved hunting! Who could remember how many little birds he had shot and killed that summer!

The everyday cares and problems of his profession were set aside for the moment, but not the fact that he had turned forty his last birthday. For him, he thought, the better part of life was over and, unfortunately, he could not say he had ever really enjoyed being young. There were so many wonderful things in life! It could be so beautiful. A radiant morning like this made up for many sorrows, many disappointments.

An idea suddenly occurred to him and he paused: Should he run back to the house for his young wife? They had been married seven months now, and he would have liked to share this enchanting walk with her. But after a moment's indecision, he continued slowly along the path. No. This enchantment must be for him alone.

His wife might have felt it, had she come here to walk by herself and without his having suggested it. Together, the charm would be lost. Even now, as he thought about it, some of the radiance had faded. A bitter taste of sorrow, vaguely sensed before, rose in his throat.

He could not reproach his wife for anything, poor dear; certainly she was not to blame for the gray hair at his temples and streaking his beard. She was all goodness. But she was only twenty-two, eighteen years younger than he. He hoped the affectionate regard she had shown for him during their brief engagement would naturally turn to love once they were married and she realized how much he loved her—like a young man despite his gray head. She was the first; he had never loved another woman.

Idle dreams! Love, real love, he had never been able to awaken in his wife—and never would, perhaps. She smiled when he appeared and she showed in many thoughtful little ways that she liked him, but this was not love.

His pain might have been less poignant were it not aggravated by an incident in his wife's life which he was unable to treat with the same gentle indulgence he usually showed for most other things.

With all the fervor of her eighteen years, she had fallen in love with a young student who had died of typhus. He knew this because he had been the doctor called to the boy's bedside. And he also knew that she had almost lost her mind, locking herself in her room in the dark, refusing to see anyone and never leaving the house. She even wanted to become a nun. Everybody at the time talked of nothing else but the sad fate of those two young lovers parted by death. The boy had been popular for his easy wit and charming, polite manner, while she who wept unconsolably after him was considered one of the most beautiful girls in the town.

A year passed before her family was able to persuade her to attend a few gatherings. Everyone was moved by her demeanor, her sad expression and soft smile—especially the men. To be loved by her, to rouse her from her obsessive loss, to restore her to life, to youth, became the dream, the ambition of all of them.

But she clung to her mourning. Malicious rumors began to circulate that, for all her modesty and humility, she must take a certain pride in her grief, realizing the love and admiration it inspired. But this was idle talk, prompted by jealousy and resentment. That her feelings were genuine was proven when, within a few months, she refused four or five offers of marriage from the more eligible young men.

But two years after the tragedy, by which time no one dared present himself because of the certainty of being refused, Dr. Francesco Cima proposed and was immediately accepted.

After the first surprise, however, everyone tried to explain his victory: she had said yes because the doctor was no longer young, and no one would imagine that she had married him for love, true love; she had said yes because, as a rational man, he would not expect to be loved like a young man and would be satisfied if she accorded him affection, devoted respect and gratitude.

He soon found out how true this was, and it hurt. He had to check himself constantly to keep from blurting out some remark which might betray his suffering. It was torture to feel young and not to be able to express his passion for fear of losing her esteem.

He had been young for only one woman: his old mother, who had died three years before. She would have shared his joy in this beautiful morning, and he would have run to get her without giving it a second thought. That blessed old woman! He would have found her huddled in a corner, rosary in hand, praying for all the sick under his care. Dr. Cima smiled wistfully, shaking his head as he climbed the path up the hill. In praying for his patients, his saintly old mother had shown little confidence in him or his training. Jokingly he accused her of this once and she was quick to reply that she was not praying for his patients at all but was simply asking God to help him care for them!

"So you think that without God's help . . ." he began, but she did not let him finish.

"What are you saying? We need God's help always, my son!"

And so she prayed from morning until night. He almost wished he had had fewer patients, so as not to tire her so much. His smile returned. Remembering his mother, his thoughts resumed the airy unreality of a dream, and the enchantment of the day was restored.

Suddenly his train of thought was interrupted by the new gardener, weeding up above in a grassy plot.

"I'm here, *Signor Dottore*. Have you been looking for me long?"

"I? No, really . . ."

"It's ready—ready and waiting ever since eight o'clock," the gardener said, stepping forward, cap in hand, his forehead pearled with sweat. "If you want to see it, it's right here in the pagoda. We can go there now."

"See what?" asked the doctor, halting. "I don't know . . ."

"But, Signor Doctor—the wreath!"

"Wreath?"

The gardener looked at him, equally astonished.

"Excuse me, but isn't today the twelfth?"

"Yes. What of it?"

"You sent your maid day before yesterday to order a wreath for today. Remember?"

"I? For the twelfth? Ah, yes, yes," said the doctor, pretending to remember. "I . . . yes, I sent the maid, of course."

"Violets and roses, don't you remember?" the gardener said, smiling at the doctor's absentmindedness. "It's been ready since eight this morning. Come and see it."

Fortunately the gardener walked ahead, so he was unaware of the sudden change in Francesco Cima's face as he followed along mechanically, dazed and distressed.

A wreath? His wife must have secretly ordered a wreath. The twelfth, of course—the anniversary of that boy's death. Still such grieving, after three years? She wanted to send a wreath in secret, even now that she was married to him! She who was so timid, so modest, and yet so bold! So she still loved that boy! Would she carry his memory in her heart for life? Why had she ever married him? Why, if her heart belonged to that dead boy and always would? Why? Why? Why?

He raged inwardly as he walked along. He wanted to see the wreath, yes, see it with his own eyes before he was willing to believe his wife capable of such deception, such treachery.

When he saw it on an iron table propped against the wall, it seemed as though it were intended for him and he stood there a long, long time gazing at it.

The gardener, in his own way, mistook his silence for admiration.

"Beautiful, huh? All fresh roses and violets, you know, picked at dawn. A hundred lire, Doctor. Do you know how much work it is to put all those little violets together one by one? And the roses. They're scarce in winter and as soon as the season comes on everybody wants them. A hundred lire is very little. It's really worth at least another twenty."

The doctor tried to speak, but he had no voice left. His lips parted in a pitiful smile and finally he managed to get out, "I'll pay you for it. A hundred lire—too little. Roses and violets, yes. Here are a hundred and twenty."

"Thank you, Signor Doctor," said the gardener, quickly taking the money. "I think it's well worth it."

"Keep it here," the doctor said, putting his wallet back into his pocket. "If the maid comes, don't give it to her. I will return for it myself."

He went out of the pagoda and down the winding path. As soon as he was alone and unseen, he stopped and clenched his fists, his face twisting into a sobbing laugh. "And I'm the one who paid for it!"

What should he do now? Take his wife back to her father's house without, of course, saying anything to hurt her? That was what she deserved. Let her go off and cry for that dead boy at a distance without playing unfairly with the heart of an honest man whom it was her duty to respect, if nothing else. Neither love nor respect? She refused the younger men and accepted him because to her he seemed old, and she was sure he would not dream of claiming her love. With that grizzled beard, he would shut an eye, even both eyes, on her consuming sorrow. An old man couldn't object to anything. So she had planned to send a wreath on the sly. Now that she was married, at least she had not thought it fitting to go herself. Yet, however old her husband might be in her eyes, this was carrying things too far. She had sent the maid to order the wreath in proof of her undying love, and the maid would then have taken it to the boy's tomb.

How unjust the death of that boy had been! Had he lived, had he grown to be a man and become familiar with all the little deceits of life and had married his dear, loving girl, she would soon have discovered that it is one thing to make love from a window at eighteen and quite another to face stern, everyday realities when the first ardor cools and the tedium of daily living leads to quarrels. That's when a young husband grows bored and first considers being unfaithful to his wife. Ah, if only she had known such an experience with that young man, then, perhaps, this "old" one . . .

He clenched his hands so hard that the nails dug into his palms. Looking down at his white, trembling hands, he got hold of himself. The first shock had passed. He stood there staring; then, seeing a bench not far off, he went over stiffly and sat down.

After all, wasn't this "old" man proposing to act like any young blood—make a scene, create a situation? And all those who had so readily pieced together her reasons for accepting him would then exclaim, "For shame! What on earth for? A wreath of flowers? Why not? She always sent a wreath to the cemetery on the twelfth, but the new gardener didn't know that. This year too she remembered, naturally, because the doctor has not been able to make her forget. It was wrong of her, no doubt, but one cannot reason with the heart. And after all the boy is dead!"

That is about what it would amount to.

Then what should he do? Let it go? Pretend to know nothing about it? Go back to the gardener and tell him to give the wreath to the maid, the wreath Cima had intended to keep there to confront her with?

No. Not that. He would then have to get his money back from the man and take him into his confidence.

Well, what then? Go back to the house and demand useless explanations? Face his wife with her poor subterfuge? Punish her? How contemptible all that was! How distasteful!

It was serious, and it went deep—serious because of the ridicule it would cause were his wife's true feelings for him to become known. He must control himself and realize that it did no good to feel young as long as everyone considered you mature, almost on the shelf. A very young man might have made a scene, but at his age he must win his wife's respect another way.

He got up, perfectly calm now, yet with a feeling of listlessness.

The birds continued to twitter gaily in the garden, but where was the enchantment of a moment ago?

Francesco Cima walked out of the garden and started home. When he came to his own front door his calm vanished. Suddenly breathless, he wondered how he had ever managed the steps on such shaky legs. The idea of seeing his wife again now . . . She must be feeling sadder than usual today, but she would probably know how to conceal her sorrow. He loved her—oh, how he loved her! And deep within himself he knew that she deserved to be loved because she was good, just as good as the perfection of her delicate features showed her to be, and the depth of her velvety black eyes, the pallor of her lovely face.

The maid opened the door. The sight of her disconcerted him, for the old woman was in on the secret, a sort of accomplice. She had served his wife's parents for many years and was now devoted to her, so it was likely she would not talk. And certainly she would not be able to assess, nor even to understand, what he was about to do. In any case, she was an outsider. He wanted this to be a secret between his wife and himself.

He went straight to her room and found her combing her hair before the mirror. Between her raised arms he caught sight of her face, reflecting a look of surprise to see him home at this hour.

"I came back," he said, "to invite you to come out with me."

"Now?" she asked, turning around without lowering her arms, smiling faintly, with that lovely mass of soft black hair piled loosely on her head.

Her pale smile upset him almost to the point of tears. He imagined it held a profound pity for him, for his love of her, as well as her own sorrow.

"Yes, now," he replied. "It is so beautiful out-of-doors. Hurry. We'll go to the little garden, then farther on, into the country. We'll take a carriage."

"Why?" she asked almost unconsciously. "Why today?"

At that question, he feared his expression would surely betray him. It was already a struggle to keep his voice calm.

"Wouldn't you like to go today?" he said. "It will do you good. Hurry! I want you to come with me." He went to the door and turned. "I'll wait for you in the office."

In a short time she was ready. For that matter, she always did as he wished except where her heart was concerned, and there he had no power. She had put up that timid opposition: *Why today?* Yet even today, despite the sadness she must be feeling, she had obeyed him and was ready to go for a ride in the country, wherever he wished.

They went out and walked awhile through the small town; then he hired a carriage and ordered the driver to stop at the little garden. He went up alone, asking his wife gently to wait for him there a moment.

Dismayed when she saw him coming down the path followed by the gardener with the wreath, she almost fainted. But he encouraged her with a look.

"To the cemetery!" he said to the driver, jumping into the carriage.

As soon as they started off, she burst into tears and covered her face with her handkerchief.

"Don't cry," he said softly. "I didn't want to speak about it at home, and I don't want to say anything now. Please don't cry. It came about by accident. I had gone for a walk in the garden and the gardener, thinking I had ordered the wreath, mentioned it. Don't cry anymore. We will go and leave it there together."

She kept her eyes hidden in the handkerchief until the carriage came to a stop at the gate of the cemetery.

He helped her down, then picked up the wreath and walked in with her.

"Come," he said, taking the first path to the left and looking at the graves, one by one, along the row.

It was the next to the last grave along that path. He took off his hat to lay the wreath at the foot of the grave, then stepped back quietly and withdrew to give her time to say a prayer. But she stayed there, silent, with the handkerchief still pressed to her eyes. She had not a thought, not a tear, for the dead boy. As though lost, she suddenly turned and looked at her husband as she had never looked at him before.

"Forgive me! Forgive me, Francesco! Take me home," she cried, clinging to his arm.

THE EIGHTY-
YARD RUN

IRWIN SHAW / UNITED STATES

THE PASS was high and wide and he jumped for it, feeling it slap flatly against his hands, as he shook his hips to throw off the halfback who was diving at him. The center floated by, his hands desperately brushing Darling's knee as Darling picked his feet up high and delicately ran over a blocker and an opposing linesman in a jumble on the ground near the scrimmage line. He had ten yards in the clear and picked up speed, breathing easily, feeling his thigh pads rising and falling against his legs, listening to the sound of cleats behind him, pulling away from them, watching the other backs heading him off toward the sideline, the whole picture, the men closing in on him, the blockers fighting for position, the ground he had to cross, all suddenly clear in his head, for the first time in his life not a meaningless confusion of men, sounds, speed. He smiled a little to himself as he ran, holding the ball lightly in front of him with his two hands, his knees pumping high, his hips twisting in the almost girlish run of a back in a broken field. The first halfback came at him and he fed him his leg, then swung at the last moment, took the shock of the man's shoulder without breaking stride, ran right through him, his cleats biting securely into the turf. There was only the safety man now, coming warily at him, his arms crooked, hands spread. Darling tucked the ball in, spurted at him, driving hard, hurling himself along, his legs pounding, knees high, all two hundred pounds bunched into controlled attack. He was sure he was going to get past the safety man. Without thought, his arms and legs working beautifully together, he headed right for the safety man, stiff-armed him, feeling blood spurt instantaneously from the man's nose onto his hand, seeing his face go awry, head turned, mouth pulled to one side. He pivoted away, keeping the arm locked, dropping the safety man as he ran easily toward the goal line, with the drumming of cleats diminishing behind him.

How long ago? It was autumn then, and the ground was getting hard because the nights were cold and leaves from the maples around the stadium blew across the practice fields in gusts of wind, and the girls were beginning to put polo coats over their sweaters when they came to watch practice in the afternoons. . . . Fifteen years. Darling walked slowly over the same ground in the spring twilight, in his neat shoes, a man of thirty-five dressed in a double-breasted suit, ten pounds heavier in the fifteen years, but not fat, with the years between 1925 and 1940 showing in his face.

The coach was smiling quietly to himself and the assistant coaches were looking at each other with pleasure the way they always did when one of the second stringers suddenly did something fine, bringing credit to them, making their $2,000 a year a tiny bit more secure.

Darling trotted back, smiling, breathing deeply but easily, feeling wonderful, not tired, though this was the tail end of practice and he'd run eighty yards. The sweat poured off his face and soaked his jersey and he liked the feeling, the warm moistness lubricating his skin like oil. Off in a corner of the field some players were punting and the smack of leather against the ball came pleasantly through the afternoon air. The freshmen were running signals on the next field and the quarterback's sharp voice, the pound of the eleven pairs of cleats, the "Dig, now *dig!*" of the coaches, the laughter of the players all somehow made him feel happy as he trotted back to midfield, listening to the applause and shouts of the students along the sidelines, knowing that after that run the coach would have to start him Saturday against Illinois.

Fifteen years, Darling thought, remembering the shower after the workout, the hot water steaming off his skin and the deep soapsuds and all the young voices singing with the water streaming down and towels going and managers running in and out and the sharp sweet smell of oil of wintergreen and everybody clapping him on the back as he dressed and Packard, the captain, who took being captain very seriously, coming over to him and shaking his hand and saying, "Darling, you're going to go places in the next two years."

The assistant manager fussed over him, wiping a cut on his leg with alcohol and iodine, the little sting making him realize suddenly how fresh and whole and solid his body felt. The manager slapped a piece of adhesive tape over the cut, and Darling noticed the sharp clean white of the tape against the ruddiness of the skin, fresh from the shower.

He dressed slowly, the softness of his shirt and the soft warmth of his wool socks and his flannel trousers a reward against his skin after the harsh pressure of the shoulder harness and thigh and hip pads. He drank three glasses of cold water, the liquid reaching down coldly inside of him, soothing the harsh dry places in his throat and belly left by the sweat and running and shouting of practice.

Fifteen years.

The sun had gone down and the sky was green behind the stadium and he laughed quietly to himself as he looked at the stadium, rearing above the trees, and knew that on Saturday when the 70,000 voices roared as the team came running out onto the field, part of that enormous salute would be for him.

He walked slowly, listening to the gravel crunch satisfactorily under his shoes in the still twilight, feeling his clothes swing lightly against his skin, breathing the thin evening air, feeling the wind move softly in his damp hair, wonderfully cool behind his ears and at the nape of his neck.

Louise was waiting for him at the road, in her car. The top was down and he noticed all over again, as he always did when he saw her, how pretty she was, the rough blonde hair and the large, inquiring eyes and the bright mouth, smiling now.

She threw the door open. "Were you good today?" she asked.

"Pretty good," he said. He climbed in, sank luxuriously into the soft leather, stretched his legs far out. He smiled, thinking of the eighty yards. "Pretty damn good."

She looked at him seriously for a moment, then scrambled around, like a little girl, kneeling on the seat next to him, grabbed him, her hands along his ears, and kissed him as he sprawled, head back, on the seat cushion. She let go of him, but kept her head close to his, over his. Darling reached up slowly and rubbed the back of his hand against her cheek, lit softly by a street lamp a hundred feet away. They looked at each other, smiling.

Louise drove down to the lake and they sat there silently, watching the moon rise behind the hills on the other side. Finally he reached over, pulled her gently to him, kissed her. Her lips grew soft, her body sank into his, tears formed slowly in her eyes. He knew, for the first time, that he could do whatever he wanted with her.

"Tonight," he said. "I'll call for you at seven-thirty. Can you get out?"

She looked at him. She was smiling, but the tears were still full in her eyes. "All right," she said. "I'll get out. How about you? Won't the coach raise hell?"

Darling grinned. "I got the coach in the palm of my hand," he said. "Can you wait till seven-thirty?"

She grinned back at him. "No," she said.

They kissed and she started the car and they went back to town for dinner. He sang on the way home.

Christian Darling, thirty-five years old, sat on the frail spring grass, greener now than it ever would be again on the practice field, looked thoughtfully up at the stadium, a deserted ruin in the twilight. He had started on the first team that Saturday and every Saturday after that for the next two years, but it had never been as satisfactory as it should have been. He never had broken away, the longest run he'd ever made was thirty-five yards, and that in a game that was already won, and then that kid had come up from the third team, Diederich, a blank-faced German kid from Wisconsin, who ran like a bull, ripping lines to pieces Saturday after Saturday, plowing through, never getting hurt, never changing his expression, scoring more points, gaining more ground than all the rest of the team put together, making everybody's All-American, carrying the ball three times out of four, keeping everybody else out of the headlines. Darling was a good blocker and he spent his Saturday afternoons working on the big Swedes and Polacks who played tackle and end for Michigan, Illinois,

Purdue, hurling into huge pile-ups, bobbing his head wildly to elude the great raw hands swinging like meat-cleavers at him as he went charging in to open up holes for Diederich coming through like a locomotive behind him. Still, it wasn't so bad. Everybody liked him and he did his job and he was pointed out on the campus and boys always felt important when they introduced their girls to him at their proms, and Louise loved him and watched him faithfully in the games, even in the mud, when your own mother wouldn't know you, and drove him around in her car keeping the top down because she was proud of him and wanted to show everybody that she was Christian Darling's girl. She bought him crazy presents because her father was rich, watches, pipes, humidors, an icebox for beer for his room, curtains, wallets, a fifty-dollar dictionary.

"You'll spend every cent your old man owns," Darling protested once when she showed up at his rooms with seven different packages in her arms and tossed them onto the couch.

"Kiss me," Louise said, "and shut up."

"Do you want to break your poor old man?"

"I don't mind. I want to buy you presents."

"Why?"

"It makes me feel good. Kiss me. I don't know why. Did you know that you're an important figure?"

"Yes," Darling said gravely.

"When I was waiting for you at the library yesterday two girls saw you coming and one of them said to the other, 'That's Christian Darling. He's an important figure.'"

"You're a liar."

"I'm in love with an important figure."

"Still, why the hell did you have to give me a forty-pound dictionary?"

"I wanted to make sure," Louise said, "that you had a token of my esteem. I want to smother you in tokens of my esteem."

Fifteen years ago.

They'd married when they got out of college. There'd been other women for him, but all casual and secret, more for curiosity's sake, and vanity, women who'd thrown themselves at him and flattered him, a pretty mother at a summer camp for boys, an old girl from his home town who'd suddenly blossomed into a coquette, a friend of Louise's who had dogged him grimly for six months and had taken advantage of the two weeks that Louise went home when her mother died. Perhaps Louise had known, but she'd kept quiet, loving him completely, filling his rooms with presents, religiously watching him battling with the big Swedes and Polacks on the line of scrimmage on Saturday afternoons, making plans for marrying him and living with him in New York and going with him there to the night clubs, the theaters, the good restaurants, being proud of him in advance, tall, white-teethed, smiling, large, yet moving lightly, with an athlete's grace, dressed in evening clothes, approvingly eyed by magnificently dressed and famous women in theater lobbies, with Louise adoringly at his side.

Her father, who manufactured inks, set up a New York office for Darling to manage and presented him with three hundred accounts, and they lived on Beekman Place with a view of the river with fifteen thousand dollars a year between them, because everybody was buying everything in those days, including ink. They saw all the shows and went to all the speakeasies and spent their fifteen thousand dollars a year and in the afternoons Louise went to the art galleries and the matinees of the more serious plays that Darling didn't like to sit through and Darling slept with a girl who danced in the chorus of *Rosalie* and with the wife of a man who owned three copper mines. Darling played squash three times a week and remained as solid as a stone barn and Louise never took her eyes off him when they were in the same room together, watching him with a secret, miser's smile, with a trick of coming over to him in the middle of a crowded room and saying gravely, in a low voice, "You're the handsomest man I've ever seen in my whole life. Want a drink?"

Nineteen twenty-nine came to Darling and to his wife and father-in-law, the maker of inks, just as it came to everyone else. The father-in-law waited until 1933 and then blew his brains out and when Darling went to Chicago to see what the books of the firm looked like he found out all that was left were debts and three or four gallons of unbought ink.

"Please, Christian," Louise said, sitting in their neat Beekman Place apartment, with a view of the river and prints of paintings by Dufy and Braque and Picasso on the wall, "please, why do you want to start drinking at two o'clock in the afternoon?"

"I have nothing else to do," Darling said, putting down his glass, emptied of its fourth drink. "Please pass the whisky."

Louise filled his glass. "Come take a walk with me," she said. "We'll walk along the river."

"I don't want to walk along the river," Darling said, squinting intensely at the prints of paintings by Dufy, Braque and Picasso.

"We'll walk along Fifth Avenue."

"I don't want to walk along Fifth Avenue."

"Maybe," Louise said gently, "you'd like to come with me to some art galleries. There's an exhibition by a man named Klee. . . ."

"I don't want to go to any art galleries. I want to sit here and drink Scotch whisky," Darling said. "Who the hell hung those goddam pictures up on the wall?"

"I did," Louise said.

"I hate them."

"I'll take them down," Louise said.

"Leave them there. It gives me something to do in the afternoon. I can hate them." Darling took a long swallow. "Is that the way people paint these days?"

"Yes, Christian. Please don't drink any more."

"Do you like painting like that?"

"Yes, dear."

"Really?"

"Really."

Darling looked carefully at the prints once more. "Little Louise Tucker. The middle-western beauty. I like pictures with horses in them. Why should you like pictures like that?"

"I just happen to have gone to a lot of galleries in the last few years . . ."

"Is that what you do in the afternoon?"

"That's what I do in the afternoon," Louise said.

"I drink in the afternoon."

Louise kissed him lightly on the top of his head as he sat there squinting at the pictures on the wall, the glass of whisky held firmly in his hand. She put on her coat and went out without saying another word. When she came back in the early evening, she had a job on a woman's fashion magazine.

They moved downtown and Louise went out to work every morning and Darling sat home and drank and Louise paid the bills as they came up. She made believe she was going to quit work as soon as Darling found a job, even though she was taking over more responsibility day by day at the magazine, interviewing authors, picking painters for the illustrations and covers, getting actresses to pose for pictures, going out for drinks with the right people, making a thousand new friends whom she loyally introduced to Darling.

"I don't like your hat," Darling said, once, when she came in in the evening and kissed him, her breath rich with martinis.

"What's the matter with my hat, Baby?" she asked, running her fingers through his hair. "Everybody says it's very smart."

"It's too damned smart," he said. "It's not for you. It's for a rich, sophisticated woman of thirty-five with admirers."

Louise laughed. "I'm practicing to be a rich, sophisticated woman of thirty-five with admirers," she said. He stared soberly at her. "Now, don't look so grim, Baby. It's still the same simple little wife under the hat." She took the hat off, threw it into a corner, sat on his lap. "See? Homebody Number One."

"Your breath could run a train," Darling said, not wanting to be mean, but talking out of boredom, and sudden shock at seeing his wife curiously a stranger in a new hat, with a new expression in her eyes under the little brim, secret, confident, knowing.

Louise tucked her head under his chin so he couldn't smell her breath. "I had to take an author out for cocktails," she said. "He's a boy from the Ozark Mountains and he drinks like a fish. He's a Communist."

"What the hell is a Communist from the Ozarks doing writing for a woman's fashion magazine?"

Louise chuckled. "The magazine business is getting all mixed up these days. The publishers want to have a foot in every camp. And anyway, you can't find an author under seventy these days who isn't a Communist."

"I don't think I like you to associate with all those people, Louise," Darling said. "Drinking with them."

"He's a very nice, gentle boy," Louise said. "He reads Ernest Dowson."

"Who's Ernest Dowson?"

Louise patted his arm, stood up, fixed her hair. "He's an English poet."

Darling felt that somehow he had disappointed her. "Am I supposed to know who Ernest Dowson is?"

"No, dear. I'd better go in and take a bath."

After she had gone, Darling went over to the corner where the hat was lying and picked it up. It was nothing, a scrap of straw, a red flower, a veil, meaningless on his big hand, but on his wife's head a signal of something . . . big city, smart and knowing women drinking and dining with men other than their husbands, conversation about things a normal man wouldn't know much about, Frenchmen who painted as though they used their elbows instead of brushes, composers who wrote whole symphonies without a single melody in them, writers who knew all about politics and women who knew all about writers, the movement of the proletariat, Marx, somehow mixed up with five-dollar dinners and the best-looking women in America and fairies who made them laugh and half-sentences immediately understood and secretly hilarious and wives who called their husbands "Baby." He put the hat down, a scrap of straw and a red flower, and a little veil. He drank some whisky straight and went into the bathroom where his wife was lying deep in her bath, singing to herself and smiling from time to time like a little girl, paddling the water gently with her hands, sending up a slight spicy fragrance from the bath salts she used.

He stood over her, looking down at her. She smiled up at him, her eyes half closed, her body pink and shimmering in the warm, scented water. All over again, with all the old suddenness, he was hit deep inside him with the knowledge of how beautiful she was, how much he needed her.

"I came in here," he said, "to tell you I wish you wouldn't call me 'Baby.'" She looked up at him from the bath, her eyes quickly full of sorrow, half-understanding what he meant. He knelt and put his arms around her, his sleeves plunged heedlessly in the water, his shirt and jacket soaking wet as he clutched her wordlessly, holding her crazily tight, crushing her breath from her, kissing her desperately, searchingly, regretfully.

He got jobs after that, selling real estate and automobiles, but somehow, although he had a desk with his name on a wooden wedge on it, and he went to the office religiously at nine each morning, he never managed to sell anything and he never made any money.

Louise was made assistant editor, and the house was always full of strange men and women who talked fast and got angry on abstract subjects like mural painting, novelists, labor unions. Negro short-story writers drank Louise's liquor, and a lot of Jews, and big solemn men with scarred faces and knotted hands who talked slowly but clearly about picket lines and battles with guns and leadpipe at mine-shaft-heads and in front of factory gates. And Louise moved among them all, confidently, knowing what they were talking about, with opinions that they listened to and argued about just as though she were a man. She knew everybody, condescended to no one, devoured books that Darling had never heard of, walked along the streets of the city, excited, at home, soaking in all the million tides of New York without fear, with constant wonder.

Her friends liked Darling and sometimes he found a man who wanted to get off in the corner and talk about the new boy who played fullback for Princeton, and the decline of the double wing-back, or even the state of the stock market, but for the most part he sat on the edge of things, solid and quiet in the high storm of words. "The dialectics of the situation . . . The theater has been given over to expert jugglers . . . Picasso? What man has a right to paint old bones and collect ten thousand dollars for them? . . . I stand firmly behind Trotsky . . . Poe was the last American critic. When he died they put lilies on the grave of American criticism. I don't say this because they panned my last book, but . . ."

Once in a while he caught Louise looking soberly and consideringly at him through the cigarette smoke and the noise and he avoided her eyes and found an excuse to get up and go into the kitchen for more ice or to open another bottle.

"Come on," Cathal Flaherty was saying, standing at the door with a girl, "you've got to come down and see this. It's down on Fourteenth Street, in the old Civic Repertory, and you can only see it on Sunday nights and I guarantee you'll come out of the theater singing." Flaherty was a big young Irishman with a broken nose who was the lawyer for a longshoreman's union, and he had been hanging around the house for six months on and off, roaring and shutting everybody else up when he got in an argument. "It's a new play, *Waiting for Lefty;* it's about taxi-drivers."

"Odets," the girl with Flaherty said. "It's by a guy named Odets."

"I never heard of him," Darling said.

"He's a new one," the girl said.

"It's like watching a bombardment," Flaherty said. "I saw it last Sunday night. You've got to see it."

"Come on, Baby," Louise said to Darling, excitement in her eyes already. "We've been sitting in the Sunday *Times* all day, this'll be a great change."

"I see enough taxi-drivers every day," Darling said, not because he meant that, but because he didn't like to be around Flaherty, who said things that made Louise laugh a lot and whose judgment she accepted on almost every subject. "Let's go to the movies."

"You've never seen anything like this before," Flaherty said. "He wrote this play with a baseball bat."

"Come on," Louise coaxed, "I bet it's wonderful."

"He has long hair," the girl with Flaherty said. "Odets. I met him at a party. He's an actor. He didn't say a goddam thing all night."

"I don't feel like going down to Fourteenth Street," Darling said, wishing Flaherty and his girl would get out. "It's gloomy."

"Oh, hell!" Louise said loudly. She looked coolly at Darling, as though she'd just been introduced to him and was making up her mind about him, and not very favorably. He saw her looking at him, knowing there was something new and dangerous in her face and he wanted to say something, but Flaherty was there and his damned girl, and anyway, he didn't know what to say. "I'm going," Louise said, getting her coat. "I don't think Fourteenth Street is gloomy."

"I'm telling you," Flaherty was saying, helping her on with her coat, "it's the Battle of Gettysburg, in Brooklynese."

"Nobody could get a word out of him," Flaherty's girl was saying as they went through the door. "He just sat there all night."

The door closed. Louise hadn't said good night to him. Darling walked around the room four times, then sprawled out on the sofa, on top of the Sunday Times. He lay there for five minutes looking at the ceiling, thinking of Flaherty walking down the street talking in that booming voice, between the girls, holding their arms.

Louise had looked wonderful. She'd washed her hair in the afternoon and it had been very soft and light and clung close to her head as she stood there angrily putting her coat on. Louise was getting prettier every year, partly because she knew by now how pretty she was, and made the most of it.

"Nuts," Darling said, standing up. "Oh, nuts."

He put on his coat and went down to the nearest bar and had five drinks off by himself in a corner before his money ran out.

THE YEARS since then had been foggy and downhill. Louise had been nice to him, and in a way, loving and kind, and they'd fought only once, when he said he was going to vote for Landon. ("Oh, Christ," she'd said, "doesn't *anything* happen inside your head? Don't you read the papers? The penniless Republican!") She'd been sorry later and apologized for hurting him, but apologized as she might to a child. He'd tried hard, had gone grimly to the art galleries, the concert halls, the bookshops, trying to gain on the trail of his wife, but it was no use.

He was bored, and none of what he saw or heard or dutifully read made much sense to him and finally he gave it up. He had thought, many nights as he ate dinner alone, knowing that Louise would come home late and drop silently into bed without explanation, of getting a divorce, but he knew the loneliness, the hopelessness, of not seeing her again would be too much to take. So he was good, completely devoted, ready at all times to go anyplace with her, do anything she wanted. He even got a small job, in a broker's office, and paid his own way, bought his own liquor.

Then he'd been offered the job of going from college to college as a tailor's representative. "We want a man," Mr. Rosenberg had said, "who as soon as you look at him, you say, 'There's a university man.'" Rosenberg had looked approvingly at Darling's broad shoulders and well-kept waist, at his carefully brushed hair and his honest, wrinkle-less face. "Frankly, Mr. Darling, I am willing to make you a proposition. I have inquired about you, you are favorably known on your old campus, I understand you were in the backfield with Alfred Diederich."

Darling nodded. "Whatever happened to him?"

"He is walking around in a cast for seven years now. An iron brace. He played professional football and they broke his neck for him."

Darling smiled. That, at least, had turned out well.

"Our suits are an easy product to sell, Mr. Darling," Rosenberg said. "We have a handsome, custom-made garment. What has Brooks Brothers got that we haven't got? A name. No more."

"I can make fifty, sixty dollars a week," Darling said to Louise that night. "And expenses. I can save some money and then come back to New York and really get started here."

"Yes, Baby," Louise said.

"As it is," Darling said carefully, "I can make it back here once a month, and holidays and the summer. We can see each other often."

"Yes, Baby." He looked at her face, lovelier now at thirty-five than it had ever been before, but fogged over now as it had been for five years with a kind of patient, kindly, remote boredom.

"What do you say?" he asked. "Should I take it?" Deep within him he hoped fiercely, longingly, for her to say, "No, Baby, you stay right here," but she said, as he knew she'd say, "I think you'd better take it."

He nodded. He had to get up and stand with his back to her, looking out the window, because there were things plain on his face that she had never seen in the fifteen years she'd known him. "Fifty dollars is a lot of money," he said. "I never thought I'd ever see fifty dollars again." He laughed. Louise laughed, too.

CHRISTIAN DARLING SAT ON THE frail green grass of the practice field. The shadow of the stadium had reached out and covered him. In the distance the lights of the university shone a little mistily in the light haze of evening. Fifteen years. Flaherty even now was calling for his wife, buying her a drink, filling whatever bar they were in with that voice of his and that easy laugh. Darling half-closed his eyes, almost saw the boy fifteen years ago reach for the pass, slip the halfback, go skittering lightly down the field, his knees high and fast and graceful, smiling to himself because he knew he was going to get past the safety man. That was the high point, Darling thought, fifteen years ago, on an autumn afternoon, twenty years old and far from death, with the air coming easily into his lungs, and a deep feeling inside him that he could do anything, knock over anybody, outrun whatever had to be outrun. And the shower after and the three glasses of water and the cool night air on his damp head and Louise sitting hatless in the open car with a smile and the first kiss she ever really meant. The high point, an eighty-yard run in the practice, and a girl's kiss and everything after that a decline. Darling laughed. He had practiced the wrong thing, perhaps. He hadn't practiced for 1929 and New York City and a girl who would turn into a woman. Somewhere, he thought, there must have been a point where she moved up to me, was even with me for a moment, when I could have held her hand, if I'd known, held tight, gone with her. Well, he'd never known. Here he was on a playing field that was fifteen years away and his wife was in another city having dinner with another and better man, speaking with him a different, new language, a language nobody had ever taught him.

Darling stood up, smiled a little, because if he didn't smile he knew the tears would come. He looked around him. This was the spot. O'Connor's pass had come sliding out just to here . . . the high point. Darling put up his hands, felt all over again the flat slap of the ball. He shook his hips to throw off the halfback, cut back inside the center, picked his knees high as he ran gracefully over two men jumbled on the ground at the line of scrimmage, ran easily, gaining speed, for ten yards, holding the ball lightly in his two hands, swung away from the halfback diving at him, ran, swinging his hips in the almost girlish manner of a back in a broken field, tore into the safety man, his shoes drumming heavily on the turf, stiff-armed, elbow locked, pivoted, raced lightly and exultantly for the goal line.

It was only after he had sped over the goal line and slowed to a trot that he saw the boy and girl sitting together on the turf, looking at him wonderingly.

He stopped short, dropping his arms. "I . . ." he said, gasping a little, though his condition was fine and the run hadn't winded him. "I—once I played here."

The boy and the girl said nothing. Darling laughed embarrassedly, looked hard at them sitting there, close to each other, shrugged, turned and went toward his hotel, the sweat breaking out on his face and running down into his collar.

YOU WERE PERFECTLY FINE
DOROTHY PARKER / UNITED STATES

THE PALE YOUNG MAN eased himself carefully into the low chair, and rolled his head to the side, so that the cool chintz comforted his cheek and temple.

"Oh, dear," he said. "Oh, dear, oh, dear, oh, dear. Oh."

The clear-eyed girl, sitting light and erect on the couch, smiled brightly at him.

"Not feeling so well today?" she said.

"Oh, I'm great," he said. "Corking, I am. Know what time I got up? Four o'clock this afternoon, sharp. I kept trying to make it, and every time I took my head off the pillow, it would roll under the bed. This isn't my head I've got on now. I think this is something that used to belong to Walt Whitman. Oh, dear, oh, dear, oh, dear."

"Do you think maybe a drink would make you feel better?"

"The hair of the mastiff that bit me?" he said. "Oh, no, thank you. Please never speak of anything like that again. I'm through. I'm all, all through. Look at that hand; steady as a hummingbird. Tell me, was I very terrible last night?"

"Oh, goodness," she said, "everybody was feeling pretty high. You were all right."

"Yeah, I must have been dandy. Is everybody sore at me?"

"Good heavens, no," she said. "Everyone thought you were terribly funny. Of course, Jim Pierson was a little stuffy, there for a minute at dinner. But people sort of held him back in his chair, and got him calmed down. I don't think anybody at the other tables noticed it at all. Hardly anybody."

"He was going to sock me? Oh, Lord. What did I do to him?"

"Why, you didn't do a thing," she said. "You were perfectly fine. But you know how silly Jim gets, when he thinks anybody is making too much fuss over Elinor."

"Was I making a pass at Elinor?" he said. "Did I do that?"

"Of course you didn't," she said. "You were only fooling, that's all. She thought you were awfully amusing. She was having a marvelous time. She only got a little tiny bit annoyed just once, when you poured the clam juice down her back."

"My God," he said. "Clam juice down that back. And every vertebra a little Cabot. Dear God. What'll I ever do?"

"Oh, she'll be all right," she said. "Just send her some flowers, or something. Don't worry about it. It isn't anything."

"No, I won't worry," he said. "I haven't got a care in the world. I'm sitting pretty. Oh, dear, oh, dear. Did I do any other fascinating tricks at dinner?"

"You were fine," she said. "Don't be so foolish about it. Everybody was crazy about you. The maître d'hôtel was a little worried because you wouldn't stop singing, but he really didn't mind. All he said was, he was afraid they'd close the place again, if there was so much noise. But he didn't care a bit, himself. I think he loved seeing you have such a good time. Oh, you were just singing away, there, for about an hour. It wasn't so terribly loud, at all."

"So I sang," he said. "That must have been a treat. I sang."

"Don't you remember?" she said. "You just sang one song after another. Everybody in the place was listening. They loved it. Only you kept insisting that you wanted to sing some song about some kind of fusiliers or other, and everybody kept shushing you, and you'd keep trying to start it again. You were wonderful. We were all trying to make you stop singing for a minute, and eat something, but you wouldn't hear of it. My, you were funny."

"Didn't I eat any dinner?" he said.

"Oh, not a thing. Every time the waiter would offer you something, you'd give it right back to him, because you said that he was your long-lost brother, changed in the cradle by a gypsy band, and that anything you had was his. You had him simply roaring at you."

"I bet I did," he said. "I bet I was comical. Society's Pet, I must have been. And what happened then, after my overwhelming success with the waiter?"

"Why, nothing much," she said. "You took a sort of dislike to some old man with white hair, sitting across the room, because you didn't like his necktie and you wanted to tell him about it. But we got you out, before he got really mad."

"Oh, we got out," he said. "Did I walk?"

"Walk! Of course you did," she said. "You were absolutely all right. There was that nasty stretch of ice on the sidewalk, and you did sit down awfully hard, you poor dear. But good heavens, that might have happened to anybody."

"Oh, sure," he said. "Louisa Alcott or anybody. So I fell down on the sidewalk. That would explain what's the matter with my— Yes. I see. And then what, if you don't mind?"

"Ah, now, Peter!" she said. "You can't sit there and say you don't remember what happened after that! I did think that maybe you were just a little tight at dinner—oh, you were perfectly all right, and all that, but I did know you were feeling pretty gay. But you were so serious, from the time you fell down—I never knew you to be that way. Don't you know, how you told me I had never seen your real self before? Oh, Peter, I just couldn't bear it, if you didn't remember that lovely long ride we took together in the taxi! Please, you do remember that, don't you? I think it would simply kill me, if you didn't."

"Oh, yes," he said. "Riding in the taxi. Oh, yes, sure. Pretty long ride, hmm?"

"Round and round and round the park," she said. "Oh, and the trees were shining so in the moonlight. And you said you never knew before that you really had a soul."

"Yes," he said. "I said that. That was me."

"You said such lovely, lovely things," she said. "And I'd never known, all this time, how you had been feeling about me, and I'd never dared to let you see how I felt about you. And then last night—oh, Peter dear, I think that taxi ride was the most important thing that ever happened to us in our lives."

"Yes," he said. "I guess it must have been."

"And we're going to be so happy," she said. "Oh, I just want to tell everybody! But I don't know—I think maybe it would be sweeter to keep it all to ourselves."

"I think it would be," he said.

"Isn't it lovely?" she said.

"Yes," he said. "Great."

"Lovely!" she said.

"Look here," he said, "do you mind if I have a drink? I mean, just medicinally, you know. I'm off the stuff for life, so help me. But I think I feel a collapse coming on."

"Oh, I think it would do you good," she said. "You poor boy, it's a shame you feel so awful. I'll go make you a whisky and soda."

"Honestly," he said, "I don't see how you could ever want to speak to me again, after I made such a fool of myself, last night. I think I'd better go join a monastery in Tibet."

"You crazy idiot!" she said. "As if I could ever let you go away now! Stop talking like that. You were perfectly fine."

She jumped up from the couch, kissed him quickly on the forehead, and ran out of the room.

The pale young man looked after her and shook his head long and slowly, then dropped it in his damp and trembling hands.

"Oh, dear," he said. "Oh, dear, oh, dear, oh, dear."

LUZINA TAKES
A HOLIDAY

GABRIELLE ROY / CANADA

Gabrielle Roy

Translated by Harry L. Binsse

DEEP WITHIN the Canadian Province of Manitoba, remote in its melancholy region of lakes and wild waterfowl, there lies a tiny village barely noticeable amidst its skimpy fir trees. On the map you will find it called Meadow Portage, but it is known to the people who live thereabouts as Portage des Prés. To reach it you must cover a full thirty-two miles of jolty road beyond Rorketon, the terminus of the branch railroad and the nearest town. In all, it contains a chapel, visited three or four times a year by an aged missionary, polyglot and loquacious; a boxlike structure built of new planks and serving as school for the handful of white children in the area; and another building, also of boards but a bit larger, the most important in the settlement, since it houses at once the store, the post office, and the telephone.

Somewhat further away you can see, in a clearing among the birches, two other dwellings which, together with the store-post-office, shelter all Portage des Prés's inhabitants. But I nearly forgot: in front of the largest structure, at the edge of the rough track leading to Rorketon, proudly stands a lone gasoline pump, complete with its large glass globe, ever awaiting the arrival of electricity. Beyond these few things, a wilderness of grass and wind.

One of the houses, indeed, possesses a front door, inserted at the level of its second floor, yet since no one has bothered to build for it either a landing or a flight of steps, nothing could better express the idea of utter uselessness. Across the façade of the larger building are painted the words "Bessette's General Store." And that is absolutely all there is at Portage des Prés. It is the image of the final jumping-off place. And yet the Tousignant family lived, some twenty years ago, even beyond this outpost.

TO REACH their home from Portage des Prés, you had to continue straight on beyond the gas pump, following the same crude road; at first glance you could scarcely make it out, but finally you saw how it ran, thanks to two parallel bands of grass which remained a trifle flattened by the passage of the Indians' light buckboards. Only an old resident or a half-breed guide could find his way along it, for at several points this track divided, and secondary tracks led through the brush to some trapper's cabin two or three miles away and invisible from the main trail.

You had, then, to stick closely to the most direct road. And a few hours later, if you were riding in a buggy—a little sooner if traveling in one of those ancient Fords which still operate in those parts—you should reach the Big Water Hen River.

There you left Ford or buggy behind.

The Tousignants had a canoe to cross the river. Were it on the further shore, someone would have to swim over to get it. You then continued downstream, wholly wrapped in such silence as is seldom found on earth—or rather, in the rustle of sedges, the beat of wings, in the thousands of tiny, hidden, secret, timid sounds, producing an effect in some way as restful as silence itself. Big prairie chickens, almost too heavy to fly, heaved themselves above the river's brush-covered banks and tumbled back to earth, already tired by their listless efforts.

Clambering out on the opposite shore, you crossed on foot an island half a mile wide, covered with thick, uneven grass, mud holes, and, in summer, enormous and famished mosquitoes swarming up by the million from the spongy ground.

You then reached another river. It was the Little Water Hen. The people of the region had had no great trouble in naming its geographical features—always in honor of its senior inhabitant, that small gray fowl which epitomized all its tedium and all its quietness. Apart from the two rivers already mentioned, there was the Water Hen—

unqualified—there was Lake Water Hen. Moreover, the area itself was known as the Water Hen Country. And it was endlessly peaceful, there, to watch of an evening the aquatic birds rising up everywhere from among the reeds and circling together in one sector of the heavens which they darkened with their multitude.

When you had crossed the Little Water Hen, you landed on a fair-sized island with few trees. A large flock of sheep were at pasture there, completely free and unfenced; had it not been for them, you would have thought the island uninhabited.

But there was a house built upon it.

Built of unsquared logs, level with the ground, longer than it was wide, its windows set low, it stood upon a very slight elevation on the island's surface, bare to the four winds of heaven.

Here it was that the Tousignants lived.

Of their eight handsome children, shy yet tractable, one alone had journeyed as far as the village of Sainte Rose-du-Lac to be treated for a very bad earache. This was the nearest French settlement in the area; it was situated even further away than Rorketon, on the local railway which in some measure linked all this bush to the little town of Dauphin.

A few of the other children had from time to time accompanied their father when, two or three times a year, he journeyed to Portage des Prés to get his orders from the owner of the ranch under his management.

It was the mother who traveled the most. Almost every year she of necessity went to Sainte Rose-du-Lac. If there were the slightest hitch, you could spend days getting there; all the same, since she quit her island approximately but once a year, this long, hard trip, frequently hazardous, always exhausting, had come to be regarded by Luzina Tousignant as her annual holiday.

Never did she refer to it far in advance before the children, for they were, you might say, too attached to their mother, very tender, very affectionate, and it was a painful business for them to let her go; they would cling fast to her skirts, begging her not to leave. So it was better not to arouse this grief any sooner than necessary. To her husband alone one fine day she would announce, with an odd look half laughter and half sorrow, "My holiday is not far off." Then she would depart. And in this changeless existence, it was the great, the sole, adventure.

—

THIS YEAR it looked as though Luzina Tousignant could not undertake her usual trip. Her legs were swollen; she could not stand on them for more than an hour at a time, for she was a woman of considerable strength and weight, full of life, always on the go the moment her poor feet seemed a little better. Hippolyte Tousignant did not like to let her leave under such circumstances. And then too, it was the very worst time of year. Nonetheless, Luzina laughed when she began to talk about her holiday. In midsummer or midwinter, if it were necessary, one could get away from the island, and even without too much trouble. But in spring a woman alone could not possibly run into greater risks, dangers, and misery than on the Portage des Prés trail.

Hippolyte long tried to persuade Luzina she should not leave. Compliant under all other circumstances, in this she remained adamant. Of course she had to go to Sainte Rose-du-Lac! What was more, she must consult a doctor there about the baby's eczema. One of the cream separator's parts had got dented; she would have it fixed. And for business reasons she would stay awhile at Rorketon. She would take advantage of that visit to get some little idea of what people were wearing. "For," Luzina would say, "just because we live in a wild country is no reason we shouldn't be in style every so often." She gave a hundred reasons rather than admit that she took some small pleasure in getting away from the empty horizon of the Little Water Hen.

And, after all, how could Luzina ever have seen a crowd, a real crowd of at least a hundred persons, such as is to be found on Saturday nights along Rorketon's main street; how could she ever have been able to talk to persons other than her husband or her children, who, the moment she opened her mouth, already knew what she was going to say; how could she ever have those rare joys of novelty, of satisfied curiosity, of glimpses of the world, had she not had a wholly different reason for traveling—an eminently serious and pressing reason! She was not a demanding woman; she was quite willing to relish the pleasures of her trips, but only to the extent that they were proper rewards for duty done.

She left toward the end of March. The Little Water Hen was still frozen hard enough to allow crossing it on foot; the Big Water Hen, however, was free of ice at midstream. The boat was drawn over the ice like a sledge until it could be launched in the open water. Luzina was installed on its bottom boards, a bearskin over her knees, warmed bricks at her feet. Hippolyte had rigged a piece of rough canvas above her, somewhat in the shape of a small tent. Thus fully sheltered and showing no sign of fear, Luzina was keenly interested in everything that happened during the crossing. From time to time she thrust her smiling face through the slit in the canvas and remarked contentedly, "I'm as well off as the Queen!"

Two of the children, one pushing and the other pulling, helped their father maneuver the boat on the ice, and it was a job that required a lot of care, since no one could tell at exactly what spot the ice would begin to yield. Without any of them getting too soaked, they reached the river's free-flowing water. Large chunks of ice were floating in the current; they had to paddle hard to avoid them and to make headway against the Big Water Hen's rapid flow. Then the boat was hauled up on the other side—not without trouble, for the footing was far from firm.

The youngest children had remained on the little island, and this was the moment for their final good-bys to their mother. All of them were weeping. Swallowing their tears, and without the least outcry, they understood that it was too late to dissuade their mother from her journey. Their tiny hands, never still even for an instant, fluttered toward Luzina. One of the little girls carried the baby in her arms and made the infant wave continuously. All five of them were huddled together, so that they made one minute spot against the widest and most deserted of the world's horizons. Then was it that Luzina lost a great part of her gaiety; she looked for her handkerchief but could not find it, so encumbered was she with heavy clothing. She sniffled.

"Be good," she urged her children, raising her voice which the wind carried, though not at all in their direction. "Mind what your father tells you."

They tried to talk from one shore to the other, but the conversation made no sense. The children recalled the things they had wanted and begged for the whole year through; despite their grief, these things they remembered very well.

"A blackboard, Mama!" cried one of them.

"A pencil with an eraser, Mama!" another implored.

Luzina was not sure she understood what they were saying, but, taking a chance, she promised: "I'll bring you picture postcards."

She knew she made no mistake in promising postcards. Her children were crazy about them, especially those which showed very high buildings, streets jammed with cars, and—wonder of wonders—railway stations. Luzina thoroughly understood their taste.

Her husband lending her a hand, her older boys going ahead to beat a path in the snow, Luzina Tousignant reached the trail, and they all stood waiting for the arrival of the postman who, once a week, if it were at all possible, carried the mail from Portage des Prés to an Indian reservation some fifteen miles further north on Lake Water Hen.

They were much afraid that they had missed the mailman, or else that he had decided, because of the wretched condition of the road, to postpone his trip a week. Pierre-Emmanuel-Roger and Philippe-Auguste-Emile came very close to hoping for such a mishap; so even did Hippolyte Tousignant, who suggested timidly: "The postman will not dare set out in weather like this. If you were to come back home, Luzina, . . . we'd manage all the same."

"Come now, you know very well that won't do," she replied with a smile of regret, mingled with a hint of mockery, which above all seemed to reproach Hippolyte for his lack of practical good sense.

She looked fixedly up the trail, more determined than ever. After having overcome so many obstacles it would be a fine thing for her to have to return home. A very light snow, mixed with rain, began to fall.

"If only I could go with you," Hippolyte was saying, as he had said on all her previous departures.

And, just as she had the last time, she agreed: "Yes, indeed! To take the trip together, the two of us, what fun that would be! But, poor man, surely someone has to keep an eye on things and be in command while I'm not there."

They said no more.

Far away in the vast, changeless solitude a horse came into view, all in a lather, and on the seat of the sleigh behind it, a great ball of fur, from which emerged a sad yellow mustache, a thick cloud of vapor, and, held aloft, a swaying whip.

It was the postman.

He drew near. Now you could distinguish his bushy eyebrows from the brown fur of his winter hat; you could see the gleam of the silver thread which always hung from the postman's nose in cold weather; you could make out his tobacco-stained teeth when he gave his mare a throaty order. Having reached the little Tousignant group without a word of greeting, his frowning glance fixed on Luzina alone, he tightened the reins, stopped, and waited. For this Nick Sluzick was an odd character. In a country where people were often silent for lack of anything new to talk about, he beat everyone for taciturnity. He was said to have managed his business, accepted errands, done favors, fulfilled his postman's duties, made love, and procreated children—and all this without ever having uttered more than a scant dozen sentences.

Luzina was installed alongside this unsociable companion, he moving over a trifle to make a little space for her to sit down. Talkative as she was, Nick Sluzick's amazing uncommunicativeness ever remained her principal—indeed, her sole—trial throughout the journey.

Pierre-Emmanuel-Roger had brought a lantern, which he now lit and slipped under the covers at his mother's feet. He spread a bison skin over her and on top of it a piece of oilcloth to prevent the fur from getting soaked. With all her coverings, Luzina had almost totally disappeared, save for her eyes, which peered out from above a heavy muffler. They were clear, blue eyes, rather large, full of affection, and, at that moment, moist with sorrow. All four of them were looking at each other with the same expression of sad stupor, as though these Tousignants, so united in their isolation, were almost unable to conceive of being apart. And suddenly these people, who thought they had long since exhausted every subject of conversation, discovered a wholly new one and began to chatter.

"Do be careful, all of you, about fire," urged Luzina, lowering the scarf which covered her mouth.

"Yes. And you be careful not to freeze on your trip," said Hippolyte.

"Above all, don't starve yourselves," Luzina added. "There's plenty of flour and lard. Just make pancakes if you don't feel much like cooking; and you, Pierre-Emmanuel-Roger, be a help to your father."

The two eldest were not the only Tousignant children to have compound appellations. As though better to people the solitude where she dwelt, Luzina had given to each of her children a litany of names drawn from the pages of history or from the occasional novel that came her way. Among the children who had remained behind were Roberta-Louise-Célestine, Joséphine-Yolande, André-Aimable-Sébastien; the youngest, a fifteen-months-old baby, answered to the name of Juliette-Héloïse.

"You'll be very careful that Juliette-Héloïse doesn't swallow any pins," cried Luzina.

It was the last advice she gave her loved ones. Nick Sluzick couldn't waste any more time. Of all human actions, none seemed to him more useless and unnecessary than saying good-by. Either you did not go away or you went away; in the latter case, the event itself was explicit enough not to require comment. He spat over the side of the sled. With one hand he twirled his long yellow mustache, with the other he picked up the reins. And they were off through the soft snow, lying uneven on the ground, here in hummocks, there in hollows, which was the road to Portage des Prés.

TO DESCRIBE the difficulties of Luzina Tousignant's journey, seated next to her unsociable muzhik, who only once opened his mouth and then to ask her to stay put on her end of the seat since otherwise the sleigh might upset; to tell how, when she reached Portage des Prés, she had to wait for a week before the next mail left for Rorketon; how she spent those seven days at the store-post-office, which also after a fashion served the settlement as an inn, since in case of need it could afford people who had no other place to go a single room, practically unheated and with little or no furniture; how bored Luzina was while she waited, exasperated at this mischance and greatly fearing that she would get to Rorketon too late; how, when she finally left Portage des Prés, there was a cold wind blowing which grew in violence and froze one of her ears; to recount these few mishaps might be interesting were it not that her trip home was to be otherwise rich in vicissitudes.

—

ONCE THE serious purpose of her trip had been accomplished and her business finished at Sainte Rose-du-Lac, Luzina's most pressing desire was to get back by train to Rorketon, where she hoped to find promptly some means of returning home. She was made that way; all year long it seemed to her, shut off on her island, that never would she have her fill of seeing Rorketon's brightly illuminated shop windows, the electric lights which burned all night along its main street, the many buggies that thronged there, the plank sidewalks and the people moving about on them—in short, the intense life afforded by this big village with its Chinese restaurant, its Greek-rite Catholic chapel, its Orthodox church, its Rumanian tailor, its cupolas, its whitewashed cottages, its peasants in sheepskins and big rabbit hats— some, immigrants from Sweden; others, from Finland or Iceland; still others, and they were the majority, come from Bukovina and Galicia.

At Rorketon Luzina gathered the material for the tales she would tell her family for month after month, practically until her next trip.

Yet once she had spent a few days at Rorketon, she had had all she wanted of it. Nothing seemed to her warmer or more human than that lonely gray house which, atop its mound between the willows, looked out upon nothing except the quiet and monotonous Little Water Hen.

She worried about the children. She wondered whether, while chopping holes in the ice on the Little Water Hen in order to fish for pike, as was their custom in spring, they might not all have fallen in and perished as they attempted to save each other. She pictured to herself a flood which might cover the whole island and force her husband and her poor children to clamber up upon the roof of the house. Hers was a mind extraordinarily adept at imagining, the moment she was away from home, all the mishaps which could befall her loved ones and to which reality, harsh as it was in that land, lent a certain verisimilitude.

She was on edge.

But the coming of spring had been unusually delayed that year by heavy snowfalls followed by rain and finally by renewed cold. The wretched road between Rorketon and Portage des Prés had become impassable. Even the mailman refused to chance it. Now in those countries of the North, everyone takes it for granted that when the mailman cannot get through, no one can get through. The mail in that awesome wilderness remains the great, the most important business, and only obstacles truly insurmountable can stop it.

Nevertheless Luzina everywhere made inquiries—at the post office, in the stores, at the hotel—to see whether someone might know of a person who was going to try to reach Portage des Prés in spite of everything. At that moment the town was full of travelers, detained in Rorketon precisely because of the bad condition of the roads. And so Luzina made a number of acquaintanceships; to some few of these she would even send letters later on, giving news of her return and of events at the ranch, so interested in her had these people seemed and so anxious to wish her well.

Because of her affability Luzina had made a number of friends during her travels; she still wrote regularly to an old lady who had grown most affectionate toward her during the short train ride from Sainte Rose-du-Lac to Rorketon ten years earlier, a Madame Lacoste who lived in the province of Quebec. In fact Luzina said that meeting likable people was the real pleasure of traveling. She enjoyed being helpful to those who happened to be at hand, and to such good purpose that rarely did she fail to find in her journeying agreeable people ready to do as much for her. This time, however, no one could help her. She was advised to speak to the postman on the Rorketon–Portage des Prés route, who would deliver her to the place where Nick Sluzick took over the mail.

Now this Rorketon postman was the most baffling fellow of all. Ivan Bratislovski nearly always said he was going to do the opposite of what he did, a kind of peasant's stratagem against fate, which perhaps he thus hoped to best. And probably for the same reason he complained endlessly. At all hours of the day he was to be found in the Chinese restaurant, eager to pick a quarrel with anyone who might have dared deny that he, Ivan Bratislovski, lived a dog's life. Were you only to agree with him on that point, the little Ruthenian could prove himself most useful. Luzina was unaware of this method of appeasement.

Having sent a small boy twice to ask the Ruthenian whether he would be leaving the following morning, she had been informed that "Ivan Bratislovski's horse had been injured, that the sleigh was very small to carry a woman traveling with a lot of belongings, and that, in any case, he was on the point of offering his resignation to the postal authorities." What this meant was that Ivan Bratislovski would shortly take his chances and start for Portage des Prés, which, of course, was beyond Luzina's guessing.

Meanwhile a Jewish merchant from Dauphin arrived at the hotel where Luzina was staying. He was in a hurry, anxious to get to Portage des Prés with an eye to a deal in muskrat skins that might at any moment be snatched away, right from under his nose. He rented a horse and sleigh. The next morning he left, Luzina with him.

———

THE TWO TRAVELERS had scarcely passed Rorketon's last farmsteads when they found themselves in a lonely expanse, entirely covered with a thin layer of sparkling ice. The fine-grained, shifting snow was wholly imprisoned, as though in an envelope of brilliant cellophane. No breath of wind disturbed this frozen whiteness. Here was the hard and perfect motionlessness which the cold in its full virulence demands.

The road was as completely frozen as the fields, as all the countryside, flat and lifeless. At times it stretched out like a congealed pond, blue and level; the runners of the sleigh began to slide to and fro as though they were waltzing; in other places the frost had solidified the hollows and unevennesses of the road into a surface so rugged that the vehicle plunged, reared up, crashed down again in a straining effort strange to behold in a landscape so broad and unfeeling.

The horse was soon in a lather. The ice shattered beneath its shoes in long sharp splinters which cruelly wounded it. Luzina could scarcely bear watching the poor beast, and despite her desire to get home as soon as possible, she kept urging the Jew to spare the animal.

It took them hours to cover a few miles. The ice grew smoother and smoother. At one corner they took a little quickly the sleigh upset, tumbling Luzina, her suitcase, and all her bundles some feet off the road. Abe Zlutkin ran to her help. Her heavy clothing had protected her, her and her most fragile gift, which as she fell she clasped within her arms.

She had not even a scratch. She began to laugh, and, after a thoughtful moment, Abe Zlutkin did too.

He was a small, swarthy man, active, thin, always worrying and calculating. He had barely left Rorketon at daybreak when he began regretting that he had taken this woman with him. She might be injured if they had an accident; were that to happen, her husband would probably claim damages. Because he had wanted the three dollars Luzina had offered, Abe Zlutkin half foresaw that he would lose hundreds. He had been shaken by that very fear when Luzina stumbled back to her feet, more nimble than ever, and began to laugh. At once optimism replaced anxiety in Zlutkin's changeable soul. Such a woman, healthy and fearless, could not bring bad luck to him who helped her. On the contrary, he should make the best of it, put himself under her star, which was certainly a fortunate one. A half an hour after the accident Zlutkin was still chuckling over it, filled with amazement and henceforward certain that his good deed would be repaid a hundredfold, in fine furs, in choice skins which he would acquire at small expense in Portage des Prés.

Seeing him so well disposed, Luzina began to chat. She was on her return journey; the horse's every step, however hesitant, brought her nearer home; she was grateful to Abe Zlutkin; she could not prevent her generous nature from offering what she had to give, which amounted to the stories of half-a-hundred adventures in her life that might have been tragic and that always had—she never gave herself any reason why—the happiest possible endings. In the goodness of her heart she really hoped that by means of all her tales she could distract her companion from the dangers continually confronting them both.

Yet she feared she might seem selfish if she talked only about her own good fortune. She asked the fur merchant whether he was married. Stout Luzina's motherly kindness, her warm, inquiring eyes, her eager interest in others, her whole nature invited confidence.

Abe Zlutkin took advantage of an interval when the road was a trifle less slippery to show her a photo of his wife. It portrayed a plump young Jewish woman of dark complexion. Abe bethought himself that he loved her dearly. For a moment the business he was in such a hurry to transact ceased tormenting him. Such was Luzina's power. She disposed people to become aware that they had reasons for being happy.

When they were tired of talking, they rested by reflecting on the pleasant things that had been said. Her life, at the only times when she could give it much thought, while she was jolting along on her travels, seemed truly wonderful. Dwelling so far from all the world, she had encountered human beings of all races and characters. The most exciting romance could not have offered her so great a variety of people: little old bearded Poles, Slav postmen, half-breed guides, Russian Orthodox; once she had even made the trip home with the post-office inspector. No one of them had ever treated her disrespectfully; Luzina had only to put herself under a human being's protection for him to behave toward her exactly as she wished. Moreover, traveling in itself had taught her lessons of an unexpected sort: it had shown her that human nature everywhere is excellent. The Jews were one of the few folk she had had no opportunity to study; yet, deciding on the basis of her fur merchant that they were rather on the likable side, she let herself drift into a feeling of vague benevolence, lazy and easygoing, which embraced very nearly the whole human race.

But she had to resume the conversation. Zlutkin was becoming uneasy again; the road continued to be just as bad; the horse was limping. And, before they had covered much more ground, the sky began to cloud over. Strange red streaks, low on the horizon, foretold a change in the weather. The two travelers were obliged to find a stopping place.

It turned out to be one of those solitary farms such as were to be found every three or four miles along the Portage des Prés road. The house was poor; it contained only one room, furnished in back, behind the stove, with a number of beds. Yet the moment Luzina entered their home, shivering with cold, the man and woman of the house came forward to greet her, smiling, their arms extended to relieve her of all her bundles. They led her to the stove and at once offered her food, all this with so much alacrity that she could not harbor the least doubt of the sincerity of their welcome, even though it was expressed in a foreign tongue. It was just as she had always thought: every human being, the moment necessity forces us to seek his kindness, eagerly offers it in our behalf.

After supper Luzina settled herself for an interesting evening.

The family were Icelanders, a people with whom she had not yet had occasion to become acquainted. She noticed that they constantly drank very strong coffee and that, instead of putting sugar in their cups, they placed a lump on their tongues or between their teeth before drinking the burning liquid. When they began talking in their own language, she was even more delighted. Peculiarities, customs, and a language that were foreign to her, rather than putting her off, seemed to give life an inexhaustible attraction.

She did not want to be outdone in amiability by such kindly hosts. So, even though she had no assurance that they understood her, she began giving an account of the road she would have to travel to reach her home on the island in the Little Water Hen. Visiting was what gave them the greatest pleasure, said she. Laughingly she granted that it was the habit of living so far away from people that made her become so talkative whenever she had a chance. When she laughed, through politeness the Icelanders pretended to want to laugh also.

Thereupon she dug into her purse, seeking some little keepsake she might offer their children. She had only the crayons and the postcards bought for her own offspring; she hesitated a lot, but reflecting—and with good reason—that her own would not have hesitated to share their crayons with the young Bjorgssons, she beckoned to them, and the crayons were duly distributed. Seemingly the parents were touched, for they arose again to offer everyone coffee.

The next morning the travelers had a slightly less slippery road; the clouds, however, hung low; the sky was mottled. A little snow had fallen during the night. The wind swept strongly through this fresh snow, and there was reason to fear that a real gale was in the offing. They did not reach Portage des Prés until midafternoon, having twice wandered off the track, and they were pierced with cold, famished, their eyes scorched by the wind. The worst of the trip was still ahead of Luzina.

—

THAT NORTH country, with its vast, sparse forests and its equally vast lakes, that land of water and dwarf trees, has, of all regions, the most capricious climate. From one day to another the ice melted on the trail between Portage des Prés and the Tousignant ranch; you could almost see the snow disappear.

Another cold wave had been expected, but during the night Luzina spent at the settlement store a south wind had blown up. Almost warm, soft and damp, a wind swollen with hope—at any other time it would have rejoiced Luzina's heart. With this wind returned the fast gray teal, the green-necked mallard, the wild goose and its plaintive cry, the gallant little silver-bellied water hens, many sorts of duck, bustling and winsome, the whole great aquatic tribe, exquisite companion of spring and of man's assurance throughout these faraway realms.

In less than twenty-four hours, however, the whole countryside had turned into a kind of perilous marsh, deep and treacherous. Under the flaccid snow a man's foot found water everywhere, everywhere seeping water.

All the same, Luzina decided to leave. Either she would succeed in reaching home that very day, or else she would have to wait idly for weeks until the road dried out. For her children she still had some postcards, and, herself childlike, she could not wait to give them their present, so that she might watch their guileless eyes brighten with joy. For Hippolyte she had a handsome necktie, which he would have a chance to wear on his next trip, within a few months. She was itching with desire to tell about how the Bjorgssons had received her. Above all she had with her, this year like the other years, the gift of gifts, so precious that Luzina dared not entrust it to anyone and kept it scrupulously wrapped. This gift was supposed to be a great surprise for her family, which, truth to tell, rather expected it, since Luzina, ever generous, would surely come home this time with as much as she had always brought before. Her happiness, no more than the wind of springtime, the warm wind, alive and friendly, could wait to spread abroad.

Hippolyte would scold her for having taken to the road on so bad a day. So much the worse! Today you could still chance the trip; tomorrow opportunity might be lacking, or the trail might be even worse. She gathered her things together and through the store window began to watch for the moment when Nick Sluzick, lately arrived, would be ready to depart. As a matter of fact, she had not saved any time by journeying with Abe Zlutkin rather than with Ivan Bratislovski, because, whatever happened, Nick Sluzick had to wait for the mail brought by the latter before he could begin to distribute it over his own territory.

At last Luzina saw that the mail bags had been piled up on the back of the sleigh. Immediately, she rushed over to take her place beside a Nick Sluzick more gloomy than ever; without good-day or greeting, without comment or question, the ancient Ukrainian cleared his nostrils with his fingers, then briskly gave his mare the whip.

Today he was especially out of humor; he had had all the trouble in the world getting through certain stretches of the road, and he suspected that the return trip would be even more disagreeable. Not that Nick Sluzick feared the water holes for the sake of his own tough hide; it took more than an icy bath to disconcert him. But he did not like to see a woman running such risks. In general he had no fondness for lugging women along with him—women, children, breakable objects, in short anything fragile.

In danger he preferred to be alone. When it came down to it, he always preferred to be alone. A man needed to be alone to ponder his own affairs. What was more, if this Water Hen country were to be any more settled, in the end he, Nick Sluzick, would have to seek refuge further north.

They reached a veritable slough. Bella refused to venture into it. The old man raised his whip; from the tip of his red nose flowed the usual silver thread; to his mustaches clung the remains of the garlic sausage and bread he had devoured standing near the stove in the store, knife in hand, even though the merchant had invited him to share his own meal. Bella seemed to be measuring the water's depth with her bent leg, which she drew back up under her belly. The water came halfway to her body, about half the height of the sleigh, flush with its floorboards.

Luzina lifted her most precious package above her head, thinking less of herself than of this irreplaceable gift. They had, however, passed through the deepest of the water. Luzina, her arms laden, quietly sank back into the seat.

Toward the end of the afternoon one of the Tousignant children, posted on the Little Water Hen shore, heard the summons on the bark trumpet whereby it had been agreed that Luzina would indicate her arrival at the bank of the Big Water Hen.

Immediately Hippolyte and Pierre-Emmanuel-Roger launched the boat. At that last moment two more children clambered in; Hippolyte had not the heart to send them back, so eager were they to see their mother again. They rowed quickly; they raced across the little island. From afar they could already see the motionless sleigh and two human figures, one of them peevish, annoyed at the delay, and the other waving, excitedly perched on the seat.

They crossed the Big Water Hen; now they were within hailing distance, and they cried out to each other. And then, a bit thinner, a trifle pale, but laughing with shyness and emotion, her face wrinkled in joy, Luzina stepped out upon the ground. And in her arms, as happened whenever she returned from her business trips, Luzina carried the baby she had gone to Sainte Rose-du-Lac to bring into the world.

BIOGRAPHICAL NOTES

SHOLOM ALEICHEM *1859–1916*

Solomon Rabinowitz, who was born in the Ukraine and spent his later years in the United States, took as his pen name the Hebrew salutation "Peace be upon you!" His novels, plays and more than three hundred short stories have been translated into many languages, but he is most widely loved for his humorous stories of life among the oppressed and poverty-ridden Russian Jews of the late nineteenth and early twentieth centuries.   Page 376

CORRADO ALVARO *1895–1956*

Alvaro lived much of his life in Rome, yet some of his most outstanding stories concern the simple country people of Calabria, in southern Italy, where he was born. A prolific novelist, he was also esteemed as an editor and journalist.   Page 196

MAX AUB *1903–1972*

Despite his name, Max Aub was thoroughly Spanish in education and culture. His work ranged from lyrical folk fantasies such as *The Launch* to novels set against the background of the Spanish Civil War. He lived toward the end of his life in Mexico.   Page 740

MARCEL AYMÉ *1902–1967*

Born of a humble family in the French provinces, Aymé became a confirmed Parisian; and because he hated school, he was almost entirely self-educated. His sense of the ludicrous combined with a skeptical realism brought him great popularity, and many of his stories and plays have been translated into English.   Page 264

NIGEL BALCHIN *1908–1970*

A highly regarded British author of suspenseful novels, Nigel Balchin was also a trained scientist who rose high in the British scientific establishment during World War II, an experience responsible for perhaps his best book, *The Small Back Room.* "Patience" is from his *Last Recollections of my Uncle Charles.*   Page 593

ROBERT BENCHLEY *1889–1945*

Robert Benchley enjoyed multiple careers as author, playwright, actor, critic, columnist, and as one of America's most beloved humorists. Very much like the bemused and often maladroit subjects of his sketches, he stood in constant bafflement at modern technology, and this spirit is reflected in such hilarious collections of his humor as *From Bed to Worse* and *My Ten Years in a Quandary, and How They Grew.*   Page 454

SALLY BENSON *1900–1972*

Sally Benson began her writing career as a newspaperwoman, doing interviews and movie reviews. After some years of this she wrote a short story and submitted it to *The New Yorker*, which, to her complete surprise, accepted it and asked for more. Her best-known works are her stories of Judy Graves, of *Junior Miss* fame, and *Meet Me in St. Louis*, a nostalgic novel about her own hometown.   Page 303

BERTOLT BRECHT *1898–1956*
One of the towering figures of twentieth-century drama, Bertolt Brecht was born in Augsburg, Germany, and studied science and medicine, but he soon discovered that his major interest was the theater. In the United States his *Threepenny Opera*, written in collaboration with Kurt Weill, has had an astonishing success.   Page 290

PEARL S. BUCK *1892–1973*
Pearl Buck grew up in China and acquired a love of that country that found expression in the Pulitzer prize-winning novel *The Good Earth*, as well as in a host of other distinguished books. A person of great causes, she worked tirelessly in behalf of retarded and displaced children. She is the only American woman to have won the Nobel Prize for literature.   Page 44

ALBERT CAMUS *1913–1960*
At the time of his death in a sports-car accident, Albert Camus had won for himself a preeminent position in the world's intellectual community. Born in Algeria and raised in dire poverty, Camus grew up with a deep rage against injustice or oppression of any sort. Active in the French Resistance during the darkest hours of the Nazi occupation, he later edited its underground newspaper, *Combat*. After World War II his novels and essays dealt impressively with the tragic and absurd in life and man's need to fight and dominate them, an achievement recognized in 1957 by the award of the Nobel Prize for literature.   Page 579

TRUMAN CAPOTE *1924–*
A native of New Orleans but a colorful citizen of the world, Truman Capote lists writing only after conversation, reading and travel as a "preferred pastime." He is, however, a writer of extraordinary versatility whose works have won him international acclaim. His novel *Breakfast at Tiffany's* was made into both a Broadway musical and a movie. With *In Cold Blood* he created a journalistic nonfiction style that reads like suspense fiction.   Page 612

ANTON CHEKHOV *1860–1904*
The grandson of a Russian serf, Chekhov was educated as a doctor and continued to practice medicine all his life. Although he considered much of his own writing to be of minor importance, he has won lasting fame as one of the world's leading dramatists and short-story writers.   Pages 31, 632

COLETTE *1873–1954*
Sidonie Gabrielle Claudine Colette, whose stories rank among the greatest in French literature, was born in the provincial town of St.-Sauveur-en-Puisaye. Her early novels were written at the insistence of her first husband, a man much older than she, who as her literary "mentor" published them under his own name. Her later works included *Chéri* and *Gigi*.   Page 191

JOSEPH CONRAD *1857–1924*
Teodor Józef Konrad Korzeniowski was born in the Ukraine of Polish parents. He shipped as a merchant sailor at the age of sixteen, and spent much of his life on the high seas. At thirty-seven he settled in England and began to write. Though his native tongue was Polish, he wrote in English, producing such masterworks as *Heart of Darkness* and *Lord Jim*.   Page 220

STEPHEN CRANE *1871–1900*
The fourteenth child of a New Jersey Methodist minister, Stephen Crane died before his thirtieth year. Yet within that short span he wrote novels, short stories and poetry that fill fourteen volumes. Best known for *The Red Badge of Courage* (a classic novel of combat experience in the Civil War that he wrote without ever having seen battle), Crane was one of the earliest and among the greatest of the realistic school of American writers.   Page 134

ISAK DINESEN *1885–1962*
This is the pen name of Baroness Karen Blixen-Finecke, a Dane who wrote equally well in English. She spent nearly twenty years on a plantation in East Africa, the genesis of her memorable *Out of Africa* and

of many superbly crafted stories. While living in Denmark again during the German occupation in World War II, she continued to write and is reported to have smuggled out the manuscript of "The Sailor-boy's Tale" by way of Sweden.   Page 56

F. SCOTT FITZGERALD *1896–1940*
It has been said that Scott Fitzgerald, with his tales of flappers, speakeasies, bathtub gin and flamboyant youth, single-handedly created the Jazz Age, the frantic, pleasure-bent pace of which is so successfully chronicled in his masterpiece, *The Great Gatsby.* Born in St. Paul, Minnesota, and educated at Princeton, Fitzgerald became a legend in his own time—a legend that has a renewed vogue today.   Page 393

ANATOLE FRANCE *1844–1924*
The son of a Parisian bookseller, Anatole France grew up to become a master of the French prose style and a dominant figure in French literature. Known as the "prince of letters," he was elected to the Académie Française in 1897 and received the Nobel Prize for literature in 1921. "The Procurator of Judaea" shows this subtle satirist at his favorite work of demolishing accepted assumptions.   Page 322

RUMER GODDEN *1907–*
Though English-born, Rumer Godden spent much of her childhood in India, the scene of many of her novels. These and her short stories and books for children are written in her home in the picturesque village of Rye, England.   Page 494

NADINE GORDIMER *1923–*
Nadine Gordimer grew up in the goldmining country of South Africa and graduated from the University of the Witwatersrand in Johannesburg, where she now lives with her husband and children. She has written several novels, but it is her fine short stories on the theme of the troubled relationship between the races of her native land that have won her a wide following overseas.   Page 201

MAXIM GORKY *1868–1936*
It was considered dangerous in Czarist Russia to educate the children of the lower classes, so Maxim Gorky, son of an upholsterer and grandson of a Volga boatman, was refused entrance to Kazan University. But he studied on his own, and by his early thirties his *Sketches and Stories* had made him a prominent literary figure. During the rest of his life he wrote prolifically, becoming a dedicated spokesman for the Russian Revolution.   Page 734

GRAHAM GREENE *1904–*
Born in Berkhamsted, England, and educated at Oxford, Graham Greene comes of a long line of teachers, statesmen and authors. He began writing while still a schoolboy, and since then has produced stories, essays, plays and more than a dozen novels, ranging from thrillers like *The Third Man* to serious studies of moral crisis like *The Heart of the Matter.*   Page 367

ERNEST HEMINGWAY *1899–1961*
The bullrings of Spain, the big-game hunting grounds of Africa, the glittering pleasure haunts of postwar Europe, the humble fishing villages of Cuba and Mexico—these are the stuff of Ernest Hemingway's novels and innumerable short stories. The son of a country doctor in Illinois, Hemingway learned his craft as a reporter and later as a foreign correspondent in Paris. In 1953 he was awarded a Pulitzer Prize for his novel *The Old Man and the Sea*, and in 1954 the Nobel Prize for literature.   Page 165

O. HENRY *1862–1910*
Once employed as a bank teller in Austin, Texas, William Sydney Porter was later convicted of stealing money from his employer and was sentenced to a term in prison. It was there he began to write stories under the pseudonym O. Henry. Upon his release he came to New York, there to write affectionately about the clerks, secretaries, aspiring young artists and actors who comprised *The Four Million*, his finest collection of stories.   Page 717

PAUL HORGAN *1903—*
A perceptive writer on the Southwest, Horgan has won both the Bancroft and Pulitzer prizes for his two-volume history of the Rio Grande, *Great River.* He is a novelist of note, but his short stories are particularly effective.   Page 562

ALDOUS HUXLEY *1894–1963*
The grandson of Thomas Huxley, the grandnephew of Matthew Arnold and the brother of Julian Huxley, Aldous Huxley was surrounded from birth by eminent men. Following his education at Eton and Oxford, he produced a series of novels whose brilliance and erudition stunned the critics. The most famous of these, *Brave New World*, is a visionary nightmare of a totalitarian state set in the future.   Page 67

SHIRLEY JACKSON *1919–1965*
Because of her preoccupation with the darker regions of human consciousness, Shirley Jackson's friends claimed she wrote with a broomstick instead of a pen—and her acknowledged classic, "The Lottery," tends to support such a belief. But she could also write uproariously about the commonplace, as in *Life Among the Savages*, a collection of informal and engaging essays about life with her children. She was born in San Francisco, California, and lived most of her adult life in rural Vermont.   Page 274

M. R. JAMES *1862–1936*
Though he was a distinguished English antiquary and provost of Eton College from 1918 until his death, Montague Rhodes James, with his taste for the macabre, was a great teller of ghost stories.   Page 458

JAMES JOYCE *1882–1941*
Perhaps the most important literary figure of his time, James Joyce developed a "stream of consciousness" style that influenced the art of the novel in the twentieth century. Born in Dublin and educated at Jesuit schools, Joyce nonetheless held political and religious views that caused him to exile himself from Ireland for most of his life.

Publication of his famous novel, *Ulysses,* touched off an international furor as well as a historic court case on freedom of the press in the United States.   Page 213

LEO KENNEDY *1907—*
Although he was born in Liverpool, England, Leo Kennedy and his parents emigrated to Montreal, Canada, when he was still a child. As a student at McGill University he was active as a poet, writer and literary critic, and his writings have since been widely anthologized. Mr. Kennedy now lives in the United States.   Page 709

RING LARDNER *1885–1933*
Ring Lardner gained early celebrity as a sportswriter, but it was not until the publication of his collection, *You Know Me, Al*, about the time of World War I, that his true gifts were recognized. He was born in Niles, Michigan, in the American heartland, and few writers catch so well the flavor and spirit of American speech.   Page 479

D. H. LAWRENCE *1885–1930*
David Herbert Lawrence was the son of an English coal miner and a schoolteacher mother to whom he was devoted. One of five children, he was brought up in an atmosphere of poverty, brutality and drink, much of which is reflected in his partially autobiographical masterpiece, *Sons and Lovers.* Enfeebled by sickness and pursued by controversy, he spent much of his life wandering through Europe, Australia and America seeking health and the ideal place to live. Still a young man, he died of tuberculosis in a French sanatorium.   Page 438

HENRY LAWSON *1867–1922*
Born in a gold miner's tent in New South Wales, Australia, Henry Lawson had little formal education and lived a wandering existence for many years as a painter at pitifully low wages. In 1887, however, his first poem was published in a Sydney newspaper, and thereafter he was continually writing the poetry and short stories for which he is remembered.   Page 554

DORIS LESSING *1919—*
Like the child in her story "The Old Chief Mshlanga," Doris Lessing grew up in Southern Rhodesia, the daughter of British emigrants. She moved to England in 1949. A strong sympathy for the poor and dispossessed, at least partially derived from her African experience, is felt in all her work. She is best known for her novel sequence *Children of Violence.* Page 511

GREGORIO LÓPEZ Y FUENTES *1895—*
Born and reared among the Indians of Mexico, López y Fuentes has unusual insight into the texture of their daily lives. A poet and journalist as well as a writer of fiction, he won the National Prize of Mexico in 1935 for his novel *El Indio.* Page 188

MACHADO DE ASSIS *1839–1908*
The son of a Negro house painter of Rio de Janeiro and a Portuguese mother, Joaquim Maria Machado de Assis worked as a typesetter, proofreader and translator before his own fiction and poetry established him as Brazil's foremost author. But it was not until 1952 that he became well known to American readers with the publication in translation of his novel *Epitaph of a Small Winner.* Page 625

KATHERINE MANSFIELD *1888–1923*
Born in Wellington, New Zealand, Katherine Mansfield was sent to England to be educated. Her first story was published when she was only nine, and by the end of her brief life she was famous for short stories that capture beautifully the subtleties of human relationships. Page 723

W. SOMERSET MAUGHAM *1874–1965*
William Somerset Maugham's early ambition was to be a doctor. He abandoned it, however, after gaining recognition as a writer, and went on to achieve international fame for his novels and short stories. Pages 24, 678

GUY DE MAUPASSANT *1850–1893*
Guy de Maupassant wrote novels, plays and verse, but no other writer is more completely identified with the short story. A consummate master of the form, who learned his craft from Flaubert, Maupassant wrote some three hundred stories, many based largely on personal recollections of his youth in Normandy. Page 121

ALBERTO MORAVIA *1907—*
A native of Rome, Moravia achieved international stature at the age of twenty-two with the publication of his novel *The Indifferent Ones.* He has written many other novels, as well as short stories, plays and essays, and their down-to-earth manner and pungent view of life have won him a worldwide following. Page 237

LILIKA NAKOS *1905—*
Born in Athens, Lilika Nakos was educated in Geneva, Switzerland, where her interest in writing developed early. After graduating from the university there, she returned to Greece, where she has since worked as a journalist and has had many short stories and novels published. Page 244

FRANK O'CONNOR *1903–1966*
Born of a poor family in Cork, Ireland, O'Connor put together a "collected edition" of his work at the age of twelve. He wrote in Gaelic as well as English and was once a director for the famed Abbey Theatre. A novelist, poet and playwright, he is best known in North America for his evocative short stories. Page 153

JOHN O'HARA *1905–1970*
John O'Hara was born in Pottsville, Pennsylvania, the eldest of eight children. Prevented from going to college by the death of his doctor father, he worked as everything from ship steward to movie critic until 1934, when the immediate success of his first novel, *Appointment in Samarra,* established him as a writer. His novels regularly made the best-seller lists and at least three of them—*Pal Joey, Ten North Frederick* and *Butterfield 8*—were made into popular films. But many critics prefer the "clean and sure style" of his short stories. Page 544

DOROTHY PARKER *1893–1967*
Described by Alexander Woollcott as "so odd a blend of Little Nell and Lady Macbeth," Dorothy Parker is equally well known as satirist and poet. A stringent wit and an uncanny gift for monologue are her particular trademarks in the short-story form, of which one of her best-known collections is *After Such Pleasures.*   Page 768

S. J. PERELMAN *1904–*
Perelman has written successfully for the stage and screen, notably as a gag writer for the Marx Brothers; but his most devoted audience is composed of readers of his wildly zany sketches. Perelman lived for many years on a farm in Bucks County, Pennsylvania, but he has recently become a permanent resident of England.   Page 550

LUIGI PIRANDELLO *1867–1936*
Before he emerged as one of the giants of twentieth-century drama, Pirandello had been chiefly a poet, novelist and writer of short stories. Born in Sicily, he was educated at the University of Rome and later took a German doctorate in philology. His was a life of struggle and adversity before honors and international recognition finally came, culminating in the Nobel Prize for literature in 1934.   Page 745

KATHERINE ANNE PORTER *1890–*
Katherine Anne Porter was born in Indian Creek, Texas, and some of her finest stories have been set in the Southwest; but her view of life is too universal for her to be considered a "regional" writer. Her great reputation has been achieved with a relatively small output of material, most notably stories like *Pale Horse, Pale Rider* and the novel *Ship of Fools.* Her *Collected Stories* received a Pulitzer Prize in 1966.   Page 339

THOMAS H. RADDALL *1903–*
Born in England, Thomas Raddall came to Nova Scotia as a child and has lived there ever since. Twice during the 1940s and again in 1957 he received the highest official award available to a Canadian writer, the silver medallion of the Governor General's Award. He has contributed numerous stories to magazines, documentary scripts to television, and is the author of several novels, including *The Nymph and the Lamp.*   Page 307

SANTHA RAMA RAU *1923–*
East and West are happily blended in Santha Rama Rau, who was born in Madras, India, schooled in England and at Wellesley College in Massachusetts, and married an American journalist. With a skilled and sensitive pen she interprets the country of her birth for Western readers.   Page 524

GABRIELLE ROY *1909–*
Gabrielle Roy was born and educated in St. Boniface, Manitoba, a French-speaking community in the English-speaking world of the Canadian prairies, and began writing stories when she was twelve. Today she lives with her husband, a doctor, in Quebec City. Her first novel, *The Tin Flute*, was awarded the Prix Femina in France, and her work has twice won her the Governor General's Award.   Page 772

DAMON RUNYON *1884–1946*
Reared in Colorado, Alfred Damon Runyon lied his way into the army at the age of fourteen and went off to fight in the Spanish-American War. Later he became a sportswriter and then a highly regarded general newspaperman whose assignments took him to France during World War I; but it is on his stories about the antics of Broadway's "guys and dolls" that his fame rests.   Page 92

SAKI (H. H. Munro) *1870–1916*
As a master of humor as well as of the chilling and macabre, H. H. Munro (or "Saki," as he is universally known) has very few peers. Born in Burma but educated in British schools, he learned the craft of writing first as a reporter, then as a foreign correspondent in Russia and France. What had already become a brilliant career ended tragically with his death in battle during World War I.   Page 336

DOROTHY L. SAYERS *1893–1957*
One of the first women graduates of Oxford, Dorothy Sayers took honors there in medieval studies. Beloved among mystery fans as the creator of the aristocratic amateur sleuth Lord Peter Wimsey, she was also a detective-story anthologist, and in her later years a writer on religious subjects. Among her best mysteries are *Murder Must Advertise* and *The Nine Tailors*. Page 105

IRWIN SHAW *1913–*
Before he was firmly established as a writer, Shaw had tried his hand at many occupations—from semiprofessional football to tutoring—which in turn provided material for a wealth of short stories, novels, plays and screenplays. His first novel, *The Young Lions*, earned him a solid place in contemporary American fiction. Page 754

HJALMAR SÖDERBERG *1869–1941*
An acknowledged master of Swedish prose, Söderberg worked for a time as a government clerk before he began his career as a writer. His best-known works are *Martin Birck's Youth*, a novel, and *Little Histories*, a collection of stories. Page 490

JEAN STAFFORD *1915–*
Born in California and educated in Colorado, Jean Stafford was recognized as an important young talent for her 1944 novel, *Boston Adventure*. She has since published several other novels, a children's book and much critical writing, but she is perhaps most widely known for her subtle and elegant short stories. Page 656

WALLACE STEGNER *1909–*
Wallace Stegner spent most of his youth in the American Northwest and in Saskatchewan. He was early attracted to the craft of writing, and for his M.A. thesis he submitted a collection of short stories. Stegner has the unusual distinction of being a three-time winner of an O. Henry Memorial Award. He is currently director of the creative-writing program at Stanford University. Page 412

JOHN STEINBECK *1902–1968*
The Salinas Valley of California, where he was born, provided John Steinbeck with the materials for some of his best writing, including American classics like *Of Mice and Men*, *The Grapes of Wrath* and *The Red Pony*, from which "The Leader of the People" was adapted. In 1962 Steinbeck was awarded the Nobel Prize for literature. Page 9

RABINDRANATH TAGORE *1861–1941*
This splendid Indian writer, composer not only of the Indian national anthem but of that recently adopted by Bangladesh, was awarded the Nobel Prize for literature in 1913. Known as poet, dramatist and novelist in both English and Bengali, Tagore was also a universal humanitarian revered throughout the world. Page 359

HERNANDO TÉLLEZ *1908–1966*
The distinctive bittersweet quality of Spanish literature is present in the work of this fine Colombian writer. Téllez set his stories in his native country, pitting an often brutal reality against the warmth and resilience of ordinary human beings. Page 428

JAMES THURBER *1894–1961*
A specially gifted cartoonist before he began to write, Thurber's drawings and humorous writings won him an international audience. Most of his work first appeared in *The New Yorker,* of which he had been a staff member for a time. Both *The Secret Life of Walter Mitty,* one of his best-known stories, and *The Male Animal,* a highly acclaimed stage hit of 1940 written with Elliott Nugent, were also successful movies. Page 433

LEO TOLSTOY *1828–1910*
As a young man Count Tolstoy lived like a gay blade in Moscow and St. Petersburg and served in the czarist army, but in 1862 he married and settled down to look after the serfs on the family estate of Yasnaya Polyana. There his children were born and his finest novels, *War and Peace* and *Anna Karenina*, were written. There, too, he came to believe deeply in nonviolence, rustic sim-

plicity and Christian love. Because he dared to preach and act upon his beliefs, he was excommunicated by the Russian Orthodox Church and forsaken by many, but he is revered today as a towering literary figure and a saintly human being.   Page 256

MARK TWAIN *1835–1910*

Exuberant, full of wit and blessed with a native zest for life, Samuel Langhorne Clemens was very much a product of the young nation in which he grew. In his early years, working as riverboat pilot (the source of his pseudonym), unsuccessful silver prospector, and reporter, he was able to see much of America, and it was from these experiences that many of his stories came. His two most enduring masterpieces are *The Adventures of Tom Sawyer* and *The Adventures of Huckleberry Finn*.   Page 283

JOHN UPDIKE *1932—*

Born in southeastern Pennsylvania, the part of America that supplies the background for much of his work, John Updike graduated from Harvard and then went to an art school in England. For two years he was a staff member of *The New Yorker*, to which he is still a regular contributor. He is the author of best-selling novels and many distinguished short stories and poems. In 1964 he won the National Book Award for his novel *The Centaur*.   Page 469

H. G. WELLS *1866–1946*

Certainly one of the most prolific writers of modern times, H. G. Wells averaged a book a year for the better part of his lifetime. An honors graduate in science, he developed a reputation as a master of science fiction—*The War of the Worlds, The Shape of Things to Come* and *The Time Machine* are famous examples. He wrote other more realistic novels as well, and for many years no respectable bookcase could be without his encyclopedic *Outline of History*.   Page 639

EUDORA WELTY *1909—*

In that distinguished tradition of Southern writers that includes William Faulkner, Truman Capote and Carson McCullers, Eudora Welty is regarded as a major talent. She was born in Jackson, Mississippi, and educated at the University of Wisconsin. Her writings have been acclaimed for their sensitive and penetrating evocation of life in her native South.   Page 669

JESSAMYN WEST *1907—*

Bedridden by tuberculosis, Jessamyn West began to write about what she knew best—the direct and gentle Quaker people among whom she first lived in Indiana. Eventually her stories were published in a book she called *The Friendly Persuasion*, and since then her stories and novels have had a devoted following.   Page 248

OSCAR WILDE *1854–1900*

Irish-born Oscar Wilde was a debonair young man widely known in London for his wit and eccentricity. He had some success as a poet and lecturer, but the publication of his novel, *The Picture of Dorian Gray*, and the production of a number of his plays—among them *The Importance of Being Earnest*—established his fame. Wilde was later convicted on a morals charge and sentenced to two years in prison, the genesis of his most famous poem, *The Ballad of Reading Gaol*. He died, a broken man, in Paris.   Page 35

MIKHAIL ZOSHCHENKO *1895–1958*

Next to Chekhov, Zoshchenko is Russia's most popular humorist, comparable in style and use of the vernacular with the American writers Damon Runyon and Ring Lardner. His acid portraits of Soviet establishment types, however, eventually got him in trouble with the authorities, and before his death he was officially denounced as "a brainless scribbler."   Page 476

ACKNOWLEDGMENTS

THE LEADER OF THE PEOPLE, copyright 1938, © renewed 1966 by John Steinbeck, is adapted from *The Red Pony*. Used by permission of The Viking Press, Inc. MR. KNOW-ALL, copyright 1924 by W. Somerset Maugham, is from *Cosmopolitans*. Used by permission of Doubleday & Company, Inc., the Literary Executor of W. Somerset Maugham, and William Heinemann Ltd. VANKA, © 1963 by Alfred A. Knopf, Inc., is from *The Image of Chekhov*. Used by permission of the publisher. THE OLD DEMON, copyright 1939 by Pearl S. Buck, renewed, is used by permission of Harold Ober Associates Incorporated. THE SAILOR-BOY'S TALE, copyright 1942 by Random House, Inc., is from *Winter's Tales* by Isak Dinesen. Used by permission of Random House, Inc., and Putnam & Company Limited. YOUNG ARCHIMEDES, copyright 1924, 1952 by Aldous Huxley, is from *Young Archimedes and Other Stories* by Aldous Huxley. Used by permission of Harper & Row, Publishers, Incorporated, and Chatto & Windus Ltd. BUTCH MINDS THE BABY, © renewed 1957 by Mary Runyon McCann and Damon Runyon, Jr., is used by permission of Raoul Lionel Felder, Executor of the Estate of Damon Runyon, Jr. SUSPICION, copyright 1939 by Dorothy Leigh Sayers Fleming, is from *In the Teeth of the Evidence and Other Stories* by Dorothy L. Sayers. Used by permission of Harper & Row, Publishers, Incorporated, and David Higham. My ŒDIPUS COMPLEX, copyright 1950 by Frank O'Connor, is from *Stories of Frank O'Connor*. Used by permission of Alfred A. Knopf, Inc., and A. D. Peters & Company. THE SNOWS OF KILIMANJARO, copyright 1936 by Ernest Hemingway, © renewed 1964 by Mary Hemingway, is from *The Short Stories of Ernest Hemingway*. Used by permission of Charles Scribner's Sons. A LETTER TO GOD, copyright 1940 by Gregorio López y Fuentes. Used by permission. THE LITTLE BOUILLOUX GIRL, copyright 1953 by Farrar, Straus and Young, Inc., is from *My Mother's House and Sido* by Colette. Used by permission of Farrar, Straus & Giroux, Inc., and Martin Secker & Warburg, Ltd. THE RUBY, © 1955 by W. J. Strachan, is from *Modern Italian Stories* edited by W. J. Strachan. Used by permission of Philosophical Library and Associated Book Publishers Ltd. SIX FEET OF THE COUNTRY, copyright 1953 by Nadine Gordimer, is from the collection *Six Feet of the Country*, published by Simon & Schuster, Inc. Used by permission of Shirley Collier Agency. THE BOARDING HOUSE, © 1967 by the Estate of James Joyce, is from *Dubliners*, originally published by B. W. Huebsch, Inc., in 1916. Used by permission of The Viking Press, Inc. THE BRUTE, from *A Set of Six* by Joseph Conrad, is used by permission of J. M. Dent & Sons Ltd. and The Trustees of the Joseph Conrad Estate. A DOUBLE GAME, © 1963 by Martin Secker & Warburg, Ltd., is from *More Roman Tales* by Alberto Moravia. Used by permission of Farrar, Straus & Giroux, Inc., and Martin Secker & Warburg, Ltd. MATERNITY by Lilika Nakos is used by permission of the author. LEAD HER LIKE A PIGEON, copyright 1944 by Jessamyn West, is from *The Friendly Persuasion*. Used by permission of Harcourt Brace Jovanovich, Inc. GOD SEES THE TRUTH, BUT WAITS is from *Twenty-Three Tales* by Leo Tolstoy. An adapted text, used by permission of Oxford University Press. THE WALKER-THROUGH-WALLS, copyright Editions Gallimard 1943, is from *Across Paris and Other Stories* by Marcel Aymé. Used by permission of Harper & Row, Publishers, Incorporated, Editions Gallimard, and The Bodley Head. THE LOTTERY, copyright 1948, 1949 by Shirley Jackson, originally appeared in *The New Yorker*, and is from *The Magic of Shirley Jackson*. Used by permission of Farrar, Straus & Giroux, Inc. THE McWILLIAMSES AND THE BURGLAR ALARM, copyright 1922 by Mark Twain Company, copyright renewed 1950 by Clara Clemens Samossoud, is from *The Mysterious Stranger and Other Stories* by Mark Twain.